Mia Gallagher was born in Dublin, where she lives and works. Her debut novel, *HellFire*, was widely acclaimed and received the *Irish Tatler* Women of the Year Literature Award in 2007, while her award-winning short fiction has been widely published and anthologised. Mia has received several Literature Bursaries from the Arts Council of Ireland and has been writer-in-residence in many different environments, both at home and abroad. In a parallel universe, Mia works as a professional actor, performing in theatre, radio and occasionally film. *Beautiful Pictures of the Lost Homeland* is her second novel.

Praise for *HellFire*

'Gallagher depicts a culture in despair and a society in irreversible meltdown with tremendous compassion and energy.... Remarkably done; as is the unexpectedly weighted power and beauty of the imagery.... The vernacular rhythm is perfect.... An extraordinary ambition; a grand achievement, too.'

The Guardian

'... there are echoes of early Irvine Welsh in the energetic joy of her language ... *HellFire* is a powerful revenge tragedy, a glorious depiction of Dublin in all her dirty glory, and an unusual love story.... There have been few better debuts in the last year.'

The Observer

'Gritty realism interjected with poetic surrealism is not an easy stylistic feat. However, this is something that *HellFire* does effortlessly... unique and innovative... takes the reader on an exhilarating narrative and stylistic journey.'

The Irish Times

'I am reminded of Laurence Sterne's *Tristam Shandy*... a magnificent achievement, bursting with energy, full of wonderful creations and telling a compelling, if unorthodox, love story. It is a novel of Dublin to rank with James Plunkett's *Strumpet City*.'

Irish Examiner

'Brilliant... easily compared to Irvine Welsh with its energy and raw, compelling narrative. You find yourself hearing Lucy in your head, telling you her shocking story and you find yourself staying up all night to be with her.'

Sunday Independent

'... a striking talent for storytelling and a subtly enchanting narrator... *HellFire* has the kind of episodic character that gives endless classics their power, the element of stories within stories.... Mia Gallagher [is]worth getting excited about; something special, something different, something completely new, readable, talented and relevant.'

Sunday Tribune

Beautiful Pictures of the Lost Homeland

Beautiful Pictures of the Lost Homeland

Mia Gallagher

NEW ISLAND

Beautiful Pictures of the Lost Homeland
First published in 2016 by
New Island Books
16 Priory Hall Office Park
Stillorgan
County Dublin
Republic of Ireland

www.newisland.ie

PRINT ISBN: 978-1-84840-506-6
EPUB ISBN: 978-1-84840-508-0
MOBI ISBN: 978-1-84840-507-3

British Library Cataloguing Data.
A CIP catalogue record for this book is available from the British Library.

Typeset by JVR Creative India
Cover design by Anna Morrison
Printed by ScandBook AB, Sweden

New Island received financial assistance from The Arts Council (*An Chomhairle Ealaíon*), 70 Merrion Square, Dublin 2, Ireland.

10 9 8 7 6 5 4 3 2 1

For Seán

and in memory of my grandmothers,

Lisa Gerhardt and Maureen Doran

Ich habe Tote, und ich ließ sie hin und war erstaunt, sie so getrost zu sehn, so rasch zuhaus im Totsein, so gerecht, so anders als ihr Ruf. Nur Du, Du kehrst zurück; Du streifst mich, Du gehst um, Du willst an etwas stoßen, daß es klingt von Dir und Dich verrät....

Was bittest Du? Sag, soll ich reisen? Hast Du irgendwo ein Ding zurückgelassen, das sich quält und das Dir nachwill?...

Bist Du noch da? In welcher Ecke bist Du?

I have my dead, and I let them go and was astonished to see them so content, so at home in their deadness, so cheerful, so different to their reputation. Only you, you return; you brush past me, you hang around, you try to knock on things so they sound of you, betraying your presence....

What do you want? Tell me: should I set off on a journey? Have you left a Thing behind somewhere, that torments itself, longs to have you back?...

Are you still here? What corner are you standing in?

Rainer Maria Rilke, *Requiem for a Friend* (1908)

Startpunkt/Inpoint

With the hissing sound of a seventies' Schweppes commercial, the doors open. Mind the Gap, calls a clipped voice.

At the ferryman's command, some of us scatter, dispersing in different directions; others stay put; the rest clamber on, swarming into the gaps left by the displaced.

Sschussch.

The doors close; on us, the chosen, packed like fish in a can.

Some of us are sitting; some standing. In front of us we hold things. Newspapers. Bags. Satchels. Books. The twisted muscle and bone of our crossed arms. Wheelie-cases, most of them black, branded with airline stubs and totemic stabs at identification: a blue ribbon, a white criss-cross sticker, a tiny teddy-bear, a decal of a silhouetted cityscape. *Praha.* Our eyes are focused on neutral territory: smartphone screens, headlines, Tube schematic, advertising copy. Nobody's talking.

We're hot. It's spring, not yet April, and up on the surface it's grey and wet and cold, but down here, hurtling along the bed of the underground river, it's always hot. Our hands are damp; our palms prickling. We all have sweaty, prickly palms, even those of us who aren't nervous. Our hands, our hands of saviours, our hands of warriors, our hands of the saved, clutch the buckles of our rucksacks. One of those hands is already on its way to do God's work, feeling under the canvas fabric of the combat jacket as it inches towards the black oblong of the miraculous device. Our hands, our hands of the blank, of the never-to-be-saved, of the uncomprehendingly-at-war, rest on our laps, leak moisture into our leggings, toy with the edges of our jackets, the cotton frills of our TopShop blouses, the ribbons on our luggage handles, rub our travel-weary eyes, grab for balance to the rail, the ceiling straps, the edges of other people's seats.

We are packed tight but obeying the formalities; our eyes avoid each other, notwithstanding the millimetre-thin membrane between arse and cock,

1

tit and elbow, mouth and forehead. We drink in each other's scent. We all smell, some of us distinctively. One of us, one of the baggage-laden travel-weary, the one with the golden earrings and the hair of lustrous steel wrapped in cheesecloth, is perfumed with Chanel Gardenia. Some of us fantasise. One, the one that smells of gardenias, thinks of *home* – the thought surprises us – our little flat on Turnmill Street, right across the road from the next station, three minutes away.

We muse, we drift, we dream. Here, in the land of the underground king, we are ripe for the taking.

Many of us have busy fingers. Watch as they play with our clothes, our jewellery, our hair. As they tinker with our machines: pushing buttons; sweeping screens, tapping keys. Sharing pictures, songs, words, thoughts, excuses, apologies, small, meaningless affections. With all those intelligent little devices, those buttons, those flashing lights, those *i luv u*'s those *cul8r*'s those *sorry cant mk it*'s, one more motion won't stand out. One more finger, inching towards one more button.

Our eyes meet and, for a moment, the chamber holds its breath. But we, the warriors, the soon-to-be-saved, are the only ones in this 'we' whose eyes are meeting. Do the rest of us notice this instant of communion? This moment where it could stop, where – if our spirit was not willing to do this, for justice, for the greater good, for ideas and God and nation, or only ideas, or only nation, or only God, for the sake of doing it because we said we would, because we have to, because we want to, because—

Do any of the rest of us notice the point at which things could be different?

Different? How? A rugby tackle? A swift blow to the head? A gunshot? An appeal to reason?

Reason? Whose reason?

Do any of us, especially the steely-haired one with the Prague-stamped wheelie-bag, have an intimation? A sudden whiff of almonds, an unexpected image of a loved one – an ageing mother, a grown child, an ex-lover? A feeling of *now, Ands, is it coming now?* Do we raise our cheesecloth-wrapped heads to see if the rest of us feel the same?

We ask.

We answer.

We reach the surface.

Our fingers find the button and—

Jump

Humpty Dumpty sat on a Wall
Humpty Dumpty had a great Fall

Nursery rhyme, Anon.

(   )

Visitors are reminded that they have just entered a floating *Raum* ('space/room') outside normal spacetime conventions. Please take note of the following:

- Like all lost territories, this space refuses to answer to a single name. Terms such as *Kunstkabinett, Wunderkammer, Sondersammlung, Theatre of Memory, Cabinet of Curiosities* and *Picturehouse of Intriguing Objects* will pop up from time to time as monikers. Please regard these as, to all intents and purposes, interchangeable.
- This is not history/herstory in any factual sense, but, like all *Art Cabinets*, a stab at creating a semblance of order out of chaos via subjective curatorial choices. You may submit your own interpretations at any point where you feel our perspective is a little off. Feedback forms are available on request.
- We remind you that the *Wonder Chamber* is a complex and sometimes volatile collection of Objects, with many possible Portals, Circuits and, of course, Dead Ends.[1] Visitors interested in exploring their own routes through our *Treasurehaus* are, of course, free to take them. However, if you do leave The Path, **we will not take responsibility for what happens**.
- Some of you may experience our Tour as a Journey that both surfs around and traverses back through a series of concentric Waves, as if heading towards their common Centre. We wonder:
  - ➤ Does every ripple of History have the same Source (✺ Boom!)?
  - ➤ If Herstory is a wave, what is the Medium through which it ripples?
  - ➤ Can waves of a specific Ourstory (and its variants history, herstory, theirstory, yourstory, astory, as well as the Holy Grail: thestory) ripple through other Mediums?
  - ➤ And, crucially, what happens once we reach a Medium's End?[2]

---

[1] Smiley-face!
[2] Smiley-face!

07:47:03–09:28:24

Wow, said Mar once, holding up a photo. Is that you, Geo?

We'd been packing for one of our panicked moves, from Berlin to Lausanne, and while he'd been digging through our stuff, he'd found a picture of me as a student. Funny, how something like that brings you back. I looked, unsure. Saw a tall, rangy shape; broad-shouldered, with a formless mop of auburn hair, delicate nose and wide mouth, dressed in a geeky yellow polo shirt with an alligator logo on the left breast.

I'd been eighteen in that photo, at that awful age where I'd convinced myself I'd be able to fit in, as I was, with no intervention. Some joke. It was then, hoping to rid myself of the puppy fat I'd hoarded since I was ten, that I began to diet, extremely and on the sly, because our kind wasn't supposed to do that sort of thing. I joined a rowing club too and started running and, to cap things off, began to wear Lacoste. I'm not sure what put that into my head; an ad, maybe? I had an idea that people who wore Lacoste were organised. Sophisticated. Fitters-in. It wasn't a bad strategy. I'd chosen a media course at a new Dublin college that specialised in tech subjects and my class had been full of people like me. People like you, or how I remember you: nerds and swots and hicks, mainly from the country, all only tentatively beginning to carve out their identities. If I'd gone to art school, as Mar later insisted I should have, I'd have stood out among all those goths and neo-punks of the mid-eighties like a sore, preppy thumb.

It would have been way too flash to go around in Lacoste top-to-toe, but I tried to wear at least one item a day. A knitted pullover, a subdued cotton T, a pair of well-cut slacks. I took care of those clothes. They were talismans, of sorts. When I was flush, I got them dry-cleaned, and when the grant ran low,

7

I washed them by hand, drying them on a flat stand at my bedsit window and ironing them when they were still damp. God, I loved that smell – crisp and warm and clean. Like fresh toast, like that blurred childhood I can still only partially recollect.

One day I was ironing something, a polo shirt, I think, and had lifted it to my face to smell it. At that moment, the alligator caught my attention. I hadn't noticed it before. I knew it was there, I'd bought the clothes because of it, but I hadn't *seen* it. I reached my finger. One small step.

I closed my eyes and let my finger move along the humps and bumps of the little amphibian's fabric body, his long snout, his single bright eye. *Softly*, I thought to myself, imagining him twitch in his sleep.

What if he wakes? I thought. What if he wakes and bites me?

Oh, wake, alligator, wake.

I could come up with lots of reasons for why I'm talking to you now. A story on the TV, the timing of your gift. But that ignores the elephant still crashing around our familial sitting-room. What did you expect by sending me that? What am I supposed to do with it?

God, this is hard. But—

Are you listening carefully?

Not knowing what else to do right now, I'm going to talk. I have no plan, no story in mind. Let's just see what comes out.

Then – as they used to say on that old radio programme – we'll begin.

The sirens, howling.

Not right, I kept thinking. And for ages, that was all I had space in my head for.

Gradually things started to make sense. The sweaty hollow of my pillow under my head, my body's weight on the mattress. The air-raid siren turned into something real; the alarm on my smartphone, screaming and rattling downstairs on the kitchen worktop. I pushed my face into the pillow. Ignore anything long enough, they say, and it'll go away. Who, I wonder, are *they*? The screaming stopped.

I was in pain. My limbs were aching as if I'd been running all night; my nose was blocked, my head stuffed with the beginnings of a headcold.

I unglued my eyes and hauled myself up, feeling for my teeth with my tongue. They felt sore, as if I'd been eating sand in my sleep. From the narrow slice of light over the blind I couldn't tell what kind of day it was going to be. The weather had been terrible all winter, cold and grey with snow and floodings, a perfect backdrop to the bone-deep misery of the recession.

I crawled to the edge of my bed and rolled up the blind. Scattered showers, sunny spells, some wind. It was a day straight out of my childhood, straight out of those radio forecasts you used to listen to, Irish to its marrow. Grey clouds were chugging over the pewtery roofs of my adopted townland. To the west, I could see shreds of blue in the sky, against them the branches of the sycamores in the church grounds, clawing like the fingers of famine victims. Beyond that, out of sight, lay Dublin's Wilder West. Graffiti, dogshit, hoodied teenagers, burnt-out cars and the occasional, lethal shooting. Inchicore, Isle of the Snout, the townland the Tiger had ignored.

All the houses had their blinds down or curtains drawn. The neighbourhood felt eerily silent; as if everyone in the world except me was still sleeping.

I slumped back on the bed. I was finding it hard to move. The dream the sirens had interrupted was still in me, clinging on like the smell of an old lover. I don't dream much, haven't since my childhood, but this one was different. It had left a residue of fading images, sticky as slug-trail. A railway station. People. Some sense of a war. The whole thing had felt shadowy and old-fashioned, like a scene from a thirties noir set in some lost borderland in the bowels of a long-gone Mittel-Europe. Steel and glass, wrought iron, arches, steam. Bandages, long coats, trilby hats. Anytime I'd tried to catch somebody's face, they'd dissolved. There'd been a dark shape on the opposite platform: male, enormous, shadowy – the more I tried to remember him, the more indistinct he got. Maybe I hadn't dreamt him at all, just mixed him up with something else, a story I'd once read.

My phone started screaming again.

Okay, you stupid machine. I hear you.

I groped my way downstairs, feeling uneasy, out of sorts. It was a familiar sensation, but off, like a once-loved suit that used to fit but I hadn't worn for ages. Things weren't right, and not just because of the obvious – though I suppose, in a way, yes, it was. Of course it was. At the time, though, all I was aware of was how irritated I was with my phone. It was a smartphone; it wasn't supposed to have gone off. I had planned to have a lie-in; a day of calm and pampering, so I could build up strength for whatever was lying in wait for me over the hump of the next night. What had possessed me to set the alarm? I couldn't remember doing it. Maybe it had a default setting I'd forgotten to switch off.

I pulled the cord beside the landing window and the blinds snapped open, striping the stairs. I pushed two of the slats apart and peered out. Under the hustling clouds, the street looked small and hopeful and chilly. Nobody was around, though lights were on in the house opposite where the Chinese people lived and I could see some movement through their net curtains. Probably getting the kids ready for the parade. I let the blinds fall. In the striped light, the landline phone on the wall of the stairwell gleamed, a tiger-pearl at the bottom of a dirty sea. My smartphone rattled again, then gave up.

The place was a mess, gloomy in the half-light, still crowded with the crap the plumbers had taken out of my attic when they were fixing the hot water tank. Bits and pieces from past lives prodded out from the murk. A broken whip, a flattened Swiss ball, a blonde wig, a rubber zip-up dress, a set of golf clubs, a pile of what looked like coats. The higgledy-piggledy innards of a *Wunderkammer*. A cloud passed the window and the heap seemed to breathe. Glamour. From the old English, meaning *magic*. I imagined the pile shifting shape, all its chaotic bits organising themselves into a single form, a hulking patchwork beast that needed the love of its maker to bring it to life. Frankenstein's sad creation. The mud-doll Golem that the sorcerers of Prague turned into an avenging demon.

A trick of the light. I shook my head, and the heap was just a heap again.

Reconfigure. I was up now, so I might as well make the best of the day. No point sitting around feeling grumpy, or worse, sorry for myself. I could have some breakfast, read the last of yesterday's paper, then attack the crap in the hall, sort it into what was still useful and what wasn't. I could bag the rubbish and dump it in the charity shop down the village. Not today, because of the holiday. It would have to be—

Tomorrow. And that was when the obvious stopped me, flooding into the corners of my mind.

I walked into the living room and picked up the remote. Because that's what I do when I'm stressed. I don't need the sound – haven't since those last tricky years with you and Aisling – but I like having pictures to look at that aren't the pictures in my head. Martin used to hate that. *Jesus, Geo, can ye no go one fucking day without staring at a screen?* Jesus, Mar, no, I can't. I used to claim it was work, that I had to keep an eye on the competition, but we both knew that was a lie.

The TV winked on. Sky News, its default channel. I pressed mute. My eyes went straight to the picture. It was a street scene. Syria?

No. Rain, rubble. Western Europe. In the foreground, firefighters. Behind them, behind the yellow and black stripes of emergency tape, a lot of angry-looking people. It looked like—

An accident? The image cut. A glossy anchorwoman with a glowing face standing under the U of a Tube station. London.

Breaking News, said the cap-gen, scrolling across the bottom of the screen, and it was only then I realised what it was saying. Black type on yellow backing. *More Bombs on Underground.*

More? I thought, because I was still groggy, still slow. But there hadn't been bombs since—

My landline rang and I jumped. Silly, I know. Sillier again that I hesitated before picking up. Even before Mar left, we hadn't got a call like that in years.

'Georgia. It's Brid, from Momentum.'

Work. 'Oh. Brid—'

'Sorry for bothering you so early, I know it's the holiday and all, but I couldn't get through to your mobile and—'

Holiday? I gapped, then remembered. St Patrick's Day. March the 17th. 'No, no, it's fine.'

She tutted. 'Terrible about London, isn't it? Scary business. I mean, you'd think with everything else going on in the world—'

I looked at the screen. The anchorwoman with the glowing face was interviewing a baggy-eyed politician in a pressed suit. *Foreign Minister*, said the cap-gen. They didn't have a key light for him; his skin was grey, like ash. The association disturbed me.

An expectant silence at the other end of the line. Brid had stopped talking.

I turned away from the TV. 'Sorry, what was that, Brid?'

'Just wondering how's your availability the next sixteen weeks?'

She had two projects: a weekly magazine show that I'd edited for her before and – 'you'll love this, Georgia' – a three-parter on the Troubles, funded by the Broadcasting Commission. I'd heard about that. A prestige project, hyped to the hilt. Drama-reconstruction, lots of archive, a strong editorial line and a rake of interviews from people who'd never talked before. They'd finished logging and were all set to get into the suite. Only then Brid got a call from the editor's girlfriend to say he'd broken his collarbone snowboarding in Austria. Brid had been rationalising like crazy since the recession and had allocated everyone in-house to other projects. At a pinch she could get someone to cover on the magazine, but she needed good eyes – sensitivity, she said – for the series.

She hesitated. 'You know who's directing?'

I twisted the phone cord. 'Yeah.'

A good director but a wanker. Full-on coke habit; nasty reputation for making homophobic comments when he was off his head. So far he'd been alright with me, but then again, so far, I had never cut for him.

'Georgia, there's no worries if—'

Brid's voice was getting distant. I pictured her scrolling down a list on a screen, the highlit names of the freelance and the newly unemployed. A familiar surge of panic; one of those Madden things I've inherited from you. 'Wait. Sixteen weeks?'

At Christmas, I had promised to give myself time. Time to think about doing something new with my life, time to start doing it. I'd taken on no long-term projects since the New Year, but it seemed like all I had managed to achieve was more of the same. The new, whatever it was, had yet to make its presence felt.

'Like I say, Georgia, I can try someone else....' I heard Brid's fingers begin to tap on the keyboard. I thought of the blank notebooks I was supposed to be journaling in, the blanker sketchbook I'd bought the week before on a whim. I thought of the money I still owed for my surgeries; my mounting credit card bill, my shrinking savings, the hole that had been eaten up by Martin's debts.

'If it's the money, Georgia....'

I thought of the day lying ahead, filled with nothing. I thought of the hospital appointment, waiting for me the next morning in Merrion. At the worst, lovely Jessica-the-GP had said, it'll take a week for the results.

What if... a treacherous little voice inside my head began to ask. *What if that's the something new?*

'Okay,' I said. 'I'll do them both.'

What if nothing. If the worst came to the worst, I would cross that bridge, but only if I had to.

We did some haggling and agreed a price. Breakfast meeting Monday. In the meantime she'd send me the scripts for the three-parter so I could get a sense of the stories we'd be putting together.

You know me—

Funny. *You know me,* I was going to say, then realised you don't, you haven't for years. But I wonder what choices I would have made, if I hadn't been so freaked out by the thought of that empty day looming in front of me? *Jesus, Geo*, Mar used to say, *can you no just take it easy?* Jesus, Mar, no, I can't.

I hung up. On the TV, Sky was still on the bombing story. Vox-pops.

We've been focusing on the victims, Brid had said. *The hole that was left in people's lives after, you know, the shit happened.*

Breaking News. More shit happens. A heavy man with a moustache and sallow complexion, essence of London cabbie, was jabbing his finger at the anchorwoman. I read his lips. Vis is facking disgasting. Vis is facking ow of facking awda. Facking Moslims—

But we're giving it a positive spin, how they've managed since, come to terms. You know, all that peace and reconciliation stuff. The viewers will love it. Feelgood.

Sky cut to World News. *Crisis in Eurozone. More Dead in Middle East. North Korea War Threat.* I stared at the screen; the tumbling euro, the khaki tanks rumbling through dust, the demagogue raising his fist.

We got some amazing people, families that moved away. Canada, the States. The stories, Georgia. They'd break your heart.

Back to the cabbie. He was shaking his head now. He looked helpless.

The Troubles. Jesus. Maybe I should have said no. Screw the money. Uneasy again, I glanced at the phone. But it stayed where it was, unmoving, and so did I.

Condensation dribbled down the inside of the window, making melting wax out of the greenery crushed up against the other side of the glass. Since Mar had left, our garden had gone to the dogs. I sat on the loo, listened to myself pee. Out of habit, my hands reached for my belly. It gave way, soft as a marshmallow. I let my palms slide down till they were holding the outer sides of my thighs, the fleshy bits near the hips. That shock, again, of finding things exactly as they were supposed to be. My nose was still blocked; I couldn't smell my scent. All I could smell was the inside of my own head.

That out-of-sorts feeling I'd woken with had got worse. I felt dull and stupid, like I hadn't in ages – weeks, months, years. Worse than in secondary school when everything, including my voice, began to betray me, dropping and spouting and spurting, worse than Berlin, just before I came out, or thought I did, worse even than the worst of the bad times with Martin. It was how I used to feel when I was a child and didn't know what was going on. Troubling, to sense her in me again; lost little girl Georgie.

Such delicate creatures we are, as my friend Sonia says. Hard to remember we're only growing up now.

I blew my nose, stood up, stepped on the scales. I looked at the mirror and the body I was born with looked back at me. The body you helped make, with variations. My belly seemed flatter. Maybe the new diet was working. Or maybe, after all the years, those hormones were finally starting to do their job and shove the fat down to my ass, where it belonged. I squinted; saw a long-legged oblong. Tilted up my chest, sucked in my gut, squinted again; this time, saw a wide-waisted hourglass. Either way, an Amazon.

Against my palm, my left breast was small and soft. I couldn't feel any grit, much less a lump. Had lovely Jessica-the-GP been imagining things?

I stepped into the shower. Water drummed on my head, needled my body. The room filled with steam; little curling shapes frosting on the glass walls of the cabinet. I closed my eyes and willed myself to meet the day.

The day was mean and cold, damp with a nasty bite that wormed up the sleeves of my bathrobe. I regretted not having got dressed first, but I hadn't seen the Invader for a few days and didn't like the thought that something might have happened to him. I rattled the tin.

'Puss?'

He's not mine. I don't know who he belongs to; if he belongs to anyone. He appeared on our back wall a few years ago, just after Mar and I moved to Dublin. We'd brought our own cat with us from Brighton, our little tabby, Jennie, so we couldn't encourage other cats to hang around, even though we did like the Invader. He was bold as brass but friendly; whenever, behind Mar's back, I'd go to stroke him, he'd push his ginger head against my palm with the bouncy confidence of a young lover. Sometimes, for Jennie's sake, I'd try to scare him away with some half-hearted clapping, but he always looked back with such cheery insolence I couldn't follow through. Then Mar took over the border control with a water pistol and that did it.

A month before we split up, Jennie disappeared. We never found out what happened to her. I still pray that she left on purpose because she couldn't stand the arguments, and didn't get herself run over or something. She was a sweet little cat.

A week after Martin left, the Invader turned up again.

He looked terrible. His marmalade coat was sparse, his body a rake. All his cocky bounce had gone. The only thing that hadn't changed were his eyes – a beautiful green-flecked amber. I approached him carefully, hunkering down and holding out a handful of Jennie's biscuits. The illness had brought caution; he gazed at me for ages, tail twitching, before lowering his head and munching. Since then I've fed him regularly and he's begun to fill out again, though he's still a long way from the bouncing Romeo he used to be.

He's your furry baby, Sonia said recently, teasing me.

No, he's not, I said. If he was mine I'd have given him a proper name. She looked surprised and I realised I'd sounded rude. Sorry, sweetheart, I said, remembering your mother. I just don't want to, you know, turn into one of those batty old biddies with a house of cats.

She laughed. No chance of that happening, girl.

I dunno. I shrugged, remembering the twelve years with Martin, the eighteen months since he'd left.

Oh, come on, Georgia. Plenty more fish in the sea.

Who says I want fish?

She laughed again. Then we ordered more wine and the Italian waiter seemed to be flirting with me, but not in a cruisey way, and I looked at Sonia, to be sure I wasn't imagining things, and she nodded and I flirted back, and was surprised by how okay it was, to feel gauche and embarrassed, flattered at the attention, even a bit scared; fourteen again, but not in a bad way. Such delicate creatures we are.

The air was bitter. Goosebumps were coming up on my arms. 'Puss?' I left the Invader's plastic bowl beside the bamboo plant and scurried back indoors.

More Bombs on Underground repeated the cap-gen, though there hadn't been any bombs there since '05. Was Sky up to something; shifting focus, inventing bogeymen? *No group claims responsibility. No figures yet. No names released.* Behind the nodding anchorwoman, the U of the Tube station glowed, nameless. Everybody's mouths were moving, talking about how shocked they were, but they didn't seem shocked. They seemed wild-eyed, elated almost, like they'd won the Lotto; like Mar used to look on a lucky week. I flicked to the Beeb. They were already in Washington, with a reporter on Capitol Hill. I read his lips.

response demanded to this appalling action—

He widened his eyes. An expert interview was on the way. I left the screen and headed upstairs.

As I passed the landing window, something snaked out from the pile of junk lurking there and caught my feet. I stumbled, banging my hip against the banisters. Swearing, I kicked at the snaking thing and limped up the rest of the stairs.

In my room, I unpeeled my towel and examined the damage. There was a mark on my right hipbone, red and tender; it would be a bruise by the following morning. I thought of my endocrinologist and his warnings of osteoporosis.

Begone, sir.

In recent years I've enjoyed getting dressed, but that morning it was hell. Nothing matched, everything was in the wash. I kept dropping stuff, like a leper discarding bits and pieces of themselves. In the end, I settled for something simple. I smoothed my hair with anti-frizz, then did my face, taking care with my make-up. Look after the little things, they say, and the big things will look after themselves.

Have you ever wondered, I asked Sonia once, what you would have looked like, you know, naturally?

She'd shrugged. This is natural, girl.

I looked in the mirror and smiled. What smiled back seemed fine. A little tired. A tad red around the nose and the eyes, and under the foundation, where only I could spot it, the flush of the headcold. Otherwise intact.

I lie. Up close, above the smile, I could see her clearly, little Georgie; the same wary expression that used to look back at me when I was a kid.

Had she been there the last time Jessica-the-GP had given me a warning? I couldn't remember, didn't want to try. My sinuses were killing me.

The Internet connection was slow; too many families bit-torrenting illegal movie downloads, trying to keep the kids happy during the holiday. I turned back to the telly, where the Beeb were holding a panel discussion on what had happened in London. An endless stream of tweets scrolling under the main picture, everyone in the world wanting to have their say. The mediator was that condescending guy with the shark's smile who Mar always hated. The panel was the usual suspects: a couple of British politicians, the obligatory lady in a hijab, a man in a sheik's headdress and another man in his sixties; white, designer stubble, slouching in a Ramones T-shirt and suit jacket. It was Blessed Eoin the Marxist, that old photojournalist who'd been big in the seventies for his portraits of radical youth in hotspot areas. He'd made a recent comeback taking pictures of suicide bombers in Palestine. I pressed the mute button, got sound.

No, Blessed Eoin was saying in his mixed-up Dublin-London accent. *We have a chance today to answer some important questions. Over ten years of bloodshed and rhetoric and nobody's asking why this stuff is happening, much less who it's benefiting. . . .* They cut to a book jacket; his latest coffee-table offering. A photo of a handsome boy with sideburns lobbing a flaming rag at a phalanx of British soldiers. It looked like Belfast.

Unbelievable. One of the politicians, fuming. *People are dying down there and—*

You can't just blanket ban and round up whoever you want, said Eoin. *We're heading towards the same conditions Europe had in the 1930s and—*

He was looking well. Blue eyes; very bright. Off the drink, rumour had it. Tapping into the old outrage seemed to suit him. For a while there'd been some talk that Brid was going to cast him as a presenter for her Troubles series.

Please, said the woman in the hijab. *We have to stop making those sort of comparisons. The important thing is—*

They cut to some pictures of the location. A close-up of the road sign: Turnmill Street. Then a long shot. They had the camera positioned differently to Sky, so I could see the name of the Tube station. Farringdon. It seemed familiar, in an off-kilter way, though I couldn't remember ever being in that part of London.

The Marxist reappeared. Angry now. *Look, if we don't face up to our own part in—*

Christ. More of the same. Blame and recrimination. Nobody with the bottle to say, It's not my fault, I know, but hands up, I still shouldn't have done it. I pressed mute again and flicked to UTV. A woman in Bangor, County Down, had just won the Euromillions. I flicked again, to an Irish channel. A politician was standing outside the GPO, her chest festooned with shamrocks. In the background were flashes of floats, kids in costumes, tiered seating. The politician spoke fast, seriously. I guessed she was commenting on London and trying to express how sorry she was. But she had shamrocks all over her and even without them, her eyes were too bright and elated for sorrow, just like the shocked people milling around the Tube station.

I switched again, chose another Irish channel, the commercial one. Tom and Jerry were chasing each other around a 1950s' living room. Tom had a fish slice in his paw. And for a moment I stopped, suspended in a parallel universe.

Brid's scripts hadn't arrived but my inbox was full of the usual rubbish. Penis extensions, hoax identity checks, Viagra offers, friend requests, Facebook debates on what had happened in London, a rake of new petitions and some stupid *is this sik?* link to what claimed to be a nasty snuff movie posted in the early hours on YouTube. A virus, I assumed, and deleted it. The only interesting thing was an email from Sabine Wiedemann, a director I'd worked with in Berlin during the nineties. She was making a one-off doc about German migrants in postwar Britain and was over in the UK finishing some interviews. She was doing the last one now, three days with an old lady in Wales, originally from Reichenberg, whose son had got involved with the German radical left in the seventies. She'd sent me the email the previous night, before news of the London bomb had broken, and had attached a link to an article from *Die Zeit*. *You may find this interesting.*

I scrolled past the link. I couldn't place Reichenberg, couldn't remember what part of Germany it was in. Maybe it was like the Tube stop where the bomb had gone off; somewhere I only thought I knew.

Sabine wanted to come to Dublin for a few days after she'd finished in Wales. She'd love to see me, hang out a little, catch up, if I was into that? The *hang out* made me smile; Sabine had always loved those American turns of phrase. I clicked Reply.

The screen froze, broke apart, turning Sabine's message into a mish-mash of nonsense. Truncated, overlapping, isolated words, scored through with horizontal lines.

I pressed Return. The screen died. I began to swear—

My phone beeped. *1 message.* An English number I didn't recognise.

So strange, those hardwired connections between sight and thought and action, especially the ones you think you've outgrown. For a moment I thought it might have been Martin. Only a moment, but that's all you need to push a button.

Hooray! said the text. I stared at it blankly. *We're tying the knot!*
Knot?
Afters in The Queen. A date. A time. *RSVP if you can come xxr+b.*
r+b? Who were—
Hard to disentangle, those connections between sight and thought and action. I swore again, properly this time, and then, before I knew what I was doing, I'd flung the phone away from me, as hard as I could.

Ray and Ben were a couple Mar and I had met in Brighton during our last disastrous flirtation with the bear and leather scene, those pressure-cooker years between running away from Berlin and landing in Dublin. Ben was Irish, an ex-Blackrock College boy with a GP practice in a men's clinic; Ray was a Scouser working as a barista in the Lanes who liked the odd flutter on the gee-gees. Martin always told me he'd met Ray in a club, but they might just as easily have hooked up in a bookies or – because Mar had had a handle on things then – at a meeting. Afterwards, Mar said we'd only become friends with them because we had the same queer cross-class vibe going on. Miscegnation. He had a point. But for a while I'd liked them, as much as I could. Ray was sharp and funny and Ben had a sexy big-man thing about him that almost made up for the privileged vowels.

When things started getting strained again, with Martin, with my new business, with my partner, with me, the four of us fell out of contact. One blustery April afternoon – it was a Sunday, I remember – Mar and I went walking on the pier and ran into them. I had dressed up, a little. Mar was working with it. It was before I'd begun to transition formally, so I suppose I was working with it too. To be fair to the boys, they didn't do a double-take, but they did look. I told Mar to walk on. He was on an E-comedown and unmanageable. I can't remember what he said to them, but Ray hummed and hawed as the rain ran down our faces and into our collars and then he said something about people selling out.

Come on, I said.

Martin shook off my hand. Colour was rising in his face. I turned and started walking. Behind me I could hear Mar starting to shout and Ben butting in, saying in his snotty counselling voice that he'd seen this before in Dublin—

This? said Martin. Dublin?

You know, said Ben. I imagined his own meaty face reddening. This type of thing, people wanting to, you know, conform to straight norms because they're not able to handle being gay—

You stupid cunt, that's not the fucking point, shouted Martin. Then there was a thud. Oh, my hero.

Some skateboarders began to clap and hoot. I pulled my collar as high as I could, hiding the lace blouse, and walked faster.

Afterwards, in our beautiful apartment with its view of the sea, I poured myself a drink and watched Martin as he cleaned the graze, put cream on the bruise. His hands were shaking; I was surprised to see mine weren't.

Fucking bufty, he said, more regret than bravado. He held out his hand. The bruise looked obscene amongst his cheffing scars; too fresh, too purple, too raw.

You shouldn't have done that, I said.

19

His head jolted back. I suppose he was hurt but I didn't see that. All I could see was how bloody angry he was, how bloody angry he always was.

Fuck off, Geo. Thought that was the idea of coming here—

The idea?

You can be what you want in Brighton and nobody cares.

Oh. No no no. I shook my head. The *idea*, Mar, was to get away from the shit you dumped us in and for me to be my own boss and make some decent money and you to get your act together and—

And we did. We have. He shook his head, frowning, like I was the stupid one. You're saying we shouldn't have come here.

Ah, don't act the thick, Martin, I wanted to say – even though he was right – but I didn't, instead pressed on, trying to stay calm and reasonable, because someone had to, using the voice that worked with indecisive directors and lying production companies and hard-nosed union techies. No. I'm saying if you say *That's not the point*, you're agreeing with him.

Fuck you mean by that? I nearly broke that bastard's jaw, Geo. Like to see you do that for me.

Don't come over all butch on me, Mar.

Thought you liked that. He started to smile.

I'm trying to say – and that's when my voice rose – that *that's not the point* is not the same as saying *You're talking through your hole, Ben, she's not doing this because she's afraid of being—*

I didn't hesitate. I swear.

Gay? he said. That vein pulsing in his forehead.

We stared at each other.

He grabbed my wrist. For a moment I thought he was going to hurt me, though that was a stupid thing to think because he never had, not that way, and I went to block him. But he pulled me to him instead, pushing my palm against his chest, clamping it there with both his hands. I didn't soften; I didn't uncurl my fingers, but I could feel his heart beating under my skin.

I meant what I said that night, Geo. I know what I'm doing.

On the telly, the commercial channel had cut to O'Connell Street. News round-up. Their stab at the parade. I watched the cameras swoop over the samba bands and the stilt walkers. Frenetic chopping. Too many jump-cuts. Some reporter was getting cheerful sound bites from kids with special needs on a charity float. Their mouths moved, enthusiastic, slow, determined. I could tell the reporter was a cub; he kept interrupting them, trying to finish their sentences.

My phone had survived the fall. Stupid machine; it would probably survive Armageddon. It was in my hand again. I didn't know how it had got there. My chest was tight; my sinuses were aching again. I was finding it hard to breathe.

The TV cut to a new story. A shot from under a bridge, one of the Royal Canal locks. An unfinished apartment block looming up on one side and a dogshit-and-needle-infested walkway on the other. In the background was a humped shape on a stretcher; beside it, a group of uniformed Guards standing around looking young and useless. One of the station's crime reporters was in the foreground; he seemed a little shook. *Body found in canal* said the title. The reporter began to speak, his chin tilting. Up-right, up-left. The reassuring tells of an experienced hack.

Hooray! The gall of them. No salutation, no *hi geo*. I might have been anyone. No mention of the bomb in London. Hadn't they seen the news? Weren't they worried for their friends? Were they so tied up in their personal bullshit that they couldn't give a moment for the bigger picture—

Down-left, down-right. I felt my gaze slip away from the reporter centre-screen, ooze towards the stretcher. A shape under a navy blanket. A limb – an arm, naked, white – had flopped out and the hand was trailing on the ground. It was a man's: bitten nails, marks, what might have been old scars, or maybe tattoos. I tilted my head, peered. Gangland? Long shot. Impossible to make out the details.

I looked back at the text. They'd probably Sent to All, forgotten I was in their fantabuloso contacts. Why hadn't they deleted me the way I'd done them? Maybe they'd stored me under Mar's name. They'd always preferred him. Homosexual intifada, I started calling them after that day on the pier, trying to get at Mar, see how far I could push him. I pressed Delete.

Movement on the TV. A gust of wind picked up a corner of the blanket. A glimpse of shoulder. A black mark on a wiry white neck. Tattoo? The blanket flapped. Up-down. Up. Throat. Head. Hard to see. There was something wrong with the face. Wrong colour. Wrong texture. No—

Skin?

Watershed! The camera swerved before I could see properly, caught the crime guy looking shocked. A jump-cut to the studio. The presenter, confused. A screenshot behind her, the YouTube logo over a night-time shot of something dark and swirling. Then, without warning, another jump and we were back in London. Farringdon. Turnmill Street. Again, that weird sensation of familiarity, though I couldn't recognise the street, couldn't ever remember going there whenever Martin and I had visited—

Britain Crackdown

Was that where he was now, Britain? I'd always assumed he'd gone back to Europe, or maybe stayed here and tried to lay low, but—

My hands were shaking. Somehow my Contacts list had got itself open, right in the middle of the M's. Mar's mobile number was staring at me.

My sinuses throbbed. He couldn't be there. He hated London. And besides….

I should delete him, I thought. No good hanging on to things that don't belong to you. Get rid of it. One tap and—

A sudden crackle of static. I froze. The TV fizzed, cut back to *Tom and Jerry*. Music exploded through the walls; the Wolfe Tones, a rebel classic, courtesy of the Traveller family next door. My chest was hurting again, worse than before. Outside, something flickered. Was someone standing there, near the crossing at the corner? No. Just the light. A breeze had cracked open the clouds above the rooftops, sending a shaft of sunshine down onto the black armour of my neighbour's 4x4.

A momentary blank; old and familiar as my own bones. Then—

Executive decision. But who was executing, I still don't know.

I saw myself, as if from outside my own body. Saw a tall, auburn-haired, well-groomed woman in her mid-forties standing in a very tidy room, smartphone in one hand, remote in another. She seemed oddly paralysed, stuck. Then something gave and she pressed a button and I don't think it was the right one because the pictures on the TV shrank to a point and died.

She moved. I wanted her to stop but she didn't. She half-glanced at a pile of junk in front of a window, picked up something – a coat? – and made towards the door. I wanted to say, No, excuse me, please, leave that behind, that doesn't belong to you—

But I was too sluggish that morning. Too groggy, too slow, too sleepy. Too Georgie. And the woman – me – was already picking up her keys and purse and punching in an alarm code and sweeping out of the house towards a waiting red Fiat, and me, I had no choice but to follow.

Lognote # 1

We start with a dinky little Object which occupies a rather special place in our collection; close to its heart, as it were. At eye-level, a book. A5 format. Bound in card, covered in green fabric. On the front and the spine is gold-embossed lettering in Gothic script.

Schöne Bilder der verlorenen Heimat[1]

For protection, the Object wears a paper dust jacket that, according to some visitors' feedback, has the texture of worn, fine velvet. *Note*: We advise visitors to refrain from handling this Curiosity, unless they feel compelled to by a neurochemical pull which indicates that they have a valid 'connection' (either ethnographic or empathic) with its content.

On the front of the jacket is a black-and-white photograph of a scenic Mittel-European village. On the back, a list of other titles by the publishers. Inside are one hundred and twenty pages; sewn, not glued. The pages have been thumbed but are not dog-eared. In our view, this is a book that someone has held open and gazed at, a book whose pages careful fingers have smoothed, as if stroking the window of a departing train.

The first seven pages are text. After this, each page contains one or more black-and-white photographs which, according to one of our earlier curators, pre-date the Object's publication by at least two decades. There is a pearly, warm cast to the tones of all the photographs, and an elegant, modern, sans-serif cast to the typeface used inside the book, contrasting nicely with the Gothic type on the dust jacket. Each photograph is captioned and all captions include the name of the relevant district in **bold** type.

---

[1] Approx: 'Beautiful Pictures of the lost Homeland' (© Wunderkammer Inc.)

For an inanimate object, this Exhibit feels curiously warm to the touch. Alive, almost. Precious, like the body of a beloved pet, or a child's much-played-with toy. It is possibly, though we don't want to run the risk of being sentimental, a Thing that, like a dead lover's letters, might even have been cried over.

Interpretation

Clearly, this Exhibit is the key to a storehouse. Witness the imagery: mountains, rivers and woods. Small towns. Snowy peaks. Cobbled streets. Spires. Elegant town squares, impressive boulevards. Statues, railway stations. Architecture, sweet as gingerbread. As the photographs are monochrome, visitors are encouraged to imagine the colours: red-tiled roofs, brown thatch, white gables, cream render, tawny sandstone. Patterned Byzantine mosaic. There are some traces of industry; factory and cottage. Women in traditional dress. Tilled lands. Blown glass. Lace and linen. The captions point to unseen mountain treasures; gold, silver, uranium. Cobalt, named for a local goblin.

    <u>Note</u>: There are no photographs of graveyards, defaced or whole, in this Exhibit. Also, the town of Lidice – yes, that Lidice![2] – is not mentioned. A glaring omission, you might think? Is Lidice *not* considered to be part of the disputed region, i.e. the 'lost homeland' evoked by the Exhibit's title? This raises further questions: What is a region? What is a homeland? And who, indeed, has 'lost' it? As a way of continuing the *Wunderkammer* experience, we suggest visitors pose these questions to each other, themselves and/or their children when – or, more accurately, *if* – they get home.

    On the flyleaf you will see three inscriptions:
- *An Fr. Anna Bauer. Mit herzlichen Dank, Ihren J.*[3] [undated]
- *Für meine Tochter. Ein Schätzchen. Alles Liebe, Juni 1976*[4]
- The third dedication, as you can see, is impossible to make out, although some visitors have claimed to identify the shape of a shimmering upper-case 'O'. In our opinion this dedication appears to be the trace-foretelling of a handover which has not yet happened but will, sooner or later, be on the cards.

---

[2] For starters, try http://www.outsideprague.com/lidice/lidice.html
[3] 'To Mrs Anna Bauer, with heartfelt thanks, your [formal] J.'
[4] 'For my daughter. A little treasure. All love, June 1976'

Publication date is not given on the Exhibit itself. However, research indicates that it is probably around 1970, well after the purge has taken place.[5]

Most curious feature

If you put your nose to the pages and smell, you get this:

The bittersweet aroma of pyriodl, the region's cherry jam. The golden warmth of straw. Sweat and secretions. Fear and longing. The metallic taste of rusting ploughshares. The acrid residue of artillery fire. The almond warning of nitroglycerine. The scent of shit. The trace of betrayal. The cheddar-sharp tang of a violated cunt.

Welcome, *meine Damen und Herrn*, to Bohemia!

---

[5] See Introduction: *Man hat uns aus dem Land unserer Väter verjagt*. Literal translation (courtesy *Mutti-Kustosin*/Mummycurator a.k.a. Anna B.): 'One has us out of the land of our fathers hunted down.'

Mermaid

☼

Iris in. An in-camera edit, an old trick. A tiny dot of colour, shouldering away a mass of black. The dot starts pink, blood-and-spit-stained tissue paper, and as it grows takes in a face, hair, reflections, clothes, fingers, background. Scene.

A child is sitting in the back seat of a battered blue Ford Prefect, her cheek pressed against a cool window. A plug of folded tissue paper is in her mouth. Every so often, she takes it out, looks at the bloody wadding, folds it again, and sticks it back into the raw hole where her milk tooth used to be. The tooth itself is in a pocket of her navy corduroy jeans. On her lap is a travel chess set, its magnetic pieces laid out all wrong for a game, no matter how crazy the strategy, but completely right for a made-up story about kings and queens and princesses and knights.

In the front seat is a man, tall, fair, and fine-featured, wearing glasses and a worried expression.

The car is heading west along a narrow road beside a lough; they are skirting the border between Louth and Down, just about to enter the Wild West frontierstown that is Omeath. Ahead of them, past the crotch of the Lough, lies tangled, congested Newry; behind them Carlingford, with its oyster beds and historic castle and pretty harbour and medieval streets, and behind that, lonely Greenore and the grey expanse of the Irish Sea. To their right is Narrow Water and the Mournes, and the North; to their left the Mournes' sisters, the Cooleys, still crowned with trees yet to be butchered in retaliation for the death of Captain Nairac. They've taken a roundabout route, staying in the Republic as long as possible, steering clear of Ravensdale and its roadblocks. The roads are bad, full of potholes. But so far the plan has worked. No soldiers – though once they get past Omeath, they'll be stopped for sure.

For anyone who cares to look out the car window, there is plenty to see: boats chugging into the Lough; cars and armoured trucks speeding out of Warrenpoint, along the far bank of the invisible border that stretches like a humming wire through the water; the flash and whirr of British helicopters; the shining glints that are the Flagstaff towns, Warrenpoint, Rostrevor, Ringmackilroy and Ballymaconaghy; over to the east the golden ruin of Greencastle – *castrum viridis in prostratum* – where on a fine day there are plenty of mussels to be picked from the shore. And lurching up behind all that, the Mournes themselves, their woody flanks green-black like something from a German *Märchen*, bits of fog already beginning to steal out from the trees like wolves.

The two in the car, however, aren't paying much heed to the view. The man is listening to a crackling radio broadcast, a mixture of chat and news. Every so often one of the news stories catches his attention, at which point he twiddles the knob, loses the band and swears under his breath. The child is oblivious. Her attention is torn between the clotting process going on in her mouth and the chess pieces on her board. She takes out the bloody wadding for the umpteenth time, inspects it, pokes inside her mouth, replaces the tissue. Then she sighs and lifts her White Queen. You are Lady Guinevere, she whispers into the Queen's featureless face. You have to be quiet, otherwise the Black Knight will wake up and then there'll be hell to pay. Her voice sounds funny to her own ears; lispy, because of the missing tooth. It is Holy Thursday, Easter 1974. Georgie Madden is so big for her age she looks like a nine-year-old. But she's only seven, three weeks away from her First Holy Communion.

In the rearview, her father's eyes flick away from the road, watch her, then flick back.

Granny and Granda Bell's house is on Ameracam Lane in Cranfield, up from the caravan park and the second last house from the point. It's on the beach, as close to the sea as you can get without actually being in it. It is a well-built old place, like most of the houses up North; two stories high with lovely views front and back. From the front you get the beach and the lighthouse and the Irish Sea, and, down along to the right, bits of the Republic's coastline on the far side of the Lough. From the back, you get the jagged Mournes, where at night you can see cars making their darting way across the mountainy passes, mad Red Rooney from Silent Valley speeding the fastest of all, and, if you're unlucky, you might also spot the strange, green, flickering Binion Light which lures travellers astray. Georgie hasn't seen that yet.

You can't actually view much of the sea from inside the house because of the lace curtains Granny Bell keeps over the windows. Looking at the sea, Granny tells Georgie, makes her feel lonely. That's why she prefers to sit at the back, in the sitting-room where the telly is, and in the kitchen, her warm, fragrant territory.

When they get into Cranfield, it is still bright, in that late spring way just after the clocks have gone forward. A teenage couple are pressed against the seawall, hands everywhere, tongues lunging down each other's throats, but when they see the Ford, they separate, patting their clothes and hair straight. Perhaps David notices this but Georgie has eyes only for the road, the gate, the open door. Granny Bell is already running down the path.

'Come in, come in,' she says as they unpack themselves from the car. 'Are your feet on fire, Georgie? Pins and needles from— Oh my Lord, what happened to your wee face?'

Georgie looks up at her from under a tousled clump of hair. 'I lost a tooth.'

'Well now, isn't that something? Come here and give your Granny an Eskimo kiss.'

Granny lowers her face, touches Georgie's nose with her own, rubs. She smells lovely, of talc and rosewater.

The usual rituals follow. Upstairs first, to the big front bedroom where they leave their things. David doesn't bother unpacking; he'll be driving back to Dublin the next day, so he has just brought an overnight bag. Georgie folds her T-shirts and jumpers in the top drawer, hangs her extra pair of jeans in the wardrobe and places her book on the bedside table. It's *The Turf-Cutter's Donkey* by Patricia Lynch and is a present from her aunts in Clonmel. Georgie would have preferred to bring *The Knights of the Round Table* – an enormous hardback she'd borrowed from the children's library with a lovely picture of a Lady in a Lake on the cover – but Aisling said it was too big and, besides, what would happen if she lost it?

Her bed looks empty without Rupert; she's testing herself to see how she'll do without him. Helen Woods in school says only babies bring their teddies on holidays with them.

In her pocket she can feel the small hardness of her fallen tooth. She wants to ask David if the Tooth Fairy will find it if she puts it under her pillow here or if it's better to wait till she gets home. But he seems distracted, so she decides to leave it where it is. If the Tooth Fairy is any good at her job, she'll know where to find it, jeans pocket or no.

Next stop is the bathroom where they 'freshen up', as Granny puts it. The bathroom is cramped and chilly; it smells of Glade and the toilet brush holder has a ruched skirt, like a ballet dancer. David pours a glass of water and puts some Dettol in it and gets Georgie to swish it around in her mouth. It's painful and makes her gum start bleeding again, but That's the job, old bean, says David. No smoke without fire, eh? which means she has to nod and act brave. Then they go downstairs for tea.

Aisling is Georgie's mother. Her absence drifts over the house like the trace of old perfume. She is at a conference in the Mater Hospital; something very important she couldn't get out of. This is not the first time Georgie has gone up North while her mother has stayed in Dublin. But there is something different about this visit which she can't help noticing. Maybe it's the fact that David has come too, or that Aisling didn't talk much about the conference in the weeks leading up to it, even though it's supposed to be such a big deal. When Granny says something about what a shame our wee girl isn't here, the weather so lovely and all, David shrugs and smiles, in a way that doesn't quite get rid of his distractedness, and says, Well, you know Ash, not so easy keeping her from something once she has her mind set on it.

For tea they have a salad, followed by apple tart and cream. It tastes nice even through the Dettol, and Georgie has second and third helpings of the salad. She would have more tart too except she's too full. After tea they go into the good room at the front of the house. David sips a G&T and Georgie does some drawings while the grown-ups chat.

'So, David, how are things proceeding with the money-lending business?' asks Granda in a wry, jokey tone.

David flushes. 'Oh, well. Not, eh, bad actually. Stops and starts, but you know yourself, sir—'

David's way of calling Granda *sir* is meant as a joke, the same way he calls Georgie *old bean* or *old chap*, like they do in *Dad's Army* – which Georgie doesn't mind, mainly because it's David.

'Aye, well,' says Granda. 'That O Bocalla fellow, he still making enemies? Can't move these days but his face is all over your newspapers.'

David laughs. 'You keep yourself very well informed, sir.'

And they're off, talking about Ó Buachalla, who isn't David's boss because he's an architect, not an engineer, though he sort of is too – your Daddy's hero, Aisling calls him, which annoys David, though Aisling doesn't seem to notice – and Mr Lyons, who's the head of all the engineers in David's firm and *is* David's Boss, and the Bank, which is David's New Project.

Georgie has met Mr Lyons, who is neat and friendly and smells of tobacco and whose first name is Arthur, like the king. She hasn't met Ó Buachalla – he never gets a 'Mister' in front of his name, probably because of his Ó – but because David has talked quite a bit about him and he's always in news stories on the radio, she's come up with her own image of what he looks like. This owes much to the illustrations in *The Knights of the Round Table*, especially the one of the Black Knight guarding the crossroads near Astolat. It's unclear why Georgie has made this association; perhaps it's all the talk of the enemies Ó Buachalla has. But there he is, in Georgie's imagination, wearing dull armour the colour of stormclouds, sitting on top of a blinkered, ebony charger with steam coming out of its nostrils. In the book, you can see Astolat in the distance, a tower with sticking-out ledges which David says is called a ziggurat, and at the crossroads where the Black Knight is waiting, there's a creepy-looking tree behind him, with the heads and legs and arms of his enemies dangling from its branches. In Georgie's version, there are no dismembered body parts, but she has left Ó Buachalla with the tree – and a sword and shield, just in case.

Ó Buachalla is Irish but he went to Germany to design buildings and after that lived in America for nearly eight years before coming back to Dublin. He has a wife who looks inside children's heads, Aisling says, and a little girl who's almost exactly the same age as Georgie – though Aisling didn't know that at first because she only met Ó Buachalla a couple of weeks ago, that night she got sick in the loo after going out to the party with David. Before that, Georgie had asked Aisling to ask David whether Ó Buachalla had any kids, but – surprise surprise – he didn't know, so he had to ask Norma the receptionist and that was how they found out about the daughter. She and her mum are still in America, but they'll be coming to Ireland as soon as Ó Buachalla has got a house for them. Georgie's wish is that maybe she and the girl will become friends, but only if the girl is nice and Ó Buachalla isn't too frightening in person. She hasn't said this out loud, mostly because it sounds like something a baby would say, but also because she doesn't want to annoy Aisling, who's been cross lately. She did ask Aisling what Ó Buachalla was like at the party, but Aisling looked surprised, as if she'd forgotten she'd even met him. Then she laughed, very bright, and gave Georgie a big hug and said, Oh, fine. Which meant boring.

'...what we're trying is new, you know, eh, revolutionary, but a lot of people don't want that in their backyard.'

'Oh, I know. Not me, they say! How about that fellow over there? Try it on him!'

The men laugh.

'People,' says Granda, shaking his head. 'Always so sure a wee bit of distance between themselves and a problem will work wonders—'

'And it does,' says Granny, coming in with a plate of coconut creams. 'Now, can you two men take your complicated conversation out into the fresh air while someone I know fills me in on everything that's going on in school?' She winks at Georgie.

They drink milk and eat coconut creams, which are easier to eat with a gappy mouth than digestives. Granny asks Georgie about school, and how she likes her teachers, and Georgie says she doesn't like Sister Germaine much because she slapped her hand with a ruler, but she loves art, and she shows Granny her drawings, and Granny says, 'My goodness, what's that?' and Georgie tells her it's a mermaid. Granny asks about Georgie's friends, and Georgie tells her about Sinéad Cowen who is what you might call a best pal, and Anne Geraghty who lives two streets away and Helen Woods who only plays with them at lunchtime and the two boys, James and Liam, who are nice and sometimes join in. She doesn't mention Alison O'Meara who lives on the Green and is sometimes mean because Aisling says the best way to treat people like that is ignore them, even though David always gets a bit annoyed if he hears because he thinks you should always stand up to a bully. Then Granny asks if Georgie is all set for the blessed sacrament of her Holy Communion and Georgie says, yes, except for the rosary beads. She doesn't say David's joke about the sacraments, two down, five to go, because Granny doesn't find that sort of thing funny. And she doesn't talk about the Dress, because she knows talking about the Dress is not encouraged and she has no answer for *Who put that notion into your wee head?* and she's figured out by now it's easier if she says nothing. Besides, dresses aren't important, and nor are beads, not compared to other things, like having friends. Granny doesn't ask Georgie if she's looking forward to September, when she'll be moving out of the nuns to big school. Georgie's glad about that.

They watch the telly programme Granny's picked out. It's an adventure story on the BBC, about a boy and girl who find a secret passage behind a wall in a big house in the country. The passage reminds Georgie of the lane that runs down the back of the road she lives on in Dublin, in the way that it's there all along but hard to get to. 'Won't this be a terrific way to send messages,' says the girl in her English voice, 'especially ones we don't want the grown-ups to discover!' Just as she says that, they meet another girl, dressed in old-fashioned clothes, who opens a door and beckons to them. *Come over to my side*, she says. The children take a step – and then the episode ends.

31

At that, Georgie feels cheated. She'll never find out what happens to those children; at home David and Aisling only have RTÉ, the Irish station, and there's never anything good on that.

Upstairs, in the colder part of the house, there are four bedrooms. Granny and Granda have a room each, one at the front and one at the back. The big guest room is at the front, beside Granny's bedroom; and, at the back beside Granda's, looking out onto the mountains, is the lovely room that used to be Aisling's. The Girl's Room, this room was called when Aisling was still living in Cranfield, before she 'flitted away', as Granny puts it, for Dublin and Trinity College and her degree in Medicine and her marriage to David and, eventually, the birth of Georgie. Granny keeps this room beautifully. It's full of pink things. Eiderdown, curtains, lampshades. Georgie usually prefers purple, but these pinks are comforting, and she likes the fact that she's normally put sleeping there, even though it is no longer called the Girl's Room.

Tonight, she's sharing the front room with David. No point in wasting the heat, says Granny. And you'll have the whole big space to yourself after your daddy goes back to Dublin. Won't that be nice?

The double bed is for David and Granny has made up a camp bed for Georgie near the window. That way, she says, you can both get a better sleep. The camp bed is flat, oddly unstable and too close to the floor.

Granny has taken the edge off the chill by putting on a two-bar heater, so getting undressed isn't too uncomfortable. David's bed has an electric blanket – the EB, Aisling calls it – but because EBs aren't safe for children, Georgie has a hot water bottle instead. She clasps it to her belly under the damp weight of the eiderdown and watches the beam of light from the lighthouse push in through the grey curtains and wash across the ceiling, lengthening as the lamp rotates, before disappearing and starting up all over again. There's a rhythm to it, like a dance. Outside, she can hear the wind and the sea whispering to each other. On the bookshelf in the corner, filled with emerald-spined murder mysteries by Agatha Christie and Ngaio Marsh, ticks the pale green alarm clock.

Downstairs, they are laughing about something. The space where Georgie's tooth used to be has started hurting again.

Later, the door opens. Georgie listens to her father pull off his clothes and get into his pyjamas. There is a creak as he sits on the bed. He takes off his glasses and sighs and across the room Georgie smells the minty scent of his toothpaste. Another creak as he gets into bed. A click as he switches off the EB.

'Dad?'

'Mmn?'

It's a sound that says *I'm tired, I don't want to talk.* Georgie gets out of her bed and walks over to his.

'Dad?' She pulls at his blanket.

David groans, a small crackling sound in the back of his throat, but moves over and raises the covers. Georgie crawls inside. The bed is toasty. David puts his arm around her shoulder and gives her a squeeze. Then he shifts away and curls over onto his side, facing the wall. She sticks her thumb in her mouth, making sure to avoid the gap, and listens to him breathe, aware of the warmth of his body inches away from hers. The dip in the middle of the bed, the legacy of thirty summers of visitors, feels comforting, as if she's in a boat, rocking on the ocean.

In the morning, she feels in her cords pocket as soon as she wakes up, but there's no penny there. The Tooth Fairy must prefer to find teeth under pillows. After they've dressed, Granny drives her to the Good Friday service in Massfort church, nestling at the crossroads on the way to Kilkeel. It's not Mass, she tells Georgie. We don't have Mass on Good Friday. We have service. As the priest drones on about Jesus dying on the cross so *we have to live with the consequences of our actions,* and Holy Communion and *not until we face the glory of the Lord will our sins be forgiven blah blah blah,* Georgie stares at the statues shrouded in purple and traces her finger along the names of the dead, engraved into the brass plate on the pew in front of her. Why, she wonders, are some letters always in red?

David hasn't come to the church because he is still asleep. The poor man needs a lie-in with that big drive ahead of him, says Granny. I'm sure he can go to the service when he gets back up to Dublin.

But David won't. David doesn't like church. He always acts too jolly before it's time to go to Mass, whistling under his breath, pretend-happy. Georgie knows it's only pretend because when he whistles like that he makes Aisling's shoulders tight.

Granda Bell never goes to Mass. That's because he is a Protestant. Granny had to get permission from the Pope so she could marry him. Her family were fairly annoyed about it at first – Aisling says people can be funny about things like that – but when they met Granda, they were thrilled. That, Aisling says, was because he's so nice. Granda comes from Derry, which he sometimes calls Londonderry, and Granny is from Annalong, farther north up the coast than Cranfield. They chose to live in Cranfield because it is pretty and beside the sea and reminds them of Newcastle where they met, when Granda was a young doctor staying in the Slieve Donard hotel and Granny was working as a maid there. And because, at the time they married, there were enough southern visitors coming to Cranfield to take the sea air that the town was able to cast a blind eye to a quietly spoken doctor; even if he was a Black Prod, even if he was from Derry and called it Londonderry, even if he was married to a Fenian, and a simple uneducated country Fenian at that.

The tale of how her parents met and married is a favourite of Aisling's, trotted out at family get-togethers, usually after everyone has had too much to drink. Imagine, says Aisling, being so much in love with someone you wouldn't let anything, not even religion or family, stop you from being together. At that she usually looks at David, just as Granny Bell looks at Granda when she tells the story. But unlike Granda, who always looks back at Granny, proud as anything, and keeps looking until the whole table laughs, David just smiles, embarrassed, and changes the subject. Something happens to Aisling's mouth then, twisting it as if she's swallowed a lemon. Blind as a Bat you are, Davey, she says later, in a voice that's drunk and far too loud, when they're in their bedroom and Georgie's supposed to be asleep. Though sometimes Georgie wonders if it's Aisling who's the Bat, because only a Bat wouldn't notice the way David looks at Aisling when there's just the two of them in a room and nobody to be proud in front of.

Breakfast is freshly squeezed orange juice, followed by cornflakes and milk, finishing with soft bread instead of toast, because of Georgie's tooth, and a boiled egg that Granny has timed so it's perfectly tacky – not too soft, not too hard; just right. David has an egg too but his is hard. He prefers them that way. There is an edge to him this morning. His jaw is tight and he's whistling under his breath and his fingers drum out little tunes on the scarred yellow kitchen table. Granda reads his paper and, every so often, glances at David from under his bushy eyebrows.

'Right, troops.' David stands and the sudden movement jolts the table.

At the gate, they say goodbye. David hugs Georgie, hard. She can tell he's trying to be comforting but he feels too jittery for that. He rumples her hair, then stretches out his hand to Granda Bell. 'Goodbye, sir.'

'Safe home, now,' says Granda Bell. His big doctor's hands, veiny and liver-spotted, engulf David's.

David kisses Granny on her soft perfumed cheek. They stand and wave until the Prefect has disappeared around the corner of the road.

Georgie goes out onto the beach, but it's not as warm as it looks and she gets bored being on her own, so she returns to the house and, after asking permission, sits at Granda's desk in his surgery and draws more mermaids. After she got the *Round Table* book from the library, she started copying its illustrations, hoping she could find a way of bringing her mermaids into a different world, not just the grey sea they usually inhabit. So far she hasn't managed it. The *Round Table* copies are fine, but every time she's tried to put a mermaid in them, they look wrong. As for the mermaids, they don't seem to want be anywhere but the sea, and they don't seem to want anything else in the sea with them. Not knights, not castles, not poor lost ladies looking down from towers. Her pencil scratches; grey sea, grey body, grey tails, long grey hair.

Through the walls come thin threads of conversation.

don't see why... come up all the way here... go off like that without saying what's

now, George, don't be

can't ask his sisters to take care

George, hush, please

Georgie frowns and bites her lower lip. This mermaid is a scary one; she has long nails and sharp teeth.

Granny has made a special Good Friday lunch of fish and chips and Georgie eats everything. She's getting used to working around her missing tooth; it's almost easy now. There's no dessert because it's a holy day but she has two Mariettas soaked in milk so she doesn't have to chew. After they've finished, Granny says, 'So pet, why don't you go find wee Adam and Judith? They've been plaguing us for weeks, asking when you're coming.'

Wee Adam and Judith live on a farm – more like a couple of fields, says Granda – out past the caravan parks, near the old airfield that was used in the war that David always calls the Emergency as a joke. Their Daddy's uncle owns most of the caravan parks round Cranfield and, says Granny, is on his way to being a very rich man. Granda Bell calls Judith and Adam a 'real handful'. Only the year before he had to treat them both for the mumps and, Let me tell you, he said to Georgie, it was worse than trying to tie up a litter of kittens in a sack. Georgie didn't like the idea of kittens being tied up in a sack but knew what he meant. Although Judith is two years older than Georgie, she's very approachable. She doesn't call Georgie names and she loves inventing games, not boring ones like hiding, but made-up stories, almost like plays, where everybody has a part and gets to act stuff out. Georgie likes those games, especially the way Judith turns everyday things into magical objects and places. For all his giving out, Granda Bell likes Judith too. She, he says, will 'go far'.

Wee Adam, Judith's brother, is okay.

The air smells of gorse, coconut-sweet and warm, dirt, rain and cow poo. Georgie's wellies squelch through mud. The back of her neck is hot under her yellow mac. Brambles pull at her, blocking her path. She pushes her way through, shoving them out of the way with her elbows, trampling them underfoot where they snap like bones. She likes going along the back path, not just because it's safer than the road, but because, with all the twists and turns and the brambles growing over, she never knows what she's going to meet next. It's like walking into an adventure. She likes it too that she can hear things through the hedgerows – tractors and dogs and sometimes even people chatting about the weather outside their caravans – though they don't realise she's there. It makes her feel as if she's something magic, a sea-creature swimming under a ship with a one-way mirror for its floor.

'Ho there, wee Georgie,' says Judith's dad as she reaches the gate. Judith's dad talks funny, more like Granny Bell than Granda, all up and down and around. Mountainy men farmer-talk, Granda Bell calls it. They all talk like that in Down.

'You looking for Adam?'

Georgie shrugs.

'He's over there yonder with Judith.' He nods towards the back field behind the farmhouse.

Georgie makes her way over, cautious. She doesn't mind the mud or the wet, but she's afraid of the Conynghams' sheepdog, Patch. He's always jumping up at her and barking. In the near field, Judith is riding a pony that Georgie hasn't seen before, while Adam swings himself off and on the gate. A grubby football lies on the ground beside him.

'Ho, Georgie!' Judith's face lights up as she pulls the pony's rope, wheeling him around. 'See what my daddy got me! Isn't he beautiful? His name's Lightning.'

'He's mine too,' shouts Adam.

'Isn't he adorable?'

Georgie draws closer. The pony is tiny and dirty, with a rough white coat and brown eyes yellow at the edges. He seems a bit miserable.

'Georgie, Georgie—' Adam jumps off the gate. A moustache of thick green snot is coating his upper lip. 'Wanna play racing? I'll race you to the end of the yard and back?'

'Eh….'

Judith looks at Georgie.

Georgie shrugs. 'Later?'

'Okay.' Adam wipes his nose with his sleeve. Some of the snot comes away, clumping like a baby slug to the ragged end of his jumper. The rest lingers on his lip, streaked with navy fibres. 'I made a bow and arrow and we can shoot with that. And I got Subbuteo for Christmas. It's magic. We can play—'

Judith snaps her fingers in Adam's face. 'Oh, go away, will you?' He flinches. 'You know Georgie detests football. Go, go. Shoo.' Adam snuffles, hesitates, then picks up his football and begins to do keepy-uppys.

'You want to say hello to the pony, Georgie?' Judith brings the animal closer. 'Go on, get up on the gate and give him a wee caress. That means rub.'

Georgie clambers up the rails. Her fingers brush coarse white-grey hair, a damp velvet muzzle. The pony ducks his head. His legs are trembling

'See, Lightning, Georgie's nice. Now, Georgie, bring your hand in really soft and just leave it there, he won't—'

'And – he – scores!' There's a thud as Adam's ball bounces against the gate, unbalancing Georgie. Lightning jolts, jerking his head.

'Oh for the dear Lord's sake!' Judith wheels around. 'Can you not give me and my friend a moment's respite?' Re-*spite*.

'Georgie's my friend too! That pony's shite.'

'You are in so much trouble, Adam Conyngham! I'll tell mummy you're using bad language – and on Good Friday in front of Georgie which is a bad thing in their church – and she'll wash your beak out with soap.'

'Church is shite! And so are the Fenians, and Good Friday, worst of all! You want to play Subbuteo, Georgie? I bags Man United. I bags Bestie as my striker—'

'Go away!' Judith swipes again. Lightning paws the ground, tugs his head. 'I told you. Georgie doesn't want to play! Do you, Georgie?'

Adam's mouth, slack and open. His eyes protruding, staring at her.

'No,' says Georgie.

Adam blinks. Then he bounces the ball hard at the gate again, and, with a grunt, runs off. Judith shakes her head and smiles. It's a grown-up smile, wise and sad, and the fact it's being shared with Georgie makes her feel quite important.

'Do you want to ride him?'

Lightning's tail twitches.

The wide back of the pony comes to meet her. The world tilts. Beneath her, everything is unstable. Georgie's fingers scrabble, find the rope. Behind a haybarn, she can hear Adam playing, making shooting sounds – *tuff tuff tuff* – as he takes on a horde of imaginary Indians.

'Magic!' shouts Judith. 'Just—'

Somehow, Georgie shifts her weight and the world rights itself.

'Champion!' Judith's face is glowing. She twitches the rope and Lightning begins to walk. Beneath her, Georgie feels the world sway again.

'Easy, boy. See, Georgie, that's a walk, and it's much slower than a trot. It's real gentle so you just sit there. You don't have to do anything, just give him a wee nudge now and then with the rope to show him who's in charge. Think of him as your trusty steed, like the donkey wee baby Jesus met in the manger or – oh, I know—' Judith's eyes gleam '—you and him are joined together, you're the magnificent Two-Headed Centaur, Ruler of the Crevasse, and I'm Scaramouche, your slave.' She lifts her arm, saluting an imaginary crowd. 'Behold, subjects! All hail the Centaur! Wave your arm, Georgie.'

Georgie waves.

'No. More regal.' *Ree*-jal. Judith stops, gasps. 'Oh! See that scurvy vassal?' She is staring at a twisted bush near the hedge. 'That's a foul traitor and he's plotting mayhem.'

Georgie makes an appropriate grunt of dismay.

'We must stop him. Should I smite him with my spear, Majesty?'

'Yeah,' says Georgie. 'Or—' remembering the *Round Table* '—your lance?'

'Oh, aye. A lance. That's good.' Judith shakes her imaginary lance. 'See, your Mightiness, how the coward flees!'

As the play continues, Judith weaves characters and places out of thin air; inventing hazards and obstacles, desperate maidens, threatening foes. Georgie's role is to back up Judith and go along with everything she says – unless, of course, Judith has decided to play an enemy, in which case Georgie has to fire invisible missiles or cast curses, worded by Judith, until the enemy dies, usually horribly and loudly. It's easier than Georgie had thought, to play the game on horseback, the world rocking around her, and as it progresses, a parallel story starts to form in her mind, the account of this adventure she'll tell David when he comes to collect her on Sunday.

'Judy! Judy!' It's Adam.

'Quick!' Judith pulls Lightning and Georgie behind a small tree. 'Duck your head, Majesty!'

Georgie obeys. Her legs have melted into Lightning's body. She can't tell which of them is trembling more. Judith squashes in beside them, shoulders tense.

'Judy, come here!' Adam is starting to sound upset.

Georgie glances at Judith.

'JUUUUU-DITH!'

'Oh . . . sugar!' Judith straightens and—

Phuttt! the make-believe world dissolves. Centaur, Scaramouche, all gone. Leaving only two children, one pony, a dirty field.

'Sorry. I've got to go or he'll plague us all afternoon. Be good now for Georgie, wee Lightning.'

Georgie, peering through the leaves, sees Judith racing across the field, Adam climbing over the gate.

'Get away, you maggot! You'll scare Lightning.'

'Where's Georgie?'

'Gone. Says you're too much of a baby to play with.'

Adam bangs the gate. 'But you promised we'd— Where's Lightning?'

'I lent him to Georgie.'

Adam frowns. 'Daddy said you shouldn't—'

'What do you want, you stupid wee pup?'

'Mummy wants you to help her with ...' He looks around, gives up. 'I'm not a baby. Georgie shouldn't say—'

'Shut up, you!'

Judith shoves Adam over the gate. As she climbs to the top, she glances around. Her mouth moves. For a second, Scaramouche is back. *Careful, my liege. I will return.*

Georgie nods in as Centaur-like a fashion as she can. The two children jump down from the gate and run across the yard, disappearing behind the barn.

Georgie waits. Around her hum the sounds of the farm. Her own breath. Lightning's. The uneven thump of her heart. The bubbling of her blood in her veins. The pony's light footfalls as he shifts under her weight. Farther off, the clamour of the Conynghams – Adam shooting make-believe Indians again, Judith arguing with her mother, their dad calling for Patch. Farther still, across the flat fields and towards the coast, a dull chugging which might be a ferry, the swoosh of cars heading towards the beach, the cries of seagulls, the low rackety buzz of a tractor. Behind her, in the small copse, the uneven cackling song of crows and thrushes.

Lightning takes a step.

'Hush, now,' says Georgie, copying Judith's calm tones. The pony stops. 'Good boy.' Georgie bends to pat him. There is a cracking sound in the bushes behind her. Lightning jerks his head, knocking her off-centre. Her foot twitches, makes contact.

A bend. A crack. A kick. And he's off.

Afterwards, Judith, running to the gate, will say it wasn't her fault, that Lightning wasn't galloping, he was only cantering and any fool could tell the difference and if Georgie had remembered what Judith had taught her, and tugged on the reins instead of yanking them, then he would have slowed down, and besides, it was Adam who'd started everything by frightening the poor beast. And Adam will say it wasn't his fault, he was miles away from them and so what if he was in the field, he wasn't trying to do anything wrong, he just wanted to check that the pony was okay, and anyway, it was Georgie who'd kicked Lightning in the ribs and made him go off like a rocket.

All Georgie will see is harsh greens and greys, shuddering and crashing around her, freeze-frames from a war photographer's camera.

'Good God!' cries a man's voice. 'I told you, Judith Conyngham—'

Something flies past the pony's ears. A ball, red striped yellow. Lightning stops, sending Georgie flying over his head. A second of strange, exhilarating freedom before the crash. Then a whir of navy. Judith, running. 'Lightning, Lightning!'

As Judith grabs the rope and calms the animal, Georgie picks herself up. The world is still spinning. Her jeans are covered in muck, her bum is aching and her eyes are stinging. She orients herself and comes face to face with Adam. He looks scared and guilty and breathless all at the one time, and under that is a hot glint of some confused feeling that she doesn't quite recognise.

'No, no, no,' says Judith's mother, gripping Georgie's arm. 'There's no question of you going back to your Granny in that state. You're in shock, you poor wee thing.' Judith's mother used to be a nurse; that's how she knows about shock.

'And your poor tooth. That's awful, what'll your mummy say?' Georgie opens her mouth to explain that her tooth has nothing to do with Lightning but Judith's mother isn't listening. 'We'll get you a fresh pair of trousers and sort out those grazes and then we'll have some tea. Won't we, Judy?'

Judith's eyes slide away from Georgie and meet her brother's. Adam makes a loud raspberry sound. The two children snigger.

'That's enough of that,' says Judith's mother. 'Why don't you take Georgie and Adam into the barn and have a wee feast there after I've got Georgie cleaned up?'

Judith makes a face.

'Oh, go on. You can have some fun and make up your wee lovers' tiff in peace, away from us grown-ups.'

Adam's clothes are too small for Georgie, so their mother goes into the big bedroom while Georgie waits in Judith's room, looking at the rows of dolls on the top of the wardrobe, the stacks of books beside the bed.

Elinor M. Brent-Dyer.

Enid Blyton.

Noel Streatfeild.

Frances Hodgson Burnett.

Ballet Shoes. Chalet School. First Term at St Clare's. A Little Princess.

Inside Judith's wardrobe hang her clothes. Jeans, blouses, skirts. A red tartan kilt. The lilac gleam of a flower-girl's dress; dry-cleaned and covered with silky, see-through plastic.

The bed is full of stuffed toys. Beside the pillow lurks an ugly-looking doll in a nightie, the sort that has a hard plastic torso and softer plastic limbs and rubbery cheeks that push in if you squeeze them. Queen Bess, this thing is called. Judith *adores* her. *I know she's an odd-looking dolly, but she's my favourite. I'd die if anything happened to her.*

'Oh,' says Judith's mother, coming in, surprising her. 'Are you alright—'

'Uh.' Georgie turns, holding her mac to her chest.

Judith's mother laughs. 'Oh, no. Look at the poor sad wee face.' She sits on the bed and pulls Georgie close. 'Now between you and me, none of that palaver out there was any of your fault, so you're not to take on. A lot of what my wee girl says is rubbish, so it is. I'd never forgive myself if your Granny thought coming here was making you sad. She's an awful kind person and has never done anything bad on anyone round here, no matter what people say.' She rumples Georgie's hair, then stands up. 'Look what I have for you.'

41

She's brought out a pair of the dad's jeans, turned up at the ends with a tie through the belt hooks so they won't fall off. Georgie puts them on and looks at herself in the mirror. She looks ridiculous with her puffed-out face and red nose and gappy mouth; she looks like a silly fat clown from the circus, the one that's always first to fall out of the broken-down car.

'Aren't you handsome, with your daddy's lovely eyes? Now, go on with you. Put a smile on that sweet face and don't take any more guff from my weans.'

The haybarn has a rusting corrugated roof and it's nearly empty because almost all the straw has been used up feeding the animals. Judith has laid a check cloth over the remaining bales. On it she's placed biscuits, cake, sandwiches and a flask full of hot sweet tea which, Judith's mother says, is the very best thing for shock. Judith digs in her anorak pocket and takes out a packet of what looks like butter.

What's that? Georgie wants to ask, but doesn't.

Judith unwraps the package and a strange smell, oily and sweet, drifts up into Georgie's nostrils.

'Is that marzipan?' says Adam.

Judith smiles sweetly. 'Aye, wee boy.'

Adam's tongue slips out, moistens his upper lip.

Judith lifts the bar to her mouth and nibbles a corner. 'I *adore* marzipan, Adam. Don't I? It's my weakness. I could eat it for ever. Only then I'd be as fat as a house.'

Adam glances at Georgie and makes a rough snorting sound, halfway between a laugh and a sneeze.

Georgie looks at Judith, trying to work out whether an insult was intended. But Judith is still nibbling at the marzipan and doesn't seem aware of what she's said, so, unsure, Georgie helps herself to a fairy cake. She moves a little bit away from the Conynghams, but not so much as to make it obvious, and chews as slowly as she can, trying to imagine that she is on her own, far far away, with knees that aren't hurting from a fall. She is in Astolat, with the lovely Lady Guinevere, in the upper storey of a ziggurat, and outside, at a creepy crossroads, the Black Knight Ó Buachalla is using his sword to fight enemies with the faces of Judith and Adam, a fight that has nothing whatsoever to do with her. Whoosh. A head falls. Whoosh. A leg. The enemies gasp and splutter, die horribly. She swallows the last of the fairy cake, helps herself to a second. Through the stiff fabric of her mac pocket, she feels plastic, some hard, some soft, rub against her leg with every movement she makes.

'Adam!' calls Judith. 'Come up here beside me.'

Adam drops the pitchfork he's been banging against the side of the barn and clambers up beside his sister. Georgie looks at the space between them and is not sure what she feels.

'Okay.' Judith touches the tip of her brother's nose. 'This is the story of the ghostly green Binion Light and where it came from.'

Georgie shifts her weight. Her belly aches; too many fairy cakes.

'Now, you know the mountains past Silent Valley, near that big gap you can see from the back of our house where Mad Red Rooney goes speeding round late at night? Well, once upon a time there was this woman who lived there. She had a wee infant child who she loved more than anything else in the world. But one morning, she woke up to find it sick. What'll I do? she said. The wee baby wasn't baptised and the minister was away up in Kilkeel, so she was in mortal terror for its soul. She went around knocking on all the doors, begging the mountain people to help. One man told her to dip the baby crosswise under a donkey. Another told her to tie a red scarf around the infant's neck and that would keep the plague away. But nobody let her indoors because they were terrified of the sickness. Then word came from the minister there was plague in Kilkeel too, so he wouldn't be home for a week. So out of desperation thon woman came down out of the mountains, and the first place she got to was the Fenian Church at the Massfort crossroads. But the priest there wouldn't let her in. Go to the sea, he said. Find your own kind there. She put the child on her back and came out here, to Cranfield, and one by one, knocked on the doors. Still nobody would help her; not her own kind, because they couldn't, and not the Fenians, because they wouldn't. Each night she slept in ditches, and out on the rocks on the beach, and the child tormented her with its crying, its voice getting softer and softer....' Judith's own voice lowers. 'Until one night she crawled into a haybarn and slept there, and that night, the wee child didn't cry at all. And when the woman woke the next morning, she found it lying dead, cold and blue beside her.'

Adam whimpers.

'Ssh! It's not over.' Judith's voice is a whisper now. 'The poor woman cursed those who hadn't helped, oh, she wished them ill, and the very next evening, she herself was found dead. In this very haybarn. Hanging from—' Judith's eyes scan the barn '—yon length of wood up there.'

Georgie glances at the thick beam across the roof. She knows it's just a story, but she still can't help feeling scared.

'They say she chose this place to die in because it was the last farm where she'd sought help. When the farmer saw her hanging here, oh, how he yammered, oh, how he wished he hadn't done that deed. He could feel that curse coming on him and his family and he knew he had to get it off him. So he took her body across the water to the South so she wouldn't be able to curse this side of the Lough. And that night, he and his Fenian family buried her way up in the hills over Carlingford, in a ditch, and that's why it's called Long Woman's Grave. But…' Judith turns her gaze, green as the sea, on Georgie. 'You know as well as I that you can't get rid of things that easy. For just before she hanged herself, she'd buried the baby's rattle right under this haybarn, and that's why it's here she continues to roam.'

'That's rubbish.' Adam's eyes are wide with fear. 'There's no ghosts in this barn.'

'Unfortunately, there is.' Judith's gaze leaves Georgie. 'The only reason I never told you, Adam, was because our mummy doesn't want you wetting the bed.'

'I don't—' starts Adam, outraged.

'I take it back! I'm only joking!' She grabs Adam and kisses the top of his head. 'What about you?' She doesn't look at Georgie. 'Do you think my story's rubbish?'

Georgie shrugs.

'What's that mean?' Before Georgie can answer, Judith laughs. 'Och, don't be such a baby, Georgie! It's only a wee ghost doesn't mean anyone any harm. A poor mummy who lost her child. Nothing to be scared of – cross my heart and hope to die. Anyway, she only haunts full Fenians, like thon farmer, but your granddaddy's one of the saved, so you'll be alright.'

Adam sniggers.

'Get off me, you pest.' Judith pushes him away and pats the straw beside her. 'Come here, Georgie.'

'But what about the Binion Light?' Adam starts to whine. 'You said—'

'Shut up. That's only a wee tale. Come on, Georgie.'

Georgie hesitates, then obeys. Judith picks up a piece of straw and breaks it in two. 'Here. That's a compact between us.' Unsure, Georgie takes the straw. It feels strong and clean and dry. 'When did you lose that tooth? You look adorable, so you do, with your wee gappy mouth. When are you going on your summer holidays?'

Adam bangs the side of the barn. 'When are you going on—'

'I said shut up!' Judith picks up something hard and throws it, ignoring her brother's yelp. 'We're going down South at the end of the month. To Monaghan, for my great-auntie's birthday. She's ninety.'

Georgie turns the straw in her hand. 'Dad says we're going to Greece. It's a surprise for Mum. I had to promise not to tell. She has a friend there and—'

'Gree-eece,' sneers Adam. 'Greasy, greasy—'

'Shut up, Adam! Greece? Oh my dear goodness! That's exciting. I'd love to go to Greece. I *am* going to Greece. I'll go next year, so I will. I bet you my mummy has a friend there too.' Judith turns over onto her front and props herself up on her elbows. 'Can you eat marzipan with that tooth, Georgie?'

'I want some—' starts Adam.

'Buzz off, you pest!'

Adam glares, then retreats, banging on the barn walls all the way down.

Georgie opens her mouth. She feels a grainy, crumbly texture land on her tongue; behind it the hard tips of Judith's fingers.

'Nice?'

The marzipan tastes like it smells. Sweaty, sweet and not in a good way. Georgie nods.

Judith's finger slides along the top of Georgie's teeth, stops at the gap. 'Nice?'

Georgie's throat tightens. She nods again.

The finger descends, touches the open wound. Saliva floods Georgie's mouth.

'Euw!' Judith's finger retracts. 'Go on, swallow. I've a ton more here.'

Georgie swallows. And again, bit by sweet crumbling bit, as Judith feeds her marzipan, and somehow the spit and the sugar help her wound to clot, and Judith talks, about Greece and her great-auntie's party and the secret hideaway which she and Georgie will build together on a Greek island, away from everyone else, because they're best friends, and always will be, till the day they die, like the sisters in *Little Women*, and the rain starts to fall, drumming on the corrugated roof, and at some point they stop hearing Adam banging on the barn, and a wind blows up over the Lough, ripe with the scent of seaweed, and Georgie's face grows red from eating too much fat and sugar and her belly tightens and her empty gum is throbbing and her nose burning with the cloying smell of almonds, but that's alright, because she's with Judith.

'Ho, Judy,' calls their dad from outside. 'Need some help here.'

Judith scrambles up. 'Coming! See you soon, Georgie!'

Georgie waits for a few minutes till she's sure Judith's gone. Then she lifts her leg and lets out a long, bubbling fart. It smells horrible. She zips up her mac and climbs down the haystack. As she jumps to the ground, there is a sudden shiver of light – lightning, somewhere off the coast – and she sees a dark silhouette at the edge of the barn. Fear sends her heart pounding. Thunder cracks. Her eyes settle. She's looking at Adam. His nose is running, a fresh translucent stream, and in his eyes is the same spark she saw earlier, after the fall, but now it's cold instead of hot, and no longer quite so confused.

'You're stupid,' he says. 'I'm never going to let you play with my Subbuteo or my bow and arrow ever again. You're a stupid fat—'

Georgie stares.

Adam's tongue darts, searching for the word. His fist twitches.

Georgie pulls up her hood and pushes past him, her face burning. Violence hums between them, a telephone wire of missed opportunity.

She goes home the short way, by the road. She's not afraid or anything. It's just it'll be faster that way, the short way, by the road.

'Oh, my, that's a brute of a night,' says Granny. 'A bad one to be out on the boats.'

On the news, someone has been killed. Granda coughs and shakes his head. 'The things people do. How can anyone put that behind them?' Georgie's gum is aching.

At nine, Granny makes Georgie cocoa; Fry's, with the sugar added separately. She winks at Georgie. 'Now, there's a wee surprise in your suitcase that I think the Tooth Fairy might have had something to do with.' Georgie feels suddenly sick.

'Och, it's nothing to be worried about, wee Georgie. She came by while you were out playing and told me she didn't want to leave it under your pillow because it's a special present to do with your Holy Communion and you're not to look at it till you get back home.'

Georgie tries a smile. It seems to work because Granny laughs and tousles her hair before giving her an Eskimo kiss.

The ceiling brightens, darkens, jittery with lightning. The eiderdown presses down on Georgie's chest, clammy and heavy. The two-bar heater was on earlier, but the room is cold again, the air damp and tasting of salt. Outside, the wind is wild. The sea crashes, ragged, like a fit of sneezing.

Ah-choo.

Ah-choo.

If I die before I wake, I pray the Lord my soul to take.

Georgie's knees are still throbbing from the fall and her stomach feels too full, like a balloon filled with poison gas. She wants to pee but Granny Bell forgot to put a potty under the bed and she doesn't want go down those dark stairs to the bathroom on the next landing. She wishes David was still in the big bed on the other side of the room, so she could crawl in and lie beside him. She wishes Aisling was there too and she and David were getting on like a house on fire, the way they do after they've been to a party, David putting on silly voices of people and Aisling laughing, fit to burst. She wishes, more than anything, that she was at home, in her own bed, with the loo just beside her bedroom.

The windows rattle. Downstairs, the phone rings: once, twice, three times, then someone – Georgie can't tell who – answers it. A door closes; the phone conversation disappears. Underneath Georgie's bed, a scratching sound begins; light, barely audible.

Georgie clenches her jaw and stares at the ceiling. There's a crack in the plasterwork she hasn't noticed before. It's a twisty shape, like a thin, broken river with smaller rivers, almost like spiderwebs, coming out of it. There is something mesmerising about it, creepily familiar – as if it means something, but she doesn't know what. The thing to do when you're scared is what Aisling told her to do when she's having a bad dream; you say, in the middle of your dream, I'm dreaming. Then you imagine yourself doing something happy and the bad thing stops. It takes practice, says Aisling, like riding a bike, but once you get the hang of it, you can do it whenever you need. Right now, the bad stuff Georgie is trying not to think about is that poor dead baby in Judith's story, the one who died only a few days old, without being baptised and with its rattle buried under the barn. I'm dreaming, she says, quiet, and tries to imagine herself doing something happy, like getting money from everyone for her Holy Communion, and that works for a while. But then she starts thinking about the rosary beads left by the so-called Tooth Fairy, lying in her suitcase beside the thing she took from Judith's bedroom, the rosary beads which weren't left by the Tooth Fairy at all, because the real Tooth Fairy knows who Georgie is and what she wants, and what Georgie wants is rosary beads like the ones Aisling has had since she was a wee girl, pearly and silver with a picture of someone that looks like a princess at the centre, not one that shows a little boy with short hair and a blazer instead.

I'm dreaming, she says again, this time in her head.

Light begins to creep in from outside, the slow, reassuring sweep of the lighthouse. Except—

Something's wrong. The light is the wrong colour. It's green and shuddery, like something alive, and when the beam from the lighthouse sweeps out of the room, instead of going with it, the green one stays. Georgie tries to say, *I'm dreaming* again, but the green light doesn't listen. Because it's the Binion Light, the light that lures travellers to their doom, and it doesn't matter that it should be shining in through the back window, not the front, because it's not just a wee tale, no matter what Judith says. It's the ghost of that poor dead baby from the story, and more; it's the ghost of all poor babies who die without the sacraments and never get their Holy Communion, and it's coming for Georgie because it's sick of being in Limbo, which Judith doesn't believe in because she's a Protestant, but which Granny Bell has told Georgie is where all the babies without the sacraments end up.

The wind rattles. The air gets colder. The scratching sound under the bed is back; the room is filling with a green mist. Georgie scrunches her eyes shut and tries to summon the Black Knight and – yes! he comes into her mind, and she realises she should have thought of him much earlier, when she was looking for a happy thought, instead of her stupid Holy Communion and the rosary beads and the thing she took from Judith lying under her bed. But instead of comforting her, the Black Knight is staring at her from the back of his horse, staring from the middle of his creepy crossroads, as if she's done something terribly, terribly wrong.

Thunder bangs. Georgie whimpers. Her nostrils fill with the stink of almonds. The scratching starts to tear through the mattress. Georgie's bladder strains. Lightning flashes; the jagged afterimage of the crack on the ceiling sharpens against her retina.

And it's then she feels them, coming for her – babies, lots of babies, in old-fashioned dresses. She grinds her eyes shut but it's no use; she can feel them in the clammy air of the room, floating towards her, their yellowy-green hair brushing against her, their eyes black hollows, their fingers reaching, dank on her skin. The crack hums. Something jumps onto her lip.

Georgie's eyes pop open. She starts to scream and three things happen: she swallows a spider, she coughs, she wets the bed. And in that spurt of shame as her bladder releases, she understands what the crack in the ceiling is. It is death, her own creepy crossroads, an ugly black rip in the grey grey grey of life, waiting for her at the end of each and every spidery, shrinking path.

She gasps and, with an effort, sucks everything back in. The pee stops.

The dip in the middle of the big bed is cold without David, but she can get traces of his smell from the pillow and that's almost as reassuring. Teeth chattering, she pulls the sheet over her head. Sleep is yawning over her, insatiable as the sea. As she slides under, a brief spark flickers; a memory of the Black Knight, staring at her. What was it he was trying to….

say

Too late.

Her head drops. She's unaware as her thumb creeps into her mouth, her mouth begins to suck. While under her bed gleam watchful plastic eyes, in an ugly, rubbery head.

Lognote # 2

This Curiosity is, in fact, not singular, but several: a sequence of Maps. Some include topographical details, while others don't. Like the Curiosity described in *Lognote # 1*, they are well-worn, though, unlike the first Exhibit, they appear to have been roughly handled. Brown with the spit of centuries of disputation, their edges are ragged and, in some cases, missing.

Most curious feature

Where to start? These maps are full of *Sonderheiten* (unusualities); sounds and textures emanate from them, little figures and hyperlinks are embedded in their weave. Some of them even smell. However, we suggest the following activity for truly curious visitors: lay the maps on top of one another and the only thing that will remain the same is the distant coastline, uneven and jumpy. While we urge you to immerse yourselves in them, please take care; as our staff know all too well, some of these little Objects have been known to swallow entire populations whole!

Map One: date?

A ragged bowl, jagged on the edges. This map is the *Ur-Karte*, the original of the species; short on political borderlines, heavy on topographical features. Visitors are alerted to, in no particular order:
- the mountainy rim, useful for defence and natural resources
- rivers, essential for transport and communication
- a central plain, good for farming

Across the centre, someone has scrawled 'citadel' or 'cauldron'.[1] The map also contains traces of dyed fabric and tufts of hair; these have been identified as mummified relics of the Boii, the Germano-Celtic tribe who first settled the region and gave it their name.[2] Note also the fabric, similar to stretched vellum, that the map is made from. This appears in all the maps in the *Lost and Found Art Museum* and appears to have been left by another German tribe, the Marcomanni. DNA testing by our experts shows that this material shares the same genetic markers as human skin.

Map Two: c. 500 AD

Is this a second map, or simply a variation on the first? We draw your attention to the north-west edges of the region – the 'Sudetes' mountain range – where blurred lines have appeared. These are undefined in colour and hazy, as if caught in motion. The Marcomanni and their heirs, the Germanic Quadi, have departed west to Bavaria, leaving the region free for the Slavs (Czechs), who move in.

Map Three: c. 800–900 AD

The *Kunstkammer* staff would like to alert visitors to the sudden appearance of dotted black lines extending the charted area to the north and east. The region (which we will henceforth refer to as 'Bohemia') has now become part of a large Slavic state – Great Moravia. The upper edges of the map are torn, and reddish-brown stains are smeared across the borderlines. (? / **alert** ! /— Oops! One of our curatorial systems has been disturbed. Move away, please, and don't touch these smears, though younger visitors can entertain themselves by trying to guess the nature of this substance; we've had some interesting answers over the years! A cloud of green-and-red-striped warpaint to the east indicates the imminent arrival of the Magyars, who will split Great Moravia, pushing out the Czechs and taking over 'Slovakia'.

Map Four: 1000 AD

Following the Magyars' triumph, the mapped region has shrunk. It now resembles the shape of a slightly flattened human heart, defended by heavy

---

[1] Of, we infer, Europe.

[2] 'First', according to some sources only, c.f., Wiskemann, *Czechs and Germans* (Oxford: 1938).

black lines. Holy St Wenceslas,[3] King of Bohemia and Moravia, has set up Prague as a bishopric of the German branch of the Roman Church under Mainz![4]

Hurrah! Or (depending on your outlook) *Boo!*

Intermission – a shadow-play

Such a kerfuffle! Visitors, note the multiplicity of entrances and exits as, during the first three centuries of the new millennium, the Kingdom of Bohemia is consolidated and the *Wunderkammer's* Key Curiosity, the region's 'Identity', is formed, reshaped, merged and tempered. In a flurry of dangerous liaisons, Czech nobles are marrying German princesses, forming the 'transethnic'[5] Přemyslid dynasty. Listen to that babble – Bohemian towns are bustling with German merchants! And as if that wasn't enough, King Ottakar II, Wenceslas's descendant, has invited German settlers[6] – farmers, miners, craftsmen and artists – to come over the borders to live there, so adding to his (already considerable) wealth and status. What a stroke of genius!

In 1306, the Přemyslides die out, and are replaced by the Luxemburgs.

Map Five: 1330s

Heavy lines appear (red-white-blue mixed with black-gold-red), extending the region to the east. Poland has ceded the strongly German Silesia to Bohemia. Pay particular attention to the mysterious gleam coating these new borderlines. This gleam, which some visitors have called a 'glamour' (though the staff of the *Kunstraum* are reluctant to endorse any suggestion that magic exists) is often referred to as the 'mystical unity of the Wenceslas lands', the right of Bohemia,

---

[3] Yes! He of '*on the Feast of Stephen … poor man … gathering fuel*' etc.

[4] See Everywhere: Divine Right of Kings as justification of ownership/control of property/land/resources/people.

[5] We are aware that 'transethnic' is a rather woolly term and might not even exist, but in the absence of anything more precise, we suggest it will do.

[6] We would like to remind visitors that the Germans invited by Ottokar are not from 'Germany' (that notion/nation doesn't exist yet), but from the principalities of Saxony, Bavaria and Upper Silesia. However, it is important to admit the existence, at that time, of the rather looser concept of 'Germania' (*Deutschlände*, roughly translated as 'lands of the German-speakers').

Moravia and Silesia to be united as one state.[7] Future Czechs will call on this historical 'fact' when claiming the territory as theirs. For now, however, please note that the Czech nobility remains 'Czech' not by resisting the German influence, but by partially absorbing it.[8]

Map Six: 1340s–1500

Exciting! This map is distinguished by a web of multicoloured lines, sprawling in a rather tentacle-ish fashion across central Europe. The Luxemburgish Charles has become Holy Roman Emperor of the German Nation, with Prague as his capital!

Hurrah!

One curator has described Map Six as the 'cultural high-point' of the Bohemian *Wunderspiel* and, indeed, younger visitors have remarked on an exciting 'fizz' emanating from it, similar to the tickle of sherbet. Some visitors have also noticed a rather sour scent when approaching this Exhibit. For an explanation, we suggest taking a closer look at the reverse of the map: on its edges you will see residues of three distinct mould cultures. These have been identified by our *Wissenschaftsabteilung* as sauerkraut, camembert and beer (of German, French and Czech origin, respectively), which have combined chemically at the centre; *voilà* – 'fizz'! However, the *Theatre of Selected Memory* would like to remind visitors that in all chemical reactions, something has to dissolve so something else can sparkle. In this case, the dissolving/diminishing element appears to be Slavic/Czech privilege, while the Germans, educated and wealthy, get to glitter.[9]

Observant guests will see a tiny stick figure near the town of Husinec/ Hussinetz[10] at the southern border. This is a 'mini-me' of Jan Hus, Protestant Reformer and Czech Revolutionary![11] Under the microscope, the figure

---

[7] a.k.a. '*Staatsrecht*' (State's Right).

[8] For comparison, see Ireland: Fitzgerald, Garret Mór, and the Norman invasion. Catchphrase: 'More Irish than the Irish themselves.'

[9] We ask: What about poor and uneducated Bohemian Germans? Do they get to glitter too?

[10] For more about confusing Bohemian town names, see *Lognote # 5*.

[11] To avoid confusion, it may be useful for visitors to view the Hussite Revolution as both an expression of Protestant identity *and* a marker of Czechness, not one or the other. See Ireland (and lots of Other Places): conflation of national/ethnic and religious identity. See also Ireland: the refusal of some Anglo-Irish nobility to Protestantise under the Tudors as a statement of independence. See also, for contrast, Ireland: Butler, James a.k.a. 'Proddy turncoat'.

clearly has two faces: that regarding the Czech name for his hometown is heroic, while the face observing the German spelling has a more brutal aspect. One man's freedom fighter is another man's terrorist? We apologise for the cliché, but do remind visitors that most clichés have a kernel of truth in them.[12]

Moving on!

This map is noted for its many spatters, oozes and pools of that strange reddish-brown substance indicated earlier (??! / **curator alert ! /**— Keep your distance, please, visitors! Suffice to say, the baby-golem of Hus is drenched in it and also significantly charred. Now, quickly, bring your attention to the border regions, particularly the towns of Saaz, Aussig, Leitmeritz, Komotau and Budweis. Our *Vorsprungdurchtechnikstaffel* has embedded a hyperlink in each of these towns: click to replay how, during the Hussite Revolution, the population, as if by magic, transforms from German to Czech![13]

Many visitors have remarked that the map smells less sour the longer they look at it. Perhaps this is owing to the influence of the tiny coin-stamp of Martin Luther's head, just inside the north-western border – reflecting the Protestantisation of many Bohemian Germans and the resultant calming of national/ethnic/sectarian tensions.

Warning: Before observing the next map, we urge visitors to don protective clothing: flak jackets, shields, kneepads and face-masks are available at any Time from our Staff.

Map Seven: 1500–1618

The boundaries to the south, east and west have been rubbed out, replaced with new lines of a startling red-white-red stripage. The (Catholic) Ferdinand of Habsburg has been elected King of Bohemia!

Hurrah! / Boo!

To the distant east a hazy golden crescent is visible. Is bringing in a Habsburg a strategic choice, allowing Bohemia to muscle up against the

---

[12] For more on this, see West Germany and Ireland: 1970s (ancillary activity), 'Blessed' Eoin; the *Ohne Titel/Untitled* collection of Andreas Bauer und Sybille Henkel; also the 'Newspaper Statement', June 1975. See also London, 201— [***error**/circular reference – footnote corrupted]

[13] What, you may well ask, happened to the Germans who used to live in these towns?

Turks? If so, beware. As all schoolboys know, every protection racket has its price. Indeed, hyperlinks reveal that, under Ferdinand, the royal administration is rapidly becoming more German and, significantly, more land is also falling into German hands.[14] Whatever way one looks at it, it's disaster for the Czechs! Some visitors have been known to cover their ears owing to the rather relentless refrain playing over this map ('*Let German be spoken in Germany*[15] *but Czech in our country*' for those who want to sing along).

<u>*Warning*</u>: *We alert visitors to the two flashing red buttons under this map.*

1. The button labelled '1615' refers to the banning by the Bohemian Diet of anyone who cannot speak Czech from acquiring Bohemian land. If incautious visitors press this, the refrain mentioned above will play at a deafening volume.
2. The second button is altogether more dangerous. Labelled '1618', it refers to the forcible election of a Habsburg to the throne of Bohemia. Press this button *only at your hazard* and only if you want to relive the following horrific events in detail:
   • the Defenestration of Prag/Praha[16]
   • the execution of the twenty-seven Czech Martyrs responsible for same
   • the humiliating defeat of the Bohemian nobility at the Battle of White Mountain[17]
   • the ensuing and rather bloody (?!— **alert! alert!** / *[curator kinaesthesis (flicker) triggered by concept of 'blood' /]* Thirty Years **sad-face icon** War

<u>*Note*</u>: We apologise for that momentary Glitch, visitors, and will be taking a short *Pause*/Rest from the Maps Cycle to allow our technical team to attend to the problem. In the meantime, we offer you some conundra:

---

[14] Technically, the 'Germans' getting their mitts on the resources of the region include both *Böhmendeutsch* (Bohemian Germans who have lived in the region for years) and *Auslandsdeutsch* ('foreign' Germans, fresh from German provinces like Bavaria and Saxony or, predominantly, from *Österreich* – Ferdinand's turf, a.k.a. 'Austria').

[15] Even though, as we have seen, there is no unified 'Germany' yet, and besides, isn't it Austria posing the threat? See Hitler, A., for later comparison.

[16] At which two Catholic governors were thrown from a window; surviving, according to some apocryphal sources, by landing on a pile of Bullshit. For contrast, see *Mutti-Kustosin/* Mummycurator: tales of Wonderland, Dumpty, H.

[17] For parallels, see Ireland: Battle of Kinsale and (later) Flight of the Earls.

The Battle of White Mountain (or BWM, as we in the *Wonder Gallery* affectionately call it) has often been seen as the 'defining' birth moment of Czech/German hostility. Here's some teasers for younger visitors:

1. Birth moment? Really?
2. Cause or effect? Chicken or egg?
3. Speaking of eggs, a much-loved and familiar query: How *did* Humpty Dumpty fall?

Deformation

The lights are getting dimmer again, the tunnel shrinking around him as he creeps forward on his belly. Around the next bend, he thinks, like he always does, that he'll see something. But there's nothing; there never is. No silhouettes of Paddy's motorbikes meshed with their riders into bionic centaurs. No sidekicks crouching behind them, trapping the tripod to keep the drill steady, their shadows shuddering as they hack away at the mountain's innards. No signs of the dead or wounded either. Even the broken rocks and twisted scraps of metal prodding into his flesh as he crawls forward are invisible.

He keeps expecting to hear sounds: generators, water, steam, shovels, dynamite, locomotives, the ganger shouting and, thumping over everything else, the bassline melody of the tunnel, the bone-jolting clack-clack-clack of the drill. His ears are crying out for noise but they're getting nothing. This isn't quiet, but absolute stillness. Does that mean he's in a vacuum? Or have his ears packed up on him? Does he even have ears?

He wakes at the usual point, just as the lights are about to go off completely and the tunnel contracts to a singularity – that moment where, Brother Sheridan used to say, one thing turns to another and you don't know what the hell you're looking at. As usual, he doesn't know if he has made himself wake, terrified of what the blackness might bring, or whether the blackness itself is the waking moment. Some night, he thinks, like he often does, his heart will speed up so fast with the fear that he'll frighten himself to death down there. An awful fate; to be stuck in nothingness, no way out.

He used to find himself shouting when he woke. Curses, sometimes; but usually no words, just formless animal noises, half-roar, half-groan. In the early days of their marriage, the sound would often wake Aisling. Davey? she'd say, drowsy, reaching for him. It's alright, he'd say. Just a dream. The same one? she'd ask, though he'd never told her about it, not properly. He'd grunt a yes. My poor boy, she'd say, and pull him towards her.

When Georgie was born, he stopped the yelling. Not consciously. It just happened, as if fatherhood had its own intelligence; a way, like motherhood, of claiming your body for itself. Some days, he would wake to find Aisling still asleep, curled into him, exhausted from a night feed. How, he'd wonder stupidly, could anyone sleep through that? On the bad days when she retreated into herself, refusing to talk – baffling, because they'd done it, made their baby, wasn't that supposed to make everything alright again? – she would be on the far side of the bed when David woke. Sometimes awake, but pretending she wasn't; if he went to touch her, she'd turn away, shrugging him off with a grumbling sound she never made when she was properly sleeping. That bothered him, but not as much as when he'd wake to find her really under, the gap between them worse for having been there through the night. A bit of distance was natural, he told himself. They were tired; they were busy; they had Georgie. Trying not to remember his parents in their separate rooms; his father raging, his mother weeping, the splintered architrave beside her never-used lock.

Today, without looking, he knows she's on the far side. There's an aching grey emptiness all down the edge of his arm. Aisling's breathing is even, but he can't tell if she's awake yet, or still sleeping, turned away from him, her right shoulder raised in protection, like it's been raised since she had the op. He imagines the back of her neck, the strands of red-gold hair clinging to her damp skin. He has always loved that about her; her blood, how it boils when she sleeps.

He stares at the ceiling. He can feel the weight of the tunnel on his chest; in his nostrils, the gelignite stink of almonds. There's a knot in his stomach and something is itching under the surface of his mind, like an equation he needs to solve, or a formula he should apply, except he can't remember the context or any of its components. An unpleasant sensation. He shakes his head, trying to dislodge it.

He should check on Georgie. That thing last night, after the argument. And Georgie had been part of what they'd been arguing about – how the bloody thing had started. David trying to bring up the thumb-sucking again, Aisling not listening. Oh, it's fine, it'll be fine, it's only that school. He hadn't been able to help himself; he'd started to get thick with her: I know. What do you think I am, Ash, bloody blind? But what if he forgets and does it there, with the other lads watching? Then it kicked off. The school and Georgie needing friends and money and David's sisters, and before they knew it, she was needling him about the bloody bank again, and the hearing, and—

Christ, he thinks, and flings back the covers. It's only a building.

Dull light is bleeding in across the hallway through the small window at the turn of the stairs. It's what his father used to call a rank day; rain coming in from the east in a slow, cold drizzle, all wrong for the dying end of November. Georgie's door is half-open. In the gap, his bedroom is warm greys, the colours of ghosts. When Georgie was an infant, David used to lean against the doorframe and watch him sleep in his cot. Just watch: the soft curve of the tiny cheek, the fan of lashes, the fiery corona of hair on the pillow. He would feel the bite of the doorframe against his arm, and his heart would get so tight in his chest he thought it would burst. Pride, of course, at making such a small, perfect thing, but fear too. The old uselessness, magnified into a new terror: that this shouldn't be happening to him, that one day, without fail, he'd mess it up. Now, without leaning, he feels it still. That grip, deep in the bone, that tightness in his chest.

The room is stuffy. Georgie's breathing is ragged. He's got some sort of headcold. It started with a dose of the shivers the other evening, when David caught him coming in through the front door and thought he'd been out playing in the lane again, though Georgie swore blind he hadn't. Since then, he's been dog-tired. Rings under his eyes, impossible to get moving in the mornings. Not interested in anything, not even his scrapbook on the bank, the one he'd started after finally finishing with those funny old drawings of the octopuses. Complaining that his chest was hurting too, though when Aisling asked, Where, pet?, he couldn't say.

Last night, in the wee hours, still wound up after the argument, David had just managed to drift off when he'd heard a noise coming from Georgie's room. A ghost dragging at its chains, he'd thought drowsily. Then he realised it was real and lurched up, terrified, thinking, *Robbers*. But Georgie was fine; fast asleep. The room had been cold, though, and that was strange, because when David checked the window, it was exactly as he'd left it: catch down, secured against the night. There was nothing untoward outside either, just the streetlamps playing on Mrs Kelly's apple tree across the boundary wall, but David had sat with Georgie a while, to be on the safe side. When he got up, he saw the box under the bed where Georgie kept his old toys was shoved out at an odd angle. Ah, he'd thought. Georgie had probably knocked it in his sleep and it was that made the noise.

Now his son is deep under; it seems almost a shame to wake him. He's flushed and hot-looking, though at least he's not sucking his thumb. Normally the sight would bring David relief. But today it just reminds him of the argument, so all he feels is tired and vaguely defeated.

'Georgie?' He shakes his son's shoulder.

Georgie grunts, weasels his face into the pillow.

'Come on. Rise and shine, like a good man.'

David pulls back the curtains, opens the window. Under the drizzle, Marino is a gloomy maze of pebble-dash and grey roofs. Something catches his eye; he missed it the night before. Mrs Kelly has left her garden door unlatched, the little wooden one that leads out to the communal lane. Bloody woman. She'll forget her head next.

He turns. Georgie is swinging his legs out of bed. He's still grumpy, that shadow over him. Maybe – David groans inwardly – he heard them arguing last night.

'Right,' he says, putting on his best fake Boy Scout smile. 'Let's get you some breakfast.'

The room looks different that morning, in a small, almost imperceptible way. David will register the fact, but not the nature of the difference. Not till Christmas, when their nosy neighbour, Joanie Flynn, over for the Stephen's Day drinks, will say how unusual it is for a little boy Georgie's age to keep things so organised, so very neat and tidy.

In the bathroom, David pisses: an arc of golden sparks. Dung-a-lung-a-lung. The ammonia flushes away the last vestige of the dream, the sweet scent of almonds.

He checks his watch. Grand.

Outside, his feet pound the pavement; drizzle slides into his eyes. His chest tightens, his knees ache.

It's alright, he tells himself. They can have a chat after breakfast, sort things out. Anyway, he shouldn't be worrying about that; he has enough on his plate with the hearing. But at that, his stomach begins to knot again, so he turns back early, unwilling to invite full-scale cramps.

When he gets in, there's a letter on the floor of the hallway. He recognises the handwriting: Maura, the eldest of his five sisters.

'David?' calls Aisling.

He grabs the letter without opening it and stuffs it in the pocket of his mac.

Breakfast is quiet. He'd turned on the radio when he'd come in, but some bright spark had put the hearing at the top of the news and a Fine Gael TD was picking the thing apart. Bleating on about how easy it was for cases like this to damage the nation's reputation. All it took was personal hubris, mixed in with professional incompetence, and.... Jesus, thought David. Then Ó Buachalla came on, sounding more confident than ever, if that was possible, and David steeled himself for Ash to start sniping with her little digs: the Not-the-bloody-bank-again's and how maybe this was the end of Mr Ó Buachalla's glittering career, which would be perfectly fine with her as long as he didn't bring other people down with him, but at least now maybe he could ruin some other engineering company or go off and bore another country to death with his buildings.... Except it was Georgie who interrupted with a weary sigh – though he'd been obsessed with the bank for months – before starting to read the back of the cereal packet in a loud monotone.

'Shush, darling,' said Aisling. Then, too bright, not looking at David: 'Why doesn't Daddy switch over to the BBC?'

At which point David leant over and turned it off.

A mistake. Anything would be better than this silence, even the BBC banging on about the miners or OPEC or, God help them, the Troubles. Now he's on edge, wound up again. He's about to leave the table to get his new Arthur C. Clarke when music starts next door. Joanie Flynn's radio, playing pop at that ridiculous volume she uses when she's being neighbourly: not loud enough to hear properly, not quiet enough to ignore. David glances at Aisling, but she's lost in her work now, frowning over a case study. As for Georgie, he's off in a world of his own, listlessly spooning his rice crispies into his mouth. At the start of breakfast, Aisling took his temperature, but when she suggested he stay in bed, he got into a sulk instead of what they expected, jumping at the chance to keep away from the Brothers. Well, said Aisling, it's only Friday, so—

'I *knew* that,' Georgie said, and the snappiness of his tone surprised them both.

There's something odd about Georgie's place-setting today. He has all the breakfast things arranged around his bowl in a pattern. Spaced, balanced, weighted. It's neat; geometric, almost. David stares. The look of it has put him in mind of something. A chemistry diagram? Molecular structure? The formula he's forgotten niggles again.

$a + b + 2(ab)^2$

If X = a, Y = b, then—

He glances up. Aisling and Georgie are looking at him. Georgie is grinning. His missing milk teeth give him a rakish cast.

'What?'

'You're talking to yourself, love,' says Aisling.

Relieved, David laughs. He winks at Georgie. 'First sign of madness, old bean, eh?'

The joke misses its target. Georgie's face goes blank; he frowns. 'Dad, you know when baddies do something and….'

Fuck, thinks David. What if they ask me about the fireproofing?

Aisling reaches across the marmalade and takes his hand. Her skin is warm, her grip strong. She squeezes his fingers. Grateful, he squeezes back and nods at Georgie, frowning and making sounds of agreement, mmm, mmm, though he's no idea what his son is talking about.

Has he always been like that? Joanie will ask. Meaning: terribly neat and tidy.

No, David will say, without even having to think. Remembering the breakfast things in their pattern, remembering the tiny difference he had registered in Georgie's bedroom.

'I'll bring him to school today.'

Aisling looks up, surprised. 'But—'

'Ash.' Before she can object, he pulls her close. He's expecting her to resist, and she does, but only for a moment. Then she softens. Under the dressing gown, her fragility still surprises him; that brittle delicacy, like one of those glass figurines his mother used to collect. He breathes her in. During the treatment, a sourness entered her waters, altering her scent. It was something that fascinated him as a schoolboy, how tiny adjustments in internal structure can lead to massive changes on the outside. Tweak the molecules in an apple, and it becomes a banana. Take away a strut and a building falls. Mess with a person's chemistry and…. Today, the sourness is still there, just a trace, even though they've practically given her the all-clear.

Practically.

That's just doctor-talk, she keeps saying. Professional caution. The important thing to remember is, it's just a scare.

Christ. Guilt floods him.

'I'm sorry—' he starts, but she's speaking too, over him.

'What?'

'I said, what have you told Art, Davey?'

'About what?'

'The Christmas party.'

His arms around her stiffen. 'The what?' Upstairs, he can hear Georgie brushing his teeth, singing to himself in that odd, tuneless, unselfconscious way of his. 'I … eh.' His throat clicks; that old hesitation, strangling him. 'I haven't said anything, Ash. I, eh, haven't thought about it.'

'I don't want to go, Davey.' Her voice is low, her face anxious.

He stares.

'Sorry.' She's flushed now, her eyes bright; frightened, guilty-looking, almost. 'I shouldn't have brought it up. You're up to ninety about this stupid thing today, of course, and—'

'Jesus. No. Ash—' He tries to hold her again, but she's slipped away, turning back to the sink and the waiting dishes, her uptilted shoulder pointing to him like an accusation.

He steps back, tries to busy himself. 'Mrs Kelly's taking Georgie today?'

'Mmm.'

'Maybe he can have a nap there, make up for all the sleep he's been missing.'

'Right,' she says. Then, as he's about to leave, 'You didn't see my rosary beads anywhere, the pearly ones my mummy gave me, in the wee purse? I think I've lost them.'

She's biting her bottom lip, her face drawn. Irritated, he says nothing; pretends to think. Frowns, shrugs, leaves.

Outside, it's got colder, the drizzle congealing into large, hard drops that slither like icy sweat down David's collar. Shoulders hunched, he runs to the car, a second-hand Cortina he'd traded the Prefect for during the summer. He glances back. Aisling is standing on the doorstep. The rain spits on his glasses, making her face indistinct.

'I'll ring you,' he shouts. 'Let you know how it went.'

She smiles a tight smile and nods, and he slides into the driver's seat. Mrs Kelly is out on the step next door, picking up her milk bottles. David thinks about calling out a Hello, but it would be pointless; she's as deaf as a post. In the rearview he watches Georgie come to the door, Aisling kiss him. David flicks on the wipers, rolls down the windscreen. 'Come on!'

Aisling gives Georgie a little push and he turns towards the car, lumbering under the weight of his schoolbag. A siren begins to scream. David cranes his neck, peering through the rear windscreen. Blue lights flash, reflected in the upper windows of the houses across the road. The sound fades, disappearing, Doppler effect, around the Green.

David glances at Mrs Kelly's house. The old woman has vanished, but she's left her front door open. Aisling is already leaning over the railing to close it.

'She'll forget her head next,' says David as Georgie clambers in.

'Huh?'

'Mrs Kelly,' says David, expecting Georgie to laugh, as he usually does at this one. Instead his son frowns, as if he's been presented with a new, sudden thought.

'Never mind.' David starts the ignition.

'Who's dead?' says Georgie.

'What?'

'In that ambulance?'

'I....' David thinks. 'Nobody, old chap.' He glances in the rearview, but Georgie is looking out the window, blank again.

They turn towards Fairview. Involuntarily, David takes a quick look down the big Georgian crescent where Ó Buachalla has bought his new home, the street Aisling used to dream of moving to when they first got married. The scaffolding is up and the men are already out, handing up buckets to each other. Ó Buachalla is doing a complete refit, restoring the period features in the upper stories and knocking down the back wall in the basement so he can build a glass extension to let in the light. The plan is to have it ready for next summer, when his wife and child come over from America. It's a big job; more than a job, a labour of love, says Arthur Lyons. Ó Buachalla even sleeps there, rolled up in a sleeping bag, when he's not kipping in the North Star. When it's done, says Art, it'll be a beauty.

A muscle pulses in David's cheek. What she said last night. And today, that thing about not wanting to go to Art's Christmas party. What sense is he to make of that? What in hell is that supposed to add up to?

He glances at Georgie, silent in the back seat, and pulls out onto the coast road. In his wing mirror, the architect's mansion shrinks to nothing.

It had been their ninth wedding anniversary. Not even a special one, but, on impulse, David decided to pull out all the stops. The bonus for the bank contract had come in; we should celebrate, he had thought. It had been too long since they'd done that. He had been meticulous, organised it all behind Aisling's back: hired a babysitter, ordered roses and chocolates, even booked them a table in that Greek place on South William Street, the one Ash loved because it reminded her of her friend Lynne, who she'd gone travelling with at the start of the sixties. Then, at the last minute, Arthur Lyons landed him in it. We're having a few people round to toast the Waterford contract; we'd love it if you and Aisling came along. By the way, there's a possibility that Mr Lloyd from London may be there too.

David had felt that hateful tug he used to feel as a child, fraying between forces he didn't understand. The firm was everything to Art, more important than family. If you were one of his senior men, if you had any sort of ambition for yourself, you were supposed to see it that way too. And now, as if that wasn't enough, this chance that Morgan Lloyd, head of the firm's Computer Group, the man David had been lobbying Art for months to get over to Dublin, would be there as well? Aisling liked Art well enough, and knew how he worked. She was always quick enough to say David should be doing better out of the firm than he was, she would understand him wanting to get his spoke in with Lloyd before anyone else did. But to spend the whole evening there, on their anniversary?

His father's ghost began to jeer. Fuck off, he told it, it's not about the money. He knew he could figure out a compromise – keep the babysitter and use her to cover the party instead of the dinner. But he couldn't bring himself to cancel the restaurant. Instead: I'm taking you on a surprise, he told Aisling over breakfast and, softened by the roses and the chocolates, her eyes widened.

Och, don't look so worried, Davey. I love surprises!

When he came home from work, she was all dolled up, in the clingy silk dress he loved on her, though she said it made her look fat. Halfway to Art's she realised where they were going and the shutters came down. He heard himself whistling behind the wheel; stiff, stupid, pretending nothing was wrong. Once they got to Art's road in Dean's Grange, he stopped the car. She was staring straight ahead. Fuck it, he thought, and right then, Ó Buachalla swept past in the Jag.

Who's that? said Aisling.

Ó Buachalla, said David. The architect. Look, Ash, let's—

Forget it, she said, opening the passenger door. We've been seen now.

At the party she went straight for the drinks. Punishing him for making a balls of it. He couldn't blame her. Dubonnet first, followed by the vino. Her social face on, the one she used around his mother and his sisters. All nice wee Northern girl and soft, bright laughter while he stewed near the window, sipping at Art's warm Chardonnay, longing for a stout.

Only there a few minutes when Art tapped him on the shoulder. David, allow me to introduce you to Morgan Lloyd. A quick wink. As you know, David, Mr Lloyd is chief High Priest over in Blackfriars. Morgan, this is David Madden, one of my top men, the fellow who's been at me to get you to wangle us some hours on the mainframe.

Lloyd was a dapper fellow, skinny and restless. Welsh, and, according to company legend, almost impossible to win over. As Art plied him with drink and *plamás*, David watched Aisling grab a skewer of cubed cheese and pineapple. Someone brushed past her, knocking her arm, and her drink spilt. She looked up. Uh oh, thought David, and would have gone over, only he realised the man from London had just directed a question at him. He forced himself back into the conversation.

Automation, complexity, efficiency. Lloyd nodded. Job done, Art drifted off.

We're an, eh, you know, international outfit, David said, it, eh, won't do if one link is eh, weaker than the rest. He knew this stuff, had practised it in anticipation, yet here he was, talking too much, stammering like a schoolboy, but instead of stopping, he kept bloody going, powered by a nameless anxiety in his gut. It was Ash, he thought. He was worried about her. Later, he would wonder if he'd had some sort of premonition.

Call it national pride, he went on, but I think it would be, eh, um, gratifying for our lads over here to get to grips with the technology. You Brits have been crowing about it on the mainland long enough—

Art looked over. Shit, thought David, and stopped. But Lloyd only laughed – I admire your chutzpah, Mr Madden – and perhaps it would have been alright, except then Niall Rourke, the other senior engineer, barged in. Sent by Art, no doubt. Shoving his hand forward with his best don't-mind-me-I'm-just-a-harmless-bollocks palaver and making a quip about Lloyd being sure not to mind David's cheek and....

David sank back, scanned the room. Aisling was at the piano, in conversation with Art's wife Marion and Ó Buachalla, of all people. Even at that distance you could smell the architect's cologne, expensive and foreign. Ash was all politeness again, nodding, listening. Not her social face, though. She seemed awkward. Nervously pulling at her dress, the way she did when she got self-conscious about all the weight she'd put on after having Georgie.

She glanced up. *Let's go*, David found himself mouthing. He nodded towards the door.

Surprise on her face, then relief. Later, it would gall him, that surprise; her shock, almost, that there would be a Part Two to the evening, a part David had fashioned himself.

He made the excuses: special anniversary, big deal. Oh, said Marion, and you came all the way over here? You're very good, David. He was still expecting Aisling to let rip at him once they were in the car, but she let out a big breath and started giggling, making cracks about the people at the party. Marion's new hairdo, the awful furniture – though David couldn't see what was wrong with it – the music. James Last, for god's sake, Davey. She was drunk, he realised. Did you see Rourke muscling in there? he said, emboldened, and started on his best Niall Rourke impression, all Clongowes vowels and barking laugh. She looked at him, sharp. Then she laughed. No. Mr Buckley was too busy boring me to death in there. Buckley? he'd wondered, forgetting that Ó Buachalla hadn't always used his Irish name. I thought you'd be more impressed, he started, but she'd already twisted the dial of the radio. Listen, Davey – your favourite! Glenn Miller! Though David's favourite of the big band men was never Miller, but Benny Goodman.

At the restaurant they got twisted. She nervy and giddy, him flooding with relief. Ouzo first, then retsina, then some sweet peach schnapps that tasted of summer. At one point he remembered thinking: would she have preferred French food? But she'd eaten tons, for once not worrying about her diet. Stuffed courgettes and lamb and green beans swimming in tomato-flavoured oil. He'd stayed with moussaka, close enough to shepherd's pie to fool his gut. Tiny changes in chemistry; big changes on the outside.

Oh my God, she kept saying, this is lovely. We could be on Paros right now!

Which was when he told her about the other thing he'd bought with the bank bonus, the surprise summer holiday he'd booked with BlueSkies.

Greece? Her eyes widened. An awful wet light in them, like she was going to cry.

No, he wanted to say, panicking. I don't mean it. It's a joke. We're going to Ballybunion. But, Yeah, he said instead. A package. Corfu. Two weeks. Meals included. There'll be, eh, kids there for Georgie. He knows, but I told him to keep it secret—

His throat caught; the words stopped.

Okay, she said, smiling with that awful bright cry still behind it. *Yiamas!* She raised her glass. Then they started on the raki.

They walked home. She wanted to, and it made sense because they were so hammered. She kept bumping into him, on purpose, that wild lemony smell in her hair like the night they made Georgie, and, pissed as a fart, relishing the lush impact of her body against his, he threaded his fingers through hers and started laughing, stupidly, at nothing. When they got to Fairview Park, she began talking again, messy, slurring, *Davey, I'm sorry, I'm so... you know I've always loved—* Afraid of that nonsense, worse, that she was going to cry again, he pulled her onto a bench and she didn't resist and they kissed, like they hadn't for too long, and he lost himself in the familiar, strange taste of her tongue. After they got home and dismissed the babysitter, he'd poured them each a glass of Baileys and she'd sipped hers slowly, tilting her head back and looking at him through slitted eyes, her pupils huge and unreadable like in the old days. Come on, lover, she said, and at that, the *lover*, he was a boy again, nineteen and aching for it. She led him upstairs and drew him onto the bed, opening the top button of her dress. Slowly, teasingly, he started to unpeel her, his senses filling with the feel of her skin under his, the scent of her hair. She started to speak. *Davey, I want. . . .* He remembered thinking, Another baby? Alright, let's do it! when—

to tell you something

'What's that?'

This is what he would remember: on its way to her breast, his hand had stopped moving. Before he spoke, it stopped, then moved again, but in the wrong direction, away from her. He would feel that action inside his bones for years; that backward lift of the wrist, the syncopated, unconscious start of the recoil. It was already on its way back, his treacherous hand, by the time she glanced down and saw the pearly bead of moisture oozing from the tip of her nipple.

The wipers flip, clearing a W-shaped patch on the windscreen.

'All set now, old bean? Remember, Mum's working today, so you'll be going to Mrs Kelly's after school.'

'Oh.' Georgie blinks.

'You can have a rest there. She won't mind. There should be a picture or two today in the papers. I'll bring you back one—'

'Seeya, Dad.'

And his son is off, with a sudden urgency, as if an elastic band has released.

David keeps the motor running and watches. A gang of boys are huddled around the mouldering trunk of an ancient sycamore just inside the gates. They're the same size as Georgie, but a few years older; David has been keeping an eye on them. Seeing Georgie, one of them hoots. Georgie's pace falters. You have to learn to stand up for yourself, David has said, countless times, but so far, Georgie hasn't managed it. If it would do any good, he would jump out of the car himself and—

David blinks. Something is wrong. Georgie has disappeared. The pack are exactly as they were, though the ringleader is looking confused. David's eyes dart, trying to follow the whirl of boys-concrete-and-uniform that might contain his son. Rattled, he thinks of science fiction entities and the dual nature of photons; of his science teacher, Brother Sheridan, the one who'd pegged him for greatness, trying to explain to the thicks down the back how matter and energy were, at their core, the same thing. There's a rational reason, he tells himself. A trick of the light. Maybe Georgie's just—

His heart skips a beat. His son has materialised again, near the bicycle shed beside a skinny boy with dark hair and spectacles. David has spotted this lad before. He seems to want to make friends, only Georgie hasn't let it happen yet. He says the boy is weird – talks about nothing but car engines and numbers. The boy doesn't seem surprised to see Georgie appear. He nods and Georgie nods back, and they start to talk.

A new pal. Good news, surely? So why has the knot in David's stomach tightened again?

A shrill peal. The bell. The Brothers pour out, a black river swirling with books, canes and belts.

Schnell, Schweine, schnell!

Oh? Joanie will say. Meaning: so when did he start getting so neat and tidy, this boy of yours?

So many answers: the day I went to court. The day I made a friend, and so did he. The day he disappeared in the schoolyard. The day the panic attacks started. But the answer that David will give Joanie, without knowing why, is this:

The day he was so relieved to find out he could have a sleep in Mrs Kelly's after school.

Either side of the Liffey, the crumbling docklands stretch towards the bay, stinking of seagulls and petrol. Some attempts at revival are visible: a lone tug, the Guinness ships down at the Basin, jaunty in black and cream. But on the whole, the city looks as dismal as ever, more so under the rain. David cuts across Pearse Street, passing ancient buildings with boarded-up windows, a milk lorry, a street-sweeper wheeling a cart. He wonders again at the paradox: intelligent people, like Aisling, clamouring for change, then railing at Ó Buachalla and his like, the ones who bring it. Holles Street is clogged – a taxi, stopped outside the maternity hospital. David watches a pregnant woman climb out of the cab; a man is waiting for her, holding up his coat to shield their heads. He remembers driving Aisling there, the night Georgie was born. Ash moaning in the back seat, clutching her rosary, praying that, this time, everything would go alright. The taxi indicates, moves on; it's a Cortina Mark III four-door, the same generation as David's, but with mismatched panels. Stolen, he guesses, and his father's ugly phrase rings in his mind. *Cuckoo in the nest.*

Merrion Square is gloomy; the evergreen sessile oaks dripping under the rain, Government Buildings making a weak attempt at bravado as it shoves its one grubby tit at the unappreciative sky. One day they should clean up that whole square, thinks David, as he often does; as he often says to Aisling and Georgie when he takes them on a drive past. We'll light it up like they do in Europe, that'll give us something to be proud of. But without the familiar response – *aye, Davey*; *yeah, Dad* – the thought seems hollow; fraudulent, somehow. He turns past the squat brown bunkers of the new ESB building, another of Ó Buachalla's designs, then onto Baggot Street, where the tall Georgian terraces always remind him of Clonmel, the damp weeping through their rendered façades like sores.

He and Aisling had rented a garret flat in one of those houses just after they got married. They'd had no central heating, just open fires, made with coal that had to be carried up five flights of stairs. The landlady was a gentrified Wicklow type, an arrogant West Brit, all fur coat, no knickers. They'd no telephone, barely any electricity. It had been an adventure, at least up until the miscarriage, five months in. Aisling had cried her eyes out at that; David tried to comfort her, useless. Feeling like someone had taken a knife to him and scooped out all his hopes, flushing them down the toilet with that small, dead thing. He still remembers the awful weight of guilt, as if he had made it happen. *Charade*, he kept thinking. A stupid word that wasn't even his, that had no bearing on anything. He's always tried not to dwell on that night, him and Ash huddled together outside that Wicklow bitch's shoddy bathroom, though whenever he does, it seems to him it was then things started going—

Wrong.

Shocked, David brakes, slamming his hand against the horn.

The car stops inches from the woman. She is wearing a bright yellow mac and her hand is up, a foot from the windscreen, warding him off.

He lifts his eyes, meets hers. She is furious. A shock of dark curly hair, sallow skin, crooked teeth; tombstones in a red mouth. His breath hisses.

First the word, then the girl.

Jesus, he wants to say. It's not my fault. Leave me alone—

But in the back of his mind, a different pattern of words is rising, repeating in a loop.

A loud beep. David glances in the rearview. A bus, right up his arse. He nods at the driver, signals, pushes the gearstick forward.

He sat on the edge of their bed, his hands pressing into the mattress, and listened to her vomiting in the bathroom. The sound travelled down the landing in waves; he prayed it wouldn't wake Georgie. *Get used to this.* Did he think that at the time? Or was his thinking locked simply to a physical sense of what was: the mattress ridge pushing against his calves, the bumpy pads of the eiderdown under his palms, the rancid aftertaste of Greek food and too much alcohol in his throat. As he listened to her, he pictured it regurgitating; their un-special anniversary, rewinding from final retch to first troubled entrance through Art Lyons' front door, like an old Super 8 film played backwards for a prank.

The tap stopped. A click as the landing light was turned off. When Aisling came into the bedroom, she was pale, her freckles stark against her fine skin. She sat beside him. Something shifted inside David, a need to put his arm around her, the way he used to when they were first going out and they knew it was time to stop talking, except she was too nervous and could never, not until he made the first move. But that night he didn't – couldn't? – and in the gap left by his inaction, she began to speak.

'Let's not say anything to Georgie for the moment.' She was using her bedroom voice, the hushed tones she used to discuss Georgie and money problems. It had an unconvincing, brittle edge. 'It might be nothing. I mean,' she looked up, squinting as if assessing an invisible chart, 'there's no history in my family. It's probably just a cyst.'

But there's no lump, thought David. Aren't cysts lumps?

'I'll ring Mummy tomorrow. Maybe....'

She trailed off.

He cleared his throat. 'Would it be a plan, Ash, to em, take Georgie away for a couple of days?'

'That's a good idea.' Her face brightened, or tried to. 'We can bring him to Mummy and Daddy at Easter and....'

'What about Clonmel?'

'Your sisters?' An appalled sound that might have been a laugh.

His head filled with a rushing noise; the River Suir hurtling itself under the Gashouse Bridge, pummelling the streets of his hometown brown.

He grabbed her wrist. She looked down and stared, as if their hands belonged to strangers. 'What's wrong with me, Davey?'

Jesus, he thought, and turned towards her, arms opening to take her in.

'Oh, Mr Madden,' says Norma the receptionist. 'I didn't realise you were coming in today. I thought Mr Lyons would have you with him?'

Fuck, thinks David, confused. Did he get the time wrong? 'Eh— No. It's fine, Norma. Art said he wouldn't need me down at the Alamo till three.' Christ. The Alamo. Where did that come from?

'The Alamo! Mr Madden, you're a scream! Butch Cassidy has nothing on Mr Ó Buachalla, that's for sure!'

David usually likes Norma's laugh. It has a nice sound, husky from all the cigarettes she smokes, the big crate of Benson & Hedges David and the other engineers give her every Christmas. Today, though, it grates.

She leans closer. 'Seriously, though, Mr Madden, we all know you'll do fantastic. Mr Lyons said he's very confident of the outcome.'

She's wearing a high-neck blouse. The fabric is sheer; her bra-straps push, defined, against it.

'That's great, Norma.' His smile feels wrong, too tight.

'Do you want a coffee, Mr Madden? I can buzz Mrs Joyce?'

'I'm grand. Thanks.'

'She's doing lamb today, for the lunch. Cutlets with gravy. And apple pie for the sweet.' Norma rolls her eyes. 'Lord help me, I'll never fit into the dress at this rate.'

David can't think of the right thing to say that wouldn't sound wrong, so he makes a humphing sound instead and nods goodbye. In the back of his mind, a phrase from Mass begins to play. *Lamb of God, you who take away the sins of the world, have mercy on us.* He walks up the stairs to the first-floor offices, past the return and the back room where *Lamb of God, you who take away the sins of the world, have mercy on us* the secretaries are hammering

73

out their letters and memos and reports and specifications and responses to claims and order forms and accounts, and *Lamb of God, you who take away the sins of the world, grant us peace* just as he's opening the door he realises these were the words that popped into his mind after almost knocking down the young woman on the bridge.

He shakes his head, sweeping the supplication from his mind.

The office is noisy. Morrissey, the younger draughtsman, is crouched over his table, a cigarette clamped between his lips as he moves the eraser drill over a drawing of the new currency centre in Sandyford. Like David, Morrissey is one of Arthur Lyons' finds; a former office boy, bright with potential. He's a bit messy – at the start he destroyed a couple of Rapidographs by not cleaning them properly. But he's a quick learner, and unlike O'Hanlon, the other draughtsman, has never hinted once about getting backing from Art to upgrade his qualifications to a full degree. Switching off the drill, he leans back and surveys his work.

'Careful with the fag, Brian,' says David. 'You don't want to undo the hard labour.'

Morrissey starts, takes the cigarette out, looks for an ashtray.

'Hands,' says David.

The young draughtsman looks down at his inky fingers. 'Sorry, Mr Madden.' He scrambles out of his chair, all limbs.

Niall Rourke laughs. 'Fighting form today, Madden, what?'

David makes a non-committal sound, but Rourke is already whooshing forward on his chair. 'I've been counting my blessings they picked you for the shenanigans. I've no *grá* to be hauled over the coals with the whole of Ireland looking on.'

O'Hanlon laughs. He's watching them, wolfish eyes sharp.

Rourke clicks his fingers. 'Eyes back on the job, lad.' The draughtsman makes a slyish twist with his mouth and bends back over his board.

Rourke leans closer. His breath smells of coffee, sulphuric and nauseating. 'Come on, David. Scout's honour. It's a mess. We don't have a chance.'

David feels his jaw tighten. 'Art thinks it's still up for grabs.'

Rourke snorts a laugh. 'You know me, I'd never say anything bad of Art, David. If it was some other boyo who was the artiste on the job, maybe. But that fucker, he'll be the ruin of all of us.'

Fucker? Twelve months ago, Rourke was singing Donnacha Ó Buachalla's praises, so far up the architect's arse you'd think he wanted to live there.

'You don't get the planners' backs up and expect them to take it lying down. That hoor, though.' Rourke shakes his head. 'He'd eat his young for a headline.' He claps David on the back. 'Chin up, Trigger. Remember, you're only the bit player.' Humming under his breath, he whooshes back to his desk.

Bit player? Sourness fills David's mouth. Above Rourke's head, Farrah Fawcett-Majors is looking over, mocking him with her postergirl fellatio pout.

He has the best spot in the room, beside the window with its grand Georgian view onto the large back garden. In springtime, he loves to watch the birds building their nests in the beech tree, constructing tough, flexible homes out of the sappy twigs, while the buds quicken, sharp green against the solid blue sky. Today the branches are bare, apart from a few grey scraps clinging on, and the sky is miserable, the hue of soiled cotton wool. David switches on his anglepoise and the figures on his foolscap jump into life. They're calculations for Ó Buachalla and Art's next big project: a hotel in Waterford, overlooking the new bridge across the Suir. Another controversial, high-profile concoction of concrete and steel.

There's a flaw; he can feel it. Somewhere in all Ó Buachalla's artistry, a slight but significant imbalance of forces, a potentially lethal mismatch between load and strength. Normally it calms him to scan the calculations, figure out what's missing. But today he can't settle. The knot in his stomach has contracted into a point of tension and the rest of him feels too loose, unbiddable. He closes his eyes and tries to focus. Picturing the hotel's structure as a thing made of rubber, sensitive to the smallest overload. Picturing it as himself – swaying in the wind, shuddering under footfall, subsiding, millimetre by millimetre, down the precarious cliff.

The night after she got the results, that Good Friday after he'd driven down from Cranfield and waited for her at the Mater and brought her home, neither of them talking much, she'd rung her mother and explained what was going on in her warm, bright, doctor's voice, her fingers all the time working her rosary beads, and said, No, don't wake the child; no, don't tell him anything, we'll talk when he comes home; after she'd been passed on to her father and – *yes, Daddy, aye, I know* – reverted to a little girl again, surrendering to his greater authority, they went to bed. No sex, just holding. David felt her ribs move under the weight of his arm, and wondered what it was doing inside her during the dark hours when it thought nobody was watching. The shadow, the oncologist had called it, but David didn't see a shadow; he saw a crab.

A crab, come out of the blue, like the famous picture of the goddess who'd always reminded him of Aisling, rising from the ocean, naked and gorgeous on a seashell. A crab was the right animal, wasn't it, for what was happening to her? A piece of seafood was all it was, a slug with pincer legs wearing armour, that right now was clawing through her ducts, sucking at her milk, dropping pearls in her glands.

Could a crab suck? Doubt surfaced. Maybe it was an oyster. Did it matter? Something small and insignificant, easily crushed.

He remembered his father Fergus, dying on a narrow bed in Waterford Hospital, eaten up by rancour and self-loathing. That's a punishment, his mother had said on one of her lucid days. A penance for all the sins he's done. His sisters casting black glares at her. What would *she* know of sin? But sideways glances at David all the same, and something scared underneath the blackness.

He rolled onto his back. Aisling made a small moaning sound. It was substantially different, in timbre and pitch, to the grunts she made when she was pretending.

Q.E.D., he thought, and hated himself.

Did you always want to be an engineer? she had asked once, soon after they'd started going out. They'd been sitting by the Grand Canal, near the bridge at Percy Place, throwing bread at the swans because, carried away with each other and the thing that was happening between them, neither of them had much appetite for their sandwiches. She'd just finished her training, working as an intern at the Children's Hospital. He was beginning his degree, the one Arthur Lyons had got the firm to sponsor.

It's just, she said, digging, I'd have thought, with your daddy's business being so successful, you'd have followed in his footsteps?

He hadn't lied; just dissimulated, been careful with the truth. There's money, he'd told her, panicking that a girl like her wouldn't want to keep seeing him if there wasn't. We have a family business. Letting her imagine the rest.

Oh, he said then, at the canal, as if only just copping on to what she meant. Trying not to remember the wasted months before his father died. Eh – well. I suppose, I, you know, just fell into it.

Aisling gazed at him, puzzled and a little hurt. But how—

He reached out, pulled her close, silenced her with a kiss.

He started making excuses. She could meet his mother and his sisters at the wedding. There'd be plenty of time to visit once they were married.

Meanwhile, smelling a rat, she prodded and, under the pressure, bits of the truth trickled out. His father a publican, not the big-shot factory owner she'd imagined. It's a good business, he said. There's money in it. It'll go to me, to us, Ash, our kids.... Heard his voice pleading, defending the inadequate life he'd fled from.

God, Davey, she'd said, laughing, holding up her hands. I don't know why you're so worried. It's perfectly respectable.

She started calling him the Great Pretender, and that was the joke for a while, though she couldn't quite cover up the sneer when he finally brought her down to Clonmel. The sawdust floor, the grubby shopfront. *Maddens*, no apostrophe, in fading yellow letters over the grocery entrance. His mother all made-up in the good room of their damp house, trying to be grand in front of the doctor's daughter. His sisters, awkward and lumbering; he snapped back into his former self, the gruff, unpolished lounge-boy. After that, she stopped asking.

It wasn't till a few years later, the summer evening they'd found out she was pregnant with Georgie, that he'd gone anywhere near answering her question. They were lying on the new bed he'd bought to make up for the fight they'd had the month before, the nasty one when she'd stormed off, raging at him because they couldn't do the two things at once: buy a house and have a Continental holiday. It was the honeymoon all over again, only worse. What's wrong with Wales? he'd kept saying. It's not that, she'd said, it's just.... Ash, he'd wanted to say, don't you know how tight things are? But his throat kept catching on the *tight*, because he could hear his Da in that, whinging on about the price of fucking everything. You know, David, my daddy was right, she'd finally shouted, red in the face. I could have had anyone. I should have known better than to marry someone from the shopkeeping classes. He'd frozen, unable to speak. The next thing he knew the door had slammed and she was gone.

He'd sat in the kitchen, seething. Drinking the Jameson left over from the house-warming, telling himself he wasn't going to do anything because there was no bloody point. I'm going up to my mummy, she'd said. She was probably on the train to Newry, probably already there. At midnight, he jumped up, grabbed his car keys; he'd drive all the way to fetch her back if that was what she wanted. He'd just rounded the Green, bleary from the drink, when he saw her, walking home. He braked and jumped out of the car and she fell into his arms and, when he held her, she felt different: fragile, full of apology. A shining, wet openness in her face. A scent in her hair, in the fringes of her Afghan coat, a scent he'd never noticed before, and wild for it, pulling at his zipper in the car, pushing him onto the kitchen table as soon as they got in. No time to even ask, Where did you go, Ash? Her ferocity only made him feel worse, more so when she fell apart during the sex and started crying, the terrible way she'd done after the miscarriage. Let's get a new bed, he'd said, panicking. We can pretend we're in a hotel. It won't be a holiday but it'll be a—

Compromise? she said, and began crying again.

Christ, he'd thought, but the next day he'd ordered it. Blown the last of the wedding money from his sisters on a feather-mattressed king size from Clerys.

Ah, she said when she saw it. Nothing more.

For weeks, she'd been tense, jumpy, and all the wild sex and awful crying in the world wouldn't make it go away. He had no idea what to do. The jokes and the silly voices didn't work anymore. He felt like he used to as a child, lying beside his mother in her honey-and-mushroom-scented bed, terrified of being rolled onto and crushed, even more terrified of moving away in case he'd hurt her feelings. Then, on that glorious summer evening, Ash called him upstairs and told him she was expecting again and, for a moment, all the trouble vaporised.

She had pushed up her blouse so he could rest his hand on her belly. *Ours*, she kept saying, urgent, trying to convince him that this time it would survive; long enough to grow from an *it* to an *ours*. Her eyes bright; defiant, like she was staking a flag in the moon.

She had felt soft under his hand, no sign yet of a bump. Please, God, he found himself thinking. Please, whatever you are, let this one live. He closed his eyes and imagined their skins dissolving; his pulse merging with hers to feed the tiny tadpole inside. We. Are. Family.

My mother wanted me to be a doctor. He'd said it without thinking. Later, he would realise he had wanted his child to know these things.

A doctor?

Whatever he'd expected, it wasn't that: that Aisling would laugh.

He stiffened and she stopped, and maybe he would have done what he usually did when it came to the grubby parts of his past, change the subject, or maybe he'd have tried to continue, but he would never know, because she was already hoisting herself up onto her side and looking at him with that serious, sympathetic expression she'd started using on her patients.

Something wrong with my wee boy? She reached for his face. He twitched, shrugging her off.

She withdrew. Oh, I'm sorry, Davey. I didn't mean to upset you….

Upset? He hated this type of talk. He laughed. God, no, Ash. I'm – it's grand.

Grand?

Her eyes filled. I didn't mean any harm, Davey.

Don't call me that, he wanted to say. I'm not your child.

It's just, I mean. I know your mummy is, but how could she have ever thought you'd make a good doctor? I mean, you've…. Aisling stopped.

Some wiser impulse told David to stop too, cuddle her, talk about the baby, their plans, anything to forget this stupid line of conversation, but, God knows why, he ignored it.

I've no what? His voice surprised him with its calm, equable curiosity. This was the voice of a logical person, he thought. This was the voice he should have used the day of the fight, the days of all the fights.

She shook her head.

Go on. I've no what?

She laughed. I didn't say you'd no anything, Davey. I just think you wouldn't have….

Wouldn't have what?

God, David. She flushed. For the first time, he noticed the new short haircut she'd got that afternoon. It made her look like a nun. You're like a dog with a bone. Can you not just—

You're the one started it, he thought. But: Fine, he said, and laughed, a mean little laugh like she was the one making the fuss, and rolled onto his back and began to whistle under his breath, a speeded-up version of 'The Cliffs of Dooneen', the same stupid tune his father used to whistle when he was raging.

No what, Ash? No backbone? No breeding? No brains?

Aisling stared at him. He didn't trust himself to look at her, but he could feel her eyes raking his skin. At last she turned away, and started playing with the tassels of the bedspread.

To hell with your doubts, he thought. I am going to be a father, and I am going to be a good one. And that time he was the one staking the moon.

Excise. Such a clean word. After the cut – scheduled for the start of May – they would blast what was left of the breast with radiation, in fractional doses for six weeks. Fractional, meaning what? David went to the library in University College Dublin and asked for medical journals, anything to describe symptoms and treatment for ductal carcinoma. 'Cancer,' said the librarian. 'Well, no, not exactly,' said David. 'More the, eh, non-invasive kind. A shadow.' 'Oh. Pre-cancer,' said the librarian. 'Mmm,' said David, thinking why did it have to be *pre*, why did they have to use that word? He sat beside a window and steeled himself. He could feel his buried self squirming inside him again, that six-year-old shivering in a dark room packed with heavy, ill-chosen furniture and delicate glass figurines; that skinny, long, mollycoddled boy staring, sickened, at his mother's ambition made into pictures. Illustrations of diseases in medical textbooks. Failing tissues, rotting flesh. Sores, ulcers, growths and scabs. It would be different now, he told himself; he was an adult. He could work out the principles, the hard science that would keep the crab contained.

To his surprise, he was comforted by what he discovered. Whatever might have been left of the crab after the excision would not stand up to radiation. It would be killed at source.

Stirb, Du Krebs. Die, Crab!

Fractional meant one dose a day, five days a weeks. Greece would be out. He felt an uncomfortable dash of relief at that and prayed it wasn't just the stinginess of the shopkeeper's son, hoping the travel agents would be generous with the refund.

In the middle of May, Aisling's mother returned up North. Two weeks later the radiotherapy started, just as they began to dig the foundations for the bank and Ó Buachalla started nosing around Marino for his new house. If David was a superstitious man, he might have looked for something portentous in that; all those changes coming together, like reflections in a hall of mirrors. But he wasn't, and could see them for what they were: coincidence, nothing more. In July, he took up jogging. It was one way to keep the anxiety at bay, better than the drink or lashing out at people, like his father might have. As the summer drew on, and Aisling grew tireder and thinner, shedding all the pounds that marriage and Georgie had brought, and her hair lengthened, growing out of its nunnish crop into the style she'd worn when they'd first met, loose and pretty, David went out for longer periods, rising earlier so he could get back in time to make the breakfast. By September, when the foundations of the bank were finished, he was up to forty minutes, and that at speed.

Everybody kept talking about how manageable it had been. Aisling's parents, the consultants, all his sisters except the eldest, Maura; even Aisling herself. Was there, David wondered, a better word? Everybody kept praising them, how well they'd pulled together as a family. Aisling returning to work so soon mightn't have been the best idea – nobody said that, but everyone thought it – but at least she'd only gone back in October, when the consultant said it would do no harm. It must be very hard for her, said David's second eldest sister Bridget, the jealous one. Cutting down on all those social engagements. But the only one David could remember was the annual Engineers' Dinner in July. It had felt off to be there on his own, as if he was missing a leg. He'd wanted to tell Aisling, but wasn't sure how she would have taken it.

A change had come into them. Less of the moods and the digs and the silences and David having to bite back his temper. Something tender again in how they touched; something *pure*. Was that the word? She began sleeping closer to him until, more often than not, he would wake to find her in his arms. We're starting over, she'd said at the end of August. Moving on. She even began talking about trying for another baby. Let's wait till we're out of the woods, said David, wondering if the fear he felt was not a sign of weakness, but a good thing.

Aren't ye great, said Bridget, how ye're managing?

Greece had been hard. Ash started crying when she realised they wouldn't get there. Heartbroken, like a child. It's fine, David found himself saying, trying to curb the panic. We'll do it next year. Go through Athens, stay with Lynne, do some of the islands, not just a package. We'll have a real, eh, adventure, all three of us. As he'd spoken, the plan had grown wings in his mind, become real. Aisling squeezed his fingers. Promise, Davey? Promise.

Very tough on the lad, they all said. Being told to be careful all the time, don't pull at her arm, no, she doesn't want to see your scrapbook, go out and play with the ball, leave Mum be, she's resting. For any little fellow, that would be tough. Especially when a Mum one minute strong – better than strong; a lady doctor, invincible in a white coat – had turned into something else. A not-Mum; an invalid, frail and easily damaged. But they'd all praised Georgie too. They didn't want to know about how tricky it had been for him, starting that school. They didn't need to know, Aisling said. As for that business with the thumb-sucking: It'll change, Aisling kept saying. Once we get this behind us. You wait and see, Davey.

On the first day of September, the same day they started filling in the cores of the bank, the seeds of all their managing appeared to bear fruit. The consultant told David that Aisling had responded exceptionally well to the treatment. Nobody said *remission*, but it was from then on that Aisling began, deliberately and especially in company, to use the word *scare*.

81

'Call for you on line 3, Mr Madden,' says Norma, jolting him. And, like a fool, he presses the button without asking who it is.

'Did you not get the letter?'

It's not Ash. Was he expecting Ash?

'Oh,' he says. 'Maura. I....'

His sister sighs. 'Thought you'd have got it by now. Mammy had a turn a few days back.'

'Turn?' He feels sick.

'No. Not that, Davey. She fell. Gave her head a bang off the bathroom door. She's grand, though. No concussion. Doctor Flanagan says it's the blood pressure. He's given her the tablets for it.' She pauses. 'She's asking for you. Will you able to get down soon? I know you've that big court thing on today, but....'

'I'll try.'

'How're ye doing?'

His throat tenses. 'Fine.'

'Aisling sounded terrible cranky on the phone last week. Are you sure that job's not too much for her, on top of the housework?'

He says nothing.

'We're happy to help. You can always send the boy to us for Christmas, Davey. You know Mammy loves to see him. All ye have to do is ask.'

He pictures his sister standing in the dark hall in Clonmel, twisting the black cord of the phone between her fingers.

'Maura—' he says suddenly. Remembering, for some reason, the woman on the bridge with the crooked teeth who'd reminded him of that girl – Lily? Rose? – the one he and his sister had used to secure their futures.

'What is it, Davey?'

His throat jams. He can't speak.

'Right,' says Maura. 'I've got to go. The shop's fierce busy. Mind yourself in court. They're lucky to have you. And say a prayer for Mammy, would you? She'd like that.'

No, she wouldn't, he thinks. What she'd like, and we both know it, is Count John McCormack, crooning love songs in her ear.

'All set for battle?' Rourke is in the doorway, dressed in his waterproofs.

David bares his teeth. 'Never better.'

Rourke laughs, and David places the receiver back in its cradle. As he does, he sees his mother's head falling to the floor; in slow motion, soft, like feathers. When he looks up, Rourke is gone.

He eats lunch alone, at a table at the back. He has no appetite, though Mrs Joyce's food, as always, is excellent. He's picked up an *Irish Times* from Reception and brought some notes so he'll look busy if anyone wants to talk to him. But there's only a bunch of lads from the print room at the next table, smelling of ammonia and regaling each other with their plans for the weekend.

On the front page of the newspaper is a big feature on the bank. David has no intention of reading it; he knows it will be galling and confusing and technically imprecise. But they've included one of his front-sections as an illustration and he promised to bring Georgie back a picture. Maybe he should leave the paper out in the kitchen tonight, with the illustration half-hidden, as if he hasn't seen it – let Georgie discover it for himself. A few evenings ago, he'd done just that, only not on purpose. It turned out they had put one of his drawings on page 3. He wouldn't have even known except for Georgie telling him. *Dad, Dad, look! Can I bring this up to my room for my scrapbook?*

At the bottom of the front page is a story on the Troubles. He remembers to skim through it, just in case there's a mention of what happened in May. It's been three months since the Bells told them, but Ash is determined Georgie doesn't get a whiff. *Not over my dead body*, she'd said, and only for that made the hairs on David's neck stand up on end, he would have pushed it. Funny, how easily they swapped places on that one; Ash saying they had to keep it a secret, while David felt Georgie needed to know, not the details – Jesus, no – but something.

He remembers the schoolyard that morning, the jolt of fear when he thought Georgie had disappeared. That poor family. The most terrible thing in the world, to lose a child.

Town is packed, but he eventually finds a parking space near the top of Capel Street. The rain is still coming down, colder now and turning to sleet, so he walks fast, hunched up against it. As he passes Brereton's jewellers, his eye catches on something in the window and he stops, arrested.

When he gets to the courts, he asks for directions from a Garda in uniform with a wide country face. Once in the right building, he waits in the corridor, unsure, though he's been through this rigmarole before, if the usual protocol will apply.

'Mr Madden?' The solicitor beckons.

David stands, straightening his suit. The first time he came to court he expected it to be more like the films. Trilby hats, popping bulbs, dark-lipsticked girls with shoulder pads, shoving microphones into his face. But it was a disappointment: a green baize chair, a row of benches, ugly fluorescent strip lights.

The usher shows him in. Arthur Lyons is sitting in a row near the front, the giant shape of the architect beside him. Lyons glances up. He looks utterly defeated.

Jesus, thinks David. The knot in his stomach plummets to his gut.

They ask him everything he's been expecting, everything Lyons has drilled him on over the last three weeks. Did he see the initial drawings? Could he describe them? How detailed were they? He skirts the truth. It's common knowledge that the first drawing for the bank was only a few lines in biro, scribbled on a piece of graph paper by Art, over pints with Donnacha Ó Buachalla in the gloomy winter of 1971, but David knows to fudge this. He talks instead about concepts, and general principles. He's sure Art has already waxed lyrical on the innovations, but the smart arse questioning him, a fellow he doesn't recognise, asks him to, Please, Mr Madden, expand. So he gives a bit of guff about the inspiration, from the firm's first big cantilevered project, the hotel in South Africa, and says again how revolutionary the design is, first of its kind in this country, blah blah blah. Bore them with the technical stuff, Art said. He digs into the details then, about the cantilevers translating the force through the cores so you don't need supporting pillars for the floors and with the narrow base you can have a piazza at ground level, and….

'Piazza?' A smirk from the smart arse.

'Yes,' says David. 'They're a sort of, eh, open space. A modern thing. In this country anyway.' Why is he starting to hesitate? He shouldn't have said 'this country' again. He sounds like a Brit. 'The, um, architect wanted to do the same thing here.'

The smart arse checks his notes. 'The architect wanted to design a building with thirty floors in Ireland?'

He blanks. 'Sorry?' Recovers, kicking himself. 'No. Of course not. The sketch was just for ten floors, because of the planning restrictions, from before. The, eh, height.'

A ripple across the courtroom. Are they laughing at him?

'Apologies, Mr Madden, we've been hearing a lot about height today. Please tell us about the initial design again.'

Keep fudging, Art had said. So, even though his mouth is drying and his throat constricting, he goes back to what he knows: sketches and approximations, and the lack of necessary information at the time planning was sought, and how things change in this line of work, how they have to be adjusted all the time.

'It's not, eh, like making something out of Lego.' Another laugh. The smart arse is getting ready for a dig. 'It's not a,' he struggles. 'A piece of art.'

A hush.

'Oh?'

'It's a working building. For people. It needs to be safe. It needs, eh, services. Air conditioning, heating, water. All that has to go somewhere. So you build a structure for that, but that throws off the original calculations. So you adjust the structure and then you need to make that safe, so you adjust it again. It adds up. Small changes, but that stuff is, you know,' he searches for the word. 'Cumulative. Making the floors higher was the simplest solution, technically. It was an ambitious build—'

'Ambitious.'

Art looks up, intent. Fuck, thinks David.

'Would you say it was over-ambitious?'

He begins to blather. He can smell Ó Buachalla's cologne now, sharp and tangy across the courtroom. He talks about the cladding. How it was part of the overall, eh, modern look of the building. He's losing them. He talks about having to make the granite thicker so the slabs wouldn't split. Too much detail, but the smart arse isn't stopping him. He talks having to manage the load, adjust the trusses, then adjust the umbrella—

'Umbrella?'

'The cantilever structure. That's what we called it. It had to be made deeper to take into account, the, eh—' That fucking word, what is it?

'Cumulative?'

'Yes.'

The smart arse grins.

They were right. Rourke, the Fine Gael TD on the radio. Aisling. It's a mess. All he can do is fall from the Alamo, as the Mexicans look on, hooting. David's awareness lifts up, out of his body squirming on his chair, and bobs around the courtroom, aimless as a balloon on a windless day. At the back of the room, he sees a long-legged figure in the shadows; the comedian from the telly, on the look-out for impressions for his new show. Near the front, an artist is scribbling sketches for a newspaper, and over at the door is a group of conservationists, long-hairs in tweed jackets and cord trousers. The enemy, Art calls them. The same crew Ó Buachalla hacked off when he tried to build the car-park on the Viking site, the ones who keep mouthing platitudes about the brutality of modernisation and the ugly forces of commerce scarring the golden face of our Georgian heritage. *Ours*? Molloy, the busybody from Planning who started the whole fiasco, is in the middle of the room, and two seats from him is a small man wearing a bow tie and making notes on a foolscap pad, and he's somebody who knows his stuff, David can tell, and, even upside down and at this distance, David can make out the lines of triangulation and is he, Jesus, is he inverting the fucking thing, putting the cantilever on the penthouse and what's that about, do they want us to cut the bloody thing in two?

Is that what it boils down to? Us. Them. A caricature on the editorial pages. The thuggish boys in Georgie's school, crowing. Is that your *da*, Madden? Years later, when David starts to understand, the only word that will fit this moment is *schism*. But at the time, it feels far messier than that; an overwhelming sense of something to prove or test, something to check, something right in front of him, if he could only *see* – that bloody equation again, that stupid formula – while at the same time a deeper impulse is warning him No no no David don't eventrytoadditup

Them ≠ *Us*

Us = ?

∴

He looks up, across the courtroom. Ó Buachalla's cologne fills his senses. The equation—

■■■■■■■■

His mind shutters, snapping it, whatever it is, out of his consciousness.

The light flickers. For a moment, David has a sense of something inhuman crouching before him. A whirl of matter and energy, devouring everything in its wake. Then he blinks, and all that's in front of him is a man; bigger than average, with wild black hair and fleshy, mobile features, but still just a man.

Pain shoots into David's eyes. He feels dizzy, cold, sick to his core.

'It's the best we could have hoped for,' says Lyons. 'They'll stall it but the client has weight. Six months' time, that little prick in Planning will be on his knees, begging for a compromise.'

Ó Buachalla grunts.

'You'll live, Donnacha. It's only a building.'

The corridor is freezing. Someone must have left a door open. David can hear his breath suck in through his teeth, too fast. His body feels jagged and shrunken; the left side of his chest is hurting, as if he's ripped some essential muscle he didn't even know he had. He wishes he was somewhere else, somewhere warm. He could murder a pint. Though he should check on Georgie first. He—

Art is talking to him. Something about taking him off the hotel. '…we'll give it to Rourke, put you on the new bridge. That's not one of Donnacha's, so nobody's likely to make a fuss.'

The architect laughs.

I want that mainframe, thinks David. If you're pulling me off the hotel, I want access to Morgan Lloyd and Blackfriars before Rourke—

Art is looking at him, puzzled. Did he speak out loud?

'So who's going to pay?' says Ó Buachalla.

Oh, Christ, thinks David. Did he – oh, fuck – did he admit any liability?

Art shakes his head. 'It's a State building. The big boys will fork up.'

'Jar, Daithí?' Ó Buachalla looks at David. He's impatient to go, clapping his hands, rubbing them together. All that movement is blurring the boundaries between him and his surroundings, making David's eyes hurt even more.

No, David wants to say. I need to go home to my son. His mouth moves. 'Maybe.'

'I'll be expecting you. I owe you a pint, *mo chara*.' Ó Buachalla's teeth bare in a grin. 'For the piazza.'

Mo chara. My friend.

'We'll be in O'Neills.' Arthur Lyons takes Ó Buachalla by the elbow and they leave, taking their pungent, fearful courtroom smells with them.

'Keep your friends close, eh?' David turns. Molloy, the man from Planning, is behind him, holding out his hand. David looks down at it.

Molloy laughs. 'Give me some credit. I didn't come up the Liffey in the bubble. You obfuscated well in there. I only hope Buckley appreciates your efforts.'

Ah, fuck off with you, thinks David, and almost says it, except Molloy has already set off; small, trotting steps, like a pony.

Outside, the chill is turning the sleet to snow; the worst sort, sticky and wet. Shivering, David goes into a public phone box on the quays to ring Aisling. The phone rings out; and the second time he tries, and the third. Is she still at work? He can't remember when she said she'd be home. Maybe she's out with Georgie. No. Georgie's with Mrs Kelly. Should he ring there? Someone has scrawled *No Smoking* on the wall above the phone. Fag butts litter the floor, mocking the warning, and there's a damp patch near the door that could be vomit. David stares at the phone, heavy in his hand. He's panicking about Georgie. That's all. And it's probably for the best, not getting through to Ash. What could he say to her? What would she, only *I told you so*?

He crosses the river and heads up under Merchant's Arch. It stinks of piss and pissed-out drink, like his youth, like the back of his Da's pub on a Friday night. At the newsagent's on the corner of Fleet Street he buys a packet of ten Major and, out of habit, picks up an *Evening Press*.

Bank: Stalled For Years. Front page. They would have needed the story by lunchtime; a late, inconsequential entrance for the bit player. As a sop, they've featured two more of his drawings: front and side sections. A final offering for Georgie's scrapbook, if he still has any use for it.

Outside Bewley's, a tinker woman is begging, two scrawny, blue-lipped kids by her side. David tosses them a few coins and walks around by College Green and onto Dame Street, passing the old buildings that once held a Parliament.

He stops. And is surprised, almost, to find the site still there.

For the whole of September – that strange, beautiful month when Aisling's vitality began to return and the promise of *starting over* took on the feeling of something real – David had gone to the bank every night. He left the house once Georgie and Aisling were asleep and drove straight to the site, staying from midnight till six in the morning to check the levels as they'd poured the concrete into the slipform mould to make the twin supports for the building. First one core, then the other. As dawn broke, he would go home, prepare the breakfast, wake his family, and they'd all eat together before he got some sleep. It had been a warm month – an Indian summer; they'd been blessed with the weather – and there had been something magical about being at the site in the dead hours of night, when everything else was at rest. Something wonderful about participating in this big, visionary job of work, this glass-and-concrete dream of Ó Buachalla's, this marvellous suspended structure of Arthur Lyons', this building that yes, would hold itself up by its own bootstraps, a gleaming exclamation mark for a modern European city's expanding centre. The air had been balmy with the last traces of summer. Around him had risen a cushion of comforting, familiar sounds. Men shouting, lorries beeping, welders droning, the constant hissing rhythm of the hydraulic jacks. David's legs had ached from crouching on the top platform of the slipform; his eyes had fizzled with tiredness and the strain of checking levels, making sure that the tiny apertures for the spigots were in the right place for each floor as the grainy grey river rose inside its steel cage, transforming by the millisecond from liquid to solid. But it had been worth it. For that small window of time, it had been worth it.

Is this how a life is made? he had thought one night, watching the concrete rise while the moon echoed its ascension in the sky behind him. Is this how I've been made? How Georgie will be? Shaped by time, bit by slow bit, so nobody can tell anymore where the start is? And the thought had struck him with such a profound sadness he'd thought his breath would stop.

At the end of the month they had erected the steel umbrella. First the columns, then the diagonals, then the trusses for the plant floor. In October, when Aisling went back to work, they began raising the floors, using twelve jacks placed around the roof. By then, effort was creeping back into David's home life, Aisling's insistence on starting over taking on a ring that unsettled him. She began nudging him. Maybe they should start to look farther afield. Ireland wasn't the only country in the world. That firm has offices everywhere, Davey. Why don't you put some pressure on Art – God knows he owes you – to find you a position in London? That man from London liked you, didn't he? An edgy brightness to her voice that only did the opposite of convincing him.

As the weeks went on, the nudging became carping and the carping threatened to spill over into full-blooded argument, though David did his damnedest not to rise to it, determined to retain that equability he had tried to cleave to since his son's conception. When he felt his will begin to crack, he started taking to the site for solace. He watched the massive slabs of steel and concrete climb, glinting in the autumn sunlight, carrying their loads of glass and granite and wood, and thought of a giant steamship, hurtling towards tomorrow. Maybe that's like us, he thought, Ash and me. Maybe we're still on track. Knowing he was clutching at straws. And that was how it was going, yet another triumph for the unstoppable architect, returned prodigal Donnacha Ó Buachalla – formerly Denis Buckley of Blackrock, County Dublin – when, one afternoon in early November, Molloy from the Planning Office looked out his window and noticed that the landmark building was on its way to being a good thirty foot higher than the original specification.

Donnacha wants you in court, Art said. Someone who knows how to keep their cards close to their chest.

I can't see why, Ash kept saying. Her November refrain. Why can't it be Rourke? He's a bulldog. Why does it have to be you, Davey? They'll only throw you to the wolves.

It's okay, Ash, he said – trying for reassurance, easy tack first. I've done this before. I know how this works. Harder and harder to keep his cool, though, as the weeks went on. Then, last night, he lost it.

That bloody architect will be the ruin of you, she had said, almost shouting. You're no match for that sort, David. You don't know what he's up to. What he's capable of.

Oh, no? he'd roared. Just wait and see. You know fucking nothing, Aisling, so stop pretending you fucking do. Who are you trying to fool with your fucking—

The word began, hissing on his tongue. Her eyes widened. He saw his father's face, raging. And – just in time – he clamped his stupid mouth shut.

Scare, he'd been about to say, with all the contempt he could muster.

He opens the pack of Major, takes out a cigarette and lights it. The smoke fills his lungs; the taste of his wayward, hopeless teenage years.

He looks up. Unfinished, the building is obscene: a woman with no skirt, a man with his trousers round his ankles. In a couple of weeks' time, the street will be rainbow bright with Christmas decorations. Whether it's left half-finished, or destroyed, or even started up again, compromised in some backroom deal, people won't notice the bank any more. They'll have eyes only for the big Christmas tree on College Green and the display in Switzers window. We wish you a merry Christmas and a Happy New 1975.

A gull swoops down, weaving through the danger signs on the hoardings.

In his coat pocket, David can feel the package he had bought before the hearing. The jeweller had put it in a blue velvet box for him, wrapped in brown paper. Even through the sleet, it had caught his eye. Torque, the jeweller had called it, not necklace. Funny, David said. I work with torques. I'm an engineer. Ah, said the old man. Perfect, so.

It is made from silver pieces, inlaid with turquoise and held together by woven golden wires. It was the delicacy that appealed to him. Like something broken and put back together again. As soon as he'd seen it, he'd imagined it on Aisling, glamorous and protective in one. Who would want rosary beads, he'd thought, when they could have that? He had pictured her opening the package, had even imagined her wearing it to the firm's Christmas party; social face on, all nice Northern girl and soft, bright laughter belied by the pagan magic streeling from her chest. Taking the eyes out of every man in the room. His red-gold Venus, his unassailable prize.

He takes another pull on the cigarette.

90

Stress can exert terrible pressure on materials; stretch or strain them, crumple them beyond recognition. Deformation, this is called. Small wonder it can do things to a man's mind. Make you see monsters in a schoolyard or a courtroom, or make you feel like you've lost your child, or left part of your soul behind, hovering for perpetuity over a green baize chair. Make you – almost – say something unforgiveable to the mother of your child; then try to convince you that there is something fundamental you should know that made you – almost – say it, some ridiculous two and two scraping at the tip of your thoughts that you should be putting together. Except you shouldn't, and you won't, and you never will, because the simple fact is you don't need to. Because the only thing that's wrong is you're freezing cold and tired to your marrow, so tired you can't even see straight, not just from an afternoon talking to a bunch of smart arses, but from a year you wouldn't wish on your worst enemy. Technically speaking, only nine months, but to hell with technically speaking.

Manageable? What a fucking lie.

He'll go for a jar, not because he said so, but because he needs one. He'll have a couple. Maybe three. He doesn't have to talk to anyone; not Art, not Ó Buachalla. He might pretend to listen, but only if he feels like it. As for Aisling, he'll come home when he's good and ready. And if she's in a snit— Let her. She was the one who wasn't there when he phoned.

He feels his shoulders ache. He knows that's probably just the tiredness speaking. The weight of her illness, the strain of the hearing. You're not good enough for me, she'd said last night, if not in so many words. Truth is, he doesn't trust himself to face her, not in this state.

They can make up tomorrow. Patch up, get on with it, like they always do. It mightn't be starting over, her grand plan, but it will have to do. He'll give her the torque in the morning and she can take it however she wants. As a peace offering, or an early Christmas present, or, if the fancy takes her, something more savage than that.

His chest is hurting again; a deep pain, like a stitch. He should ring Mrs Kelly, make sure Georgie's okay. He knows he's probably fussing, but he should still ring. He'll do it from the pub. If everything's fine, he'll stay for a pint. No more than that.

Promise, Davey?

The gull swoops past the penthouse floor of the unfinished bank, circles through the sleet, then disappears.

David flicks his cigarette butt away. It spirals, a red kiss against the night. Hunching his shoulders, he turns towards the city.

*'**Ausland/Otherland'**. Regie/Director: Sabine Wiedemann. Datum/Date: 15/03/20— Ort/Location: Aberystwyth. Befragte/Interview Subject:'Anna Bauer'* (<u>**Sitzung/Session 1**</u>).

Yes. Thank you. I am comfortable. You had a *gute Reise*? You came by the valleys, the Devil's Bridge. Good, yes. It is beautiful. To have the three bridges in the one, it makes one imagine all sorts of differents times, laid over on themselves in the one spot....

Yes. Of course. I am *bereit*. So.

...

I came in the summertime and you know, that was a city that stinked. It was the Georges brewery and the cut into the harbour that they called New, low tidings and the water dropping. You dear goodness, it stinked. Of the shit and pigsty and rotting cabbage.

I had nothing but noises in my head, you know? The noises of the mill, clackety-clack and whirr-whirr-whirr. Dust in my nose and noises in my brain. I sat on a wooden seat in the train and I look out and see England go pass me. Foreby. I had the mothertongue in my head too, all those girls that did the working in the mill with me, none of us had the good English, we all spoke *auf Deutsch* together, and after the work we lived and cooked in the same house, so that, the German, was playing the song in the inside of my head with the clackety-clack of the mill. There was still dust from the mill in my nose, in my clotheses, in everything. In Rochdale, I would in the evenings take off my dress and shake it out and see the cotton dust falling, like snow or cherryblossom off the trees and the bloomings.

The dandruff, we called it. The itchy scalp. Told ourselves
to wash our hair *gut* with lemon juice and the grapefruit
seeds! A joke, you know. A witticism.
Excuse me? My hearing is—

Why it is I—? Is it not… Is it—

Excuse me? Is it not that one you want me to talk of? I am
sorry, please, excuse me. There gives so many leavings,
you see, so many crossings from one place to the other,
at times they mix together in the head and it is difficult
to, you know, untangle. But—

See you. If I put out the fingers of my hand and look, I can
see, *also*, that one is for such a reason, and that one is for
money, and this because we had to, and this leaving because
he, the Man, came from there. But with this I'm talking of,
the leaving of Rochdale, there is no good reason.

. . .

Also. I had enough of the dust. I wanted to leave it. Enough
of the clacking of the mill and yes, perhaps the mothertongue
in my head. And, of course, I was pregnant, but....

[laughs]

Oh, no. No. That I will not talk of.

. . .

So. I smelt Rochdale and the mill in me as I come down
the back of England, and watched the fields and towns
and sometimes even the sea. It was a priest who put in
my head the idea of going there. Father Joseph. Or as
we called him, *Josef.* One writes them similar, but they
sound different in the two tongues, the names. He had a
motorcycle. He was a young man, out of Bavaria, with the
dark hair. He looked of the south. He took the motorcycle
to where we were, in Rochdale, to say the Mass at the
German church for our community, because in England it
was on the most part Protestant Churches, and then he
rode it, the motorcycle, down to Bristol. You would like

Bristol, Anna, he said. Oh, yes, it has mountain ups and downs and there is a harbour, so pretty.

All I see when I come are the holes, you know. Holes the Germans made. Luftwaffe. People talking all the time about the holes and where they were, and how they were eating and in what park they sat or in what bed or under what floor they hide as the bombs fell. It would be simple, an easy thing, you know, to feel the responsibility for such holes.

Do I? Feel such?

...

I come in the station, Temple Meads, and it is very nice to look at, with glass and the iron framing such as one I saw in the big town near the village where I grew. I walked. I did not know what else to do. I had no plan. Father Joseph had told me of the city and it flew into my mouth, the name of it, Briss-toll. As you know, *toll* is *auf Deutsch* the name for great, fantastic and also crazy, like a lunatic, and yes, it was funny how the word came in me as I stood in the station to buy the ticket. What else I would do there once I came I did not know. There was not such the community of us there. There was a POW camp outside the city but to that time many of the men were already gone home or married or so further.

Did I, excuse me? No. I liked the other girls, the ones in the house, we spoke the same dialect, we knew us. But to care what they were saying, such as, dear goodness, what must the Anna have done, why she left so suddenly, the gossip, was I pregnant and so forth, that was never important to me.

No. I don't think that. To leave because of other people's talk, that is not a brave thing to do. I wanted to leave the dust.

I became lost for an hour, perhaps. I had the happy feeling to first, of being new, in a new place, and being close to a new person. It stinked more than I wanted, but there was no dust. I ate an ice and watched the ladies in their hats walk through the streets with the holes.

There is a long, rising street in Bristol, you know, Park Street, so beautiful. In the high heels you must walk very carefully. Then I came to the Queen Square, quiet it was, and to the front of the harbour, and I saw Redcliffe and it, as you say, pulled me. It was how it looked out, what is the word, perching, over the city as a mother bird on the branch. The spires of the cathedral, St Mary's, and the tall narrow of the houses on the high wharf. It made me feel quiet in, you know, here.

Yes, Sabine! Exact. No more clacking. No more words, so much in the mothertongue as any.

I was heavy, you know, seven months, and it was hot. I was small, a miracle with two in me, like it had been with my mother, so it happens, one generation to the next. I could hide the lump, with some effort, but heavy. Later, I told the children that, how hot it was, how the place stinked, how heavy I was, when I came here. How I walked for hours, around Redcliffe, because although I grew in a small village, nothing like a city, there was a, sensing, in the air up on the red cliff that was like a home. I had not that in Rochdale. Rochdale was always other. Elsewhere. But Redcliffe seemed to me to be somewhere I knew. Though I did not grow in a city or near a harbour. How is that? That a place feels as oneself and is quite not the same as what one knows? That a place is home but not too? Later, I found Hotwells and that pulled me also. It was somewhat as the towns on the Baltic, pictures I had seen. And Clifton also, very lovely, the colours of the houses, as ice cream. It was, I believe, one of the most lovely places I have fled to. Is that correct? Fled? The correct word?

The children, Lotte und Andreas, they made a game, a, no, a, *Spiel*. A playing-out, as theatre. When they were little. They played a meeting between I and the Doctor, as if I came like the Holy Mary to Bethlehem watching for the Christchild bed and the Doctor was the kind innkeeper. But in the realness it was quite other. Not so romantic. In the fact, I found the position advertised and attended an interview and the Doctor Brooks was, as you would say, open-minded. But for the twins, no, that would not be enough. They wanted so much more. An adventure!

They readed, you see, they readed so many books, and joked at me always, how bad my English, how like a country-peasant I spoke, like a child. But I was always proud on them. To go to the university, to read such books. And the works my boy made, the art. Yes, the strange, um, *Kunstkammer* – yes, the one he made with that girl, the beauty – with the, you know, samplers and such stating such angry things. Such angry things, all woven in hair. *Ganz völkisch, ja.* The other workings he made with her, more disgusting, those I did not care for. But that *Kammer*, which he thought I did not understand, yes, even that made me proud.

Lotte too. So clever. It was her named my boy's work the *Kunstkammer*, she loved that sort of things. Though the girl of Andreas, the beauty, she did not like that name.

Did I...? Excuse me?

...

To talk more of my son? But you see—

Ah. No. Maybe the next time. I am losing the concentration, you see. An old lady.

[laughs]

That is a joke, to say I am old, because my heart is young, you see, and to speak of the past makes me younger. Here, inside me, yes. Though these days, perhaps, it is not so much of a joke as it used to be.

[rises, removing mic]

Now. I must to my room to view the News programme. Always at this time I watch, before the *Essen*, the lunch. It is better then. Not so hard for the mind to um, yes. Digest. *Bis gleich!* as we say *auf Deutsch*. Though, yes, of course, that means in the very soon moment. *Bis der nächste*, I mean. Till the next.

Cross/Dissolve

Budweisers were not the only group that failed to conform to nationalist visions of identity.... Others, so-called 'renegades' or 'amphibians,' were able to move between [Czech and German] national categories. Recently, scholars have turned their attention to these national outcasts as a way to underscore the flexible rather than the fixed notion of nations....

David Wester Gerlach, *For Nation and Gain* (2002)

((   ))

Important Note
In reponse to visitors' concerns regarding the use of parallels with Curiosities from Elsewhere, as suggested in some of our Footnotes ('See Ireland…' etc.):

As we all know, Herstory and its variations (history, itstory, theirstory, etc.) never repeats itself; it just mimics, badly. We therefore suggest that you visualise our 'parallels' as loose/wavy, not (Fig. 1) straight lines. Think of them as strings on a musical instrument; carrying sound waves which travel at different frequencies. At times, when the vibrations are pitched just so, they appear to reach for each other (Fig. 2), almost, one might fancy, as if searching for connection. Occasionally, they may even intersect – an unintended mimicry, perhaps, of a double-stranded molecule of DNA.

Some visitors have suggested that, if these 'parallels' are a struggle to make unified sense of something that perhaps cannot be made sense of, should we not learn from Einstein and the failure of his Grand Unified Theory? Drop all attempts at resonance, focus instead, as many have and will, on one specific trajectory?

One land, one folk, one leader?

Maybe not.

Fig. 1 'True' (geometric) parallels   Fig. 2 Our curator's parallels

09:32:16–13:18:58

Cars, an astrologer once told me, *are ruled by Mars.*

Ares, I'd said, surprising him, and myself. Then I backtracked, explaining. He was Greek first. Mars was his Roman name.

Huh, said the astrologer. He was American, slight and attractive. *Inneresting....*

He was my first shrink, though I doubt he'd have called himself that. I met him in Berlin, soon after I moved there. The same place I found Martin, but ten years earlier.

I'd gone to Berlin straight after college because Berlin, people said, was cool, especially now the Wall had come down. My first job came to me easily enough; a three-year contract with a small post-production company in what had been the East, cutting music videos for death metal acts. I had started editing in uni and enjoyed it. I still do; there's a quietness to it, a listening, even if you're cutting death metal.

It was the early nineties, when all that New Age stuff started getting mainstream. Someone at work had gone to the astrologer and said he was a genius. He can read you like a book, they said, tell you why you do things. I had money, I was living in a cool city, I had work I liked doing. So why was there so much wrong with me? I was having problems sleeping; I was having problems controlling my eating. I didn't know why I wanted to fuck the people I wanted to fuck. I liked what astrology seemed to offer: something big, outside myself, that I could hold to account for everything that wasn't working. A system that might even explain that sleeping amphibian inside me; better still, give me rules to help me contain it.

The astrologer's graphs and charts were beautiful; he made nice gestures when he spoke. But most of what he said went over my head, except for that bit about cars and their ruler, Mars.

God of power and passion. Fucking and fighting. Pure testosterone. He'd looked meaningfully at me then, as if we were brothers in arms. *You don't have a car, do you?*

No, I said. Do I need one? Because Berlin is like London, good public transport.

Well. He looked at his chart. *Your Mars is in Libra, so I can't see it happening soon.*

He'd smiled. Then he'd asked me on a date.

Me? I'd said. Oh, God. No. Sorry. I didn't mean to. I mean, eh, I'm not, eh—

What shocked me most was how like you I'd sounded. Unable to get to the point, one stiff stutter after another.

He was right. I didn't start driving till my early thirties, after I'd met Martin, and then only reluctantly. I told Mar I didn't want to learn; it was politically incorrect, ecologically unnecessary. He didn't buy my excuses. *If it bothers you that much, Geo, why don't you go live in a yurt?*

Mar loved cars, everything about them, could tell a make and model streets away, just by the sound of the engine. The upside, he used to joke, of being a Ned. *You're born in Govan knowing how to do three things. Get a bird up the duff, sign on the Giro and hotwire a car.* I used to watch for hours, fascinated, as he tinkered around with the insides of our bangers. Those capable hands, pocked with knife scars and scald marks, twisting wires, testing bearings; those light hairs on the back of his wrists staining blue with oil.

God of power and passion. Fucking and fighting. Mar was right; it had nothing to do with eco-guilt. Nothing to do with Libra either. Martin's hands weren't the first I remembered tinkering with the insides of a car. I didn't want to drive because I didn't want to be like you.

Is this what you're expecting, what you want from me? Is this information concrete enough? I keep forgetting. I forget and then I remember and – this might sound stupid, given all the distance and time between us – but it still comes as a shock, how much you don't know.

I know I've asked before, but I'll ask again. What made you send me that?

'Georgia!'

I turned. Dolores, my neighbour, was trotting around the corner, shouting to make herself heard over the Wolfe Tones' music, still belting out from the Travellers' house. Usually I make time for Dolores. She was good to me after

Mar left, and that has to count for something. But that morning my head was thumping and I hadn't the patience to exchange *Hello*'s for the sake of it, much less get into the full Irish chat about the terrible weather or the dreadful news on the telly. So I gave her a big smile, a hasty nod to show I was in a hurry, then, quick as I could, shoved the coat I'd picked up on my way out into the back of the Fiat and slammed the door. I opened the driver's side and started to clamber in.

'Wait!' Dolores speeded up, her shamrocks bouncing against her green tweed chest. She was waving something at me.

'Sorry, Dolores! Got to go!' I shoved the key into the ignition.

'But the postman told me....' It was a jiffy bag. I recognised the stamps first – America. Then the handwriting.

'I'm in a rush!' I turned the key. The car revved.

Your handwriting. Even worse, if that was possible, than the last time.

'It says valuable—' She was screeching now.

'Just stick it in the letter box!' I yelled back. Christ's sake. If it was that valuable, you could have sent it by registered post. I slammed my foot on the gas. The car lurched forwards. I rammed the stick into second.

As I reached the corner I saw Dolores in my rearview, still holding out the jiffy bag. Her mouth was open and her eyebrows were raised, stark against her pale skin. A mask from a Greek chorus, one of those plays where the sins of the parents fall upon the children. Crunching the gears, I took the corner. The chorus disappeared.

Left first, then right. Right again, at the lights. Left, onto the Canal. As soon as I got out of the warren of tight, grey pebble-dashed little streets, something in the back of my head eased and my nose began to run. I reached for a tissue in the glove compartment, but there weren't any, so I used the sleeve of my top. At a garage – not the next one, somewhere farther away – I'd stop and get some. I had no idea where I was going. All I knew was I needed to get out.

It was still early, but crowds were already forming, hustling towards the tram stops and swarming there in messy impatient queues. They looked like refugees from another dimension. Everyone seemed to be wearing green and fright wigs and leprechaun hats, clutching giant plastic shamrocks, their faces a mass of tricolour. The first bolts of Paddy's Day mania were crackling through the air. Laughter just that bit too loud, kids crying, crumpled cider cans lying in the kerb. And, the big giveaway: teenagers up too early, all curling lips and young offenders' stubble and acres of exposed flesh, jigging away on the platforms, yowling bad R&B/punk mash-ups, getting geared up for the party ahead.

I thought of that news story playing out on Sky, all the other news stories it had pushed to the background. All those invisible agendas unfurling into action; those bodies, blasted under rubble, fermenting in the heat. I thought of the dying, the ones still alive. What thoughts were playing in their minds? Did they even have minds anymore?

I pushed my foot down on the gas. The bridges of the Grand Canal flashed past. No reds; an easy run.

I still wasn't sure where I was going – straight on, perhaps as far as the coast, or just to leafy Milltown and the river – when, at Harold's Cross bridge, my finger flicked the indicator. The car swerved to the right, catching the lights just before they changed. Ahead of me lifted the road, flanked by the hilly suburbs of south Dublin. The car had decided for me. We were heading for the mountains.

When I was a child, my Dublin was compassed by the coastline, those two headlands crouching at either end of the bay. Howth to the north, and, off to the south, distant Bray. The suburbs south of the Liffey always seemed like mysterious, unknown quantities to me; not as grand as the Georgian centre, but – with some exceptions – way more impressive than the northside flatlands where we lived. I used to love saying their names under my breath. Did you ever hear me? *Ranelagh, Rathmines, Rathgar. Harold's Cross, Terenure, Rathfarnham. Donnybrook, Merrion, Dean's Grange, Foxrock. Dundrum. Ballinteer. Stillorgan.* Those were the places you would take us through on our way to the Mountains, capital M, or, less often because we'd beaches of our own on the northside, the Sea. But when you took us to Clonmel, to visit my aunts and your mother, my batty Granny, we went inland, passing through the other southside. The uglier one, the southside that looked like the northside. *Inchicore, Drimnagh, Bluebell, Walkinstown.*

Inchicore; Island of the Snout.

It was an accident Mar and I ended up there. We'd landed in Dublin in 2005, the height of the Boom, and we'd both got work quickly enough – me back freelancing again, Mar in a swish fish restaurant in the Docklands. I still had some money, from what your sisters had left me and the remains of my sale of my share of the post-production business. But between Mar's debts, my medical bills and the Boom, we couldn't be picky. Inchicore seemed like a smart move. I hadn't minded the grungy, down-at-heel feel of the place; it seemed real, somehow, dirtily authentic among all the gloss and polish of the Boom. Anyway, it was all going to change, the estate agent told us; new money was putting the 'chic' into Inchicore. But the new money never came and it wasn't long before Mar began to hate it. The litter, the insularity, the violence and, worst of all, the betting shops, a constant, nagging reminder of his own addiction. He always got mopey when we went on drives through the prettier suburbs of the southside, bitching that I should have brought us back to Dublin sooner and bought somewhere decent.

How would that have happened? I'd said. I never wanted to come back here.

So why now?

Ah, you know why now.

Don't avoid the fucking question—

Don't you—

And on. And on.

I told him he was petit-bourgeois, Hyacinth Bucket with a skinhead, secretly aspirational in spite of all his down-with-the-people Socialist Workers cant. He told me I was a hypocrite, getting my kicks living in Coronation Street with a Glasgow Ned, knowing I'd never have to face real poverty with my smart degree and multi-page CV and two modern languages and country pub inheritance and dinky little facilities house buy-out prize money. I told him if he felt that strongly about things, he shouldn't have immigrated with me. He told me if I felt that strongly I shouldn't have asked him to come. I told him I didn't ask him; we'd agreed it, like adults. It was the next logical step.

Logic? he said. Don't do that.

Do what?

You know. Make it look like I'm the irrational one.

Irrational? I said, and laughed.

He told me I was freezing him out, like I'd frozen out my company, my business partner, my friends in Berlin, in Switzerland, in England, everywhere. I told him he was an idiot, I'd kept in contact with everyone who mattered; besides, I needed some space, I needed the buy-out, I'd got stuck in a rut in Brighton, I needed to do new things in a new place, and there'd never been a better time for change, a better time for freelancing, a better place than Dublin. He said I was at it again; avoiding his question. Moving to Dublin had nothing to do with work, he said, otherwise I wouldn't be back stuck in front of a screen all day, tidying up other people's stories because I hadn't the guts to tell my own.

Guts? I said.

Yeah, he said. All you want to do is test whatever you're turning into in a place that's got no risk for you.

I told him he was stupid; my life was full of risk. If it wasn't, what was I doing with him?

What did you just say? he said, his face white. I started to answer but he wouldn't let me.

He told me that was unfair, he told me that wasn't the fucking point. He told me I was a liar, I was terrified, I was such a control freak I had to tidy away and put a lid on anything that didn't make sense, including my past, including my own fucking imagination. I told him hang on, he was the one being unfair, using that stuff against me, that was a step too far, and besides, he was a fine one to talk about putting a lid on things when he was the one bottling everything up, and if he wasn't, if he was such a big fucking hero, then why was he so afraid of the smell of my neck?

After stopping at a garage for petrol and tissues, the car and I kept heading south, over the river Dodder and up through Rathfarnham. South again up Willbrook Road, the fastest route to the mountains. The roundabout at the top was packed; suburban dads in Chelsea tractors bringing the kiddies out for the Big Day. I let them swirl in front of me, filling the open spaces like piranhas. I had no choice; the dads were white-knuckled, warped into Curly-Wurlys with anxiety, the terror – remember? – of missing the Good Spot at the parade. Eventually I found a gap and forced the Fiat through.

We lifted up over the new motorway, past the empty zombie estates, the gates of the burnt-down Big House at Massey, the scalped entrance to the HellFire wood. At the summit, we ignored the car park with the ice-cream van and swung right instead. Darkness closed around us as we entered a long tunnel of trees, blue-green conifers that have always reminded me of Germany, before emerging, small and exposed, on the Military Road.

Around us, the curves of the hills were purple and brown, bruised with the colours of the early heather. I twisted the wheel. The Fiat pulled into the lay-by above the reservoir, a few hundred yards from the memorial for the executed Old-IRA man.

The wind was up now; cold and fresh. Inky clouds were hustling over the city. The patches of blue sky I'd seen earlier were being chased away, eastwards, towards Britain. Rain was coming. The ferns and bracken danced. I reached for a tissue just as the pressure behind my nose built, peaked, exploded.

I have hazy memories of going to the Military Road as a child, with you and Aisling and then just you. After moving back to Ireland, I collected new associations; sharper, cleaner, that lay like a camera filter over what had been there before. I love the borderland wildness of that part of the Dublin mountains; the new perspectives I get each time I look down over my hometown from a height. Strangetown, oldtown, newtown. *Call these mountains?* Mar used to say. *They're oany wee baby hills, Geo.* He used to say he only came along for the ride, for the fresh air, so he could blow away the week's excesses. Liar. He loved it there too. I could tell from the way his breath used to slow, his chest lower; the way he let his eyes get just a little sad.

Sundays and bank holidays are still popular on the Military Road. The lay-by with the view is often so packed it's hard to find a parking space. During the glory days of the Boom, it was all macho 4x4s, clumpy people-carriers, nifty hatchbacks. Young couples, bustling families, oldies. Dublin slowing, just for a second, to take in the big picture. Martin used to make fun of the people we saw, inventing secret lives for them.

See him, Geo, he'd say, pointing out a frail pensioner in a tweed jacket; OAPs, he used to call them, one word. *He's into BDSM. Goes to London every month for the fetish parties. Bet you he wears restraints.* In his mouth even the primmest word sounded filthy.

He used to turn off the ignition and the lights and we'd sit for ages and watch. Life unfolding in time-lapse, fast-slow-fast like those quality nature documentaries on BBC4. Fast-slow-fast the cars pull in, stop, and people do their small human business: bicker, kiss, change nappies, share a flask of tea, look at the view, pull off again. While we stayed, unmoving, growing more and more mismatched by the week: two little sparks of nothing in a little red Fiat, stuck like a boil on the face of the world.

I laid my head on the steering wheel and closed my eyes. A slow snakey lowness had entered me, climbing in through the soles of my feet, rising up my legs and swirling around the basin of my guts.

I longed for sleep. It was the last thing I wanted.

When I opened my eyes, a feather was dancing in front of my windscreen, carried by the breeze. I remember the thought; it was clean and fast as a knife-cut. Wherever that feather goes, I'm going to follow.

The feather shuddered, shimmied, flew.

Naked, the Gap, and huge. I watched the scorched landscape pass; its stunted trees, its scrubby bush, all ash browns and muddy blood-reds. Martin used to say going over the Sally Gap was like travelling across the moon. It's not, Sonia corrected him once, on an ill-planned outing, just the three of us. Iceland is far closer, geologically speaking. Isn't it, girl? I don't know what irritated him more, the correction or the *girl*, delivered to me in her Cork lilt. She was right, but I know what Mar meant. The Gap does feel like an alien place, free of any sign of humans, and that morning, I could sense it working its old magic on me, the same magic big empty places always work on the small human mind. Geological glamour; the illusion that landforms, unlike us, never change. That this is how it is, was and always will be.

Bullshit. It's always changing, just slower. You taught me that. Mass, structure, pressure, collapse. The weight of sand and rain, the weight of air. The push of fire from below. Shifting plates, drifting land masses. Big, messy explosions.

Somewhere before the turn-off for the Gap, I had come up with a plan. I would use the outing to make a pilgrimage: take the day to visit Glendalough, go for a long walk, have a meal in the hotel beside the lakes and aim to get home just before sundown. Then I would have a shower and go to bed. No telly, no distractions, just nature. The plan had a quiet clarity to it; it seemed almost talismanic. Even my headcold had eased off. I wondered why I hadn't thought of it sooner.

A pilgrimage. Like the last time I'd gone through this?

Would I go *through* anything this time round? That I pushed away before the obvious could get its claws into me again.

By the time I arrived in Laragh, the sky was the purple of meths, heavy with rainclouds. In spite of that, there was already a queue at the ice-cream shop and as I drove up to the car park, I could see a couple of buses near the lakes. The tourists who'd travelled on them were hovering near the prefab café, all sensible rain gear and tiny cameras. What sort of tourists would want out of Dublin on the day of the parade? They looked confused, as if they were in the wrong place, and a little frantic, as if Glendalough was going to disappear at any moment. I caught the eye of a heavy woman, face pale and doughy.

See her, Geo? Bet she uses a whip.

I parked and swung my legs out of the car. The air was damp, colder than it had been in Dublin. I opened the back door and reached for the coat I'd picked up on my way out. And then, for a second, everything turned into a blur.

'Fuck!'

The coat jumped back as if it was alive. The door snarled, bouncing.

I swore again, louder, and lashed out, smashing my arm against the door. My elbow screamed. I bit my tongue, held back the curse. Enough tourists were looking around already; eyes wide, like startled meercats.

The open door mocked me. A corner of the coat was sticking out, stopping it from closing. I slumped against the car and stared.

I have always hated that coat. Martin picked it up in a flea market near Alexanderplatz a couple of years before he'd met me. He used to wear it all the time in Berlin, saying how cool it was. Cool? Forgive me, but— My hole. It was a dog of a thing, a battered black leather monster, lined with a woollen undercoat that smelt like it hadn't been washed in decades. Martin used to claim it was army stock, worn by some poor bastard who'd served on the Eastern Front. A Prussian, maybe, from a noble military tradition. Someone who'd survived the mud and the frostbite and the unspeakable brutalities only to return home, missing a few toes and a good chunk of his faith in human nature, to find his woman a multiple Soviet-rape victim or an Ami-whore, selling herself for a few ciggies. The worst thing about it was its collar. It was a hunk of moulting sheepskin that looked as if it had been stitched together by that psycho from *Silence of the Lambs*; not Anthony Hopkins, the other guy, the – of course; how clichéd is that? almost as bad as the wrongbody bullshit – crazy tranny.

After we'd moved to Brighton, I'd kept on at Mar to get rid of it. He told me I was being paranoid.

It's oany a coat, Geo. Don't know what you're so threatened by.

Threatened? Don't be ridiculous.

I couldn't explain why I hated it so much, but *oany a coat* was a lie. The way he'd clung to it, you'd think it was part of his soul. He'd worn it less in Brighton, though, and when we moved to Ireland, hardly at all.

How had it got into my car? I was sure he'd got rid of it, or I had, when he'd left. There'd been a rake of stuff he'd put out for the bin and I could remember folding it, pushing it into the warm smelliness of a refuse sack. Hadn't I?

I closed my eyes and imagined the thing vanishing, like magic. Silly, of course, because when I opened them, it was still there, sprawling on my back seat. Why didn't I dump it now? The thought appealed. I could throw it on the ground and drive away. Leave it there like a gangland killing; unmourned, unburied.

Gingerly, I lifted it out. The leather felt oddly warm against my fingertips; dry and scaly, like the skin of a lizard. I brought it to my face and sniffed. My sinuses were blocking up again so I couldn't get any smell. No mothballs, no leather. No Martin. I glanced around. There was a bin behind me.

A wind gusted, stiffening the hairs on my arms.

You can't get rid of things that easy, Georgie.

This was ridiculous. It was bitterly cold, and likely to rain, and if I wanted to go on my pilgrimage, did it matter what I wore? I slid my hand into the right sleeve. It felt okay. Then the rest of my arm. That felt okay too. Of course it did. It was only a coat.

I hoisted it up, put it on. The man it had been made for had been wider in the shoulders than Martin. It fitted me well. Too well? I looked at my reflection in the car window and saw a dark shape, enormous, blank and menacing. Hurrying a little, I rooted in the pockets and found a belt. Cinched around my waist, the coat took on new definition. At a pinch, I could let pass for one of those forties ladies. Rosalind Russell or Jane Greer, maybe, in *Build My Gallows High.*

I smoothed down the collar, trying not to think of fleas, and as I did, I noticed a bulge in the left breast pocket. I fished out a cap; it was the black beret Martin used to wear when he first got his skinhead. Very revolutionary, the radical bloc kids from Prenzlauer Berg had said. Very RAF. They'd meant Meinhoff's crew, not the Royal Air Force, but Martin loved it. *Fairry Airr Eh Eff.*

Is that what you are, I used to ask him, my fairy revolutionary?

Och, don't be so literal, Geo.

Shoving the beret back in the pocket, I locked the car and headed towards the lakes.

The churchyard was empty, but huddled around the interpretive centre was a sprinkling of Americans. They were talking in loud, cheerful upspeak about Saint Kevin and what a, like, complex, man he must have been, maybe even autistic, huh, to choose such a, like, isolated, retreat? On the other side of the bridge, at the south edge of the upper lake, a signpost marked the scenic paths. Four arrows; red, yellow, blue and green. Ludo. I'd forgotten which colour went where. There was no text on the arrows and the map showing the codes was back near the tower.

I felt your irritation surface in me. A difficult sensation. Even after all the therapy I've been through, I have tried not to think about you very often, much less identify with anything you might have felt or thought. But there have always been situations, like when that astrologer asked me on a date, that remind me of where I've come from. It's a miracle, genetics. One trigger and whoosh, sense-memory surfaces, fast as Pavlov's dog.

Two weeks ago, my birthday had been. And your packet only arrived that morning? Valuable. What a fucking joke.

I chose blue.

In spite of the headcold, I took the swooping curves of the lower forest at a good pace. The dark patches of conifers calmed me; I could see the first sparks of spring on the broadleaves, little prickles of green pushing through the brown nubs on the branches of the birches and ash. As I climbed up the stairs of railway sleepers that led to the cliffs, my pace started to slow. I'd forgotten how many steps there were; how far it was to the top. By the time I pushed through the bracken and emerged out in the open, I was sweating and my legs had begun to shake. Ahead of me, I could see the place where the wooden path gave out, near the source of the stream that fed the lakes. If I wanted to keep going, I'd have to cross the stream using the stepping stones and clamber down through rubble till I reached the path on the other side. There were a lot of boulders that way and on a damp day the moss and lichen would make them hazardous.

I looked up. The clouds were still full of rain, but hadn't spilt yet. I decided to play it safe and at the little platform they'd built near the hawks' nest I stopped for a breather. Hunkering down, I took in the view.

Gleann Dá Lough. Valley of the Two Lakes. Double Water, Cleft. I've always liked the word *cleave*; how, like an editor's cut, it means two contradictory things. Stick to; split from. Of course, one of my therapists had said when I'd told him. He hadn't meant to be patronising, but still. I'd felt as if I'd just neatly folded myself into a box labelled *all trans stop here.*

From above, the valley looked like a child's drawing, one of the drawings I used to do when I was little. I peered down at the snowman-shape of the two lakes, the paths along their banks, dotted with the tiny moving forms of people and dogs. The black masses of trees leading up from the water, the dirty-white cliffs scarred with the marks of old quarries. Funny little shapes stuck out from the grey silhouette of the crest facing me. If I squinted, I could make out the slanting oblong of a water reservoir, the broken thumb of a mineshaft. The colours and shapes hummed, playing tricks on my eyes. At the back of my mind, neurons buzzed, aching to connect.

I thought again of Farringdon, the station where the bomb had gone off, and Turnmill Street, the road it belonged to. The names were tugging at me, like individual features belonging to a face I used to know, that were refusing to come together as a whole. They say the human brain remembers every single thing the eyes register, like those baroque princes who used collect oddments for their cabinets of curiosities, but we let ourselves forget because otherwise we'd go mad. Had Martin ever talked about that part of London, said he knew people living there? Still no connect. I let it go.

If everything goes well tomorrow, I said to the view, I promise I'll—

I stopped, unable to think of an decent enough pledge.

'Och, in't this place really lovely?'

Hillwalkers. I stood; fast, awkward. Back the way I'd come, flashes of red were appearing through the bracken.

'Aye, Celsus, it's a grand wee spot.'

They were Nordies. What were Nordies doing in the Soyth, copping out of the Big Green Celebrations taking over their Victorian streets?

'Och, it's beautiful down here.'

Prods?

The bracken near the turn of the path twitched. No place to hide. I powered forward, away from the Northern tourists speaking in my mother's voice.

I'd brought Martin to Glendalough only the once, and that had been just before the end. Maybe it's more honest to say he'd brought me. He'd suggested it and only when we were in the car did he tell me why: he'd thought it might help.

Help? I said.

You know, he said, get a bit of space, like a sort of meditation.

Meditation?

It's a pilgrimage, he said. Isn't it?

A pilgrimage? I'd stared at him, my rational other half suddenly turned mystic.

Look, why don't you just give it a wee try, Geo? There's more to heaven and earth than—

Sure, I'd said, raising my eyebrows, raising my hands. Whatever.

We'd taken the long way round, braving the rubble and the hazards, and up on the height I did stop and think a bit, though I'm not sure I went so far as to meditate, much less make a prayer. After we'd crossed the stream one of us had started running, and the other followed, and there we were, racing like kids to the bottom, pushing, trying to trip each other up. I'd started laughing and couldn't stop. Mar was so serious, in that competitive boy way of his, so terrified of losing. Once we'd reached the safety of the path down near the water, he'd grabbed me and put me in a headlock. Punishment, of course, because I'd won. I twisted free and then he shocked me by taking my face and kissing me on the mouth, full, the way he used to when we'd first met, dancing scared, excited circles around each other in the clubs off Nollendorfplatz.

I've never— he'd started, then stopped. Fuggerstrasse neon flashing behind him, making an inferno of his face.

I'd had no idea what he wanted to say. I had no words to call it out of him or push it back. All I had was the feeling, like I used to get sometimes as a kid, with the odd babysitter or friends or your mother or – oh God, yes, you remember, Lotte, yes? – of being somehow *seen*. So, tentatively, I'd offered him my mouth and steered his hands to where I'd wanted them and, to my surprise – he'd seemed like such a tough little guttie, stuck in his club-queer ways – he hadn't tried to resist.

Don't worry, I'm not going to get graphic, tell you who stuck it in who.

What's your name? he'd asked later, when we were lying on his bed, in the big room with the black-speckled mirror, in the squatty hinterhof off Oranienstrasse. His head, rough with its dirty-blond crewcut, lay in my lap. My palms already aching for the feel of his skin. He'd had acne in his teens and the scars on his face and on the back of his neck where he had the tiger tattooed made him even more beautiful; he felt worn there, with all those ridges and puckers, but in a good way, like Rupert, the teddy I'd loved as a child. I realised I didn't know what I wanted him to call me.

When I was a kid, I'd said at last, I was … Georgie. Strange, to feel that name again in my mouth.

Georgie? He'd looked up, grinned. Like the football player? No!

I shrugged, glanced away, caught myself in the mirror. I'd arched my back so my chest stuck out: make-believe décolletage. It was a habit I used to practise then, thinking it would make me look more like myself. I was in a skinny phase, the dangerous one where I'd been borderline anorexic, and my hair was longish again, framing my face. Under the black dots my shape blurred, soft-focus. Rita Hayworth in *Gilda*.

Hey, he'd said, bringing his hand to my face. You know, you don't really look like a Georgie.

I don't know if he'd meant that, or just said it to make things okay, as if it would. I can't remember how he happened on *Geo*. From a note, maybe. Geo, gone to get some milk, back soon. *Gi-o*, he'd said, pronouncing it in two syllables, as if it was Italian, the name of one of Caravaggio's angel-renter models.

Geo? I'd raised my eyebrows, playing like I didn't care. Thinking, you call me what you want, soldier, and I'll come running every single time.

By the time I returned to the car park, it was two hours later and I was in rag order. Whatever the so-called pilgrimage was supposed to have done hadn't happened. No mystic space around me; no inner harmony. I felt sicker than I had setting out. Sweat was pumping through me, the hip I'd banged against the stairs was aching, my left ankle groaning from where I'd turned it on a bit of rubble and my sinuses were like cement. I hadn't managed to even contemplate meditating; all I'd done was try not to think about Mar. It had been a terrible idea to leave the house. I should have just grinned and borne it, put on a box set, or had a long bath, or got on the blower to Sonia. Forgotten Brid's stupid scripts. Talked to Dolores. Thrown that bloody jiffy bag in the bin. Anything.

The place was filling up. A new group of Yanks, fresh from the parade, were crowding around their tour guide. Hordes of people from other countries were swarming over the church grounds. I couldn't help thinking of locusts. I felt suffocated. Feverish, too clammy to want to eat anything heavy. It was no longer a headcold; I was coming down with a flu. The best thing, I decided, would be a quick cup of coffee and a snack to keep my energy up. Then I'd hit the road, get home, take a couple of sleepers and throw myself into bed.

Inside the café was just as packed as the grounds. Most of the tourists were wearing colourful anoraks that hurt my eyes, apart from a group of Italians in padded black and dark glasses herded round a Formica table near the window. They looked wrong, too stylish for inside, like they should have been out with all the smokers. Up on the wall was a small flat-screen TV, vomiting out the day's news.

I didn't want to look at it, so I kept my eyes on the queue and shuffled up with the rest of the tourists. I was swimming in sweat. The sooner I got back in the car and rid myself of that damned coat, the better. Behind the counter a thin blonde with Polish cheekbones was feeding rubbery scones to a microwave. She had that surly, Eastern European thing going on; probably got up the duff by a Paddy, stuck there while all her compatriots had gone home to Krakow. There was no sign of a coffee machine, just a jar of instant Nescafé, a grubby kettle and a percolator jug full of thin brown liquid that looked like diarrhoea. Pish, Mar had called it, that time we'd come here. Someone – the Polish girl? – had put green food colouring in the milk to remind everyone of the day that was in it. It coated the teas and coffees with a layer of verdigris scum, making them look as if they'd been dredged from a canal. The sight made me nauseous. I bought a black coffee and a scone anyway and took them outside, away from the condensation and the foul heat of other people's breath.

Voices rose around me. German, French, American, Italian, Chinese, Russian. A wall of sound, a – what's that word? – polyphony. Oddly comforting but isolating too, as if I was the only one on the other side. I started to shiver: hot shivers, flu shivers. The coffee tasted of nothing. Behind me, someone was listening to news on a smartphone. The voices faded in and out of static.

unprecedented... terror... need to radically rethink... National Front protests

I pushed away my cup and moved to get up, but a heavy American woman opposite got there first, hauling herself up and jolting the bench with her thighs. Teas and coffees sloshed everywhere, sending green streams of froth down the grooves of the table, spattering all over Martin's coat.

'Aw, shoot!' said the woman. Her eyes were small and raisinish in her doughy face. She was the same woman I'd seen in the car park. I could feel everyone looking at us. 'I'm so sorry.' Shut up, I thought. Just fucking move. She jolted the table again, making it worse. 'Gawd... I am so sorry.'

Someone giggled, soft and girlish. My skin crawled.

Let me share a trans secret. Rule number one: self-preservation. Be safe, be unseen. No sudden movements, no gender- or otherwise-inappropriate behaviour. Be confident, but not brash. Stand proud, but only in a crowd of like-minded people. Choose your companions wisely. Don't invite trouble; melt when you need to. When in doubt, when necessary, call for help. Since I was a child – though you may not recall this – I have prided myself on my nose for danger.

Fighting the urge to look back at whoever had laughed, I gathered Martin's coat around me. The leather was dripping with green scum; I would wipe that off later, once I'd got away. With a grunt, the American heaved herself free and shoved past me. She was heading towards the toilets. I gave her a few seconds, then I slid out from the table in the opposite direction, away from where the laugh had come from. There was an emergency exit at the back of the interpretive centre. If the people who were giggling had spotted me, if it looked like they meant trouble, I could nip out that way and disappear.

At the door of the centre, I glanced around. I wasn't sure what I'd expected, young ones, maybe, out for a bit of happy-slapping, or a few lads, ones whose voices hadn't broken yet but who thought they were real men, hard chaws, the sort that pick on queers and faggots and shirtlifters and lezzers and niggers and polacks and aul ones and junkies and knackers and babies and small animals and chicks with dicks and every other soft target you can think of. They were sitting a couple of tables behind my seat. A teenage couple, a girl and a boy. That surprised me but, as Sonia says, you never can tell.

The girl was unhealthily thin, a long marsh reed in black lace and an ugly motorbike jacket. Goth get-up – or maybe emo, one of those youth trends. She was wearing chalky foundation and heavy purple eyeshadow that hid her eyes. Silver baubles dangled from her front pockets. Skulls, I guessed, or daggers. Something suitably witchy. Around both wrists she had wound rosary beads; they were blood-red, bright as pomegranate seeds. Her hair was long, dyed purple at the front. It looked like it needed a good wash. The boy beside her was around the same age – eighteen, I guessed – but overweight, with heavy features that were sensuous but somehow indistinct. His sandy-blond hair was plastered up into a fin and his skin was blotchy with purple acne marks. They looked close, like a couple, but in a weird way, not like a couple who had sex. He was holding a can of Diet Sprite and whispering into her ear. They hadn't been looking at me or the American woman at all. They were playing some app on her smartphone.

The girl's head lifted. Her eyes brushed over me, stopped.

The boy did something on the smartphone, whispered again. The girl glanced down, recoiled. Then laughed, making a big fake face of outrage as she tossed her hair.

Something in the sky rumbled. I needed to get away but I couldn't move.

Rain began to fall, big, soft, heavy drops that would be vicious in seconds. The girl with the goth make-up and eyes I thought I'd left behind in my childhood moved to go, pulling at the boy's hoodie sleeve, and all around them tourists were rising from the cheap wooden tables, zipping up their too-bright raincoats and popping open their umbrellas. Come on, said the girl, tugging again. I couldn't hear her but I could see her mouth move. The boy drained his Sprite, tilting his can upwards, and as he did, I caught a flash of something on the exposed soft skin of his lower arm; striped marks, orangey-brown. Suicide attempt? Maybe he was a cutter. He dropped his hand, crumpling the can. Then he rose, dragged by the invisible leash the girl had on him and, finally, my feet let me move.

The rain began coming down in buckets, pounding my face as I ran towards the Fiat. I felt unhinged, not in the mental sense but physically, as if part of me was still there, standing outside the interpretive centre, my eyes glued to the girl who looked like Elaine but couldn't be and wasn't, of course, and the boy who looked like me or something I used to be, but wasn't, of course, and the thing they made together that was a nonsense but not, and I was back on the wrong side of the wall again, searching for a portal that I didn't want to find; a gateway into that lost, irretrievable dimension, my own bloody past.

You don't talk much about that time.
   Time?
   Yes. My first proper therapist, consulting her notes; also in Berlin, two years after the astrologer. Knowing Virgo was my ascendant hadn't helped with my insomnia, my eating disorders, my uncontrollable lusts. Sometimes I wonder, Mar used to say, if all those therapists failed you, Geo, because there's something in you doesn't want them to succeed?
   The time that your mother was ill. You don't talk about those years much.
   Oh?
   ..
   (silence)
   Oh. Yes. I was very busy. I was very busy during that time. There was a lot going on…. I was, I suppose, keeping my head down. Under.
   ..
   (silence)
   unsaid: under what?

The air inside the car was bone-cold, raw with damp. I tried to smooth my hair but my hand was shaking too much. I was shivering, worse than before. My face felt as if it had been grated; every bit of heat in my body was escaping through its pores. I managed to turn the key in the ignition and flicked on the air conditioning. Bits of Glendalough began to emerge in ragged lines in the back window. I laughed, and the sound shocked me. The teenagers from the café had appeared again, walking between the rows of cars. They were the same height, but she seemed taller because she was so skinny. He was one pace behind, as if he didn't want to go too close in case he'd damage her. They were soaking. Her hair hung around her face in long purple strings. He'd pulled his hood up against the rain, but kept his eyes on her, like he was scared of losing her, or himself.

117

She slipped into the narrow space behind my car, passing through like a strip of seaweed. Then it was his turn, but he was too fat, and got stuck behind the bumper. He glanced towards her. The condensation made his face in my rearview mirror melt, as featureless as a burn victim's. She floated on towards the bus stop, not looking back. For a second I thought of starting the car and inching it forwards to give him space, but—

He looked up and saw me. His expression changed, two patches of red flaring in his cheeks. I slunk back. He tugged himself free, banged his fist on the hatchback and the car shuddered. Then he lurched off to join the girl, who was waiting for him at the gates, swaying on her long, willowy legs.

You know, I said suddenly, and my therapist straightened up. It's weird but I don't actually remember much of that time. From the inside. I can say what happened, dates *et cetera*, there was a lot that happened, there was a lot I did, people I met. School and friends and…. And Aisling and David and all that with your man that stupid architect coming in at breakfast and later and then bloody Jan, sorry, Jan, arriving. It wasn't a fugue; it wasn't like I wasn't there. But I can't remember *feeling* anything. I look inside, and there are no feelings. It must have been stressful. But I can't remember feeling stressed, so I think I must have, you know, blanked it? Those, um, emotional aspects of it. Like when you let your eyes go out of focus and the thing you're looking at splits. Parallax. Isn't that something you see a lot in your line of work, people, you know, forgetting things….

Forgetting….

..

(silence)

.

(unsaid: so when did you start to remember?)

Alright, I thought. You win, Mar. It's all my fault. Everything.

He didn't answer. I didn't expect him to; I knew I was being ridiculous, talking to myself. But I still peeled that stupid coat off me, and pushed it into the footwell behind the passenger's seat, stuffing it and its dried coating of canal scum as far down as I could.

My reflection in the rearview looked terrible. Feverish, done for. Time to go home.

I turned the key, changed gear, drove down my foot.

Lognote # 3

Cognisant of the recent Glitch encountered during the Maps Cycle, we now steer you to a homelier Object, which, we have been assured, is free of any disruptive resonances. A cork board, vaguely 1970s in feel, to which is tacked a shopping list. The list is on blue-lined paper, apparently torn from a schoolchild's jotter. The ink is faded but legible. The handwriting is rather spiky and, at times, difficult to interpret.

Things to bring back from Bohemia

- Pretty coloured glass objects and jewellery
- Uranium
- The original word for 'dollar' (*thaler*)
- The Kobold (mountain goblin)
- 'Cobalt' blue pigment
- Textiles
- Kafka
- Rilke[1]
- Picturesque settings for movies (e.g. *Mission Impossible*)
- Budweiser beer
- Pils lager
- Beautiful views of sandstone streets
- The word 'bohemian', meaning artistic, poor and consumptive
- People! Lots of them! Hungry, marching people!

We advise visitors to pay special attention to the small print at the bottom of the list:

---

[1] See Ireland, 1976 (Christmas). *To Lotte, for all you've done to us.*

The small print

Not all products are currently available for export, please check with the supplier or try futher afield. Germany, Britain, the US and the former Soviet Union are all good starting points.

Most curious feature

A red button beside the Exhibit allows visitors the option of listening to an audio loop for a full 360˚ multimedia experience. For your convenience, we have supplied the text of the speech (below). Try speaking along with the audio; you may find it easier if you pretend you have 'bulldog jowls' and a plummy British accent. Another tip is to emphasise the last word in each phrase or sentence, e.g. 'for-expulsion-is-the *method*', etc.

The audio loop[2]

'For expulsion is the method which, so far as we have been able to see, will be the most satisfactory and lasting. There will be no mixture of populations to cause trouble.... A clean sweep will be made. I am not alarmed at the prospect of the disentanglement of population, nor am I alarmed by these large transferences, which are more possible than they were before through modern conditions.'[3]

---

[2] For the origins of this audio, see the records from the British House of Commons, December 1944.

[3] See, Ireland: Cromwell – catchphrase: *'To Hell or to Connacht'*. However, please treat this reference with caution as it throws into relief the somewhat 'blurry' quality of our curator's parallels. According to these:

Protestants/Czechs ≈ Catholics/Irish/Nationalists (Colonised) – or, as we shall see in
Lognote # 4, 'good'
Catholics-becoming-Protestants/Germans ≈ Protestants/British (Colonisers) – or 'bad'
Be aware that conflating 'ethnic', 'sectarian' and 'political' identities has been known to create more problems than it solves. Moreover, as some of our other Curiosities show, being Colonised or Coloniser (thereby 'good' or 'bad') is not a fixed state. For example, in the case cited here, Churchill (from the 'Coloniser' tradition) is representing the Czechs (from the 'Colonised' tradition), raising the question: What Happens When Boots Gets Put On Other Feet?[*]
[*] As a Footnote to a Footnote, we wonder: What happens if one is English *and* German? Does that make one Doubly Bad? Or does one instance of Badness cancel out the other, like two minus signs multiplied?

Domestos

She pulls the lever to release the paper, scans the page for typos, and places the sheet on top of the pile. She tries to yawn, but can't, so she tilts her head instead, stretching the muscles in her neck. She's sweating. The day has only just started but the heat is already lying in wait, a predator twitching its tail on a high branch. It's June 1976 – the year of the Dragon, the season of the great British and Irish heatwave, the month of Juno, jealous Queen of the Roman Gods, the day the Twins become the Crab – and Lotte, wandering Lotte, has been up all night.

Sunlight is slicing in through the bay window, shooting hazy shelves of motes across the interior of the double room. This part of the flat is classic Georgian Dublin: high-ceilinged, grand in scope, though the colours and textures are muted. The floor is bare-boarded, raggedly stained a white that might be limewash, or, more likely, the leftovers of a bad paint job by the previous tenant. Empty shelves. Ugly furniture: a round table, two mismatched chairs, a sideboard – all originally dark brown but now also stained patchy white. Facing the wrought-iron fireplace is a rickety sofa, hard, uncomfortable, over which she has thrown a jazzy Indian cloth, one of the few splashes of colour in the flat. Through the double doors peek a mattress, two tea chests, one supporting a small black-and-white portable telly, and a clothes rail with wire hangers. A few nondescript garments in muted colours – grey, taupe, khaki, olive – are on some of the hangers; the rest are bare. A battered brown suitcase in the corner, as if to say, look, I'm just about to leave. On the windows are bamboo blinds, rolled up. Cheap rush mats on the floors. The lone concession to luxury is a red velvet curtain at the bay window. Through this window is a pretty view, of a long, tree-lined residential Georgian road.

A half-drunk cup of coffee sends its outworn scent towards her. On a saucer are two softening slices of Ryvita, each decorated with a scraping of honey. Stubbed around the Ryvitas are fag ends; they look like rolled-up, pus-stained Band-Aids. She scratches her neck, raises her arms and reaches towards the ceiling.

Some day, she promises herself, I will take up Yoga. And stops, still reaching, surprised at the conjunct of *some day* and *will.*

She upends her money jar, a French pâté pot the same colours as crème caramel. She has just enough to get her through to the end of next week. Today's will be the last dissertation for a while; the summer has already started sending the students away in droves, abroad to work in fruit-canning factories, home to the provinces to leech off their parents. The cleaning job will keep her going for the moment, though she has no idea how long that *moment* will be.

Concern gnaws at her. There may be other cleaning jobs; she could ask the Maddens for a recommendation. And she hasn't even begun to look for translation work. Not a good time now, with the universities and colleges slowing down, but....

She thinks of the money Dr Brooks left Ands. It's still in her Halifax account, every penny of it: a layer of slime coating an underground riverbed, untouchable.

If it gets really tough, she supposes she could go somewhere else, though it's hard to think of somewhere cheaper. Back to Greece, maybe? To hell with the Colonels: she could sleep on beaches, dance on tables, mend nets, get a job showing English-speaking tourists around the monuments. The thought bubbles for a moment, reflecting a rainbow of possibilities, then – fuck strangers, smoke pot, talk about means and ends, actions and intentions with the last of the drop-outs, the dregs of the revolution she was always, they insisted, too young for – implodes.

She sighs, rubs her eyes, swallows the rest of her coffee.

The bathroom mirror shows her sallow skin, curly hair, amber eyes flecked with green. For a while, these features haven't seemed to belong together, let alone to her. She dots Oil of Ulay on her cheekbones, forehead, nose, chin.

You should always put cream on like so, Lotte. Gentle, in circles.

A draught – impossible in the heatwave – seems to curl around the part-open door. Her head turns. 'Caliban?'

No.

She shivers –'Fuck off, Ands' – and returns to the mirror, showing the ghost her back.

Two drops of olive oil in the middle of her right palm. The women on the Pelopponese told her they used it everywhere: hair, skin, inner thighs. Keeps you young, they said, pointing at her, meaning, Lovely girl, you don't need young-keeping. Then they laughed; knowing laughs that crinkled their eyes, seeding wrinkles everywhere.

She threads her oily fingers through her hair, separating it into wiry strands that curl and buckle.

Finishing touch: a drop of Chanel Gardenia, from a sample bottle stolen from the posh department store on Grafton Street. One smear on the inside of each wrist.

Her skin is darker than it usually is; the heatwave.

Where you from, then? You a black? Schwarz? *Türkin*? *Algérienne*? Jew?

She'll wear white today, to make the contrast more startling. The door shudders a little. She bares her teeth in a grimace, curls her fingers in mock claws and snarls at her reflection. You heard what I said, Ands. Fuck bloody off.

When she goes out the back to get her bike, Caliban is lying on the top step, sunning himself. His slitted eyes are the same colour as the yellowing garden and, as he looks up, they narrow even more against the light. He begins to purr, his ragged boxer's ears vibrating with the sound. She pushes her toe against his warm black side.

'Mind the fort, monster. And don't catch any more sparrows, please. I've had enough of your killings.'

He makes one of his funny growling sounds, turns a paw to his face and attentively studies it.

She had arrived in March, month of Ares, Greek god of war. There had been no heatwave when she'd arrived; the city – though Dublin didn't feel like a city, not after London, and Paris, and Berlin and Athens – was grey and flat, hunkered down over itself. Behind it rose purple hills; above it a restless, punch-drunk sky. For a week, she'd walked in unplanned, concentric circles, negotiating the capricious weather. On her seventh day, exploring a leafy road that people here call Baggot Street – though, according to the map, it's Pembroke Road – she saw a piece of ragged paper taped to the inside of a magnificent, if grubby, ground-floor bay window.

Flat to Let. Tidy person wanted. No Dogs.

Caliban had walked in off the street one wet Sunday evening a few weeks later. A draught had been blowing in under her door; it's full of draughts, this ancient house, as if the merchants who built it are still prowling, kept from their sleep by the random, senseless carving-up of their territory. At first she tried to ignore it, but eventually, cold and cranky and unable to sleep, she went out to the hallway and found the front door banging softly against its frame. It had been left on the latch. She assumed one of the other tenants had come in sozzled and forgotten to close it properly. The old queens from the first floor, maybe – one of them, the actor, had had an opening that night; or Beatrice, the sad lady dipso in the basement; or the other drunk, the guy who lived in the garret flat, the one she has taken to calling the Poet. She had shut the door and was about to go back into her room when she saw him. An enormous black cat, sitting in the shadows under the phone box. He was drenched and his left ear was torn. He had huge paws, awkward joints, a boxer's hulking shoulders, but his green eyes were gorgeous and the sweeping curve of his profile could have belonged to a panther.

She'd crouched, offering him her hand. He nosed out, sniffed, nudged her fingertips, then eased his battered head along the blade. God, she said, you're beautiful.

He began to purr. And that was it: love at first sight.

She'd called him Caliban after Shakespeare's monster; Browning's amphibian philosopher. Knobbly on the outside, noble on the inside. Ands, she'd thought, will adore you.

The thought had come so slyly she hadn't been aware she'd formed it. A split second: the void. Then the correction followed, as automated as the Speaking Clock.

Would have.

After hoisting the bike inside, she locks the back door and closes the kitchen windows. Because she's feeling a bit bolshie – no sleep, too hot – she leaves the little window in the bathroom open, even though it's against house rules. She is fumbling with the keys of the hall door when it's pushed open from the outside. The movement is sudden and should surprise her, but the heat has slowed everything, including her reflexes. Spears of light outline a silhouette. The Poet. She's not sure if he really is a poet, but the name fits. He's dishevelled in that Irish way – she knows he's Irish; she's heard him talk on the phone – long-haired, bearded, with a distracted look in his puffed-out eyes. Today he's wearing dirty jeans and a scruffy T-shirt printed with an overblown Celtic motif. Through the cotton she can smell his sweat, mixed with something chemical.

He sees her and, in a sloppy, fluid movement, leans against the doorpost so she'll have to walk past him to get out. With the beard, it's impossible to tell if he's good-looking, or even what age he is; she's assumed he's older than her, late twenties, early thirties. In idle, dangerous moments, of which she's had too many recently, she's started to make up things about him. Imagining he has a weak chin, which is why he's covered it up with all that hair. Or some shameful congenital defect – a missing testicle, or six toes, or an extra nipple beside his bellybutton – which has forced him to take refuge in the bottle. Otherwise, it would be all too predictable. Pickled Irishman takes a fancy to mysterious English stranger. His gaze drops to her breasts.

She pushes the bike forward, deliberately wheeling it over his foot. He grunts. His breath is pungent, a mix of alcohol, cigarettes and sugary tea. His mouth twists to speak, but today of all days she really doesn't have an inclination for conversation.

She walks out. The heatwave encloses her like a glove. The front door is still open behind her and she can feel the loose smear of the Poet's gaze on her naked, halternecked back as she bumps the bike down the crumbling steps. Come, come, sisters. Come, come the revolution. It would make her laugh if she wasn't so fucking tired.

The ride across the city is invigorating, sending sweat streaming down her sides, blood coursing through her veins.

She takes a little detour around that beautiful Georgian crescent that's just off the main road. The houses there are in pairs, accessed by granite stairways which curve up and around from the gates to the side, meeting at the centre. They remind her a little of Bristol in their faded grandeur. Most of them are falling apart but lived-in, like the house where her own flat is. A few have been carefully reconstructed: clean grouting, sanded-back brick, new windows, doors painted deep rich colours and studded with ornate brasses. She sniffs, suddenly aware of the scent of bergamot. Behind her, a car honks; it's the rather showy golden Jag that belongs to one of the houses, and she's standing in its parking space. Lotte resists giving the driver the V-sign. Instead she pulls the bike away from the kerb, taking longer than necessary, hoping she's irritating him.

As she cycles into the little development beside the Green where the Maddens live, her heart sinks. It still weighs on her, this poky suburbanity. Not even the blazing sun or Madonna-blue sky can elevate it; these windows are still too squat, these gardens too small, these pebble-dashed walls – custard yellow, avocado green, shit brown – still the wrong colours.

She slows as she approaches the empty house next to the Maddens, the one Aisling and Georgie still call 'Mrs Kelly's', though, Lotte gathers, it's been over a year since Mrs Kelly went to her Maker. There is something curious about that house. The day of the interview, she'd heard a strange sound coming from the garden as she'd turned the corner. A rattling, creaking. She saw nothing odd when she looked, but as she passed the house, she felt one of those draughts again, and in the corner of her eye saw a flash of something white flicker in one of the upstairs windows. Instantly, cold fingers had walked up her spine. Ands, go away, she'd thought – maybe she'd even muttered it out loud – before looking over properly. In the garden there'd been a For Sale sign, half-hidden by the leaves of the cherry blossom tree. The gate had been left open a little. Ah, she'd thought, elementary, my dear Watson. Rattling branch. Creaking gate. The estate agent must have forgotten to lock up.

She knew it was none of her business, but things not left in their place have always bothered her, so she leant her bike against the railings and tried to shut the gate. It was rusty, hard to budge. The open gap was just big enough for a child, or a slim adult, to squeeze through. For a second, she'd been tempted to try it, but common sense prevailed.

As she'd stepped back, a thought struck her. She looked up again at the window and moved her head, slowly, trying out different angles until – yes – she saw the flash of white again.

It was her own face, too small to be more than a blur; reflected in what must have been a mirror, hanging in the darkness of that empty upstairs room.

Elementary. Still, every time she passes that house, she can't help stopping and looking up, just in case that face, appearing again, will do more than reflect her own.

'Lottie?' The voice is husky and enervated, the pronunciation slushily Irish. *Losh-ee.* Lotte picks up the key from under the plant pot near the door and straightens up. Her smile feels stretched, false. 'Hello, Joan.'

'Joanie,' says the neighbour, waving her hand in front of her face. She's draped against her doorway as if she'll melt into a puddle without its support. Through the open door, Lotte hears the inevitable disco music playing on a transistor radio.

'Gorgeous, isn't it?' A pencilled eyebrow rises, vaguely in the direction of the sun. 'God knows how long it'll last, though. I mean, our summers are atrocious. You get a lovely May and then maybe a bit of sun in June and then....'

'Well.' Lotte laughs and starts to move away. 'We may as well enjoy it while we—'

'Oh – eh, Lottie?' Fingers move, languid as canned asparagus. Lotte stops. 'I'm nearly after forgetting. The heat has me head melted. Ash told me to tell you to hang on.'

'Sorry?'

'She said, wait after you're done till....' Joanie sighs, too heat-struck to finish the sentence. 'I think she wants a word.'

'Oh.'

Something flickers in Joanie's eyes. 'Ah, love, it's nothing on you. She's thrilled, poor thing, with you. Sure they both are.' She unpeels from the doorway. 'Tell you what – why don't you come in for a cuppa before you start? You must be parched.'

This isn't the first time Joanie has offered Lotte tea and, with it, the promise of gossip. Her offerings are heady with Dickensian melodrama. *Little mite, god bless him* is how she describes the child, though the child is far from little. The husband, whom Lotte hasn't met yet, is *A saint.* Aisling is always *Poor thing,* often followed by a *But....* At every opportunity, Joanie drops hints: *What they been through... patience of Job... God only knows....* And those irritating, inconclusive *But's....* Joanie is the mistress of the knowing ellipsis, the hanging sentence. Her gaps and trailings-off are rich with what they don't say, barbed with expert plays for connection: pity, shared disapproval. It would be amusing, if it wasn't so exhausting. Ironic, that such a nosey parker can't figure out that Lotte has no capacity, right now, for pity or disapproval, that she's carrying so much weight of her own – what's that word in the popular psychology books? Baggage, yes – that the last thing she wants to be roped into is somebody else's melodrama.

So why, today, does she struggle to say No? Could it be that she is regaining, if not pity, then a smidgin of her old curiosity?

'Em. Well, thanks very much, Joanie—'

Thanks? Always you must be so polite.

'But actually, I'm grand.' *Grand?* Since when has that word entered her vocabulary? 'I've quite a lot on today. I'd better—'

'Oh.'

'I'm sorry, I—'

Joanie's fingers move again: dismissal. 'In anyways, she said they'll be back round one. So….'

'Thanks.' The door begins to close. Lotte forces another smile. 'That's very kind of—'

The door sucks itself shut, its faded striped sun cover a reproach. Fuck off with you, you stuck-up English cunt.

Inside it's quiet, apart from Joanie's music bubbling through the party wall. It's her usual thing: disco, all groovy bass and wah-wah and light, soaring, female vocals. The walls are thin enough to conduct the melody and rhythm, but some denser material in the structure is blocking the lyrics. Rainbow-coloured light bleeds in through the stained-glass window in the top half of the door. Lotte feels like a fly, struggling across petrol-tainted water. The place has got so dusty again. By now, she thinks, bits of her own skin must be there too, floating in the atmosphere, mingling with the family's detritus. In person, the Maddens – mother and child, anyway – are neat enough. However, apart from Georgie's bedroom which is almost unnaturally organised, their house is always messy. Even with all Lotte's scrubbing, a sense of disorder still spikes out of it; as if the building's default position is to teeter on the edge of chaos, drawn towards it without ever falling over the brink. How much energy, she thinks, must it take to maintain that balance; how many tiny adjustments have been made over the years to keep the chaos just so far away, but no further? Though perhaps those adjustments haven't been tiny. *After all they been through….* Perhaps they have been enormous: seismic shifts that she arrived, like everything else, just a fraction too late to witness. Maybe her arrival itself was one of those shifts, part of what's kept everything teetering on that edge?

Oh, always such many questions, Lotte.

Somewhat irritated – at Joanie for piquing her interest, at herself for being piqued – she walks into the kitchen. With the windows closed, it's stifling. Unwashed plates beside the sink. Breakfast things still scattered on the pine table. A jar of raspberry jam: Chivers, with a gollywog on the label – wonder what the Black Panthers would say about that – its lid off. A bluebottle, buzzing. Milk still in a jug, souring by the second. Butter melting into a yellow lake on a pretty ceramic dish. Newspapers, letters, bits of the child's Lego, a colouring book; a science fiction novel, one of the husband's. It's the same one he's had out for the last two weeks – he's rather a slow reader, Lotte has noticed.

She opens the back door to let in air and pours herself a glass of water which she drinks at the doorway, smoking a ciggie and looking at the wilting buddleia. In spite of the ciggie, the irritation remains, spiking under her skin like a hangover. She realises it's not just because of Joanie and her hints; she's bothered by that invitation. Stay later than usual, because Aisling wants a *word*. But about what?

Lotte's mind begins to race, a zig-zag swallow's path. Maybe she's put things in the wrong place? Or broken something? Maybe it's the books. Though she's been very careful not to—

She groans. If there's something wrong, if she's overstepped in any way, they should have left a note. That would be the civilised thing to do. They shouldn't have asked her to wait. After all, she has things to do, stuff to look after....

What stuff? What thing, Lotte?

It's the thought of the effort that's bothering her most. Except for the interview, it's been months since she's exchanged more than a few sentences with anyone; more than Thanks, Yes, I understand, Yes, I'll do it, That's fine. Even with the Maddens, she's made sure to time her cleaning stints so she has the minimum of interaction. Gosh, I have to dash. No problem. Yes, next week. Bye, then. That arrangement seems to have suited Aisling too. To Lotte's surprise, it hasn't been difficult, keeping quiet.

You always such a talker, Lotte.

But really, it's been fine. No. Correction. It's been bloody fantastic. Not having to talk has made her realise how much fucking time she's wasted pushing pointless air out of her mouth. The silence has made a space around her, a bubble to keep out bad thoughts. And now they want to ruin it all with a *word*.

She finishes her cigarette and is about to throw it away when she remembers and, instead, stubs it out on a desiccating buddleia leaf. She puts the butt in her pocket.

This could be a sign, this word, like the disappearing students and her dwindling coins. She thinks, uneasily, of her reluctance to resist Joanie's invitation. Maybe it's time to get out, while the going is good. Maybe whatever she is supposed to do here is done.

Tch. So quick you are to give up, Lotte. Your brother, now, he—

Sshh, Ands. Quiet.

She presses her fingertips against her eyelids. Breathes in, breathes out.

When the globe had stopped spinning and she'd opened her eyes, she'd thought she was seeing things.

Dublin? Ireland?

First thoughts; old ones. Backward. Donkeys. Priests. Leprechauns.

Then ... poor. Cheap. Good.

Then: IRA. The Cause. Bombs. Children with their heads blown off. And they hated the English. Eight hundred years. Did they even have electricity? Had any of them heard of Liberation?

Except ... James Joyce, she'd thought. Didn't he write....

Exile. No divorce. No Pill. No abortion. No blacks. Rain.

Samuel Beckett.

Rain.

Did they even know what the oil crisis was?

She stared at the globe, the compass end sticking into Dublin. She could try again. Greece was backwards too, and it had the Colonels, but at least there was sunshine. She imagined the globe spinning, the compass landing. Paris. Too bourgeois, worse now they'd squashed the students. Marseilles. Too many drugs. Toulouse. Too redolent of the Cathars; another failed resistance. Berlin—

No.

She supposed she could have done worse. She could have landed on Palestine.

Apart from what everyone knew, she hadn't a clue about Ireland. There had been children, at school, the first school, in Bristol, a long time ago; and there'd been nuns and priests too, but she couldn't remember what they'd told her, and if she did, who was to say if it was the truth because who was to say anymore what was the fucking truth in the first place?

Someone had told her it was beautiful. Very green and lush and.... Someone she couldn't remember. Was that good? She didn't know anyone there; that she was certain of. And with their own problems, their – Troubles; the euphemism surfaced, lazy, insulting – why would they give a damn for anyone else's?

In the end, she'd told nobody where she was going. Not that there were many people to tell; not now, not after Ands. The only person she'd had any contact with was Charlie, sweet Charlie from the Chelsea School who'd let Ands break her heart when Sybille had come along, who'd let Lotte sweep up the pieces afterwards. Maybe it was that: payback for an old favour, why Charlie had been so—

Understanding.

Or maybe it was just Charlie's nature, to understand.

They hadn't seen much of each other since '71, when they'd gone their separate ways. Lotte had to admit she'd been touched by the way Charlie had tracked her down last year, through Julia's first guesthouse, the one she'd run with the Captain in Morecambe. Lotte had been suspicious at first, but Charlie didn't mind that they didn't talk much about what had happened, or why. Maybe it was because of that: payback for a new favour, why she'd told Charlie she'd send her a forwarding address once she'd left London – a PO box, nothing definite – as long as she promised to keep it to herself.

Not even your Mum, Lotts?

No. Not even Julia.

On the day she'd left England, Charlie insisted on bringing her to Euston Station, though Lotte refused to tell her what train she was taking. They'd sat together, nursing paper cups of Nescafé from the kiosk and sharing a packet of cigarettes while the rain drummed down outside. Lotte could feel something brewing. Charlie was rubbish at hiding things. That was how everyone had twigged how she'd felt about Ands.

'Go on,' she said.

'Sorry?'

'Spit it out. What you're thinking.'

'Oh.' Charlie flushed. 'I'm not—'

'Come on.'

Finally Charlie spoke. 'I know this is none of my business, but….' She hesitated. 'Is this owt to do with your dad?'

'What?' Blood rushing in Lotte's ears, pinpricks of light flashing before her eyes.

'You know,' Charlie's voice a long way off, 'because of Ands and everything, are you trying to find him so….'

'Why would I…?' started Lotte. Then she realised what Charlie was talking about. She laughed and the station pulled back into focus. 'Him? Gosh – I mean – I never – Christ, what on earth put that into your head, Charlie?'

'I'm sorry.' Charlie shrugged. 'I just thought, with Ands, you know, gone, you wanted….'

Family.

'Gosh,' said Lotte. 'No. That didn't even cross my mind.'

They smoked a couple more ciggies and Lotte watched the light glinting from Charlie's ring finger as she lifted the fag to her mouth. Rich, the boyfriend Charlie had turned to after Ands had broken her heart, steady Rich who worked in Lambeth Council, had popped the question in September.

131

To everyone's surprise, Charlie had accepted. 'You see, Lotts, I want kids, I really do.' She'd said it candidly, no flicker of shame at betraying la vie bohème or the sisterhood for the sake of two-point-five kids, a two-up-two-down in Hounslow and a Rover 3500, and Lotte couldn't blame her for that.

The loudspeaker belched out some unintelligible garbage. Wheels screeched. The train was still an hour off, but Lotte stood.

Cover your track; sometime what you needs, Lotte, is to hide.

They hugged. Lotte picked up her bag, a canvas army surplus thing that held nothing of importance.

'You look after yourself, love,' said Charlie.

Love. It was like something an auntie would say. Except Lotte and Ands had never had any aunties. Lotte walked down the platform, and without looking back, let her arm lift straight up into the air, her fingers curl in a wave.

She knows it's impractical, to start with the floor; she'll have to mop it all over again when she's finished the surfaces. But disorder underfoot has always made her nauseous, ever since they were children. It's like one of those imaginary games where you have to step over the cracks; if there's dirt or grime or bits on a floor, she becomes paralysed, can't step on it, can't do things. She's sure a psychiatrist would have something to say about that. Funny Dr Brooks never had; though when it came to matters close to home, Dr Brooks never was very observant.

She dunks the mop, squeezes out the excess liquid and drags the head across the lino. Long, rhythmic movements; a figure-of-eight, the never-ending leminiscate of women's work. The grey fronds undulate like seaweed. On her first day in the Maddens', they'd caught strange fish: flakes of old vegetable peelings that had fallen beside the gas cooker, forgotten grains of sugar, washing powder and breadcrumbs that had spilled in the awkward corners between the food presses and the Flatley heater. How strange, she'd thought, for a doctor to let things get so dirty. Today, thanks to her previous ministrations, all the mop is soaking up are the slightly grubby traces of the Maddens' feet, though, under its sparkling surface, the deep stuff of the floor still feels grimy.

The pattern on the lino gleams: a right-angled stripe in mustard yellow and burnt ochre. A Greek key. A meander, named after a river in Turkey. Greek, Turkish; the duality had always confused her as a child, though in another way it made perfect sense.

Once the floor is done, Lotte fills the sink, squeezing Fairy Liquid and Milton's Sterilising Fluid into the steaming water. The Milton's is hers; when she'd started, the only bleach in the Maddens' kitchen had been Domestos and she didn't fancy the thought of the family ingesting molecules of that along with their tea. On her first day, she'd had to boil a kettle because there was no hot water in the tap. The oversight had puzzled her. Maybe, she thought, they were careful about things like that? Economical. Saving on the heating bills. He was the right age to have been a war baby. She'd worried about how to bring it up, decided in the end to leave a note. *Not sure how to work immersion so I boiled a kettle.* Exclamation mark. The tone was jolly but, she hoped, not bossy. There'd been a time, not too long ago, where such worries, such hopes, would have been inconceivable.

So charm you have, Lotte. But peoples don't live on charm.

They've put the sink under the back window, so as you wash the dishes you can look out at the garden. It would be a nice idea if the garden was worth looking at.

She wipes the draining board. The day is eerily still. No wind. Sweat is trickling down her back, between her thighs. God, she could do with a bath.

After re-mopping the floor, she makes a cup of tea. She would prefer coffee but the Maddens have only instant. She reminds herself to bring over some ground next time, from that shop in Grafton Street with the nice smell.

If there is a next time.

Jobs not easy to find, Lotte. Not easy for one with no qval-if-i-cation.

Lotte's hands around the mug are hot and damp, her veins protruding. In India, someone told her once – Ands? Sybille? someone from the commune? – they drink tea to cool themselves down. But there's nothing cooling about this stuff; it's brackish and malty and tastes, she imagines, like the peaty heart of this island. Some day, before she leaves, she must get out of the city and see those sights people she doesn't remember have talked about. The sea, the mountains, the bogs; the cruel limestone bareness of the west.

She lights another ciggie, making sure to stand at the door so she can wave the smoke out into the garden. Maybe – the realisation is sudden and needling – that's what Aisling wants to talk about.

Are you a smoker? It was the first question at the interview. No, Lotte had said, and wasn't surprised at how easy the lie came.

Good, said Aisling. I can't stand it. Then, as if proving a point, she coughed. It was a nasty one, chesty and rattling, suffusing her cheeks with red. Her right hand closed into a fist, knocking against her slender chest, the ribs just above her heart. Like a penitent, thought Lotte, begging for forgiveness.

The child in the garden had stopped playing and was looking in at them, intent. Aisling finished coughing and smiled through the window at the child. Then she looked at Lotte.

'So.'

It had been relatively easy at the start, as interrogations go. Aisling had done most of the talking. Lotte answered her careful questions with a Yes, Of course, or No, Goodness, no, keeping to the facts, lying when necessary, inserting her own little prompt (You mean? or Really? or Is that...?) whenever she sensed an opening that might keep the other woman talking for a while.

'Have you been to Greece?' said Aisling suddenly.

'Oh.' Lotte was taken aback. Despite the attempts at colour, the woven rugs, the cheesecloth blouses, she hadn't pegged this neat, slim woman as a bohemian. 'Well, yes, actually, I—'

Aisling was already interrupting, excited. 'I've a friend who— Oh, I'm sorry, I didn't mean to—'

'No,' said Lotte, relieved, waving away the apology. 'Please. A friend?'

Lynne. A paediatrician, an English woman who'd worked in a hospital in Dublin. They'd gone to the Greek islands together, twice. Once in '61, back again in '62. They'd made an adventure out of it, climbed mountains, hitch-hiked to Corinth, viewed the monuments, drank retsina, eaten tzatziki, slept on beaches. Lynne had moved to Athens in 1966, the year Aisling got married. She'd met someone in the restaurant business over there, got married herself a couple of years later. Aisling had kept meaning to—

'Go back?' said Lotte, unprompted.

Aisling looked right at her, and for a moment her eyes were the sea, turquoise and horizonless. 'Yes.' She made that funny little gesture again, that soft knocking of her fist against the bones of her upper chest, and her eyes turned inwards. 'It used to drive me mad, this country. How small it gets. I used to think, if I could only get away....' Her face changed. 'There's a view from a hill in Athens. You can see right out over the sea. Someone I went there with said it was like eternity up there. He's right. You look out and it's like you're there, back at the time of the Trojan War, looking out over the Aegean towards the Pelopponese, and nothing has changed. Just you and the sky and the sea, and it's like your soul has just....' Her hands separated. A light glowing in her face, as if a candle had been lit under her skin. 'I always wanted to show Davey. But.' The candle went out, the eyes turned in again. 'Timing.' Her mouth tightened. 'Anyway, can you ever really do it? Go back, I mean. Don't you just spoil it, if you try? And everything else too.' An odd bitterness, almost anger, in that last question, though she hadn't said it like a question.

There was an uncomfortable silence. Defeat gathered in Lotte's gut, sludgy as concrete.

See what you make of yourself, Lotte. No good for nothing. Not even a silly housemaid job.

Through the back window, she could see the child playing on the swing. Again, watching the large, sensuous limbs, the sulky mouth, the messy hair, she was reminded of one of Caravaggio's angels, those mysterious androgynous creatures that, for a while, had obsessed Ands.

So much a waste, Lotte. To give up so quick. When I was your age, to have the possible-it-ee of university education. Leastways your brother—

'Sounds like fun,' she said, and was shocked by the rawness of her voice.

Aisling looked up.

'Greece, I mean. That view.'

'Aye.' Aisling smiled. 'That's it. Fun.' Case closed.

Aisling leant forwards and reached for her mug; her fingers landed carefully, tipping the china as if feeling a child's neck for swollen glands. Lotte prepared herself.

Thanks for coming, but we don't really think....

'So, Lotte.' It was the first time she'd used Lotte's name. She said it delicately, as if tasting a strange fruit, and pronounced it correctly, in the German fashion. 'When can you start?'

According to Carl Gustav Jung, Dr Brooks had announced once, the rooms in a house, when appearing in a dream, may reflect the different compartments of the dreamer's psyche. To pursue this logic, continued Dr Brooks, we may assume that the attic signifies what Freud called the superego, or Jung the persona, the basement the id – or in Jung's terminology, the libido – and so forth. This had been a preamble to one of Dr Brooks' lengthier lectures on why the *esoteric* was such an unreliable method of scientific enquiry. But Lotte had been taken by that, the curious idea that something inanimate, like the chambers of a house, could map so neatly onto something as alive and fluid as a person.

Dr Brooks had never explained what a *lounge* might signify, and Lotte hadn't asked. The house in Guinea Street did not have a lounge; it had a drawing room. But *lounge*... what a word; slouchy and chewy as the goings-on that might take place in it, dripping with the unsavoury connotations of the ginhouse. A room where less-educated people – like the Poles and the Irish the twins went to school with – sat in front of televisions and would one day watch men land on the moon and pass around glasses of Dubonnet, tinkling with ice, and bowls of nuts and car keys in lieu of their wives' private parts. Lounge: a room, Lotte would later think, that signified the part of the mind that excels in doing nothing.

The Maddens' lounge is small, with a single squat window looking out onto a patch of front garden and an overgrown, un-topiaried hedge. It's an awkward space; not quite hexagonal, not square. A many-cornered room which has sacrificed bits of itself to make the porch and hallway: a sanctum that in Bygone Years might have been used for significant acts: asking for daughters' hands in marriage, announcing insolvency, reading wills. The Maddens have installed a cheap-looking gas fire in the art deco fireplace, which is rather a shame. Above the mantelpiece is a six-sided mirror, oblong, unframed, with bevelled edges. Its shape echoes that of the room; the overall effect is, in spite of the clutter, pleasing.

Here, the disorder in the house is at its most tangible; probably because of the books and papers. They're everywhere, strewn, stacked, squashed on shelves, heaped on the sofa and the brown-glass-topped coffee table, spilling over the TV, piled in tottering ziggurats beside the fireplace, swarming over the record player and the rag-tag collection of LPs.

Sorry, said Aisling the first day. I know – this place is shocking. Don't worry too much in here. Just a wee spit and polish.

Along with the cameras, including the one Dr Brooks had given her and Ands, Lotte had sold all her books before leaving London. She needed the money, she'd told herself; what good were books anyway? What was the point of printing and reprinting so many misguided ideas, of reading and re-reading so many unhappy tales? But seeing them in the Maddens' lounge, sprawled louche and disorganised as prostitutes in a cheap brothel, had dissolved something tight in her chest she hadn't even known was there.

She hadn't intended to disobey Aisling. It was an instinctive thing, the need to order, and once she realised she had begun, she slowed herself down, so any changes she made would be gradual and subtle. She started with the non-fiction because, at first, that was all she could see. First, a gathering-together of the obscure technical tracts that she assumed belonged to the husband. An assembling of what looked like his work: large sheets of perforated green-backed paper that she guessed must have come from a computer; on it, endless lists of numbers and formulae. Some badly Xeroxed copies of what looked like technical drawings for a bridge. There were things written on the printouts and Xeroxes, in a neat black script which she rather liked. It had flair. She hadn't expected that. She traced her fingers over the shapes, following the patterns of the equations and the handwritten scrawls. $R = (\Sigma_e k^e)r + \Sigma (Q^{oe} + Q^{te} + Q^{fe})$. *Virtual work? Plates. ?overdetermination.* This last word underlined, three times.

She had put these documents somewhere obvious; they looked like they shouldn't be lost. Then followed a sifting and collating of Aisling's work references: medical encyclopaedias, back issues of *The Lancet*. On her third day she found a German dictionary and phrase book buried under a stack of *National Geographic*'s. She wasn't sure who those belonged to. Aisling hadn't said she spoke German, or was learning to. They looked as if they'd been tucked away for safe-keeping, so she put them back exactly where she'd found them.

Next she turned to the books. First, artfully arranging them so it would seem like coincidence, the popular science paperbacks. He – she assumed it was him, the husband, the *saint*; Davey? – seemed interested not just in engineering but in wider scientific matters: Einstein and Bohr and Heisenberg, Oppenheimer and the Bomb. The history she organised in triplets, by period, interleaving them with other non-fiction so it wouldn't be too obvious. Aisling's non-fiction tastes – another assumption – included an array of travel books and some quasi-scientific titles that veered towards Dr Brooks' *esoteric*. Koestler, Jung, Desmond Morris. They had no poetry; the only signs of the classics were some faded Penguin paperbacks – English translations of Homer, Plato and Euripides. Lotte had almost given up on the fiction when, on her third day, she found the first lot: a complete set of Hardys, hidden behind a stack of *Irish Engineers*. It was the same set Dr Brooks had had in her library: narrow, blue-bound volumes with cracked cream dust-jackets, and that had stopped her in her tracks.

When they were little, she and Ands had taken it on themselves to make puppet shows of all the Hardys, starting with *Desperate Remedies* and finishing with *The Well-Beloved*. They'd put on the shows in their den, the narrow annexe they'd found hiding behind their bedroom wall on the same sort of rainy day the children in C. S. Lewis' books found Narnia. They'd been peeling off the wallpaper out of boredom when suddenly the wall underneath began to crumble and they realised – Ands realised – it was only daub and wattle and there was something behind it. A secret passage? They'd excavated a hole and crawled through it and there they discovered not a passage, because it didn't lead anywhere, but a sliver of space that wasn't really a room, eight foot long by one and a half-foot wide, lined with broken bricks and the soot of ancient trains, with a cast-iron stove sunk into the corner, where a Victorian lodger might once have boiled a kettle for his tea. Their own personal *Wunderkammer*, ripe for the filling with curiosities.

They'd done quite a good job of the Hardys. They'd made puppets from the usual things; empty bottles and cans and, most dangerously, an unexploded grenade they'd discovered in the bombed-out tannery near Bedminster, which Ands had transformed into the Mayor of Casterbridge using wire, buttons and scraps of fabric. They'd got all the main bits of the stories in, even though they hadn't understood any of the parts with sex. After their tenth birthday, when Dr Brooks gave them the camera, they planned to do it all over again, only this time make films; Ands would direct, Lotte shoot. Except then boarding school came along, for Ands, and, for Lotte and Julia, Captain Evans.

There were no books in Captain Evans' house, let alone a *Wunderkammer*. He preferred magazines and the *Reader's Digest*. Not that that was an indication of anything.

Gradually, as she imposed order, the rest of the Maddens' fiction hoard revealed itself. The French: Zola, Maupassant, Flaubert. The British: Somerset Maugham, Orwell, Huxley. *Brighton Rock*. Shakespeare; the only plays the Maddens owned. She was surprised one day by a Nabokov and Anaïs Nin, which, in a perverse gesture, she placed either side of Louisa May Alcott's *Little Women*. *Ulysses*. They had other novels she didn't recognise; mostly things by Irish writers, large-format children's books and, dotted at random like tourists from a newer, brasher country, those thick science-fiction doorstoppers with garish covers which she assumed belonged to the husband. Philip K. Dick. Robert A. Heinlein. Arthur C. Clarke. Ursula K. Le Guin. That lone initial in the middle fascinated her. Was it, she wondered, a rule of the genre? For a slow reader, he seemed to have got through quite a pile.

After finding the Hardys, she'd almost taken *Tess* away with her. She hadn't cried once about Ands, and for some reason thought that revisiting Wessex would do the trick. She'd picked up the book, opened it, almost turned the first page. The leaves smelt like they hadn't been read in years. But then it rose in her, the sheer bloody pointlessness of it all, so she let it be.

Now, six weeks on, only a discerning eye would identify the underlying new order in the library. Apart from that, Lotte has followed Aisling's instructions, satisfying herself with a quick hoover and dusting, a light wipe-down of the bits and bobs on the mantelpiece, the jazz and classical records, a flick of the chamois across the framed photographs. There are three that she's particularly fond of. A wedding portrait, where a plump, long-haired Aisling – rather beautiful, actually – stands beside her husband. He is slender and fair, tall, with delicate, boyish features. They both look very happy – Aisling facing the camera, radiant; he shyly looking at her, as if he can't believe his good fortune. Beside that is a silver-framed print of a somewhat intimidating Edwardian couple, grandparents, probably. Perched on the telly, balanced against a vase, is an unframed snap of Georgie and Aisling on a beach. Georgie is waving a spade, while Aisling, close-cropped, overweight and almost unrecognisable, kneels behind, arms open, grinning. This picture is Lotte's favourite. The lab made a mistake while printing and the area around Georgie is brighter than the rest of the picture. It looks as if the child is encased in a celestial glow, about to be beamed up to another planet. There is something unbearably nostalgic about the faded colours in that part of the photo, the way they highlight the curve of the child's cheek, the pale skin, the full mouth.

She's still reluctant to use a pronoun, even though she knows her initial assumption was a mistake. Georgina? she'd said, then, quickly, because as soon as she said it she knew it was wrong, No, I know. Georgia. Had she just imagined it, the child's response? A flicker in the eyes; a sense of things settling, somewhere, as if a spell had been cast, or maybe lifted? Then Aisling appeared.

Oh, no. That's Georgie. Georgie's a boy.

Had there been a trace of something unsure in Aisling's eyes as she said that, a hesitation before the naming? Or had Lotte only imagined that, so she could make sense of her own confusion? She'd almost said it: *You know, I had a twin brother once and people used to think we were the same—*

But stopped, thank goodness, just in time.

Master bedroom. Change sheets. Vacuum. Dust. Clean mirrors. Leave laundry basket out on landing. Ignore the mess of papers on his side of the bed. More diagrams, probably.

Georgie's room. The only neat space in the house. Not a lot to organise. Change the sheets. Dust the toys: cars, Meccano, Lego, colouring books. Plump up and replace in its position of privilege on the pillow what she has assumed is the favourite toy, a soft brown teddy with a broken eye and a worn, furry coat that smells of cake and affection.

Lotte works quickly. The tea and ciggie break was longer than she intended. Usually not a problem, but with this chat she's supposed to have, this *word*.... In the back of her mind, a plan is half-forming; to finish, to leave early, to plead ignorance. *Sorry, couldn't stay. Lots on.* Exclamation mark. They would understand. And it's the right thing to do; after all, she didn't get a wink of sleep the night before and—

Maybe Aisling wants to talk to her about money.

Always, always, it is about the money, Lotte.

Shut. Up. Gritting her teeth, she pushes the vacuum under the bed. The push is harder than she intended and the nozzle hits the side of the long wooden box underneath, where Georgie keeps winter clothes and old toys. After the first day, when she'd pulled out the box and opened it up—

And nosed around, Lotte.

And nosed around, yes, she'd felt a bit guilty. She wasn't sure what she'd expected: something, obviously, or she wouldn't have opened it, but the box was like everything else in Georgie's room: neat, organised, ordered. Folded sweaters and trousers and pairs of gloves; old colouring books, old jigsaws, rattles. The only thing that was even halfway interesting had been tidied away neatly, right at the bottom of the box, buried under a stack of jigsaws. It was a somewhat battered library copy of an illustrated children's book, *The Knights of the Round Table.* Hardback and quite handsome, though the title page was torn and crumpled, as if it had been the object of a panic attack, or violent rage. May 14 1974 was the last return date. It didn't seem like Georgie, or Aisling, to hold on to things that didn't belong to them. Although that was an assumption; she didn't know the family then. They'd probably just forgotten it, let it slide.

After replacing the book under its sarcophagus of jigsaws and pushing the box back under the bed, she'd felt uncomfortable, as if she'd tried to take the lid off Georgie's skull and look inside. Later she realised what was missing, or, more accurately, what she'd expected to be in the box: something made by the child, from the child's own imagination. A story, maybe, scribbled on a jotter, or drawings. But there was nothing, not even a scrapbook.

Not everyone have to be creative, Lotte.

Since then, she's avoided cleaning under the bed, satisfying herself with a cursory whisk around the box's edges. But today, for some silly reason – tiredness, or too much tea, or coffee, or some illogical need to compensate for the fact that a *word* needs to be had; does Aisling want to give her the sack? Is that it? – she switches off the vacuum cleaner, gets to her knees and hooks her fingers in under the wooden edge. She pulls. The box resists at first, then rolls out.

Pushing it to one side, she shoves the vacuum cleaner under the bed and presses the switch. The machine groans as she drags the head back and forth, sucking up the dust. At the corner, where the walls meet, it changes its tone to a high-pitched whine and the head sticks. It's jamming against something. Annoyed, she pushes off the switch with her foot and pulls at the machine. The vacuum slides out but the head is still stuck. She drops to the floor and looks under the bed. It's dark; she can't see a thing. She pulls at the tube. Now she sees; the head is stuck in what seems to be a hole in the skirting board.

She pulls harder. Something cracks; dust. The hole is a ragged punch in the plasterboard, just big enough for a small animal to crawl into.

A mouse? Ugh.

Quickly she pulls out the tube of the vacuum. There's a rattling inside; the machine must have sucked up something too big to swallow. She screws off the brush head and shakes harder, holding the open nozzle over the carpet.

A cough. Dust, carpet-fluff, a Lego piece, something that looks like a tuft of blond curly hair, then—

A small grey thing tumbles out, its contents rattling like little teeth.

Pig's ear, thinks Lotte.

She hesitates. This is important, she'll later think: the hesitation. She didn't just jump on it. When she picks it up, she sees it's a purse, made from some soft fabric that might be silk, fastened shut with a popper. A grubby, dusty little thing that might once have been white.

Downstairs, the front door opens.

'Hell-oo!' calls Aisling.

Lotte stuffs the purse in her shorts pocket, pulls the vacuum away from under the bed and shoves the box back in, hard. This whole sequence of actions can't have taken more than ten seconds, but when she looks up, Georgie is standing in the doorway.

'Well!' says Lotte. The breathless insincerity of her voice appals her.

Georgie's eyes have already flickered down to Lotte's knees, the floor beside them, the detritus coughed out by the vacuum cleaner.

Lotte is surprised to find that her hands are shaking, her breath short.

Caught in the act.

'I'm—' she starts.

What? *Sorry?*

But whatever it is she wants to say, she doesn't get the chance because footsteps are lumbering up the stairs and a voice is calling—

'Uh, Georgie? Your Mom says our snack is ready?'

Georgie's head lifts. Something shifts in the child's face; a return, Lotte will later think, a collecting-together, though she won't be sure exactly what it was that went away, what exactly fell apart.

A doughy, flat-featured face adorned with thick pink-rimmed spectacles peers around the doorway. There is an awkward silence. 'Uh, hi.' The newcomer glances at Georgie, then Lotte. She makes a decision and steps into the room. 'I'm Saoirse.' She thrusts her hand at Lotte.

'Seer-sha?'

'It's Irish,' says Georgie, not looking at the other child.

'Yeah, it means freedom. Donnacha, that's my Dad, he called me that.' The girl glances at Georgie. 'He says names are really important. You should change them if they don't fit.'

The girl's voice has a slight American twang and an adenoidal quality. Her waiting hand is dimpled, plump and white. Feeling slightly ridiculous, Lotte gets to her feet and leans past Georgie to shake it. The child's palm has a damp, gritty feel, as if she's been eating a melting ice cream and hasn't washed up afterwards.

'Saoirse's a neighbour,' says Georgie. 'Her dad's a architect.' This said flatly, as if architects and planks of wood belong in the same boring genus.

'Donnacha and David are really good friends. They work together, but only sometimes. Donnacha—'

'She lives in Dracula's house round the corner,' says Georgie, as if Saoirse hasn't spoken. 'This is Lotte.' The pronunciation is nearly right. 'You don't know her. She's been here a while.'

'I'm their....' starts Lotte, then stops. What is she, exactly?

'She's kind of a cleaning lady,' says Georgie.

'Huh.' Saoirse frowns. 'Cleaning ladies are an oppression. Jan – that's my Mom, I call her Jan because—'

'We have tongue,' says Georgie. This, directed at Lotte, takes her by surprise.

'Sorry?'

'For lunch. Mum says you're to stay and have lunch with us.'

'Oh.' Something ancient chews at Lotte's insides. 'I don't think....'

'You can have mine,' says Saoirse. 'I'm a vegetarian. Jan's a vegetarian too. She's—'

Georgie sighs, loudly. Saoirse stops talking.

'You should go downstairs,' says Georgie to her. The suggestion doesn't sound as rude as it might. There is something almost considerate in it: resigned, weary, adult.

Saoirse blinks. 'Um.' A glance at Lotte. 'Uh, okay.'

They listen to her heavy footsteps clumping back down the stairs. Georgie lingers at the doorway, half-looking at Lotte, right foot softly kicking at the wooden rider.

'Aren't you hungry?' The question is sudden.

'Sorry?'

'It's lunchtime.'

'I….' Lunchtime. How long has it been since she had what anyone would call a lunch? 'I don't know.'

A weak Ling you are, Lotte.

Georgie nods. 'Then you are. It's like when you're tired and you don't think you are but you're sort of cross which means you are.'

Despite herself, Lotte laughs. 'I suppose that makes sense.'

'Okay. I'll say you'll be down in two shakes of a lamb's tail.'

No, thinks Lotte, suddenly frantic. Stop, that's not what I meant. But the child has turned, the door has closed, the deal is sealed.

Lotte sinks back on her hunkers and presses the heels of her hands into her eye sockets. Breathe out, breathe in.

Before she goes downstairs, she scoops up the dusty vomitings of the vacuum cleaner, wraps them in a tissue and flushes them down the loo.

'Hope you've all got a good appetite now,' says Aisling. She's at the counter, slicing a Vienna loaf. Four plates are laid on the kitchen table. Tongue, ham, halved tomatoes, gem lettuce, sliced cucumber, pickled onions, cubes of cheddar, potato salad.

'Um, Aisling. I don't eat meat anymore,' says Saoirse. 'Can I—'

'Och, Saoirse, don't be silly. I told your mummy I'd feed you. If you don't eat your meat, how are you going to get your iron?'

'But Jan says—'

Georgie's knife scrapes loudly against the plate.

'Georgie! Come on, Saoirse, have a try. Think of the wee brown babies in Africa.'

Saoirse sighs, digs in her fork.

Always works, Aisling mouths at Lotte. Then, brightly, as if Lotte is one of the children. 'Now, Lotte, hope you'll get this into you. It's not the grandest of offerings but….'

'No, it's.' Lotte is aware of the dust streaks on her halterneck, her grubby knees. 'It looks very tasty.'

143

'So sit, sit.'

They eat, Georgie ravenously, Saoirse less so, though her vegetarian ethics seem to be disappearing rather quickly. Aisling spears a fork with potato salad, brings it to her mouth. Lotte cuts her slice of tongue into small pieces. She forces herself to chew. The tongue tastes of nothing; all she can sense is texture, spongy, like bits of brain.

'The place is beautiful, Lotte,' says Aisling. 'You've done a great job. We don't know ourselves, do we, Georgie? It was like a pigsty before you came.'

Georgie makes a snorting sound, like a pig. They laugh.

'Jan says if a person's house is too clean, it means they didn't learn how to poop right when they were a baby,' says Saoirse.

'Poop?' Georgie frowns.

'She's a child psychologist so she knows that stuff. If you poop right—'

'Saoirse, please. We're eating.' But Aisling herself is only nibbling, carefully, as if the food might hurt her teeth.

The tongue, masticated, slides down Lotte's throat. Bile rises to meet it. Where is this *word*, she thinks, that we're supposed to be having?

'Um, may I be excused, Aisling?' says Saoirse. 'I need to go to the bathroom.'

Georgie glances at Lotte and mouths. *Bayth-rum.*

'Certainly. You know where it is.'

Saoirse scrambles off the chair, out of the kitchen. Aisling shakes her head, smiles. Lotte smiles back, though she's not sure what she's supposed to be complicit in.

'Mum?' says Georgie, eyes boring into Aisling.

'God, Georgie. Okay.' Aisling sighs, pushes her plate away. 'So, em, Lotte, I'm sure you're wondering why we wanted you to stay on for a bit?' The question is friendly – a little too friendly – and bright.

'Well—'

'You see, it's such a lovely day, we thought it might be nice for you to come to the beach with us?'

Lotte's mouth opens, like a fish.

Aisling glances at Georgie, her finger tapping the edge of her plate. 'After all, you've been helping us out for a good while now. But we've hardly had a moment to get to know you.'

'Actually—'

Georgie makes a small angry sound.

Aisling stops tapping. 'You finished, pet? Why don't you go out the back and play and Saoirse can join you.'

'But—'

'Come on, Georgie, be a good boy now, I've got one of my headaches coming on.'

Georgie sighs, slides off the chair and leaves.

'That's awfully kind,' starts Lotte, but Aisling is already leaning across the table, her voice different, low and urgent. 'Look, I'm awful sorry for landing this on you, Lotte. That child….' She glances towards the stairs, in the direction of the absent Saoirse. 'See, her mummy's been very good to me, a dear friend, but she rang me at the last minute asking me if I could take her for the afternoon, and really, you know, it was the least I could do?' An odd plea in that, as if looking for confirmation. Her fingers toy with the crumbs on the table, worrying beads. 'Then Georgie said let's go the beach and I thought, well, at least they won't be killing each other like they would here, and then he said why doesn't Lotte come and—' She takes a breath, stops, coughs. They both wait for the cough to finish. Aisling laughs. 'Listen to me, gabbling away.' Her voice is huskier now, rustling with phlegm. Her face becomes serious again. 'I know it's very short notice and it's not how I planned it, but it would mean a lot to him.'

Planned what? So close, Lotte sees that Aisling has lost some weight; her cheekbones are sharp, her skin taut and sallow.

Aisling's eyes widen. 'Oh my God. I'm sorry. Is it a money thing?'

'Gosh, no—' Lotte flushes, and is appalled at herself.

'Oh, goodness.' Aisling shakes her head. 'I'm so embarrassed. I should have said. Of course I'll give you something extra on top of your usual. I mean, I know it's work for you and—'

Lotte is shaking her head now too – No, no, that's not it, it's not that – but that doesn't matter because Aisling isn't listening, or at least not understanding; she's offering more money, on top of the extra, and guaranteeing fun, and a nice day out, and a lovely opportunity to get to know each other, and she'll lend her a swimsuit, and it'll be a great help having her there, it'll take the pressure off the kids, who don't really get along, and too tired now to protest, and worse, worried if she does, she'll set off another coughing fit, all Lotte does is nod, saying in that polite, prim, stuck-up voice she hates herself using, No, no, really, that's fine, I, no, yes, that would be, really, no, yes.

On their right hunkers the sea, petrol-blue, slothful. Palm trees line the road; on the promenade, people are walking, cycling, running, dark against the sunlit-bright cement. Lotte stares out through the other window, the glass cool against her cheek. She is struck again by Dublin's lowness. So drab and flat. So many straight lines. Its Georgiana so narrow, grey and uniform; its Victoriana dried-blood brick painted in such shocking, wrong colours. So full of gaps; sad gaps, made by neglect. She finds herself yearning, with a longing that sickens her, for Bristol. Stupid. She hasn't been there in years.

Always you complain, Lotte. You make your bed, in it you lie.

They are sitting upstairs, at the front of the bus so the children can pretend to be driving. Down the back a group of teenagers are playing a transistor radio. Lotte half-recognises the tune. Something about being back in town.

'See, Georgie, there's your new school!' says Aisling. 'Look, Lotte. There's where he'll be going in September.'

Lotte looks, reluctantly; sees a church, a yard, trees, a pretty gingerbread building with a red roof and diamond-paned windows.

'Saoirse goes there,' explains Aisling. 'Her mummy helped us get Georgie into it. Didn't she, pet?' This to Georgie, who she hugs. Georgie ignores Aisling and the school, keeps staring out towards the sea.

'It's Protestant,' offers Saoirse. 'I've been there for a year. Donnacha, that's my dad, he used to be a Catholic but Mom's an ath—'

The bus takes a curve in the road, hard.

'Look! Dollymount!' says Georgie, pointing to a causeway sticking out into the bay; behind it a low green landmass bumpy with sand dunes.

'That's where we're going for our swim, Lotte.' Aisling's speaking again with the same bright, cheerful tone she'd used in the kitchen. 'It's called Bull Island. It's—'

'It's sandy,' says Saoirse. 'I was there, like, last summer when we first came here. Before that I lived in New York City which is the biggest city in the world. I ate a bacon sandwich and it was real windy and the sand got stuck in my.... Hey!' She laughs. 'Sandwiches!'

Georgie glances at her.

'Get it, Georgie? Sand. Sandwiches!'

'Ha,' says Aisling, humouring her. Georgie says nothing. Aisling bends her mouth to Georgie's ear, whispers.

Georgie shrugs, shakes Aisling off. 'Can you swim, Lottie?'

'Lott-*eh*,' says Aisling.

'That's what I said.'

'That sounds foreign,' says Saoirse. 'Georgie said you're English.'

'Och, Saoirse, don't be rude—'

'Well actually.' She is surprised to find herself speaking; even more surprised that her voice sounds normal, like that of a real person. 'Actually, my mother came from Czechoslovakia.'

146

'Wow,' says Saoirse.

'I didn't know that.' Aisling is curious now. 'I thought Lotte was—'

'Czechoslovakia?' says Georgie. 'Where's that?'

'It's beside Russia,' says Saoirse. 'Poland's in the way, but it's right beside it. It's in the Iron Curtain.'

Georgie frowns.

'See the Russians made a curtain to keep the Commies out—'

'In,' say Lotte and Aisling at the same time. They look at each other.

'Can you speak Russian?' says Georgie.

Lotte flushes. 'Well....'

'She's not Russian,' says Saoirse. 'She's....'

'Can you?'

Oh, why the hell not. '*Alzo perfeelykte kann iss Roosky spricken.*'

'That's not Russian.' Saoirse shakes her head. 'Jan—'

Georgie groans.

Aisling glances at Lotte. 'Maybe it's Czechoslovakian, Saoirse—'

'Nadia Comăneci is a Russian,' says Georgie, looking straight at Lotte. The words seem to have come out of nowhere. 'She's really good at gym. Did you know that?'

'Em,' says Lotte, thinking, Hang on, isn't she Romanian?

'Huh! Donnacha says the Commies are evil. He says the Russians are going to blow up the world and—'

Georgie sighs. This time there is no attempt at consideration. 'Are we there yet?'

'Soon, pet,' says Aisling. She is frowning. Her headache must be getting worse.

The sea scoops over Lotte's head, blurred greeny-blue; a salt sting in her eyes. The muscles in her shoulders and back unfurl. She thrusts forward under the water, seeing herself a shark, unstoppable, submarine-tough, until a swell from a ferry far out in the bay sends a wave rolling up against her, breaking her stride. She lifts her face, sucks in air and light. Her nose is streaming. It's a nice feeling: the cold, the blood, the oxygen, even the snot. For the first time today, for the first time in what seems like months, she feels awake. Is that a good thing? Behind her, closer to the beach, are the children. Saoirse is wearing armbands. They are orange and somehow talismanic, giving her more energy in the water than Lotte would have expected. Georgie is fluid, fishy, powerful. Hands wave, white teeth flash. Saoirse suddenly jumps onto Georgie's back. A snarl, a whiplash, sudden violence. Thrashing water. *At least they won't be killing each other here.* Saoirse screams, disappears. When the children emerge, Saoirse is chastened, her hands making panicky flapping movements. *I'm sorry I'm sorry I'm sorry I give up.*

Georgie stands. They are not out of their depth. Saoirse heaves herself up. The children look at each other. Saoirse says something. *Sorry* again. A jerk through Georgie's body: a shake of the head. Saoirse's shoulders slump. She turns and walks away, back towards to the beach. Behind her, Georgie's hands lift, as if to offer an apology, then jerk again, as if realising something is wrong, and lower again. Saoirse reaches land and hunkers down, arms wrapped around her knees.

Her mummy's been very good to me. Good in what way? And why, if Saoirse's mother is such a dear friend, does Georgie flinch every time her name – Jan – is mentioned?

Lotte looks towards where Georgie was, but the child has disappeared. Back in the water.

She swims out farther, stopping when she feels the cold rush of the deep tide. Treading water, she looks over at the jagged skyline; the lighthouses, the humped cliffs, the harbour where she came in on the ferry, the cluster of high-rise flats to the north, the red-and-white clown-striped chimneys to the south. She takes a breath, closes her eyes, sinks. Coldness snakes around her legs and the soft flesh of her belly. Bladderwrack drifts towards her. She feels it brush her hands, her hair, her face. Her eyes open. She sees nothing.

If she was to sink now, if she was to let go....

She opens her mouth, releases bubbles. Her lungs contract, collapse.

For a second all it feels is empty and all that feels is familiar.

Then panic seizes her and she kicks herself up, breaks the surface, gasping. Between her isolation and the shoreline bobs a lone figure in green trunks, arms outstretched, hard white belly facing the sky. Georgie.

'I'm sorry,' says Aisling suddenly.

'Hmm?' Lotte stops towelling her hair. They are lying near the foot of a dune. Aisling has kept on her cheesecloth blouse and has a soft white sheet over her legs. 'I brought you here on false pretences, I'm afraid, Lotte.' Her voice is light, but not in the same way as it had been in the bus. Under the wide-brimmed hat and black sunglasses, her expression is unreadable. 'I, em. I wanted to tell you, you see, before telling him.' Aisling nods towards Georgie, still bobbing out on the sea. 'But then Jan foisted Saoirse on us and … I'm not well, Lotte.'

This is what Lotte feels: warm sand under her legs, seawater-cold all the way through to her bones, heat blazing inside her head.

Poor thing. Little mite. A saint. The disorder in the house. All that bloody coughing. For so a clever girl, how stupid can you be, Lotte?

'We've had a long fight on our hands. Up and down, a few close calls. There were a couple of times where I even thought, okay, that's it, we can, really, you know, get through this without….' Aisling's hands separate, then fall in towards each other. 'Silly. Unforgiveable, really.' Her mouth twists in a smile. 'Anyway, we've known for a few months now, but kept it to ourselves. I mean, of course, the doctors and nurses, and David's sisters have some idea, but…. We're starting to tell people, so I thought you should know. Up to now it's been fine, I've been able to do lots of things. But my, em, energy isn't going to be the same.'

At the water's edge, Saoirse is on her knees, building a sandcastle, face furrowed in concentration.

'I'm sorry,' says Lotte. Horribly inadequate.

'It's not, I, I'm not asking you for anything, or. It's just, we'll be telling Georgie soon, so he'll be prepared, and because I'll be at home a bit more from now on, and he will too, if he's acting funny or anything, I just wanted you to….'

So this is the *word*.

'He really likes you.' Aisling laughs, coughs, laughs again. 'It's funny. He's only met you the few times, but he really likes you. I've heard him showing off to his pal, Jeremy – you know Jeremy, the funny wee boy with the glasses, you might have met him once? – he says, wait till you and me get to play with Lotte, Jeremy. We'll have loads of fun with her. We've had other girls in, to help with the house, but he's never taken such a shine before.'

'Oh. Gosh, I. I don't think….'

Aisling makes a small sound; half-laugh, half-sigh. 'Just please don't, you know, say anything.'

The globe spins, stops.

Should have got out when you can, Lotte. Always good, to know when to make exit.

On the bus Saoirse starts sneezing; she has, it appears, allergies. Right then, says Aisling, we'll drop you off pronto. They turn off the main road, onto that beautiful Georgian crescent with its hotch-potch of renovated and gone-to-seed houses. Saoirse's home, the so-called Dracula house – which, Aisling tells Lotte, is actually next door to Bram Stoker's birthplace – is one of the renovated ones. There's no sign of the showy Jag and its impatient owner.

'I wonder....' Aisling hesitates at the gate. Georgie is gripping her hand, as if trying to hold her back.

'Yes?' says Lotte, too eager.

See how easy, Lotte, you play the second-guess. So good a little helper.

'Nothing,' says Aisling. She squeezes Georgie's hand, slips out of the grip. 'Come on, Saoirse, let's get you up to your mummy. Georgie, you wait down here with Lotte. We'll only be a sec.'

Georgie, eyes averted, begins to kick at the black-painted railing as Aisling and Saoirse climb the stairs. The door opens. Saoirse's mother is inside, out of sight, but her nasal New England twang is clear and carrying.

'Hey, honey! Hi, Aisling. So good to see you. You guys had a fun time?'

Saoirse begins to speak excitedly. 'It was neat. We swam and—'

'Aw, I'm so happy for you, honey. You say thank you? Hey, Aisling, you wanna come in for a while, we can catch up? It's been too long.'

Georgie looks up, towards the door.

'Saoirse can take Georgie to the den and maybe they can do some art or—'

A small, animal sound. On Georgie's face is an expression Lotte hasn't seen there before. It almost looks like terror.

Aisling steps back, shakes her head, says something inaudible.

'Aw, what a shame. Next time, huh?' Jan steps forward into sight. She is heavier than her voice sounds, tall and imposing with sallow skin, long black hair and thick black-framed spectacles. Lotte's not surprised to see she's wearing a kaftan. She grips Aisling by both arms. 'So good to see you, honey. Don't be a stranger, okay?'

Aisling nods, smiles, extracts herself.

'Come *on*,' says Georgie, tugging at Aisling's hand.

You don't mind bringing Georgie home, do you? I've forgotten to get something in the shops. I'll settle up with you next time if that's okay.

Well—

Thank you. Her fingers hard on Lotte's, unexpectedly strong.

Georgie is quiet, humming an almost soundless tune, walking in zig-zags across Lotte's path, like a shadow. Opening gambits for conversation trickle through Lotte's mind. She seems funny, Saoirse. Are you going to be friends in the new school? You don't have to be friends, you know. You don't have to like everyone. You're a good swimmer, you know that? Are you good at gym? Did you ever want to do gym like Nadia Comăneci? Because you know, if you really want to do something, you—

Trickle in, trickle out.

When they return to the Green, a dark-green Ford is parked outside the Maddens' house and the front door is ajar.

'Dad,' says Georgie, and rushes inside.

Lotte hovers outside. She can smell frying oil, hear the sound of something sizzling in the kitchen.

'Come on,' says Georgie, reappearing on the doorstep.

The finger click, Lotte. You come. You a dog, then, to follow the master?

It takes her a few seconds to adjust to the darkness. She sees stars first, dancing in front of her, and wonders if she's sun-struck. Then her eyes focus and he's there, a tall man, standing stooped at the cooker, frying fish fingers. Her first impression is: *Crikey, you're handsome.* Then: *You've changed.* Ridiculous, of course, because she's never met him before.

He turns, sees Lotte and frowns.

'Sorry,' she says, though there's no good reason to.

'Oh.' He smiles awkwardly. 'You must be, the, eh...'

'Help.' *Help?* 'Lotte, yes.'

His eyes are the same as Georgie's; she hadn't noticed that in the photo. He shares his child's skin too. Translucent and delicate, the type that's always threatening to flush.

'You're the—' She stops herself, just in time, from saying *saint*; pushes down the giggle that threatens to follow. Is she nervous? 'Georgie's dad.'

'Yeah.' He frowns again, rubs his right arm as if he's cold. His eyes have clouded over. He seems pained now, irritated.

Why isn't Aisling there to introduce them, smooth over all this silly, unnecessary interaction? Lotte is about to make her excuses and go, except Georgie pulls at his sleeve and begins telling him about the swim, the ice creams, the Coke they drank in the coffee shop in Clontarf, and it would be rude to interrupt.

'Isn't that right?' Georgie turns to Lotte.

'Mmm,' Lotte nods. So polite you are. 'Terrific fun.'

David – this man isn't a *Davey* – rumples Georgie's hair. 'Sounds like an, adventure, what?' There's a funny, clipped quality to his voice, as if he's modelled himself on a not very assertive sergeant-major. 'Did, em, whatshername, have a good time?'

Saoirse, thinks Lotte.

'Yeah,' says Georgie.

'Great.' David drains the peas, switches off the gas, takes off a lid. His actions are precise and considered. Another uneasy counterpoint to the house's lurking chaos. Steam rises. Rice.

'Dib dib dib,' says Lotte.

'Sorry?'

'The Boy Scouts.' She gestures to the pots. 'I assumed that's where you learnt to cook.'

'I was never in the Boy Scouts.'

'Oh. Sorry.'

'No, it's not....' He takes off his glasses, rubs the bridge of his nose. 'I had asthma.' Freed from the lenses, his face is naked, more like the wedding photograph; younger, vulnerable.

Georgie looks puzzled. 'What's asthma?'

'Pains in your chest, old bean. It means you can't breathe. I don't have it any more.'

'Does Mum know you had—'

David replaces his glasses. 'Oh-kay. Grub's up.' He starts to ladle Georgie's food onto a plate. 'Where is she? Mum?'

'Getting messages. Jan,' Georgie says the name deliberately, almost like an insult, 'wanted her to stay and have a drink with her but she said she couldn't.'

'Oh.' David looks at Lotte, then Georgie's plate, then Lotte again. 'Sorry.' He is irritated again, tense. 'Did Ash give you any nosh, or.... Would you like—' He gestures to the pots.

'Oh. No. Thanks,' says Lotte. 'Though it looks lovely. Actually, I'd better dash. I have some—'

They begin to speak over each other, then stop.

'Sorry,' she says. 'I should go. Nice to meet you.'

She offers her hand. He takes it.

'Good. Em. See you again?'

'Yes,' she says, and could kick herself.

This is what lingers: long, strong fingers, humming with electricity, the vestiges of the day's work. Tired grey eyes, fine skin. A boyish smile, worn at the edges.

Older, of course, than the wedding photograph; no longer a boy. But that's not what was most different. She thinks of his clipped fake-sergeant-major voice; the effort in his shoulders, that awful tension in his eyes. *We*, Aisling kept saying at the beach, and after. *We've had a long fight on our hands. For a while there, we thought we'd beaten it.* Emphasising the first person plural, speaking for him as if they'd become one, merged through the illness. Is that what happens to couples? Something builds between them, a collective persona that absorbs their individualities, until they come into focus only when they're together? Except there had been an *I*, hadn't there, down at the beach, when Aisling had talked about something or other being unforgiveable?

Poor thing, Joanie kept saying. *Poor thing, but....*

But what?

Enough. None of your busyness, Lotte.

As she reaches the top step, she can hear someone talking inside, so she stays there until she hears the endless Grand, bye, seeya, yeah, grand, grand, seeya, yeah, bye bye bye of an Irish phone call's conclusion. She still mistimes it, though, and, as she opens the door, she catches the Poet's dishevelled shape walking up the stairs. He half-turns; she ducks her head. But after she opens the door of her flat, she finds herself listening, not for the sound of his feet starting up again on the stairs, but the silence of his continuing regard.

So vain, you are, Lotte. Even after all.

When she's sure he's gone and the hallway is clear, she goes into the kitchen and feeds Caliban. Then she opens the fridge and takes out her precious bottle of gin. Her reflection looks back at her from the window. Hair sticky, near-dreadlocked, from sea and sun; skin glowing, eyes bright. Her legs and arms are outside the reflection's frame but she knows they're in good shape too, humming from the swim. If you were an adman and you wanted a picture, for a Coca-Cola campaign maybe, or summer holidays, or health insurance, or a new university, something to sell the essence of what it is to be young, alive and healthy, and with everything to live for, then she, Lotte Evans ex-Bauer, would fit the bill.

She pours a good measure of gin into a tumbler and drinks it neat.

She doesn't want to think about what today means. She is too tired. It is too soon. On the way back from the beach, before Saoirse started sneezing, Aisling made her an offer. In the coming weeks, they – *we* – will need someone to mind Georgie, someone to come twice a week, maybe three times, depending on how things go. Nothing too onerous, just a helpful, friendly eye to make sure everything is alright. No dates have been mentioned. It won't be for ever, said Aisling. He'll be starting the new school in September. You should see September in Dublin, Lotte. It's gorgeous. We – *we* – love an Indian summer.

Lotte pours another measure, adds tonic water and ice, sips it, and brings the glass and bottle into the front room. The post she picked up on her way back is sitting on her white-stained table, beside the now-mushy Ryvitas.

She takes another sip.

Julia has sent a parcel, brown paper tied with string, with three addresses on the front. Two of them are crossed out: the flat that Doctor Brooks' money bought in Farringdon, just across the road from the Tube station, and, underneath that, Charlie's Brockley address. The only intact address is the Irish PO Box, written in Charlie's looping script. Inside is a Hallmark card with a horrible illustration on the front and a money order for ten pounds. Under the printed legend, in Julia's careful, elementary-school lettering, is a message. *Happy Birthday! Love from all here. Please get in touch. We love to hear what you're up to!* That phrasing, so familiar, so carefully casual, almost colloquial. *We.* But no *would.* It doesn't sound like the Captain's English lessons have stuck.

She has also sent a book. Seeing the dedication inside – *Für meine Tochter. Ein Scätzchen. Alles Liebe, Juni 1976* – makes Lotte feel she should weep. She supposes she should put it inside the tea chest in her room, along with everything else. Not just yet, though.

Charlie's card is homemade, with a oil pastel drawing of the constellation of Cancer in a night sky. Inside, she has folded a piece of cobweb-fine silk which unfurls into a beautiful, batik-printed scarf, all swirling, sea-ish patterns in turquoise, lilac and umber, the colours Lotte used to love wearing. Charlie has also sent a letter, on onion-skin paper, with little doodled illustrations in the margins. She and Rich have found a house – in Hackney. Dead cheap. With a garden. Yard, really. But still. How hilarious is that? Up North, things aren't good. More strikes and power cuts and Charlie's nan couldn't get candles and....

Come back soon, Lotts, it finishes. xxx. Miss you.

Music drifts down from the Poet's flat. It sounds like David Bowie, except rougher.

She tilts the glass, lets gin slide into her mouth, then slides herself onto the wonky sofa. Caliban miaows and jumps up onto her, purring, kneading her belly with his paws. Something is digging into her shorts pocket, inside the crease between thigh and hip. Her fingers reach, close around something soft; the silk purse she found in Georgie's room. Under her fingers, the contents roll, innocent and unsettling as missing milk teeth.

In 1957, the year Lotte and Ands celebrated their First Holy Communion, Dr Brooks made one of her grand philanthropic gestures, not quite as dramatic as when she'd joined CND and got them all to come on the marches, but still significant. She gave Lotte a present of buttons, tiny seed pearls that glimmered under artificial lights. Lotte had whined for months for rosary beads, pearl ones, like the ones Mary O'Callaghan had got from her granny in Ireland, but You have to admit these are far more practical, dear, said Dr Brooks, think of all the ways you can use them afterwards. With hindsight, it made sense. Dr Brooks couldn't have given rosary beads; that would have been a step too far in the support of Papish superstition.

Julia spent days sewing the buttons to the front of Lotte's Communion frock, making sure they were lined up perfectly. *Wie eine Prinzessin siehst Du aus*, she'd said, in the language Lotte hated and loved. Like a princess, you look. The dress was so beautiful Lotte almost didn't want to wear it. In the nights coming up to her Communion, she'd prayed that the other girls from school, the Polish and the Irish, wouldn't squash into her on the day or deliberately walk into puddles, ruining her frock out of spite. It's alright, Ands had said, reaching across the space between their narrow beds. I won't let them.

He wouldn't have been able to protect her, though. They would be separated for the ritual; girls on the left, boys on the right. She will always remember the tug of anticipating that parting, as if a bit of herself was going to be ripped away.

On the morning of their Communion, Lotte woke to find all the buttons on her dress gone, as if a bad fairy had crept into the room at night and hacked them off. She'd been about to burst into tears when she caught Ands' expression. There was a curious gleam in his eyes; excited, proud, important. He was holding something behind his back. With a sinking feeling Lotte opened her palm. *Geb her.* He dropped whatever he was holding into it and his skin against hers had the same excited feel as the light in his face. She knew before she saw it what he'd made: a set of rosary beads from Dr Brooks' pearl buttons, strung together with wire and thread; the crucifix a chicken wishbone, wrapped like a sailor's canvassed corpse in a slender silver chain.

She held the gift, not knowing how she felt.

You said it was Unfair, he said, or thinks she remembers him saying, the Unfair pronounced Germanly with the emphasis on the Un.

No, I didn't. That's not what I meant.

She would have said that, except Julia came through the door and, without thinking, Lotte flicked her wrist, sending the present flying under the bed.

Something hurting in Andrew's eyes: a baffled incomprehension.

Julia had dressed up in her good clothes: houndstooth coat, tilted hat. She had curled her hair and made up her face. She had been smiling. Pretty. Proud, Lotte would later realise. She said nothing when she saw that the buttons were missing.

The day itself went well; the other girls weren't cruel, and nobody called them names – nasty, Nazi – and Julia said nothing, just smiled with the other mothers and nodded proudly, and acted as if it was normal for a Communion dress to have no ornamentation on it, just tiny holes down the front where the button-thread had been, and when they went for tea afterwards to celebrate, in the Victorian Tea Rooms on the Downs, Lotte had felt only a little bit embarrassed at being so obviously from the wrong religion, clothed in a wedding dress and aged only seven.

Displaced person.

That night Julia brought Lotte into the kitchen at the back of the slave trader's house and asked her to take off her dress. Her voice was soft. She smoothed the dress as if it was something alive and carefully hung it over the back of a chair while Bobbi, the sweet-natured black-and-white mouser the twins had found in an alleyway, looked on. Then she asked Lotte to sit. Up to the point of her death, Lotte will remember the coolness of the air around her bare arms and legs; the bite of the knicker elastic against her belly; the meaner bite of her good white socks into her calves; Bobbi's calm, compassionate gaze. She sat on a three-legged stool and Julia put a towel around her neck. Her touch was gentle.

Siehst Du, Lotte. See, Lotte. *Wenn Du Keine Prinzessin sein willst, dann müssen Wir Dir Prinzchen nennen.* If you don't want to be a little princess....

She was calm, tired; resigned, Lotte thought later. She stated the penalty as if it was a fact, not something she'd been musing over all day; agonising over, even.

Lotte still remembers the feeling of the scissors, cool against her nape. How Julia held them there, for hours it seemed, without moving, the first long strand of curling hair slipping between the blades, alive as an eel. The gritty promise of not-yet biting metal. The bead of sweat sliding down her mother's powdered forehead; the shine in her eyes, like tears. The sickly, nervous churning in her own belly. Something else – hotter, wetter, more tickly, more excited – in the bit down below.

The release, like wee, when the blades finally bit.

Followed, instantly, as the hair fell, by a crushing sense of disappointment.

Oh.

No.

There was no drama when she finally got up to their room and Ands saw her. No lyrical little moment; them facing each other, mirroring each other's gestures, like something from a modern ballet. Oh, said Ands. That was all. He looked disappointed too, as if this new reflection was lacking in something. Bulk; substance; conviction. As if the consequences of his action were a pale shadow of what he'd imagined. No world changed; no wrong put to right. No Un made fair. Just a husk; a cropped, smaller version of himself. Even his disappointment seemed muted; less exalted, less leaden than her own. But he pulled back his covers, inviting her in, and she lay beside him and he put his arm around her, and at some point in the night, they ended up wound round each other, limbs indistinguishable. *Hänsel und Gretl.*

All summer, Julia had her wear Ands' clothes. *Das Gleich, wollt Ihr? Also, gleich, Prinzchen.* You two will be the same? Then be the same, little prince.

Rilke wrote something about the rosary once, didn't he, comparing art to a prayer or—

She can't remember it. All she can remember is what Julia told her. We Germans have five lots of mysteries in our Rosary. One more than elsewhere. That fifth lot, the Comforting lot; that is ours. It belongs to the people.

She expects to hear the ghost's voice, scoffing. Prayers? Mysteries? Rubbish, Lotte.

But he's quiet, for once. All she hears are her own thoughts swirling in her mind, oily and sweet-sour as the gin, the mother's ruin, oozing down her throat.

Lognote # 4

Welcome back to the Maps Cycle (first encountered via Lognote # 2*)! We have been advised to inform you that this Cycle may, on occasion, trigger volatile responses for which we cannot be held responsible. Your exploration of these Objects from Now On is therefore taken at your own Risk.*

Map Eight: 1648–1750s

Thick gold lines, twisted with red-white-red bunting and ornamented with baroque cherubs, encircle central mainland Europe. There is a faint smell of fireworks as—

Hurrah! Or, depending on your outlook, *Boo!*

—the Thirty Years War ends and Bohemia is now officially part of the Holy Roman Empire, ruled by the Catholic Habsburgs!

Visitors will notice a multitude of hyperlinks and a plethora of tiny figures on this map, referencing yet another spinaround in the ethnolinguistic mesh of the region. As control of Bohemia's finances moves from Prag/Praha to Vienna, the nobility with their vast estates are becoming increasingly German,[1] while Czech, formerly the language of kings, has now reverse-alchemised into the language of peasants.[2]

Tiny blackboard icons are also visible, celebrating Empress Maria Theresa's introduction of public education to the region. Observant visitors will notice that the text on the blackboards contains both Czech *and* German words. In

---

[1] *Mainly* German (curator's emphasis). There are still Czech nobles *in situ*. For contrast and similarities, see Ireland: post-Flight of the Earls.

[2] *Dirty nasty things.* For the source of this Footnote, see (1927–) *Mutti-Kustosin*/Mummycurator: unconscious self/class-judgement, later queried by Andreas Bauer a.k.a. 'Ands', co-curator with Sybille Henkel of the 1970s' work *Ohne Titel/Untitled*, a.k.a., this collection's reference only, '*Antifascistenkunstkammer*'.

spite of the audible mantra (*Eine Sprache, Ein Volk!*)[3] rising from this map, the Empress has introduced the study of Czech to the University of Vienna![4]

Hurrah! / Boo!

Many visitors have observed a distinctive clackety-clack (the sound of textile production) coming from the mountainous border regions where the German-speakers live; also the appearance of rather toxic-smelling factory fumes. Please contrast these with the smells of manure, hay, agricultural animals and silage emanating from the Czech-speaking centre. Note that the longer we immerse ourselves in this map, the louder the clackety-clack and more toxic the smoke become and the more both start to encroach on the grassy centre.

A faint scarlet haze is also visible in the air. This is connected to the introduction of land reform by Maria and, later, by her son Joseph. It suggests the birth of yet another borderline, an 'Identity' based on class. Unfortunately (or fortunately)—

Musical interlude

Aux armes, citoyens,
Formez vos bataillons,
Marchons, marchons!....

Blood flows— (! / **alert** !— ⊕ops – take a very quick look, visitors, just a glance, towards *Chambre Vivela*, where Madame La Guillotine is eating nobles' heads for dinner!

Hurrah! / Boo!

Map Nine: 1806

Plus ça change. Although the cherubs are gone, the borderlines stay just as thick, just as red-white-red. The Holy Roman Empire is dead. Long live the Austrian Empire!

Map Ten: 1815

Octopussing out to the north and west are sturdy new lines; dark blue, mixed with red-white-red. Austria and Prussia, along with lesser states, have formed the German Federation. Bohemia, as part of the Empire, joins the club!

---

[3] One Tongue, One People! See Hitler, A., for comparison.
[4] Smart move. For contrast: see Ireland: Penal Laws and the criminalisation of the use of the Irish (Gaelic) language. Visitors may also be interested in Googling 'French Revolution: build-up to' to gain a clearer sense of the strategic reasoning behind the Empress's apparently generous policies.

Interlude: A thought experiment

At this point, visitors will notice a certain haziness in the *Kabinett*'s atmosphere as, during the new century's early decades, the Bohemian aristocracy struggle to clarify a Key Curiosity: their – and the region's – Identity. Under the haze, it is also possible to hear a whispered refrain: '*neither Czechs nor Germans, but Bohemians*'. Inspired by the ideals of the Enlightenment and the Romantics, the aristocrats are reviving the medieval literature of the Czechs, hoping to locate a 'pure' Bohemianism personified by the mythical figure of the noble Czech savage.[5]

Listen to those sibilants, read those strings of consonants! All around, German nobles are learning Czech, reading about Czechs, celebrating Czechness! Digging Their Own Grave?— (! **/ warning !** /— Visitors, please move away immediately from that dangerous turn of phrase and bring your attention instead to Moravia, birthplace of František Palacký, a.k.a. 'Father of the Czech Nation'. Palacký has just finished rewriting Bohemia's history in German. According to him:

- Hus and Protestantism and the simpler Slavic life are good.[6]
- German feudalism is bad.

Honestly! In all this confusion, it's easy, even for Palacký, to lose sight of the many Czech peasants with German names, and vice versa, because, noble savagery aside, does anybody really care about peasants?[7]

Map Eleven: 1848 – The Year of Revolutions (Side 1)

Red! Red! Red!

This map has been ripped from the much larger *Generaleuropakartezyklus* (the Great Eurowide Map Cycle). Our little segment is horribly burnt and features large patches of carmine; both fabric dye[8] and, in the most damaged

---

[5] See Ireland, 1900s: the Anglo-Irish, Yeats, Lady Gregory, J. M. Synge et al. and the Gaelic Revival. See also, for contrast, Britain: Shakespeare and Elizabethan notions of 'England'.

[6] Refer back, if you can, to *Lognote # 2* for issues arising from the conflation of sectarian/ethnic/national identities. See *Lognote # 3*, Footnote 3 for the mutability of 'goodness' and 'badness'.

[7] *Nasty dirty things*. See Footnote 2. For further commentary on this issue, see Berlin, 1970–1973: *Ohne Titel/Untitled* (a.k.a. '*Antifascistenkunstkammer*') © Andreas Bauer und Sybille Henkel.*

*A Footnote to a Footnote: We would like to remind you that, unlike the present *Wunderkammer*, the Bauer-Henkel collection did actually (materially) 'exist'. Please also be aware that the term '*Kunstkammer*' as applied to the Bauer-Henkel work/s has limited historical validity, not having originated with the collectors/creators themselves.

[8] See 'Red Flag': history of, Ancient Rome to present day.

areas, traces of that reddish-brown substance we came across earlier (?! / **alert !!** /— Visitors, please don't touch! Instead, focus on the *Year of Revolutions* soundtrack, a death metal extravaganza featuring 'found' noises of splintering timber and rusting iron. Like an ancient bridge, the Austrian Empire is creaking under the weight of conflicting forces: the need to modernise, the need to hold its centre, the fact that most of its population is now Slavic, the fact that the lower down the class ladder you go, the more Slavs you see.

Demokratisieren! (Democratise!) urge the chorus, that stalwart band of leather-and-hair rockers we recognise as the German Confederation. But, as our curator knows all too well, 'democracy' can mean different things depending on where the line is drawn – and who draws it.[9]

Interlude: The Great Bohemian Democracy Conundrum

Riddle me this and riddle me that! Here's the dilemma:

- Infected by the heady thrash-metal of the *Year of Revolutions*, Bohemian, Moravian and Silesian Germans have decided they now want democracy inside the *German Confederation* – a move which would make the Czechs a tiny minority in a sea of Germans.
- Band-Battling them in the other corner, the Czech subjects of the same regions want a federalised *Austria* with regional autonomy – a move which would make *them* the biggest player in Bohemia.
- Meanwhile, in the live-chicken-swallowing mosh pit, some Czechs are starting to make noises about a *Great Pan-Slav Nation*[10] – a construct which wouldn't include any Germans at all.

What will our lost homeland – or rather, those who govern her – do?

(a) *Split along ethnic lines.*
(b) *Choose democracy (within reason).*
(c) *Try to work out something with which everyone is happy.*

All bets on a postcard, please! Address:
'The Black Box'
Turnmill Street
Farringdon
London EC1

---

[9] See Ireland: partition of; also Ireland: Battle of the Bogside; also Ireland: Bloody Sunday.
[10] See Stalin, J., for later contrast.

Map Eleven: 1848 – The Year of Revolutions (Side 2)

In April, the Empire seems to back Option (b) Democracy (Within Reason), accepting a proposal for a moderate democratic constitution which guarantees the autonomy of the Historic Provinces (Bohemia, Moravia and Silesia) within Austria.

Hurrah—

Sadly, the deal falls flat. The Moravians don't want to be outnumbered by the Bohemians, the Bohemian Germans don't want to play second fiddle to the Czechs, and the Czechs are terrified of ending up in Greater Germany. Please note the gunpowder residue in the area of the map closest to Praha/ Prag, traces of the demo staged by Young Czech radicals which ultimately stymied this proposal.

For a brief moment, Option (c) Happy Compromise becomes a runner. A small, luminous dot beside the town of Kremsier is the sign of a convivial campfire. In November, moderates from all groups confer here, hoping to transform Austria into a democratic federal state where local government would be divided along 'national' lines!

Hurrah—

However, we also draw your attention to the sprinkles of gunpowder (date, March 1849; source, arsenal of Emperor Franz Josef) which interrupted the conference, obscuring the dot's luminosity and staining it a familiar dirty reddish brown (?!!! / **caution** ! /— Quickly, visitors, move away from the surface of this map and focus instead on the rather subtle dotted red lines[11] hovering above it. These celebrate the decision to free all peasants in the Empire from forced service and make them masters of the land they till.[12]

Hurrah!

Map Twelve: 1850s

To the west, the borderlines are becoming darker blue as the Prussians flex their muscles, while in the east, a thin red-and-green line is forming across the Empire, a sign of increased Magyar demands. The thrash-metal of the previous map has been drowned out by the drumbeat echo of marching songs and Magyar cries of '*Nekem! Nekem! Nekem!*'[13] In spite of all this,

---

[11] Related, perhaps, to the red haze of nascent class 'Identity' spotted in Map Eight?
[12] See Ireland, 1870s: Parnell, Davitt and the Land League.
[13] *Me! Me! Me!* Translation from Hungarian © Wunderkammer Inc.

you may notice a rather nice smell of fresh banknotes coming from this map. Meanwhile, the smoke plumes, clackety-clack, chink of coin and enthusiastic cries of *'Ja! Ja!'* in the borderlands are getting stronger as the German-led forces of market capitalism, free trade and industrialisation march forwards. Listen closely and you'll also hear the civilised patter of an emerging Czech bourgeoisie. Is the playing field finally beginning to level off?

Sadly – but not altogether unexpectedly – no.

Newsflash: Winning answer to the Conundrum:

Option (a) ☺ *Ethnic Partition!!!* ☻

Under the Prussian threat, the notion of a split-up, federalised Austria is now anathema to the Habsburgs. A freshly printed ballot paper serves as proof of a new voting system – one which gives big landowners and urban areas more deputies than the provincial, mainly Czech areas. German privilege is now enshrined in law![14]

Boo! / Hurrah!

Map Thirteen: 1866–1870

Trouble in the west, where a fresh batch of red-white-red lines are strangling the once-thick dark-blue octopus tentacles of the German Confederation; Austria and Prussia have fallen out. Meanwhile, to the east, a powerful green-and-red striped line has snaked through the Empire, dividing Germans from Germans and Czechs from Slovaks.

The Austrian Empire is dead! Long live the Austro-Hungarian Empire!

Boo! / Hurrah!

A rubber stamp near the bottom of the map indicates that the Empire has also finally got a constitution, thanks to the German Liberals.

Hurrah!

The Liberals (mainly from the Bohemian and Moravian borderlands) have replaced quasi-military police power with legality and have acknowledged Jews' rights.[15] In 1870, the Liberals also accept *Staatsrecht*, the 'historic' claim of Bohemia, Moravia and Silesia to unify in one state. However, rip-marks under the stamp indicate some conflict about their

---

[14] See Ireland: Penal Laws; also Northern Ireland: gerrymandering: the Law as used to control and limit 'democracy'.

[15] In light of this, visitors might wish to reconsider received wisdoms about Germans/German speakers: (1) *They are all in thrall to the idea of authority*; (2) *They are all anti-Semitic.*

proposals to recognise Czech as an official language and give Czechs a form of Home Rule.[16]

Map Fourteen: 1879–1900

This is a particularly difficult map to navigate, since it is covered with a brambly thicket of scrawlings; in Czech, crossed out, rewritten in German, and vice versa. A shifting, animated quality to the crossings-out and the raucous hubbub of dissenting voices suggest that the key borderlines in this map are not geopolitical but more abstract in nature – linguistic, ethnic, ideological – as the people of Bohemia are driven to forsake their tenuous amphibian identity and choose one 'nation' over another. Visitors are urged to take particular care around the jets of steam which can rise without warning from this map, a sign of the region's intensifying tensions.

In the borderlands, the clackety-clack of the mills and factories and the chink of coin passing through German hands are continuing to grow louder. Yet click the forest of hyperlinks and another picture emerges. Visitors examining the tiny group portrait of the 1879 cabinet will notice Pražak, a Czech, amongst the politicos. Lured by jobs, Czechs are also migrating into the prosperous borderlands which the Germans have always thought of as theirs.[17] For a millisecond, we identify thick dotted red lines pulsating through the mess. Could this be, at last, a confluence of class and ethnolinguistic Identities – Czech worker versus German employer? No! The Czechs are passing through that scarlet barrier, entering the bureaucracy and the hitherto German domain of the craft and shopkeeper castes.

Listen to those beeping sounds, similar to Morse Code! Linguistic dispute, bane of the nineteenth century, has raised its head. The Czechs want a bilingual civil service; but many Germans don't.[18] In 1880, the first Language Decrees allow Czech to be used alongside German in some civil service offices. The Germans are outraged. Why? shout the Czechs. Most of your lot choose the army anyway! But look – what's that crawling all over the

---

[16] Note that the first to protest against Czech rights are the Hungarians.

[17] 'Always'? See *Lognote # 2*, Map Five: the 'mystical unity of the Wenceslas Lands'. See also Ireland: 'Who was there first: Firbolgs vs Tuatha de Danaan vs Celts' (with the caveat 'what is/was a "Celt"?'). See also Northern Ireland: Dalriada, 'Irish' settling of 'Scotland' vis-à-vis 'Scots' later Plantation of 'Ulster'.

[18] In contrast to their Enlightenment forebears, many fin-de-siècle Bohemian Germans do not speak Czech, thinking it beneath them. See Ireland: 'Peig'.

borderlands? Maggots? (!!!!/ **alert! alert!** /— *curator psycho-sensory association—* Visitors, collect yourselves! Those nasty little things are only the so-called 'national' societies, the ethnically segregated gym clubs which have begun to burgeon all over the region. As the young Bohemian Germans turn in their droves to the *Turnverband*, the Czechs join their own organisation, *Sokol*. [19]

My, how twisty those dotted red lines first seen in Map Eleven are now! Class fronts are shifting – the Czechs have got their own bank, their first national theatre, the Czech University. They're the modern ones, pushing for federalisation, democracy, liberty, equality, fraternity, while the Germans are on the back foot. Is it any surprise to visitors that the voice of Pan-Germanism, strident to begin with, becomes almost unbearable at this point?[20]

For ease of use, our curator has installed a series of flashing buttons under this map. Press each to experience, in high-definition 3D, moments from the region's 'roaring nineties':

- ❑ *1883:* Cheers and stamping feet as Czechs win a key district and Germans walk out of parliament.
- ❑ *1890:* Quiet conversation, the start of cheers, interrupted by gunfire as moderates on both sides try to make an agreement, only to be thwarted (again) by a Young Czech uprising.
- ❑ *1897:* Cheers, shouting, explosions as the government introduces the Badeni Language Decrees, the German Nationals resist, riots break out between Czech and German gym club members and the Empire teeters on the point of civil war.
- ❑ *1899:* Boos, hissing, cheers as the government withdraws the Decrees.[21]

Warning: we urge those visitors reckless enough to press any of these buttons to don protective gloves and eyewear. The *Kunstkammer* takes no responsibility for damage caused by shards of broken glass, live ammunition, explosive devices and sudden eruptions of blood— (!!!!!!!!!! / **Oops!** *[acutely 'present' curator kinaesthesis triggered by concept of 'blood' →* reality-perception *'blood' →* cognition-flash: **'I am bleeding. Why?'**] /

garbagegarbagegarbage and/or bone spl)(nters. *[neural circuit fades]*

---

[19] See Ireland: Pearse, P. and the GAA.
[20] See Northern Ireland: Orangemen and siege mentality.
[21] See Canute and the Sea.

<u>Not</u>   <u>**e**</u>:
Visitorssss, pologies for the *breakkkkk* in Transmission. A key pathway through the *Kabinnnnnnnnn* e T has irreversibly FFFailed. We will liaaaiseeee with our Cur

        a

                tor nd rtrn to the Tooooo

u

      r

                     as sooooon as pssib   l

Chimera

☼

Outside the house, the moon suspends, hugged by the warm cobalt of the late August sky. It is huge and pink, nearly full, raw as a face burnt in some unspeakable explosion. Lughnasa, the Celts' harvest, seeps out from every pockmark on its surface. There is a rattling sound on the bedroom window, like hailstones or the feet of a small bird. Too close to sleep to notice, the child grunts and turns onto her side, pulling the sheet over her head.

She topples over. The rattling stops. In the overgrown back garden next door, the branch of an apple tree shakes. A small green fruit, hard as a sweet, falls to the ground.

Today is Georgie's first day back at school. Though, as David says, back isn't quite the right word; technically speaking, she's moving forward. Her shoulders are sore, sagging under the weight of her new satchel, and her toes are bumping against the front of her new shoes. Mr McCarthy in the shoe shop in Fairview left some growing room, but this means the shoes slip a little with every step she takes. Although the uneven rhythm adds to the discomfort she's already experiencing about the day ahead, there's something in the extra space in front of her toes that makes her feel vaguely hopeful. What's not in question is the wonderful swish of her jeans, the freedom of not having to wear a uniform. Georgie hates wearing shorts, especially once summer is over. They make her feel exposed, marked out as wrong.

Beside her David is walking quickly, his shoulders hunched. He's not whistling; it's been a while since he's done that. He has the bike with him. Too nice a day, he says, to waste in the car.

It feels odd, like they should be going in the other direction, towards what is now her *old* school, Scoil Choilm, and the familiar things there: the boys in her class, her friends Jeremy and Paul, the predictable layout of the day. Georgie never thought she was going to miss cranky Brother Doyle or the gloomy yard, but she did manage to get herself organised there and, now it's gone, she feels a bit, as Lotte would say, off. Is it going to be worth all the arguments, she wonders – people making such a fuss saying one thing only to turn around and say exactly the spit-bang-wallop opposite – to send her somewhere else just because it's different?

Correction: because *Jan* said it was different.

Why should different, especially Jan bloody Ó Buachalla's version of different, be any better than what already is?

When they reach the school, the yard is swarming with children. The pretty Hansel-and-Gretel gingerbread windows shine in the late summer light. The enormous trees, their leaves just turning copper at their edges, bend over the peaked, striped roof of the hall, as if protecting it.

'Right there?' says David.

Georgie shrugs.

'You want me to come in with you—'

'Uh uh. Seeya later.'

They hug. Georgie can tell he's half-thinking of giving her a proper hug, big and close, like he never used to at Scoil Choilm, but she makes it short on purpose. Just because *Jan* says things are different here, doesn't mean they are. David gets on his bike. Georgie hopes he won't be bringing her to school every day; this is too small a place for that stuff to go ignored. It's not that she doesn't want him ever to bring her, or even to hug her, that would be even more weird, it's just....

'Hi, Georgie!'

Too late, Georgie realises that she is standing in the empty part of the yard, beyond the gate where the parents and children are saying their goodbyes. She is on her own, in full view, an easy target for the focus of the other children, and the person who's coming towards her is the last person she wants to be seen talking to.

'I was inside already.' Saoirse's had her hair cut since the summer and it makes her flat face look even more doughy. 'And I picked us out a really cool seat. It's near the top of the class but not at the very front.' She blinks.

Please go away, thinks Georgie.

Saoirse rummages in her shorts pocket. 'Look, I got this for you.' She shoves a piece of folded newspaper towards Georgie. Georgie's skin crawls.

'It's like, your babysitter. Lotte.' Saoirse unfolds it and holds it up. 'I saw it in an art magazine and thought you'd like it.'

It is an article of some sort, with a big picture of Lotte in the middle. She has her fist raised and is shouting at the camera. She's with some other people and they're all surrounded by placards and big banners with ugly writing on them, but Lotte's is the only face in the photo that is sharp. Her eyes are wild and she's fuller-faced in the picture than she is in real life. Beside her, arm twined around her, is a slender person, not shouting but also with long curly hair, so like her you might think it was a mistake, that the camera had shaken when the photographer clicked it, taking two pictures instead of one – except that at second glance you can that they're different; girl-Lotte, boy-Lotte. To the other side of Lotte's double is a tall girl with long blonde hair who, even through the blur, is probably the most beautiful person Georgie has ever seen in her life.

'She looks pretty there,' says Saoirse. 'Lotte. Not so um, skinny. I guess that's her boyfriend.'

Georgie says nothing.

'Take it.' Saoirse waves the newspaper cutting. 'Please. Mom won't notice. She's got hundreds of magazines.'

Sissy. Georgie doesn't want to look around, but she can feel the word beginning to rise around her, like smoke rings, out of the cracks in the yard's surface. Are they looking at her, the other children? Are they staring, the boys, witnessing the exchange?

Without taking the newspaper, she walks past Saoirse towards the open door of the classroom. As she does, *Sissy* begins to fade. In its place, hazing up around the spongy, disappointed features of the architect's daughter, another warning has formed. It's in writing too and it's old-fashioned, like the map of Wales that Lotte showed her during the summer. Here Be Dragons.

Georgie knows that dragons aren't real, they're just mythical animals, but she still tries not to stick around Saoirse too long when she feels that warning start to take shape. That's because Saoirse's dragons, if they ever came into being, wouldn't be like normal ones. They would come all the way from Ancient Greece and be way, way nastier. Ugly little monsters with three heads, each spitting its own dangerous, chimerical little flame.

The classroom is empty and silent. The air is clean, not spoiled yet by the smell of softening apples or the rotten-milk fug of children's farts. There are three columns of desks. The two on the left are for fourth class; the one on the right is for third. Georgie remembers this from the meeting she and David had in August with the head teacher, a tall scary man with a shock of white hair who wears a black cloak that flaps like a crow's wings. He reminded her of the headmaster in *The Best Days of Our Lives* but he wasn't half as friendly. Georgie is in fourth class, so she needs to find a seat somewhere on the left. The sinister side, Lotte calls it. Georgie scans the room. She'll sit in the row nearest the door, so she can get out quick if she needs to; but not near the front where Saoirse said she'd be, or down the back where the teacher will probably get her to answer loads of questions. She reckons she'll get on okay with whoever's in the middle.

The desks are old-fashioned, a wooden seat and table joined by an iron clasp. Georgie sets down her bag. A bell begins to ring. She returns to the yard and, doing her best to avoid Saoirse, mingles with the crowds of children jostling to form lines. A lot of the kids in the infant lines look scared; some of them are even crying, though a few are giggly and excited. One tiny boy has his tongue stuck out. His eyes are darting, looking for a victim; he finds one, sticks his tongue out farther. The victim cries. The tiny boy laughs.

Georgie is the tallest in her line. She hunches her shoulders, sticks her hands in her pockets and does her best to look uninteresting. The teacher stops shaking the bell.

'Fourth – class!' she calls.

The line begins to move. Someone bumps into Georgie from behind. There are giggles. Sorry, says a familiar voice farther down the line. Saoirse. Georgie glances around, but casually, so as not to draw attention. Near the very end of the line, a stocky, neatly dressed boy with a blunt-cut fringe and wide face is staring innocently into the middle distance. Saoirse is in front of him; she seems confused and is putting her glasses straight. Despite his innocent demeanour, the boy with the fringe reminds Georgie of Alison O'Meara who lives on the Green; she used to go to school with Georgie and is a real so-and-so. Just as Saoirse gets her glasses on, she stumbles again. The boy with the fringe has pushed her; but this time with his knee, so the teacher can't see. Sorry, says Saoirse again. The boy with the fringe looks right at Georgie.

Georgie makes her eyes go dull. The line shuffles forward. Georgie's gaze drifts skywards. The sky is blue, the sun a tough ball of gold, the moon only a shadow of a shadow, a thin outline of silver that she has to stare hard at to find.

I wonder what the stranger is doing? she thinks. And it's only then that she realises that with all the upheaval, she hasn't thought of her new – *friend* isn't the right word – playmate, then, for at least three or four days.

When she was much younger, Georgie had been fascinated by the lane that ran along behind the houses on their road. It was quite private; cars didn't go down it, and it didn't have any streetlamps, and, even though it was so close, you couldn't get into it directly from her house, because the Maddens' back garden, unlike most of the others on the road, didn't have a door that led onto it. Instead, you had to walk the long way round, out the front door and to the top of the road, past the corner where the rubbish bin was with *Brúscar* written on it, then, just before that intersection that was more like a spiderweb than a proper crossroads, turn left again. All that effort made the lane seem even more mysterious; so close, but so hard to get to. It was like a secret backbone, Georgie imagined – connecting everything up through the places you couldn't see. Even when she was very little, she used to wonder what was in there, what hidden things were going on that nobody knew anything about.

When Aisling got sick the First Time Round, two-and-a-half years ago when Georgie was only seven, it was important to find new ways of playing that wouldn't annoy people, Aisling least of all. Georgie had thought the lane would make an ideal place for that; she wouldn't be in anybody's way and she'd finally get a chance to explore its mysteries. But Aisling and David wouldn't let her go there, David especially. He said the lane was dangerous. *You don't know what you might find in there, old bean.*

Wasn't that the point?

But she didn't say that. Instead: It's only round the *corner*, she'd whined, knowing she was whining and hating herself for it, but still not being able to stop; *everyone* plays there. *Everyone* wasn't a lie, but it wasn't exactly true either. There weren't many other kids on their road, none her age except Alison O'Meara, the C-O-W, and Georgie had never actually seen her playing there.

In the end, it was simpler to do what David said, so Georgie didn't go into the lane at all that first summer Aisling was sick. Sometime after that, she'd lost interest, and it wasn't until a good bit later, after *Jan* had come over from America, in fact, and started prying with those questions, that she'd started thinking of it again. She's never been sure exactly what put the lane back into her mind, but it began to seem interesting again; though she still didn't go into it. Soon after that, Aisling got sick Second Time Round; only this time, with so much happening – the chemotherapy and Aisling being so cross and tired and all the different babysitters coming and going, and Auntie Bridget staying, and bloody *Jan* coming over and so-called helping and driving David round the twist and making him give out to Georgie, which was why he started going to the office all the time, Working Himself to the Bone, as Auntie Bridget put it – that it made sense when finally, Georgie was let go play in the lane. As long, Aisling wearily insisted, as she went with a friend.

A friend? But who? By then, Georgie was pretty well ensconced in Scoil Choilm, so she didn't see Sinéad Cowen any more who'd been her best friend in St Bernadette's, her first school, and Anne Geraghty only came around once in a blue moon. It had been clear from the off that Saoirse Ní Bhuachalla wasn't the right sort of material for a friend, which was a relief, what with her dad being so boring and *Jan* being so nosey, apart from all that other stuff. In Scoil Choilm, Georgie had at least got to know Jeremy Higgins quite well and Paul Cantwell, who'd joined in second class, and she was palling around with them, so they seemed like the obvious choices to share her new playground with. However, in the boys' company, the lane seemed much less exciting than Georgie had imagined. She thought at first it was because of the games they played – after all, you didn't need to be in a *lane* to play chasing and ball or chess or Meccano or Lego; you could be anywhere. Then she wondered if it was the boys themselves who were making the lane less interesting, so one day she sneaked off and went in there on her own. And hey presto. Nothing exciting happened, but it felt much more like she'd imagined. Private; mysterious again. After that, she stopped bringing anyone with her; she just headed off on days when she was on her own and played there without telling a soul.

She played pretty simple games to start with; handball or sevens, or tennis against a wall. At some point during Aisling's second illness, she started to make up her own games, stories, really, based on things she'd begun to read. Sometimes she'd pretend she was running errands with the Artful Dodger and Nancy; or solving mysteries with the Hardy Boys and the other Nancy, Nancy Drew; sometimes she was in Narnia with Aslan and Lucy and Susan and Peter, though there was far too much magic in that and it wasn't exactly what you'd call factual, so she tended to stop those stories before they got too silly. Sometimes she pretended she was in *The Secret Garden*, which she'd picked up in the library and read in one go because she hadn't wanted to take it home with her, in case the librarian said something, like he had ages ago over *A Little Princess*. It wasn't bad, making games out of stories; though she did wonder if maybe that sort of thing was best left to babies.

It was only towards the end of last year, before Aisling started to get better Second Time Round, that Georgie became aware of how special the lane really was. Something weird began to happen when she went in there; all the noise outside stopped. It felt like she'd pushed through an invisible curtain and was somewhere else, a place where nobody else could see her. Later she would think of it as going through a *portal,* which, Lotte said, was a magical doorway which could bring you to another *Rowm. Rowm* was one of Lotte's Czechoslovakian words; it meant two things – space, like outer-space, and room, like bed-room. The thing that happened in the lane wasn't magical, though, because nobody except babies believed in magic. It was scientific. A *phenomenon* was the word David used, in that distracted, stiff voice he'd started putting on ages ago, after Aisling had got better First Time Round.

Phenomenon is a Greek word, Lotte says. It means something that happens that you can see and feel.

Georgie had a theory that the phenomenon in the lane had to do with dimensions. David had explained dimensions one Sunday at the end of February, right before Aisling found out The Thing, though Georgie didn't know it at the time. He'd taken the salt and pepper cellars and balanced them on the edge of the table, like a see-saw, and explained how, if you were made up of two dimensions, flat, like the bottom of the salt cellar or the surface of the table, that was all you could see. Flatness everywhere, in all directions. You wouldn't see the body of the salt cellar or the legs of the table, all you'd see was flat shapes. So you would think that everything in the world was like that; two dimensions too, flat like you. It was the same with humans. Imagine, he said. There could be people going around with four dimensions, but we'd never notice, because all we can see is three! The point where three slipped into four was called an event horizon, he said, like the horizon at sea. You can see everything up to the edge and then you can't. It was quite interesting and David sounded more normal as he spoke, not so stiff or distracted. Even Aisling was listening properly, watching David like she hadn't in yonks, a funny little smile playing around her mouth. Though David didn't notice that because he was concentrating so hard on the salt and pepper.

And the fourth dimension, he said, sweeping the cellars into his hand, is time.

Q.E.D., said Aisling. David looked up. He saw Aisling smiling and laughed, surprised, and Georgie joined in because that was David's joke and they all used to laugh at it before First and Second Time. It was nice to have that happen for a change, probably because Jan and you-know-boring-who weren't around. Then lunch finished and – Best get cracking, said David – they were all back doing their own things. David checking the sums for the bridge he was building, Aisling listening to music and Georgie thinking about the lane.

Georgie's theory was that the lane had an extra dimension, and there was an event horizon that only she could get over, and that was why all the noises stopped when she went in there. She wasn't sure exactly how it happened, but she'd tested it by doing a Thought Experiment. Which, Jeremy Higgins said, was what all the Great Minds did whenever they had a new idea. Her Experiment was simple: all she did was go into the lane, wait for the phenomenon to happen and then, once it did, imagine someone passing by at the top of the lane except – this was the experiment bit – they couldn't see her. The first day she did it, Kerrie Grogan who was lovely and a teenager walked by and Georgie waved, quite big, from the middle of the lane, and Kerrie didn't look around. Doing an Experiment once isn't enough to prove it, Jeremy had said, so she repeated it a few times – with Mrs Kelly's daughter and Joanie Flynn and the man who'd looked after Mrs Kelly's garden after she'd died, and even on Alison O'Meara, the B-I-T-C-H. And nobody saw or heard her, not even the dogs. All they did was walk past. After that, she wrote her theory down as a sum, like the ones David used, because Jeremy said Great Minds did that too.

lane+Georgie=invisibility

She didn't tell anyone else about her theory, not even Jeremy. She had a feeling that if she did, the whole thing would go doo-lally, as Lotte might say. The invisibility she and the lane conferred on each other would disappear. Not like a spell being broken, because spells and curses and things were magic and everyone knew they didn't exist. No; somehow, the phenomenon would be dis*proven*, like the two men with the periscopes who said you can change a thing by looking at it; or the story David used to tell about the poor cat who was dead when they opened the box but dead and alive right up until the minute before. Once or twice, before the stranger had turned up, she'd thought of telling Lotte. Lotte was different to other grown-ups. She called Georgie 'monster', which was okay in a strange way, and she kept things organised but wasn't interfering or bossy like the Aunts, or nosey, trying to find out everything about you, like bloody *Jan*, and she didn't do that horrible poor-Georgie-poor-David-oh-you-poor-things-blah-blah-blah thing like everyone else. Even David seemed to cheer up around her. Georgie had a feeling that Lotte would not just understand, she would *see* what happened when the lane and Georgie came together. Lotte had a way of looking at a person that was the opposite of the lane; it made them seem sharper at the edges, revealing bits of them that had been hidden before.

But....

There was a but and Georgie wasn't sure why, except that Lotte was almost but *not quite* the perfect person to share the mystery with, and that *not quite* was crucial.

The seating arrangements are new for everyone, not just Georgie, so there's some confusion at the start. 'Come on, come on!' calls Mrs Allen. 'You don't have to sit beside the same person this year!' But her voice is friendly, not cross like Brother Doyle's. The head had said Mrs Allen was a wonderful educator; Georgie assumed this meant she'd be very strict and they'd be doing loads of sums. But, instead, she's pleasant and quite young and wearing really with-it clothes: high-heeled platforms, a scarf around her neck and a skirt called a maxi, which swings near the hem when she moves.

Georgie takes advantage of the confusion to slip into her seat quickly, before anybody notices she's already put her schoolbag there. Saoirse trundles up, little raisin eyes hopeful, and for a moment Georgie's heart is in her mouth. But thankfully a boy with dirty-blond hair pushes past Saoirse and plumps himself down beside Georgie. Two girls sit in the desk in front of her, and behind her she hears the voices of a boy and girl. Saoirse, despite what she said earlier, has found a seat beside the teacher, right at the top of the middle column.

A swot. A lick. A scab.

The boy beside Georgie doesn't introduce himself, but during roll call he says '*Anseo*' when Mrs Allen calls the name 'Timmy Nelson'. He has a horrible voice. It's hoarse and sounds like he needs to clear his throat all the time. Hearing him makes Georgie want to clear *her* throat, and she does, a few times, but he doesn't take the hint and copy her. His voice sounds like a cheese grater, and at that she gets an awful picture in her head of how if she keeps having to listen to Timmy Nelson, the sound will grate away all the skin on the inside of her neck until there'll be nothing left, just knobbly bits of bone, and blood, and strings of muscle dangling like spaghetti someone has sicked up.

Mrs Allen reads out her name as Georgie, which is different to Scoil Choilm, who always called her George or Madden. Some of the other surnames are familiar from her visits up North. Robertson, Wilson, McKim, Johnson. There are other Englishy-sounding names, like Lotte's: Jones, Woods, Jacobs – though Aisling says Jacobs is actually an Irish name that belongs to a type of Protestant called a Quaker. There are some normal ones, like her own, and some real Irish ones like Ó Dálaigh or Ó Súilleabháin. Saoirse is Ní Bhuachalla because she's a girl.

The girl sitting behind Georgie is called Sarah Hannigan. She has a slightly vacant expression and raggedy hems to her jumper sleeves. The boy beside her is the one with the innocent wide face who pushed Saoirse and he is called William Robinson. Georgie hadn't expected he would sit so nearby. William Robinson doesn't seem like the type who belongs in the middle of a row; from Scoil Choilm she knows the natural place for boys like him is down the back, where he can get up to all sorts without being seen. At first she tells herself to give him the benefit of the doubt. Just because he looks like Alison O'Meara and pushed Saoirse with his knee doesn't mean anything. However, as the morning goes on, and William Robinson continues messing – farting, belching, punching Timmy Nelson in the back, making whispered jokes about the other kids, saying really rude words that set Sarah Hannigan off on fits of nervous giggles – she realises there is no benefit of any doubt to give him. William Robinson is trouble, with a capital T.

Georgie's not worried about him picking on her – she's got good at avoiding that sort of thing – but she doesn't like the fact that she's sitting directly between him and the teacher. Every time Mrs Allen calls 'William Robinson!', which she does a lot because of his messing, she has to look at Georgie, which means the rest of the class do too. He probably chose that seat because Georgie is so big and he can hide behind her. She makes a mental note to keep her head down and her bum at the edge of the seat so she's out of his sightline as much as possible.

Strangely enough, when the embarrassing thing happens, it's not William Robinson's fault or even Saoirse's. It's when Mrs Allen asks who'll be exempt from Religion. For some reason Georgie gets confused; she knows she has to go to a special class on Tuesday afternoons with the other Catholics, so she puts up her hand. As soon as she does, everyone looks over and she knows she's made a mistake. She might as well have switched on a flashing light saying, *Newcomer! Newcomer!* William Robinson snorts a laugh and even Timmy Nelson looks up, his moo-cow eyes vaguely troubled. But luckily, she's not the only one with her hand up for long. Saoirse joins in – of course; bloody *Jan* is an atheist – then a boy with curly dark hair and brownish skin, followed by a girl from third class, who, it later turns out, are both Jews. 'Great,' says Mrs Allen. 'You can all go to the hall while we're working here.'

William Robinson sniggers. 'You can all go to Hell while we're working here.'

Georgie feels his finger land on the soft fat bit of her upper back. Saoirse has half-turned round and is staring at her, sad almost, like she knows something Georgie doesn't.

Fuck off, thinks Georgie. She moves her head so she's looking away from Saoirse, slightly over her own shoulder but in a way that the teacher won't notice. She catches William Robinson's sniggering dark gaze.

His finger pulses, heat pushing into the middle of her spine. She keeps looking. His snigger fades, becomes something altogether less obvious. Slowly, with inhuman patience, his finger retreats.

She had first started seeing the stranger in July. It was after they went to Dollymount with Lotte, but before Aisling said The Thing. There was nothing definite at first, just glimpses. A skinny little girl with scabby knees passing them on the street. A flash of blonde hair reflected in a shop window. Laughter trickling out of a back garden. The sound of footsteps outside the Maddens' house in the evenings, during the musky, dusky hours before the sunset. But any time Georgie tried to catch sight of her – by turning around, or running into the shop she thought the little girl had gone into, or looking out the window towards the source of the footsteps – she'd found nothing. For a while, Georgie thought the stranger wasn't real, she was what Aisling called a mirage, the sort of thing thirsty people see in the desert, but that changed the day Georgie spotted her going round the corner into the lane and followed her.

The plan that day had been for Aisling to take Georgie into town to get schoolbooks and have a treat afterwards. But Aisling had been too tired to get out of bed that morning and Georgie guessed then it wasn't going to happen, because this wasn't First Time or even Second Time Round, this was The Thing; and before she'd even asked David, he was shaking his head. She almost said, Well if you *knew*, why didn't you warn me? But even just thinking that made Georgie feel uncomfortable, so, before he could speak, she asked him to ring Jeremy's mum, Mrs Higgins, to see if she would take her into town. Eh, um, said David, but he went ahead and rang. Nobody home. Just as well really, said David, we don't want to, eh, impose. Even though he and Georgie knew that Mrs Higgins was okay that way, not nosey, even if she didn't like people getting too close to her. Then David looked at Georgie and, exactly at the same time, Georgie said 'Lotte!', because that was the Ideal Solution. But Lotte was out too and at that David ended up getting really irritated. Georgie knew he was worrying that maybe he'd have to take her into work with him, but the last thing she was going to agree to was the Alternative, which was going over to bloody *Jan*'s to be minded or, worse, have bloody *Jan* come into town with her to buy the books – which she'd offered to do tons of times, even though Aisling had said, No thanks, we'll be fine. It was jaw-dropping, how some people just couldn't Get the Message. But David didn't say anything about Jan, just went pink in the face, which meant he had decided to bring her into work after all and was trying not to show how much he was fuming about it, though Georgie could see the curse words – Jesus and Bloody and even Fuck – starting to buzz like fireworks behind his teeth.

David hadn't been keen on Georgie coming into the office for ages, though until March and that stupid test, he'd been quite good at covering it up. Aisling said he didn't hate Georgie being there, he was just planning a big top-secret suprise for them that involved Germany and he was worried everybody in the office would spill the beans if Georgie went in, and until Georgie found out the Thing, she'd believed that. If David had any eyes in his head, he would see that Georgie herself had no *grá*, as Auntie Bridget would say, to be stuck in his office, pretending to be good, that man with the sharp smile looking at her like he could see something nobody else could. But David couldn't figure that out, and probably never would: Blind as a Bat. So Georgie said really fast, before he could suggest it, that actually, she'd be fine on her own at home. She was big enough to look after herself, and anyway she wouldn't be alone, she'd be with Aisling, and they could get the books another time. David stared at her and she thought he was going to say No Way. Then he sighed. Okay, but you're not to bother Mum. At which Georgie felt like exploding because she *knew* that; even when Jeremy came over, they never did loud stuff in the house. David said he was going to call the Nurse to come in for a few hours and Georgie was to promise to be on her best behaviour. Okay, said Georgie. Then David burnt the toast and she couldn't eat it, and he went off and she was on her own, except for Aisling, upstairs, still in bed.

The kitchen door was open; outside, the sun was making everything look tired and scratchy. They'd all got so used to the heatwave, it had stopped being fun ages ago. Georgie didn't want to go out the back because she was tired of being sunburnt, and she couldn't watch telly, even with the sound down, because RTÉ had no cartoons on during weekdays, except bad ones from

Czechoslovakia – funny, how Czechoslovakia, where Lotte's mum Julia came from, could sound so interesting in some ways, but be so boring in others. She didn't want to read because none of her books seemed interesting any longer. Colouring-in might have been an option, but the last time she'd tried to do that, she'd ended up ruining the picture like an eejit.

Eventually she got a brainwave and decided to make Aisling minestrone soup from a packet. She added mace at the end which Aisling liked and brought it upstairs, and Och that's sweet, said Aisling, you shouldn't have. Georgie was glad to see she was awake, but annoyed too, because if Aisling was awake, why couldn't she get up and go into town and get schoolbooks with her? Then she felt bad for thinking that, and then even more annoyed with herself for feeling bad. Aisling took a few mouthfuls of soup before putting down the spoon. That's lovely, darling, but I need to get some shut-eye. Aren't you going to have the rest? said Georgie, meaning the soup. In a while, love, which meant *No*. Aisling moved her face on the pillow, looking for a kiss, but Georgie pretended she didn't see and went downstairs again, and it was still only eleven.

The sun was higher now, but inside the house was dark and sticky. Georgie was running out of ideas. She could have tidied her room, but she'd tidied it the night before and Lotte had hoovered on Wednesday afternoon, which meant there wasn't anything that needed organising. So she sat at the kitchen table and closed her eyes, and kicked the leg of the table and counted up the number of kicks and divided them by eleven. When she'd done enough of that, she thought of the long words in the book Lotte had given her – *Greek Mythology for Children* – and counted up the letters in each of them. Chimera. Seven. Arachnaea. Nine. Heracles. Eight. Orpheus. Seven. Hades. Five. Eurydice—

Aisling had gone quiet when Georgie unwrapped Lotte's present, even though she was the one who'd always talked about Greece and how great it was. It was an okay book. The stories were quite good, though the pictures were weird; realistic but messy-looking, reminding Georgie of those stupid drawings of mermaids she used to do before she'd realised there was no point in doing things like that. Georgie already knew some of the stories in Lotte's book. They were called myths, Aisling said, which basically meant – though Aisling didn't say it that way – lies that people believe in to make themselves feel better about things. Georgie herself had decided a while back that she didn't believe in myths. She understood that while a woman in a myth could have a lion's head and vice versa, scientifically and technically, as David would say, it was nonsense. The pictures in Lotte's book unsettled her, though. They didn't make her believe that the myths were true, but some were so realistic they did make her wonder if it would ever become scientifically possible to do that – stick a cow's head on a man's body, a goat's head in the middle of a lion, have snakes grow from a woman's scalp.

Despite herself, she'd quite enjoyed reading about the gods, who seemed like real people; they were good at getting their own way and weren't afraid to be horrible to other gods and the heroes, like how Alison O'Meara was, only way more serious because they caused dangerous things like the Trojan War. Aren't these stories great? Aisling had said. Don't they remind you of King Arthur and his knights in that lovely wee book you used to take out from the library? But Georgie ignored that question, because it wasn't relevant to anything. Oh, said Lotte quickly, in an embarrassed sort of way, I didn't think of that. Which didn't make sense at all, only then she started talking about how different the Greek gods were to knights or anything else, really, because there were female gods too, and they were just as important as the male ones and did just as much fighting and plotting and killing. Isn't that interesting, monster?

Interesting? Lotte was great most of the time, but, as Georgie had to keep reminding herself, she was still an adult.

After she got bored with counting up the letters in the Greek names, she rummaged in the kitchen cupboards, hoping Lotte had left some treats. But Lotte hadn't been since Wednesday and they'd eaten all the salty twisted snacks she'd brought then – bretzels, they're called, and they're from Europe. Czechoslovakia? Georgie asked hopefully; but Lotte just smiled, which meant *I'm not saying* – so there was nothing in the cupboards, except glacé cherries which Aisling had bought for a Christmas cake but never made because Mrs Kelly always used to give them one instead. Georgie went ahead and ate most of the cherries anyway. Then she felt sick and her chest started hurting, so she took out Lotte's book and, for the want of anything better to do, looked at the drawings for a while.

Sphinx. Minotaur. Dryad. Cerberus.

At midday the Nurse came. Georgie didn't like her; although she tried to be kind, she treated Georgie like she was really young instead of nine and a half, which was a right pain in the arse. The Nurse went upstairs and bustled around and when she brought down the soup, Georgie saw that Aisling hadn't eaten any more of it and it had got a skin on top. Georgie sat with Lotte's book in front of her and watched a bluebottle land on the soup and buzz there, its small black legs paddling furiously through the noodles and orangey-red liquid and thick disgusting skin. A jimmy-joe dandelion head wafted in from the garden. It floated around the lightbulb for a while, then began to drift down towards the table in figure-of-eight loops.

The Nurse went back upstairs, and Georgie heard her squeaky rubber soles singing on the bathroom lino. Georgie hoped she wasn't annoying Aisling, touching her hair or calling her 'dear'. God in heaven, I hate that, Aisling had said, loudly, to Lotte, one afternoon when they thought Georgie was outside playing, and the wet hurt in her voice had gone through Georgie's insides like a knife. The bluebottle buzzed, drowning, and Lotte's book with the mishmash people stared up at Georgie accusingly, as if hating her for having burnt all those pointless mermaids which only a baby would draw in the first place, just because bloody *Jan* had said at that stupid Sunday dinner where they'd first met her, her stupid boring husband sitting beside her, a big gap of blankety-blank nothing, Oh, so you're creative, Georgie? That's Neat. Your Mom tells me you used to draw. You get that from your Dad. Same Hands, huh? I bet you have some Imagination!, and stupidly Georgie blurted out, Yeah, I mean, I used to do mermaids. Mermaids, huh? said Jan, leaning in. That's unusual. So what made you decide to stop doing them—

And too late, Georgie had stopped, understanding, though she had no idea why, No. No. No. Here Be Dragons!

The jimmy-joe landed on the soup; a tuft of child's hair sticking to a smear of blood.

At that Georgie couldn't take any more. I'm going out to play round the back, Mum, she called, making sure not to say the Nurse's name. She took her ball with her, having a notion that at some point she would play sevens.

The leaves of the box hedge were singed, the grass in the front garden was straw-yellow, thin as Aisling's hair when had it started falling out during the chemotherapy Second Time Round. Georgie mooched towards the gate, shoulders heavy, feet dragging, slouching the way David always tried to make her not do, even though he wasn't exactly Mister Straight these days, and she was half-thinking maybe she should just go back inside and ask the Nurse nicely if she could sit in Aisling's room and read, when she caught a glimpse of something at that odd little crossing, disappearing around the corner of the road behind the bin, and knew immediately it was the stranger.

She steps into the shimmery mirage of wobbling air. The lane breathes out and the sounds of the neighbourhood fade, leaving her quarantined in a hidden dimension of silence. Under the sun's glare, the images around her sharpen: hotch-potch limestone render, a patchwork of doors leading to other people's back gardens, scruffy dandelion heads and parched green weeds in tiny triangles of dirt. Halfway down the lane gleams the disintegrating carcass of the stolen Cortina the robbers dumped there at the start of summer. Something percolates up through her awareness; something is not right. The broken and whole bits of the car are bouncing back white splinters of sun that hurt her eyes. The tyres are flat and droopy, as if melting into the ground. The crack in the back windscreen, extrapolated into a frosty, glittering spiderweb, stares at her. From its crazed glass eye comes the sound of music.

It is a tinny sound, faint but recognisable. The sound of a transistor radio playing pop, the type of music Joanie Flynn listens to, the type that makes your feet want to tap and your bottom and shoulders shake. Curious, cautious, Georgie draws closer. A flicker of movement behind the windscreen. She stops. The lane breathes in. Georgie finds herself looking into a pair of cool, heavy-lidded eyes reflected in the rearview mirror.

They stare at each other, Georgie and the skinny little stranger, as Joanie Flynn's disco beat rises its chic freak over the lane and the suburb and the city poised on the brink of a troublesome secular European modernity, and the flies buzz and the heavy leaves in people's back gardens sigh and the buddleias creak in a non-existent wind and the Nurse's shoes keep singing, singing on the linoleum floor. Then, at the same time, the children break eye-contact and somewhere, deep in the lost dimension, the lane laughs.

Bouncing her ball with hard, determined strokes, Georgie made her way round to the side of the car. The stranger was in the passenger seat, slouchy and indifferent. Through the broken windscreen, Georgie could see she was wearing a dustyish pink T-shirt, too big for her, with a faded cartoon of a girl's face on the front. The cartoon was like the cover of the *Mandy* annual Sinéad Cowen had got for one of her birthdays and it reminded Georgie of Lotte – beautiful, all swirling hair and long lashes. Below the T-shirt, the stranger was wearing denim shorts, which seemed to be cut-off grown-ups' jeans, secured around her middle with a man's tie. Her legs were bony and effortlessly brown, nonchalantly crossed so one foot dangled while the other tapped to the music. On the tapping foot, Georgie caught a glimpse of a sandal, brown leather, also too big.

Georgie bounced the ball. She wasn't going to be the first to speak. It was her lane and her Cortina and the stranger owed her an explanation. A boundary had been breached and it was important to make people aware that this wasn't okay.

'Hiya,' said the stranger eventually. She had a croaky voice and a Dublin accent like Joanie Flynn's; what Paul Cantwell would call a knacker's voice. She shifted on her seat, drawing closer to the passenger window. The movement made it look like she was apologising for taking up space in the car; but it also made it look like she was inviting Georgie to join her, and that felt wrong.

Georgie bounced the ball again. She couldn't get into the car because that would be accepting the invitation; worse, it would be saying that the girl had the *right* to invite her. The stranger was staring ahead of her and, not quite in time with the music, was chewing gum. Georgie couldn't tell if it was Juicy Fruit or Spearmint. She seemed oblivious to Georgie, which means you don't know anything or care what people think, but Georgie knew this was an act. Every so often she would blow out a breath and her blondish hair would rise from her eyes. Georgie had the feeling she was waiting for something, but it was anyone's guess what. So she stared straight ahead too, pretending to be equally oblivious.

Eventually, the girl looked at Georgie. Georgie shrugged. Bouncing her ball, she turned her back on the girl, to show she didn't care, while staying close enough to the car to show she was still in charge, and started playing sevens. On the fours, while she was turning, she saw the girl had climbed out of the car and was leaning against the wall, beside the door that led into Mrs Kelly's back garden. She was holding her radio close to her, as if it was a baby, and was tapping her foot. Georgie saw that Mrs Kelly's back door was slightly open, just enough for a thin person or a child to get through.

Ah, thought Georgie, that's where she lives.

Georgie did her last throw. She bounced the ball without looking at the girl. 'D'you want a go?'

The girl nodded and put the radio on the ground. She took the ball and started playing and only then did Georgie get in the car and sit in the driver's seat. The girl was good at sevens but not as good as Georgie – though Georgie wondered if she was only letting on to make Georgie feel better. Georgie had another go, and then they swapped names and Georgie didn't even think how funny it was, that the stranger was called Elaine and they'd met in a lane. Elaine played again and then, suddenly, in the middle of a throw, she said, 'Have you ever played this with tennis balls?', and Georgie could tell she'd asked it not because it was an important question, but to show that she knew Georgie was in charge. At that point, Georgie realised she needed to be magnanimous, which was what all good leaders were, like Hector in the Siege of Troy. So she shrugged, as if to say, Maybe. Then one of them, Georgie would never remember who, said 'Or golf balls?' And the other shrugged and said 'Or ping-pong balls?' Georgie saw they were staring at each other, really hard, as if looking for something. And when the stranger said, 'Or boy balls?', not even an eyelid flickering, no sense that what she said might disturb her leader, because there was no reason for it to disturb, Georgie finally allowed herself to smile, magnanimously, and the girl did too.

In the three weeks since, they've met regularly, always on Georgie's terms; when Jeremy isn't around, or when there isn't stuff to do with Lotte or Aisling, and always in the lane. Elaine is patient; she doesn't seem to mind hanging around waiting for Georgie to find time to play with her. Georgie has developed a theory about her new playmate. She reckons Elaine is a runaway, and that's why she's hiding in Mrs Kelly's house. Elaine hasn't said anything about where she's come from, but she looks like runaways look in all the books: cast-off clothes, sleeping in an empty house, trying to keep out of adults' way. There may be another explanation, but if so, Elaine hasn't offered it and Georgie certainly won't ask. That would be breaking the rules. In their not-quite friendship, the only one who does the asking is Elaine.

One thing bothers Georgie. The last time they were playing, Elaine asked Georgie what school she was going to and Georgie told her. Then Elaine surprised Georgie by saying, 'Yeah, well, I'm going to St Bernadette's. I've binned there before. I know *loads* of people there.' She said it in her usual way, tossing her hair, sort of blasé, which, Lotte says, means bored and like you don't care. Elaine sounded so confident, it seemed inconceivable she would be going anywhere other than St Bernadette's or wouldn't know people there, and it took Georgie a moment to realise, Hang on, that can't be true. For how could Elaine know people in St Bernadette's when she didn't know anyone else in the neighbourhood, or even the street names or the best shop to get sweets? Later, Georgie started thinking about how Elaine had looked when she'd said St Bernadette's. She'd glanced under her lashes at Georgie, as if daring her to contradict her. Something in that look had made Georgie very uncomfortable; she'd felt hot and got a stitch in her chest thinking about it afterwards. But to challenge Elaine about it would push something in their not-quite friendship, and that's one thing Georgie is not up to. Not yet, anyway.

Break is fine. Georgie finds a largish group, mainly boys, who are kicking a ball around, and mucks in. She is okay at football though not brilliant, but there are no visible paths into the games the girls are playing – tag and chatting and some made-up thing about spies – and she doesn't want to go near the bike-shed, where Saoirse is hanging around on her own. Although Georgie feels sorry for Saoirse, just like she did the first time she met her, she knows she's doing absolutely one hundred percent the right thing in keeping her distance.

'Here, here!' shouts William Robinson, gesturing to Georgie for the ball. Georgie throws it his way, avoiding eye contact.

She realises it's stupid, but when the bell rings, she finds herself imagining that Aisling will be at the gates, waiting. Instead, as the crowd separates, Lotte is standing there. She's wearing a silky mauve dress and looks nice. It's the first time Georgie has seen Lotte in a dress, or wearing anything that isn't grey or brown or faded green. She doesn't stand out as much as she might have if she was collecting Georgie from Scoil Choilm; enough of the other parents and minders here are young-looking too, with flicked hair and jazzy clothes, and that's a relief.

As soon as she sees Georgie, Lotte waves and gives a big smile. She doesn't rush up to give her a hug like Aisling would, but when Georgie gets to the gate, Lotte nudges her in the side and ruffles her hair. Lotte isn't a huggy person, though she makes other types of contact easily, almost absently, touching people's forearms, patting their backs – the only person she doesn't do that with is David. Once, embarrassingly, while they were watching telly, she even let her hand drift over and smooth Georgie's hair from her forehead without seeming to know what she was doing.

'So?' As usual, Lotte smells nice, rich, of summer flowers. The dress has thin straps that make the bones at the top of her chest look very sharp. 'Any news, monster?'

Georgie shrugs, thinking of the newspaper cutting Saoirse showed her. 'Uh uh.'

'You want me to take that?'

'Okay.' Georgie hands her the schoolbag.

'Must be nice to finish school early.'

'Hmm.' Georgie shrugs.

'You can show off to Jeremy when you see him. Imagine, he's probably still doing his maths or—'

'Nature studies,' says Georgie. 'Lotte, I'm hungry.'

'Alright, matey, no worries,' says Lotte in a jokey way, like she's an Australian. 'I've brought you a sarney and an apple and we're going to have fish and chips later on and—'

'Okay.' Georgie takes the apple and bites. 'Can we go now?'

Georgie has been hoping that *Jan* won't be coming to collect Saoirse. So far, there has been no sign, but as luck would have it, just as they get to the gate, that boring Jag pulls up on the other side of the road with you-know-bloody-boring who in the driver's seat.

Come *on*, thinks Georgie. Lotte, though, like everyone else, has stopped to look at the Jag. Georgie can't see why; it's just a car. Big and flashy with stupid green windows that you can't see out of. People love it, though; even Jeremy got excited when he saw it. Wow! he said, you know that's an XJ-S, Georgie! Way more aerodynamic than the E-Type! Unbelievable!

Unbelievable, alright.

The horn honks. In the yard, Saoirse detaches herself from the other children and races towards the gate.

'*Isteach, a stór*!' The front passenger door opens, sending out a wave of sharp scent. Jungle smells, sunshine smells, man smells. *No, Denis*. Georgie blinks. On her retina, the afterimage of a man's arm, white-skinned but covered in dark hairs, the rolled-up edge of a shirt, its colour hidden in the shadows.

'Georgie!' Saoirse skids to a halt, losing her balance and knocking into Lotte.

'Goodness!' says Lotte.

'Uh, sorry!' Saoirse is completely out of breath. 'So I guess I'll seeya tomorrow, Georgie. Maybe we can sit together then?'

'Saoirse! *Isteach*!'

A head emerges from the driver's window. A halo of wild hair, a sharp-collared shirt the same colour as the golden car. His face is silhouetted by the sun; a black blank. They're not here, Georgie thinks. Neither of them are. And if they were, they wouldn't want to talk to you. What's unbelievable is how can anyone be that big and still so bloody boring *useless*.

'Oh,' says Lotte. A funny sound, almost painful, as if she's stubbed her toe.

The engine revs. 'Saoirse! *Anois*!' Saoirse ducks her head and runs, clambering into the car.

The engine roars, shoving the Jag into motion. A gust of wind swirls the last of the driver's scent around them and lifts the hem of Lotte's dress, making it billow around her thin brown legs. The driver's head turns, his enormous black shadow shifting behind the green-tinted back window. Lotte's chin lifts. The car beeps again and speeds off, leaving tiny spirals of dust in its wake.

When the dust clears, Elaine is standing in the road, right in the middle of the crossing. A car stops, masking her body from Georgie's view. Over the shining metal, her head appears to float, staring.

Something tight grips Georgie's belly.

Elaine's mouth opens and she begins to call, yelling soundlessly over the traffic, *come here, come here*, and before Georgie gets a chance to think how strange that is, Elaine coming here, Elaine, who never asks for anything, calling her over, Lotte turns and – 'Right, Georgie?' – starts to walk towards the bus stop. Georgie shakes her head at Elaine.

Later, she mouths. *In the lane.*

For a moment Elaine looks terribly sad. Then her expression changes.

'Georgie Porgie!' sings a taunting voice.

Hackles rising, Georgie turns. William Robinson is standing at the gate. He must have slid up while she was distracted. She ducks her head. Through the blur of the other kids passing between them, she can see William Robinson's neat tanktop, underneath it his ribs, moving up and down. His hands are rolled into fists and stuck in the pockets of his neat, ironed trousers. She's expecting an attack, even though he'd be stupid to do that with all the grown-ups around, but when he moves, it's only to open his mouth. In the edge of her vision, she sees his tongue poking out over his bottom lip. It's small and pink, not forked, but still....

His tongue retracts. His lips purse, he jerks his head back and, before the worst can happen, she runs.

'Hunh,' she hears him say. A rough sound, low and empty, that follows her all the way to Lotte.

Lotte half-turns, but keeps walking, and as Georgie draws close, she stretches her hand out behind her, palm open to take Georgie's. Georgie doesn't look round to see how far the spit has travelled, but she can still feel William Robinson's baleful eyes on her, so she lets Lotte's fingers stay where they are, drifting in the air.

'Who was that, Georgie?'

'Hmm?'

'Outside school?'

'Oh.' For a split second she considers. After all, Elaine looked like she really needed help. Then Georgie remembers: you can never ever tell a grown-up about a runaway child in case they pass it on to the wrong person. Anyway, Lotte has her own secrets. 'Just a friend.'

The nun in the special hospital is small and smells of flowers. She presses Lotte's hand and holds it a little longer than Lotte is comfortable with. Georgie knows this because Lotte's smile goes very bright but doesn't quite reach her eyes. 'She's in the garden,' says the nun, lowering her voice and looking sadly at Georgie as if it's a jesus bloody fuck off secret, and Georgie makes a cross sound with her breath like David does when he's trying not to swear, but the nun doesn't look any less sad. Instead she turns and leads them down the corridor, her rosary beads clacking by her waist. The lino-covered floor shines in the afternoon light, reflecting the glass-framed holy pictures on the wall and the shadows of Georgie and Lotte, which here are somehow never shadows but something alive and three-dimensional, and Georgie thinks of David's salt cellar and the lane, and wonders if the floor of the hospital is a portal too, into another dimension, and if so, which one.

The special hospital was Granny Bell's idea. She and Granda Bell and the aunts in Clonmel are paying for it. Georgie is not supposed to know this but she'd have had to be deaf not to pick up what was going on from the tense phone conversations conducted in the hall too loud and too late at night, when she was supposed to be asleep and Aisling resting. How people think they can argue about stuff like that, especially stuff *the child* isn't supposed to know about, and think you won't hear, is beyond her. The point of this hospital is to make everything easier on David and Aisling and her. Georgie hates it. It's supposed to be special but it smells just like all the other hospitals; of disinfectant and wee.

At least the little garden at the back is pretty. There are roses and a fountain but the fat red petals look parched, and the nuns haven't been able to put on the water all summer because of the heatwave.

Aisling is sitting in a wheelchair near the big glass doors, which are called French windows, even though Lotte says the French call them English ones. Her eyes are half-closed and the bag of stuff on the metal stand beside her is glowing, like the insides of a goldfish bowl. Georgie is relieved to see that the tube leading from the stuff is going straight into Aisling's vein. The day before, her arm had been swollen out like a balloon. When he saw that, David started shouting; it was like those fireworks building up behind his teeth since springtime had finally gone off, like they hadn't since Don't-Mention-The-Bank. Didn't those nuns know how bloody serious this was? Didn't they have anyone keeping an eye on things? What were they, fucking blind? He only stopped yelling when Aisling said, in that new, quiet voice which sounded like she'd always had it only nobody had heard it before, 'Davey, please.' Afterwards, when David was talking to the doctor, his back hard and tight again, Aisling explained to Georgie that the swelling was because they couldn't find the vein, so the stuff had gone into her tissues, which means her fat and muscles, instead. The reason they couldn't find the vein was because of her blood pressure. It's so low, the veins have stopped sticking out. See?

Georgie didn't want to see; she already knew all she needed to know about blood pressure. Granny Madden's was very high and made her have what were called strokes, which was why, David said, only not in so many words, she could seem a bit crazy sometimes. Auntie Bridget said that everyone knew Granny Madden had been crazy long before she ever had a stroke, but Georgie wasn't quite so sure about that. Some of the things Granny Madden said would make you think she was one of the few not-crazy people in the world.

Today Aisling's arm is still swollen but not as much. Georgie hopes that by evening, when David comes to visit, it will have gone completely back to normal. People can be a pain in the big-hairy-arse when they get angry about things that they so-called can't fix when actually if you look hard enough you can always find ways of making things a bit better, even if it's just organising your own bloody room.

Aisling calls the stuff in the bag her miracle cure. With this miracle cure going through my veins, you could hug me like Mr Universe, Georgie, and it wouldn't bother me. Georgie knows it's neither a miracle nor a cure; that's just one of Aisling's little white lies, like saying people don't want you in their office because of surprises in Germany. The stuff in the bag is a drug called morphine and what it does is make Aisling numb, the same way as the anaesthetic in the dentist's when you need a filling. Georgie feels better for knowing this, and glad that she asked David what the stuff was without saying either 'miracle' or 'cure'. Glad, most of all, that she asked him in front of Lotte, because that meant he would tell her, instead of making up something that they both knew was a lie. It's important to know what things are, what people really mean.

As they approach the wheelchair, Aisling's eyes open. Georgie's not sure if that's a good sign. She hates it when Aisling won't wake up and they have to sit by the bed or wheelchair and say nothing for the whole of visiting hour, just wait, like they did on Sunday, not knowing if she would wake up at all. But she hates it too when Aisling *is* awake and trying to talk and not being able to and forgetting stuff, like the new school or the names of Georgie's friends or anything.

'Come here,' says Aisling, and smiles. She hasn't cut her hair since it started to grow back after the Second Time Round. It's hanging past her shoulders now, straw-gold in the light. It's pretty and looks like it's just been washed. The nuns, she says, are good that way. Her face is gold too. That's because of her liver and the lumps growing on it, eating it up.

See, that's The Thing. You can't live without a liver.

Georgie goes over and hugs her.

Lotte leaves. She has an errand to do. They talk. They say nothing. Silence falls, thick as custard. Aisling hovers on the brink of sleep. Georgie waits. They talk. They say nothing. Georgie needs to pee. Aisling is holding her hand, rubbing Georgie's little finger between her index finger and thumb like she's rosary beads. The pee demands an out. Aisling's eyes half-close. Georgie waits. The pressure of built-up pee becomes everything she knows. Aisling's fingers release, just a bit. Georgie rises, leaves.

On her way back from the loo, just before she reaches the French windows, Georgie gets a funny feeling in her back, as if someone is following her, but when she turns around, nobody is there. It's then that the decision pops into her head, clear as anything. She has to tell Aisling about Elaine. Aisling will know what to do. She steps up to the open door, stops.

Lotte has returned from her errands and is hunkered down on the grass beside Aisling's wheelchair. At first Georgie thinks Aisling is still asleep and Lotte is leaning on her shoulder, like a cat might sit on you, comforting. Then she realises that Aisling has woken. Her mouth is bent towards Lotte's ear and she's saying something really quiet, over and over, and Lotte seems confused, but is nodding, Yes, Yes, and then she's crying, and Aisling's right palm is flat against Lotte's cheek, tender, like she's holding Georgie's face, and her other hand is holding Lotte's and Georgie can see how hard her hold is, because Lotte's skin under Aisling's fingers is pink.

But I didn't even get to tell her about William Robinson, thinks Georgie, and for some weird reason this really matters, but with everything else they'd talked about she'd never got round to it.

And Elaine? Slipped from her mind.

Lotte says something and presses Aisling's hand back and at that, Aisling stops talking, suddenly goes quiet as if she's remembered something. Lotte keeps watching her. Then Aisling looks up and smiles. Oh, I do, she says, clear enough for Georgie to read her lips, and Georgie sees that same rare thing that she saw once in her mother's eyes, a long time ago, a light that's so bright it hurts to look at and it's sad and frightened at the same time, and what's the worst thing of all is that Georgie may as well not be there, standing just inside the stupid French windows a few feet away; she may as well be down her lane shouting and waving at the passers-by who walk on, oblivious, stuck in their own piggy little dimensions. Georgie must have made a sound then, because Aisling's head jerks and she looks over at the door-window, full of surprise, as if she's only just remembered she has a child who sat with her talking and saying nothing all afternoon in the garden.

I hate you, thinks Georgie, and the hate is a sea-swell in her chest.

Aisling flushes, her yellow skin suffusing with the same colour as the roses near the fountain. Lotte turns. Her eyes land on Georgie and the stupid sad kindness there makes Georgie's teeth ache with fury.

You hungry, monster?
  You know I am. Thought, not said.
  Well, we'd better—
  Bye.
  Bye, love. Come here....
  This hug is stiff and hard and Georgie loathes herself.
  Something tells her not to look back as they leave the garden. She disobeys. Aisling's face is tilted at the last bit of sun and looks as if it's on fire. Her hair is glowing.
  Look away, they told Orpheus. If you don't look away from Eurydice, then....
  Georgie keeps staring; afterwards she would think of herself at that moment like a piece of photographic film, burning her mother's image onto the inside of her soul.

The fish and chip shop is crammed. Lots of people have the same idea; mums and dads whose kids have gone back to school and who've decided it's easier to get a takeaway than make proper tea. Georgie knows from the neat clothes William Robinson wears that his mother is not the sort to go to a fish and chip shop for his supper, but she still finds herself glancing around, just in case. The girl serving at the counter is wearing lots of make-up and has her hair flicked up either side like Charlie's Angels. She looks a bit like how Elaine will look like when she grows up.

If she grows up. The thought sends cold fingers trickling up Georgie's spine.

  'I forgot to ask you,' says Lotte. 'Did you enjoy the Greeks after all?'
  'Huh?'
  'The book I gave you?'
  'Oh. Yeah. It's okay.'

'That's a relief. Have you read about Odysseus yet?'

'In Troy?'

'Yes. He's my favourite. When we were little—'

'Next, yeah?' interrupts the girl behind the counter.

'What d'you want, monster?' says Lotte.

'Fish and chips.' Suddenly, Georgie gets a brainwave. 'And a burger. And a spiceburger.'

'Fish *and* a burger?' says Lotte. 'Are you sure?'

Georgie sighs and looks at the ceiling.

Lotte's tongue makes a little clicking sound. 'Oh-kay. Two haddock, two chips, and a burger, please.'

'And a spiceburger.'

Lotte stares. For a moment she looks just like any other adult who's ever looked at Georgie. Then she shakes her head and laughs, and that's even worse. 'Right. We'll take a spiceburger too, please.'

The made-up girl calls the order back to the kitchen, where the Italians are dunking the chips in the deep fat fryer. Lotte begins to whistle under her breath.

The bell on the door rings and Alison O'Meara walks in. She's wearing her new St Bernadette's uniform – she gets a new one every year – and looks as grumpy and C-O-W-like as ever, though, seeing her up close like that, anyone could tell she's no match for William Robinson. Georgie turns her back and melts into the queue. She's had enough to manage today without anyone else coming along and making problems.

'Salt'n'vinegar?'

'Yes, thanks,' says Lotte.

The girl shakes the salt and vinegar over the chips, bundles them up and hands them to Lotte.

'Coming, Georgie?'

Georgie follows Lotte. The door of the fish shop swings open, reflecting the line of people waiting for their chips, and suddenly, at the counter, instead of Alison O'Meara, Georgie sees Elaine, waiting in a too-big uniform. Her head is cocked, her eyes half-closed, her hand on her hip, her foot tapping in time with Joanie Flynn's inaudible music. And it's right then that Georgie realises exactly what her grubby little playmate is looking for.

The moon is rising, just visible through the gap of Georgie's bedroom curtains. It is full, giant, peach-coloured, oozing with scald-burns. A finger's reach away, it seems; as if, were Georgie to poke through the glass of her bedroom window, she might even touch it. The sky is hazier than the night before; but still powdery, still cobalt, still warm.

Downstairs, Georgie can hear David banging on the telly. It's like music. First the sound of the telly, then a buzzy crackling sound, then David gets up and bangs and says Feck, loud, like a gunshot, then the sound of the telly comes back. Usually David jiggles the rabbit's ears while he's banging. Georgie pictures him jiggling, the images coming and going in a sea of white snow.

I saw your friend today, Lotte had said to David as she was leaving for home, and guessing who she meant, Georgie concentrated hard on organising the things around her dinner plate so they were all in the right place. She didn't hear what David said back, but she still got a horrible feeling after Lotte left, sick and anxious. Then the phone rang.

David's voice in the hall was quiet and gulping. He put down the phone, then came into the kitchen to tell Georgie he'd be going out; he'd forgotten to do some stuff with Mum in the hospital and needed to go back there for a bit. His face was thin and pale. 'Old chap….' he started to say and Georgie got that sick feeling again. Then he changed his mind and just told her to start getting ready for bed. Mrs Lynch down the road was coming in to mind her.

Georgie couldn't believe her luck. Mrs Lynch was ancient and her hips were sore; she hated coming up the stairs. 'Did you ring her?'

'Who?'

'Mrs Lynch?' She was surprised to hear how grown-up her voice sounded.

'Oh,' said David. 'Eh. No. Just get ready for bed, Georgie.'

He took off his glasses and rubbed his eyes. His shoulders were very tight, but his face seemed different: cold, sharp and afraid.

Georgie's room smells of salt and vinegar. She'd opened the window earlier so Lotte wouldn't notice. She would have preferred to have kept the burgers warm in the oven, but that would have meant going downstairs again when she needed them and that would have meant answering questions. Luckily Lotte didn't make a big fuss when Georgie only ate the fish. Other people would say, Told you so. All Lotte said was, Well, maybe your Dad would like them. Georgie had offered to tidy up the kitchen while Lotte watched the news and that was how she'd been able to sneak the food upstairs.

The noise of David's banging downstairs stops. The front door opens. David says something in a low voice and Mrs Lynch answers. Blah blah. Poor-you-oh!-poor-her-oh-the-poor-wee-bloody-bloody-bloody-fuck.

The front door closes. Heavy footsteps on the stairs.
Mrs Lynch's grey sheep's head peeks around the door.
Georgie pretends to be asleep.
The bedroom door closes.

She gets up, making as little noise as possible. The window is already open, so she squeezes out onto the sill. From here it's an easy enough slide to the roof of the extension. She'll have to jump from there to the garden wall between her house and Mrs Kelly's, then she'll climb along the wall and get down into the lane that way. She's never taken this route before, but it feels familiar, if backwards, somehow; like looking into a mirror and watching your finger trace the reflection of your own skin.

Halfway along the wall, she hears low, urgent voices coming from over the roof, from the street-side. Then—

'Here.'

Georgie turns. Elaine is perched on one of the lower branches of the apple tree in Mrs Kelly's back garden. She gestures. 'Come on.'

Georgie hesitates.

'It's okay,' says Elaine. 'Swear. It's safer in here. There's lads and all in that lane at night. They do hang around that Cortina and....'

Georgie bites her lip, makes a decision, hoists herself up onto the tree. The branches are scratchy and hard to navigate. She will have scrapes and bruises in the morning.

Elaine slithers down first. 'This way.'

I'm not going inside, thinks Georgie. No way am I going into that creepy house and no way am I going upstairs.

'We can stay out here,' says Elaine. 'If you want.'

Georgie nods, jumps to the ground. In the darkness, the difference between her back garden and Mrs Kelly's seems even greater than it does from the wall. Trees, bushes, long, uncut grass. Mrs Kelly's garden is *enormous*. She looks up. The black windows of the empty house stare back like horrible science-fiction eyes from the cover of one of David's books. The bathroom one is cracked. She shivers. There is no sound from the lane. She stares at Elaine.

'There *are* lads. They do come here later, with the black night. I get a warning that something is wrong. I do hear them slinking around, sniffing like dogs, but they slink off again when they think you've got their number. They're rough.'

Georgie takes her Dick Whittington knapsack off her back. 'I got you some food.'

'Ah, thanks. That's great.' Elaine opens the bag of cold chips and burger and starts tearing into it.

'I didn't get you fish. I didn't think you'd like it.'

'Ah, no. This is lovely.' For such a small, dainty girl, Elaine eats like a savage.

'You want a uniform,' says Georgie.

Elaine looks up.

'You need a school uniform so you can go to school and fit in and people won't know that you're hiding here.'

Elaine stops chewing. In the corner of her mouth is a crumb of gold; a piece of chip, its grease shining under the moonlight.

'If you're in a uniform, they'll think you're living with your mum and dad and that you're okay. You won't stand out.'

Georgie pulls at the grass at her feet. It comes away easily, like hair. 'But you're not to let on, Elaine. I can get you more food and I'll get you the uniform, and a bag and even some books—'

Elaine swallows and her eyes light up. 'Books! No way! That'd be a great help. Can you get me an adventure story, with a tower and a maiden and a black horse and—'

'Yeah, okay.' That wasn't what Georgie meant; she was thinking of schoolbooks. 'But if you breathe a word to anyone that I'm helping you, especially William Robinson, you're dead. I swear.'

Elaine blinks. She finishes chewing the last bit of burger. The little lump in her throat shifts. Then she lunges across, breaking the distance between them. Georgie thinks of William Robinson, lying in wait, singing her name with his forked, forked tongue. But Elaine has no baleful intent. Her skinny arms soften as they close around Georgie.

Oh, thinks Georgie. All she wants is a hug.

Elaine is very small and light, even smaller and lighter than Georgie had imagined. She is warm, though, and alive, and her skin is soft like nothing Georgie has felt in her life. Her back is shaking. Georgie hopes to God she's cold, not crying. Georgie couldn't stick another person crying today.

'It's okay.' Georgie's hands lift, pat Elaine's shoulders. 'Sshh. You're not to worry. I'm here.'

Lognote # 5

With the Maps Cycle temporarily closed for business, we bring your attention to one of the more stable Curiosities in our collection. A foolscap piece of paper with a typed list of town names. The list is in three columns, created with what appears to be a 1960s' electric typewriter.[1] All accents and special characters are in type, indicating that the device has been designed for widespread 'Mittel-European' use. Observant visitors will notice that the lowercase 'e' is rather faded; there is also a fault with the lowercase 't' which is positioned higher than the other lowercase characters.[2] Our curator would like you to take special note of the middle column, which contains approximate etymologies for many of the town names. (Note that in some cases, we have been unable to find an etymology, while in others, the entry is not strictly etymological, but rather a 'loose association'.) In general, this Exhibit favours the German root. Our curator would like to stress that this is a reflection of our *Übersetzungstaffel*'s translatory limitations, rather than evidence of any nasty *Herrenvolk* (master-race) ideas about ethnolinguistic superiority.

Activities

- Internet fun for kids: Why don't you and your friends split into two teams? One take the names on the left-hand side, the other those on the right. Google all the names on your list and see how many you get Wikipedia entries for! The team with the most entries wins!

---

[1] A hand-me-down 1969 Olivetti Valentine, traceable to *Mutti-Kustosin*/Mummycurator a.k.a. Anna B. See Morecambe, 1969–1971: 'Silver View Guests' paperwork, preparation of; also Aberystwyth, 1972–1983: '*Moranned* (Seaview) Guest House', ditto.

[2] Perhaps, we wonder, this character has notions? Upwardly mobile aspirations towards Teutonic hegemony?

- Did you know that
    - 'sinister' comes from the Latin for 'left', while 'dextrous' comes from the Latin for 'right'?
    - we[3] read from left to right?

What happens if you switch the lists around – put the left on the right and the right on the left? Take notes of your feelings, even the unpleasant ones.

- Teaser: Which came first, the chicken or the egg?[4]
- Trick question: When does ethnic cleansing *not* lead to 'sinister' results?

The list/s

Děčín	*settled by Slavic tribe, Děčané*	Tetschen
Ústí nad Labern	*on the river Labern/Elbe*	Aussig
Teplice	*up in the mountains*	Teplitz-Schönau
Most	*'bridge'*	Brux
Chomutov	*on the banks of the river Chomutovska/Komo*	Komotau
Karlovy Vary	*'Charles' bath'*	Karlsbad
Cheb	*from river Eger*	Eger
Mariánské Lázně	*'Mary's bath'*	Marienbad
Plzeň	*Pils!*	Pilsen
Klatovy	*…*	Klattau
Česky Krumlov	*Bohemian 'Krumlov/Krummau', on the banks of the Vlatva/Moldau*	Krummau
České Budějovice	*Budweiser!*	Budweis
Třeboň	*…*	Wittingau
Jindřichův Hradec	*'new house'*	Neuhaus
Lanškroun	*…*	Landskron
Hradec Králové	*'castle of the queen'*	Königgrätz
Trutnov	*?by the river Trauten/Trutn?*	Trautenau
Janské Lázně	*'John's bath'*	Johannisbad
Liberec	*'empire mountain' a.k.a. 'the Manchester of Bohemia'*	Reichenberg
Česká Lípa	*'Bohemian Leipa/Lípa'*	Böhmisch Leipa

---

[3] Should we ask who *we* are?
[4] Are we ever going to answer this question?

Terezin	*'Theresa's city'*	Theresienstadt
Kladno	...	Kladno
Karlštejn	*Charles' stone*	Karlstein
Tábor	*now 'camp'/originally named for Mt Tabor (see Jesus, Transfiguration of)*	Tabor
Kutná Hora	*'mountain of monks' cowls (Kutten)'*	Kuttenberg
Pardubice	...	Pardubitz
Mladá Boleslav	*founded by King Boleslav*	Jungbunzlau
Praha	*from Slavic 'praga', meaning ford*	Prag

Most curious feature

It has come to our attention that this Exhibit is extremely hot, as if boiling with a never-ending fury. We have clearly underestimated its capacity to trigger a violent reaction. Please put the Object down as soon as possible – i.e. Now.

199

***'Ausland/Otherland'**. Regie/Director: Sabine Wiedemann.
Datum/Date: 15/03/20— Ort/Location: Aberystwyth.
Befragte/Interview Subject: 'Anna Bauer'* (**Sitzung/Session 2**).

No, Sabine. There was nothing of interest on the News. So
rarely these days. Just complaining.

So, to your other question. I have thought on it.

It impresses me as comical, you see. For most of my life
as a grown, since coming to Britain, one might say, I have
lived in a town near the water, yet I was born in a land
with no seaside. We had mountains, where I was a child. Our
village was in the mountains, and the fields and the farms
and the little houses and so on. And the big town nearby, a
spa town it was, with many fine ladies and gentlemen before
the war, and the demesne of the Count which later became
a government building, and then, after, in the wartime,
a hospital for the invalids of the war, which is where I
did em, a placing? For the war effort. But that, the town
and demesne, that too was by the mountains. So as child
or young person, one would look out to the horizon and
always see a, what is the word? A form. A shaping of land.
Some Thing. The sea I have never liked. It moves, always
changing. Like clouds, but more dangerous. For me always,
I see things underneath. The big fish, or monsters. The
children laughed at me for having fear. But Julia, it is
only water. Look, touch, see – only water! It can't hurt,
there is no danger! Water-babies, they were. Born in Juni.
Under the sign of the crab, if one believes such.

. . .

Excuse me? No. I. I laughed with them. It was simpler.
Andreas, Andrew, if I did not laugh, he would fight. And

200

he could fight, you know, for always. He would have an idea in the head, quite fast there, and once it was in, it was impossible, dear god, to move it. My daughter, Charlotte, Lotte, she was more em, fluent? Like water. She would always change the mind. So it goes, I think. One gains the strength of will, the other the em, flexibleness.

No. I was not a fighter. Never. I liked fun! To laugh, to have the jokes, to dance. Oh, I loved to dance! That was the Captain's gift, also, what, you might say, blinkered me to him. You know, I am a very simple person. And as the *Mutti*, when the twins were quite young, there was so much to do, so much busyness, I did not have the lust in me for a fight.

. . .

[long silence]

Excuse me? No, it is alright. I understand. You wish to know about the leaving.... Yes, yes, I understand the question you ask, was it sad to look back at home and to know one was going away? But you must understand, that was not how it was for me, or any of us, really. We were going for perhaps a year, or maybe two, and in besides that, we were not leaving home. The homeland was far away; we had left that in forty-six, or forty-five. There was no homeland more. But to leave in forty-eight, on the Westward Ho, that was quite other. We were going on an adventure. We were young, all young girls, nineteen, eighteen, twenty-two. Only at the beginnings of our lives.... We had new dresses for the journey. Some had coats, and hats. My dress was made out of a curtain with a, you know, ziggy-zaggy pattern, very beautiful. I made it in the house in Hamburg, where I must stay with six other girls until the permits arrived. It was important to be well-presented in going to the foreign country. We were the lucky ones. We had work already, in the cotton mills in Lancashire, and many of the other girls had not – or it was, you know, for them, the arrangement, very loose. Perhaps in a hospital, or cleaning for a lady. But we were Westward Ho and that was a good work. When we came to Britain, it was clear that cleaning for a lady was not the good job, from the girls we met, the ones who had a position as domestics. Although, of course, it's funny. Because that is what I did in the end, with Doctor Brooks and then with the guest houses, cleaning, cooking, looking after people, and I liked it.

...

Can you say that again?

Yes. Yes. I understand. It was perhaps a little sad to leave the elders – parents, yes – and the cousins, but not so much for me. For me, it was only my mother because my father had died in the camp, and my mother.... She was in fact only my stepmother, you know, and was living in East Germany with her sister, so.... There was some discussion of perhaps her joining me later, so, you know, it was not very sad, and there was money, we all needed money, and food, we were hungry, and clothes, and there was nothing of this in Germany.

...

Yes. I understand. Germany I do not think of as home. I am German but Germany is not my home. The village I grew in, in Czechoslovakia, that was my home, and where I live now, here, in Aberystwyth, not this place with the other oldies, but where I lived, my guesthouse and so on, that is my home.

Yes. The money of course. We all needed money. We were hungry. Many people had died. My father of dysentery. The people in the camps were good, the Czechs and later the Americans and then the English, they were all good people, I have the luck to be able to say I met only good people on my journeys, but—

Yes. Of course, we wanted to go.

...

Can I say again? You mean—

Yes, naturally. I wanted to go. Sorry? Again? Yes. Of course. For to make this clear on the television. It is not good to have your questions. I understand.

Ah. So. I wanted to leave Germany as it was no longer my home. Though, you know, as I said, that is not perhaps the true wording. It was never really my home in the true sense.

You know, I told a little lie at that time, when they were getting me the papers for the Westward Ho. I grew in a village, by a mountain, so I did not ever work in a cotton mill like the girls from Reichenberg. I had a cousin who did and she had told me of it. I knew how to look after invalids and I understood machinery, from the farm, when the men went to fight, my brother went to fight, I used the machinery and I was good at it. But, you see, the girls in the camp were speaking of Britain, how good it would be to have a new life there, so I took the opportunity, and told them the untruth, that I had worked in the mill.

Do I feel guilty? For what? That? No.

...

Oh. Oh! But I—

[tries to stand; out-of-shot] No, no, it is not the bathroom. You see, I remember, I remember. You will see! I—

Oh, yes. Of course. Excuse me. Of course.

[is helped to sit again]

You see, this I had forgot, but it is such a.... Such an odd thing. *Hör mal, als ich*, as I left Hamburg I saw a strange thing. I was on the deck of the ship, looking back, and I saw an odd thing, a very strange thing on the water. You must understand, we were travelling towards the west, away from Germany and to Britain, along the, you know, North Sea. So the setting sun was in front of

203

me. But as I looked back, to Hamburg and the port, I saw
red lights on the water, as if a sun was setting there
instead. It was very comical. No, I mean strange. Very
strange. The red light blinks on, like so, as if it is
coming from the underneath of the ship, and then it stays,
on the water, just underneath, like a chain of red beads.
A form of *Rosencranz*, *gel*? A rosary? I imagined to myself
that maybe the ship was dropping the lights in the water
so it could find its way back, you know, like a fancy tale,
Hänsel und Gretl. Or perhaps there were mermaids, holding
red lights, and that was to wish us farewell. And later,
with the Captain, in Morecambe, he loved to go to the
cinema, the movies, yes, and so did I. We saw many films
and there was a, you know, rule, that to show a journey
in the movie, one would show a map and a little toy ship
travelling with the lights coming on behind the ship to
show its journey. And that was how it was, little mermaids
showing me the way back so I would not get lost.

So?

I – yes. I understand.
No. I never took it, the backgoingway. Not even when
Andrew did the stupid thing.

...

Anyway.

Wipe

With regard to the surpassing disaster, art acts like the mirror in vampire films: it reveals the withdrawal of what we think is still there.... Does this entail that one should not record? No. One should record this nothing, which only after the resurrection can be available.

Walid Raad and Jalal Toufic, notes from seminar
'The Withdrawal of Tradition Past a Surpassing Disaster', 2007

((( )))

Please ignore any comments from previous visitors suggesting similarities between the 'circular' nature of our Route and those evoked by Dante Alighieri in describing his *Inferno* (see *Divine Comedy*, written in exile, 1302).

13:25:31–17:55:09

I have a memory for you. They've been coming a little faster and sharper since I started talking to you, but this one I think you'll appreciate:

Oxygen destroys.

You told me that – do you remember? Early that spring, after she'd gone. It doesn't seem like a big deal, you said, but once it starts, it's hard to stop. Take suspension bridges. They're walking death traps, Georgie. All those steel wires – rust, waiting to happen. You gestured: A wire goes – ping! A cable snaps. Crash, bang, wallop – and the whole thing is gone, old bean. I remember watching your hands move as you spoke; you seemed very alive to me in that moment. Most bridges can take the loss of a few cables, you said, but after what we call a critical point, you get a chain reaction. More and more of the wires start to spring free, and then the beams collapse, folding in on each other like a, you know – you gestured again, your hands elegant as a conductor's, and I saw a house of cards, falling.

Iron, see, it always wants to go back to the earth, Dublin. Another memory; another time. You'd put on one of your voices and when Lotte said *What?* – she was there, do you remember? – you told us a Scotsman had said that, a man from Aberdeen. A ganger, I imagine; my aunts later told me you'd done a stint navvying in Britain before you became an engineer. *It's weak, iron,* you continued, in the Scotsman's accent. I remember Lotte laughing at that. She had a beautiful laugh, crackly.

Frail as a girl, iron, you said. *One kiss from the air and it turns red as any virgin.*

At that, my memory of the story fails, falls back into the blur again. I imagine you flushed, realising what you'd said – *virgin* – and stopped. Because of me, not wanting to put dodgy ideas into your child's head. Or maybe because of Lotte – you liked her, didn't you? A lot. Until she disappointed you,

Christ knows how. Did you flush then, further back in your past, in front of that ganger? You callow teenage Mick. Why did he call you Dublin? I always wondered about that, but never asked. You were from Tipperary.

I like that picture of iron you wove. How something so strong can weaken under the cumulative effects of something so apparently fragile as air. Flushing, blushing, crumbling. Falling, weak with love, back to where it belongs.

Concrete buildings are prey to rust too. You know that, of course; you probably told me. The steel mesh that's supposed to reinforce the concrete, prevent it from cracking under loads, snapping in shock, will eventually corrode. Over time the reinforcements will flake, generating layers of rust that expand, fattening up the skeleton so it creaks and heaves, pushing at the flesh, devouring it from within.

Wood gets eaten from inside and out. Microbes rot. Termites gnaw. Steel bends and stretches and buckles. Deformation, this is called. Splinter, creak, crash.

I read a newspaper article a while ago that said if you talk to people who are facing serious things – like illness, for example, or the threat of it – and if you ask them to journal about something, they won't focus on that serious thing. Instead, they'll go into other stuff: family, relationships, career, ambition, lost hopes, unexplained dreams. The psychologist who wrote the article said that was normal behaviour, healthy even.

So this, me talking to you; is that what I'm doing, skirting the unspeakable? Or am I just being normal?

Oxygen destroys. It rusts, it ages, it withers. It kisses molecules and out of that kiss makes free radical babies, and once freed, the radicals make mischief. This is metastagenicity. This is progress.

Ashes to ashes, rust to rust, you said to me and Lotte. And then you laughed, as if at your own private joke.

The green tunnel in my rearview squeezed to a point, swallowing houses, people, cars. Laragh turned toytown, then disappeared. Banks of vegetation flashed past, the conifers and broadleaves striping it light and dark like a tiger's coat. Through the canopy the sky had darkened into a bloody mercury. The rain was coming down hard now, sweeping across the windscreen, racing in streams along the ditches.

My face was on fire; rivers of heat were running through my limbs. I hoped it wasn't swine flu. Maybe it was the 'mones acting up, sensing the time bomb in my chest that could, right now, be getting busy.

That could, I corrected myself, might not even exist.

I passed a signpost, too fast to make out what it said.

Flip-flup, flip-flup, went my wipers. An uneven sound, like a child with a lisp. My left wiper wasn't working properly. It trailed a loose bit of rubber that squeaked against the screen and left a stripe of dirt in its wake. I should sort that out, I told myself. Next week; once I got the all-clear and my first instalment from Brid.

Pain began to throb up my right leg. A repetitive strain injury that had been building since I'd changed the way I'd held my foot on the clutch. It was that mechanic's fault. If I hadn't gone to him, I wouldn't have had to change anything.

What's the problem, love? he'd said. His face was raw and purple, his hands swollen and his belly sagged out over his waistband, but still, I'd been charmed, a bit, by the *love*. I'd smiled, not too coyly, I'd hoped, and told him how, when I was driving in fifth, I'd begun to hear a rattling sound, followed by a jolt from the gearstick. Then the engine would make a loud noise, screaming, almost, and it would feel like the whole car had gone out of control.

Ah, said the mechanic. He lifted the bonnet and peered in.

It's fine in fourth, I said. Is it the gearbox?

He closed the bonnet and wiped his hands on his overalls.

Do you ride the clutch, love? Rest your foot on it when you're driving?

Didn't everyone? Sometimes, I said.

Ah, no, love. That's the problem. Too much weight on the clutch – you're wrecking the gearbox.

So it *is* the gearbox?

It's slipping into neutral, see. That's where you get the screaming sound.

So—

You'd want to change that, love. Keep riding the clutch and you'll drive it into the ground. Probably need to take the whole box out sooner or later.

Not trusting him, I'd asked him for a quote and, shocked at the price, found myself, once again, doing the stuttering thing I learnt from you.

Great. Em – great. I'll get back to you on that.

You're such a coward, Geo, Mar used to say when I did that. Was he right? Am I one? You should know; I got the habit from you.

Flip-flup, flip-flup. Bits of forest dirt, pine needles and broken leaves gathered at the edges of the screen. The bit that was clear made an uneven double helix. Sound waves intersecting each other. Parallel lines gone all curvy. DNA strands. A number eight turned on its side.

211

My neck was aching, my sinuses had released and my nose was streaming. I would have killed for bed. I let my foot fall back on the clutch. Go on, take it, you little bastard.

On the slopes young ferns were pushing up through the remains of winter. Pine cones, cracked sticks, the lacy skeletons of leaves. Fairy-tale stuff. The books I loved as a child. Grimm, Narnia, Tolkien.

When you're older, monster, I'll give you *The Lord of the Rings*. You'll love it.

Does it feel odd to you, hearing Lotte's voice rise in mine? Have I got her right? Another thing you passed on to me: a gift for mimicry. How long has it been since you thought of her? Be honest. I hadn't remembered her for years, not even in therapy, and then, on that road from Laragh, she popped into my head, just for a moment, as if to say Hello.

She never kept that promise. Of course she didn't. Why would she? But you – or should I say, your other half – sent me the trilogy for my twelfth birthday.

Get rid of them, I thought when I opened the parcel. They were silly books; childish. Worse, they'd come from you. As soon as I'd got that thought – *Get rid of them, Georgie* – I'd frozen. Then, carefully, I placed them on the little desk in my room, the one that used to be your mother's, in plain sight, so if something happened to them I'd know straight away. A week later, they were still there.

I didn't open them for ages, not until a boy in school told me he'd read *The Hobbit* and it was very good actually and then, cautiously, I entered Middle-Earth. It turned out okay; better than that. It turned out that was what we could do, the ones who were quieter than the others and not so good at football; we could read *The Hobbit* and *The Lord of the Rings* and then we could move on to fantasy, if we liked that, or pure sci-fi, if we preferred to follow our fathers' footsteps, or, if we had ideas about ourselves, the great magic surrealists: Kafka, Márquez, Borges.

She'll never know it, but Lotte was right. I loved Tolkien, even though you'd given him to me. My favourite character – apart from Gollum, who didn't count, because he was everyone's favourite – was Éowyn, the cross-dressing horsewoman. No surprises there, girl, Sonia said. She liked Éowyn too, but for different reasons; she thought she was hot.

You're not into that fascist crap, are you? Martin had asked the first time he'd stayed over, in my apartment near Wilmersdorf. We'd finished fucking and he'd got up, was prowling around my place naked, sniffing, already on the way to another erection, an alpha dog leaving his scent all over my stuff. He'd picked out the Tolkien from the bookshelf. I remember feeling surprised, then worried, then more surprised at that.

Fascist? I don't think so. Wasn't it a, you know, protest against the Nazis?

Martin laughed. Read between the lines and it's all white supremacist pish. Keep the nignogs out and the unions off our lawns and make sure those wild fucking Celts stay where they belong, behind the gates of Mordor.

I was still dazed from the smell of him around me. I – where does it say anything about black people?

Everywhere. See?

Then he'd started reading passages, deconstructing the Orcs, and that was that.

Later, he'd spoilt Narnia for me too, told me it was fundamentalist far-right Christian polemic. That Aslan, he's Hitler. All blood-sacrifice and annihilation prophecies. If you don't fit in, bam. We'll take away your voice first and then it's off to the gas chambers wi ye.

I'd never thought of things that way. Since the end of those blurred years with you and Aisling, I'd made my peace with myths, or thought I had. I knew that fantasy was not reality, that magic was a poor substitute for science, but as an adult I had also learnt – or thought I had – that that was the point of art. To go beyond the constrictions and compromises of realpolitik, to *mean* something. Besides, Middle-Earth had never struck me as particularly English. It was always somewhere more European to me; Bohemia – the Czechoslovakia I was obsessed with as a child – wooded and dangerous. *Here Be Dragons.*

Who's David? Mar had asked, looking at the inscription you'd put on the flyleaf. Your first boyfriend?

Jesus, I'd said, shocked. Then, not knowing what to say, because, in truth, I didn't know who you were to me any more, No one.

For Georgie. Love, David. None of those silly names you used to call me, *old bean* or *old chap*, like we were comrades in our own little army. No *Hope you'll enjoy this.* No *Dad.* And—

Love.

When did you ever learn to feel comfortable saying that word?

I thought we had a deal, Mar. You were to get out of my head if I went home. I didn't speak that out loud, just thought it, forcing myself away from the suck of our shared past. Flip-flup, flip-flup. Above me criss-crossed the branches of ash and beech trees; living doodles, brown and green. I thought of the Art Brut museum I'd visited in Lausanne in my twenties, long before Mar and I moved there. Weird rags twisted into voodoo dolls, stained with shit and blood.

Outsider Art; made by the bad, the sad and the mad.

Flip-flup, flip-flup.

I thought of the drawings I used to do as a kid, the ones I'd stopped after I'd seen death in a cracked ceiling, though I didn't know how real that death would be. The ones I now realise I regret never showing Lotte, because a year before she came to us, I'd burnt them in the gas fire of our lounge and stuck the ashes in the bin in our kitchen, frightened by questions from a nosey American woman that were going somewhere bad – *So why did you stop drawing, Georgie?* – somewhere, in that moment, I couldn't fully understand.

Flip-flup, flip-flup. I forced myself back into the present but all I could think of was the new thing I was supposed to be doing with my life, only I hadn't been able to find it.

You're gonnae hae ta bite the bullet sooner or later, Geo, Mar had said. You can't go around telling everybody else's stories for the rest of your life.

I thought of Sonia's reassurances. What we're doing, girl, with our bodies, that's our narratives. If there's any other story left to tell, don't worry, you'll have plenty of time.

Time? In five years I'd be fifty. If I was lucky.

I thought of Elaine's immortal eyes in the face of the girl at the lakes.

I pushed my foot harder on the accelerator.

I thought of Turnmill Street and Farringdon. The pundits outside, baying for war. The bodies underground, their mouths filling with dirt. Their memories, their lives, their ancestors, all collected mish-mash in the bottom drawer of their minds, looping in ever-tightening circles.

I thought of Brid's phone call, her series on the Troubles. Of Sabine Wiedemann's email, cracked into a million pieces.

I thought of that stupid letter, birthday card, whatever, from America. You useless, useless prick.

I thought of Martin's coat, waterlogged as a drowned body, sighing in the footwell.

A figure was standing in the crossroads, huge and dark.

Flip—

It took a second after the light-green-dark-green tiger stripes froze for my mind to wonder, Why has everything stopped? But by then my head had flung itself forward and my chest had smashed into something hard, and water had turned to broken ice and the red of flayed meat and then it was cold.

'Jesus Christ!' shouted a man's voice. 'Jesus Christ!'

Strange accent, I thought. I had my fingers up at my face, tipping at the air around me, and my scalp was stinging and through the red film blurring my eyes – where had that come from? – I could see my fingers were shaking, making jerky little movements that approached my skin but never quite touched it, and I felt my guts stiffen with something I couldn't understand and then one of my hands left my face and drifted down, shaking like a moth at the side of my hip, and the other followed, and the fingers started doing something near my hipbone and I understood that they were trying to unlock my seatbelt and—

'Jesus Christ! Didn't you even look where you were going? Were you asleep, you silly bitch?'

Asslup, you sully butch.

I heard this shouting in an accent I wasn't familiar with, but I couldn't pay it that much attention because all I could think about were my fingers, trying to undo the buckle of the seatbelt, because the buckle of the seatbelt needed to be undone because otherwise the car would explode and I would go up in flames like—

Something banged the windscreen on my right.

My head moved faster than I thought it could. My fingers froze. My guts were hard and shaking at the same time. I blinked. My vision smeared. Through it, I saw the windscreen, and trees, and a dark blue metal shape and in front of that a man's sallow face. His mouth was open and his teeth were sharp and angry and his fists were opening and closing like some underwater plant and I understood that he wanted to hit me. The man's mouth faltered and he said, 'Oh… Christ,' I couldn't hear the sound but I could see his lips move and could read them, and I realised he was seeing how ugly I was. His fists relaxed and his body jerked away from my window.

Cold wind blowing around my face. Odd. My chest was really sore, but the headcold or flu or whatever had evaporated. I looked down at my fingers. They were red. I looked up.

My guts gave way. I folded forward and heaved but nothing came out.

The windscreen a fractured spiderweb. In its centre, someone had punched a hole, its edges smeared with strawberry jam.

If the farmer hadn't turned up, I think we might have stayed there forever. Him saying, 'Oh, Christ... Oh, Christ', his hands opened like a saint explaining a difficult theological proposition, his feet shifting in a little foxtrot on the tarmac; me hunched behind the wheel, my useless hands still feeling for the seatbelt. But then we heard the clatter of an engine and too-big wheels trundling down the road and then there was a 'Jesus!' and a braking sound and the farmer jumped out of his tractor and everything started moving again.

'Are ye alright?' We both looked at him, helpless.

'Jesus,' he said again. He shook his head a little, as if he had Parkinson's. 'Do either of ye have a mobile on ye?' Mo-*bile*, like it was something recently invented.

We looked at each other. 'Oh,' said the other guy. He sounded surprised. He started patting his body.

Why, I wondered, was a farmer working on Paddy's Day? Silly question, came the reply. Farmers work every day. Freelance. Like me.

I started to laugh, had to blink again.

'You ring the Guards,' said the farmer. '999.'

That's stupid, I thought. That other guy should know the number for the Guards.

'Jesus,' said the farmer as he looked at the Fiat. He leant down so his face was peering through the shattered windscreen. 'Can you move?' His voice was loud, his eyes wide. He had little hairs growing from his nostrils. I think I nodded.

'Okay, so.' He went round to the side and started pulling at the handle of my door.

It took me a while to realise that the safety lock was down. I watched my finger drift towards the central locking button, shaking, and push.

The door opened. 'Jesus!' The farmer lost his footing, surprised. 'Right.' He scanned my body, the inside of the car. 'Can ye move your legs?'

I stared at them. My right knee lifted a little. It was shaking violently.

'Can ye – is your head hurting? Can ye see me? Can ye hear me?'

I looked at him. I think I nodded again.

He shook his head. 'Jesus.' He bit his lip. He looked as if he was making a decision. 'Alright, we'll get you out of there. Just in case the engine goes—'

Obediently, my fingers went back to the buckle of the seatbelt. There they stopped, not sure what to do.

'Can ye not get that open?'

I looked down at the seatbelt buckle and shook my head.

'Excuse me.' The farmer bent in through the door and leant across me.
'Careful,' I said. 'I've a bruise.'

He nodded and undid my seatbelt. His hands were white and hairy with long, thick fingers. They looked fascinating and repellent at the same time. I wondered whether he had a wife.

'There you go.' He gestured to the open door. I did nothing. 'Come on,' he said, louder. 'Out ye get, now, sir.'

Sir?

My chest started to hurt again. I shook my head, 'No, no.' He took my right arm. His touch was surprisingly gentle.

'Come on, now, sir, outta that seat.'

Tears prickled behind my eyes and I bit my tongue to stop them. 'No, no,' I said again, and I wanted to say, Not sir, it's Ma'am, Ma'am, or Ms, or even Miss, or *Fräulein* or *Mademoiselle, Señora, Señorita*, if you must, but I didn't have the words in me. All I had was 'No, no' and that shake of my head, even as my feet were swinging out of the glass and metal box and searching for the hard comfort of the road and my legs had uncrooked themselves from around my seat and my hands were leaning on the door, and somehow, miraculously, I was up, standing, out of the death trap.

The farmer guided me to a gate and left me there, leaning against it for support. He bustled around to the other guy's car, a monstrous black Hummer, and started making 'ooh' and 'aah' sounds about the damage, even though I couldn't see a scratch anywhere. The other guy had his back to us and was saying loud things to Emergency Services on the other end of the line.

Why does he have his back to us? I thought. We're all in this together. That made me laugh again.

'Where's your man?' I asked. 'Your man in the crossroads?'

The farmer looked up; he seemed confused and a bit angry with me. The other guy turned around. His phone had a jazzy cover on it. It looked nice.

'We've got to stay where we are,' said the other guy. I decided he was a prick. Where did he think we were going to go to – the fucking moon?

They both looked at me oddly and I realised I'd said it out loud, and said it in Martin's accent, full-blown Glesga, the way I've been doing here, replaying him for you, the way I used to do with him when I wanted to annoy him, channelling his voice through my face, his inflections in my mouth, his intonation on my tongue, the shape of his sound across my cheekbones, the nasal buzz of it, just so I could get him where it hurt, because he hated the sound of his voice, thought it was common.

I shook my head. 'I'm sorry.'

The other guy shook his head too. I saw that his eyes were wide and frightened. 'It's okay. It's the shock.'

Maybe he wasn't such a prick after all. I began to shiver uncontrollably.

The other guy looked at me blankly. 'Don't you have a coat?'

No. He *was* a prick.

I started to laugh again.

In the reflection of the unshattered window I saw my face. It was a mask of red, dusted with something glittering, made worse by the rain. I looked like I'd looked when they'd beaten me up on the Ku-Damm, during the bad months before I met Martin, when for the first, the only time, I'd dropped my guard, lost my trans radar, paid the price. Like I'd looked in Thailand, after the surgery in 2006, when they'd lowered my hairline and softened my jaw and broken my nose and lifted my eyelids and left my mouth alone, because my mouth, they said, was gorgeous, easily the most feminine thing about me.

My bottom lip was split and swollen: a purple ridge of pain. Blood was pouring down from the side of my head.

A scalp wound. They're the worst; a bitch to heal.

The farmer used his own mobile, an oldish Nokia, to call his wife and we, me and the guy from the other car, looked at each other at that. But in five minutes she'd come down with a flask of tea with brandy shot through it and a few minutes later the Guards were there and the AA and an ambulance which I thought was a bit over the top.

'It's okay,' I kept saying, trying to resist the helpful hands of the paramedics. 'It's only superficial damage. I need to get home. I have an appointment tomorrow and I need to get some rest.' But they wouldn't let me alone and kept gently pushing me down until I was lying on a hard board with one of those hard white comedy collars round my neck. An ironing board, I thought. I remember thinking that, I'm lying on an ironing board and they're going to iron me because I'm an alligator but—

The Guards took our details. I can't remember if that was before or after the ambulance. We told our stories. They sounded very different. He said I'd been speeding. I said he'd come out of nowhere, hadn't stopped at the red sign. I didn't mention your man at the crossing because nobody else did. It must have been a trick of the light. I had to keep making an effort not to speak in Martin's voice.

I'd forgotten to bring my driving licence with me. The Guard with the notebook pointed at the car. 'I'll take a look inside, Miss. Just to be sure.'

The Guard was young and strong with blond hair and wide shoulders, and I really wanted to fuck him and not just because he called me Miss. It bothered me, because I hadn't felt horny like that, thinking of sex three times a minute, since I'd started on the T-blocker, but then I realised he was straight and I was too and that made everything okay. My face was doing something funny, under the stinging pain, and I realised I was trying to smile, and that I still hadn't answered his question and he was halfway over to the car.

'There's no point,' I said. Did I shout? 'The licence. I never bring it with me. Bad girl.' Then I laughed again.

'Sshh,' said the paramedic. That must have been when they were getting me on the board.

The Guard shook his head. 'You know there's a fine for that. You're supposed to have your full licence on you at all times.'

I tried to nod but the collar wouldn't let me.

The bonnet and front passenger door of my Fiat were buckled into accordion folds. The windscreen had shattered when my face hit it.

The paramedics started closing the ambulance doors. 'My keys,' I said. 'My house keys.'

One of the paramedics was a woman. She ran over to my car and came back with my keys. She held out my purse. 'This is yours too, Miss?'

I smiled; out of gratitude, I think I smiled. Pathetic. The doors closed. 'No,' I said, because I knew this was wrong, getting into this ambulance was all wrong, not at all what was supposed to happen. I tried to move my head. My back on the board was sore.

'It's okay,' I said. 'It's okay. I need to get home. I don't need—'

'Yes,' said the woman paramedic. 'Yes, it's okay.' She patted my arm as if I was a child. 'Nothing to worry about.'

It was then that I burst into tears. Fucking hormones.

Someone in the ambulance was holding Martin's coat. For the first time that day I could smell the thing. It was rank. Dead meat.

Outside, we could hear the guy from the other car complaining to the Guards about some dent near his front bumper.

'He's South African,' said the woman paramedic. The ambulance revved. The paramedic nodded, as if she'd just uncovered an interesting fact. 'You know, I've never been to South Africa.'

I let out a breath and it was like I hadn't been able to do that in months. Then I started crying again.

They brought me to the new hospital outside Wicklow town. It was one of those places that had been built during the Boom, all tasteful glass corridors and low lighting. There was shamrock bunting up in the main reception area and some diddly-eye band was playing live trad for the patients. They were all standing and sitting around, looking lost. Dressing gowns, casts, bandages. Quite a few had drips.

'We're taking you to triage,' said the woman paramedic, and I started saying, Yes, okay, because the last show I'd cut before Christmas had been for one of Brid's competitors, *A&E Under the Knife*, emergency services in the recession, and I knew all about triage, but they were already calling for help to get me off the board. Someone held my head and three of them held my body. I didn't like it. Rolled like a log onto a trolley. The world rolled too; the floor came to meet me. For a sickening moment, I thought I was going to land on my face, but my right hipbone, the tender one, made contact first. Before they rolled me back, somebody passed their fingers down my spine. Does that hurt? No.

They pushed me through the reception. All I could see was the ceiling and the shamrock bunting, and in the corners of my vision, people – queuing up at desks, lying on gurneys, sitting on chairs, wandering around in dressing gowns, listening to the diddly-eye. There were new people like me, bleeding, bruised, missing bits of themselves, looking anxious, uncertain, unfinished, holding onto their bags and stuff as if that would fill the gaps. Up in the corners Sky News was on. Blessed Eoin the Marxist was being interviewed, but I couldn't hear him under the diddly-eye. He was starting to look exhausted. *No bodies recovered yet*, said the cap-gen. The firefighters were still fighting. They cut to the British Prime Minister, offering his deepest sympathy to those who feared for their loved ones. *Attack will not go unpunished*, said the cap-gen. *No stone left unturned*. Back to the Marxist. He was trying to argue with someone. The stud in his left ear glittered. The skin above the neck of his Ramones T-shirt was sagging a little.

Was that what happened to punks when they got old? Maybe that was why Brid hadn't cast him for her series. Too saggy. I wondered why he didn't wear a cravat. Johnny Lydon did.

Farringdon, said the Tube stop. Turnmill Street, said the street sign. The names grabbed again at my mind. Stop it, I told them. You don't mean anything.

There was no sign of the man who'd been hauled out of the canal. Too local for Sky. I was relieved by that, but a bit bothered too. I mean, he'd died too, hadn't he, not just people in London—

Blessed Eoin shook his head. I recognised his expression. He was sad.

In triage there were more people than I had expected. The space was too small. The nurse didn't seem bothered by my face. This is an expensive face, I wanted to tell her. Wouldn't you like to know how much it cost; shouldn't you be more upset? She took my pulse, checked my breathing, blood pressure, temperature. Vital signs. She pursed her lips. She was categorising me, deciding how much danger I was in. Someone else asked me for my name. I tried to tell them I couldn't remember the number of my medical insurance policy but the other person told me it didn't matter. I was an emergency. Everybody gets treated the same in an emergency. There's no difference.

What about my face? I said. I think I said.

They didn't seem to think my face was important. I wanted to touch my wounds, but they kept pulling my fingers back.

Are you allergic to penicillin?

Can you tolerate a tetanus shot?

How is your short-term memory?

Do you walk in your sleep?

Someone said something about X-rays. Then they moved me again.

The journey to the cubicle couldn't have taken more than a few minutes but in my head it lasted hours. They brought me down a corridor, past a row of rooms, the doors half-open like those little religious objects – monstrances, I think they're called, didn't Lotte tell me that? – that show medieval tableaux. Morality plays; the nine Circles of Hell. In one of the cubicles was a man with a leg shoved out at a weird angle, sitting beside a much younger woman. She had her hand on his knee, the one that didn't look broken. Was she his daughter or his lover? Another man, younger, on a trolley, holding his hand to his face and swearing. Blood dripped from between his fingers. It looked like he'd lost an eye. In another room, a lot of people huddled around a dull white shape heaped on a bed. The face was turned away. Short black hair, curly; silver roots. Through the row of backs I saw the vulnerable inch of an exposed neck. They brought me into the next room. It was painted a dull peach and smelt of disinfectant and air freshener and it reminded me of Mrs Kelly's house, where I had brought Elaine to hide.

But I hadn't brought her. I had—

Something was wrong. Since when had I been able to smell again?

'No,' I said, trying to sit up. The orderlies in charge of the gurney wouldn't let me.

A female nurse trotted in. She had plump downy skin and a French manicure and was wearing a shimmery blue eyeshadow, very misty, quite glamorous.

Glamour. Mermaids, monsters—

Here be Caliban, I wanted to say, but stopped myself in time.

'Insurance?' she said.

A long window stretched above me, high on the wall. Yellow fluorescent light shone through it.

I thought that didn't matter, I said. I thought I was supposed to give you all that at reception. I thought I was an emergency.

She nodded, wearily, like she got this all the time. 'VHI?'

I nodded. Then I realised I couldn't nod because of the fucking collar. 'Yes,' I said. My voice sounded childish and sulky.

Grow up, Georgie.

'GP?'

On the other side of the wall I heard a funny sound, gurgling and breathless.

'GP?'

I had too many doctors. Christ. Why did I need so many doctors? I closed my eyes, summoned my GP's name. Jessica. Gave it to her. Then I remembered.

'I don't want—'

'Next of kin?'

Voices raised suddenly. The sound of machinery being wheeled.

'Martin,' I said. 'Martin Canney. No. Shit. Sorry. I don't. Have any.'

I gave her Sonia's name.

She nodded cheerfully at me. 'Grand.'

'Can you call her?'

'We'll get someone to bring you down to X-ray. It'll be a while. Very busy today.'

I don't want an X-ray, I wanted to say. I don't want anything here. I haven't broken anything. I don't want anything. I just want to get my face cleaned up.

'Georgia.' She was looking at her notes. Was that a smirk? Did she hesitate before the *a*? 'Lovely name.'

She trotted out.

The noise next door had calmed down. Someone was crying. Whoever it was sounded like a child. Around it rose a low rumble; waves of reassurance from the more contained, or repressed, or whatever members of the family. The fluorescent light flickered. My sinuses were starting to block up again. The shock, probably, wearing off. I stared at the ceiling and wondered why they'd put the window in my cubicle so high. Were they afraid of people seeing what was going on next door? But how could anybody see if they were lying flat on their back? Had they designed this place like a prison, where the windows were there only to hammer home the point that you were being seen, that you could never not be seen, that incarceration meant you, your whole bloody image, belonged to someone else? Or was it just some stupid aesthetic design idea invented by some idiot architect like my idiot engineer like—

You?

I was suddenly very cold, so cold I couldn't think straight.

I sucked in breath, loudly, pushing it into my lungs.

Out for a few minutes. Wished it had been longer. On my return, things were worse.

The crying steadied, rose, fell. The rumblings eddied around it. Underwater sounds. I heard the nurses' sneakers squelching on the tiles, doors banging, the whirr of gurney wheels. In the distance, someone shouting. The siren of an ambulance.

My back was aching. My chest was throbbing. My nose was hurting. I wanted to move. There was a draught from a window or door and it was crawling down into me, past my collar, gripping my throat like a corpse's hand.

A Filipino nurse in green scrubs came into my room. I thought he looked quite attractive and for a split second I wanted to fuck him like I did with the policeman but that disappeared almost before I registered it and then I just felt weepy and exhausted. He was carrying a file and wheeling a blood pressure machine.

High-heels rattled up the corridor. The door to the room next to us opened. The rumbling paused. There she is, said a low voice. Oh, Jesus, said a woman. Her voice sounded like oranges being squeezed.

'Okay, madam,' said the Filipino. Did I look like a madam? He pointed at his eyes, rolled them upwards. 'Look up.'

I did what he said. It felt grainy, like sand was caught behind my lids.

Next door, a broken thud; feet stumbling under the weight of a body. The scrape of chair legs being pushed back. Exclamations. Catch her. Is she – I've got her. Take it easy, Mary. Take it easy.

The Filipino flashed his torch in my eyes. He wrote something down on his file. He seemed not to be hearing what was going on in the next cubicle.

A long, low, bubbling keen. 'I'm sorry, Mammy. Oh, Mam, I'm sorry. Oh, Mam.'

'Now,' said the Filipino, and wheeled the blood pressure thing over to me.

Maybe he'd heard those sorts of cries so many times before, he'd managed to blank them out.

'I've done that already,' I told him. 'They did that in the first place I went to. Triage.' I pronounced it right. 'Can I go now?'

'We've got to get you to the X-ray?' He left a question mark at the end, one of those mid-Atlantic markers everybody uses nowadays, not just the people you live among. Then he smiled, bland, rolled up my sleeve, put the blood pressure bandage around my arm and began to pump. I felt the belt tighten, squeezing my flesh.

It's okay, the voices next door were saying. You came as quick as you could. She didn't suffer. She knew you were coming. It's okay. It's okay.

The Filipino released the air from the machine. He took another note.

'Do you need to use the toilet?' he said. 'I can get you a bottle?'

I shook my head. I realised I did want to go, but only a bit and only because he'd said so. If I used my willpower, I'd be able to hold it in. They give you a catheter if you have a penis. In the grander scheme of things, not a major inconvenience, but—

The door of our cubicle opened. An African doctor came in. At least I assumed he was African. Maybe he was Irish.

'Well,' said the doctor and smiled. 'What do we have here?' His skin was very black. It reminded me of a chocolate mousse Martin used to make for dinner parties. Deliver us not from temptation. He sounded English.

There was, apparently, some equivocation with the X-ray. My sternum had taken the brunt of the steering wheel. Bruised, no fractures. I had no double vision, no concussion, but above my head, they were talking about giving me a CAT scan. Maybe even an MRI.

MRIs are loud, Sonia had told me. Her mother had got one; she'd been in for high blood pressure but they ended up giving her the works. It's like being in a tunnel, she'd told Sonia, a mine. Except it's all happening inside you.

'How long—' I started saying but they weren't listening.

'Do you have a list?' said the doctor.

The nurse made a face.

'Try and squeeze her on the list.' He looked at me. 'You'll need to stay overnight.'

Overnight?

I started to move.

'Quiet now,' said the Filipino nurse. 'Until you get the scan….'

'I don't want a scan,' I said. 'I'm fine.'

'Your insurance will cover it,' said the nurse. 'Do you need to use the toilet?'

I gritted my teeth. 'No.'

The Filipino nurse brought me back to the cubicle where I'd waited before. He gave me a painkiller and took out a tweezers and I was confused for a moment before I realised he had to clean the glass out of my face. It took a while; the pieces were tiny. 'It's okay,' he said. 'Nothing in your eyes.' As soon as he said that I felt the sand again, and didn't believe him. Then he put some gooey stuff on me and tape on the worst cuts and a bandage on my scalp. I was lucky, he told me. No stitches. His touch was very gentle.

He put all his stuff back on his trolley. He was going.

'Excuse me.'

He turned.

'Can I have my phone?'

I pointed at Martin's coat. He went through the pockets.

'Sorry.'

'Sorry?'

'No phone.'

I asked him to double check, it was an expensive model and I needed it, and he did. Sorry. 'There's a phone in the lobby,' he said. 'We can get somebody to call your family?'

'No, I don't, I just, I mean—' but he was already out of the door.

Any other little lumps or bumps? the doctor had said. *While we have you here, we can test you for anything.*

A benefit of my insurance apparently. And the fact that I was in a new hospital, full of new equipment, screaming for use.

Not here, I wanted to say. Not now. Not here. I've made my own arrangements. I'm going to a clinic tomorrow where they specialise in that stuff. But instead, all I'd done was shake my head.

I closed my eyes. Next door, they were still at it. Somebody was saying prayers. A rosary. It sounded like the entire extended family had turned up to join in.

225

Did you hear that noise last night, Davey? Sounded like someone walking around?

My eyes were open, staring at the ceiling again.

The prayers had finished. The family were talking – a low, gentle hubbub of noise, punctured by occasional giggles and sobs. The roller coaster of bereavement. Remembrances, anecdotes, the collecting-together of a life into a story to be passed on to the next generation. I'd been thinking of that, before the accident. Hadn't I? But I couldn't remember why. Who would be my next generation? That I didn't want to think about. The door to their cubicle opened and closed. In the corridor outside I could hear sobs. Someone had a radio on; the news was crackling, low as a prayer.

I want my mother, I thought.

I felt as if something had broken me into little pieces. Each piece knew what it was feeling, but I hadn't a clue how to bring everything together.

You can blame what happened next on the concussion, even though I wasn't concussed. Or on my straining bladder. Or you could say that when I sat up on that gurney, I knew exactly what I was doing. That whatever I needed to face, through whatever tests, mammogram, ultrasound, FNA, whatever medicine or illness or recovery or not-recovery would put me through, had to be on my own terms, not a whiplash side-effect of a stupid, senseless accident. If I'd faced that test before, in more trying circumstances, then I could do it again now.

It was strange to move after being still for so long. My chest twinged and something in my spine groaned but it felt like a normal groan: weariness, or the flu – not damage. I would live. Would I? Hush. I swung my legs over the edge of the gurney. The collar around my neck felt horrible, tight as a stranglehold.

I stepped towards the half-open door, feeling sneaky and guilty and half-excited, like a kid doing something they shouldn't. It was an unfamiliar feeling. Had I been that rule-bound as a kid? Tell me: even transgressing, had I still followed orders?

Why do you always have to be so *good*, Geo?

But I'm not, Mar.

I peered out. An old man with a stomach like Humpty Dumpty's was standing with his back to the wall, staring at the floor; beside him a scrawny fellow in his thirties was crouching on his hunkers, tugging at his long ginger ponytail. They weren't looking at each other, or speaking, but I assumed they belonged to the woman – *Mam, sorry Mammy* – who had died next door. They had that vague resemblance families get, the same things you and I share. A detail of nose, curve of lip, sweep of forehead.

Double doors flapped open. I ducked my head back in. The scrawny fellow stood, too fast, too polite. A female nurse swept past. She was walking very quickly and carrying a tray with sandwiches and a teapot. The doors flapped closed.

I stepped out. The corridor was lined with the family of the dead woman. They were hugging, holding hands or in small oases of private pain. Nobody looked up. I glanced around, clocked a sign for the toilets, and began to walk towards the doors. A mobile ringtone went off, polyphonic, stereo-sound-perfect. *Where do you go to, my lovely?* Someone who didn't see me got out of my way and the world stopped.

Lotte was standing before me, her back turned, her face pushed into the corner of the wall. Her hair was wild and dark and curly and she smelt as I'd always remembered her smelling, of Chanel Gardenia. Her shoulders were shaking but she wasn't making a sound. Agony was humming around her, a forcefield of static. *Repel All Invaders!* My hand lifted. It seemed very important that I make contact with her. Her head jerked around. Her face was wide and freckled and nothing like how I remembered Lotte's, and her eyes were a dull blue, not amber.

Rubbish phrases rose in my mind. I'm sorry for your trouble. I know, it's awful. It'll be okay. But all I could do was stare, disappointed.

Something flashed in her eyes. She laughed a bitter little laugh.

Reichenberg? I thought. That German town in Sabine's email. Is that not in Czechoslov—

Then: Fuck, I thought, remembering. Martin's coat. I can't leave it. Someone might throw it out.

I turned and walked back to the cubicle, as quickly as I could. The coat was lying on a chair. I was shocked at the relief that flooded through me. It's only a coat, I told myself. But I grabbed it and pulled it on as fast as I could. I think I had enough presence of mind to search the pockets, check that my purse and keys were still there, before leaving again.

Under the harsh blue-white bathroom lights, my face was purple and swollen, my lower lip a mess, the worst of the cuts covered with white bits of surgical tape. Lucky, the nurse had said. I would have laughed, except my chest was too sore. I felt tired, woozy again; the flu was back. I leaned forward until my forehead touched the mirror. It was cool, comforting. I closed my eyes.

I had forgotten something. I had remembered it, almost, but now it was gone. Did it matter?

I lifted my head, looked into my own eyes. Saw yours: dark grey marbles, ringed with red-veined white. I felt in my pockets, cursed myself for not bringing concealer, then wetted my fingers and ran them through my hair, teasing the strands around my face, trying to hide as much of the damage as I could.

The door to the bathroom opened and I caught the smell of hospital food. Roast meat, mashed potatoes. Smells of my youth. Then – how did that happen? Reflex? – my nose blocked itself up again and I smelt nothing.

Taking off the white plastic collar – it was an effort – I put it in the sink next to the one I'd been using. Standing there on its own, it reminded me of a Frida Kahlo painting: a woman's corset, empty.

As I walked over to the main entrance, as casually as I could, a few people looked at me, but not as many as I'd expected. In the kingdom of the damaged, only the whole are freaks. At the doors, I hesitated. I had to get home but I had no idea what trains were running, whether trains were running at all.

'I know,' said a familiar voice, heavy with Wicklow inflection. 'Sure with the cutbacks, we can't….'

The woman paramedic who'd brought me in on the ambulance was walking down the stairs, straight towards me. She was with two young nurses and an older man and had a duffel coat over her paramedic anorak. Off duty.

I saw a flash of yellow light outside the main doors; a line of cabs waiting for business. Tucking my chin down to hide my face from the paramedic, I walked towards the rank; Martin's coat flapping around my shoulders, shielding me from the rain.

Junket

Con-cen-tra-tion!
   Are-you-rea-dy!
   If-so!
   Let's-go!

The poplars, sighing.

Four days in, he makes the decision.

'Oh,' says Art, sounding surprised. 'Well, I suppose, if you think you must....'

As soon as David hangs up, he feels sick. Georgie is sitting on the stairs, eyes down, forehead furrowed as if working on a sum.

'So what about that, old bean? Munich. An adventure, eh?'

Georgie shrugs.

Fuck, thinks David, and is about to lift the phone again, when his son looks up, suddenly curious. 'Is Munich in Czechoslovakia, Dad?'

On the evening he leaves, struck by one of those panicky urges, he rummages through the papers on his side of the bed – can he call it that anymore? – and pulls out Georgie's old scrapbook, the one he'd used to collect all of David's press cuttings from work. David had found it that bitterly cold night he had come back from the bank hearing, Ó Buachalla in tow, the pair of them blind, buckled drunk. Course you have to stay. Can't have you sleeping on a building site, old sport. Old sport? Donnacha laughing, almost pissing himself. You're a hoot, Daithí. A fucking panic. Messy on the drink, hardly able to see, David had been shunting a stack of newspapers off the sofa to clear a makeshift bed for the architect when the scrapbook had fallen out, its cover torn and crumpled.

What's that? Donnacha said, lumbering back into the lounge, that heady aftershave of his filling the house like a cat's spray. Nothing, said David. He would remember staggering, the room swimming. Somehow getting his fingers, boneless as butter, to curl the book into a loose roll and push it into his pocket. Till the morrow, what?

Amárach, mo chara. The architect collapsed on the sofa.

Before stumbling in beside Aisling, David had put the scrapbook on his bedside locker, thinking, through the whiskey, muddled thoughts of keeping it safe and giving it to Georgie whenever he asked for it. But Georgie didn't ask, so the book stayed there, slowly getting buried under David's papers, two years of work and research and futile attempts at distraction.

Now, on this dark October evening, he lets it fall open. A page bearing a legend – *Dad's Bank. 25th November* – in Georgie's careful, wobbly seven-year-old script. Above that, four globs of dried glue, but no picture. The paper is crumpled, just like the cover. All the pages after it are blank. David tries to smooth out the crumples, but they spring back; too heavily creased by the weight of those two years.

Something stings the back of his eyes.

'Davey!' shouts his sister, Bridget. 'Taxi's here!'

He closes the scrapbook quickly and puts it into his suitcase, laying it carefully under his two new shirts in their cellophane wrappers.

The hostesses in their green suits are walking up and down the aisle, self-conscious as bridesmaids as they check the passengers' tabletops and seatbelts. One, wearing scarlet lipstick and a wedge of curls that reminds David of his mother in her Rita Hayworth glory days, leans in, offering a plate of boiled sweets. David takes one and pops it in his mouth. A rush of synthetic lemon hits his tongue. The overweight man fidgeting in the aisle seat beside him refuses the sweets, but makes some crack with the hostess about when they're ever going to bring out the hard stuff and be sure to make his a double, won't you, pet? His attempts at flirtation ring false, too aggressive to be charming, too eager for a man his age. He's a sap, and the worst kind – the sort that doesn't even know it. Yet in spite of his oafishness, he's nimble enough. As soon as he'd sat down, he'd forced his elbow onto the armrest, expertly ousting David. He is a salesman. Brochures for pocket calculators had fallen out of his over-stuffed briefcase as he'd run towards the gate. Cascaded, like the leaves of an accordion.

Commandeering the other armrest is a sleek Continental in the window seat. A businessman, judging by the sheaf of typed reports stacked in the pocket before him. Some big shot from the EEC, probably, fresh from a visit to the Department of Poverty where he's warned a small nation of the costs and consequences of belonging. He smells of an expensive cologne which claws at David's nostrils and his skin is a glowing caramel, his hair a silvering mane. Too flamboyant for a German. Maybe he's Danish. The air hostess sparkles as she hands him his sweet; her eyes shine, her chest under its emerald casing swells.

Bile rises in David's mouth. He looks down at his conference schedule. *Computing and Design in Structural Engineering: What Lies Ahead*. What is he doing here? It's all wrong. That feeling comes on him again, of being an imposter, a pretend version of himself. He should be anywhere but here, on this over-packed plane. As he'd been going through the gate in the departure lounge, turning at the sound of the calculator salesman's briefcase bursting open, he'd had the same thought. *Go back now*. What would it have taken? To retreat, run back along the corridor with its windows looking onto north County Dublin, shouting, *Wait! Wait. I made a mistake!*

The hostesses begin their demonstration. The plane trundles forward, the fields of north Dublin spool past the windows like halting frames of film.

The pressure builds, the engines scream. The hostesses seat themselves.

The city dives away, a Christmas-tree string of lights in a sea of black. The sky tilts, adjusts itself, finds the horizon; becomes a mass of deep blue, streaked with slate. David sucks his sweet. His ears pop. Reflected in the window he can see the face of the salesman; nose twitching, fat lower lip making silent prayers. The sweet rolls around to the front of David's mouth. He bites, hard. Lemon crunches into splinters of bitter sunshine.

They had contacted him at the start of March, three days after the doctors had given Aisling the results of her test. *That* test, the only one, in the end, that would ever mean anything. The invitation had come by post, forwarded by Morgan Lloyd, the Welshman who was head custodian of the firm's mainframe in London. *Dear David, I think your work on the Boyne Bridge would be perfect for this*. Since early 1975, when David had been granted access to the mainframe, he'd had enough regular communication with Morgan and his team in the Computer Group to know that the other man thought well of him, in an uncomplicatedly British way that was different to Art and the rest of the Dublin office. But – *perfect*? – this came as a surprise.

Instinct told him not to open the letter at his desk, but he was all over the place, unable to think straight. It took him a moment to understand what he was reading. Enough for wolfish O'Hanlon, now elevated from draughtsman to Rourke's junior, to clock it. What's that, Mr Madden? he said, eyes sharp as ever. Later David would wonder why he'd answered, not just batted O'Hanlon off with some excuse. Maybe it was the oncologist's report, only three days old, or Aisling, moving around in a trance, unreachable. Maybe it was Joanie bloody Flynn with her *Oh David, you gave me a shock there, I thought you were already at home, I just saw—* Or maybe it was simply that, to put the little pup in his place.

An invitation, actually, he said. To a conference. In Germany.

O'Hanlon's nostrils flared, the envy coming off him rank as cowshit.

A junket! Niall Rourke had come in without them noticing. So how did you swing that, Madden? Your buddy Ó Buachalla, I suppose?

O'Hanlon grinned, looking straight at David.

What do you know about it, David wanted to say, his fists tensing. But Rourke was on him then, clapping his back, shaking his hand. You cute hoor! Wait till Art finds out, hah!

Art? thought David, blanking for a stupid second before he remembered.

One of the founders of the Dublin office was retiring in December; a directorship would be up for grabs in the New Year. It would come down to David and Rourke, everyone knew that. There was enough at stake. Money, standing. Certainty. Rourke had three kids, two in university. Law and Medicine. Expensive. O'Hanlon was always asking about them in front of Arthur Lyons, though he never mentioned Georgie – just looked at David any time his son's name came up, all false-pity under his wolf's eyes. Beneath his rough-around-the-edges bonhomie, Rourke was a tough nut and since the bank mess, he hadn't been slow to elbow himself into Art's favour. Lots of cracks about some projects – bridges, for example – being Also-Ran's while others – Rourke's own, of course – were what you'd call First Division. Always followed by the quick backtrack: Sure, I'm only slagging, David. Art would hardly take Rourke's digs at face value, but he liked ambition in his men; would like it even more, David knew, in a company director.

We've scheduled the event for mid-October. Perhaps you can let us know by the end of spring?

Are you alright, Mr Madden? said Morrissey, the young draughtsman who was still just a draughtsman.

Eh, grand, Brian, said David, and put the invitation away.

That evening, as he cycled home against the wind, he tossed imaginary coins in his head. I tell her. I tell her not. October was a little over half a year away. The oncologist had given Aisling six to eight months.

I tell her.

I, eh, haven't made up my mind yet, he said.

A beat of something unreadable passed behind her eyes. Then—

But of course you should go, Davey. Why ever....

Not hovering between them, barbed and savage.

The next day, the whole office knew. A pre-emptive strike. Rourke – or O'Hanlon, on his behalf. Art popped in to congratulate David. Great stuff. I had no idea. Mr Lloyd certainly kept that one up his sleeve. It'll do wonders for our public image, having a man at the forefront. David couldn't tell if Art was genuinely pleased, or irked at Morgan for organising it behind his back. Lately, he felt he no longer knew how to read Art – though, really, had he ever been able to?

Who'd have pegged Madden for the academic type, Art, hah? said Niall Rourke.

Yeah, grinned O'Hanlon. Maybe he missed his calling.

You hoors, thought David. So this was how it was going to play?

Well, you know, he heard himself saying, in an awful voice, airy and casual, that didn't belong to him. It's not in the bag yet. I still have to write the shagging paper. They all laughed, himself included.

Would you like me to do you up your thank-you now, Mr Madden? said Monica from the typing pool. It won't take me a tic.

No, he thought, panicking, seeing the reality of the situation. Consequences exploded, grew teeth and claws. Thinking, write a paper? Thinking, give it? In public? The thought made him cold. Then thinking, stuff the paper and the public – six to eight months? What was he, mad? Thinking, why did she not say that? The timing was wrong, it was the worst possible timing in the world. She would need him around, and if she didn't, Georgie would. More to the point, he knew that. Why hadn't he said it?

He saw Joanie Flynn again, standing on her doorstep, hand flying to her mouth. Oracle of fucking Delphi.

Art was watching him, poker-faced.

Great, said David. Thanks, Monica. And followed her down to the typing pool, watching the letters appear on the creamy headed paper as he dictated God knows what in that awful stranger's voice, while the machines chattered around him, the women's fingers shoving at the keys as if they were wounds.

Monica pulled out the letter. Perfect. Now, if you can just mark it with your X, Mr Madden.

He took out his fountain pen and signed. Fast, before he could change his mind.

At that stage, he had told nobody at work how bad things were. From time to time, Art would ask – How's Aisling? How's the home life, David? – but everyone else had been too polite, or squeamish, to pry. It had been simpler to keep to the party line. *She's on the mend. It's been rough, but things are looking up.* Occasionally, he found himself using that other word, the one everyone else used to use: *manageable.* He hadn't told anyone about the weight that wouldn't go back on after the chemo had finished, the coughing late at night and first thing in the morning, the specks of blood in the bathroom sink. Why would he? There was nobody to tell outside family, except the Ó Buachallas: and he assumed, until the last test, anyway, that Aisling had told Jan everything. He and Donnacha didn't discuss those things; he couldn't remember what he and Donnacha discussed. Mainly they just drank.

The night he'd signed the letter, Maura rang. She gave him some guff first about their mother needing proper care and Eileen not being up to it anymore and running up and down them stairs and changing dirty underthings not being right and....

Tch, she said, stopping. The sucking of her spit through her teeth a ghostly echo of their father's. How's Aisling? Did ye get the results of that test yet?

He didn't answer.

She sighed. You know we're here for you, Davey. Ye can have Bridget anytime you want. We'll give ye the money for her bed and board, so don't worry there. We can take the little fellow either if it gets too much. He can even stay the summer with us if....

Who's that? Aisling called down the hall.

Nothing, he said, and hung up.

She was in the lounge, on the sofa, her legs tucked under her. The gas fire was on, the telly off. She wasn't coughing; her lungs had eased off for a couple of hours, though it would probably start up again after she went to bed. With her hair growing out and all the weight gone, she reminded David of a fashion model from the front of a magazine. It felt like years since he'd looked at her in that way and that old impulse rose in him again, a craving for the feel of her skin against his palm. But he couldn't seem to act on it, so he leant against the doorframe instead, welcoming its cold nudge.

What do you think about getting some help, Davey?

A stitch, stabbing, just above his heart. Help?

She looked at him. With the house, I mean. Or. She chewed her lip. Maybe even Georgie? I know I'm not gone yet, but—

Jesus Christ, Ash.

She laughed; the sound hurt him.

Eh. He tried to regroup. Funny you should say that. I mean. Maura was on just now and—

Christ, David! I'm not talking about your sisters. This thing might be heading for my brain but it's not got there yet. A, she struggled. A cleaning lady.

Cleaning lady? The phrase felt alien in his mouth.

They'll give us the money. Your sisters. That's what Maura was ringing about, right?

I— He shrugged. Yeah.

I don't want to waste what's left of my time messing around with a stupid hoover. I want to spend it with Georgie. She blinked. And you, of course.

And you, of course.

David felt one of those compulsions again to go upstairs and see if Georgie was alright.

We should, eh, make up our mind about that school, he said. He saw Aisling prepare herself for a fight. He couldn't stomach a fight; he kept talking, hands up. I've been thinking. You're right. Let's send him to the other place, the place— He blanked. Whatshername, Donnacha's daughter, the place she goes to. It'll be better for him.

She looked away. Have you thought any more about that conference thing, Davey?

Thing?

Ah, he said. I'm still, eh, undecided on that one.

Something sparked in her eyes. He forced himself to see it, not look away. He couldn't tell what it was. His teeth began to hurt.

Here, she said, patting the sofa next to her. *Hall's Pictorial Weekly's* on in a wee minute. We could do with a laugh.

In a sec, he said. I just want to check on Georgie.

So many things he never shared with her. Wouldn't, at the beginning, because he was ashamed of where he'd come from, and afraid of losing her; then later, when things got bad between them, couldn't. In the early days, she used to joke about it. Picking up not just on the small dissimulations he had practised when they were first going out, but the way he had of sitting back at family gatherings, staying quiet, letting others tell the stories, or, if he said anything, only generalisations, shaving family anecdotes smooth of any individual barbs that might have brought his life before her and Georgie into clearer definition.

But didn't we all eat turnip jam during the Emergency? Didn't we all gasp at our first taste of a banana? Didn't we all smoke Woodbines and dance to 'The Hucklebuck' and kiss a girl on the Gashouse Bridge—

No? Right, then. Must have been someone else.

The Great Pretender, she called him first. Then: International Man of Mystery. You've got me wrong, Ash, he wanted to tell her. I am a simple person. I have nothing to hide.

Yet: What have I done? he thinks now, sitting at the window of his hotel bedroom, watching the Olympiapark yawn dark under the dirty-red sky while Munich sleeps. How, he wonders, could he have ever hoped to set up a life with someone – stayed together, made a child, weathered the storms – with such dissimulation at its core? Words from a poem he learnt in school creep into his mind. *The centre cannot hold. Things fall apart.*

A wave of exhaustion had hit him as soon as the plane landed. Great, he'd thought. I'll sleep tonight. But once they showed him to his room, the tiredness vanished. Now everything – the room, the bed, himself – feels wrong again. Too small, too hard, too different. He had a shower, but he can't get rid of the stink of the Danish man's cologne and it's turning his stomach. He looks at his briefcase, perched on the chair beside the unfamiliar wardrobe. Inside are his notes for the presentation on Thursday, thirty-one hours away.

Open me, says the briefcase. *Crawl in here and let me take your mind off things.*

He gets up, but as he does, the exhaustion hits him again. He catches sight of himself in the hotel window. A bathrobed ghost hovering over a green leather chair, trapped in the light-sprinkled blackness of a sleeping city.

Jesus, he thinks. Is this what falling apart looks like?

Herr Fuchs is young, Morgan Lloyd had written in the letter accompanying the invitation, *but very good. You'll enjoy working with him.* Morgan was right; Klaus Fuchs, the academic organising the conference, is young. His first welcome-on-board letter to David oozed youth and its bastard by-products: enthusiasm, vision, conviction. He wrote in a way that was fresh and exhilarating, about the field for its own sake; a change from Art's strategic positioning, Rourke's brusque wheeling and dealing. *I want our event to bring the arguments to a new, international realm. Our profession should be communicating – not just sharing technical expertise, but talking about the difficult issues. Bias, national prejudice, problems....*

Fuchs' insistent inclusivity – all those *our*'s and *we*'s – unsettled David. He told himself he would probably back out. He told himself it would make sense to have something prepared, just in case. Two days after receiving Fuchs' letter, he started the abstract. The words poured out, slow and unstoppable as cement trundling from a mixer. As if, he later thought, he would never have been able not to write them.

I like it! wrote Fuchs. *The ill-conditioned problem. A very hot topic.*

David had encountered the problem through his work with Morgan's team in London, when he'd used the mainframe to run a finite element analysis on the plate and weld components of the Boyne bridge. He'd chosen it as a topic partly out of a certain satisfaction in the idea of bringing one of Rourke's Also-Ran's to the attention of the international engineering community, but also because the issue in itself was interesting. How do you ensure you have enough elements in your model to create a close approximation of your structure without overloading computer memory? Get the balance right and you'll achieve a robust result, a safe structure. Get it wrong, and it's disaster. With too many elements, you'll choke the computer so it can't generate any results at all – as David had found out to his cost three weeks into his analysis. *Perhaps,* one of Morgan's men had suggested tactfully over the phone, *we might try reducing the number of elements, Mr Madden?* But compromise too far in the other direction and it's even worse. You end up with garbage, your handful of elements stretched so thin across your structure that even a tiny error in input will lead to an avalanche of error. Welcome to the Planet of Ill-Conditioning.

Even as he wrote, he knew he was compartmentalising, and it was artificial, and wouldn't last.

He still hadn't told Aisling he had said yes to the conference. Nor had he told Morgan, or anyone at work in Dublin about Aisling, though Art probably had some idea. They had agreed to keep it to family-only until Georgie knew. But who else could they have told? They had no friends outside the Ó Buachallas, and Jan had stopped visiting in April. *I'm too tired for company,* Aisling had said, and it was easier not to challenge that. Apart from everything else, Donnacha's wife was a weapon; always upsetting Georgie with her stupid, blindingly obvious observations. *Huh, so you like playing with girls as well as boys, Georgie? Huh, so you're creative, Georgie? Well, we all know where you get that from!*

He didn't explain to Aisling why he no longer went out drinking with Donnacha, and she didn't ask. Instead she talked about the cleaning lady or, more accurately, the lack of one: the women she had interviewed, had tried out, let go. Because Georgie didn't like them, or she didn't, or they just didn't suit.

That evening in May, he had been at the kitchen table. Dinner was over and he was dreading the hours ahead of them – the pottering, the distance, both of them trying to be normal and not doing very well, the questions starting to writhe and hiss in his mind again – when Ash came up behind him and put her arms around his neck. For a moment, the nonsense in his head shushed. God, he thought. All this, what if it's just shock? A way of dealing with—

His hands lifted, held hers. She felt very frail.

I said yes to Munich, Ash, he started, but she didn't hear because she was talking too.

Sorry?

I said she's lovely.

Who?

The girl I found today. Georgie hardly knows her and he's already mad about her. Lotte. She's English, but she's a gem.

Year of the Heatwave (Spring–Summer): The Ill-Conditioned Analysis (1) / Questions Thought But Never Asked

Did something happen, Ash?

How long did it go on?

A night? Three? Months?

When did it start? The night I brought him back to the house?

Or—

But at the *or*, he would feel something in him

■ *o* ■ *r* ■ ?

separate, like yolk from an egg, his mind stalling, paralysed, the feeling of missing a fundamental part of himself, it being left behind somewhere, and besides—

You gobshite, he would tell himself. How can you even—

atatimelikethis

You crass, you petty little man.

Sometimes disbelief: You eejit. You girleen, imagining things. She didn't even like the man. What had he to go on? Things he hadn't even seen, feelings he wasn't sure of, nothing more than—

Except at *more than*, the uncertainty itching under the surface of his mind would stop suddenly. A sickening feeling of *déjà vu*, followed by a spark of something more

■ *s* ■ *u* ■ *r* ■ *?*

vicious. He had been made a fool of. He was a sap, and he didn't even know it.

Then, catching himself, appalled: How could he—

sixtoeightmonths

You crass, you selfish, you petty little man.

At some point the Scotch he ordered from room service must have kicked in, granting him sleep, of sorts. Fitful, restless. Fragments of dreams, not joined up, the usual thing. A woman. A star. A lemon tree. A clock, ticking its ours away. Except— This is new: he's in his Da's Plymouth, but it's yellow, not black, and he's surrounded by his sisters, even Noreen, the dead one, and they're all fat, all of them, even his Da. Association (just a flash): a man on a plane. They're all crunching sweets, him included, and outside the car is his mother, veiled in black, walking slowly, inches above the surface of the Suir.

She turns. My son, my son, is drowning, she says, and smiles.

Now he's in water, and it stinks of ammonia and something else, musky and distinctive, that he should be able to place, but can't, and—

David splutters, pushing at the cloths winding his body, and wakes. He is on his back, staring at an unfamiliar ceiling. He's lying not on a bed, but a floor, and the shroud twisted around him is only a sheet, reeking of bleach and too many washings.

Munich.

For a moment, a strange, weightless sense of possibility rises in him. Then:

Aisling—

Christ.

Reality lands, a punch to his gut.

At the back of his skull, a headache begins to throb. Shaking off the sheets, he pushes himself up from the floor.

The wind, crying.

Breakfast is downstairs, in an overheated room stuffed with heavy dark-brown furniture and lots of people. Munich is busy this week. As well as the conference, there's a construction trade fair in the Messe and a big concert on in the Opera House. We're sorry, Herr Madden, Fuchs' secretary had said. This is the closest we could find for you. She had left a little gap. It took him a moment to realise what she didn't want to say: we were expecting you to withdraw.

He doesn't recognise anyone. It seems he is the only delegate from the conference staying here. The thought offers some relief but then that instantly makes him feel – *imposter* – fraudulent again. There are no single tables free, so he sits at an empty table for four beside the kitchen door.

'*Tee? Kaffee?*'

The waitress is blonde, buxom and cheerful, like a propaganda poster-girl from the 1930s. He orders coffee. The breakfast is continental. Cold ham and cheese, cake, yogurt flavoured with odd ingredients: nuts and citrus fruits. The coffee arrives in a porcelain pot, accompanied by shards of pumice-hard croissant and small tight rolls that look nice but, on closer inspection, turn out to be riddled with caraway seeds. David loathes caraway seeds; they have always reminded him of rot. He cracks open a croissant.

'Excuse me?'

A pleasant-faced woman on the wrong side of thirty-five, wearing lime-green trousers too tight around the crotch, is hovering at David's table. Behind her is a frail, elderly man, stooped like a question mark. The woman smiles. Her smile doesn't match the rest of her. It is surprisingly attractive, the sort that lights up a person's face. 'Would it bother you if we…?' A soft voice. American; from somewhere in the South, David guesses.

He shakes his head, gestures. The woman guides the elderly man into the seat beside him.

'Now, Poppa, you tell me what you want and—'

Her father makes an impatient whooshing sound. 'I can order for myself, thank you.' *Sank you.* His accent is Billy Wilder's, heavy with history.

David opens his guidebook. In the corner of his vision, he sees the elderly man pick up a caraway roll from the plate on the table. The daughter, busy catching the waitress's attention, doesn't notice. Her father begins to rip the dough from the inside of the roll. His fingers are long and elegant, like a piano player's, but his movements are slow, arthritic; trembling; like the little skeletons of mammals in the National History Museum that David once showed Georgie. Only three years ago, though it feels like an age now.

'Oh, Poppa,' says the woman, seeing. Her father ignores her, slathers the eviscerated crust with butter.

'I am so sorry,' she says to David. Then, as if it's an explanation: 'We're here for Dachau.'

'Excuse me?'

'Dachau?' She points to David's guidebook. Lowers her voice: 'The Nazi camp? The memorial.'

'Oh.' He looks down. The ache in his head gets heavier; the musky smell intensifies.

She glances at her father. 'I dunno if it's such a good idea to go. But this is the first time he's been back here since—'

'Ugh!' The old man brings his napkin to his lips and spits. 'The seeds, Helena. I hate to eat this. You should have told me.' His eyes land on David.

'So.' The daughter is smiling again. 'What brings you here?'

I don't know, David wants to say. Please tell me.

'Sorry.' He is rising, clumsy, too fast. 'I have to, eh. I'm late.'

The hotel lobby stinks of an artificial air freshener that makes his headache even worse, so he decides to set off on foot without waiting for the bus. It's a practical choice, he tells himself. He needs some air.

'*Ja, klar,*' says the receptionist. 'I will inform the driver you will walk.'

Outside, the sky is a pale chilly blue, streaked with the snail-trails of aeroplanes. The air is cold; properly, continentally autumnal. David reaches for his guidebook to check the route, and as he does, hears a beep behind him. The bus has arrived, two minutes early. With a slow hiss, the pneumatic doors open. Through the windows David sees faces; mostly strangers, but some he half-recognises, engineers from the firm's other offices in Britain and Europe.

'Herr Madden?'

Reluctantly, he climbs up and sits in the first free seat he can see, a single one directly behind the driver. Across the gangway, a slim Asian man, also on his own, is leafing through a sheaf of papers. He looks up, sees David; smiles, nods. Awkward, David returns the courtesy.

The bus lurches off. Under the watery sun, the city is an ugly-beautiful patchwork of reconstituted post-war streets, glass-and-concrete towers and snatches of an older, *kitschier* place. Tiled roofs, sandy gables, cobblestones; scraps of Bavarian charm lingering like soapscum on the forward-rushing wave of modernising Germany.

Is *kitsch* a real word? Georgie had asked a couple of weeks ago. Whatshername – the Ó Buachallas' child – had introduced the term at school and nobody, not even the teacher, had believed her when she'd said she wasn't making it up.

I don't know, said David, *Let's ask Mum* crouching unspoken behind his teeth.

Yes, said Lotte later, arriving to do weekend duty. David could have hugged her. It means cheap and sentimental, monster. Nothing you'd care for.

Outside, a dull sound of shouting that gets louder as they approach a red light. The bus brakes. At the intersection, a group of people are holding placards and chanting slogans. The engineers stop talking.

'Bloody hell,' murmurs one of the Englishmen. Stephen Flitch, from the firm's Manchester office. 'Can't go anywhere without running into the Angry Brigade.'

The protestors are picketing what looks like a newspaper building. They're all sorts, young and middle-aged, men and women, wearing rag-tag clothes. Most of the men have long hair and beards. One of the younger women has a peace sign painted on her face. They glare at the stopped traffic, shouting in through the windows.

Fa-shiss-ten! Shvine-err-eye!

'Like bloody Belfast, in't it? All we need now are the flaming IRA.'

Fascists! Piggery! The chant is in three-time, a leaden staccato that reminds David of that word game Aisling used to play with Georgie. Concentration! Are You Ready! Some of the placards have text on them. *Ulrike: wir vergessen Dich nie.* Ulrike, we will never forget you. Others are just pictures, familiar from the news; a grid of empty-eyed, dead-skinned faces, most crossed out in thick red ink. The girl with the peace sign sees the engineers watching and thrusts herself forward to jeer at their driver. She is inches away from David. The driver's nape reddens. He starts to tap a tune on his steering wheel. Four-four, defiantly military. The girl bangs on the chassis, laughs, turns.

Lotte? thinks David. Then, immediately – her fingers are claws, her teeth crooked – No. Lotte is beautiful.

He recoils.

The girl's mouth slackens. For a moment, she looks desperately young and lost. Her face twists and she flings up her head. The lights change. She falls back into the throng. On David's window drools a trail of white spit. The girl recedes. She laughs, arms waving, mouth still moving.

You bourgeois pig. You fascist prick. You capitalist reactionary scum.

'So young,' murmurs the Asian engineer.

You fucking hoot. You useless father. You terrible husband.

charade

David grinds his eyes shut, trying to ignore the pain drumming behind their sockets. He would kill for an aspirin.

His mother was forty when her wits began to curdle, the same age David would turn the year of the heatwave. The warning signs had been there for some time: the weeping, the elated insistence that her son was destined to be a doctor, the – I know, Davey! – plans and plotting, the secret presents, the medical textbooks ordered up from Dublin behind his father's back. His Da had different plans: forget university, the idea of a Profession. David was going to take over the business, run the grocery bar when he was gone. Fergus Madden had waited seven years for an heir; he wasn't going to be swayed by a woman's silly notions.

The things David never told Aisling: the evenings of cold disregard between his parents. Their separate bedrooms. The jibes, the bullying, the tugging this way and that. His sisters, stuck in the middle, making noise, unheard. The tales his sisters used to tell. You know Daddy used to sleep on the sofa, Davey? If you sleep there, you'll turn into him. You know Daddy used to make Mammy walk to Mass, though we all went in the car? If you don't behave yourself, he'll do the same to you. You know Daddy broke the lock on Mammy's bedroom door the year before you were born, Davey? One night, when he was a rage. So whatever you do, don't make him angry.

A domestic Emergency raging in a tall, damp house in Clonmel while Europe fractured itself in war. Can a child be an Emergency itself without knowing it?

At six, his father perched him on a high stool behind the shop counter and tried to teach him commerce. Doing sums with an abacus of boiled sweets. The smell of sawdust. The glass-paned door leading to the pub; the mysterious sounds of men's conversation trickling out on a Guinness-scented haze. Can you not get anything into your head? his father roared at him. You useless little shite. You runt. You cuckoo in the nest. In retaliation, his mother pulled David into her parlour, placed her presents in his lap. Read this, she would say. It'll help. Help what? It didn't. He couldn't read. He was only six. The pictures disgusted him.

That summer was the year she became ill, and David fell sick too – the start of the asthma, a chest infection that confined him to bed. You're only copying Mammy, said jealous Bridget. Years later, during the nights of the heatwave, as the unasked questions coiled tighter and tighter in his mind, David would be plagued by that same fear. Was he only copying her again, but this time for real, curdling his wits into a pathetic imitation of hers?

His mother's illness was a bane. She would spend weeks in bed, then, when the spirit lifted her, would burst into the little box room and wrench

David away from his own sick-bed. He would rest better with her, she said. The two of them could cosy up together, make each other well. This picture David would always try to keep from Georgie: a long-limbed child in a darkened room, lying beside the warm bulk of his mother in her honey-and-mushroom scented bed, terrified she would roll onto him by mistake and squash him to death.

On days when she was better – more like herself, she said – she would go the kitchen and make cakes and listen to the radio. David's father hated the BBC but she loved it because they played music and in hard times, you needed music. Count John McCormack for when she was feeling melancholy, dance music for her jolly moods. Not jigs and reels, only the knackers of Irishtown danced to that muck, but foxtrots, waltzes, the daring, knee-baring Charleston. Dance with me, come on, dance. How can you not dance to that, Davey?

Whirling across the floor, fingers walking quick-steps into her child's skin. Until—

We interrupt this broadcast—

—she would moan, a sound from the melting pit of her, and switch off the depressing, unnecessary news of bodies lost and bodies found, broken cities and shifting fronts, the crisp British tones of the announcer promising victory at all costs. At night, he would hear her crying; sobbing, like a wounded creature, into her pillow.

Year of the Heatwave (Summer): The Ill-Conditioned Analysis (2) / Output from Thought-but-Not-Asked Questions

1. A yearning for the tunnel, because at least he knew it. But he hadn't had the nightmare in years. Flash images instead; fragments that refused to join up. A crowded room. A woman on a table, legs spread, wet with desire. Lemon trees. A star, cold and bright, in the north sky.

2. More of the panicky impulses around Georgie, the ones that had started a couple of years back. He would wake, terrified there'd been a break-in, that someone had taken Georgie away, and the only thing that would settle him was to go to his son's room, lie on a blanket on the floor, like he was nineteen, working the mine again, and keep watch.

3. Physical sensations. Though sometimes he thought he was imagining them too. That stitch in his chest, like he'd torn a muscle. Heartburn. Cold sweats. Aching, deep in the bones of his arm. Eyes stinging, blurring, out

of focus. Some weeks he'd wake every morning, freezing. The next, he'd boil. No sleep.

4. A feeling of missing something that was almost the same as the panic around losing Georgie, but not quite.

5. The sense that each second was an opportunity wasted, though David no longer knew for what. For talk? For questions? Like what? Those questions?

6. Suspicion.

7. Rage, suspicion's ugly offspring. You fool. You sap, and you don't even know it.

8. Recrimination, rage's equally ugly sister. You eejit, imagining things. You gobshite. You useless prick.

There had been good things. You must meet her, Davey, Aisling kept saying. Lotte's so interesting, isn't she, Georgie? But David hadn't wanted to. This girl, this *cleaning lady*, was none of his business; and when they did, sometime late in June, he had been too on edge to take her in. All he had registered was a slim girl, little more than a teenager, with dark shadows under her eyes and a posh English accent. Someone far less capable, less – maternal, was that the word? – than Aisling's descriptions had implied. But in one way, Ash had been absolutely right. Georgie really liked her.

There was this too: strange, precious moments of intimacy. Hand-holding, jokes. A brush of her fingers across his face. Other days she would be angry, or folded into herself, or only wanting Georgie, or something scientific to read, and sometimes he found that a relief. As if, in rejecting him, she had taken the burden of recrimination from his own shoulders. As the summer deepened, burning the grass in their back garden brown, and the crab clawed up her body into her brain, she started to forget things. Began asking for Jan. One morning, Jan vanished; and the only person she wanted near her was Lotte.

In August, she grew demanding. Told him to sit with her and sponge her mouth and tell her things. No dark secrets, she would say, the old glint back in her eye to show him she didn't think he had anything dark to share. Do your voices again, Davey. Do Jan. Do Rourke. Do Joanie. Do Bridget. Do Art. Do Lotte. Oh, yes. Do Lotte.

Hard not to read into the omission; hard not to offer, just to test.

Where's Denis? she asked once, just before dawn. Sitting straight up in bed. Eyes bright with a terrible, wet light.

245

Who? he said. She looked through him and he realised she wasn't awake.

His beloved jazz helped, but only sometimes. His sci-fi books didn't; it had been months since he'd finished one. Work did a little, but not much. Writing the paper for Munich did, and didn't. By then, he had decided he was going to back out, let Morgan down, and Klaus Fuchs, but he still needed something to do. He would feel the danger signs start: his mind racing, looking for things under its own surface, and he would grab something – foolscap, or a page of calculations, drawings, computer printouts sent over from London, a notebook. These, at least, he understood. These were real; things he had lived through, made happen. It didn't matter that his analysis hadn't always been successful. What mattered was it was there. He didn't need excuses to work on his paper – like the directorship or the fact that Aisling had been at him for years, pushing him to make a mark, to provide better for Georgie and herself. Some days it was enough to just face the problem, the ill-conditioned analysis, and ask: *What is this?* And if he was lucky, an inch of space would scrape free in his mind.

As August crept forwards, and Aisling retreated, the compulsions began to intensify. He would find himself halfway up the stairs to Georgie's room, or, if he was at work, thinking he should phone home, not once or twice a week but as many times a day. He wished he knew what to say to his son. *It's going to be alright.* How could you say that? Curbing the panic as best he could, he would try to convert it into a gesture; something normal, something comforting. A hug, or a rumple of hair, casual so Georgie wouldn't feel too overwhelmed, but it was as if his son could recognise the terror behind the attempt, and didn't want to have anything to do with it. Instead, he grew slippy, evasive, spending all his time outside, playing in the lane.

David felt himself grow more and more brittle. Two-dimensional, flat. An imposter in his own body. Everyone else acted as if he was being perfectly normal. You poor thing. Must be terrible. Only Lotte, their cleaning lady, didn't. No attempts at comfort, no pats on the shoulder, or silly offers of cups of tea. Like she knew enough to keep her distance, read the spikiness, a mirror of his son's, radiating out from him. Here be Maddens.

The wire, looping.

Under the forced intimacy of the lift, the engineers' chatter has subsided again. The conference is on the fourth floor of the Engineering Department, a new build designed to complement the eighteenth-century silhouette of the university. Someone is whistling under their breath and Stephen Flitch is jingling as he shifts his considerable weight, hands stuffed in his trouser pockets, kneading his loose change as if it's a lover's flesh. David avoids his own reflection in the stainless steel walls. He has no desire to dwell on his puffed skin, his broken veins, the jowls collecting under his jawline; that awful stoop of his shoulders.

Every old man I see reminds me of my father.

'Alright there, Dave?' says Flitch, glancing over.

Dave?

David nods, looks at the ground.

The lift tings, releasing them into a bright corridor. The walls are covered with an orange patterned wallpaper, hardly visible under all the noticeboards and student posters. At the end of the corridor is a long trestle table, behind which a shapely brunette in a clingy, flame-coloured dress is checking names.

The corridor is already full of men, humming with the sounds of their greetings: back-slapping, hand-shaking negotiations of status and power, wary overtures, professional enthusiasm, competitive jousting, strategic obeisance. At the door to the lecture room David sees Morgan Lloyd. He's talking to MacLean from Bridges, two of the team from Blackfriars and a younger man David doesn't recognise, a student-type with longish hair. Stephen Flitch pushes past David to greet them. Morgan pats Flitch's back, opening his other arm, Christ-like, to introduce him to the fold.

David thinks of school, those Gaelic matches he never played because of the asthma. Some men would love it. Big men with too much hair, men that stink of cologne and call themselves your friend. *Mo chara*, Donnacha.

'David?'

Morgan Lloyd has extricated himself from the group at the door. He looks just the same as the last time they met, two and a half years earlier, the night Aisling discovered the shadow. Lloyd's grip is strong. In it, David's hand feels like a child's; crushable, insubstantial. He withdraws as soon as is polite.

'I am so sorry to hear,' says Lloyd. 'Your son, how is he?'

David shrugs. It's an effort. 'Holding the fort.'

'Brave little chap. You'll be here on Friday?'

'Just the morning. My flight's at lunchtime.'

Lloyd looks disappointed. 'Shame. A colleague of mine who lives here, chap I met in Oxford, is taking me on a day trip to the Mannheim Garden grid shell. Three hours of autobahn-bashing, a spot of lunch, back for dinner at his home. If you were still here....'

David imagines grey asphalt, green embankment, blue skies, a hundred miles an hour, too fast for thought.

'Well. Can't be helped. Have you met Klaus yet?' Morgan takes David's elbow. 'Let me introduce you....'

No, thinks David. Please don't.

'Mr Lloyd?' The secretary in the clingy dress is behind them.

Lloyd releases David's elbow. 'Sorry, David. Must dash.'

The hum turns to a hush as the long-hair who had been in the group at the door bounds onto the platform and raps on the pulpit-like stand. Is this *child* Klaus Fuchs? Up on the podium, he seems even younger; all soft brown colouring and large, moist eyes that remind David of a Labrador that belonged to the pavees who camped on the Dublin road outside Clonmel. The lads in his school used torment it on their way down to the river, entice it with scraps of food, then kick it. One day David found it belly-up in the Suir, drowned.

'Ladies and gentlemen,' says Fuchs, though there are, of course, no ladies present. 'I am honoured to welcome you here. I hope our time together over the next three days will be fun – if that's not too much to ask – but also, of course, enlightening.' A ripple of laughter. Fuchs smiles. His accent has American inflections, a leftover of his PhD years in Stanford, blazing trails. 'As you know, our Department's aim is to establish meaningful connections between practice, testing and research. Before this decade ends, our profession will be seeing unparalled opportunities. Sooner than we think we will be carrying out extraordinarily complex calculations on structures that early generations would have thought impossible....'

David's attention starts to drift.

We.

Us.

Our.

With a start, he realises that Morgan Lloyd, three seats to the right, is observing him. Uncomfortable, David flushes, looks away.

The speakers have come from universities, research teams, institutes and professional bodies, consultancies, contractors and government agencies. Britain, Italy, the DDR, Switzerland, Poland, France, West Germany, Japan, the Antipodes, the US of mighty A. Two are from Czechoslovakia and that makes David think, with a pang, of Georgie. He is the only Irish representative.

The coffee break is full of conversation. The morning had been well planned, each topic seguing into the next, designed to provoke debate. David hovers near the refreshments table, pretending to read a poster on the wall. It's in German, too complicated for him to follow. Behind him, he can hear Stephen Flitch holding forth about the limitations of graphics capabilities while someone from California enthuses about a new type of pointing device designed to mirror the human kinaesthetic. The Californian will be presenting that afternoon on the same subject. David wonders why he doesn't just save it. Then he thinks of his own talk the next morning, and his head begins to pound again.

A hand on his shoulder. He jumps, spilling his coffee.

'Sorry, David.' Morgan Lloyd is behind him, along with the slender Asian from the bus. 'Just wondered if you'd met Mike Ai yet?'

'Oh,' says David. 'Yes. Well, sort of.'

'Mike's from the Hong Kong office. He was on the team who recommended the recent transport upgrade over there. He's now one of the consultants for the metro.'

They shake hands. 'So how's that going?' says David.

'Good.' Mike Ai nods. 'On track.'

They laugh.

'We expect to be open for business the year after next.'

'Hong Kong is where it's, as they say, "happening", David,' says Lloyd.

'So little space. All we can do is go up.' Mike Ai gestures to the ceiling.

'Speaking of which,' Lloyd glances at David, 'I believe the embargo on the bank has been lifted. Arthur must be happy about that.'

The thumping in David's head gets louder. 'Well. We've had to, eh, compromise. But better that than, you know. Pulling the whole thing down.'

Mike Ai is looking puzzled.

'They had a problem,' says Morgan. 'Someone had a bone to pick with the architect.'

'Oh.' Mike Ai makes a face. 'Architects.'

A priest, a lawyer and an engineer are in jail awaiting execution. On the first day, the executioner leads the priest to the gallows. Nothing happens; the trap doesn't work, the priest doesn't hang. The priest claims divine intervention and says it would be a sin to try to hang him again. The jailers, fearing God, release him. Next day, they try to hang the lawyer but again, nothing happens. The lawyer claims double jeopardy and says it would be illegal to try to hang him again. The jailers, fearing the Law, let him go. On the third day, they lead the engineer to the platform. He stands there for a minute looking.

'Ah,' he says. 'I can see what your problem is.'

It's an old joke, the engineer willing to Build his Own Grave, and familiar to most of the audience, but they still laugh. Morgan Lloyd has them in the palm of his hand. Didn't I tell that one recently, thinks David. Then realises that he's still laughing, but everyone else has stopped.

They take the lift back down to the ground floor, where lunch is being served in a glass extension that reminds David of a fishtank. It is a buffet; a choice between one of two hot meals or a cold plate with meat and salad. David, head sizzling from the central heating and too much coffee, chooses the salad.

'Do you mind?' says Mike Ai, indicating the seat beside him.

Stephen Flitch is at the next table, arguing about politics with a group of academics from the States and two local PhD students. 'It's a travesty.' He's talking about the North. 'We should have acted sooner. Sent in the troops as soon as we bloody could— Excuse my language. But make no bones about it, it's one thing banging on about civil rights. Killing innocent people, though—'

One of the PhD students begins to argue back. 'But you must understand the roots, please. My generation, we were not spoken to. The war, our parents told us nothing. It was disremembered. How can you fix the problem if you bury the causes? Those on the left opened the grave, brought the bodies to light. It was good—'

'Lad, you can try to argue black is white but—'

'I am looking forward to your presentation,' says Mike Ai.

David looks up. 'Sorry?'

'The ill-conditioned problem. I'm interested to hear how you managed to contain it.'

'Oh. I. Wouldn't call it containing. More like….' He struggles. 'Trying to get a, um. Picture of it?'

Mike Ai nods, cutting his meat into small, precise pieces.

While he's in one of the cubicles in the gleaming new bathroom, he overhears them. Two men from one of the firm's English offices, talking about him. One sounds like Stephen Flitch, but he's not sure. It's hard to tell with all the other noises. Water running, hand-dryers howling, the gurgling of a new, German building. This is what he hears, what he thinks he hears:

the obvious choice shoo-in not just because of the wife you know terrible business poor sod or even this yes of course morgan's new pet hah say no more lyons will want to nip that in the bud but far better choice than down to the architect mr you know flash o bockley good word left right and friends in high places not just because of the wife you know rumour has it terrible business poor sod—

The cubicle door clangs behind him. He sees their heads turn, doesn't look back.

The panic. Always the panic. He is shivering, the pale Munich sky a freezing blue weight above him. The city is full of traffic and people, too full, but everything feels noiseless, farther away than it should. His eyes are hurting again; he can barely see.

Something calls to him across the street. A green neon blur. A chemist? David takes a chance, braves the traffic. Forgets what direction to look. Hears beeping, swearing, but somehow keeps going, gets across, enters the pharmacy. A young woman is behind the counter. She is wearing heavy brown-framed spectacles; that's all he notices. She can't speak English and her German is incomprehensible, thick with what David guesses is a Bavarian dialect. She realises he is lost, slows down.

Uh. *Bitte. Bitte.* Please. Please.

He squeezes out bits of German, trying to recall what he learnt from his phrasebook. She nods, somehow manages to understand. She opens a drawer, wraps the aspirin in a green paper bag and passes it to him.

'*Wollen Sie ein Bisschen Wasser?*'

Water? Does he look that ill? '*Um* – yes. *Ja. Ja, bitte.*'

She disappears into the back of the shop and he tears open the packet. She returns, hands him a glass. He sips, swallowing the aspirin. Thank you, kind girl, he wants to say, but can't find the words.

As he leaves the chemist, he feels the bitterness of the aspirin coating his mouth. Please God, he finds himself praying, make it work. He needs rid of that awful pain in his head, that musky stink that's been in his nose since he woke. If he doesn't get rid of them, he'll go mad. He knows this as surely as he knows his own name. Tiny changes in chemistry, big changes on the outside. The clock tower over the main entrance to the university chimes. Forty-five minutes left before the second session starts. *Networking time,* Fuchs calls it.

He stalls, insubstantial again, sickened by that. Movement catches his eye. An olive-skinned man in overalls is scrubbing at a wall, removing a poster.

It's the same type as the posters the people protesting outside the newspaper building were carrying that morning. The brush scrapes at the faces of the dead and incarcerated, removing them in bits and pieces like stubborn nail varnish.

David thinks of Aisling's fingernails, ten days ago, before they closed the coffin lid. Someone had removed the varnish she'd worn right until the end. Her nails looked wrong without it, too naked and grey against the white satin lining, the jet rosary beads that her mother had got blessed specially and wound around her wrists, forcing her daughter's fingers into a final clasp of prayer against the mutter of the sorrowful mysteries.

Where did you go, Ash?

The man in the overalls has stopped scrubbing. He is looking at David, a question forming in his face.

Making some animal noise he doesn't recognise, David wrenches himself away.

He is rushing. He has no idea where he's going. Just away. Past the sixties' towers, the five-story shopping centre, into what looks like the older part of town. Beer-kellers, restaurants offering schnitzel, wurst and sauerkraut, bookshops, ticky-tacky purveyors of lederhosen and pewter steins. Tourists and shopping. Women everywhere, cramming his vision like a reproach. He doesn't think he's ever seen so many before in the one place wearing such heavy make-up, such tight trousers, carrying so many bags. If it wasn't for the bags, he thinks, they could be prostitutes. The thought makes him want to laugh, crass, like a schoolboy. He forces it down. Food halls, clothes shops, a record store. The crowds swarm, then clear, revealing a cobbled square. At its back is a cathedral, its twin domed towers, half a foot in the difference, jabbing at the sky. A name from the guidebook pops into David's head. *Frauenkirche.* He looks up, craning his neck.

The women's church. Frailty, thy name is—

Pain stabs his eyes. Black dots dance before him; grow, coalesce, fragment. The compulsion: Where's Georgie? He needs to phone home—

He turns. A bollard crashes into him, bashing his thigh. He staggers, reaches, finds a lamppost. Clings to it, hyperventilating. His legs are shaking. His teeth are clenched. He gasps; thinking, if he could see himself from the outside he'd be reminded of someone, but he doesn't know who. His father? Georgie? The thought makes the dots dance faster. He tries to unclench his teeth but they don't budge. He realises they've been clenched for weeks. No,

months. No. Years. How ridiculous he must have looked, smiling at everyone
for the last two years through clenched teeth. Why didn't anyone say anything?
Why didn't Georgie? Or Donnacha? You fucking panic. How ridiculous he
must have looked this morning – what a hoot – to that international family
of engineers, as claustrophobic and controlling in their petty hierarchies as
the Tipperary town he ran from in 1955. How stupid he must have seemed
to Morgan Lloyd and Mike Ai, and to Stephen Flitch, he of the unshakeable
convictions, and that other unnamed engineer in the toilet who knows as
little, and as much, or maybe more than he does.

He forces his jaw open. Air floods his mouth. He gulps. The pounding in
his head begins to decelerate. The musky smell is back.

'Poppa?'

He looks up. Helena, the American woman who shared his table at
breakfast, is standing twenty yards away, her back to him; hands on her lime-
green hips, facing the cathedral doors.

'Come on. Pop.' Her voice is plaintive. Against the lime-green, the lines of
her underwear stand out like sine waves. 'We gotta....'

In the gloom, David makes out a small figure, stooped like a question
mark, placing his foot on the Devil's Step.

'Poppa, we'll miss the train....'

Helena not-of-Troy bends towards her father, hands on her hips,
imploring.

Later he might understand it as this: some subliminal connection
between repressing root causes, degeneration and protest. Right in that
moment, though, all that goes through his mind is a string of phrases, half-
remembered from his guidebook.

It was the first; the model, built in 1933. Work makes you free.

Structural engineering is the art of designing structures to withstand loads
that we cannot predict, using materials whose properties we cannot measure,
by methods of analysis that we cannot prove, and to do so in a manner that
ensures that the public and client are ignorant of our shortcomings.

Did you always want to be an engineer, Davey?

In the autumn of 1942, when they realised his mother's illness was there
to stay, David lay in bed, phlegm building at the bottom of his lungs, and gazed
at her presents, the grotesque medical textbooks ordered up from Dublin.
One afternoon, he turned a page and found a diagram of a skeleton and it was

then – Eureka! like that poor foolish Knight in the library book that Georgie used to love, King Arthur's scrawny little Parzival, the one who saw the Grail – that he got his first inkling. To begin with, the skulls frightened him; then he realised they were only stripped-back versions of his own head: no gooey, putrefying flesh, no slimy, mysterious, vulnerable grey matter. He counted up the vertebrae on each diagram and was intrigued to find that they added up to the knobbly bits on his own back. But what was it, this interconnection of knobbles? What did it do? If you didn't have one, what would happen? He had no words for what he was learning. It didn't matter. Do you need words for things like that? He started carrying out tests. Do skulls always balance on backbones in the same way? Do all people have the same things in their knees? What would happen if you took – say – this bone away, and replaced it with something else? He would creep out of bed, push his feet onto tippy-toes, crane his neck, bend and straighten his elbows, analysing each movement. At this point easy; at this hard. Load and stress. Degrees of freedom. *Structure.* He forced his fingers back to the place where they couldn't bend any more and wondered what a break might sound like.

At night, he started to dream of them: the bones from his mother's books turning shiny as steel, dancing foxtrots with each other, merging into new, unimaginable constructions. During the dank, wheezy daytimes, he began to make his own models, using matchsticks and pencil nubs and pebbles and bits of Meccano poached for him by his confidante and oppressor, his oldest sister, Maura. How aborbing it was, how difficult to get right. Warp and torque and bend and thicken. Add, stiffen, make elastic, more supple, less plastic, more robust. Could you, he wondered, ever make a box that would hold a person's very – whatchamacallit, who they were, their very self – in it?

In 1963, that day on the bank of the canal, he evaded Aisling's question. Four years later, the evening he learnt he was going to be a father, she laughed when he started to answer – You, a doctor? So he shut her out.

Now, on his way to the death camp, he finds himself offering her – his memory of her – not a different answer, but a continuation, as if he has begun to travel back through the shells of dissimulation to something that might, at least, approach a truth.

Always want to be an engineer? No. He first saw the Grail when he was six, though it took him years more to figure out what he was looking at.

Countryside flashes past. Red roofs, sandy buildings, neat fields. Crows. Trees, their branches emerging from tattered gold sleeves.

David's palms are sweating. A low excitation is bubbling in the pit of his stomach, an echo of that strange weightless sensation he felt on waking. He knows the feeling is completely inappropriate, given where he's going, given everything. But that just makes it worse, like trying to bite back laughter in school, or at Mass, or in your own sitting room, where people are gathered like vultures around the funeral meats.

The woman across from him has been peeling an orange. The discarded peel lies in spirals on a paper napkin, a pocked miniature tower of Babel. She separates the fruit, pops a segment sideways between her teeth. Her lips spread, wrapping the fruit in a bizarre smile. David fights the urge to smile back, the more dangerous impulse – where did this come from? – to tell her a joke.

Hey, German lady, did you hear about the Cork mother? Help, help, she screams. My son is drowning. My son the Engineer.

The friendly old man at the gate tells him he is just in time. They will be the last tour of the day. Four people only.

David counts two young women who sound Australian, and a thin, middle-aged man, slightly effeminate, with dyed black hair and a bushy moustache. He looks around again, but Helena and Poppa are nowhere to be seen. He is surprised by his own disappointment. They weren't on the train. What had he expected?

'Follow me, please,' says the guide.

They step through. Narrow avenues. Shadows and lowness. Coils of snaggle-toothed wire against a pale sky. Colours of earth; colours of death.

'It was in 1968 that the memorial site was built. The committee was set up after the War, and it took time to agree on the protocols. The camp was, of course, built initially for political prisoners. Röhm—'

'Who?' says one of the young Australians.

'Ernst Röhm,' says the guide. 'He set up the SA, better known as the Brownshirts, and was assassinated in 1934, on the Night of the Long Knives. There were rumours that he was a homosexual—'

morgan's new pet hah say no more

David flicks the thought away.

'—but, really, it was as a political opponent that he was targeted. His men were interned here, then later, others, from Austria, Sudetenland, which is now of course Czechoslovakia, then, after the War, the Poles. After the liberation, Dachau was used for years by the Allies. Many people came and stayed. Refugees from the *Flucht*, the—'

'Flood?' asks the Australian.

'Flight,' says David, surprising them all.

'Exactly.' The guide nods in something like approval. 'But by then, of course, the camp was a sanctuary. Unlike the Nazitime, which is the time of the collective guilt, the time we now choose not to forget.'

Schubraum. The guide waves his hands, trying to find the word. 'Pushing-space. Like you push a, you know, drawer, into a chest.'

Shunt. The word rises into David's mouth; stays there, sour.

On each side of the room, between the pillars, are long tables. These, the guide explains, were where the prisoners had to place their possessions: clothes, jewellery, anything they'd brought with them was taken, leaving them naked, ready for the shearing, the divesting of names, the allocation of numbers. David thinks about those multiple eradications. One second you're a person with an identity; intact on the outside, smooth as an egg – look, here I am, my clothes, my stuff, my family, tell you, the world, what I am, consistent, a thing that makes sense – but on the inside ruptured, like everyone else, with contradictions. Your ceaseless battles with your own failings, your needs to prove, your hopeless efforts to be a better father, a better husband, a better self. The next second it's been reversed. Your private fault lines are there for everyone to see – your warts, your veins, your gammy leg, your boils, your hidden creases – while the only thing that makes you you, that thread of consciousness, that field of electrical activity, the only thing that endures from moment to moment, has been shoved somewhere else, deep inside. Invisible, intangible, hardly there. An event horizon of being – blink and you'll miss it – teetering forever on the edge of oblivion.

His eyes are drawn to the writing on the wall behind the tables. Double lines, like symbols on sheets of music. Confident swerves where the block of type changes direction. A beautiful script, he thinks first. Then he understands what it says.

Rauchen verboten. No Smoking.

Déjà vu. Cold. Soiled. Shivering. That weightless, floating feeling.

a sense of something in him separating, missing, left behind—

o ▪ o ▪ o ▪ o

His vision blanks. What— Then it's back and he realises rage is surging in him. No smoking? Is this how it begins? Annihilation? With a single small, apparently civilised request?

'Sir?' calls the guide. 'We are over.'

David looks down. His hands are fists. No, he wants to say. Wait. Sorry. I have something I need to find here, something I lost and have to bring home—

But the moment is gone, and he is back in the leaden chambers of his body, following the group out the door. It is only then, as they leave the grim little room, *Rauchen verboten* flashing in the corner of his eye, that David recognises it, the smell that's been haunting him since he woke.

By the end of August, the last of his compartments had disappeared. Aisling was in the hospice. That wasn't something that could be hidden away or not spoken about.

Art told Morgan straightaway, though David had asked him to wait. That evening, Morgan phoned him at the office. Everybody else had gone home. There were only the birds, singing the last of their summer songs on the beautiful beech tree outside his window. Under the long-distance crackle, David heard a delicate undertone of worry in Morgan's musical Marcher-lands voice.

I can let Klaus know, David. If you want. It's really, you know. Up to you. He will understand, of course. In the greater scheme of things, none of this is....

The line faded.

Important, thought David.

Although— The line was back. One never knows, of course, what one is capable of.

She started going downhill – properly downhill, the real thing – the day Georgie began at the new school. The school Jan had plagued them so much about the year before, those hellish five months when Aisling had railed at the cancer for coming back, into her breasts and her lungs, because she didn't deserve it, she'd done nothing to be punished like that. Railed at him, David, for not being there, for not understanding, because only Jan understood, only Jan could help.

That evening, Georgie had been badly out of sorts. Christ, thought David, doubt starting to gnaw at him. He should have stuck to his guns. That school had been a terrible idea. Something savage yawned inside him, began to stretch its claws. The nuns rang shortly after Lotte had left. As soon as David hung up, he went upstairs and stood outside Georgie's door. The landing smelt of chip fat; he would remember that for years. He wanted to knock, but what could he say? He wanted to hold his son, drink up his scent, crush him to his chest, absorb him into his own body, keep him safe there. Tell him: I know, I know, old chap, but I'm here. But what good would that do? Then Mrs Lynch arrived, but instead of heading for the car, David found himself swerving right, straight up Joanie Flynn's path and onto her doorstep.

Year of the Heatwave (End of Summer): The Ill-Conditioned Analysis (3) / The Asked Question

Oh, God, David. Joanie's face went pale. Is Aisling—

Who did you see? The words bursting out of him.

Sorry?

That day in March, the day I came home early to bring Ash to the consultant.

I don't. David—

I caught you on the step.

Caught. Wrong word.

He batted it away. You've seen things. You said someone was visiting Ash. That day. You thought I was there. At home. Already. A man? Was that why you were surprised. Who was it?

I…. She looked frightened. Nobody.

Was it him? My – he fought to get the word out – my friend? The big man? The one who used to come up for dinner here all the time with his wife, the American? Was that the first time—

Jesus, David. Calm down, it's—

When did it start?

It was— David. Nothing. Nobody. There was no one there, just— Listen, you're upset. In shock. Nobody would blame you. Come in for a cup of tea—

He said something that wasn't words, jumped into the car and drove down to the crescent. Sat in the driver's seat, stewing, watching the lights go on in the Ó Buachallas' mansion. He punched the steering wheel, heard a crack; imagined the broken thing his head. Pictured his brain, mangled by suspicion, oozing out onto the seat leather.

What do you do with that?

Bite down, bury it deep. Stick it in the shunt-room, turn the key and pray that nobody remembers there's a body in there.

By autumn, she was barely present. Occasionally, a spark, mainly around Georgie. *Have you got any of your drawings for me, pet?* You know he doesn't. *You know I don't.* Any time David took her hand, her eyes would flicker.

Sometimes she would flinch, twitching him off. Sometimes dig her nails into his skin, as if to say, *Wait. I have something to say.* He didn't know which was worse. Mostly, she just seemed puzzled when she looked at him. As if trying, through the morphine, to remember something that had once been painful, but was no longer important, something they had both forgotten long ago.

The smoke, rising.

Streaking clouds are front-crawling across the cold, soured-milk sky. The sun is on its way down over the long low shapes of the killing chambers. The tall trees lining the avenue have turned colour. It's an unspectacular sight. The leaves are dull colours, crisped at the edges. As David watches, he sees a beige shape fall from a branch, followed by another. Soft, erratic movements, like snow.

He walks the narrow path down to the town and the train station. As he walks, he thinks of the SS barracks, now turned into classrooms. Of Nandor Glid's sculpture for the forgotten, the political prisoners. A screen of barbed-wire geometry; people contorted into screaming triangles. He thinks of his own work, his models for the Boyne Bridge, those finite triangular elements stretched past the point of usability.

When he was a boy he couldn't understand why, every Sunday night – the only night his father didn't work in the bar – his mother used to spend half an hour washing her husband's feet. His sisters said it was to stop him from going out for the *poitín*, but David was baffled as he watched the ritual. How could a woman be so tender with a man who had broken the lock of her bedroom door in a rage? Years later, as a young father himself, he used to love watching Aisling and Georgie at bath time. He would lean against the bathroom door and look in as his wife covered their son with suds, ruffled his hair, rinsed him off.

Eskimo kiss, sweetheart, she'd say, and rub Georgie's nose with her own.

Mine, David would think, with a fierceness that staggered him.

The ill-conditioned problem: without enough information, a small error in input leads to an avalanche of error. Take, for example, a splinter in a bedroom door: unless you've witnessed the act of splintering, how can you say that it's not just wear and tear? That it's an indication of anything resembling frustration, much less a pattern of force in a marital bed?

Take a neighbour's statement:

I just saw… said Joanie Flynn that blustery March afternoon an hour before the doctors would hand Aisling her death sentence. That was all Joanie said. Then she stopped. She could have *just seen* anything. When David turned to look, he *saw* nothing. No broad architect's back, no mane of black hair. The only thing he registered were footsteps, as whoever it was disappeared around the corner, but that wasn't *seeing*.

Words are words and sometimes they're hard to understand, especially when you're in a strange, foreign, busy building. Who is to say that what he heard in the toilets wasn't just hearsay? Who is to say that anyone, least of all Donnacha Ó Buachalla, has been using his influence to nudge a directorship towards a man he once called his friend? And even if he has, who is to say he's been doing it out of anything other than the memory of that friendship?

The train station is empty. David feels chilly again. His eyes are blurring. It is cold over here, he tells himself. He is in Germany. He is in shock. He is tired.

'You have a message, Herr Madden,' says the receptionist, giving him a folded piece of paper. 'Herr Lloyd came by, said it was very important you received this. Also, this.' She hands him his guidebook. 'A lady brought it to the desk this morning. She told us you had forgotten it at breakfast.'

'Thank you.' David skims through Morgan's note, then asks if he can use the telephone in the lobby.

When he gets through to home, Bridget answers. Georgie's asleep, she tells him. Dead to the world. Good as gold, not a bother. Playing on his own, mainly, outside, the usual stuff, brings a ball, comes in for his supper. Had a bit of a temperature last night but he's grand now. Eating. Oh my God. Eating like a horse. He's found a new friend.

'Oh?' says David, surprised.

'At school. William something, he's always talking about him.'

'Oh.' David has encountered William Robinson. He didn't think Georgie liked him.

'Your boss dropped in, Davey. Lovely man. Spoke well of you, actually.' She lays on the surprise, makes sure he hears it. 'Said to tell you if there's anything he can do, they're all thinking of you. And the grandparents, they've been—'

'Right,' says David, not able for any of that now. 'I'll be back early, tomorrow night. I'm coming home straight after my talk. I changed my flight.'

A sharp intake. Then she's on the offensive, like he expected. 'Ah, Davey, no. You know, Maura and I and Eileen, we agreed the little fella needed—'

He cuts her off. 'Thanks Bridgie. Best though, if you head back at the weekend. Ye're alright for food?'

She says nothing.

He feels the compulsion stir again. 'Is Georgie—' He stops, wills it down. 'Tell him I'll be home early, will you? I want him to know.'

She grunts an assent and hangs up.

He glances again at Morgan's note. An invitation to dinner that evening. Just four of them: Morgan, Klaus Fuchs, Mike Ai from Hong Kong and David. *Only, of course, if it suits.* No mention of Stephen Flitch, or anyone else from the firm.

Four days in and he'd thought: Christ, is this the best I can do? Bridget snoring in Georgie's room, Georgie on a camp bed. The burnt toast, Georgie listless and unresponsive. The digs at breakfast, about boys needing shorter haircuts and what would our daddy have said about his only grandchild going to a Protestant school, and a mixed one at that, with girls and Jews and God knows what. And all the time, hammering away in David's mind, the calculations: how much a live-in housekeeper would cost and directorships and three offspring against one, two already in university, and Niall Rourke blustering on about how much extra responsibility could take out of a man if he wasn't up to it, and O'Hanlon mentioning articles in the *New Scientist*. You know, Mr Madden, they've just found out living with stress for protracted periods can impair the nervous system, affect the judgement and everything....

One can be surprised by what one is capable of. Morgan, he'd said, his voice too airy and casual, like an actor reciting lines. Tell Herr Fuchs to count me in.

Leverage, he'd imagined. *A man at the forefront.* Yet all he'd done since he'd got here was flee. He remembers the fat salesman at the airport with his bursting briefcase. His own reaction: get me out of here. What was that word Mike Ai had used at lunch? *Containing.* Better to stay where you are and contain, surely, than to waste your life spilling fear out of every pore, fleeing from what's in front of you out of some misguided instinct that there is a better answer to it all somewhere else?

The only thing that matters now is Georgie. He thinks of his son in the church, gripping his arm.

Triangles, the engineer's friend; strongest of strong structures.

He takes a breath, dials.

'Hello?' On the other end of the phone, Lotte sounds young, as young as he'd thought she was the first time he'd met her. He almost puts the phone back.

'Ah,' he says. 'Didn't know I'd, eh— It's David. David Madden.'

A nervous girl, he'd thought the first time he'd seen her. Cagey, hiding something, but with a habit of talking over people when she was ill at ease. The only time she didn't was after the funeral, when they were smoking her illegal marijuana cigarette; hiding in the parched buddleia away from the other mourners, sitting together in tense silence and bursts of giggles, the musky smell of her joint rising around them. It had taken David a while to relax; too anxious listening out for other people. The randy cousins with their bottom-pinching fingers and worried Maura and his other sisters and Aisling's angry, cheated parents. They had stared at him all through the funeral, the Bells, *it's your fault* lurching from their eyes, and though he knows that's rubbish, that cancer is just cancer, a set of miscreant cells multiplying without warning, not anything to do with how well one person loves, or doesn't love, another, still, given how everything had gone between himself and Ash, he couldn't blame them. As for the grave, there was nothing he could have done about it; he'd explained, countless times, it had to be that way for Georgie. His son needed somewhere safe where he could visit his mother or – he didn't say this: whatever was left of her – somewhere close, not off in an unreachable, dangerous part of the country that wasn't really their country at all. He knew Annie would never forgive him for that, but: *Fuck you*, he'd wanted to say, *there's enough I'm carrying unforgiven without adding you to it*. At the house, Joanie Flynn kept hovering, gee-eyed on gin. Oh David, I wish I could have helped, you know, said something earlier— Shut up, you useless bitch, he thought. Said instead: Ah, Joanie, you're very good. Have another drink, Bridget will look after you. Fussy adenoidal Mrs Lynch starting to bang on about kids making noise down the lane. And all the time, that pair. Jan coming too close, cloying, clinging, trying to hug him, I really loved Aisling, you know, I really did. Donnacha crashing around the kitchen like a bear, opening presses, grabbing a whiskey bottle. Daithí! *Cá bhfuil mo chara?* Where's my pal? Come to me, my friend, so we can drown our sorrow.

He'd fled into the garden, hidden between the shed and the buddleia like a child. That was where she'd found him.

Oh, she said. Anyone else might have said sorry. An awkward little silence. He was the one who broke it, surprising himself. So what are you hiding, Lotte?

She started, shocked almost. Then laughed, pulled out her pouch. Guilty as charged. A small hesitation: Would you like some? I know it's *verboten*, Aisling hated the habit, but—

Go on, he said. Let's break all the rules.

They huddled in the corner, giggling uncontrollably – wrong, so wrong – like two idiotic schoolkids on the mitch. At one point, during a taut, silent hiatus, he heard his mother begin to croon and his body flooded with fear. Sick in case Jan would hear too, butt in with one of her sweeping statements, upset Georgie. Hush, he prayed, but his mother didn't. Instead her voice rose, calling for her grandchild. *Come here, alanna. Oh, aren't you the beautiful little thing, will I teach you to dance, a stór, so you can dance with all the boys, come on, alanna, dance, aren't you the little beauty, who'd have thought, Davey, you'd have been able to make such a dote—*

She can see under the surface, your mum, Lotte said. Serious suddenly, and for a moment, she'd seemed unbearably sad. David had nodded, though he normally hated that kind of talk. *When I was a lad, she used to say she could see right through me, into the valley of my heart.* Had he said that aloud?

'David?'

'Sorry,' he says now, gathering himself. 'Look, I know it's, eh, been a bit frantic....'

Frantic?

'And with the, eh, my, you know, his aunts in place....'

In place?

'Yes—'

'Thing is, he needs, eh, continuity. You know, time to just—'

settle

'And eh, good news, you see, there's em, something coming up for me at work, a promotion, you know, nothing definite, but, eh—'

'David—'

He keeps going, right through her, afraid that if he doesn't, he'll change his mind. 'Anyway, Georgie would be thrilled if you collected him after school on Monday, like usual.'

Thrilled?

A flash thought; the same one he'd had on the bus that morning, staring out the window at the snaggle-toothed girl. *No. Lotte is—*

Stop. He forces his attention back to the phone.

Silence, and he's messed it up, he's sure of it.

'Oh,' she says. 'Okay, then.'

He hears his own breath let out. He thinks he says Thank You, or Great, or something, and she says You're Welcome, or It's Fine, then one or the other of them hangs up.

As he crosses the lobby, the receptionist glances up. She is about to call to him when the doors of the hotel open, releasing a new wave of guests. The receptionist puts away David's guidebook, with the bright purple American notepaper peeking out from under its cover, and polishes her *Guten Abend* smile.

A shower, a shave, a change of tie.

David glances up at his reflection. Something feels strange. He turns his head, half-expecting to see another version of himself – that bathrobed two-dimensional ghost – hovering beside him above the tiled floor. Then he realises that what is strange is that his headache has gone, though he can't remember when it stopped.

The woman's leopardskin-print top is straining against her breasts, her legs in their stockings are sinewy and long. When they get into the room, he sees, through his drunken stupor, that she's about fifteen years older than he'd thought.

She presses a switch with her shoulder. The overhead light flicks off.

'*Also, jetzt, Jungs*.' Now, Boy.

Her cleavage is freckled, her skin tanned. She is Moravian, she'd explained on the street – why, he can't remember; did he ask her? She said her parents came to Munich during the Flight. They'd stayed in the camp, in Dachau, then moved to the city. Nowhere else for them to go. They never felt fully German, she said, and laughed. '*Keine Reichsdeutsch*.'

Funny, he thought. Would have said, only he didn't want to talk about Lotte behind her back, spilling what she'd started to tell him in the garden before Maura interrupted them: *I know a girl from Bohemia. At least her mother was. She doesn't talk about it much....*

'Okay?' The woman's fingers have stopped tugging. She is looking at him.

He grunts. Pushes her head down, feels her mouth close around him, her lips move, the helmet press against her soft palate. Through the curtains the neon blinks on and off. He wonders what time it is. They left the restaurant before midnight, then he and Mike went for one before he started the real drinking, on his own. One bar, two, maybe three....

He feels her tongue search, probe, then plunge. He feels his behind grate against the nylon bedclothes, his sweat trickle between his shoulderblades. I'm sorry, he wants to say. I'm really sorry. But all he feels is—

The ash, falling.

—absolute nothing.

Lognote # 6

Our next Exhibit, while not the most volatile in our collection, has been known to evoke tricky maternal associations for some visitors, so please take care when approaching it. An inventory, filled in by hand on what appears to be a stained and rather grubby official form entitled '*Freiwild – Baggage Allowance*'. Visitors may be interested to know that '*Freiwild*' means literally 'fair game' and was a term used to describe German women during the liberation.[1] Beneath the inventory is a placard:

Placard

Most of the Baggage detailed above was taken by German women during that stage of the liberation of Czechoslovakia traditionally known as the 'wild' expulsions (May–August 1945).[2] However, be aware that Inventory Forms such as this were never filled in by any administrative body of any ethnicity/nationality to account for Baggage taken. Perhaps it is therefore reasonable to wonder whether such Baggage ever actually existed in the first place?

---

[1] A.k.a. 'expulsion' or 'purge'. Or, more recently, 'ethnic cleansing' (see Naimark, 2001), although we agree that the use of the term in this context does raise some tricky questions. See, if/when we get there, *Lognote # 8* for a more detailed discussion.

[2] The 'wild' expulsions were led in some regions by the Czechs (the Revolutionary Guard a.k.a. *Revoluční Garda* or the special police a.k.a. *Sbor Národní Bezpečnosti*) and in others by the Red Guard (Russian Army). According to Naimark (2001), the Czechs' speciality was plunder and violence, while the Red Army, as in other German-populated areas, favoured rape and pillage. It is debatable to what extent the brutality experienced during the 'wild expulsions' was a result of popular fury (the traditional interpretation) and to what extent it was deliberately orchestrated by the military (new or 'heretical' interpretations; see Gerlach, 2002).

Most curious feature

Above the inventory is a three-dimensional visual aid, suspended by what looks like a noose. The aid is a plastic doll, c.40cm tall, with shorn hair, designed to help you learn anatomy and politics in one. Please feel free to 'play' with it by touching it on various parts of its body. A scream – ! – it's fine, visitors, just our little joke! After all, she *is* 'Fair Game' – will let you know if you've struck gold!

Freiwild Baggage Inventory

- Scars on wrists from manacles, ropes, chains, cords, gripped fingers
- Whip-marks on back, chest, thighs, neck, face, breasts, feet, arms and so on
- Bleeding scalp, scars, scabs on head and face and general loss of feminine loveliness from shearing of hair by bayonets
- Bruises from stonings
- Broken and lost teeth
- Broken legs and arms
- Broken spinal columns from hangings
- Broken nails from attempting to wash swastika out of clothes
- Chafed skin on forehead from daubing of letter 'N' or swastika
- Nasal irritation from the smoke from 'human torches' (i.e. people hung by their heels on trees or lampposts, doused in petrol and set alight; common in Prague)
- Eye irritations from smoke (see above)
- Sore throat from shouting 'we are Hitler-whores'
- Sore ears from the sound of cheering, jeering, catcalls and applause
- Sore eyes at the sight of the letter 'N' (N for *Němec* = German; conveniently, N for Nazi = German also)
- Lost limbs and ripped guts from being pulled apart by dray horses
- Goosepimples from stripping off clothes
- Muscular tiredness from walking long distances, i.e. to a camp or the border
- Hunger
- Pains from dysentery, typhus, hunger
- Nausea and sickness from eating human excrement
- Sore nose from smell of urine in latrine where our babies were drowned
- Sore throat from crying
- Sore mind from trying to think ahead
- Sore neck from keeping head down

Freiwild Baggage Inventory (cont.)

- Sore face from having doors of restaurants, shops, taverns, hotels slammed in it
- Sore tongue from making friends with nice Russian soldier who will protect us from the Czechs
- Sore nostrils from making snuffling sound because we are 'pigs'
- Sore conscience?
- Sore head thinking of Theresienstadt and Lidice?
- Sore back from carrying all our worldly possessions
- Sickness in the belly, distension, waters breaking, weakening of teeth and cramps from giving birth to rape-children
- Scabs on feet from being stripped of shoes and stockings
- Ash dust from burning of homes, possessions, neighbours and all that is familiar
- Unusable/meaningless wedding rings following the beatings, shootings, killings and maimings of husbands, fathers, lovers
- Sore vaginas/anal cavities/mouths from multiple and mass rape
- Slicing apart of vaginas from having to sit on sharp instruments, e.g. an SA dagger*
- Sore lungs from holding breath under the surface of the Elbe to avoid potshots
- Rust on pram structure, rotting leather, mouldy skin, distended flesh and no eyes because the fish ate them after we were thrown with our babies into the Elbe at Aussig (now Ústí nad Labem) to the sound of cheering (see sore ears, above)

---

* Caveat: only one incident of this type was recorded and the dagger was stuck in the snatch of an SS member so she probably deserved it, the Hitler-whore.[3]

---

[3] This caveatical footnote (not to be confused with the *Wunderkammer*'s own Footnotes) is, unlike the handwritten entries on the form, in type. This gives it the quality of an 'official' comment. Our technical team has not yet established whether it was added by the person/people who never filled out the form – or if it belongs to the fabric of the form itself, an intrinsic strand in the weave of (non-)documentation about these events. A Curious Thought, indeed.

Stollen

🕐

She is in a dark space, full of corridors, feeling her way through strips of Super 8 which are hanging from some terribly high point above her. Far behind, she can hear the roar of the ocean. Someone is coughing. Aisling? No. Silly. She is looking for something, but she doesn't know what. The film strips are long, tangled, cobwebby. Too soft for film. They feel like hair, or wool. As she touches one, it changes, in that dream-way, weaving itself into indecipherable words and phrases. Coiling double helices broken down into nonsense.

She is seventeen. She is in a white space and nothing is there with her. Something should be there, but the walls and floor are pale and smooth, empty, like the inside of a gallery, or an egg. *Raum*, she thinks, and thinks it in its double, German sense: chamber + empty space. Is this where she'll go when she dies? Or is it where she's come from? Maybe the thing she's looking for is the thing that should be inside the egg.

The coughing gets louder. She needs to pee. Is this in her dream? Is it real?

Her body twitches. The cougher splutters.

Now she is at a door. It smells of beer, sweat, piss and blood. It smells of Andrew and the things he collected from himself and Sybille, the things they turned into art, his Anti-Fascist Cabinet of Curiosities, the things he didn't want Lotte filming because the way she framed her pictures, he said, made them too pretty to make a statement.

A leg stretches in front of the door, blocking her. It has been torn from its owner, separated in what Lotte knows has been an explosion, but it's still alive, like the head of a decapitated chicken. It's ragged and ugly; spurting blood, slick with pus, the toes black and gangrenous. It's Andrew's leg. Or maybe Sybille's. Or perhaps her own.

The leg laughs. Lotte's face flushes. That's because in this dream she doesn't have her own skin; she has Aisling's, fair and freckled. Does that mean she's dead? Is this where people go to, when they die – this antiseptic, putrid museum space?

'You want to go through the door?'

The leg is speaking German, but not as her mother speaks it. It's possibly not German. It might be Dutch.

'Just say, lady. If you want to go, say.'

The leg moves, making a gap. She charges forwards. Something crunches. She fumbles at the handle. She realises she is wearing a tweed coat; 1940s' style, in pink dogstooth pattern. The same colours as a used tampon. As she realises that, that's what the coat becomes. A tampon, bloated with blood. She pushes the handle. Wind blasts in. She steps out. The leg says something.

Close the door, you stupid cunt.

The sea bellows, a dirty black beast rattling against its chains. There is no moon. The deck is a slimy jade green under the lights. The smokestack belches plumes of chalky white. The tips of the waves are grey feathers in the blackness, long ostrich boas where the ship has cut into the sea. The wind pulls at her coat, whips her hair across her face. Her hair is too long. Long red hair, Aisling's hair. She opens her mouth, lets the wind tug at her tongue, pummel her lips. Her chest tightens. Her breath—

She is swaying, balancing in Julia's shoes that are somehow too big for her. She is younger than seventeen; someone – the leg? – has stolen her passport while she was trying to get through the door and she is twelve again.

No.

A man is behind her, his breath harsh against her neck. The Captain—

No.

She is dying – literally? Dying? Then she must be Aisling, except Aisling is already dead – dying to turn and look him in the face but she can't twist her neck. Her vertebrae have fused; she is paralysed, a pillar of salt wedded to the deck of a ship that is going nowhere.

'Andrew?' she calls. 'Ands? *Bish doo dass?*'

She makes a final wrench. Her neck twists. She is looking at—

She sits, gasping for air.

She stretches her neck, examining her skin for traces of a rash. In spite of her hints, he still refuses to shave his beard; she could feel it chafing against her again all through sex. Her neck looks fine, but she squirts Oil of Ulay into her palm and smooths it in, just in case. Putting the top back on the bottle, she looks at her reflection, waiting for the cabinet door to shiver, her twin's ghost to make its presence known.

Nothing.

She pulls the string, snapping out the light.

They've been lovers – is that the correct word? – for about two months. For weeks they circled each other like sharks, him looking, her avoiding, then, one drunken night, stoned and randy after Aisling's funeral – Eros/Thanatos; *quelle surprise* – she made her way up to his flat with a block of hash she'd got from one of her thesis students and a bottle of something rough and that was that. This is the first time she's let him fuck her in her place. Up till now, they've done it in his, under the low ceilings, on his table or spreadeagled over the bath, pushed up against the door, sometimes even on his narrow mattress with the smell of his socks all around them and the ghostly shapes of his drying prints dangling from the washing lines. She has never stayed in his flat; always sneaking out after he's fallen asleep. So far she's been so careful to keep things separate, not let it get messy, keep the fucking zipless. How – why? – did they end up here?

Slivers of memory begin to resurface. Drink, of course. Drink and music. And…. She groans. They had an argument. On the way home. She said something insulting and they had to make up and….

The memories slide away, refusing to coalesce.

She pours herself a glass of water and takes a cautious sip. The air is frigid. Under the false heat of her hangover, her skin is goose-pimpling. An eerie greeny-grey light is seeping through the blinds, as if the world is underwater; as if she, and every other living thing in it, is dead. She frowns. Something is missing, but she doesn't know what.

She leaves the kitchen, steps into the hall, balancing the two glasses of water in the crook of her arm as she kicks the door shut with her foot.

Oh, she said, the first time they did it, the night of Aisling's funeral, staring up at his prints on the washing lines, you take photographs.

And? He sounded defensive.

Just. That's not what I thought.

He became quiet and she thought she'd offended him, but didn't care enough to ask why. Later, when they were fucking again, he brought it up. So what did you think?

What?

What did you think I did?

Oh. A – it sounded stupid, even to her. I call you the Poet.

He laughed, a small sound. Poet.

Sorry.

No. Say it….

Sorry?

Say it. Say it to me.

I. Poet?

No. Say it like you mean it. Like it's my name.

Oh – she rolled her eyes, arched her back. Poet? Oh. Poet. Oh—

File, he said. Fill-eh. It's an Irish word, for bard. Then he laughed again, at some private joke.

She wanted to tell him not to get carried away with illusions of artistry, she'd meant it ironically, but he had his eyes closed and it would have felt unkind to put him straight. That had surprised her, her unwillingness to be seen to wound, still there after everything.

Always the bleeding heart, Lotte.

She didn't ask him anything else about his work; if it was work, and not just a hobby. The sight of his prints strung over her head caught on the back of her throat, stopped her words, her breath, made her itch, yearn to get away. She didn't want to have to look at them, decode light and dark into meaning and affect. Can't you put those somewhere else? she'd said, rather rudely, on the first night. I can't stand that stink. The next time she came up, she discovered, to her surprise, that he'd obliged. One night, he forgot and she hadn't had enough to drink and found herself sucked in, in spite of herself; analysing them, the old, critical cogs beginning to whirr again. He was busy down below, lapping away. They seemed haphazard, she'd thought, a little unfocused: too grimy for a professional snapper, not news enough for a hack. But promising. He'd taken a series of – portraits, she supposed they were; young boys riding piebald ponies on scraps of grey grass near a tower block somewhere beside the airport. Their posture was as defiant as a Mongolian warlord's, but he had found their eyes and made his way in; under the bravado they were full of fear, full of hope. He'd exposed their souls, to her and to anyone else who might look at them.

Care you must take, Lotte. Not let him turn that knack on you.

On the second night, she'd noticed books littering the floor of his flat, lying around like small, explosive conversation pieces. After that, she made sure to get hammered before going up there and once in, scattered her clothes over everything that might have once had meaning for her, blotting out the familiar names, the familiar titles. Mao, Marx, Trotsky, Marcuse, Debord, Adorno, Horkheimer.

Best not register the contents of his life, let them sink in too deeply. Best not let him register the contents of hers.

He calls her by her surname. *Lottee, Lottay, that's way too complicated. Why don't I just call you Evans?* Funny, how a Welsh name had softened things between them, dissolving the barrier of her perceived imperiality like glue in rain. She didn't tell him that the name was false, that it belonged to the Captain. She didn't tell him anything; he didn't ask. They don't talk about things.

Except for last night; she has the distinct, uneasy impression that last night they did a lot of talking.

Now, he is lying on her bed, unconscious; chest down, face turned towards her, bum exposed. He has a beautiful back. It is her favourite part of him, strong and lean, and when they fuck she likes to picture it, as if she's riding him from behind, not the other way round. He has a nice face too, or would have, if he didn't swamp it with that bloody beard. Sometimes she runs her hands over his jaw while they're in bed, feeling for the shape of him, trying to match the sensation with a plausible set of visual coordinates. His chin isn't weak; she's discovered that much by feel, but she still can't picture it fully. The beard is a statement of something: adulthood, seriousness, intent. It's a mask. She hates it. Sometimes she thinks of shaving it off while he's sleeping. Would his power over her evaporate then, like Samson's? In the dull, underwatery light she can see that sleep is encrusting his eyes; little sprinklings of gold on the tips of his lashes. She resists the temptation to pick at it. When she was little, Julia used to clean out her eyes, and Ands', like they were kittens. Lotte always enjoyed that: the gentle, insistent rub of her mother's thumb, the flick of her nail in the corner of the socket. It's a nice thing to do for someone, clean away their excess. Once, for a dare, she and Ands ate each other's sleep. Ands' tasted just like hers: salty, crunchy, like crisps.

He is younger than she'd thought; three years younger than her. Twenty-three, and already lost to the bottle. Maybe that should bother her, but she's told herself that as long as things don't get sticky between them, it will be alright, to stand on the sidelines and watch him battle his addiction, fighting to retain his self-control before, inevitably, it slips away from him, an eel sliding into the Lethe. And things haven't got sticky. Yet.

Have they?

She frowns, unsure whether to wake him. She doesn't want sex, not after that dream, certainly not with her hangover, and especially not if they argued, but neither does she want him hanging around her flat all day, becoming comfortable, drinking from her cups, snoozing at her fire, examining her things, petting Caliban.

Caliban?

Something missing. Her gut turns to a bowl of worms.

'Monster?' She crosses the room, opens the door. Her voice sounds faint and inhuman in the cold, translucent air. She calls a few more times, but there's no busy padding of paws, so she retreats into the womby warmth of her flat, leaving the door open so Caliban can get in if – when – he wants. The sight of the Poet in her bed troubles her now, so she sits as far away from him as she can, at the table beside the drawn curtains of the big front window, biting her nails, starting to remember.

She shouldn't have said yes last night. He'd broken the rules, but she'd gone along with it.

He'd knocked on her door, early, around seven, all dressed up, scarf and hat and duffel coat. He looked different. Younger. Boyish. Something shining in his eyes that wasn't just the drink.

Uh oh, she'd thought.

Ready?

She didn't say *For what*. Just leant against the doorframe and blew smoke into his face until he shrugged, irritated. Get your coat. A command, followed by the usual qualification. If you want?

She should have resisted or, even better, laughed at his attempt at machismo and slammed the door in his face, but it had been cold and she'd hadn't the fire lit and she was – let's face it – lonely. She made him wait in the hall while she dressed, though; her gentleman caller, leashed to the other side of the threshold. She didn't want him poking around, nosing through her slowly filling bookshelves, her new bits and bobs of jewellery, the splashes of colour on her clothes rack, the posters she'd bought from the Dandelion Market, the few scraps of something beginning to populate her bare white space.

He'd nodded when he'd seen her, pleased. She should think so: she'd made an effort. Abba-style crochet cap, fur-trimmed coat, new platform boots.

Outside, it had been on the verge of freezing, sharp and cold and clear.

I love this time of year, she nearly said, but caught herself in time. Said instead: Where are you taking me?

To hear some music.

What sort?

Ah… his hands waved, vague. Irish.

They took a bus from Ballsbridge, across the road from the exhibition halls. He paid for the fares. They went south along the coast, down the grand leafy streets and out onto the beach road, past the desolate bird sanctuary, then a detour into the little town with the outdoor baths, up around and past the port and the coves, right to the terminus; a pretty little village with hills and small winding streets and chocolate-boxy shops.

Dalkey, said the Poet. It's famous. A famous writer lives here.

I didn't know you could read, she said, only half-teasing. He flushed, then laughed.

She'd felt alright on the journey, giggly, a little schoolgirlish, and it had seemed odd but not wrong to hold hands and lean against each other upstairs in the front seat, swaying as the bus rounded corners, allowing gravity and centripetal force to push them together, pull them apart. She'd caught sight of their reflection in the bus window and even thought, My God, how innocent. But once they'd got to the pub, a dingy little place that wasn't that nice, a basement, really, full of smoke and the smell of Guinness, where a band in woollen jumpers was setting up in the corner, tuning fiddles and things, it changed. She began to feel claustrophobic, hemmed in, and that got worse when she realised he was meeting friends – all male, all young, or youngish, most of them bearded like relics from an older, more idealistic time. She didn't want his friends in her life. Especially not these, with their Gaelic names and their laughter when she failed to pronounce them correctly. She'd felt like leaving straightaway, returning to Baggot Street and Caliban, to – *home*: that surprised her – but before she could, the Poet came back from the bar and handed her a pint of Guinness and a whiskey chaser – I'd have got you a sherry if you weren't such a Women's Libber – and even though it was a bizarre thing for him to say, an awful joke, if even that, she could feel the awkwardness behind it, the need to please, so she decided, against her wiser instincts, to stay.

So what's it like, now you're working for the enemy, Eoin? asked one of his friends. Small eyes, close together, a shock of dirty blond hair, a bushy moustache, a heavy accent she could now recognise as working-class Dublin.

The Poet flushed, glanced at her. Jesus, Christy, just—

Working? she thought. Funny that, not *enemy* but *working*.

Leave him be, Christy, said another of the men. Dark, self-contained, with an accent she associated with Aisling.

What do *you* think of that? said the moustached one. Christy. He was staring at her.

Sorry?

Eoin taking pictures for the Brits.

Oh. Confused, she looked at the Poet.

It's not the Brits, said the Poet. It's—

The Organ of the Liberal Bourgeoisie, said Christy. His words were enunciated too clearly, like an English person speaking school French. Probably an attempt to hide his accent. He laughed. Irish. Times. Irish? That's a right fucking joke.

The Irish Times, she thought. The newspaper?

That's stickie talk there, Christy, said the dark man.

Christy ignored him, kept staring at her. I'm just asking Eoin what happened to his principles. *Tiocfaidh ár lá.*

The dark one looked at her. Every instinct telling her to run.

Evans is Welsh, said the Poet.

Oh aye? said the dark one.

Still a left-footer, said Christy. Still a Subject of the bleeding Crown.

File. The Irish for bard. The Gaelic bards, he'd told her when they'd been fucking, had two functions: to flatter the power and, if crossed, to satirise it. Since when had he been working for a newspaper?

Actually, she heard some other, airier, part of her say, I'm not. Her voice was surprisingly steady. Welsh. The Poet's head jerked towards her. I'm from Bristol. A – what's that word, Poet? – *Sasanach.*

Christy snorted into his pint.

Interesting city, Bristol. Home town of Strongbow, I believe. She lifted her glass. Without whom my Saxon ancestors may never have invaded this lovely little island of yours. *Sláinte.*

A collective intaking of breath. Funny, that: nobody corrected her, said *it wasn't the Saxons; it was the Normans.*

Jesus, Evans, said the Poet. Just—

How long had he been working there?

Oh don't get your knickers into a twist, Poet, she said, exaggerating the glottal stops she'd picked up in London. I'm not a proper English. No more than Christy – she nodded in his direction – knows the least fucking thing about revolution.

Something brutish coiled in Christy's shoulders. Ah, she thought, it's coming, and that dead part of her wouldn't have been disappointed if he'd hit her. But instead the dark man laughed – suddenly, revealing strong white teeth.

Lotte? he said. *Deutsch, oder?*

Christy looked puzzled.

Rote Armee Faktion, said the Northern man.

Fraktion, du Idiot, she almost said, but the Poet interrupted. Jesus, quiet, will ye, the music's starting.

She could see the anger flickering in his face, and underneath it something raw and uncertain, but that was a fucking liberty, because if anyone deserved to be angry, it was her, and then the music started up and people hushed, and soon even Christy lost interest in her and began enthusiastically thumping the back of the man next to him, and she drank the Guinness and the next chaser the Poet gave her, avoiding his eyes and the eyes of the dark man, and swallowed the next pint and chaser after that, and gathered, without really listening, that the Poet's friends, apart from the Northerner, were boys he'd met in the wild, dead years after he'd left school and failed to get into Art College, three times he'd applied and been refused, too thick to get the message, too bloody-minded, too full of notions of his own bloody genius, kept pestering the papers and the magazines, though, and now some uncle who was a subbie had pulled a few strings, and she had only herself to blame, she had seen the books, what had she thought she was playing at, to put her head in the lion's den like that? And they all drank another round, and somebody said something about how hot the weather would be in Belfast and they all laughed, and slapped the Poet on his back, and told him, now, Eoin, you show the Brits, you show the fat cats, you show the mohair suits in Kildare Street, show it like it is, Eoin, show everyone on this poxy island what's really going on, those Orange pricks with their property and profits and proletariat-fooling lodges and no Catholics need apply, those B-Special bollixes, those trigger-happy para bastards, those warmongering imperial fuckers in Whitehall, those murdering cunts, you show them what the martyrs of 1916 died for, what the people on the streets of Derry were gunned down for. *You name it as it is*, shouted the Northern man, anointing the Poet's forehead with whiskey, *for you are Eoin Báiste, John the Baptist! Eoin the Marxist!* shouted Christy, *Blessed Eoin!* roared another, and she thought of the music he played when they fucked, the soundtrack to their rocking and rolling:

his blues and Chuck Berry and Bowie and Velvet Underground and the weirder, brasher sounds with screeching guitars and yowling voices preaching anarchy that belonged to some new thing called punk happening in England and New York, and wondered what on earth that had to do with this, these fiddles and drums, these beards and oily jumpers, and what Belfast had to do with him or anything, especially her.

After the next whiskey, everything got too hazy to remember.

There is a small squawking sound from outside the front window.

'Monster?'

Lotte pushes the curtain. Through the chink, light floods in, hurting her eyes. Dublin has disappeared, transformed into – Dickens. Christmas. Home? No. It's just snow. She's surprised at her disappointment. That *just*. Outside is a sea of blue and peach and white, slashed by the twisting black arcs of branches. Caliban miaows again. He's up on the sill – how on earth did he manage that? – looking rather cross. His back is arched, his fur flecked with white. Behind him, the sun is peeking over the rooftops, sending shivers of pink light across the street. On the far side of the road, a milkman is unloading a crate of bottles. His breath curls away from him, eddies of white air. Caliban yowls, impatient now, up on his hind feet, pushing his front paws against the window.

Lotte heaves up the sash. Coldness hits her face. The cat takes a step, stops, sniffs, looks at her, looks into the room, at the bed beyond the open dividing doors.

'Come on, monster. It's freezing.'

Caliban makes a grumpy, uncertain sound and steps inside. He jumps to the floor, takes a few steps towards the bed, stops. Looks at the Poet, around, back at Lotte. Another yowl. Clearly, he resents being cuckolded.

'Alright, I'll get him out. Then I'll feed you.' She crosses the room and hunkers down beside the bed. 'Wake up.'

The Poet grunts. His hands rise, reach, searching for her.

'No. Wake up.' She shakes him. He rolls over, his eyes open; two slits of bloodshot sky. He has an erection. A smile starts to curl around his mouth. His hands push upwards, find her breasts. He mumbles something. She pulls away; he pulls her back, mumbles again.

'What?'

He grabs her face with both hands, pulls it towards his. She resists. He laughs and his fingers soften. At that she gives in, even though she knows

277

she shouldn't. He turns her face, brings her ear to his mouth. His beard is sandpaper at her skin. She's expecting him to speak again but he gives her his tongue instead and her resolution withers.

'So when am I going to meet your brother?' he says, watching her as she dresses.

The room seems to pull away; shifting perspective but retaining dimension, as if she's a camera on tracks, wheeling back and zooming in at the same time. She's aware that her hands have stopped what they were doing, pulling at her tights, and realises, for appearances' sake, they should start again. Move, she tells them, and they obey.

'Sorry?' Her voice is calm; too calm, and light.

'You know,' he says. 'The film.' Laughs, like it's a joke. 'Your brother. We talked about him last night. You said he was a photographer too. Into politics. You said he'd made a film and he was in it. A statement.'

No I didn't.

'You said you'd show it to me, teach me proper revolution.'

She turns. Every muscle in her face feels tight, like it belongs to someone else. She feels her mouth moving, hears words sounding, but has no idea what she's saying.

The Poet blinks. For a moment he looks very stupid and very young.

Caliban appears at the door again, miaowing long scrolls of hunger. He butts the doorframe, steps in, butts the Poet's leg.

'The— fucking pest!'

A whiplash, a blood-curdling scream. The leg flicks; the cat jumps, halfway across the room.

'Don't you bloody dare—'

Now she is screeching too, a banshee, and Caliban is somehow squirming in her arms, hissing.

'Fuck this.' The Poet twists up and begins to pull on his socks.

She releases the cat, turns to the mirror, wills herself to keep dressing. Bra on, snap, close. In the mirror, she sees him reach for his jumper, stop. The bang of his fist on the bedhead makes her jump.

'Christ!'

'Jesus, Lotte, I'm. What do you want me to say? Sorry? Okay? Forget it. I'm sorry. But what we talked about last night—'

Out in the hall, the phone begins to ring.

'I meant it—'

She cuts across him, cold. 'You going to answer that?'

His mouth opens; something changes in his eyes. 'Don't be such a hoor.'

Without warning, he lunges towards her. She must have said something, because just as suddenly he stops. The phone keeps ringing.

She waits for him to speak, or do something, reach for her maybe, hold her, hurt her, even tell her – stupidly – that he loves her, but he doesn't, so she walks past him, into the hall, towards the phone. Caliban follows, manic now, furious, oozing between her ankles. She picks up the receiver. 'Hello?'

The man on the other end of the line clears his throat.

'Hi. Em, eh… Lotte?'

She is smiling now, a too-bright smile that has nothing to do with anything.

Always you smile, Lotte.

'David. This is a surprise.'

She hears noises in her room: a crash. Dear God, she thinks, keep him away from my stuff. All the time saying, Yes, yes, but not knowing to what. Caliban growls. More noises, quieter. David keeps talking; she lets him witter on without registering what he's saying. Yes, yes, of course. A sound at her doorway. Caliban retreating. Movement in the shadows on the wall facing her. He has come to the door. Yes. Yes. That should be fine. His eyes burning holes in her back. Caliban pushes his nose against her leg. She changes position, keeping her back to the Poet, her body huddling around the phone box. Yes, yes.

He comes close, too close, inches from her skin. She feels his mouth open. His breath is hot on the back of her neck. She is curled now, foetus-tight, into the wall.

He breathes.

Ands. Bish doo dass? Is that you?

Some fucking hope.

'Yes,' she says again, and laughs, a tinkly silly girly laugh. 'That would be a pleasure, David. No, no, of course not, that wouldn't be a problem.'

The Poet sucks himself away from her, leaving cold space around her. His steps recede, sullen on the stairs.

'Right, em. Grand, so,' says David.

Christ, she thinks, and puts the phone back in its cradle. Upstairs, loud music begins to play.

She walks into the kitchen, opens the fridge, and takes out the butter, the cheese, the salami. Opens her bread bin, takes out the soft Vienna roll she bought three days ago and has been nibbling away at, slowly, since. She slices through the bread but is careless. Beads of blood bubble up in a line across her thumb. No pain. The slice of bread is ugly, fat, its edges ragged as a wound's. Sucking her thumb, she slathers the bread with butter, cuts three hunks of cheese and wedges them on top. Caliban howls. Later, monster. She eats the whole thing, fast, unthinking. Greedy pig.

Another, then another.

She sits on the throne and lights a ciggie. Her fingers are shaking. Her bare arms are goosepimpling. She's cold now. Freezing. More than anything else, more than ever, she would love a bath, but there's not even enough hot water for a shower, so she'll have to do with a whore's wash instead.

In the mirror, her reflection is swamped in clothing, tented like those women in strange, primitive Arab societies. She lifts the silk scarf Charlie gave her for her birthday, the one decorated with swirls of turquoise, aquamarine and umber, and holds it against her face. It's all wrong; too pretty for today.

Her mind is clear now, from the purging. It is starting to make sense. Bits of memory reassembling themselves around her, like pieces from mismatched jigsaw puzzles that she has forced to fit together. They had an argument on the way home, and she told him he was an idiot. Art and politics, politics and art, bloody art, bloody politics. She should have stayed away. The animal stuff always gets complicated; fucking never stays zipless; she should know that by now. It was what she'd said to the caveman Christy: I'm not Welsh. It had undermined him, apparently. Why didn't you tell me you were born in England? he'd asked, when they were on their own, after one of the friends dropped them off somewhere between Blackrock and town. They were still hammered from the whiskey and pints and manic, mournful music. She didn't ask the question she should have: Why didn't you tell me you were in newspapers, Poet? Why did you hide that from me?

Instead, she asked the other, the more obvious one. Why didn't you tell me you were going to Belfast?

I didn't know. You never asked.

It started getting nasty at the Booterstown level crossing, that ugly concrete hospital an orange slab behind him, its incinerator belching fumes. Behind her the sea, reflected in his eyes, black and oily. You think I don't know what I'm doing, he said, going up North, and she said, Well, what are you? Doing.

What do you think I'm doing?

Expecting her maybe to say, Stirring it up, getting yourself into trouble, meddling with stuff you don't understand, risking your life. But she just laughed. Oh, just what any hack would do. You're sniffing out a good story.

He shook his head. No. No stories. The truth.

The truth? Oh, please.

I'm not a hack. That's not what I—

No, sorry, I forgot. You've got principles. You're after the truth—

Don't laugh—

Do you actually read those books, Poet? Or do you just leave them lying around so girls will think you're clever—

Shut up—

There is no truth.

What about oppression?

You honestly think your stories will stop that?

I'm not telling fucking stories. I'm taking pictures. Real pictures. Of things that are happening to real people—

Representing reality as it is, Poet? Don't forget, it's only just as long your editor lets you.

No—

Know what? Your friend Christy's a berk but I think he's right about that one – you think you're radicalised just because your poor auntie had to move from bloody Antrim to Derry or wherever the bloody hell it was, but really you're just going up there to do a job, make the middle classes feel cosy, like at least they're taking a fucking interest, but because it's all so shit they're right to stay where they are, sat in their houses, counting their savings, working for the Man, doing—

No, I'm—

No? What then? *Détournement*? Fucking it up from the inside—

Oh, look who's got the big words now, you think I don't know—

Fuck off. You think you can take it all on, get at the so-called bloody system from the inside—

Don't you dare laugh at me—

Newsflash, Poet. The system's fucking everywhere and we're part of it. There's stuff going on all over the world, killing, looting, raping, and you know what? Nobody gives a shit and no amount of planting bombs, stealing cars, robbing banks, least of all no pictures taken by no would-be fucking radical is going to change that. You're better off sticking with your pretty little snaps of your gypsy boys—

And what are you better off sticking with? Something shifted in his face. Germany? Would that make you happier, Evans, if I was sniffing out stories there?

She shook her head and started to walk on.

Why don't you tell me things, Lotte? he shouted.

She thinks she might have laughed then, and said something like *You wouldn't*, only he interrupted again—

Understand?

I don't want to get into this, she said, and he said, No, why would you get into it with some thick illiterate Paddy, and she said, You said that, not me, and Do you even know, he said, and she said, Know what, you fucking idiot? And then he went to hit her but didn't follow through and there was running and chasing and they were in Ballsbridge, down by the river, fucking in the yard of an abandoned cottage, and the bricks were damp and hurt her back, and then she couldn't bear it because of the dead look in his eyes, so she ripped herself away, thinking that's it, that's it, this is bloody pointless, except he followed her, caught up with her, and found her key when she'd thought she'd lost it and was cursing, violently, on the top step and then he pulled her indoors, gently, that was unexpected, and she started to shake but didn't – Christ, no, didn't cry – and then somehow, they were making love on her bed, love not the other, and—

Wait for me, he said. Please? I'll come back, Lotte. Just wait....

What did she tell him about Andrew? She can't remember; everything else in the jigsaw, but not that.

She places the silk scarf back on her dressing table. Her hands are shaking.

'Thanks,' says David again. 'If I hadn't this blinking meeting, I'd....'

'Oh,' says Lotte. 'No problem.'

'It's in Carlow,' says David. 'It's a hospital.' Lotte's sure she should have recalled this from their phone conversation, but she doesn't remember anything and David seems anxious to tell her again.

The pipes in the school have burst in response to the unexpected cold snap. Inadequate insulation: the Irish do not prepare for snow, for floods, for drought; not well, not at all.

'I'll be back, em.' David checks his watch. He's nervy, anxious to go. 'I can pick them up at five? I think that's when they're, eh, expecting her.' He looks at Georgie.

'Lovely.'

'So how about that, Georgie?' David keeps looking, but Georgie is distant, preoccupied. 'Be good for Lotte.'

'Um,' says Saoirse. 'Thanks for letting me come. This is gonna be such fun.'

David glances at the architect's daughter. A flicker of something, gone as quickly as it appears.

'Righty-ho,' he says to Lotte, and leaves.

Although she was aware she'd agreed to do something with Georgie, she'd missed, completely, the bit about Saoirse. David had mentioned a friend – would you, could you, mind a friend too? For some idiot reason she'd assumed he'd meant one of the boys from school, that William Thingy fellow Georgie talks a lot about or Timmy, the snotty-nosed blond from the children's home. But Saoirse? This lump, suet-fleshed and flat-faced, raisin-eyed as a wedge of stollen cake?

It bothers Lotte. Coming so fast on top of everything else, this does not at all feel right. God, why didn't she say No?

Contact between the two children has been minimal since that visit to Dollymount beach. Georgie rarely acknowledges Saoirse outside the school gates; instead, makes as big an effort as possible to avoid her, going blank whenever her name is mentioned. There was a brief resurgence in Saoirse's attempts to ingratiate herself after Aisling died – Hey, Georgie, wanna come over to my house after school? Hi, Lotte, my Mom says— but with no reciprocation from Georgie, and with Lotte not feeling it her place to pass on the invitations to David, those shoots of potential friendship have quickly withered.

So why has Jan foisted her daughter on them again? Saoirse's mother seems – as far as Lotte can tell from the handful of times that she's met her – a clever woman; domineering, but not stupid. She's a child psychologist, for God's sake. Surely she would have the nous to recognise the tension between the two children; know that it's hardly a good idea to force them to spend a whole day together outside the safety zone of school?

In those hazy days of the Indian summer after the morphine had taken hold, Aisling had often rambled about her relationship with Jan. What a dear pal she'd been, how much she'd done for Aisling, how great it had been when she'd first come over from the States and the four of them had been such good friends, before the illness had put the kibosh on everything. These remembrances had been mushed up with a lot of other ramblings, about Georgie, mainly, and Aisling's fears for her child; and David, a little; and other, unspecified worries she had voiced, that suggested she had left some important obligation unfulfilled.

The Maddens and the Ó Buachallas bosom friends? That you wouldn't have picked up, not from David. From the little Lotte has seen of him around the Ó Buachallas, he appears stiff in their company, polite in a slightly forced way, but not particularly attentive. I ran into your acquaintance today, she'd found herself saying, that day she'd first seen the architect after picking Georgie up from school. *Acquaintance*, not *friend*. Oh, said David, though she couldn't imagine he knew who she meant. That's nice.

She herself has met the architect only a couple of times since that afternoon outside the school gates when – for a fleeting, stupid second before recognising him as the owner of that showy Jag – she thought she was seeing Andrew; grown older, larger, richer. They still haven't been properly introduced. It hasn't bothered Lotte. There is something disturbing about Saoirse's father, and not just that apparent resemblance with Ands. He's the type who hurts your eyes if you look at him for too long; he has one of those mutable faces that changes in the light, reflecting, she imagines, whatever you'd like to see in it. He reminds her of an illustration on the cover of one of David's science-fiction novels. Not so much a man, but an entity; formless and voracious, conviction and certainty crackling from him like lightning. In that respect he reminds her more of Sybille. Radiating self-belief, just like he radiates that heady bergamot of his cologne. Maybe that's why he keeps himself hidden behind those tinted glasses and loud shirts and wild hair. Wanting to shield his mojo. And yet…. Poke those men and it's always a disappointment. Always something banal, like sentimentality or a desire to please, that oozes out, gooey and cloying. She wasn't surprised at how mushy he'd got at the funeral afters, calling out in his rich messy baritone for David to drink with him. At least, that was what David's sister had said. Lotte hadn't understood; it had all been in Irish.

She was shocked at how easily that picture had come into her mind in the church, watching David walk up to the pulpit to read the blessing, a long-limbed boy in his Sunday best, bowed and brittle with grief. So inappropriate, but pop! Right into her mind.

Easy to smell a rat. Just because you have so little many rats of your own, Lotte, don't infest other people's houses with them.

But she couldn't help seeing it. The two couples during that idyllic time Aisling had spoken of, playing wife-swapping in the Maddens' messy hexagonal lounge, a modern version of *The Mayor of Casterbridge*, with everyone complicit in the barter. The architect's giant form wrapping around Aisling's freckled body. David, all that terrible tension uncrooked by sex, losing himself inside Jan's large American fanny. Though fanny means something else in the States, and Jan would probably use the right word, the factual word: *vagina*.

A ludicrous picture.

If so lud-i-cris, Lotte, why you never talk to Joanie Flynn?

Was it loyalty that had kept her from Joanie at the funeral afters? The woman was sozzled, eyes out on stalks, killing to talk to someone. Was it loyalty that had kept Lotte chattering away to everyone else, in that awful bright voice that Julia used to use when people talked about the Captain and what a good man he was, taking on Lotte as if she was his own? Was that what had led Lotte, finally, out of the over-stuffed kitchen and into the garden, to the corner near the buddleia tree where David had been lurking like a hounded fox—

Unless – a thought strikes her – this whole thing is a lot simpler than her twisted imagination would have her think. It might have been David's idea, this idiotic notion to take Saoirse today. Since Germany, he's mentioned several times that he might be up for promotion at the end of the year. *Nothing's certain*, he's said. *But….* Anxiety chewing away at the back of his eyes. Saoirse's father is clearly an influential man, capable of making or breaking reputations. David has never struck her as the type who'd risk his child for the sake of a bigger pay packet, and nothing Aisling ever said made Lotte think of him as ruthless, but—

Please, Lotte. He leaves his child a week after his wife die. How well you know him?

How well, really, does she know any of these people?

Feeling nauseous now, and more anxious than before, she closes the front door, rejoins the children.

'Who wants a drink? Milk? Cocoa?'

'Wow.' Saoirse is staring at the plasterwork on the ceiling. 'This apartment is neat.'

'It's a flat, actually. Do you want to take off your wet things?'

Saoirse nods, begins to unwind a long striped scarf from her neck. 'That's real loud music.'

'Yes, it's not mine.'

'Who's playing it—'

Georgie looks up. 'The Po—'

'Georgie, d'you want to take off your coat?'

'Unh. I'm okay. I'm cold.'

'Oh?' Lotte frowns. 'Maybe I should make a fire.'

'Jan says it's not good to make fires unless you're really cold,' says Saoirse. 'It interferes with your circulation.'

'Great. Georgie, really, take off your coat. You'll boil.'

'Uh uh.' Georgie's head shakes.

Lotte begins to insist, stops. 'If you must. So what do the two of you want to do today?'

'I've homework,' says Georgie.

Saoirse looks puzzled.

'But you did your homework yesterday,' says Lotte.

'I've extra. I've sums.'

They lock eyes. Georgie's are shadowed, troubled but, as far as Lotte can tell, not lying.

'Do you need a hand—'

'No.'

'I can help,' offers Saoirse. 'I like sums.'

Georgie ignores her, starts taking out books.

'Georgie, there's no need to be quite so rude. Can't your homework wait?'

Georgie glares. What a mess. For a second Lotte considers pushing it. Only a second. 'Alright then, if you absolutely have to. Maybe you'd like to do some drawings, Saoirse. Or—'

'I got a book. I can read.'

'Fine. Would you like some milk?'

'No. I'm allergic—'

'Yes,' says Georgie. 'And biscuits.'

'I don't have any. Besides, it's far too early for—'

Georgie's eyes roll, stare at the ceiling. Saoirse glances over.

'Um, I have money?' says Saoirse. 'Jan gave me some. I can buy Georgie some cookies if he wants—'

'No, Saoirse. Sit down. We'll have them later.'

Georgie does sums, more sums, more sums again, sipping absently at the glass of milk, obstinately bundled up in the coat like a junior tramp. Weight has been lost; sleep missed. Blue shadows stain the skin under the eyes; there is an uneasy listlessness in the child's movements. Something, thinks Lotte, not for the first time, is going on. But she's still too frazzled and hungover after the night before and the fight that morning, thrown off by Saoirse's presence, and whether or not it's David's doing, and the Poet's music still pounding through the house; jumpy, distracted, starting to think, as she hasn't for a while, that maybe it's time to move on.

Saoirse drinks water, her mouth moving silently as she reads. From its jacket, the book she has brought appears to be a worthy modern tale of worthy modern children who have realistic adventures in suburban gardens with not a sign anywhere of witches, gods, monsters or magic. Saoirse is absorbed. Her Mom, she's told Lotte, helped edit it. It's for kids, she explained, so they get a super firm grasp on real life. Jan is working on the follow-up today. She has a deadline. When I grow up, I'm gonna be a writer. For TV. You can do that you know, make up stories for—

Yes, yes. Now, why don't we all be quiet for a little while?

A deadline. Is that why Saoirse is here, because Jan is too busy? That would make sense. Except— surely they have their own babysitter? It's not like they don't have the money.

Saoirse looks up, catches Lotte's eye and smiles. Lotte smiles back; hoping – always so needing to please, Lotte – it doesn't look too false.

Caliban is curled on Georgie's lap, purring. Georgie is stroking him, sums momentarily forgotten, face intent. I love cats, Georgie confided in Lotte just before the funeral. So does my Granny in Clonmel. She takes them in from the wild and everything. But Mum won't let me have one in the house because their fur gets caught in her lungs.

Won't. Wouldn't. Gets. Got.

Outside, the city sparkles as the sun creeps higher over the roofs. The reflected light travels into the room, illuminating its dark corners. Cars make slow progress up the street. Adults hurry past; children dawdle, throwing snowballs. Lotte yawns, restless; longing for sleep.

Around eleven, the Poet's music stops, abruptly, like he's taken the needle off the record. Then footsteps sound, running down the stairs. Urgent. They stop in the hallway, outside Lotte's door. Lotte half-rises, expecting a knock, maybe even the door to push open, him to stand there, hands out, penitent or demanding an explanation or surly or ashamed or. Something. But instead the front door opens, then slams shut, so loud it makes Caliban jump. Both the children look up. In the edge of the bay window, Lotte sees a slender dark shape flick down the steps and turn towards town.

What did she tell him?

'Alright. Finish up that sum, Georgie. Saoirse, mark your spot. We're going out.'

'But....' Georgie's eyes widen, forehead creasing.

'No buts, monster.'

A blank look, then a grin. For a second, Georgie-that-was is back again.

'Um, Lotte, are my things dry?' asks Saoirse.

By the time she's got the kids ready and out of the house, he has disappeared.

'This way,' she says, turning them in the opposite direction, away from town.

The park is full of people. Everybody in Dublin seems to have taken the day off. Schoolchildren chase each other around the lake; toddlers stretch curious feet towards frozen puddles, arms lifted by anxious mothers. Students stroll arm in arm, mouths moist with cold searching for each other.

Lotte's not sure who starts the fight. What happens is: a snowball lands on her face and when she looks around, Saoirse and Georgie are giggling helplessly beside each other, unlikely allies. Lotte bends, rolls, throws, gets Georgie in the face. Retaliation is sweet.

'Hey, let's make angels!' calls Saoirse after they've covered each other in white.

The snow and fresh air seem to have ignited her spirit. She finds a patch of virgin snow, flings herself, back-first, onto it, and moves her arms and legs up and down. Then she stands, carefully, a skin of snow coating her back, and shows them her angel.

Lotte closes her eyes, lets herself fall. The snow catches her like a cushion. Lying there, on the ground, moving her arms and legs like they're flippers, with the sky so clean and bright above her and the sun so weak but still visible, she feels something fill up in her and, for a moment, even after what happened that morning, even with the children around, even knowing Ands is – say it – that he's – *say it* – that he's gone, everything is nearly okay.

Her vision blurs. A shadow has crossed over her. Georgie is standing there, offering a hand.

Lotte takes it, allows herself to be pulled. A shiver of electricity runs through her; a shock of recognition. It's as if somebody else's hand is helping her up too, as if somebody else, small and frail with enormous eyes, is occupying the same space as Georgie, or overlapped, just slightly, so its muscles and skin and bone intertwine with Georgie's; a double negative, a twin strand of DNA. Georgie's chin tilts; something crosses the child's face, not a smile but something deeper. More adult. Recognition. But of what?

'Thanks, monster.'

Saoirse looks over. 'See? Aren't they cute? Georgie, yours is the cutest.'

Georgie grins, bashful; makes a funny little movement in neck and shoulders, as if shaking off an invisible hand.

Lunch is soup and bread in a little basement coffee shop off Stephen's Green. Georgie orders a sandwich too, and chips; has devoured everything by the time Lotte and Saoirse return from the loo.

'Gosh,' says Lotte. 'That's some appetite you've built up there, Georgie.' She regrets it the moment it's out. Georgie's face darkens, then becomes blank again.

She was pushing her luck, she thinks afterwards. Imagining that a couple of hours in the snow had made everything okay, obliterated the night before. Thinking that the differences between the children were resolved, that perhaps David had the right idea, bringing Saoirse over, no matter what his motivations were; that maybe the differences were not so great, never so great; thinking, okay, now they can be friends, and – this prompted by God knows what, because what bearing could a friendship between children have on a promise one makes to an adult? – but thinking all the same, maybe that promise I made, maybe it's been honoured and I can—

'What are we going to do now?' says Saoirse. Not so much a question as a challenge. The exercise and lunch have given her a glow; she almost seems attractive.

'I want cake,' says Georgie.

'Why don't we—' starts Lotte.

'We can have cake later,' interrupts Saoirse, looking to Lotte for back-up. 'Why don't we go do an activity, like visit an art gallery?'

Georgie's lip curls.

'Jan says it's really good to do activities.'

Georgie's mouth moves, scornful. *Jaan says.*

'If all you do is homework and sports, your brain goes dead.'

'Well…' Lotte glances at Georgie.

Georgie shrugs.

She should have read the signs better. But it was just a gallery; she was only taking them to see paintings. It wasn't like giving them a book with dangerous, inappropriate content, or bringing them to a film where something scary might happen. It was only an art gallery. The safest of the safe, Ands used to call them. The aesthetic justification of the fascist machine, Sybille used to add, her face glowing with certainty.

I just love the pictures, Lotte used to say. What's wrong with just loving pictures?

'No,' says Georgie.

Lotte reminds herself not to swear. 'It's boiling in here, Georgie. You're going to explode if you don't take it off.'

'Come on,' says Saoirse. 'I'll help—' She reaches, pulls at the top toggle of Georgie's duffel.

Georgie makes an inarticulate animal sound and twists around, hiding the neck of the duffel. With a shock Lotte realises the sounds aren't inarticulate at all.

'Fuck off, you cow pissy bitch!'

The gallery freezes. The nice lady behind the counter lets her mouth fall open. Lotte is aware of stares landing on her. Is that how you let your children behave, you dirty English slut? She realises she is doing that thing her mother used to do when caught out: looking at the people who've caught her, smiling anxiously, attempting to reassure, find reassurance.

'That's really mean,' says Saoirse. She begins to cry.

'Oh, come on. I'm sure Georgie didn't mean it, did you, Georgie?' But Georgie is staring at the door, teeth clenched, mouth pursed, making a distorted, soundless whistle.

Christ.

'All I was doing was trying to help. Jan says everyone needs to be nice to Georgie because David is too messed up and Dad said it was okay now to be friends again and Mom and Dad have been so sad and I just wanted...' Saoirse's face crumples into an unprepossessing tragedy mask.

Sad? thinks Lotte, but doesn't have a chance to wonder why, because—

'Can we go?' says Georgie.

'Go? We've only just—'

'You said we were going to see pictures.'

Saoirse snuffles. 'It's not fair. All I want is a....' *Friend.* The word dissolves into another squeaking sob.

Lotte reluctantly hugs Saoirse. The child is lumpy and damp in her arms. 'Okay, look, this isn't… maybe we should go somewhere else.'

'No,' says Georgie.

'I wanna go home,' says Saoirse.

'Yes, well, I—'

'How are you going to get home?' says Georgie, rounding on Saoirse. The expression and question are oddly adult, almost practised. 'Lotte doesn't have a car and your house is ages away. What are you going to do, walk back on your own?'

Saoirse snuffles.

'What if you met a tramp? Or a sex maniac?'

Oh, Christ.

'Or got knocked down? Or lost? You'd get into trouble, and so would Lotte. Do you want that?'

'No.' Another sob. Georgie looks at Lotte.

Pain is throbbing through Lotte's jaw. 'Right. Saoirse, you hold my hand. Georgie, say sorry.'

'For what?'

'Look, don't—'

'It wasn't my fault.'

'Look—'

'What good does *sorry* do? I was being sensible. She started it.'

'Oh, God. Look, just say sorry and—'

'I don't want sorry. I wanna go home. I want my Mom….'

'Yes, Saoirse. You are going home. But Georgie's right. David's picking you up later and I can't just….'

Saoirse sobs.

Fuck, thinks Lotte. Fuck fuck fuck.

She stands at the phone in the marble basement of the gallery and listens to the Ó Buachallas' number ring and ring and ring.

Okay, Plan B, says Lotte, cutting Saoirse off before she has a chance to speak. Your mum seems to be out at the moment and I can't get hold of David, so we've three options. We can all either sit here and stew and be cross, or we can go back to the flat together and do the rest of our homework, which strikes me as a very boring thing indeed, or, if we're good, we can have a look at the paintings and if we're very good, we might even have some cake and tea afterwards.

Georgie's mouth moves. *Good?*

Right, says Lotte. Why don't you two say sorry to each other and we can get on with having a nice day?

Saoirse swallows some snot, looks at Georgie. I'm sorry.

Georgie's head jerks as if it's been slapped. Then the child's face flushes, suffusing with a fury that almost scares Lotte. The words when they come are mumbled, too indistinct to hear.

They are staring at an enormous painting that takes up an entire wall on the ground floor. It's a history painting, depicting the aftermath of a battle: the canvas is packed to its edges with ruins, twilight, tattered flags, wild-eyed horses and prone, waxy bodies. The living, clustered in the centre, pose in the affected postures of the Salon; index fingers pointing, torsos twisting, limp-wristed hands touching subdued chests. Saoirse's eyes are darting from figure to figure; inventing stories, Lotte imagines, relationships, threads of love and hate and longing between the naked and the clothed. Georgie's eyes move more slowly, lingering on the nude women, their gauzy wrappings, the sheen of the men's armour, the green-tinted corpses.

The Marriage of Strongbow and Aoife. She knows it's just coincidence, but still, Strongbow.... Maybe she should talk to him when they get back and she's got rid of the children; ask him, straight out, what she said.

Georgie glances around, right hand scratching at throat. Under the duffel coat and the navy poloneck, Lotte sees a glimpse of familiar colours. Turquoise, aquamarine, lilac and umber. A drum begins to beat at the back of her head.

Georgie catches her eye, pulls the poloneck higher.

Lotte laughs and is horrified at how brittle she sounds. 'Strongbow,' she says, indicating the painting.

Why you need cover-up, Lotte? Always, you must cover-up.

'He was called Strongbow, apparently, because he was good with bows and arrows. Like Robin Hood.'

'Yeah, I know,' says Georgie. 'Mum told me.'

'Oh.' This is ridiculous. 'Georgie, is that my—'

'Lotte?' says Saoirse, interrupting.

'Yes?'

'Do you think it's wrong that the women in this picture aren't wearing clothes?'

'I—'

292

Saoirse is staring at her. Is that a look of calculation in the curranty eyes, a tinge of expectation in the damp, fishlike mouth? 'The women in the painting. They're nude. Jan says that's wrong. She says it's sexist.'

'Well, I'm not sure....'

Saoirse blinks. 'If it was fair, the men would have no clothes too.'

Georgie laughs. 'That's stupid.'

Saoirse turns. 'What?'

'What you said, stupid.'

'Georgie, don't—'

'Um?' Saoirse frowns. 'I don't get you, Georgie. Are you saying it's stupid for boys to have no clothes on but not for girls?'

'Children, come on. We—'

'Uh uh.' Saoirse blinks again; deliberately slow. 'I don't understand. Why do boys look stupid with no clothes on, Georgie?' Her eyes sharpen. 'Is it because you look stupid when you're nude?'

'Saoirse—'

'Because you're a stupid boy who thinks you're a—'

'Know what, Saoirse? You're fat and ugly and you've no friends and you piss your bed because your Mum is a crazy lesbian like William Robinson says and your dad is a stupid big stupid black fuck off blank nothing who can't warn a bloody fuck off flea and nobody loves you. You know what me and Elaine call you? Stinky-Saoirse. Stinky-Saoirse. Stinky—'

A thud. A crack. Georgie's nose is spurting blood. For a second Lotte thinks it was she who'd dealt the slap.

'Oh, hi, yeah, you're Lotte, the au pair?'

'Well, no—'

'Sorry, that was some assumption. Childminder, yeah?'

Is that what she has become? 'Yes.'

'Saoirse's fine, right?'

'Well, actually—'

'Is my kid okay? Is she sick?'

'No.'

'Did you give her dairy products?'

'No.'

'Because she reacts badly—'

'No, I didn't. Look, Mrs—' Fuck. Lie? Truth? 'Saoirse's fine, Mrs Ó Buachalla.'

'Maguire. I use my own name.' A sigh, then a laugh. 'You can call me Jan, honey. My, you got me worried there.'

'Yes. It's just, em, you see, nerves got a little frayed and....'

A tut. 'That poor kid. It's been so rough on him. I said to Donnacha, we need to help out, for Aisling's sake, and hey, it would've been no problem taking care of them here, but we know how complex Georgie is, right? Real sensitive around folks who aren't family. So when Donnacha told me David had it all under control, no surprises where Georgie gets it from, said he wanted you to take them....'

Black dots begin to dance in front of Lotte's eyes. Bloody David. 'Jan, do you think you could meet us in town? I think Saoirse wants to go home.'

'Oh?' Puzzled.

'They haven't really been getting on, Jan. Tempers are fraying a little. I think it's better for them both if you collect Saoirse now.'

A silence.

'I'm—'

'Do you have kids, Lotte?'

'Excuse me?'

Saoirse's mother laughs. It's a hollow sound. 'Guess not. Too busy taking care of your own needs, huh?'

'Sorry?'

'Come on, honey. You got a good game going there, with David so fragile right now.'

Lotte looks out through the phone box. The two children are standing shivering at the corner of the street. Saoirse is staring at her feet. Georgie's head is turned. In another universe, a hairsbreadth from this one, Saoirse's face is bleeding; Georgie's fist is bouncing.

Fuck it, she thinks. Fuck the lot of you.

'Of course, if you're too busy with your deadline to come and meet us, Jan, I can always put your child in a taxi and send her back on her own.'

The hiss of an in-drawn breath.

Oops, thinks Lotte. But it's too late. Tick, tick, tick, goes the shocked disbelief at the other end of the line.

Jan Maguire explodes into the pub and scoops up her child. A tight smile. Then she sees Georgie, face turned away, hanky clasped to bleeding nose. Surprise is followed by confusion as her *Hey, Georgie, how you doing...* fades into nothing.

'Bye, Saoirse,' says Lotte.

Jan Maguire ignores her; not even an *I'm gonna talk to David about this, honey*. Lotte watches them leave, Ó Buachalla's women; heavy and unstoppable as mountains.

'Can I've some more crisps?' says Georgie.

'Sure. Here's some money. Get them yourself. Have as many as you want.'

They walk home in the twilight. The half-melted snow, now slushy, is starting to freeze. Georgie smells of crisps and sugar. At one stage, the child slips on the ice and Lotte reaches out to stop the fall. Georgie's head ducks. Leave me alone. Lotte's hand around the child's middle feels lumps, bumps, damp parcels, the crinkle of plastic; an oddly formed belt, solid and squishy at the same time. Georgie twists away, out of reach.

Why did you steal my scarf, Georgie? Why are you hiding food in your pockets? Why won't you take off your coat?

When they get home, Caliban is crouching on the front step, looking miserable. He stands as soon as he sees them and starts yowling.

'Oh….' Georgie runs up the stairs. 'Poor cat.' The cat rubs his head against Georgie's chin, avoiding the swollen nose. Georgie's eyes close; the strong fingers knead, rub, caress the cat's whine into a purr.

Lotte sighs.

'Right, monsters. Let's get ourselves warm.'

She makes a fire, draws the curtain in the front window, and switches on the telly. A black-and-white movie is playing on RTÉ. Georgie is shivering.

'You need to get out of that coat.' Lotte's voice is decisive. 'Your clothes are drenched from all those games in the park.'

Georgie says nothing, strokes Caliban.

'I'm going to the kitchen. I'm going to get a dressing for your nose and make us some cocoa. While I'm doing that, you take off your things and put on something warm and get into the bed.'

Georgie looks at her. One eye is red and swollen; it'll be black in hours.

'It's much warmer than the sofa. You can put all your things there.' Lotte points at the chair near the window. 'Pile them up any old how. Don't worry about making a mess. When David comes, I'll need to have a chat with him. You can change back into your stuff then.'

Georgie nods. That adult recognition again, looking out from those eyes.

An impulse. Lotte hesitates, then obeys it. 'Look, Georgie. I know you don't like people saying this. But not everything is not your fault, you know.'

A glimmer in the young face. A moment where – is Lotte imagining this – things might be said? The glimmer vanishes.

'Right,' says Lotte, not sure if she's disappointed or relieved. 'Off with those clothes now and I'll get you your cocoa. Come on, it's been a long day.'

In the kitchen she strains her ears, listening for his music. Nothing is seeping down from the upstairs flat: no drums, no guitars, no howling calls for anarchy. All she can hear is the murmur of the queens' radio on the first floor and the quiet crackle and hum of the voices from her own telly, floating down the hallway. Maybe, she wonders – hopes? – he's asleep, putting the last of his hangover to rest.

As she's filling the kettle, she hears a dull crash from her bedroom, followed by a flicker, as if a light has gone off. She glances out the return window. Through the half-opened shutters, she can see that the overhead bulb in her big room has blown. Shadows are crawling up the walls, dancing in time to the zither music playing on the TV. Outside, an eerie green light is rising in the garden, hovering like mist above the snow-covered grass. It's just a trick of the moonlight, refraction, an optical illusion, but for a moment she thinks she sees the shape of a child standing there, skinny and girlish, teeth bared in a skeleton smile.

Why you must always make up stories, Lotte? Why you never stay with what is real?

After she's made the cocoa, she delays a bit in the hallway, to make sure Georgie's had a chance to hide the stolen things. Then she knocks on the door. 'Georgie?'

She turns the handle. The room is freezing, colder than it should be given the fire, and there's a strange, sweet smell in the air, like almond essence. The flickering of the TV has accentuated the fault lines of the old building. In the ceiling, there is a crack in the plasterwork that she has never noticed before. Under it, Georgie is sitting up in bed, wearing Lotte's dressing gown, hair bound up in a towel.

'Look at you, you're like—' *Not Nefertiti*. 'Something from the Bible. Did that bulb just blow?'

'Mmm.' Georgie sounds out of breath.

Caliban hisses.

'Silly boy, relax. God, it's freezing in here.' She closes the shutters and the green moonshine disappears. 'What's on?' she says, even though she already knows what the film is.

'Midweek Matinee.'

'Oh? Is it good?'

'It's okay. It's spies.'

Lotte pulls up a chair and sits beside the bed. In the corner of her eye, dignified Joseph Cotton is wending his way through the ruins of post-war Austria. 'Okay, monster.' She takes Georgie's face in her hands and gently turns it, examining the nose.

'Hold tight.'

She twists. There is a crunch. Georgie makes no sound.

'Aren't you brave?' Caliban jumps up on the bed and begins to knead the duvet. 'You'll thank me for that when you're grown up. Now, put this on, right on the skin. It'll keep the swelling down.'

'Are you a nurse?'

Lotte laughs. 'God, no.'

'You're good at minding.'

Lotte hugs Georgie, trying not to think of Sybille, lying on the bed in the prison hospital at Essen, faceless, yellow pus oozing through her bandages. 'Thanks, love.'

Caliban finishes kneading, curls himself into a pie. Joseph Cotton asks questions. People answer him in German. The zither plays. Bombsites, relics of Empire, the sewers. Something strikes her.

'Georgie, who's Elaine?'

Georgie frowns, staring at the screen. A split second later, Joseph Cotton frowns too, and moves onto the next person, searching, searching for Harry Lime.

Jesus! says David. His face seems to collapse and, for a moment, Lotte sees him as he will be when he's eighty: tiny and shrunken, long limbs folded in on themselves; a husk of a man.

I'm terribly sorry. It's—

Oh. Christ.

I—

Jesus. I mean. Did he provoke her?

I don't think it's that simple, David. I probably should have—

Christ! Sorry. It's just.... He said he'd take Georgie but— David stops. His face is grey, sick-looking.

Yes, says Lotte, not fully understanding. Your, um – don't say *friend* – Saoirse's dad mentioned....

Fuck. David shakes his head. Sorry. I should have— The teacher's been on to me, there's been reports, you know. Not bullying, not exactly, but. Jesus. I. I wasn't thinking straight.

So bringing Saoirse along for the day, even if it was a play for position, wasn't a conscious one? Lotte is surprised by the depth of her own relief.

David, I really think it's not as bad as you—

He rubs the bridge of his nose, agitated. I eh. I lost sight of Georgie. Couldn't see him. Then Donnacha was there and— I couldn't let him go with—

He lifts his eyes. They are raw, full of panic.

Yes, she says quickly. Jan. You didn't want Georgie going to Jan's house because Jan upsets Georgie. Forgetting, or blanking, what Saoirse said about deadlines and Jan being busy, because at least Jan and Georgie's distaste for her makes some sort of sense, and what they could both do with, her and David, right now, is sense.

His throat jerks, like he's being forced to swallow something. Things fighting in his face. You don't have to keep doing this. He almost spits it out.

Excuse me?

Georgie. His hands tense. Point to his chest. Us.

I….

It's. He struggles. It's a lot, I know. But it's not going to be for ever. There's that thing at work coming up for me. Now David's almost too insistent, as if trying to convince himself. It'll make a difference. For Georgie. Ash would have wanted—

I know. I mean—

David's hands bunch. I'm trying to just. You know.

Yes. Of course—

I just want to keep him—

I understand—

If we can get through to the end of the year, it'll. You know—

Yes, yes. I know. Mean something.

She has put her own hands up; a gesture of appeasement, or perhaps a warding off. She thinks of him in the garden in Marino, after the funeral, high on the weed she'd brought; giggling, hysteric, manic, almost crying. All that pent-upness had to go somewhere. He had made jokes, silly jokes, about Cork mothers and their engineer sons, and engineers building their own graves, and what's the difference between a doctor and an architect, one can bury her mistakes, the other has to grow ivy over his. Others too, not so innocent. Doing impressions of the people at the afters then, cracking her up, cracking her open, turning them both – Eros/Thanatos, *quelle surprise* – into teenagers again. Banishing the unsavoury picture of the wife-swap that had come into her head at the funeral; because a man that unknowingly *lonely*, she'd thought, wouldn't have let his wife be swapped for the world. Who had started the jokes, him or her? She can't remember. Can't remember what most of them were about. Would she have ever fucked the Poet, she wonders, if it hadn't been for that weed, those silly, unmemorable jokes?

A blurt: Can you come for Christmas?

Sorry?

Something held gives way in his chest. Just, eh. For dinner. Christmas dinner?

Won't you....

Be with your sisters, she wants to say, but he cuts her off.

We'll eh. He stalls, then it's all out, in a rush. We'll be going up North on Stephen's Day. Boxing Day. But it'll just be the two of us then. On the day itself. And you.

Oh.

Of course, if you don't want to. Just say.

He looks at her. His whole face raw now, anxious.

Promise me you'll take care of him, Aisling had whispered in her ear, that day in September, Georgie's first day back at school.

You've other things. He steps back. Well, we'd better—

No. The force of that surprises her. Yes. I mean, yes, of course, I'd love to, David. Thanks.

Georgie is dressed again, pockets bulging with stolen food and toilet paper and, most likely, the silk scarf Charlie gave Lotte and God knows what else. 'So,' says David. 'Lotte's staying for Christmas and she's going to, em, spend it with us.'

Georgie looks up; Lotte has never seen an expression of such horror on anyone's face.

'What, monster? Aren't you glad?'

'But people go home for Christmas,' says Georgie.

David blinks. 'Yes, but Ireland is Lotte's home now.'

Is it?

'Look, we'll talk about this in the car—' he starts, defeated, as Lotte says, 'Oh God, I mean, if—'

'No,' says Georgie, staring at David. 'It's not that. It's—'

The child sighs and the horror is gone, transformed into something dead and uncaring.

'Okay.'

Leave it with me, troops, he starts to say on the doorstep, already retreating into an unconvincingly blasé version of his brittle sergeant-major. But then he stops, glances at the car. Georgie is hunched in the back seat, swollen-faced under the stripes of orange streetlights.

'I'm sorry.' David frowns. 'He didn't mean it. He's, you know—'

'Yes—'

'No.' His hands lift, stopping her. 'I, eh. Really. I mean, your kindness. You know. Not just to him. I, eh. We really appreciate it.'

'A pleasure,' she says.

So polite, always. But she's not polite; she's oddly flustered.

With anyone else, she would have done her mother's thing, reached out, touched his forearm. The continental gesture. Instead, they nod at each other and he's gone, half-running down the steps, whistling to himself. What holds her back? Not Jan Maguire, surely, and those ridiculous assumptions.

Come on, honey. You got a good game going there.

Ridiculous?

She remembers the way David's shoulders changed when she accepted his invitation, as if releasing an ancient weight. Christ, she thinks. What have I done?

When she goes back into her room, she doesn't notice the end of Charlie's silk scarf, lolling out over the top of the drawer like a sea monster's tongue, put back exactly where she'd left it that morning. She won't notice that till the next day. That's because she's in too much of a hurry to get at the tea chest beside her bed. She takes off the books and the lamp that she'd put on top and turns it upside down. Then she pulls out the bundle, wrapped in its grey blanket. She uncovers it. Her twin's metal shell gleams; round, unbroken, a snail-carapace.

Caliban weaves around her legs, butting her with his nose. She bites her nails, unsure, waiting for Andrew's voice to rise in her head, mocking their mother with one of her unusable pieces of advice.

Instead, all that comes to mind is David, opening his hands, saying in his halting way, Thank you, kind girl.

Is it better to tell people the truth of who you are – truth? She can't help a little laugh at that. Or do you allow them to ferret out their own version? She thinks of the architect at the afters, blotto in the Maddens' kitchen, howling for the master of the house like a dog who'd lost its owner. She thinks of his wife, so intent on attributing blame and motivation, so eager to find her own patterns in other people's stories. Of Aisling in the garden of that hospice, digging her nails into Lotte's skin, an odd, insistent emphasis in her plea. *Please, Lotte, promise, Georgie,* our *baby, promise me you'll stay and look after him, I owe Davey that much.* You don't owe anyone anything, Lotte had tried to say. *Oh, but I do,* said Aisling, her face glowing with a sick, feverish light.

Is it better to take a risk, face the other front-on, say, Here you go, this is my story, isn't this what you were looking for? And read their response: surprise, shock, or the shamed uncertainty that means they were after that all along. Then what? Do you become another trophy to hang on their washing line? Or, once they've got their scoop, are you forgotten? What if they prove you wrong, say, No, I don't want that, I don't care about the story, I just want you.

If it was only her, it would be easier. But she's holding something else; her twin. Flesh of my flesh, blood of my blood. DNA of my curling, interwoven DNA.

> *Do chonaic mé spéirbhean mhaorga mhallrosc*
> *Mhilis bhog bhéaltais mhéarlag mhealltach*
> *Thaithneamhach tháclach shásta fhionn*
> *Ina seasamh in airde ar chlár na mionn.*

I saw a woman in the witness box, he'd said last night, whispering poetry in her ear. *The Midnight Court* by Merriman. The Gaelic first, then the English. A beautiful, fair lady, soft-lipped, beguiling. With her hair loosened down in flowing masses and sorrow in her look; vigour in her aspect and fire in her eyes; boiling with a vile temper of argument about her. Soundless in her silence. It was easy to state that death was her choice. I think I love you, he said, as they lay on her bed, melting into each other. I think I've loved you since the first day I saw you. I saw you on the stairs and I thought, Jesus. That is some woman. *Mo spéirbhean.*

But love is a joke, Poet, an illusion; the dried vestiges of fourteenth-century minstrels' wet dreams; a glamour seeded in the woods of Bohemia.

She didn't reciprocate. She thinks. She might have said, as a joke, Well, that's nice. I love Caliban.

'You'd want to be careful what you talk about in your sleep,' he'd said as he stood behind her in the hall that morning, and his breath was the Captain's, fetid on her neck.

Bloody art, bloody politics. Rilke's knots on the rosary of life.

Do you let the past trap you, pin you in its gnarl? Or do you, can you, move on?

'Eoin?'

He must have cleared out in the afternoon, while she was at the art gallery with the children. He hasn't bothered cleaning up after himself. There are dirty sheets on his bed, the floor is unswept, the sink grubby, a heap of unwashed plates piled up beside it; a room caught in mid-flight. But he's left nothing important. No clothes; no washing lines; no darkroom chemicals; no scraps of torn-up prints lying in the wastebasket. No Theodor Adorno or Walter Benjamin. Just a small, black-and-white square lying in the middle of the floor.

She picks it up. It's a 45. The sleeve is like one of Ands' early artworks, a Situationist paste-up of ransom letters against a rough collage. Snarling boys with hedgehog hair. *Anarchy in the UK.*

Auf Wiedersehen, Gudrun, he's scrawled in red crayon across the vinyl, making it unplayable.

She sits on his floor, in the cold green moonlight, cradling the can, its long strips of film coiling inside.

You win again, Ands. Blood of my blood. Flesh of my flesh. DNA of my rootless, rotten DNA.

Lognote # 7

Visitors, we are about to plunge again into the Maps Cycle. Expect disruptions. We have been informed that, as a result, the Space/Raum in which our Kammer operates will soon begin to experience Contraction. For your own safety, keep your eyes on the ball, move fast and follow our instructions At All Times.

Most curious feature

A constant hum of electronic music plays throughout the entire field of this Exhibit. Although no words are audible, some visitors have identified the tune as belonging to that old favourite, 'Let's Call the Whole Thing Off'.

Map Fifteen: 1900–08

That thick red-white-red-green coil first seen in Map Eight has grown thicker; Austria-Hungary has got in on the Empire-Building Races of the early twentieth century! This borderline is also starting to vibrate rather violently. How hard it is – as our *Kunstkammersuperego Staff* know only too well – to hold on to your core when extreme forces are pulling in every direction.[1] To the far east of the map, more observant visitors will see the start of a red haze. Perhaps you can also detect the curious shapes starting to gather there: hammers, sickles, guns, Molotov cocktails.[2]

In the borderlands, a mound of eraser rubbings is evidence that the Prime Minister's proposal to partition Bohemia along ethnic lines – separating the wealthier Germans in the resource-full border areas from their poorer Czech cousins in the centre – has just been overturned. And, nearer the Moravian

---

[1] See Ireland: Yeats, W. B. and *The Second Coming*: 'The centre cannot hold'.
[2] For more information, visit, if you ever get the Opportunity, the *RusskyOktoberRevolutionspiel*.

303

boundary, more indelible marks are visible: the German Social Democrats have pushed through the Moravian Compromise, 'fixing' the ratio of Czechs to Germans to facilitate fairer local government!

Hurrahs! all round (rarely for this *Kammer*, no *Boos!*).

Scraps of ripped-up ballots suggest that universal suffrage is proving a trickier question. Listen, and you'll hear the clamour of grumbling German[3] voices: *don't see why the Czechs should be able to have a say/vote/appear in parliament after all who's made this place what it is we were here first* etc.[4] Please note that twinkling light near Prag/Praha. Is a compromise for suffrage, negotiated by Prime Minister Beck, on its way? Or—

Warning: Vistors should be aware that a cacophony of clinking coins will sound if you press the flashing red button labelled '1908'. In addition, the border will spread south and east, as the Empire, following the money, encloses Bosnia-Herzegovina.

Hurrah / Boo! Sound of breaking eggshells as Humpty Beck falls.

Map Sixteen: 1909–14

On the borderlands those beeping sounds identified in Map Fourteen are getting louder as the language struggles continue. What on earth are those wriggling things at your feet? Maggots? (? / **curator alert !** /— V̶ẃitors, please, please keep your eyes away from that ugly little metaphor – it's only those pesky gym-clubs again. The national societies are everywhere, seeking influence in schools, youth clubs, fitness organisations, land acquisition and business. Many visitors have also reported being deafened by this map: who'd have thought one small territory would generate so many complainers? In the borderlands, paranoid mutters in German about the rising numbers of Czech schools and Czech officials.[5] Elsewhere, angry noises in Czech about the local elections still being weighted in favour of the Germans. *You're trying to make us all German! Oh, no, we're not, you're trying to make us all Slav! Oh no, we're not! Oh yes, you are!... etc.*

---

[3] *Many* German voices – curator's emphasis: the German Social Democrats aren't, in fact, resistant to change.

[4] Bloody krauts at it again, eh? See All Imperial Nations: justification for holding onto power and control.

[5] At the risk of sounding *wrong* (see, if we get there, *Lognote # 8*, Footnotes 1, 12: the 'Dresden argument'), are the Germans really that paranoid? By 1914, they'll have 5,000 state officials less than their numbers would justify (Wiskemann, 1938).

Please bring your attention to the tiny, rather festive golem figures in the map's centre, which appear to be the source of most of the noise. Closer inspection will reveal that they represent a bunch of new political parties: the German Agrarians (peasants), the Czech Agrarians (snap!), the German Workingmen's Party and the Czech National Socialists.[6] If you dare to put your ears close to the racket, you may be able to differentiate three main groupings:

- German Social Democrats, just about audible. These want a fully democratic federal Austrian state, divided along ethnic boundaries. But the Czechs don't seem to be listening.[7]
- Czech moderates, speaking rather forcefully, who think Bohemian Germans are 'hopeless' and will never give Czechs their day.
- Extremists both sides, the loudest of the lot.[8]

Above the din of the golems is a faint *cuckoo* – Harry Lime's despised Swiss clocks, sounding the chimes for an alternative model of government. However, unlike Harry, we suggest that visitors give these little clocks the benefit of the doubt. In Switzerland, even though they speak three different languages, they've managed to make something work. Which is more than can be said for—

Warning: When approaching the flashing red button labelled 'June 1914', visitors are advised to wear waterproof clothing and insert ear plugs. Pushing this button is done *at your own risk* since it will result in being splattered with an Archduke's grey matter 💣 (! / **aler**— *[cognition-flash:* **Was that a bomb?** *[circuit self-destructs]*— to 𝔡je æℳ□mpaniment of – (!!! / **alert! high-alert!!** /— move on as fast as you can, visitors! – a deafening mash-up of Franz Ferdinand's 'Take Me Out' and U2's 'Miss Sarajevo'.

Interlude: a Musical Schattenspiel (Shadow-Play)

Visitors, we suggest you contain yourselves for the duration of the War[9] in this safe corner, where you can listen to a medley of popular songs,

---

[6] Not Czech Nazis, but proper socialists who want a sovereign national identity. See Ireland: Connolly, J.
[7] Too little too late? Or perhaps it's because the Germans live in the parts that are (a) the wealthiest; (b) the most industrialised; and (c) have the best geographic defences? So – trick question – who's going to benefit most from division along ethnic lines? See Ireland: partition of, particularly in relation to the linen/shipbuilding industries of Ulster.
[8] Please note that while only Czechs understand the Czech ranters, everyone understands the Germans. Is this why German extremists get such a lasting, sour reputation?
[9] Which prompts us to raise that old chestnut: Who benefits, economically and politically, from wars? By which we mean all wars, including ones on 'Terror'?

including 'It's a Long Way to Tipperary', 'Silent Night' and 'Pack Up Your Troubles in Your Old Kit Bag', all chosen to comfort the shell-shocked ear. You may wish to shield the eyes of your little ones, as violent imagery will continue to play out on the walls of our *Kammer* for some time. Particularly distressing to the kiddies will be the sight of so many adolescent Bohemian Germans signing up in droves to become the crack regiments of the Austrian army, while their counterparts, young Czechs, join 'legions'[10] to help the Allies.[11] That tenor voice some visitors have heard across the medley is Czech politician Kramar,[12] singing his rather lovely '*that-was-a-close-one*' aria.

By now, you'll notice that the multilingual chaos of the previous map has been replaced by a soundscape with a decidedly Teutonic tone. During the war, German has been reinstated as the only official language of the Empire. Look to your West! A flicker of shadows as, in response, the smart guys, Czech politicians Edvard Beneš and Tomas Masaryk, head out of the region towards the *LalalalalAmerica!schattenspiel*, a move facilitated by none other than Woodrow 'Self-Determination' Wilson!

Map Seventeen: 1918

The *Schreckkabinett* apologises for the state of this map. It is, frankly, a mess. So many scalpel-marks, pen-strokes, body parts, burnt edges and reddish-brown stains (!!— 💣 / **alert** ! /— *[overload kinaesthetic / cognition-flash:* '**I am in pain**' */ circuit self-destructs]* i ◄'i—ignore that, visitors, time is getting Tight, eyes back on the Map— it's almost impossible to see what's going on. The familiar thick red-white-red lines tremble, appearing to strengthen momentarily as the 'Great' War ends and Emperor Karl offers federalisation to the nations of Austria!

Hurr—

Oops! We spoke too soon. France and Britain have already signed up to a new deal. Hankies, visitors, as those familiar red-white-red lines disappear, never to be seen again, banished to the shadowy corners of All Maps known as the Past.

---

[10] See literature, Czech Legionaire. Noted for, among other things, its rank anti-Semitism.

[11] For contrast, see Ireland: especially Redmond, J., and the concept of 'deal-making': Young Irish Blood for Home Rule.

[12] Sentenced to death for speaking out against the war, then reprieved. See Ireland: Casement, R., for contrast.

Good-bye Empire. Hello 'Czechoslovakia'.
Hurrah! / Boo!
Shimmering text over the border regions indicates that it is from this *Punkt* on that the territory inhabited by the Germans of the Historic Provinces of Bohemia, Moravia and Silesia starts being called the 'Sudetenland', and its inhabitants[13] get the moniker 'Sudeten Germans'.

Map Eighteen: Late autumn 1918

Don't blink as you approach this map. Otherwise you'll miss it. For six weeks, the Sudeten Germans declare autonomy in the spirit of Wilson's ideals of 'self-determination'.
Hurr—
Oh dear. Look at all those tiny guns and tanks, all with Czech names on them.
Warning: This map has now disappeared. Any visitor lucky enough to have glimpsed it, even if only for a moment, will have remarked on the absence of brownish-red stains in its fabric, suggesting that the Sudeten Germans were happy to accept the authority of the new Czechoslovakian state and therefore chose not to violently resist.[14]
Hurrah!

—

Map Eighteen (a)[15]: 1918–28

Strong lines emerge: blue, white and red. Visitors will notice a dramatic shrinkage as the region loses contact with the once-sprawling giant of Empire and contracts into a smaller area, rather humpy in shape with a funny protruding bit. Younger visitors may notice a resemblance to a small amphibian creature, an alligator, maybe?

---

[13] Including *Mutti-Kustosin*/Mummycurator a.k.a. Anna B. and her *Volk*/People.
[14] For alternative readings of the capitulation, see Any Defeated Nation: post-defeat traumatic stress syndrome, economic hardship, collapse of existing order and previous certainties, lack of foresight brought about by unrealistic wartime propaganda and so on. See, for example (at the risk of offending some), WWII: the Czech resistance to the Nazis, allegedly haphazard nature of.
[15] This '(a)' is for the purposes of clarity only. Visitors offended by any connotations of second-aryness are urged to rename this map Map Eighteen and the previous one Map Eighteen (a). As the *Kammer* still (just about) operates outside normal spacetime conventions, the very act of thinking differently will cause 'reality' to change too.

Long live Czechoslovakia!
Hurrah! / Boo!

The torn edge of a voting ballot stitched into the map near Praha/ Prag is evidence of the first elections held by the new Czechoslovak state – a 'landslide' victory for the Slavs![16] The more observant visitor will have noticed gunpowder residue and brownish-red stains (! /— **oooooops** ! /— **curator al**—/ 🔥 *[circuit self-destructs]* in the 'Sudeten' regions. This is evidence of the 1919 'massacre' of Sudeten Germans (fifty-two killed, eighty-four wounded) who protested at not being allowed to participate in the elections and were shot by the Czechs.[17] Otherwise – commendations, visitors, for staying with us – the fabric of this map appears relatively stable. There are no flashing red buttons. Instead, a few rather half-hearted blinking LEDs point to, in no particular order:

- Czech dominance of government
- The murder of a politician by an anarchist
- German initial absenteeism from, then later rejoining of, government,[18] again suggesting a willingness to go along with things[19]
- Czech dominance of government (yes, still there)
- Land reform and the nostrification[20] of businesses

A light scarlet sheen above the nostrification button indicates an idealistic agenda; the redistribution of wealth![21]

Hurr—

Not so fast. Visitors looking for traces of genuine Robin Hoodlumism will be disappointed when we rewind the 'nostrification' sequence. True, the people who lose out most during this process are the rich, specifically German landowners, financiers, company MDs and factory owners who've had their

---

[16] 50 per cent Czech, 20 per cent Slovak, 23 per cent German, 7 per cent Romanian, Carpathian & Magyar. Trick question: if you can, subtract the Slovaks. What sort of landslide do you get now?

[17] See, at the risk of confusing our previous 'parallels': Ireland: Bloody Sunday, Derry.

[18] *You put your left leg in, you put your left leg out.*

[19] Or, for an alternative reading: do some powerful Sudeten Germans (i.e. the bourgeoisie and industrialists) simply prefer to belong to an economically stable, Ally-backed Republic, rather than being part of a bankrupt ex-Empire, the capital of which is, besides, inconveniently far away?

[20] Literally 'our-ification', meaning national ownership, putting an end to centuries of 'them-ification', unless, of course, you are a German and us = them.

[21] See, if it's still possible to return there, *Lognote # 4*, Map Eight: Empress Maria and the real-location of wealth to keep the peasants happy. See also Ireland: robbing the rich to feed the poor; appropriation of Big House lands in the early years of the Free State.

savings tied up in Viennese banks. But the people who win the most are also rich; specifically, canny Czech businessmen. No peasants, either Czech or German, seem to have gained much. And while the Czech unions in the industrialised Sudetenland are grumbling about economic discrimination, nobody, especially not the powers-that-be in Prague, is listening. Because noble savages, Mensheviks and Bolsheviks aside, who cares about peasants or, indeed, working men and women? [22]

Just inside the borderlands, there is evidence of a fizzing substance far more volatile than the stable red-white-and-blue borderlines of this map might suggest – the scent of *Volkstum*.[23] This tricky material is accompanied by a slight but constant rumble of discontent from the newly 'oppressed' German population; a sound which, if the Czechs were willing to listen, might sound awfully familiar. But, as you can see from the baby golems of Masaryk, Beneš et al., most Czechs politicians are still looking for support and validation from the West – Britain, France and the grand old US of A – and are not remotely interested in rumblings from Germans.[24]

You may also notice some eerie shadow-lines forming around the borderlines. It's as if the map-maker[25] has scratched out the contours of the border's identity, then redrawn them in an ink-combination of uncertain hue (black-red-gold; red-white-red; red-black-white?). Listen to the confused patter around you, rising from the German professional and noble castes! They are now seeking to create a new 'Bohemia', the Impossible Thought Experiment described in *Lognote # 4*, rebranded here as a feudal utopia. This twentieth-century Bohemia will, ideally, include machinery, banks and all the nicer aspects of market capitalism and will, naturally, be for only the professional and noble Germans to govern – not peasants or workers. If you squint, you may just see, straddling this hazy line, the initials KB, referring to the secret neo-feudalist society *Kameradschaftsbund* (Comradeship Association).

Draw a breath (! !/— **alert! alert!**/ [cognition-flash: **'Can I breathe?'** → *neural impulse* → *sympathetic nervous system/ effort*] → 💣💣 *[circuit self-destructs]* Visitors, please keep going! Don't try to breathe, just Imagine you can! Smell that sweat! Behold those Bohemian German boys, scarred and disfigured from the War, alienated from party politics, as they fill the ranks of the gym-clubs! Watch them grunt and heave as they work out! Feel their strong Teutonic

---

[22] *Dirty nasty things*. See, if you can, *Lognote # 4*, Footnote 7.
[23] Literally, 'Folk-ish-ness' a.k.a. 'being-German-ness'.
[24] Or, for that matter, Slovaks.
[25] Who, we wonder, is that?

muscles, their gleaming skin! Applaud them as they do their press-ups, under the tutelage of their instructor: hopeful idealist and KB-fan, Konrad Henlein![26]

Final interlude: Demolition Derby, 1928–33

Achtung! Careful! Mind your littl'uns! Beware of falling Humpties, Walls and Wall Streets! The Crash may be happening in *LalalalalAmerica!schattenspiel*, outside the chambers of this *Sonderraum*, but even the most severely hearing-impaired visitor won't miss the sounds of beer-steins clinking, men shouting and window glass breaking as, far closer to home, in a parallel *Deutschlandspiel*, an Austrian with a funny moustache starts saying things that seems to make sense to the good people of Munich.

And what's that growing in the shadows of our own lost *Heimatkammer*, a few red rungs of the socio-economic ladder down from their quasi-feudal KB lords and masters, only spitting distance from Henlein's gym club?

Surprise! It's the German Workingmen's Party – only overnight, they've grown knuckledusters and earned themselves two extra initials, N and S![27]

What on earth is going to happen next?

Note: Visitors, thank you for your compliance. As predicted, our Space/*Raum* is starting to shrink. We must now leave the Maps Cycle, although a Coda of sorts may be available later in the Tour. Without further ado, we urge you to get your skates on.

---

[26] For more about Little Konrad – and what became of his Ideals – see, if Time/Pressure allows, *Lognote # 9*.

[27] No prizes for guessing what that stands for. Two syllables, rhymes with patsy.

17:57:39–20:59:03

Is there a better story I should be sharing with you? A tale from a parallel universe? One of those books you used to read when you were my father; a sci-fi epic with a big cast of characters and interwoven plots? A story that jumps from place to place and spans decades, that's packed with gizmos and technology, heroes and villains and enough alien life-forms to keep even you listening? Instead I offer you this: a hotch-potch of memories, my own talking head intercut with observational footage from a day in the life. Mar, if he was around, would be appalled. Am I avoiding something by telling you this? If I get the chance, will I move on; start talking about other things?

That elephant, still crashing around. I'm no wiser, I'm afraid, as to what I'm going to do with your gift.

I sat in the cab, a rod of tension dissolving into a brittle puddle as, behind us, the hospital and its infernal machinery, its lost souls wandering in circles, peeled away. I felt not exactly human, but animal again. Mammalian, warm-blooded; grateful for the heating, the music playing on the sound system, the support of the seat, the thin strap across my chest bracing me against sudden accelerations. Grateful too to the cabbie; for his lack of surprise at the sight of my face, for not saying something like *Jaysus, you been in the wars*, and most of all, for his body, shielding me from the windscreen and the knives hiding in it.

The flu was back, but keeping its distance. I couldn't smell but could imagine the smells around me: fake leather, pine tree freshener, stale tobacco. A faint after-tang of vomit. The cabbie was wearing a baseball cap; his face was saggy, his eyes hooded. He had Neil Young playing: 'Powderfinger', a ballad of young lives lost, sad and thin.

His eyes flickered in the rearview, met mine.

'You sure about this? I mean, I can drop you at the station.' There was a smartphone near the dash. His fingers were hovering over it. 'There's a train at nine and….'

I shook my head. 'It's grand.' My voice sounded croaky.

The cabbie nodded. His fingers had yellow tips. A box of cigarettes nestled beside his phone. Ninety minutes to Dublin, non-stop. No chance of a smoke. No wonder he was so jittery.

'Eh— I know this is a bit, em, cheeky, but could I have one of your cigarettes?'

He blinked. On the back of his seat, facing me, was the No Smoking sign.

'I won't tell.'

He made a snorting sound that might have been a laugh. 'Alright, then.'

He pushed the gearstick into fifth as we swung onto the motorway; then, without looking around, handed me the pack.

'D'you want one?' I asked.

He grunted. I slid out two fags. John Player Red, pure lung-rot. Yet another thing you don't know about me: I started smoking in college, where my aunts couldn't see me, but gave up six years ago, when I started to transition. I was worried about the risks: circulation, clotting, complexion. Typical, Mar said. Worried too, though I didn't admit it, about the other C, the big one, Aisling's legacy.

I lit a fag with the cabbie's plastic lighter and handed it to him. Then I lit my own. In for a penny, in for a pound.

My lungs filled with the familiar cushion of smoke. My chest complained, then, grateful, loosened. My eyes half-closed. Out the front windscreen, I could see the road; a blurry grey sea split by a wedge of green, dotted with red tail-lights, the pale silver of oncoming daylights. Behind it, the sludgy blue of the sky. Rain washed across the windscreen, followed by the sleazy tango of the wipers. Ah – one – two – three. The rain had slowed since I'd had the crash. The wipers were better than my Fiat's: they were intact.

A medal was dangling from the rearview. St Christopher on a blue thread. A picture of a smiling baby was stuck to the glove compartment. On the seat beside me was a paper. The previous day's *Evening Herald*. Too early for a mention of the bomb or the looming reprisals. Too early for a mention of anything.

The cab swung into the fast lane. A sudden change in my field of vision. My heart stopped, waiting for the cabbie's back to lurch towards me, the glass to break over his face.

One fag, two fag. A good distraction. I watched the world pass: sea, sky, tiny oblongs of ferries and carrier ships glinting on the horizon. The watery-green hills of Wicklow, scarred red by the teeth of JCBs and left, undeveloped, to rot. Brown signs pointing to Scenic Routes, Areas of Natural Beauty, Heritage Sites, TV Towns. Service stations begging for our custom, offering Lowest Prices Ever, Cappuccino and Hot Snacks in lime-green, custard-yellow, blood-red neon. Everything Slashed.

On the sound system, Neil Young segued into Willie Nelson, then Johnny Cash. My cabbie was a lonesome cowboy. As the nicotine worked on him, he turned chatty. He was from Dublin, he told me, outside Tallaght, you could probably guess from the accent, but he'd moved the family to Gorey at the height of the Boom. I'd read news stories about those waves of migration: working-class families, usually with drug problems, being shifted out to the sticks. Brid had wanted to do a programme about it. Ethnic cleansing by any other name would smell so sweet.

We talked a bit about the weather, then he brought up the bombing. Unbelievable, he said, and tutted. D'you know anyone over there? No, I said, trying to flick away the nonsense connection that was Turnmill Street. Oh. He sounded disappointed. Lovely place, London.

He avoided mentioning the parade or what either of us was planning to do over the long weekend. He must have had me for a loner; at best, a spinster. On the dashboard, his baby's face stared at me. It looked confused, like babies often do, and its mouth was stained with jam. Beside it, in the little digital window, I could see my fare, mounting. I thought of my shrinking savings; I thought of the fee I'd wrangled from Brid. I lit another fag. Fuck it.

Johnny Cash finished and then we were listening to the news.

'...man found today in the Royal Canal had a distinctive tattoo on his back and....'

'I thought they'd forgotten him,' I found myself saying.

The cabbie tutted again. 'Poor tosser. Destroyed. Vicious little fucks. Tore his face off and all. And to fucking film that?'

'Sorry?'

'Sick. Cops aren't saying but they reckon it was kids.'

Kids?

The cabbie's eyes flicked. 'They put it on YouTube. Has to be kids.'

It probably wasn't, I started to say. Then I remembered that weird jump-cut during the news bulletin, the website's logo back-projected in the studio. The cigarette suddenly tasted foul.

'It's all them video games. *Grand Theft Auto*, zombies. Nasty business. They spent hours at it, watching him. Who would do that? Poor bastard. You'd of hardly known about him what with everything else going on. Chose the wrong day for it, eh?'

'Mmm,' I said, and leaned back again into my seat.

As we reached the border between Wicklow and Dublin, the detritus left by the Boom began to close around us. Last-ditch attempts to push the city farther out: empty apartments, derelict malls, an unusable 500-seater arts centre. Your world; building sites and half-constructed things; hunks of glass and concrete shimmering above slatted wooden walls. Jesus, Geo, Mar had said when we'd arrived in Ireland, if they could build on the fucking sea, they would.

Had he been right? What would have happened, do you think, if the Boom hadn't burst? Would my city, that used to be yours, would all the small cities of this small island have continued growing, extending out onto the water until they were floating, like Venice, or Lake Titicaca? Can you picture it, the way you told me you could always picture things that hadn't been built yet? People living in tottering high-rises, washing their clothes in the waves, swimming everywhere, or travelling by boat. Voices calling across the water and constant interruptions to business, as all those beautiful glass ships, those office-blocks built by the Tiger, rise and fall, following the rhythm of the tides sweeping in across the Irish Sea. Mischief in the boardroom instead of malice. Unbolted tables sliding across floors, chairs tilting back like swooning lovers, pencils and corporate toys tumbling off desks. Can you picture the people too, those blithe new amphibians, with their expanding fortunes and never-falling house prices? Laughing at all the interruptions, while at night their gilly children lie in bed, rocked to sleep by the foundations of their floating cities, dreaming of a past lost to them, when people walked on solid ground and took balance for granted. Can you see their mothers, smoothing their foreheads, singing land-shanties to lull them to sleep?

Do you see her, still? In your dreams? Aisling, my own dream-mother?

Eskimo kiss, sweetheart.

We had reached the connection between the M11 and the M50. The road was bristling with signs. *60. Slow. Road Works.* Flashing lights. A blur of luminous-yellow jackets, orange diggers, white helmets, ripped-up ground.

'Sorry,' said the cabbie. 'Wouldn't of thought, with the bank holiday and all….'

'Actually,' I said. 'Can you go through town first?'

'Town?'

'Marino.' My tongue fizzed around the name, like it was sherbet.

He frowned.

'It's fine,' I said. 'I know it's out of the way. I'll pay.' I gave him the address.

The cabbie looked as if he was about to argue but something in my face must have stopped him. He shrugged, soft and helpless, and flicked the indicator.

The palms of my hands started to prickle. This was a bad idea. I leant forwards to tell him I'd changed my mind, but before I could, the traffic surged, and we were past the junction.

'You ever been to Spain?' said the cabbie.

'Sorry?'

'You know, Spain. *Viva España.*'

I shook my head, then remembered. 'Once. I was in Barcelona.'

He looked back at the road. 'I'm heading to Andalucia. Pal of mine has a bar there, so I reckon, if he can do it, you know. No money in this game anymore. Any gobshite can get hold of a plate and they're like wolves, I swear. And don't get me started on the hacks. See, where I am now, Gorey, Wexford, the odd job in Wicklow, there's fucking nothing. And nights... Jesus. They're a cunt—' he glanced back '—sorry, hard, I mean. The stories I could tell you.'

Would I be one of those stories? *Had one of them he-shes in the car the other night; Jesus, should of seen the state of it....*

'I used to rake it in. Me brothers hated me for it.'

He laughed. The traffic was slowing again, as if out of spite. I was starting to feel tired and bruised again. I wondered how much longer the detour would take.

'They all fucked off to England in the eighties. Got jobs on the black working dodgy hotels, giving three addresses to the DSS. Nice money for nothing. Wouldn't blame them. Back here it was a cunt of a place.' This time he didn't bother glancing around. 'They could of ended up getting in with the wrong crowd, the drugs, all that. I was okay, though. I was the babby, born at the right time.' He laughed; it had a dry, rattly sound. 'Used to call me Jammy Noel on account I had it so good.'

He finished his fag, stubbed it out.

'Then my luck ran out. Got busted for a hit and run in ninety-eight, couldn't drive for five years. Drunk. Fucking gobshite I was. That learns you real fast, but.'

Did I imagine it or did his eyes drift to the picture of his confused, smiling baby?

We'd stopped at the Cabinteely intersection. He gestured to the box of fags. 'Go on, have another.'

A fourth? I lit up, inhaled.

The cabbie had turned silent and was looking at me. I became aware of the roadlights picking out my features, my cuts and bruises.

He cleared his throat. 'Sorry. Gerry, that's my girl, she hated me smoking. Told me I'd get cancer and die on her. Hah.'

The lights changed. I let the fag burn itself out and closed my eyes, only half-listening as Jammy Noel told me about Gerry, the girl he'd loved, the girl who was the mother of his jam-faced baby, who'd run off with some fucking Polak or Serb or Russian gangster involved in them illegal poker dens on the North Strand, after her ma died she'd legged it, real sudden like, and they after moving to Gorey for a cleaner life because she'd been messed up before, you know, on the drugs, only he'd helped her clean up, but she hadn't listened, and in a way, he said, if she had taken him back, left that Russky mafia cunt – vicious fuckers they were, them gangsters – and come back to him, he probably wouldn't even be thinking of going to Spain. You can forgive anything, can't you, if you've a bit of love in your life?

I was feeling cold now, the same cold I had felt in the hospital, thinking about you. My chest was beginning to hurt again. Marino was a mistake. A bad decision brought on by stress. I had no business going there. Once we got to the canal, I'd tell the cabbie to hang left and head straight to Inchicore.

Swish, swoosh went the sound of his wipers. My eyelids dropped.

Martin's face loomed. His eyes were huge and hollow, his skin smouldering. Bits of it were tearing away, turning grey and flaking off, as if he was made of newspaper. Stop, I told him. Go away. But he wasn't listening. The flames licked, caught the ends of his hair, shrivelled them to tufts. Behind him was a dark shape. Broad, no head, arms stuck out like one of those cartoon railway signals at level crossings. A door opened. A labyrinth. Underground. A blur; a gap. We were in a bedroom, my old bedroom in Marino. A window was opening. No. It was already open, and I wasn't inside, but outside, on the extension roof, and I had to get in because there was something I had to find and bring to where it would forget its head and—

The world jerked. My body shook. Something was touching my right breast.

316

I opened my eyes. Jammy Noel's face was close to mine. Too close. He was twisted around, half out of his seat, and his hand was on my shoulder. No. Collarbone. Martin's coat was unbuttoned. The cabbie's mouth smelt bad. Could I smell? I tried to speak but nothing came out.

He blinked. 'Sorry about that. Didn't know you were asleep.'

Had I been asleep long enough to dream?

'We're, eh, here.'

The cab had stopped. I could see the yellow of the hazards flashing in the side mirrors; suburban gardens, pebble-dashed walls.

Jammy Noel's hand was hot, pulsing against my body. What had he— Had he been *at* me?

My skin crawled. My throat gagged.

He flushed and took his hand from me. 'I'd of woken you up sooner, yeah?'

Had he not just said he hadn't known I was asleep?

'But you looked like you needed the rest, what with the....' He gestured to his face. 'Anyhow.' He glanced at my chest. An involuntary movement. A tic.

Perve. I pulled Martin's coat closed, reached for the door handle.

'Do you want me to wait?'

I stared at him.

'Marino, right? Then Inchicore?'

Outside, a cherry blossom tree was moving in the wind. Bare branches, like a woman's arms.

Oh, fuck.

'Alright, then.' He pressed a button. 'That'll be a hundred and twenty.' At least he had the grace to sound embarrassed.

I dug around in my coat pocket. Martin's coat pocket. Found my purse, took out my debit card. He swiped it. We avoided eye contact. My chest was throbbing now, my head starting to ache. I stared at the No Smoking sign on the seat-back in front of me.

'Grand,' said Jammy Noel.

I nodded, smiled a tight smile that made my face hurt. If he hadn't been so dodgy, I might have wished him good luck in Andalucia.

Another tip for you. Trans rule number one: never alienate. Not, at least, unnecessarily.

I got out of the car. The rain had softened, was wetter now. Behind the windscreen the cabbie's face had become a fright mask: his eyes black holes, his mouth a vortex. I slammed the door. The lights inside the cab winked out, making him disappear. The car pulled off. Panic rose in me. I forced it down, pulling Martin's collar up against the rain, and turned to face the dirty grey sky and, black against it, the house that used to be ours: yours and mine and Aisling's.

Funny. Most things from my childhood shrink any time I've revisited them as an adult. Clonmel. My aunts. Your mother, my tottering wreck of a granny. My other grandparents and their two small, tidy graves, packed neatly away into two different cemeteries. But our house seemed far larger than I'd rememembered it as a kid. The windows were dark, the gate ajar. The front garden looked okay; tidier than when we'd had it, but not as nice as the rest of the houses on the road, with their uniform sandy gravel and weeping birches. I wondered who was living there now. They'd put wooden blinds on our windows and I felt a bit sorry for the house to see they'd chosen standard ones from Homebase, not the posh sort with the wide slats. For Sale, said a sign sticking out of the hedge.

This was a terrible idea. I felt unhinged again, like I'd felt at the lakes when I'd seen those creepy teenagers, as if part of me was still in Jammy Noel's car, sleeping, while the other stood here, facing—

Facing what, exactly?

It had been nearly thirty-five years. The college I'd gone to had only been half a mile away but I'd never returned to our road. Funny, said Mar when I'd told him. Classic addict behaviour. Sorry? I'd said. Keeping your fix close at hand, Geo, but not touching it. But that doesn't make sense, I'd thought. How could the past be a fix, especially a past that felt so far away?

I thought of the woman I'd heard dying in the hospital. *Mam, Mam, I'm so sorry.* Bargain-basement psychology. Shock, dying mother, possible genetic inheritance, chilling thoughts of father, sorrow. You make the links in that irrational part of your mind, and there you are, stood in front of someone else's home, trying to reclaim something that was never fully yours.

I stepped back, looked up. The blank eye of the bedroom window you used to share with Aisling looked back at me. Where was she, that ten-year-old I used to be? Lost in time, dreaming in her own, long-ago bed, or had she felt my approach and woken, crept across the corridor and the decades into your room, and was, even now, staring out at me? What was she seeing? The person she'd always dreamt of becoming, or someone else; a stranger, unrecognisable?

All the other windows had their blinds down. I had no idea what was inside. It was hard to tell if anyone was still living there, or if the owners had already decamped – to Andalucia, maybe. I imagined them departing in a rush, escaping before the banks got them, leaving food uneaten on the kitchen table, beds unmade, clothes hanging in the wardrobe. What would they have taken with them? Pots and pans, a mattress, some bread? I remembered standing in front of your wardrobe, looking at her clothes, still there after she'd gone: pressed trousers, cheesecloth blouses, office skirts; maxi dresses, swirling with the colours of the seventies, orange and brown. Her white mac, her Afghan coat. Her rings, bangles, beads. Her precious things.

Valuable.

I thought of the package you'd sent that morning, the one Dolores had tried to give me. Was that why I'd gone there? More bargain basement. Your last birthday card had been one of those jolly ones about how I was getting older, with a tacky cartoon illustration on the front. Whose idea had that been? Helen's? Sounds like her style; so cheerily American. Inside, a terse message. It could have come from anyone, except it was in your handwriting, grown shaky and illegible. An old man's hand. Accompanied by two typed pages of uninteresting bullshit from her. As if I cared. Another invitation. *Maybe, when you get a chance, honey, you could come visit….*

Yeah, right.

You'd put my initial on the envelope. G. Madden. Just a G., no name, so you wouldn't be condoning whatever damage you thought I was doing to the life you'd given me. You'd sent a postal order for a hundred dollars. I'd torn the whole lot up, letter, card, money, smarmy invitation.

Mar used to hate it when I did that. Jesus, Geo, he's only trying to— He's family, you know. He's your father.

Well you're not, Mar, so shut up.

Why d'you find it so hard to forgive him, Geo?

Forgive? You're trying to make it sound like I'm blaming him.

Well—

Christ, I'm not that much of a child. I'm happy to take responsibility for my part in what happened. I didn't give him much choice.

Doesn't sound like you're taking responsibility. Sounds more like—

What? Like I'm trying to be right again? I'm not. I'm just—

Just what?

I looked away from our house, towards the one that used to be Mrs Kelly's. Her cherry blossom was enormous now, stretching right over into what had been her front garden. The gate had been widened, the grass cleared and replaced with gravel to fit the obligatory two cars. They'd put the expensive blinds on her windows, but left them half-open so I could see into the front room, the room you and Aisling used to call a *lounge*, and so did I, until someone in college laughed at me for being petit bourgeois. It looked nice; stylish and tidy, nothing like the way our lounge used to. The blinds upstairs were closed. I could see a blue light flickering through the chinks. A TV or laptop. Maybe they were watching the news.

Turnmill Street (Farringdon).

A flash in the back of my mind; umber and turquoise, colours of the sea—

Then someone stood in the window above me, and I saw their silhouette, all angles like a monster from a German noir.

Elaine?

In the depths of Martin's coat, something trembled, vibrating against my skin.

Silly. Worse than silly. Stupid. Even stupider that sudden nagging unease between my shoulder blades, that wobble in my legs. My hand found the railings and I steadied myself. In the corner of my eye, I could see the bin near the odd little crossing. It wasn't the same bin, of course; it was black, twenty years old at the most. The wind was flirting with a piece of newsprint, sticking it to the bin's side, peeling off again. Around the corner I could feel the lane, calling to me. I stepped forward.

'Eejit!'

Hoarse voices ahead of me. Barking laughter. A group. Behind me, from the other end of the road, a scream, melting into giggles. 'Fuck off, will ya!'

Pincer movement.

Let me remind you, because it's too valuable a lesson to forget. Trans rule number one: when in doubt, when necessary, hide.

I ducked back through our gate, and squashed close to the hedge. Shielded by the branches of Mrs Kelly's cherry blossom, I watched them appear. The Sharks and the Jets: a gang of boys coming from the lane, a pack of girls heading up from the Green. The boys were lanky and spotty, the girls luscious and dolled up, faces painted, bodies poured into spray-on jeans and fluoro tops. Put it away, hen, Martin used to call out at the muffin-top pyjama girls in Inchicore, taunting them when they slagged him off for being a queer, though by then he was living with a woman.

None of them could have been older than fourteen. I felt vaguely ashamed for panicking. Still, as Sonia says, you never can—

'Headcase!' One of the boys lunged towards our hedge and yanked at the cherry blossom. I jerked back; saw a long jaw, mouth gaping like a hyena's. The branch broke. The hyena disappeared. My nose began to run.

'Jesus, Macker!' A girl stepped forward, sharpening under a street lamp. A beautiful, perfect mouth, a heart-shaped face. The boy with the branch – Macker? – grinned and tossed the branch away. He dug a plastic Coke bottle out of his tracksuit and trailed it along Mrs Kelly's railings like a xylophone.

'Scarlet!' said another of the girls: plainer, blonder, fatter. Macker barked a laugh. Making a big show of ignoring them, the heart-faced one tossed her hair, let her eyes brush over the cherry blossom, the jasmine, me.

Kids, the cabbie had said. Vicious little fucks. They'd tortured that man in the canal, torn his face off, spent hours filming it, then put it all up on YouTube.

Bullshit. Hysteria. A gangland thing, probably. But when in doubt, blame the young—

'Fuckin *cunt!*'

One of Macker's mates had grabbed him, started wrestling the Coke bottle from him. They got into a headlock. Cheers, jeers, giggles from the girls. All except Heart-Face, who was still staring through the cherry blossom. Could she see me?

Macker shrugged off his mate. 'Fuckin *rotten* here, so it is. I'm off.' He looked at Heart-Face.

She turned away, still pretending to ignore him. 'Ya drinkin that, Stacey?' A fumble in a handbag; a vodka bottle, held high. More cheers as Stacey – the fat girl – drank, her head back, flaunting her cleavage for the boys.

You've got so soft, he'd said, cupping my right breast in his palm.

There had been a strangeness in his touch. Something different in the skin-on-skin between us. Is that okay? he said. My Mar, usually so sure with his hands. I hadn't known what to say, so I'd just fired the question back at him, like I'd learnt from my therapists. Is it? He flattened his palm, sliding it away from my breast towards the hardness of my sternum. I'd felt his blood pulse, his cock soft against my belly.

Geo, I don't know if—

I'd pushed him away. Oh, fuck off, Mar.

'Come *on*, will ya!' Stacey was close to Macker now, pulling at him. But he had eyes only for Heart-Face, who had taken the vodka and was drinking, her white throat rippling, her décolletage gleaming under the streetlamps. Seizing advantage, the second boy grabbed the Coke bottle and banged it.

'Bren! Leave them railings alone, willya?' shouted Stacey. 'Fuckin *pervert* lives there!'

'Huh!' grunted Bren.

321

'Come *on*,' said Stacey.

Somehow, Heart-Face had manoeuvred herself up to Macker. An agreement got itself made. The groups' allegiances shifted, and, flocking, they headed off as one.

She turned, looking back just as I straightened up. *It's not your fault that ya look like that*, she shouted, right at me: *Scarlet for your ma for having ya!* Then, louder, *Pervert!* A laugh from that perfect mouth. The gang howled and she disappeared.

Eugh, he'd said and pulled away. Not then, the time of the *softness*, but earlier. It was before I'd been able to afford electrolysis and, even though I'd never been that hairy, another Madden gift I have to thank you for, I still had to shave, so one night there was stubble on my breasts when he'd put his face there. Eugh, he'd said, jerking his head away. Then he'd laughed. I'd stiffened.

That's a mad place to get beard rash, Geo.

At first I'd felt a bit – disgusting, I suppose. That old inbetweeny thing, that sense of having failed, that I'llneverpass bullshit I'd never felt before around Mar, because he'd always been able to *see* me, like your mother had, or, yes, Lotte. But when I looked down and saw the ginger stubble across my breasts it seemed so ludicrous that I couldn't help laughing too.

You're one to talk, I said, pushing the heel of my hand against the bristling ridge where his crew cut met the worry lines on his forehead. His throat stretched. The back of his neck corrugated, an accordion of muscle, making the tiger tattooed across his shoulders snarl.

Actually, he said. I take it back. I like it. It's kind of dirty.

Ah, g'wan, gies a wee smirk, then, I said, taking off his accent.

He opened his mouth, stretched his tongue and licked the stubble.

I pushed harder against his head. You invert, I said. You sleazy trans-fucker.

He began to fuck me and I felt my nipples harden. I glanced down. They looked like jelly tots. Jelly tits, in a sea of stubble.

He was always so *right*, you know. So sure in his actions; how he moved, how he touched. Sure too, of what he felt and thought. So hungry for argument, to prove a point. Even his humour was ferocious. *You know why Sonia's such a ball-breaker, Geo? Poor thing can't help it; she's a man trapped in a woman's body*. Winding me up in the hope I'd get self-righteous and tell him he was being offensive so he could get self-righteous back and tell me I'd no sense of humour anymore. He could be slippery too, though. Classic addict behaviour, as he might have put it. When Sonia challenged him to his face about him not liking her, he said, No, not at all, darling, don't know where you get that from. It's not personal, Sonia, just dialectics.

That working-class chip on his shoulder again. Though, if you'd asked him, he'd have said: working class? Fuck, no, Geo. I'm a Ned, King of the Lumpen Proletariats. Yet there was nothing lumpen about Mar, believe me. He worked hard; Jesus, did he work. Like you, of course, though I never told him that.

His burden, too, was just like yours; all that certainty, all that raging hunger, lay over nothing more than the need to be seen to be doing the right thing. For all his queer- and class-pride rhetoric, his uncaring sexual-predator shtick, for all his bloody addiction; boy, did Mar crave the respectability of being a family man, even if that family was just the two of us, him and me.

My head was spinning, snot streeling down my face. I kept having to wipe it away with my sleeve. Mar's sleeve. My body was hurting, but I no longer knew where. Fairview was a blur of opening pub doors, green bunting and people in silly hats; belligerent smokers holding court beside tall ashtrays that looked like pillars from Egyptian temples; diddly-eye music, streaking headlights, drunks and more drunks and more drunk again. There was a phone box near the corner of the Howth Road. I'd used it as a teenager, during my college days. It was missing some Perspex near the bottom; the wind was cold as it gusted through the gap and up around my legs.

'Sonia?' My teeth were chattering.

'Hello?'

Relief surged through me. 'Sonia, hi, it's me, I'm—'

'Hello?' Everything was noisy behind her.

'Sonia, you're breaking up. It's me, Georgia—'

'Where are you, girl?'

'Sonia, you're—'

It took us three goes and ate another hole in my purse but finally we connected.

'I was in hospital.'

'Oh. Jesus, was that today— I thought it wasn't till—'

'No, that's still tomorrow. I didn't…. I left. I had an accident.'

'Georgia, Christ….' Her voice disappeared.

'Can I stay with you?' I hadn't planned to ask that. 'It's just, it would be great if—'

'Oh, I'm sorry, girl, I'm....'

She was in Limerick for the holiday, spending the long weekend there. Family time. Christine and the kids. Of course. I'd forgotten.

'Oh.' I was horrified at how small and needy my voice sounded.

'No, no,' she said, regrouping. 'Look I have—'

She broke up again.

'...idea.'

'Yes?' I said, desperate. Was I that desperate?

'Take a cab.' She must have moved, got the phone into a better signal because suddenly I could hear her. A cab? I thought. But I've just spent—

'Don't worry about the cost. Give them my account number. I've a spare key—'

crackle crackle

'Under the what?'

'Geranium.'

'No, no,' I said. All around me were monsters in enormous gold-buckled green hats. 'I'm grand. I should go home, it'll be—'

'Get. A. Cab. You can have a bath. Remember the code?'

I didn't have a bath at home. I nodded, then remembered she couldn't see me. 'Yeah.'

'Stay there and give me a ring tomorrow morning, first thing, don't worry how early it is, and I'll give you a pep talk before you go in, and just, you know, just keep ringing, okay? I'll try to get back up early. Christine's supposed to be coming up on Monday, with the kids, but she'll understand. Help yourself to what's in the fridge—'

'Thanks....'

'If you need a change of clothes—'

'I went home, Sonia.'

'...no problem at all....'

'I went home,' I said again. It didn't sound as weird as I'd thought it would.

Behind Sonia's voice I could hear people laughing. Trad music was playing. She must have been in a pub.

'...push it a bit, girl,' she was saying. 'There's a problem with the rider. Once you get in, keep it on the latch and don't let anyone in. Okay?'

The new cabbie was Nigerian. Black. I assumed he was Nigerian. Maybe he was from the Ivory Coast. He had a set of rosary beads dangling from his rearview. I'm not sure what religion they are in Nigeria. Have. Religions, plural. Aren't they mainly born-again? Maybe he was Senegalese. He didn't speak much. We swung down the coast road into town and the rosary beads swung in front of the windscreen. Protect me from the knives, I prayed. We passed the park where I'd cruised in the eighties while I was at college, when I first explored the possibility that I might have been gay – no, when I first explored the possibility that being gay would explain why I was the way I was. It was dark and dirty, not a soul to be seen beyond the first ridge of trees. Over the Tolka, down North Strand. The same route we used to take in the Cortina when you brought me to your office, up until Aisling's last spring, when you decided you were too ashamed to bring me to work, or I was too much trouble, or something. Drunken people were everywhere, in spite of the rain, careering in messy, straggling groups, raising beer and cider cans at our windscreen. It was only 9 p.m. but the fights were already starting. Amiens Street. The North Star Hotel, all jazzed-up; remember it? That place you didn't like, frequented by travellers who needed somewhere to kip on on their way to the North.

A garda car was parked outside the Luas station at Connolly. Hazards on, blue light flashing. Across the road, outside the amusements arcade Mar had more or less lived in during our last months together, two big shaven-headed lugs, Russian or Polish or – maybe Jammy Noel was right; Serbs – were doing the no-you-can't-come-here-without-a-warrant tango with two obscenely young-looking Gardaí.

The Nigerian didn't say anything.

We crossed Butt Bridge. Over the tops of the roofs I could see the big wheel outside Government Buildings. It was lit-up and turning. The air was thick with the sounds of hurdy-gurdy music, samba bands, shouting, drink.

You've a lot of emotional past in your body, one of my earlier New Agey therapists had said. A skinny blonde from the Gold Coast in Australia. *If you don't work through it, it'll fester. That's where illness comes from.* I've always hated that sort of cant, have never been able to understand how anyone can mistake simple, scientific processes – a rogue cell, a chemical imbalance – for *feelings*. Yet I had gone *home* – was that the word? – and survived it. Would that count for anything?

The cabbie leant forward and pressed a button.

'...no, no,' said Blessed Eoin. He was on a news analysis programme; he sounded panicky. 'I'm not saying that at all. You're making me out to be some kind of conspiracy theorist. All I'm saying is, this is perhaps a last opportunity for us to understand that violent actions take place in a context and—'

325

The cabbie tutted and turned off the sound.

Up Westland Row, then a sharp left down Fenian Street, past the registry office where Mar and I used to fantasise we would one day tie the knot, that ridiculous bourgeois ritual that Ray and Ben were celebrating, maybe at that very moment, over in Brighton. Past the bridge stretched Northumberland Road. Behind it, unseen, roared the coast.

Lognote # 8

We snatch this brief opportunity to present some evidence of our collection's openness to 'official' as well as 'subjective' interpretations of Herstory. A set of certificates, printed on heavy watercolour paper and framed in a pleasant pine-effect laminate. Each certificate features a set of league tables, cross-referenced by source. Certificate 1 also has a brightly coloured sign underneath, suggesting activities for the younger visitor. Certificate 3 is longer than the others and appears to be in the form of a papyrus-type 'scroll'; the ragged quality of its upper and lower edges suggest that it is incomplete, and carbon dating implies that it originates from either a very long time ago or some unknown point/ wave/membrane in spacetime yet to leave its trace in human memory. It is worth remembering that our League Tables of Human Violence are among the most robust Objects in the *Kammer*. Therefore – while reminding you that we are under Time/Pressure – please feel free to examine them closely.

Most curious feature

Across the glass of all three certificates someone has sprayed a graffiti question: *Two wrongs make a right?* We take no responsibility for these marks.[1] Negotiations are currently in place with a reputable firm to have them cleansed.

Certificate 1: *Germans killed/displaced during the expulsions from Czechoslovakia[2] after World War II.*

---

[1] Would you blame us? See various sources, including Naimark, Botting, etc: tendency to be seen as Nazi apologist when describing bad things that happened to Germans, especially during and after WWII. See, for example, frequently uttered statement: 'Dresden? They asked for it.'
[2] By 'Czechoslovakia', understand 'Bohemia and Moravia'.

Consensus is that there were approximately 3.2 million Germans/German-speakers living in this area at the end of WWII.

Online encyclopaedia[3]	no mention how many killed
	• 1.7m 'resettled' in American zone of West Germany
	• 750,000 'resettled' in Soviet zone (East Germany)
	• 225,000 remained (50,000 later 'emigrated'/'expelled')
Naimark[4]	19,000–272,000 'killed' (depending on source) lower figures reflect those killed as direct result of violence during 'wild expulsions'; higher figures reflect those who died from other causes, including suicide, disease, hunger and exposure
	• c.2m 'ended up' in American zone
	• Over 1m 'transferred' to Soviet zone
	• 200,000 'allowed to remain'
Online Sudeten Germans website[5]	3.5m civilians 'suffered' during expulsions
Nationmaster[6]	20,000–200,000 'killed' (depending on source)
	• 1.9m 'expelled' to American zone
	• Over 1m 'expelled' to Soviet zone
	• 250,000 'allowed' to remain
MacDonogh[7]	240,000 'killed'
	• 1.45m 'expelled' to the American zone
	• 786,485 'expelled' to Soviet zone
	• 250,000 remained in Czechoslovakia

[3] http://countrystudies.us/czech-republic/36.htm
[4] Naimark, N. M., *Fires of Hatred* (Harvard University Press, 2001)
[5] http://sudetengermans.freeyellow.com/RECENT.html
[6] http://www.nationmaster.com/encyclopedia/Expulsion-of-Germans-after-World-War-II
[7] MacDonogh, G., *After the Reich* (John Murray, 2007)

Botting[8]   267,000 'killed'
                                          • 2.9m 'expelled'

Activities for the younger visitor

• Spot the differences! Which sources use 'transfer' and which 'expulsion'?
• For the more mathematically minded among you: Is there a correlation (ask your parents if you don't know what this word means) between the terms used and the numbers stated?
• For all the family: Did you know that some German families from the region killed themselves *en masse* before the partisans came – surrounding themselves with photographs, toys and garlands of flowers? <u>*Note to parents*</u>: Don't try this at home!

<u>*Certificate 2*</u>: *Germans killed/displaced during and after World War II.*[9]

Botting   10m–12m 'displaced'
                                          • 1.1m 'killed' during the War

Naimark   500,000 'died' as direct result of deportations from Poland
                                          • At least 1m 'died' from the overall[10] 'ethnic cleansing' of Poland[11]

<u>Note</u>: In recognition of the points made by our Footnotes, we encourage visitors who find the term 'ethnic cleansing' anachronistic or, indeed, offensive, in the context of this Certificate to use other wording. Acceptable options

---

[8] Botting, D., *In the Ruins of the Reich* (Methuen, 2005)
[9] By 'Germans', we mean 'German inhabitants of East Prussia, Pomerania, Brandenburg, Silesia, Hanseatic cities, Bohemia, Moravia; and ethnic German settlements in Poland, Yugoslavia, Hungary and Romania'.
[10] By 'overall', understand not just 'during deportation' but also: 'during the Russian offensive', 'en route to labour camps in the Soviet Union' and 'within camps in Poland and the Soviet Union'.
[11] Some clarification is required around Certificate 2's use of the term 'ethnic cleansing'. Since the phrase did not enter existence until the Yugoslav wars of the 1990s, it may have questionable value when applied to a post-WWII context. We must also point out that the Germans are those we usually associate with doing the cleansing (see, if possible: *Lognotes # 3, # 4* and 'badness' of Colonisers). Though we may also wonder: Who is this 'we' who makes that association?

include: 'resettlement', 'transfer', 'removal-of-people-and-their-replacement-by-others-by-whatever-means-necessary' or, indeed, the idiomatic '*Flucht*'.

Nationmaster	2.6m German speakers were still living in Eastern/Central Europe in 1950 (about 12 per cent of pre-War total)
	• Therefore at least 18m were 'killed' and/or 'displaced', including 'War-time deaths'[12]

Certificate 3: *Other major population wipeouts of the 20th century*

(i) Expulsion a.k.a. genocide of Armenians and Greeks of Anatolia 1915–23[13]

Armenians	1.3m–2.1m (depending on source) in Ottoman Empire pre-genocide
	• 800,000–1.4m 'deported' (depending on source)
	• 600,000 'died' in genocide (Arnold Toynbee)
	• 600,000 'escaped' deportation (Arnold Toynbee)
	• c.250,000 'died' in 1918–19
	• Causes of death: starvation, violence, cannibalism, disease
Greeks	1.2m –1.5m in Ottoman Empire pre-expulsion
	• 1.25m 'deported' to Greece
	• tens of thousands 'died' in process
	• 356,000 Turks 'deported' from Greece
Both	10,000–125,000 (depending on source) 'died' in fire in Smyrna

---

[12] Some of us might say: 'So what? They reaped what they sowed'. See 'Dresden argument', cited earlier, and please ignore the writings of H. Fallada and the actions of S. Scholl and other members of the German 'resistance'. For comparison, see Ireland, Northern: the 'Who did What to Whom in the "Troubles"' debates. Also do remember that, of the 18m 'killed and/or displaced' in that period, it is unclear how many actually died.

[13] Naimark, *ibid*.

(ii) Genocide of Jews of central and Eastern Europe (1933–45)

- 4.1m–6m[14] 'died' in total[15]
- 1.5m–4m people 'died' in Auschwitz (not stated how many Jews)[16]
- 200,000–350,000 prisoners 'died' on death marches of 1945 alone (not stated how many Jews)[17]

(iii) Soviet deportation of Chechens-Ingush and Crimean Tatars (1944)[18]

- 496,460 Chechens and Ingush 'deported' (entire population)
- 10,000 (est.) 'died' during deportation
- 100,000 'died' in first three years after deportation
- 189,000 Tatars 'deported' from Crimea
- Up to 85,000 Tatars 'died' during deportation and settlement

(iv) Wars in Yugoslavia (1991–99)[19]

Bosnia (1991–95)

2m (mostly Muslim) 'fled' from Serbs

- 1,000–1,200 'killed' in Srebenica in one day (July 1995)
- 485,000 non-Serbs (mostly Muslims) 'killed/expelled' from Banja Luka region
- 180,000–200,000 Serbs 'uprooted' by Croatians in 1995

Kosovo (1998–99)

960,000 Kosovar Albanians 'became' refugees

- 550,000 'became' internally dislocated
- 30,000 'killed' ('only' 2,108 bodies found)

---

[14] Now, match that to our paltry Certificate 1! Let's face it, visitors. Who in their right minds could ever claim that 270,000 dead Bohemian Germans goes any distance towards 'balancing the books'?

[15] http://www.holocaust-history.org/questions/numbers.shtml

[16] *http://www.shoaheducation.com/camps/statistics.html*

[17] Evans, R. J., *The Third Reich at War* (Penguin, 2008).

[18] Source for all figures: Naimark, ibid.

[19] Source for all figures: Naimark, ibid.

Visitors, you will notice a red button labelled *'Push me (out)!'* under the certificates. When pressed, this plays one of five audio tracks (see below). As a fun way to test your understanding of German-Czech relations in the context of post-World War II Europe, see if you can quickly match each track with its correct source (listed at random, also below). Please also mark each track, in the boxes provided, as either 'True' or 'False'. No penalties will be applied if any of your marx are wrong.

Audio tracks

- With hindsight… [it] is clear that this was not just an outburst of irrational anger but a measure which, on the basis of Czech recent experience and Czech future hopes, could be justified and rationally explained.
  ❏ True   ❏ False
- The Czechs, after all, did not suffer terribly at the hands of the Germans, certainly not in comparison to the Poles. Their economy remained in decent shape; their losses in the war were comparatively small; they were often able to maintain their communal lives without excessive interference from the occupiers.
  ❏ True   ❏ False
- This was not punishment, it was revenge.
  ❏ True   ❏ False
- A more complete definition of ethnic cleansing might read as follows: the forced removal of a group, because of its ethnicity, in order to seize the territory it inhabits.
  ❏ True   ❏ False
- *Má caitheann tú solad sa leacht samhlaíann go cailleann sé cuid dá mheáchan agus tá an cailleadhúint meáchana sin cothrom le meáchan and leacht dí curtha.*[20]
  ❏ True   ❏ False

---

[20] 'A body immersed in a fluid is subject to an upward force, equal in magnitude to the weight of fluid it displaces.' Literal translation from the Gaelic © Wunderkammer Inc, possibly traceable to (?) 'David', Dublin, 1976. Or, in common parlance: 'Shove a foreign body into a bath and you'll get a hell of a lot of splashing.'

List of sources

- N. M. Naimark, *Fires of Hatred*, 2001
- D. W. Gerlach, *For Nation and Gain: Economy, Ethnicity and Politics in the Czech Borderlands, 1945–1948,* University of Pittsburgh, 2002
- Archimedes, as presented to Irish secondary school students in the 1940s
- Z. Radvanovsky, in M. Cornwall & R.J.W. Evans (eds), *Czechslovakia in a Nationalist and Fascist Europe*, OUP, 2007
- Václav Havel, March 1990.

Hulk

☼

In some countries, Aisling once told her, people hate getting their photos taken. They think you've stolen their soul.

Outside, it's freezing, the sun invisible behind the dirty grey clouds, but inside, the heating is on too high, making everyone, even Mrs Allen, drowsy. Georgie, trying to stifle another yawn, watches Timmy Nelson pick his nose and eat his snot, his breathing harsh and snuffly. Behind her she can feel William Robinson. He's the only person who isn't sleepy, though he's pretending to be. Under those heavy-lidded eyes, Georgie knows he's alert, like a crocodile in a bayou; just waiting for the right opportunity to strike. As soon as Georgie lets herself register his presence, she feels heat throb in the middle of her spine, in the place where as an adult she will one day fasten a bra. He gave her a little nudge there the day after the Incident, when she came into school with the black eye. It was the first time since September that he'd done more than look at her – even though he's always *at* everyone else, calling them nicknames or leaving green gullies in their pencil cases, saying rude things about their Mums and Dads or pushing the girls' chests – which he calls boobs, even though everyone knows nobody will have boobs till they're in sixth class. The nudge he gave her after the Incident was lighter than the one he'd given her on their first day in school; but stronger, like he knew he'd found the right place to push. 'An accident?' said Mrs Allen, after reading the note from David, the one Georgie had to beg him to write, which said she'd slipped on the ice and that was how she'd got the black eye – because the last thing she wanted was a great big bloody fuss and bloody *Jan* having to get involved and ask more of her stupid questions again. 'Dear, dear, you poor thing. Well, that will teach us all to be extra careful in the bad weather, won't it?' Everyone had nodded, as if they were actually going to do what Mrs Allen said. Everyone except William Robinson. *Accident?* he'd whispered, his breath hot on her neck. *You're not fooling me, Georgie Madden. You got that black eye in a fight.*

Now she feels his breath again, his finger ready to push. Georgie stares resolutely ahead. In the cloudy edge of her vision, she can see Saoirse, flushed and red-eyed, looking over at her, hangdog and uncertain. And around the head of the architect's daughter are those hazy three-headed baby dragons: multiplied, swarming, open-mawed, vicious-toothed, making hungry, darting circles in the air.

Come *on*, she begs the big clock on the wall. Mrs Allen turns the page of the Christmas story, looks up, catches Georgie's eye. *Holidays!* she mouths, eyes wide and aren't-we-all-delighted. Then she remembers, and her face does a little shimmy of shock.

Jesus bloody Christ.

Advent hasn't been all bad. The snow, the day they got it, was nice, pretty and fun, up till the Incident anyway, and Georgie will be getting decent presents for a change; she's been told she can ask Santa for anything she wants this year, within reason. But from the way David's been acting, you'd think it was going to be the most special Christmas ever. Once or twice he's hinted that there's going to be a big surprise at the end of the year, something that'll be Great News for him and Georgie. He's begun to look less hunched-over and he's even started whistling again, and not as fake-jolly as he used to. Saying things like *We'll try to make this one to remember, eh, old bean?* or *This could be fun, what?* and going on about Santa, and what hotel they're going to for the dinner, though he never used to care about that stuff. He's not giving out to Georgie for stupid things, or flying off the handle the way he did Second Time Round and over the summer, but Georgie's not sure if she likes this any better. Sometimes it feels as if Christmas is some sort of experiment her father is conducting, that she's supposed to be in on too. But if it is an experiment, it's all David's and nothing to do with her. Over the last few weeks, there's been times Georgie's felt so exhausted by it all that she's found herself wishing she could go into the lane and fall asleep in its lost dimension and when she woke up, like Rip Van Winkle, the entire festive bloody season would be over and she wouldn't have to think about it, or anything else, ever again.

Lotte doesn't seem that enthusiastic about the whole thing either. At first Georgie was worried that Lotte was still annoyed about her taking that scarf, or worse, bothered by Georgie making such a big hullaballoo about her spending Christmas Day with them. But Lotte hasn't said anything about that, so maybe it's just a mood.

It took Georgie ages to sort out that mess. Okay, David had said the evening they'd come home after the Incident, which meant they were going to have a Chat. For a horrible second Georgie had thought he'd found out about Elaine. But instead he cleared his throat:

If you, eh. What I mean is— His voice sounded rusty, like a gate that hadn't been used in ages. Then all the words came out together. Look, things aren't set in stone, Georgie. I just thought we could maybe do something, not like before, of course, with—

It was then – when his breath sucked back in at the point when he should have said *Mum* – that she realised he wasn't talking about Elaine. He still thought she was upset about Lotte. It took her ages to convince him that she hadn't meant it, that of course, she'd like Lotte to come over, she'd just been tired and cranky from what had happened with Saoirse.

Well, he'd said. If you're sure….

Georgie nodded. And although he still seemed worried and not 100 per cent so sure himself, that appeared to be that.

She's still not sure what disturbed her most about the Chat; the way David had talked to her, like she was another grown-up and he was asking her for permission for something, or the fact she'd nearly let the cat out of the bag with Elaine.

Oh No.

That was what Georgie had thought when they'd said Lotte would be staying for Christmas. She'd almost said it out loud. Oh. No. Not because of Lotte, but because of Elaine.

Up until then, Georgie had assumed that once the holidays started, Elaine would be going home; because that's what people did, they went home at that time of year. David always said he was 'going home' for New Year when what he meant was Clonmel, and in the old days, before the Troubles got bad, Aisling would talk about 'going home' to the North for Boxing Day. But David's invitation to Lotte opened up a gaping black hole in Georgie's head that she hadn't even known was there. Because if Lotte wasn't going home for Christmas, did that mean Elaine wasn't either? And if Elaine wasn't going home for Christmas, did that mean she was staying for good?

It was only then Georgie realised how exhausted she was from the endless amount of things she'd had to organise in order to keep Elaine hidden and safe: stealing food, clothes, toiletries, blankets; keeping Elaine warm, doing her homework for her, making sure she got to school on time, making sure Mrs Kelly's daughter didn't drop into the empty house out of the blue and find Elaine, or any trace of her. What had started out as something interesting, something *decent*, had become, after all this time, work.

If they could only talk—

But talk about what? Every time Georgie looks at Elaine, the questions she wants to ask crack before she can find the words for them, oozing down the invisible wall of her own mind like a mess of broken shell and yolk.

She's lost count of the times over Advent she's wished she could just undo that *Oh No*. Un-think it. Close up that hole, make everything go back the way it was. But that's the problem: once you open a hole, things come out of it, and no matter how hard you try to stuff them back in, those things are there to stay.

Tick—

Tock, goes the clock.

'Right, now!' says Mrs Allen in a glad voice. 'Have a lovely time everyone! And don't eat too many mince pies!'

Desks scrape back, books are bundled into schoolbags, bags hauled onto shoulders. A hubbub of excited chatter starts.

Georgie goes to the loos instead of racing out to the gate with the others. Last Christmas, Jan had invited them over for a mince-pie and mulled-wine party on the evening term ended. Och, won't that be lovely, Aisling had said, but Georgie had loathed it. Jan watching her, waiting for her to slip up again. Boring you-know wasn't around, though, thank God, and David had chickened out, saying he had to work – though Georgie knew it was an excuse; he couldn't stick Jan – and it was just as well he wasn't there, because he'd have gone bananas if he'd seen how much Aisling was drinking, especially as she was still Officially Not Out of the Woods. She kept putting her arm around Georgie, saying, *You're my rock. My wee treasure.* Then Saoirse dragged Georgie into her bedroom to show off her books and toys. This is my favourite, she'd said, holding up a rag doll. I call her Billie. I'm like, crazy about her. At that, Georgie felt so awful she nearly puked and then they had to go home.

It's unlikely that after everything that's happened this year there'll be an invitation today. But you never know. Bloody *Jan's* been collecting Saoirse an awful lot after school lately. Probably angling to fix everything up again – as if she could – so she can go back to pretending they're all friends.

337

Georgie sits in the cubicle for five minutes, timing it on her watch. Then, casually, just in case Saoirse's still there or William Robinson is lurking, looking for Trouble, she leaves, heading across the yard to the gate.

'Ah, there you are now,' says Mrs Lynch. 'I was getting worried, so I was.'

It's not a nice day; it's freezing, rain coming down in a constant curtain of wet, but there are candles lit in people's windows, and wreaths on doors, and all the kids they pass on the street look excited. Maybe the holidays will be okay after all.

While Mrs Lynch is snoozing in front of *Playschool*, Georgie retrieves Elaine's latest food parcel from the back of the fondue cupboard which nobody has opened for well over a year, since the last time Jan and you-know-boring who came for dinner. She slips out of the house. At the corner of the road, near the crossroads where the bin is and just before the mouth of the lane, she hesitates. Since the *Oh No*, things have begun to change. Little rips have started to appear in the lane's protective shield, a couple more each time she visits, a bit like that hole in the sky the scientists have discovered, through which, Jeremy once said, the sun will one day burn everything the world over to a crisp. So far the lane's invisible dimension is holding, but Georgie can feel changes in its fabric, subtle leaks in its texture.

She steps in. The lane hushes around her; but raggedly, like an old television being switched on. When the shimmer fades, Georgie sees a slight, shadowy figure peel away from the broken-down Cortina. It's been three days since they've met.

'Have you anything to eat? I'm starving.' In the rain-drenched light, Elaine looks terrible. Her eyes are huge in their sockets, her summer tan has faded; even her hair seems thinner, with little bare patches on her scalp, as if strands are starting to fall out.

Georgie feels a bit sick, but sets her face, not wanting Elaine to see. 'Sure. Did you get what I left yesterday?'

'I thought you were never coming. I was getting very worried so I was.'

'It's only been three days,' says Georgie, stung. 'It wasn't like I was avoiding you. I left you out stuff and all and besides—' She stops.

You're the one who hasn't been turning up.

'Here.' Georgie shoves the parcel at Elaine. 'That'll do you till Christmas.'

Elaine says nothing.

'It's got to last because I'll be up to my eyes tomorrow and the next day. But I'll bring you some of our dinner on Christmas night. It'll be from a hotel.'

That should keep you going till we come back from the North. I'll bring you back stuff from there too.'

'Bring me back,' says Elaine, like it's a question.

Something tight twists in Georgie's chest. She ignores it. 'We're going to Clonmel for New Year's, but Granny Bell will give us lots of stuff so you'll be grand. Take it.'

She shoves the package at Elaine again, but Elaine doesn't budge. The freezing rain has thickened; it slides down the backs of their necks, drenching their jumpers, seeping into their socks, soaking through Elaine's school uniform that Georgie stole from Alison O'Meara's washing line and which is now far too big for Elaine. Elaine's teeth begin to chatter. They look bigger too; her gums are receding. It's as if anything that isn't bone in Elaine is wearing away.

'Look, there's no point us standing out here catching our—'

Elaine's head twitches. 'Is it them lads?' She's staring past Georgie, towards the mouth of the lane.

'There's no lads, Elaine.'

'They do be here. Near the crossing in the black of night. I hear them.'

'Look....' Georgie glances at Mrs Kelly's garden door. Someone has been at it; the gap Elaine uses to slip through has got wider and one of the hinges is coming loose. *Bren wos here* says a new bit of graffiti, right beside the *Brits Out!* that had appeared yesterday morning. Georgie sighs. 'Okay, I'll come in with you. Only for a bit, though. Otherwise David will think I'm lost and he'll get into a fuck-off bollocks humour and he's a real pain in the balls when he's like that.'

Elaine laughs softly, as if she's more than familiar with exasperated fathers and their fuck-off bollocks humours and the pains they create in one's balls, real or imaginary.

Steeling herself, Georgie follows Elaine through the gap. She much prefers entering Mrs Kelly's garden the proper way, climbing out of her bedroom window, along the wall and down the apple tree. It feels horrid going in through the back door, too squashy and tight, and she always gets a funny sweet smell in her nose. But today Elaine is showing no initiative, as David might say, and she can't leave her to freeze over Christmas with nothing to eat. Georgie forces herself through, pulling the door behind them just in case those lads do turn up.

They trudge through the garden, past the ancient marble bird bath and the crooked rose bush with its few faded roses clinging to its brown stems. The branches of the fruit trees wave against the sky; skinny fingers, grey against browny-grey. The rain turns to sleet. Both children are shivering, backs humped against the cold, but Elaine is too weak to run anywhere and Georgie – well, Georgie doesn't want to walk any faster. The longer she can keep outside that house, the better.

Since Mrs Kelly died, it's been hard to remember how things were when Georgie was younger and went over there to sleep for the afternoon and be looked after. Now anytime she's in that house, all she sees is peeling wallpaper and lino curling up at the edges, with mould and cobwebs growing in the corners of the ceiling and trailing down beside the windows. Sometimes she thinks that was how the house always was, old and cold and musty; it was just Mrs Kelly being there made it look different. Only now Mrs Kelly is not there; Mrs Kelly is not anything anymore. Whenever Georgie does go inside, she tries not to venture any farther than the kitchen. Once, when David was in Munich-not-Czechoslovakia, she went upstairs to make the bed in the front room where Elaine sleeps. Elaine had insisted, saying she was afraid of doing it herself in case she'd be seen from the road, but Georgie felt disgusting afterwards, sick and anxious, as if she'd had her head pushed into a toilet. That's not something she's in any hurry to repeat.

'Here.' Elaine, teeth chattering, points to the two chairs left in the kitchen. They're wood, painted a greeny-grey colour. One of them is missing sticks from its back and the other has a bockety leg. Georgie's never sure which is the least of a pain to sit on, so she chooses the one with the bockety leg. Elaine begins to peel open the packages Georgie has brought. The sound of her teeth chattering is really irritating Georgie, even though she knows it's mean to feel irritated, because it's not like Elaine can do anything about it.

'Where's your blanket?' The blankets had been a brainwave; she'd taken two old ones from the hotpress and brought them over one night, just after it started to get cold. 'You have to wear them, otherwise you'll catch your death. You know that.'

Elaine makes a funny little face, twisting up her mouth and looking away.

'You still have them, don't you?'

Elaine looks worried. Georgie's heart sinks.

'Oh, fuck. Did *She* come by?' *She* is their shorthand for Mrs Kelly's daughter.

Elaine nods.

'Jesus,' says Georgie. 'What happened?'

Elaine shakes her head. 'She was gone when I got back from school. And the blankets were in the bin. The bin,' she says again, gesturing to the black sack near the door. 'I'd of dug them out again only there's all sorts of weird stuff in there.'

Georgie sighs. 'Okay. I'll figure something out. I'd give you my coat only David will probably notice.'

Elaine laughs. Georgie joins in. It's a running joke between them how David hardly notices things like that anymore, though he always used to. Elaine's laugh turns into a cough.

'Right.' Georgie hoists herself up. 'Sit down and I'll make tea. There's loads of grub in that parcel. Help yourself.'

She opens the door of the press and feels around the back, taking out David's camping Gaz, which she stole in October after the hour went back, and the biscuit tin where she keeps Elaine's supplies of tea and cereal. Filling a small saucepan with water, she puts it on the Gaz, lighting it with matches she's taken from home.

Elaine coughs again. Outside, the dying sun manages to wrestle free of the clouds and, for an instant, the garden looks almost like that beautiful picture in the National Gallery, the one Georgie saw the day of the Incident before Saoirse dragged them into the big hall. The picture had had mountains and a pink sun or moon – it was hard to tell which – and a red volcano and white lightning zigzagging across the front and, weirdest of all, an unseen, white-white light that seemed to come from outside the picture and was everywhere and nowhere at the same time. But this light in Mrs Kelly's garden is not beautiful; it's dark, a burnt yellow colour, like pee.

'*She* might of put one of the blankets upstairs.'

Georgie turns and gets a fright. Elaine is on the chair, rocking. In the pee-coloured light, with her enormous eyes and jutting bones, she looks just like a skeleton.

'It could be in the front room. You could help me get it.' Elaine smiles but instead of its usual sweetness, the smile with those skull-like teeth makes her look even more ghoulish. 'I think she might of bin there, put it under the bed.'

Georgie shivers, and, as if the sun can feel her, it sinks again, back into the clouds, and everything goes dark again. She turns to the stove. 'Have the crisps first. They're soggy because Lotte got them for me in a shop and I had to pretend to eat them or she'd start wondering again.'

'Lotte?' Elaine asks vaguely, as if she's forgotten who Lotte is.

Georgie ignores her. 'You can have the sandwiches with your tea. I made them myself. The sweets were a present for Mrs Allen, but she gave them to us.'

'A present?' says Elaine hopefully. She's been talking about Christmas presents for ages.

'Yeah. From Saoirse.'

Elaine laughs.

'She's so thick,' says Georgie, encouraged. 'SO, SO stupid. A big fat eejit-head. A stupid fathead lesbian spa. A Yanky-wanky—'

Elaine's body shakes with laughter. She waves her hand, meaning *please, Georgie, stop*. Sometimes Georgie makes Elaine laugh so hard she wees herself.

'Okay. You alright? You haven't—'

Elaine shakes her head. Georgie is relieved to see there is some colour back in her cheeks; she doesn't look quite so horrible as she did a few moments ago.

'You should have the cake for supper. It's lovely. There's cream on it and jam. And you can have my dinner from the other night too. We'll heat it up. I got it all off my plate without David noticing.' She laughs. 'He had his head buried in work and he didn't see a thing. Blind. As. A—'

'Bat!' they both say. Then they smile and even in the dark, musty kitchen with the cobwebs everywhere and the smell of damp, things seem okay again.

'What's for dinner?' says Elaine.

'Chops and peas and mash.'

'Real mash?'

Georgie sighs. Sometimes Elaine gets a bit silly, blanks out like she's not really there. 'There's wee brown babies dying in Africa, Elaine, and they'd love Smash.'

'I know. It's just Cadbury's make—'

'Chocolate. Yeah. But how are you going to get your energy if you don't have your Smash?'

Elaine stops, thinking.

The water begins to bubble. 'Right, tea's up, troops.'

Elaine coughs again and Georgie adds Benylin to the shopping/stealing list in her head as she pours the water and adds the tea bag. The smell of tea rises around them, the steam making circles and figures-of-eight. Georgie thinks of Saoirse's baby dragons with their three open mouths, those warning signs keeping everyone at bay. And she thinks again of that photo she almost stole from Lotte's drawer, the one with the two little babies in it, and even though that shouldn't make her feel bad – because she didn't take it, did she?

she put it back, it's important to put things back – that tightness in her chest returns, gnarling inside her like a piece of knotted string.

Something light brushes her face. With a start she realises Elaine is standing next to her, reaching her small, ghost-thin fingers to Georgie's face. Sometimes Elaine does that; moves so quickly you don't even know she's there.

Are you okay, wee Georgie?

Georgie blinks. Course I am, eejit-head, she wants to say. But there's a ball of burning lead in her throat and she knows it won't let the words out. So instead, she lets Elaine's hand cup her face, gentle, as her arm snakes around Georgie's waist, holding her, not tight, not hard, just right.

It's okay, darling, says Elaine. Her mouth dropping Eskimo kisses like butterflies, on Georgie's cheekbones, chin, forehead and nose.

Before Georgie leaves for home, she tells Elaine to turn around.

Is it my present? says Elaine. Her eyes light up. I do hope it's a book, black as nigh—

Sshh, says Georgie. Close your eyes and stand over near the door.

Elaine does what she's told and, humming loudly to disguise what she's doing, Georgie opens the oven of Mrs Kelly's range and places the Christmas present inside, leaving the door slightly open, a tiny piece of red ribbon sticking out like a tongue, so there'll be no way Elaine will miss it on Christmas morning.

☼

They were all black-and-white, most of them yellowy around the edges. At first Georgie thought she was seeing things. How could Elaine be grown-up in ancient photographs when she was only a little girl now? But then – it took a while because she was so addled after the Incident and her own clumsiness and the fact that Lotte *knew*, not everything, but something – she realised her mistake.

In the first picture, the woman who could have been Elaine grown-up was standing indoors, posing against a curtain. She was very beautiful, like an old-fashioned film star. Blonde and pale, hair piled high on her head, lips painted a dark colour which must have been red; high, wide cheekbones. Her eyes were bright; her smile equally bright, equally wide.

In the second picture, she was standing on a pier, clutching a big flowery hat, wearing long gloves and a billowing bell-shaped coat that reached her knees. She was glancing up at a man in a dark blazer. He was wearing a

Captain Bird's Eye hat. He looked like the type who could be good at telling jokes, but there was something about his mouth Georgie didn't like. That picture was different to the first one; rough and a bit shaky-looking, but more *real* somehow. Even though the man and woman had their clothes on, they seemed sort of *nude*; not like the people in the painting which had triggered the Incident, but as if the person photographing them had crept up on them without their knowing and caught them in the middle of being themselves.

'Well,' says David. He sounds impressed. Lights from the road and the Christmas trees are turning his face all colours: green, blue, orange, pink. 'Three hundred and fifty-seven.' He spaces out the numbers. 'That's a bit of a record, what?'

'Yeah.' Georgie lets her head loll and watches David's hands grip the worn steering wheel. It hasn't been as bad as she'd thought it would be, doing what they do every year this year.

'I think we saw maybe two hundred last year?'

'Two hundred and sixty-one,' says Georgie. 'Including the ones on O'Connell Street.'

'Three hundred and fifty-seven Christmas trees in Dublin's fair city. Well!'

Music is crackling on the car radio, too low to be anything. As they round the Green, a muscle begins twitching in David's face and he starts whistling again, in that new way. The lights are on in their house, which is weird, because Georgie was sure she'd turned them off before they left. As they get closer, Georgie sees there are candles lit in the windows and the tree in the lounge looks really fantastic. Then the door opens and the smell of cooked food wafts out and for a split second Georgie lets herself almost imagine—

Dear Santa, what I would really like for Christmas is….

But it's only Lotte, standing in the doorway.

'See?' says David. He sounds surprised but relieved, as if he's only just realised he's been conducting an experiment, and that, as experiments go, it's working quite well.

Georgie closes her eyes. Small white stars burst in the blackness. Under her body she feels the car surge, stutter. Halt.

Lotte seems different this evening, chirpier than she's been for a while – since, Georgie realises, she stopped mentioning that Poet all the time who lives upstairs from her. *He takes pictures – imagine that, monster – pictures!* Any time he passed them on the steps, Lotte used to pretend not to see him, but then she'd keep dropping his name into chat, like a Disprin, only to forget and look puzzled if anyone else talked about him.

They're having a Love Affair, Elaine had said at the time. Remember how people look when they're having them, Georgie? Georgie must have looked as if she didn't, because Elaine continued, glad to explain. Their faces go real silly, happy and frightened at the same time. And they get bits of strangers all over them, dark hairs on their coats, or that smell, the No-no-Denis-it's-not-right smell, like Brut in the chemist only nicer, they get that on on their necks, and you get it too, only they push you away saying, Not now, darling, I need a wee wash— And she'd have gone on like that for ever except Georgie got a brainwave and persuaded her to play Scrabble instead.

Tonight you couldn't say Lotte is back the way she used to be, because Georgie hasn't seen Lotte like this before. But she is in good form; giggly, full of sparky electricity that comes off her like static from a nylon jumper. Maybe it's to do with that smell, sweet and heady, on her breath; the smell that Georgie knows is alcohol, though she's not sure what kind. But David hasn't drunk anything, and he's that way too, joking, laughing, messing, even doing some of his voices, which makes Lotte giggle harder. Would he still be like that, Georgie wonders, if he'd had to hear Lotte constantly drop the Poet into chat, like a Disprin? He keeps looking over at Georgie as if to say, *Come on, old bean,* like he and Lotte are the kids having fun and Georgie is the parent, needing to keep an eye on things. It's only seeing them like that, brother and sister almost, that makes Georgie realise how they usually are, cutting across each other's sentences and not listening and always saying sorry.

'Bit of a surprise, eh?' says David. 'I had to twist her arm to come over early.'

'Nonsense,' says Lotte. 'It's a treat, really. What else would I be doing, rattling around that flat on my own?'

You could be Having Sex with the Poet, thinks Georgie. But Lotte looks over, smiling, and she seems so bright and giddy that Georgie feels bad about having those thoughts; the thoughts William Robinson might have, only he'd say them out loud. 'What about Caliban?'

'Oh, he'll be fine, monster. He's a survivor.'

'Now, who's for a bit of Baileys?' says David, just like he used to say to Aisling.

'Baileys? Oooh, lovely. In for a penny!' When he brings it over, Lotte raises the glass and says, 'Here's to Good News from the firm and a turnaround in both your fortunes.'

345

David's face gets a bit tight. He glances at Georgie. 'Well, it's not all in the bag yet....'

'Nonsense,' says Lotte again, in that interrupting way. 'They'd be idiots not to give it to you.'

Georgie isn't sure what she feels about that; annoyed that Lotte seems to know more about David's Good News than she does, or happy because, as News goes, this, for a change, mightn't actually be bad.

Lotte has cooked a moussaka, which she tells them is from Greece – though David and Georgie already know that – and they eat it in the kitchen which does look nice, Georgie has to admit, with the candles and the big vase full of holly Lotte has brought over from Baggot Street. The moussaka isn't as tasty as the ones Aisling used to make, but it's still pretty good, which surprises Georgie, because she hadn't thought Lotte would be any use at cooking. Not bad, says David, pleased, and Lotte smiles, happy, like she knows what he really means is Great. They watch a Christmas film on BBC because David has finally got in piped TV, and it's miles better than RTÉ and the old man telling stories in the fireplace, and after that they listen to some of David's jazz records, the jolly ones, not the sad ones, and a couple that Lotte has brought over as a loan. Well, what do you know, says David, his foot tapping. It's a while since I've heard this one. Then he goes off and potters about in the kitchen doing things that Georgie supposes are to do with Santa while she and Lotte sit in the lounge, warming their feet at the gas fire and making jokes about what's on the telly. And all that's fine, actually. Almost—

Say it.

—normal.

'Odd.'

Georgie glances up. Lotte is looking at the Christmas tree. She notices Georgie. 'Sorry. I mean, not opening pressies on Christmas Eve.'

'Christmas Eve?' says Georgie, surprised.

'Yes. That's the way our Mum used to do it.'

'In Czechoslovakia?'

'Well.' Lotte thinks. 'Yes. Of course. When she was little. But we did it in Bristol too. It was lovely. We'd have a meal and sing hymns – even though Doctor Brooks wasn't too keen on that part – and then we'd sit around the tree and open our pressies.'

We. Our. Two babies, identical on a black-and-white rug.

'We lived in a pirate's house. Can you imagine that?'

'Yeah?' says Georgie, unsure what's coming next.

'It was very exciting, lots of secret passageways, nooks and crannies. A bit like the *Famous Five*. We had so much fun.'

We. Lotte looks at her, intent, that way she does when she's *seeing* Georgie, and there's something she wants to ask. Georgie can tell because she can feel the question under the look. It's like the questions she feels rising in herself when she looks at Elaine; the ones she can't make into words. Is Lotte going to ask again about Elaine? Or mention the scarf? Maybe she found out about the photos? Georgie suddenly feels panicky.

Lotte's eyes flick away. 'Yes, the good doctor was very tolerant.' She raises her glass. 'To Doctor Brooks.'

'I thought he was a captain,' says Georgie.

'Sorry?'

And the room is cold, as if something old and dark and wet has just crawled in from the sea.

'I mean, a pirate,' says Georgie, flushing, rushing. 'You said it was a pirate's house—'

'Oh—' Lotte blinks. 'Of course.' She laughs and rumples Georgie's hair. Then stops, eyes wide in mock-horror. 'Can you believe it? I forgot to bring in the pfefferkuchen.' She jumps to her feet.

Next door there is a swell of loud laughter as the Flynns turn up their record player. It's a Christmas song, the one where the singers tell you that you should be having fun.

Pfefferkuchen turn out to be biscuits that are sort of soft, more like cakes really. The icing looks like chocolate but is more see-through. 'One of Julia's – my Mum's – specialities. I haven't baked them in years. Try one.'

Georgie thinks of Elaine, sitting alone in Mrs Kelly's mouldy kitchen, nibbling on stale mince pies.

'Go on,' repeats Lotte. She seems anxious.

Georgie takes a biscuit. It tastes okay; spicy and not quite as good as it looks, but not bad.

For Midnight Mass, they go to the big church near the crossroads at Santry, and Georgie feels herself wedged tight, Lotte on one side, David the other, while the choir sing their beautiful Christmas hymns and the women click their beads and incense wafts around the congregation. She closes her eyes, and for a moment it's okay, almost, even feeling that the neighbours are looking over and saying things behind their hands.

David and Lotte have rearranged the beds for the night. Lotte is to sleep in Georgie's room while Georgie sleeps in a camp bed in the room that used to be David's and Aisling's until it became just David's.

Please God, prays Georgie, don't let her hear Elaine moving around next door.

☼

The third picture wasn't like the second one; it was neat and everything in it was sort of square-looking. It showed a picnic. All the people there looked very self-conscious and dressed-up, not just in their clothes but in their selves. *Cheese!* The blonde woman was wearing a checked mini-dress: dark talons, dark sunglasses, lacquer-solid beehive. The man in the captain's hat – the doctor? – was stretched out beside her, only he wasn't wearing a hat this time. His balding head was shiny, his paunch pulling at his Fairisle jersey, his trouser legs lifting at the ankles, revealing matching Fairisle socks. Tucked in beside him was Lotte, wiry, full-mouthed, regarding the camera with the same dry amusement at – ten? Fourteen? Hard to tell – that she would employ as an adult. And that was when Georgie realised that Elaine grown-up was not Elaine at all, but Lotte's mother, Julia, who comes from Czechoslovakia.

Under the early morning light, the world is frosty and magical-looking. There are little strands of white clouds pulling across the sky, and the street and the house feel open, as if there's more space for everyone.

'Good morning, old bean,' says David, giving Georgie a big Happy Christmas hug. 'Have you seen what Santa's brought?'

She runs downstairs, into the lounge, and there's her stocking, hanging over the mantelpiece. It's stuffed. There's a whole set of Lego people with hair she can put on and take off; another box of Lego for building a village and an enormous Universal Building Set with 350 pieces. There's the usual stuff too, sweets and tangerines and chocolate Santas, and, to round it off, a quite interesting-looking book called *The Next 50 Years on the Moon*.

'Goodness,' says Lotte, sticking her head around the door. 'What a haul!'

David makes toast and they have it with some nice cherry jam Lotte has brought and real coffee, which Lotte makes using a filter. Then they open their other presents. Lotte has given Georgie the whole set of Narnia books – in a box, really swish. 'I know you've already read *The Lion, the Witch and the*

Wardrobe. But there's nothing like having the whole set. Anyway, it's just a start. I'll give you Tolkien when you're older, monster.'

Older?

Lotte looks quickly at David. 'Oh, I'm sorry—' and he says 'No, eh. That's great, great,' and they both laugh, a bit nervous, and 'Well,' says David, sucking in his breath, 'this is from me.' It's a Swiss Army Knife with lots of gadgets; very useful for doing Elaine-stuff. Clonmel has sent the same-old-same-old: a stripy scarf and old-fashioned writing paper and envelopes to say Thank You. Granny and Granda Bell have posted down a big box, even though Georgie and David will be seeing them on Stephen's Day: in it is a tin of shortbread which Georgie plans to pass on to Elaine, a new pair of gloves and matching woollen hat, the type which William Robinson would probably say makes people look like spas, a carpentry set which David gets really excited about and a book of Irish myths and legends. Georgie's gift to David is one of those special pens which he likes doing his drawings with. Lotte helped her buy it in the Pen Corner. He acts like it's a surprise, which it isn't, of course, because he always gets a Rapidograph for Christmas, only normally from Aisling.

It was difficult to think of something for Lotte, but in the end Georgie decided on a long purple scarf with tassels, from the Indian shop on Grafton Street. David was embarrassed going in there with her but Georgie knew it was absolutely – no argument – the perfect thing.

'Well, isn't that something,' says David when he opens Lotte's present, a wooden box with set squares and compasses in it. He's really polite and doesn't let on he already has one that has way more stuff in it. His present to Lotte is a small, slightly tatty book with strange old-fashioned writing on the front.

'Oh.' Lotte sounds surprised. 'That's beautiful.'

'I, eh, discovered it in Greene's. The bookshop. I hope it, um, fits the bill.' He then says something in a foreign language which sounds like Lotte's Czechoslovakian but is German, because Georgie heard him practising before he went to Munich. Georgie can tell from the stopping and starting that he doesn't say it very well. But Lotte laughs and says, looking straight at Georgie, *seeing* her again: *Perhaps all the dragons we meet in life are only princesses, waiting for us to do one beautiful and brave thing.*

Later on, when Lotte and David are in the kitchen tidying up, Georgie takes a peek inside the book.

To Lotte, for all you've done to us, love David and Georgie.

Did he mean the *to,* she wonders, or was it a mistake?

Outside, the sky has stayed clean and blue and the sun is low but bright, so David suggests they go for a walk before dinner in the hotel. 'Hell-oh! Happy Christmas!' says Joanie Flynn, because she just happens to be out on her front step as they're leaving, and Lotte puts out her hand with one of those smiles that doesn't quite reach her eyes, while David whistles to himself, in a way that doesn't sound at all pretend-happy anymore, but almost the real thing. As they leave, Joanie Flynn glances at Georgie and there is something in her glance that Georgie doesn't expect, troubled and quiet; it stays with her, resting on the back of her neck like a piece of too-heavy jewellery, all the way to Dollymount.

They drive out over the funny wooden bridge and walk towards the sun. Georgie thinks of the time she came out here with Lotte and Aisling and stupid Saoirse and then does her best to forget it. It's windier than in Marino; the sea is choppy with little waves and the sand is the colours of Neapolitan ice cream. Georgie runs to the edge of the water and dares the waves to come in and wet her boots. Lotte slips on some seaweed and David goes to grab her but she steadies herself just in time and he stops. Then they both laugh, though the wind tears their laughs from their mouths before they've barely made a sound.

Georgie stands at the waterline, watching her shadow lengthen across the ice-cream sea that's getting pinker and darker-blue by the minute, with the sun already on its downward dip. The shadow of her head is so small she can hardly see it; it's stretched way, way out, almost as far as Ireland's Eye where, William Robinson says, all the rats in Dublin live. She glances back at the grown-ups, huddled together in front of the dunes, holding their coats tight against the wind. Lotte is staring northwards, up past Howth and towards the Mourne Mountains that are grey whale-backs on the horizon, and her eyes are streaming water, because of the wind, of course, and David is staring at Lotte with a raw look in his eyes that's just a little bit too hungry, and that makes Georgie feel ill, because it's exactly the way William Robinson looks when he's staring at her. Lotte turns and David swallows down his hunger with a tight smile, and Lotte brushes her wind-tears dry and goes to pat David's arm, that way she does with everyone, without thinking – except, just before she gets there, she stops. Then they both start laughing, silly again.

Goodness, says Lotte as they approach Georgie, that was fun.

Alright, old bean? David looks as if he's on the verge of being terribly pleased with himself. Georgie can't remember the last time he looked like that, so she nods.

It happens over dinner, between the turkey and the plum pudding, when both of them have had a fair amount, as Granda Bell would say. It starts over something silly and afterwards, Georgie isn't sure who's to blame, Lotte for being so rude about the lady at the far end of the restaurant with the loud kids, or David for laughing, embarrassed, and saying, *Now, now, let's not, those in glass houses, all that*, and Lotte saying, *Sorry?* and David saying, *You know*, glancing at Georgie in a way Georgie isn't supposed to see. Except it's Lotte who doesn't see – why not? why does Lotte, who's usually so good at *seeing*, not see this? – but instead laughs, too loudly. *Oh come on. I mean, I know this is Holy Ireland, but nobody forced her to produce a gaggle of brats.* At which David's head jerks, like he's been slapped. *For Christ's sake, David, you of all people should know it's a complete bloody farce. Breeding, matrimony, the works.* At which David goes a cold, painful white, then stares down at his plate, as if it's suddenly very interesting. But Lotte doesn't see that either, just pours more wine without offering any to David, though he's already shaking his head. *I mean, we* both *know that, David,* says Lotte in a voice that's got a wobble in it and is way too serious for Christmas dinner, and now David laughs, only not to Lotte, to himself, and it sounds mean. At which Lotte does take notice and says, *Sorry?*, in a way that means trouble, and David looks up and says *Sorry?* back, and though it sounds polite, his jaw is tight which means Watch It. But Lotte doesn't get it and instead says, drawling, very English, that way she does when she's making fun of people, her eyes slitted like Caliban's, *Oh my God, David Madden, don't tell me you'd pegged me as the maternal type….* And David laughs again, over the top hearty now, like he's been in on the joke all along. Except, unlike Lotte, who's produced a cigarette – out of nowhere; long and black: does Lotte *smoke?* – and started tapping it against her plate, small, angry taps, the way Aisling used to drum her nails when she was cross, Georgie knows David isn't in on any joke. That's just what he does when he wants people to shut up, he laughs and pretends he's on their side.

Lotte shakes her head. 'You men.'

David nods. His fingers are gripping the stem of his wine glass.

'You think all we're there for is to pop them out. You have your wicked way with us, you leave us in the lurch, then you expect us to mop up the mess.'

David laughs again. Under his nails his fingertips are white.

By now, Lotte's other hand has somehow got itself on top of her belly, protecting it, almost, and for some reason Georgie thinks of those photographs of Lotte with the man in the Captain Bird's Eye hat – the doctor? – and she knows, right then, if she doesn't get away, something really horrible is going to

351

be said, that might sound like it's about politics or wars or bloody science, but underneath will kick what's gone before into the ha'penny place, and Georgie doesn't the bloody shit-fuck-balls want to be stuck in the middle, being the audience the kids need so they can hurt each other without anybody cottoning on, when really, nobody would be in this situation if it wasn't for her, needing to be bloody minded as if she was a stupid bloody baby.

Without asking to be excused, she gets up and goes to the loo, praying it will have blown over by the time she gets back.

It's on her return that she sees the fur coat. It's draped over a chair at a table near the exit. Sitting on the chair opposite is an old man; his skin is green-veined like a cockleshell, his body slumped, his bald, paper-crowned head nodding towards his plate of Brussels sprouts. Drops of gravy have spilled onto the cuff of one of his shirtsleeves and he has a big napkin tucked into his collar, like a baby. The coat is on the chair facing him but there's no one sitting there, no place laid on the table in front of it. Georgie glances through the double doors. Lotte is still sitting at their table up at the other end of the restaurant, her back to Georgie, smoking. Her pose is slouchy, but Georgie knows she's still angry because of the slow way she's smoking, her mouth blowing out poisonous kisses of blue air that look as if they're coming from inside her, not from the long black cigarette. David's at the cash register, paying; he's making a big deal out of it and trying not to at the same time. It's unclear whether their fight has got over the bad bit, but at least they aren't looking her way.

It's important to know why you take things that belong to other people. There are good reasons and bad reasons and just plain stupid reasons. A good reason, e.g. taking Alison O'Meara's school uniform for Elaine, is because someone else will get better use of it. A weak reason, e.g. taking a silk scarf the colours of which are so beautiful they hurt your eyes but in a good way and make you almost want to cry, is because you want the thing for yourself. A bad reason, e.g.—

Well, nobody should do things for bad reasons. End of story.

But if the thing doesn't belong to anyone, if it's just been left there and there's someone who could use it, who *needs* it to stay warm and alive, what's the harm in that? A coat like that could keep Elaine warm and alive for ever. All Georgie has to do is get it off the chair, bring it out to the car, spring the broken lock of the boot and hide it there till they get home.

It slides off easily enough, almost like it's the chair's skin. The old man grunts a little, but doesn't wake. Georgie folds the fur and puts it over her arm.

It's heavier than she expected and stinks of mothballs. She looks down at it. Grey fur, patchy, like a balding head.

Warm and alive for ever?

Georgie's throat convulses. Dropping the coat, she runs back to the loo.

When Georgie returns to their table, the taste of her vomited dinner sour in her mouth, Lotte is standing up and David is helping her on with her poncho. They seem to be doing their usual thing, smiling and talking to each other but not really, so Georgie supposes things are past the worst. Lotte's head turns. She sees Georgie and, without looking back, goes to touch David's arm, only this time her fingers make contact. She shivers a little, like she's got a shock, but doesn't look down. Instead, it's David's head that turns, as if pulled on a string, but in the wrong direction, not at Georgie, but at Lotte. As he realises who he's looking at, his whole body stops, frozen. Georgie almost expects to see that hungry look in his face again, the same one he had on the beach. But this time it's not like that, it's way emptier, like the first time someone boring sat in their kitchen and—

this beats the North Star Hotel, bean an tí

'Christ, almighty, George! Where on earth did you get to?' His head has snapped to the left and he's staring at Georgie and now he's *fuming*.

He steps towards Georgie. But his arm under Lotte's fingers is slower to move than the rest of him, so it sticks to her as he's turning. With an effort, he pulls away, separating from Lotte like the flesh of a date pulling from its stone, and as he does, the same string that pulled him pulls Lotte. Her eyes drift away from Georgie, down to the empty space under her fingers, then, puzzled, dart up towards David, who's striding forward now, jingling his keys. Something happens in Lotte's face, pushing out the puzzlement, and then she's staring at Georgie, but not at her, through her, not *seeing* her, not seeing anything, and for a horrible moment, all Georgie sees is a reflection of herself.

Oh

No.

'No. I'm fine, I won't stay, all that wine has caught up with me. Let me just get my things and….'

David nods and shoves his hands in his pockets, as if he's afraid they'll do something unplanned if he leaves them free. He is whistling under his breath again, but in the old way, tight and fake-happy.

Lotte goes upstairs, leaving Georgie and David in the hall, both fidgeting, both hovering, neither going anywhere.

'Right,' says David. 'Just eh.... Back in a tick.'

He moves as suddenly as a cracker being snapped, taking the stairs three at a time.

Georgie waits for the voices to start – hesitant, polite, cutting across each other again without meaning to – because when they do, she knows they'll be upstairs for ages, trying to figure out how to get things back to the silly, nervous brother-and-sister excitement of the evening before. Instead, the door of the upstairs loo opens and David goes in. Georgie tries to block her ears, but the sound of his poos going into the water is very loud.

Lotte comes down first. She's holding her bag.

'So,' she says, 'you had a good time, monster?'

'Yeah. The food was lovely.'

'You didn't finish your pudding, though.'

Georgie shrugs, not bothering to remind her that none of them had any pudding.

'So,' says David, appearing at the top of the stairs, and Georgie thinks how stupid it is, people saying the same words but meaning different things. 'Ready to hit the road?' He descends the stairs jauntily, jingling his car keys.

'Please, there's no need,' says Lotte. 'You've been terribly good to me. I'll get a taxi.'

'No.' David smiles and Georgie can see he's trying his best to make it look okay but something in his face has decided there's no point. 'We'll drop you over.'

There's a wall of something invisible between them now, thick and wobbly, like jelly. They're pretending it doesn't exist, or that they're so used to it they don't care about it anymore. Georgie knows that this is how it's going to be from now on. Every so often, one of them will forget the wall is there, and move their hands towards the other, trying to get through it, but the wall will be too strong; so when the first person moves, the other will turn away, or look in the wrong direction, or something.

'Do I have to come?' says Georgie. '*The Jungle Book* is on.'

David exhales.

Don't be angry with me, thinks Georgie. It's not my fault. Even though through the walls, she can hear the sound of sobbing, lonely and afraid, in Mrs Kelly's empty house.

That night, she tries to lift her bedroom window but she can't budge it. The catch is broken. Lotte must have done something to it. She stares out at the darkness. Something is flickering in the lane. She can't see what it is, but there's a warm light reflecting off the back windows of the houses opposite. A fire? Is it those lads, those lads Elaine has been so terrified of, only Georgie never took her warnings seriously? She presses her forehead against the cool glass of the window. She can make out distant sounds: music, laughter, the creaking of an old wooden door. She imagines the cracked glass of the Cortina's windscreen, eaten alive by yellow tongues of flame while Elaine's lads tilt cans of beer into their mouths and swing on Mrs Kelly's door, forcing it open, banging it shut, torturing the gap, wrecking the hinges, pulling at the edges of the event horizon.

She falls back onto her bed. It's full of the smell of Lotte's perfume.

Elaine will be okay, she tells herself.

Just before she drops into sleep, she hears the fingernails. They're scratching at the wallpaper on Mrs Kelly's side of the wall, near the skirting board at the corner, scratching through the plaster and bricks and board and that box under her bed where she used to keep things she no longer had any use for.

Help me.

She pushes the duvet into the corners of her ears, grinds her eyes shut, imagines pleasant things happening to her. When she finally sleeps, her dreams are full of babies: identical, sad-eyed, their mouths full of pearls, silver chains between their bellybuttons, their ears tiny flaps of white silk.

☼

There were only three pictures of Lotte, not including the double. The picnic, a castle ramparts and another pier. As they progressed, Lotte's mother's beehive mounted, getting stiffer, stickier, paler, shinier. Her smile brighter; falser. Lotte's hair escaped its schoolgirl plaits, growing wilder and more unkempt. And the man in the Fairisle jersey grew ever balder, ever closer to Lotte, his hand creeping down from shoulder to upper arm to elbow to waist. Lotte's expression remained unchanged, except for a slight shift in her mouth; that dry amusement giving way to something harder, warier, older.

The fourth picture had no Lotte in it. Instead it was back to Lotte's mother – Julia – and the man, the doctor, standing outside a guesthouse by the sea, looking at each other. This picture was like the first one of them on the pier; rough but more real than the others, that same *nude* thing about it, as if it was showing something they knew was there but didn't think anyone else could see. Georgie could tell they were just about to have a fight.

The phone rings in the morning, after breakfast and just as they're getting ready for the trip to the North.

Oh dear, says David. That's terrible. I'm awful sorry to hear that, George.

It's Granda Bell, he tells Georgie. Granny isn't well. She had pains in her chest the night before and had to be rushed to the hospital. It's not serious, thank God, just a bit of angina—

What's angina? says Georgie.

David gestures to his chest. Heart. I think. She has to take it easy.

Georgie knows what this means. They're going to have to put their visit off.

But no cloud without a silver lining, eh? David says this in a way that's trying so hard to cheer her up it does the opposite. Your Granda said we could organise something when Granny's better. In the New Year, maybe, one of the long weekends. Won't that be something to look forward to?

Georgie nods. She and David both know there isn't going to be a long weekend till Paddy's Day on the 17th of March.

Now I know you're a good man, David, said Granda Bell at the funeral. He spoke quietly but Georgie, shivering in the long black car, had been close enough to hear. And I know Annie would be beside herself if she thought I was saying this, but I'll not mince my words. It's breaking her heart having her wee girl buried down here.

Leaden clouds, a bone-heavy wind; slatey, thundery skies. The only benefit of not going up North is that Georgie has plenty of opportunities to visit the lane in the daytime, bringing provisions with her. But with Elaine not budging from the house, what's the point of that?

Would Elaine be budging if Georgie had brought her back that coat?

Since Christmas Eve, the fabric of the lane has become even more fragile. More slogans have appeared on the walls. *Fuck the EEC. Bren loves Stacia. Up the IRA.* Crumpled beer cans and smashed bottles are piling up around the wreck of the Cortina. The lads have been lighting fires inside it. All the stuff Georgie used to hoard in the spare-wheel well – balls, books, skipping ropes; the things she and Elaine played with in summertime, when it was all still an adventure – have been taken out and strewn around. Many of them are burnt. Georgie stares at Mrs Kelly's prised-open door and worries about Elaine, vulnerable beyond it. But any time she tries to approach the gap, she feels sick: nauseatingly ill, with that awful smell in her nose. If Elaine was there to help her, she would go through. No problem. But on her own?

Impossible.

In an effort to distract herself, she tries to bury herself in Narnia. Yet no sooner has she opened *The Magician's Nephew*, the official first book of the set, than David interrupts, suggesting yet another walk.

Enniskerry, Howth, Glendalough. When in doubt, march in the face of mortality.

Boooooooooo-ring, thinks Georgie, dragging along behind him, trying not to think, trying not to listen as he points out the names of fishing boats, mountains, plant life, describing the types of engines they use, the rocks they're made of, the soil they grow in. Trying not to pay attention to the effort he puts into talking about concrete rusting because of all the iron in it, because that only reminds her of the story he told her and Lotte on Christmas Eve, about the man from Scotland with the funny voice. Trying not to look as he points out a car, saying in a voice that's way too hard and bright, What about that, eh, old bean? Fancy switching to a Beamer in the New Year when we get the Good News from the firm? Or a Jag, even? Rourke can put that in his pipe and smoke it. From time to time, he even tries his funny voices, doing Joanie Flynn or that mean man with the sharp eyes from work, but they don't sound as funny as usual and when he does Jan, Georgie feels like she does listening to Timmy Nelson, like David's voice is a blackboard and he's scraping his own nails down it.

In Howth, on the treacherous north pier, where ropes lie curled around the bollards like snakes, ready to trip up unwitting passers-by, and fronds of seaweed clutch the uneven cobbles like mermaids' fingers, and slimy fishscales coat the ground in silvery, slippery armour, David helps her to get up onto the high steps so they can look out at the view. As he hoists her up, she feels the force twisting through her father's arm, triangulated by gravity, and wonders what would happen if she let go. Would he let her drop, crash back down onto the cobbles while he stood there, laughing? Or would he turn white with shock and scream 'Geeeoooorgieeeee' – just like the doctor does in *Black Beauty* when something bad happens to Jenny, his daughter?

Stupid question.

The view from the steps is okay. They can see out over the Irish Sea, past the chalky lump of dull green that's Ireland's Eye where, William Robinson says, all those rats live.

'Nothing like the sea air, eh?' says David, rubbing his hands. Georgie listens to her teeth chatter and longs for Aslan, the lion-king of Narnia.

Two teenage boys, dressed in their Christmas best, are messing around at the top of the lighthouse, swinging off the railings, daring each other to jump. One looks over. David nods. The teenager yells something, but his words get whipped away by the wind.

'What?' yells David.

'I said, fishing, mister?'

Use your eyes, thicko, thinks Georgie. If we were fishing, we'd have rods.

The teenager has bits of hair growing on his upper lip, like a sketch of a moustache. His face is out of shape. He looks like Stretch Armstrong, pulled too far in the wrong directions. A sketchy Stretch. He looks like William Robinson might, when and if he becomes a teenager.

'No!' shouts David. 'Just a walk!'

The teenager swings himself over the rail. There is a flash of belly, taut and white; a line of soft dark hair rising from his waistband to his navel. Georgie wonders what the teenager's willy is like: small and mushroomy like hers, or like David's, long and purply, the hair around it fluffy, dark-ginger like old carrots. Or maybe it's like William Robinson's, gold-coloured and sort of strong-looking. William Robinson loves showing off his willy in the boys' toilets at break time; he always gets whoever else is there to show off too. Except Georgie. Georgie he only stares at while he pulls at his own, as if daring her to pull too.

'That right, Georgie?' David pats her on the shoulder. The teenager has uprighted himself. He starts to laugh, his friend too, their Adam's apples bobbling in their throats. What's so funny? she thinks. You, you stupid hairy-balled, turkey-necked boys?

'Come on.' David nudges Georgie. 'They're only being friendly. Say something.'

Like what? Georgie stares at him.

David stares back. 'Jesus—' He lifts his hands. For a horrible moment Georgie thinks he's going to hit her; though he never has, not even a smack.

He looks at his hands and turns, fast, leaving her to scramble down the steps on her own.

'Seeya Carrot-Top!' shout the boys.

By the time she reaches the bottom, David is halfway back to the car; his back rigid, his legs moving like one of those machines on *Tomorrow's World*, his feet pounding the ground like they want to break it into pieces.

☼

Clonmel is fine.

☼

The photo of the double was the last one Georgie found, because when she knocked Lotte's drawer out of the chest as she was putting back the scarf – made clumsy by the rush to put things right again, by the big dark man and his strange music playing on the telly, by, above all, Caliban and his reproachful gaze, green as the sea: *You can't get rid of things that easy, wee Georgie* – that photo landed underneath the others, as if even in an accident it would be protected by them. It was a small square snap, black-and-white, showing another picnic. Two tiny toddlers, sitting side by side. Sallow-skinned, dark-haired and clasping hands. Each wearing a flouncy white baby dress and an identical, slightly stunned expression. Behind them, two sets of women's feet; both pairs in pretty shoes with straps across the front. It would have been impossible to tell if the babies were boys or girls, except that Georgie had seen a picture of them before, grown-up, shouting on the streets of Berlin. If she hadn't seen that other picture, she might have thought the photographer had made a mistake and snapped the same baby twice; or, if she was being very silly, and a baby herself, she might have thought that every person in the world, not just her, is born with a side to them that only some people *see*. When really, nobody is *seeing* anything; all they're doing is looking for something that used to belong to them and doesn't exist any more.

They're hardly in the door when the phone rings. Georgie runs to it, thinking it's Lotte – or someone – but instead it's just Mr Lyons from David's office.

Ah, says David. Oh. Well. God, no. That's eh— Fine. No, really— Rourke's; eh. His youngest? I knew he— Bolton Street? Oh, I didn't know— Of course. Yeah, yeah. Fine. A fine choice.

He puts down the phone and stares at it. If this is the Good News from the firm, there doesn't seem to be much goodness in it.

David sighs and slumps against the wall. He takes off his glasses and closes his eyes. His face looks bare and tired, but in a weird way; young, almost.

But that's not important. What's important is what Georgie sees through the kitchen window: spikes of glass sticking out from the top of the wall they share with Mrs Kelly's back garden, glittering in the sunset like the bloodied fins of a slaughtered sea monster.

Tomorrow, she taps on her bedroom wall, using the Morse Code she'd learnt in the *Scouting for Boys* book Auntie Maura had given her as a surprise extra present.

I. Will. Come. For. You. Tomorrow. In. The. Lane.

There is no answer. That night her dreams fill with poison, black and smoking.

As soon as she gets to the crossing, she knows. But she keeps going, past the bin, and enters the mouth of the lane. As she expected, nothing happens. There is no fading away of sound, no shimmering wall between her and the outside world. Whatever hidden dimension the lane has stored is gone. The *Rowm* has burst. The event horizon is no more. The phenomenon has been disproven. The world is flat.

Georgie + a lane = nothing.

The lads have taken the car apart, ripped off its doors and strewn them around the dismembered carcass. Bits of charred newspaper are fluttering across the ground; light and fluffy, like burnt hair. Someone has added a new graffiti: HAUNTED, in bleeding red letters, with an arrow pointing to Mrs Kelly's door.

Georgie can tell just by looking that the door won't open. It's been forced back into its architrave by whoever put the spikes into Mrs Kelly's wall; closed up, re-hinged. She pushes anyway, not wanting to walk away without proving, even if only to herself, that she made an effort. But the door doesn't budge; they must have fixed new bolts to the inside. She leans against it, clapping her hands against the cold, and waits. Over the wall, she can hear old leaves whistle around the hidden parts of Mrs Kelly's garden. She pictures them: dead matter, a tracery of veins, nothing more; too decayed to even rustle properly. She knows it's ridiculous to keep waiting; if Elaine was okay, if she still wanted Georgie to help her, to do whatever thing Georgie has been too – *afraid*? Is that the word? – to ask, she would have made her way down the garden by now, new bolts or no new bolts, and be standing beside Georgie, and together they'd be planning what to do next.

As she turns to go, she sees something bright gleam inside the rusty darkness of the Cortina's shell. She peers in. On top of the stinking ruins of the chassis is a Christmas present, wrapped in holly-pattern paper and loosely tied with a red ribbon.

It's filthy, the paper torn; whatever is inside is ruined. There's a bare patch on the wrapping, as if someone, in a hurry to rip off a Sellotaped namecard, has torn away the top layer of the paper. On the patch is scrawled, in lopsided, childish writing: *To Georgie, Love Elaine. Bring Her It Back.* Through the rips, Georgie can see fragments of the present she bought for Elaine – a girl's jewellery set: necklace, lipstick, earrings and mirror.

She'd saved up for it with her pocket money. Jacob in the newsagents in Fairview had looked at her oddly, but she'd just made her face stupid, like Saoirse's, and then he didn't say anything.

She could leave it there, but instead she picks it up. The moment she touches it, she feels ill. Even after she throws it in the bin on the corner, the nausea lingers, lying in the back of her mind like a scum of oil.

That evening, before David goes out to the big party to celebrate them starting to work again on Can-You-Believe-It-The-Boring-Bloody-Bank, he gets another call. This one is from Auntie Maura. Oh, he says, as if someone has winded him in the stomach. He starts shaking his head. No. Look, Maura, we need to have a chat about it. You can't just get rid— No. I will come down. It's just. Wait. Please, wait until—

Mrs Lynch, sitting in the lounge, moves her false teeth around with her tongue and laughs at Terry Wogan. In the kitchen, Georgie finishes her fish and chips; she asked for double helpings and ate them but she's still hungry. She gets up, goes to the press and takes out some bread. Maybe, she thinks, everything that's happened is for the best. She folds a slice, shoves it in her mouth whole. Swallows, takes another.

If a photo is a stolen soul, what's a photo of twins? A twice-stolen soul, two minuses, subtracted together? Or is it theft squared, like multiplying two minuses; so the bad act cancels itself out?

What if you see a photo of twins and want to steal it? Would that be like putting another minus into the equation, so depending on whether the first theft – the photograph itself – is minus or plus, you'll either cancel it out or make it worse?

And what if you want to steal that photo, but don't, if you put it back instead? Does the putting back cancel out the wanting to take? Or does the wanting stick around, hanging over the stolen souls like a curse; minus recurring, connecting the wanter and the souls till death do us part?

☼

'Georgie?'

Caliban's head turned. On the telly, an enormous dark man fled through an underground labyrinth. In the ceiling, a spidery crack shivered, while outside, in Lotte's back garden, the eerie green Binion Light froze; the limbic ghost it had summoned hanging semi-formed, misty, above the snowy ground. Panicking, Georgie stuffed the photos back into the envelope with the crossed-out addresses on the front—

~~Hackney~~
~~Turnmill Street (Farringdon~~)

—and shoved that back into Lotte's chest of drawers, bundling on top everything else that had fallen out when she'd knocked the drawer loose. As she did, something familiar brushed her fingers. Little teeth, joined by silver links, in a silk purse that – if she'd had the presence of mind to register it – would have reminded her of Aisling's rosary beads, the ones she'd had since she was a girl, the ones Georgie used to put on when she was little and wear around her neck, as if they were a necklace, and parade in front of Aisling's mirror, admiring herself, until one day when she went into Aisling's room to find them, they were gone. But she had no time to register that, because the door was opening. All she had time for was to scramble into bed, getting there just as Lotte came in with the tray.

'Why, look at you, Queen Nefertiti!'

On their first day back, there is no sign of Jan at the school gates. Instead, Saoirse is accompanied by an awkward-looking girl in specs and dungarees; a teenage version of herself. 'My Mom's in America,' Georgie hears Saoirse say to one of the girls from their class. 'She's got this like super-busy job in a college and they're paying her a ton. I'm gonna go back there too, real soon.'

Is this what relief feels like? If so, why does it feel so empty? Georgie's fingers slide inside her schoolbag. They find the greaseproof paper around her sandwich and prise it open. She rips a chunk of sandwich free, mushing it into a ball so she can sneak it into her mouth without Mrs Allen seeing. Heat rises on the back of her neck. William Robinson, breathing there again.

362

During break time William Robinson deliberately misses the ball that Sarah Hannigan kicks in his direction. It goes straight towards Georgie. She is alone. Timmy is in the loos again, with constipation. Georgie could have side-stepped, but the ball comes out of nowhere, taking her by surprise. Her foot flicks out, automatically giving her possession.

'Hulk!' calls William Robinson, waving. 'Over here!'

Hulk?

She can't help it; she looks over. Around her, the world seems to slow down, with a long creaky chuckle like a ghost train. William Robinson's eyes are waiting: bright, alert, a crocodile in a bayou showing no glimmer of malice, only welcome.

*'**Ausland/Otherland**'*. *Regie/Director: Sabine Wiedemann.*
Datum/Date: 16/03/20— Ort/Location: Aberystwyth.
Befragte/Interview Subject: '*Anna Bauer*' (**Sitzung/Session 3**).

Well, naturally. It was a, em, big thing. To leave what
you know, to leave everything, is not easily done. Of
course we were not the first to become displaced persons.
My father had been in the police during the war—

The? SS? No, not at all. Just the local, you know, a local
bobby. He was responsible for managing the transports of
foreign workers and....

No. I did not know about the camps, not in the war-time.
I was young, and not interested in politics. I liked to
dance. In our village and the townland, there was not much
bombing; we were farms, not useful to be bombed. And with
the camps, well, you see, by us there was none for certain,
and overall in the Protectorate, not many. Theresienstadt,
of course, but that was so, a toy, a dolly *KZ Lager*, where
they played and so forth. All for the public relations. The
worst camps the Nazis made, that was in Poland. There was
a, you know, coldness to the Poles. From the Nazis. They
thought them beasts, lesser *menschen*. But Heydrich, you
know, he said the Czechs were civilised.

What I think of that? *Nun*, so, now, that is an impossible
question.

...

But, yes. By us, it was different. We were a village,
so.... I mean, there was always little fights, who owns
what land and who buys what shop and who gets the gold,
the money, from the government. But that was small-fry.

364

Typical village. People in a village will fight about
what they can. To be Czech or German, it was not that
important. When you say Czech, what you mean by that is a
big body of people. A nation, *ja*? But for us, only in the
village across the mountain, and further in, was there
Czech. Everyone in our village spoke German. We were
Germans. When I was a child, I had to speak in Czech in
the school and I found that very difficult. My mouth was,
em, not accustomed to the shapes. I was told I was stupid
because I had not the words. But, dear God, I grow up in
a house speaking German, I am four? How am I to speak
quickly in another tongue?

Excuse me? Well. Yes, *natürlich*. As a child of course, I
remember. Hitler coming to the big town near us, after
the taking over, the annexing, and the people waving and
cheering, and we, the children, had flowers. Because that
was as it was; we were to be liberated from the Czechs,
allowed to be oneself again, German. Perhaps before, I
would not have said this, because England was home, and
with the documentaries, one knows more, of course, of
what happened. But I am old now. So, yes, I had the flowers
and I waved also. Because I was to be freed. And, this
question, if I had the flowers at ten years old, was I
guilty, for giving the flowers and cheering? You want to
ask this, *gel*? The together-guilt. Am I then, as child of
ten, to blame for what is happened to me and my family?

Also. How can I say? Who is to say?

. . .

So em, the transports, that my father supervised. These
were for the *Fabrik*, factories. My father must organise
the workers off the trains and on the trains. I heard some
time, later you know, on the documentary, that Hitler
would have killed the Czechs, more of them, like the
Poles, but he wanted the factories to work, for the guns.
In any case, my father was a kind man, and the Czechs who
came to our house after the war, not the first lot in the
wild times but the second lot, after things settled, they
said how they had made inquiries about him, and had many
good stories, how he did not hit the foreign workers or

365

shoot like the others. His kindness was remembered and it was resulting from that we were allowed to stay longer—

You mean after the first lot came, in the wild time? Did I wish to leave then? But.... No. This was our home.

As I said, I was not ever interested in politics, so I did not talk to my father about that during the war, what he saw, or did. Also, I was young, yes? I was serving in the big house, the Count's house, on a scheme. The, um, region I lived was joined to Germany in that time; we were no longer Czechoslovakia, we were simply a *Gau*, a province, so the central government had many schemes and one was to send the young men into the Count's house, the invalids from the war, and that, naturally, was far more of interest to me than politics. Those young men, so handsome in bandages! But—

Yes. He came home at times, my father, very down in the face, with you know, a face like this, but saying nothing. My mother did not want to ask him what it was because she had an aunt who was married to a Jewish man. But in the end, he was kind and the Czech guards said it was because of that we could stay.

How it was, was five German families out, five Czech families in. Like a balance, you know, as you make a cake. More fruit out, more nuts in. All the people we knew from the village, they went. One family after the next, until it was only us. And you can imagine for yourself; all the friends and neighbours and cousins gone. So who do you talk to? Only strangers, or Czechs from other parts of the country. Houses and businesses and farms that were the property of a friend, or neighbour, and now somebody else was living there. And—

Am I? Can you say again?

Angry? *Tja. Weisst Du*, you know, if I say I am angry, someone will say, *na*, this happened before, in other ways. A Czech butcher out, a German butcher in. And then there are the flowers and the waving. So what is the reason for anger? What good does it do? My father always said it is good to accept, not fight. And be kind to people. That is the most important thing. But one can only find the kindness in a, you know, one time, one place. It is not a rule.

...

How it was? Yes. Of course. This is, so, the *Punkt*, *gel*, of your programme, describing the leavings? The first ones who left, before us, they had to walk to the border. I saw them passing through the village. There were mostly old people, and mothers who had no husbands because the husbands were POWs, and children. The small ones were in prams and the other children, they had to walk. That was not so easy. How many things can you bring with you if you walk? Not many, that's for certain!

Our turn was the next year and I remember that because we left on Good Friday. We were luckier than the ones who walked as we had a little van and a horse. We could take feather beds and frying pans and pots. My mother, she wanted to put more things on the wagon, but the Czechs said No, that is all. But we had our beds, at least.

No. That was not a good time for food. We had dried bread on the journey in water-soup.

Sorry?

Yes. Soup made of water, like—

Yes. Stock. Broth.

We brung the little van and the horse to the railway station and then, that was it. Goodbye to the horse and onto the train.

Was I sad? Um.... *Sehen Sie*, what use is sadness?

No, we didn't know where. We thought we were going to the border because the others had gone there, but in

the end we went the other way, back, further in, to
Czechoslovakia. The first camp was work. Sixteen hours a
day sometimes, but that is what it is, to bring in the
harvest. I lived with a Czech family, my parents in the
house next, with other old people. Then the second camp,
the one of the long waiting, where my father died. Yes,
of dysentery. Though it was not that, it was, I think,
the shock that killed him. To leave everything you know,
and there's nothing, maybe only what you fit on a wagon.
Is it a surprise that someone dies? Like a tree, taken
out of the soil. Sometimes it will grow in the new soil,
sometimes not. But that is life, *gel*?

How I escaped? Well, it was not what you call an escape,
not really. My mother had the chance of going to East
Germany, to a little town near Dresden, the city which
had been, you know, burnt. So she left first. But I didn't
trust the Russians, so I stayed longer because the papers
were not coming. Um, four, seven months, maybe? In the
end I walked over the border alone, at night, through
the forest. Then I was in West Germany. At that time the
English were talking to the Americans about Westward Ho,
to bring the girls over to England, the German girls who
knew to work with cotton, and they organised my papers.
And that was when I told the lie.

Sorry?

No. There was no nastiness to us, not from the Czechs,
not in the camps. Other people were not so lucky. And
yes, before, we were not so lucky. But I— You know, when
you watch the documentaries, can you blame anyone who was
bitter?

. . .

Yes. I mean the Czechs.

Forgive?

. . .

Tja. My mother, in the end, she was more bitter against Hitler than anyone else.

...

You know, Sabine. What is interesting is, maybe only to me, is this leaving, this *Flucht*, yes? I have not the same pictures in my, um, soul, as I do with the other leavings. It shines to me that this should be the important story, the one you fill out with all the pictures, *ganz dramatisch, gel*? You use it in, so, a trailing, to advertise the programme. The poor sad people, leaving the homeland. Rain falling, and sad faces and all the pots rocking on the little van and, later, the girl at the railway station, touching the horse's head to say goodbye. But in realness, all I remember is things happened. Even the horse, that was a dear horse we brung with us. But I still cannot reach into my soul and feel again what I felt for him that day, touching his head. Not even my father dying. I was sad, I know that. But all I feel when I think on him now, a kind man so thin in the bed, is empty.

I know what you want to ask. Is it perhaps all the other documentaries, yes? Or the films, the pictures, of what Hitler done? That our leaving is not perhaps so important—

No? Excuse me? If what happened to me before, in the wild times, was that it? *Na, also*....

You know, what is different is the forest, that night, when I crossed over to the West. That, *weisst Du*, I remember. The feeling in my soul. Fear. I was afraid. My breath, my heart, bumping. And the excitement – *mensch, nochmal!* – I was young. It was an adventure. I was starting fresh! But the times before, rocking on the little van, all the pots and pans rocking with us, it is like, *gel?*, nothing.

...

My mother? No. I did not see her after the war. She died in 1955, when the twins were little, Lotte and Andreas.

Sorry?

No. I did not write her about the children. She had begun to forget at that time. The, you know, Alzheimers. And she was my mother in name, but in fact she was a stepmother, so it was not the same. My mother, the first one, died when we were born.

We? Yes, I said that. I had a brother. Peter. He was my twin. He died in a POW camp, in the East.

Do I...?

Who is there to miss? In Germany, nobody. They are all dead. And in Czechoslovakia, there is nobody any more, nobody I know. That is not the same place anymore.

[rises]

Yes. Thank you for helping. It is not so easy, with the chair. And I must to the News. Just in case there is something to be seen. Sometimes, you know, I, I dream there is something I must see. But always, never. *Tja*. That is what it is, to be an old lady. All what is important, what plays on the television, is nothing of me. Only—

Yes! Excuse me, Sabine, for such complaining! Of course. This, what for the television we make together now, of course this of me!

Split

In all stories, when a man is faced with alternatives, he chooses one at the expense of the others.

Jorge Luis Borges, *The Garden of Forking Paths* (1941)

((( )))

Sensing the inevitable and fast-approaching opening of this *Kammer*'s Schröderingerish Box, we ask you to consider the following statements via the lens of True and/or False:

(a) it's good to know where you come from
(b) knowing where you come from can show you why you do stuff
(c) knowing why you do stuff means you don't have to do it again
(d) knowing why you do stuff means you can do it again, only more effectively
(e) if you don't face what you've done, it will creep up behind you and bite you on the ass
(f) every point/Moment of violence in human history has its own unique Source and Wave of Consequences and cannot be compared to another
(g) two wrongs can sometimes make a right
(h) we are all responsible for actions taken in the name of the nation to which we belong
(i) we are all responsible for actions taken in the name of the dominant ideology of the nation to which we belong
(j) we are all responsible for actions taken in the name of the dominant ideology of the nation to which we find ourselves belonging
(k) everything that appears horrifying may, in its deepest essence, be something helpless that needs our care (courtesy R. M. Rilke)
(l) everything that appears horrifying is, in its deepest essence, something that should be contained and, if it continues to horrify, destroyed
(m) never apologise; never explain
(n) you don't need to know why something happened: all you ever need to know is where to go next, i.e. Pack Up Your Troubles in Your Old Kit Bag and Smile! Smile! Smile!

373

21:28:40–01:15:33

The cab disappeared, soundless. The tarmac on the Rock Road used to hiss and bubble when you and I drove over it, as if it was melting. Remember? By the time I'd come back with Martin, it had become bikini-wax-smooth. Vroom.

His hand on my chin, feeling for stubble.

Rain drizzling down, soaking into my skin.

My first public failure. Latin, for the Inter Cert, aged fifteen. You could blame the Brother who taught me, already knocking into the mushy wall of Alzheimers; or my teenage hormones; or laziness, or insecurity, or the boy in my class I had a secret crush on. Or you could say, like my Aunt Bridget often did, that, whatever else I got from you, I certainly hadn't inherited your brains. Although I flunked the subject, I used to love the feel of the Latin in my mouth. The words tasted different to English; perfect, somehow. Even after I gave them up, their taste stayed with me, while their meanings dissolved like atrophying muscle tissue; like the tissue that makes erections, that you have to keep making erections with, even if you don't want to, so that when they turn that part of you inside out, it still works.

For ages, I thought *lacuna* meant 'tear' – as in weeping – until Mar corrected me. He'd been a choir boy, briefly, in Govan. That's *lacrimosa*, Geo. *Lacuna* is a gap. Later, Sonia told me he was wrong; *lacrimosa* means sorrowful, girl. *Lacrima* is the Latin for 'tear'.

But a 'tear' can be a 'tear' too. A rent, a rip. A gap. So not that stupid a mistake. Strange, how these things insist; as if to say, try all you might, lady, there will never be a bridging. Will you wonder why I haven't picked up the phone and just talked to you? Will it come as a relief that I've chosen this method to communicate? Is that what your gift is about – me, relieving you of something?

The lights of Kish swept around, bouncing off a thin band of water far in the distance, then vanished. The tide was out. Over the ooze and bustle of the city, the sky was rusty with pollution; above the sea, it was a soulless grey-black. The harbour towns of Blackrock and Dun Laoghaire glittered in the distance. The air was chilly again, poking nagging fingers under my clothes.

A set of headlamps flashed over the level crossing in front of me, then swung into the car park. The engine stopped; the lights went out. I couldn't hear anybody get out. Maybe they'd driven out to the coast to look at the sea, or to sneak a secret adulterous fuck on the front seat. Or maybe they were doggers, waiting for someone else to come along and watch before they'd start their dirty business.

I have never liked Booterstown. Perhaps because it reminds me too much of Dollymount, our beach; yours and mine and Aisling's. Like Dollymount, the water at Booterstown is never deep enough to go swimming and, worse, the air always stinks because of all the raw sewage they pump out onto the strand. Martin used to love going there. He said it was good for us to get the ions. I would drag along behind him, reluctant and sulky, moaning about the cold, while he stormed ahead, fists stuck in his pockets, chin jutting at the sky. A year or so before things got really bad, before the recession bit in, costing him his job, drawing him back to the bookies and the Internet sites and the poker dens, he started going out there on his own. Without telling me, but I knew. I saw the sand on his boots, smelt the seaweed off his jeans. He told me he liked it because it was handy; near town, nicer than the northside, easy to fit in a little walk during a split shift. He said he liked it because of the sea, the sky. Bullshit. He only went there to cruise; trying, failing, trying again to swap one compulsion for another.

Fuck you, Martin Canney, I thought. Like I'd said, out loud, during our last argument, except that thinking it felt different. Fuck you to high heaven.

Behind the gates, the closed compound of Sonia's apartment complex was floodlit. Branches above the railings, silhouetted black against the sky. For Sale and To Let signs poking out over the spikes like severed heads. Only a few windows were lit in the block itself. I had wanted sanctuary after the madness of Marino and Fairview, but this looked desolate.

I glanced back. At the level crossing, the lights had gone on in the parked car. Two heads, silhouetted. There was something about them I didn't like. They looked like cops on a stake-out; or gangsters waiting to do a hit. The same gangsters, maybe, who'd tortured that poor sod in the canal? The wind gusted. Martin's coat billowed.

I keyed in the code to the complex as quick as I could. The gate swung open, smooth, pulled by a ghost's arms.

The lobby was empty and silent. The lift hummed, flicking up past the floors. I saw myself reflected in the brushed steel. Hulking, dark, monstrous.

I picked up Sonia's spare key where she'd left it, under a geranium pot in a communal window box. Only one of the overhead lights was working, giving the corridor a sick, greenish cast. There were four apartments on Sonia's floor. A businessman from the Balkans lived in the one beside hers. He had a mistress, a hot blonde, according to Sonia, with a high ass and long legs, and a son; a good-looking boy in his twenties taking a masters in International Law in Trinity. Mar used to have a joke about that; he'd picked it up from one of the waiters in the restaurant where he worked. Along, I used to taunt him, towards the end, with crabs.

How do you know if someone's been to Trinity? They'll tell you.

A young couple used to live in one of the other apartments, but bailed out when the recession turned nasty. Negative equity, up to their necks. The apartment facing Sonia's had never been let. Sonia claimed it was haunted; by the ghost of a restless nun who'd lived in the old convent the block had been built on, or a sailor who'd run aground in Napoleonic times. Rubbish, I'd said. There's no such thing as ghosts. And if there is, they wouldn't be haunting you.

It wasn't a bad build – spacious and well-finished, if a bit impersonal. The buyers had had to pay extra for the finishings: floors, units, special lighting features. Sonia's promotion had just about covered it.

Sonia's wife Christine had decided to stay in Limerick when the multinational that Sonia worked for announced its move to Dublin. Besides the obvious reasons – Christine's design company was in Limerick and the kids were still in school – there was, I suppose, some unspoken contract between them that made it not just possible, but the right thing to do. Christine had been supportive enough; she'd fought a little at the beginning, resisting the nighties and the tights, but in the end it had worked out. Sonia was loyal and a high earner and good at persuading and Christine, by her own reckoning, was a settler, not a fighter, and if I was to wear a less cynical hat, I would have

377

to say there was probably enough love between them, of the right amount or the right variety to see it through.

Ninety-eight per cent of couples split when someone transitions. I don't suppose you know that. If you're trans, you're far more likely to stay with your partner if you're in a relationship with a woman. They give all sorts of reason for that. Women are by nature stayers. Women get used to being married and don't want to leave. Women's sexuality is more fluid than men's. We love the person, as Sonia might say; they – she meant men – need the smell and the shape.

Mar hated those statistics. Christ, he'd say. I thought you were against all that biological determinism, Geo.

I thought you were too, Mar.

I was at Sonia's door. I glanced back at the lift. The doors began to close. I saw myself run back, stop them and—

And what? Race out of the compound and over to the beach? Run through the stinking sand? Feel rain on my face; salt on my skin? Lose myself in the darkness? Howl at the moon?

Run into those two shaven-headed thugs from that car, more like.

I turned the key. The door opened a bit, then got stuck. It was the dodgy rider that Sonia had warned me about. My head began to thump. I put my weight against the door, pushed.

The apartment felt wrong. Maybe it was the flu, descending on me again like a heavy duvet, playing tricks with my senses. Or maybe I'd expected things to be like how they were when Sonia was there; music on, voices in the kitchen, the crackle of the TV, low lamps in tasteful corners, homey smells of cooking. Instead, I found myself in a labyrinth. Endless grey corridors leading to half-open doors, relieved only by the floodlit lines bleeding in through the blinds. Awkward shadows sprawled across the hallway, making everything look weird and out of place. *The Cabinet of Doctor Caligari*. I slid down the wall and hunkered against it. Through the doorway of the living room, I could see the large picture window that led out onto the balcony. Inside its frame, two masses of dull colour fought against each other; the dead sky, the oily, poisoned sea. My sinuses ached. I was sure my chest was sore again, but I couldn't feel it.

What was I doing there? I thought of the CAT scan the hospital in Wicklow had offered me, the one I'd run from, like a private eye in a cheap noir. It seemed like a pointless reaction now. What had driven to me to race from that ward and jump into a cab like a crazy person when I could have been tucked up in bed, with a nice nurse feeding me sleepers? All sorts of stuff, never mind the obvious, could be going wrong with me because of that accident. Blood clots, aneurism, stroke, twisted spinal cord....

I closed my eyes and saw the same thing I used to see after Martin left; a flash image of myself lying dead in a parallel universe. Like something from one of your sci-fi novels, as if the existence I thought I was leading was just a shadow of the original, while the real me was laid out cold and stiff on a gurney in Wicklow, broken to pieces in that collision.

The first time I got that image was that February, in 1977, after you had made us go our separate ways. I began imagining that the real Georgie had died, drowned at sea, or in a train crash, and what I thought was me was just a leftover, a ghost-recording. Maybe that's why I've had such difficulty remembering those last years with you and Aisling as more than a sequence of events – because I'd left who I was, all those emotions and feelings, behind me. Sometimes I wonder how many more *me*'s, Georgies and Georgias and even Geos, have been strewn in my wake; killed in bike accidents, or freak waves, or heart attacks brought on by using the wrong drugs at the wrong time. How many more are yet to die? Right now, I'm praying there's a rake of them, lined up to take their turn so I won't have to.

I stared at the ceiling. Everything seemed very far away. Wasn't that why I'd asked the cabbie to take me to Marino, so I could reclaim something from the time before I'd become a ghost? It had felt brave, for a moment, in the cab. Yet all I had done was end up hiding in a bush, like a silly frightened tranny from a soap show, waiting for a pack of spotty Dublin adolescents to terrorise me. I went home, I'd said to Sonia over the phone. But I hadn't. Home wasn't Marino; it hadn't been for decades.

Stupid to have done it; stupid to have come here too. I should have kept my mouth shut with that cabbie. I could have been in my real home – no bath, but at least a place that felt like it fitted.

It's your fault, I told Martin's coat, pooling around me like a black sea. If I hadn't brought you with me, I'd be fine. As soon as I spoke, I wished I hadn't.

I forced myself to my feet and pressed the switch. The corridor filled with yellow light. I wrenched Martin's coat off me. It fell to the floor.

You're nothing, I said. You're just a coat.

To drive the point home, I kicked it. It crumpled like there was a person inside and I felt immediately, nauseatingly, guilty. Fighting the nausea, I picked it up and carried it into the living room. I lay it across one of Sonia's white leather armchairs.

Stay, I told it, as if it was a dog.

Sonia's kitchen lay long and cool and white, ghostly under the lights of the compound. It was a beautiful space: all chrome surfaces and Philippe Starck appliances. Christine had designed it. It reminded me, a little, of the kitchen in the apartment Mar and I had lived in in Brighton, the one that looked out onto the sea with the view of the pretty, frothy pier. I switched on the kettle and opened a cupboard. It was stuffed with teas and infusions: too much choice. I went for one in a pink packet, the Goddess brand Sonia kept for when Christine came up to Dublin with the kids. The kettle bubbled and switched itself off. I dropped the bag into the biggest mug I could find and filled it with boiling water.

Steam rose. The packet said rose and liquorice, but I could smell nothing.

I headed to the bathroom. Tiredness had crawled into me. I could hardly keep my eyes open.

I turned the taps. The bathroom was white, splashed with bits of colour – towels, tiles engraved with seashells, marine life, mermaids.

Did you used to like mermaids too? I asked Sonia once. As a kid? She'd had to think about it. No, she said eventually. Seahorses.

Such delicate little amphibians we are.

I took a bottle of bath oil and shook it into the water. Foam began to rise. Sonia had a spare robe hanging on the back of the door, white and fluffy. It looked just what I needed. I peeled off my jeans and top and put it on. The collar came up to my cheek. It felt comforting and I was sure it smelt nice, just like the bath oil probably smelt nice. I lit a candle and stared at the foaming water. Maybe I should forget about supper—

An animal warning growled inside me; a leftover from my years of disordered eating.

I returned to the kitchen and opened the fridge. Cream cheese, salad, dressings, cherry tomatoes. I closed my eyes, stuck in my hand and found cardboard. Eggs.

One of the eggs had two yolks. Twins. Little freaks. I whisked them into the other egg, dribbled oil in the pan, lit the gas. Something beeped in the sitting room; it sounded like my mobile and for a moment I nearly went for it. But then I remembered that my phone was lost, sacrificed somewhere in the wilds of Wicklow.

I threw together an attempt at a salad and thought, not for the first time, of how beautifully my friend had transitioned – though that wasn't fair, because you couldn't even think of Sonia as in transition any more. How beautifully she lived, then. Everything was right, down to what was in the fridge. Had she liked that sort of food before, I wondered; women's food, girly food, salad, eggs, white wine, dark chocolate? Or had she been into steak and chips until the 'mones kicked in? We'd never talked about that. We should. Had it been the 'mones that changed her tastes? Or had Christine been working on her well before then, influencing her sensual preferences under the weight of time and intimacy? Had I liked to eat different things before I'd met Martin? Had he? Had he somehow infiltrated me, and me him, exchanging more than bodily fluids, swapping bits of our selves along the way? Did you change Aisling? Did she change you? Or did all your changing end up in me?

Use water, Geo. It helps emulsify, gies it that nice smooth Italian texture.

Thanks, Mar. I poured a drop in. He'd been a good cook; I have to hand him that.

I poured the eggs into the pan and watched them ease out towards the edges. And maybe it was that, that simple domestic gesture, me alone in that big empty kitchen, a sort of peace descending after all the chaos of the day, that got me thinking about him – but not the stuff I've been telling you, not my memories of how he was when he was with me, how we'd been together. I started thinking about him now. Where he was, who he was with. Imagining, questioning, worrying, wondering. The stuff I'd tormented myself with after he'd left. Not because I'd wanted to; it had just insisted, rising from my gut into my gorge, staying trapped in my head, chasing itself around in endless circles. I'd tried everything – meditation, yoga, swimming – trying to push him out of my mind. And it had worked, for a while. Did it work for you? Is that what you did with her, my mother? Push her out, push her down, pretend she didn't exist?

I stood in that over-designed kitchen and, suddenly, I wasn't able to push anymore. Questions clawed the air around me. Was he in Glasgow, in that little flat off Dumbarton Road, cooking up tatties and saussies for his sweet mother Janet? Was he in England? Had he gone back to Europe? Or farther afield? He'd always wanted to visit Thailand, learn to cook proper Thai. Was he with a ladyboy now? That would be funny. Or back in Brighton? Or still in Ireland? I'd never thought he would stay, but— Had he gone west, to Connemara? Was he in London? Or up North? He'd always loved Down when I'd brought him there. Maybe he was holing up in the house I'd inherited from my grandparents and never managed to get rid of, looking out at the sea, thinking longingly of the bookies in Warrenpoint. Was he in London, where that bomb had gone off? Or maybe he'd never left Dublin—

The kitchen looked funny and I didn't know why.

The lights went out; only a flash, then they came back on. Sound exploded; an inhuman scream, ripping at my ears. It was Sonia's smoke alarm. Black smoke was rising from the pan. I'd burnt the omelette.

I swore and grabbed a high stool. The alarm shrieked as I wrenched it out of its fitting and shoved at the battery. The screaming stopped, leaving an echo ringing in my ears.

The kitchen was black with smoke. I turned off the gas and, grabbing a towel, took the pan off the cooker and threw it into the sink.

I opened the window. In the acrid silence, something was wrong. I couldn't hear the sound of running water.

Fuck, I thought, and ran to the bath, getting to it just before it spilled over.

I sat in the hall again, close to the door, as far from the kitchen as I could. My entire body was in pain; I knew that, but couldn't feel it. My eyes were watery and blurred. I kept seeing little shapes in the lingering omelette smoke; curling tails, three-headed monsters. Through the doorway of the sitting room Martin's coat sprawled, coaly black against the white leather. One of the sleeves had flopped onto a coffee table and the cuff was almost touching the TV remote. My finger itched to press a button, switch on Sonia's flat-screen TV, but I couldn't see how I could do that without touching the coat and the thought of that made my skin crawl. It was probably just as well. The TV would only be full of shit; it was always full of shit. Mar was right. That was my job, putting pieces of shit together so they made a bullshit sort of sense. If I switched it on, I'd only see more of the same. Bombs, terror, politicians, reparations. The National Front burning houses in Bradford; Jihadis burning flags and books. And on the other channel, Lotto wins, quiz shows, soap operas and, if I was lucky, wiry tattooed men drowned in canals with their faces ripped off by a ganglord's thugs or, maybe truth was stranger than fiction and the taxi driver was right, sick ignorant kids ketamined up on a reality-Tarantino jag, snuff-movieing for YouTube – who knew? Who cared? – while the rest of the world bayed for blood.

The names of victims, unfolding in black-on-yellow on an unthinking cap-gen.

Farringdon, Turnmill Street. The address still tickled at me, but duller, as if the pulse it was trying to latch on to was fading.

I stared at Martin's coat, but it was silent.

If you're that worried, I told myself, give him a ring. Use Sonia's landline. Thirty seconds, over and out, you don't even have to talk. Just listen to him pick up.

I could remember his number; that was the scary thing. I'd had it on speed-dial for years, but I could still remember it.

Something buzzed, raising the hairs on the back of my neck. The coat shivered.

I lurched up and went back down the corridor to the bathroom. The water was heading towards lukewarm, but I was beyond caring.

I stepped in, sank.

Ack-ack-ack. Gunfire first. Then shouts. The ground was shaking. An earthquake? My eyes opened. I was lying in a white-tiled hospital morgue and the walls were moving, shuddering in candlelight. Somebody laughed right beside me. I couldn't see them. Was I dead? Was this my wake? A little mermaid winked at me across the pool of burning oil and I realised where I was.

I'd no idea how long I'd been out. The bath had gone cold; my knees and shoulders were goosepimpled. The water shivered, rippling in concentric circles. I tried to move my head again, but couldn't. My eyes were fixed to the ceiling. It was shivering too, as if people were dancing on it. That didn't make sense; Sonia's flat was on the penthouse. There was nothing above us. The shivers above me blurred, sharpened. The plasterwork in the ceiling was cracked. I hadn't noticed that before. The crack came into focus. A web of broken, spidery rivers. A crazed crossroads, each shrinking path leading only to oblivion.

Funny, said Mar when I'd told him about that ancient childhood fear.

Sorry? I'd said.

How you associate death with that. A, you know, crack.

Meaning what?

Think about it, Geo. A crack? An opening. A slit. A gap…. He'd got more uncomfortable as he'd gone on. A, you know, vagina.

I'd stared at him.

All I'm saying is it's funny you associate that, you know, with existential angst. Maybe that's why you've so much problems expressing yourself. You know, creatively. Why you got so frightened of your own imagination and what it could do.

I'd kept staring, remembering a nosey woman from my childhood and her probing questions at a dinner table. Thinking, *No, no, no. It wasn't just death or angst or some sort of stupid creative block, and it certainly wasn't down to my gender, it was—*

Alright, he'd said. Fuck this. I need a walk. Don't wait up for me, alright?

The gunfire grew louder. It was rhythmic, pulsing. It wasn't gunfire. It was music. Rapid-fire grime. More people shouted. I groaned, realising what was going on. They were having a party next door, in the apartment that belonged to the businessman from the Balkans. The bath was shaking now, Sonia's expensive oils and creams bouncing on her expensive glass shelves. The party-goers were laughing, screaming, whooping, kango-ing through the walls. I could make out words.

Roysh, Soarsha, Dod… and then she… and like you know omigod you'll never believe but—

The businessman's son, the Trinity student. He was the one celebrating.

A male voice. *Fucking WANKERS!* A bellow of laughter.

Go away. I was so tired I wanted to cry. I needed to take my eyes off that crack, but I couldn't move them. I couldn't move a thing.

Someone started hammering. It wasn't from the party, but closer. It was—

A door. Sonia's?

Whoever was hammering changed their tune.

A – G.

A – G – R.

A – G – R – O. Ag-Ro!

'Geo!' shouted a familiar voice, drilling through the cacophony. 'Geo! Geo!'

Stupid, really, those split-second connections between sense and thought and action.

I scrambled up and grabbed at the robe, half-slipping on the tiles. The candle flame lengthened. The crack in the ceiling widened, the morgue tilted. In the doorway of the living room, I saw Mar's coat, still slumped over the armchair. I righted myself.

'Geo! Geo!' An odd rhythm, not the way he usually said it. Fast. Like one name. 'GeoGeo!'

'Coming!' I shouted as I ran down the corridor, thinking, Christ, is he okay? Thinking, Christ, that fucker, I'll kill him when I see him. Thinking, Christ, how did he know I was here—

A – G. A – G – R – A – G – R – O—

One hand on the safety catch, the other pushing down the handle. The door stuck.

'GeoGeo! That you?'

I yanked at the handle, tugged. It gave way.

The bulb in the remaining overhead had blown and the only light working was the green exit sign near the stairs. My eyes adjusted and—

What the fuck.

Told you not to let anyone in, girl.

In front of me, like the punchline from some sick cosmic joke, stood the teenage couple I'd seen outside the café in Glendalough. The girl who'd reminded me of Elaine, rake-thin with her long stringy hair and starving eyes, and behind her, the boy who'd reminded me of myself – stodgy in his beige hoodie, his hair scooped up in a glittering fin, his fist still raised in a knock.

They were both drenched and shivering. In the washed-out green light they looked like ghosts of the drowned.

How in the name of anything had they ended up in this apartment block, outside this door? Dublin is small, but this was—

Shit. Had they followed me? Stop, I told myself. Cop on.

The music from the party kept thumping as we stared at each other. Something flickered in the girl's face and I realised she was frightened. Of me? Was I that scary? The boy spoke. I couldn't hear him. The music was too loud. His teeth were chattering. Was he scared too? I couldn't tell. The girl's limbs were nervy, twitching to run. She looked like a frightened woodland creature; she looked like Elaine again, the last time I'd seen her alive.

I realised I was talking. Sorry, I was saying, holding out my hands, I thought you were someone else, though why I should have been the one who was sorry I didn't know. It wasn't my fault they'd ended up here. It wasn't my fault I'd thought they were Martin. The boy frowned and spoke again, lifting his hands. It looked like an apology, but under the chattering teeth, the surface politeness, something else was beginning to creep into his eyes, something infinitely more shifty and calculating.

It was kids, Jammy Noel had said. That fella they found in the canal.

Hysteria, I'd thought. Not kids, but adults. Gangland, most likely.

Tore the face off him, said Jammy Noel. Put it on YouTube. Has to be kids.

I thought of the spam I'd got that morning. *is this sik?* Probably only a spurious connection. But—

Trans rule number one: protect yourself at all costs. If in doubt, if in danger, get out.

I stepped back, hands up. I was speaking, but couldn't hear what I was saying. Why did I have my hands up, like someone surrendering? Was I apologising again? Why? To who?

The girl sniggered; she wasn't frightened anymore. Had I said something stupid? Sticking out from her leather jacket pocket was the glinting neck of a naggin. Was she drunk? The boy's eyes were sizing me up. Why? They had the same forehead, I noticed. I hadn't seen that before. Bizarre. And the same nose.

The boy started to shout over the music. He was saying something I could hear. My name—

No. 'No-No?' he was shouting. He jutted his head past the girl so I could hear him properly. 'Where's No-No?' A name, but not mine. 'No-No?' He had a Glasgow accent; that much I could make out under the noise. That was why I'd thought he was Martin.

His face was less than a foot from mine. His lips were full. Under the healing acne marks, he had fair skin, like Mar's. Irish. Or Scots.

'I don't know,' I said. 'I don't know him. Or her. Sorry.' My throat was raw. It was hard to make the words come out. I pushed the door to close it. It jammed; Sonia's dodgy rider.

The girl's face twisted, she started to speak. Not to me, to him. I tugged at the handle, trying to free the door. Down the corridor, the music suddenly stopped.

'—like should fucking go.' The girl's voice, hissing in the silence, was Dublin, pure southside valley-girl. 'I need to piss, okay? It's like obviously the wrong fucking apartment, you dick.' She didn't sound one bit like Elaine. Of course she didn't; Elaine was gone.

Why had I stopped pushing the door?

'Don't call me a fucking dick.' Without the music, his voice was thin and high, nothing like Mar's. It was those bloody drums. They had made him sound deeper; that was what had fooled me.

Had they fooled Martin? Were they working for someone, had they— What?

I froze. There was a shout from the party, a peal of laughter. The crescendo of a drinking game. *Oh-oh-oh-oh....*

The boy looked like a renter, that soft body, those wounded eyes, all that shame and calculation simmering under the surface. Mar had been amazed by that, how I could sniff out a renter a mile away. Did he owe someone, that boy? Did both of them? Were they working for someone? Was that how they'd got to Mar—

No.

The girl's mouth pinched. She looked uncomfortable, like she did need to piss. My fingers began to tug at the door. The girl pulled at the boy, harder, but he was ignoring her, stepping right up to me. I tugged again. The door wouldn't give. The boy had a canvas bag over his shoulder. Odd shapes, pushing the fabric at weird angles. I could smell something acrid coming from it. Chemicals. It must have been strong for me to get the smell. What sort of chemicals? How had those kids torn off that guy's face?

The boy put his hand on the doorframe.

'You wouldn't let us use your bathroom for a wee second....'

The girl's eyes rolled upwards. 'Freak,' she said, in that American high school way, pretending it was a cough. The boy glanced back. A mean, silent laugh passed between them.

Oh! A round of applause.

Get out, Geo.

The boy looked back at me, smiled. 'You have to forgive Rad. My wee sister gets a bit—'

Sister? I couldn't help it. I did a double-take. The boy saw his chance and stepped onto the rider. The music began again. House of Pain. Mar's favourite track. We were nose to nose, close enough to kiss. I heaved. The door jerked free, slamming shut—

'Ow!' Not quite. The door had smashed into the boy's arm, trapping his hand on my side. On the soft flesh of his inner arm I saw tiger-stripes – burn-scars, not cuts – and a string of rosary beads, red as pomegranate seeds, wound around his wrist.

'Fucking freak!' shouted the girl.

He pushed. The door shuddered, gave, came towards me.

'Jesus Christ! We oany wanted to—'

Wanted what? To rob me? To kick me? To—

Jump Around!

—do what all animals do when they sense otherness, thrash the life out of it?

'Omigod!' shrieked the girl.

He shoved his foot through. I heaved again. The door swung shut and he swore, getting his foot out just in time. I felt the lock click.

'Fucksake!' he was yelling through the door. She too. 'Fucking cunt!' They started to hammer again.

387

A-G. A-G-R. A-G-R-O. Aggro!

I forced my hands to slide the chain across. Through the fish-eye lens I could see them, still screaming.

I returned to the kitchen and poured myself some water. My fingers were shaking. Outside, lights were strobing and flashing. The drums were pounding. Behind me I could hear the teehagers, still hammering on the door. I brought the glass into the sitting room and sat on the sofa, barricading myself behind Sonia's cushions. My chest was tight, a sore wedge of pain. I picked up the remote. It was shaking too. Be still, I told it, and zapped the TV.

Blessed Eoin the Marxist was in a studio. He looked exhausted.

Global Emergency, said the yellow scrolling ribbon beneath him. *United States Pledges Support.*

Support? For what? I flicked to the Discovery channel. Martin's favourite. He used to love it when I slagged off their programming. Hitler's Secret Underpants. World's Deadliest Snatch. Goblin Sharks Do Dallas. Three minutes of waffle stretched out over an hour; two money-shots, edited a million different ways. Cheap graphics, cheaper experts, nothing new under the sun.

An elderly man with tanned skin and a brush of white hair was speaking. He looked German. Probably a Nazi. Germans were always Nazis on Discovery. *Und dann haben wir—* Subtitles appeared across his chest.

I zapped again and found a white face, surrounded by darkness. Someone spoke in Irish. More subtitles. The face had red lips and very pale skin. Teenage vampires, Gaelgeoir style. I knew the series.

A-G... R. The hammering was starting to ease off.

My wee sister. They'd had the same forehead, the same ears, the same colouring. If she'd been fatter and not wearing so much make-up and hair dye, I would have known they were twins from the off. But they'd sounded different. Why had they sounded so different?

A nasty seventies-style wipe got rid of the vampire, replacing her with a misty long shot of Connemara. An ironic touch.

I zapped again. Found the national broadcaster. A late-night arts show. A blonde with too much Botie was holding forth. On the backdrop behind her they'd projected a murky, indistinct image. No. Not a still. Video, moving at an almost unbearably slow rate. Dark and light, in swirls. Beautiful yet disturbing, though I couldn't figure out why. My finger pushed, but instead of changing channel, the sound came on. Stupid. It was paranoia that had got the better of me on the doorstep. They were only kids, looking for a party, needing to use a bathroom. No connection. I was overwrought, because of the accident, the crazy day I'd had, and the obvious, of course, the hospital appointment waiting for me the next morning. Nothing more; nothing less. Martin was fine, and if he wasn't—

Why wasn't my finger moving?

'—fascinating, really, as a new take on snuff movies—' The blonde had a Belfast accent.

'Fascinating?' said a young man. He sounded Dublin. 'That's sick.'

'Isn't that the question he raised, though? In the title—'

'Why are you assuming it's a he? Nobody knows who did it.'

'Are you implying—'

'Look,' said the moderator in his educated midlands drawl, 'let's just—'

The party next door was going full tilt, but the hammering had stopped. Had those kids left the complex? Or were they still out there, waiting for me?

Paranoia. It can happen to the best of us, girl.

My finger pushed. The volume went up.

'I'm not going to sit here and take this crap,' said the young Dub. *Poet*, said the title across his chest. 'I mean, you've kids from Bluebell and Tallaght, and they're seeing this shit and they think, yeah, great, maybe I find a homeless man, throw him in the Grand Canal and—'

Homeless? But—

'He didn't throw the man in. He found him—' *Journalist*.

'How do you know? D'you've a direct line to the cops now?'

'Hey, hey, hey,' said the moderator. 'The point of this discussion—'

'I think our friend would have to agree it's foolish to come to conclusions before—'

'Yeah, but who's not coming to conclusions right now? You, with your feminist ideas around *he* and—'

'I'm saying we have a right to consider the cultural implications of what this child is presenting us—'

Child?

'Child? You're saying it's alright for some privileged little toe-rag with a smartphone to get their buzz filming a corpse, some poor bastard with his face eaten off by rats, just so it'll go fucking viral—'

Rats? Privileged? But—

Tore his face off, Jammy Noel had said. Vicious little fucks. That could have meant anything. It still didn't explain—

'Hey, language….'

Martin's coat leered at me from the white leather armchair. Something was sticking out of the side pocket. I hadn't noticed it before.

'—seems like you're the one now making assumptions based on class— Please, let me speak. I'm in no way endorsing what he, or she, has—'

His beret? No. I'd lost that at Glendalough.

'Yeah, but who the fuck—'

'Hey, hey, hey. I need to remind you this is a broadcast—'

The object sharpened. Jammy Noel's box of fags. I must have taken them without knowing. Once a thief, always one. Serves you right, I thought, you—

'Perve!' shouted someone at the party. It sounded like Martin; it sounded like the boy who'd tried to push his way into Sonia's flat. But Martin wasn't there; Martin wasn't anywhere.

'Well if you wanna know what I think,' said the telly; it spoke with a woman's voice, deep and authoritative, a slight American twang. The others stopped. I looked up. The woman on-screen was overweight with a heavy pale face and raisiny eyes, wearing a burgundy velvet tent: the sort of burka fat women wear to cover themselves, the sort I'm terrified of one day having to wear myself. 'Is, why are none of us talking about the victim?'

Scriptwriter, said her caption.

Farringdon. Turnmill.

The names bubbled in my mind, tried to coalesce, one last ridiculous stab at meaning, then—

boom

I saw what was in the video. A tiger's face, snarling on a dead man's back under the swirl of canal water.

'… thass fuckin mental!' shouted the person at the party.

Something popped behind my sinuses; a sonic effect, rippling in concentric circles. Suddenly I could smell again. Sewage. Sea-salt. Petrol fumes. Burnt omelette. And closer again, on my own skin, the unmistakeable reek of marzipan. Sonia's bath oils had been scented with almond essence.

I staggered up, doubled over, retching. My hands flailed, grabbing for support. They landed on Mar's coat and under the dead dog stink of that soulless object I smelt him too, as clear as if he was in the room beside me. It was then, I think, that I began to cry.

You may know what I'm going to say next. When you get rid of things, especially things that mean a lot to other people, especially people who you think you may have hurt, it's important to do it properly. You need to do it right; not fast, not carelessly. You need to make a big deal of it, honouring the things you're shedding. You can't just stuff them in a refuse bag or throw them in a bin. Because if you do, they'll come back and haunt you.

Lognote # 9

Visitors, as our Space/*Raum* is shrinking fast, we speedily direct you to what, unfortunately, appears to be our penultimate Exhibit. A theatrical Entertainment, accompanied by music, entitled *Up the Ass! A Farce About the Last Years of the Sudetenland, 1933–1938*.[1] The libretto has not been written by Bertholt Brecht, not even in a parallel universe.

Note: According to a no-longer-existing playbill, the original production welcomed audience participation, including singing along. Lyrics have been supplied, so do join in at any moment you wish.

<u>Warning</u> *(in small print):*

This Curiosity is possibly the most curious and definitely the most hazardous feature in the entire Kunstkabinett. It contains scenes of extreme violence and language which some of you may find offensive. The Wonder Chamber wishes to stress that neither its staff nor curator can take responsibility for anything which befalls visitors who watch the Entertainment for lengthy periods.

<u>The Cast</u>

Enter, stage left, the sinister side:
The Nazis a.k.a. 'Radicals'

> *The Boss of the Reich (bass baritone)* ....Hitler, A.
> *The First Wave of Nazi Opportunists (baritone chorus) who meet an untimely end at the hands of the Jets (see below)*.......Bohle, E.,
> ....Rosenberg, A.

---

[1] For more detailed information, see, for starters, *The Sudeten Problem, 1938: Volkstumspolitik and the Formation of Nazi Foreign Policy* by Ronald M. Smelser, 1975. A more extensive bibliography may be sourced from: 'The Black Box', Turnmill Street, Farringdon, London EC1 (appointment only).

*The Second Wave of Half-Nazis (tenor chorus) who want power but
aren't sharp enough to see the Jets (see below) coming.............................
....Von Kursell, O., Wehofsich, F.
The Jets (bass chorus), masters of the Dog-Eat-Dog game of National
Social(ist) Darwinism. Let's hear it for the boys! Ra! Ra! Ra!....................
..................Himmler, H., Heydrich, R., Lorenz, W., Behrends, H.*

Stage right, the dextrous side:
The Others[2] apologies, The 'Traditionalists'

> *The Good Old Boys of the Reich (baritone chorus) who only want to help
> Germans everywhere but whose dreams, sadly, get thwarted by the Jets
> ....Steinacher, Dr. H.,
> ....Stieve, F., Haushofer, K. and A., (briefly) Frank, K. H.*

> *The Good Old 'Sudeten' Boys (baritone chorus) who only want to help
> the Germans in Bohemia and Moravia, but sadly realise that the Jets
> (again) have the monopoly on the lunch money....................................
> ....Heinrich, W., Brand, W., Rutha, H.*

> *The Sharks (bass chorus) who live in the 'Sudetenland' – and may once
> have been Good Old Boys – but who deep-down really want to be Jets
> ....Haider, R., Kasper, R., Frank, K. H.*

Centre stage, on a wire from the 'Flies':
Our Hero

> *Little Konrad (lead tenor) who wants to be all things to all people (all German
> people, that is, and specifically, all German people living in the 'Sudetenland')
> ....Henlein, K.*

---

[2] Error! History does not recognise the term 'other than Nazi' when describing German politicos 1933–1945 (see, though back-referencing is fast becoming a thing of the past, *Lognote # 8*, Footnote 1: 'Dresden argument').

The Entertainment

Act I

A frozen (? / — **alert!** *[sense-kinaesthesis input* → *cognition-flash* '**I am cold. Why**—/ignore this, visitors— *[circuit resists/restarts]*

A lake in the borderlands of Bohemia, where our Hero, humble Gym Instructor Konrad Henlein, stands pondering the wake of the 1933 Nazi Takeover in Germany and the Banning of the Nazi Party of Czechoslovakia.

In a lightbulb Moment, Little Konrad remembers the neo-feudalist fascist writings of Othmar Spann. Spann isn't a Nazi – problem solved! – so our Hero calls for the Germans of Bohemia and Moravia to unite under the Umbrella of his new Political Party. This plucky Umbrella is initially known as the Sudeten Heimatfront/SHF (Sudeten Home Front), later the Sudetendeutsche Partei/SdP (Sudeten German Party) and, most commonly by successive generations, the 'Sudeten Nazi' party.[3]

Following a flurry of Absorptions, Expulsions and Controversies, and amidst roars of Popular Approval, the Act finishes with a glorious choral number as the SdP, acting as a magnet for disenchanted Germans all over the State, wins the 1935 elections with 15 per cent of the vote – the biggest party in the country!

The Sudeten Heimatfront Lyric: (Everybody, sing along!)
> *It's good to be German and it's good for all the Germans in Bohemia and Moravia to get together under one roof, especially since that Nazi lot almost wrecked our chances and got themselves banned, and Othmar Spann is really groovy with his idea for a German utopia that's, like, completely fair, man, but totally ordered too, and of course being in a secret society with vague anti-democratic ideals that are supposed to somehow benefit the entire ethnic group living in the borderlands that call themselves German, even though they're from, like, radically different social classes, of course that won't mean we'll get mixed up with that Nazi lot on the other side of the border, even though our fanbase is sort of, quite like a lot of those guys, but – hey! Forget all that, Volk, come on, let's get those Votes!*

---

[3] This name is of dubious accuracy, certainly in the early days of the SHF. While Little Konrad, like Spann, is in favour of a quasi 'fascism' based on the feudal notion of nobles' estates, he supports democracy, not National Socialist dictatorship.

Bravo! Now, surely, the 'Sudeten' Germans will finally have their Moment in the Sun? There is hardly a chance, is there, in the warm afterglow of Victory, that our Hero will be eclipsed by men with Bigger Ideas…?[4]

Act II

On cue, an ominous chord plays. A sinister spotlight appears upstage and a Wooden Horse enters from the flies – cheers for the Deus Ex Machina! What follows is a romping rollercoaster of ups and downs, progressing at a pace of such Nail-biting Tension that even the streetwise in the Stalls have been known to Swoon.

Our Hero's brave attempts to find a Democratic Foothold in the Czechoslovak state are, sadly, falling on increasingly Deaf Ears. The English in Prague, Britain and Elsewhere are fond of Little Konrad, but they don't want to upset Beneš and the rest of the Czechs who – Behind You, Konrad! (? /— **alert!** [*sense-kinaesthesis input* → *cognition-flash* '**Behind? Where is behind? Where am**—/—/ *[circuit diverts]*— time running out, move on, move on—*[circuit re-starts]*]

Let's try again, visitors: Little K, in a nutshell, is trying to get the Brits on-side to support the establishment of a democratic 'Sudeten' German *something*. The Brits like Little K, but they don't want to alienate the Czechs, who distrust him. Meanwhile, and here's the rub, the Jets and the Sharks, the Nazi Top-Dogs on both sides of the border, want to harness our Hero's popular movement to their own Nefarious ends. Drumroll!

<u>The Jets Lyric</u>:   (Sing along, if you dare)
> *Fee fie foe fum. We smell the blood of Volkstum. Divide and conquer. Infiltrate. Subvert. Collect bureaucracies. Hollow the goodies out and stuff them with our own mix. Learn from our master. Put an ineffectual pretty boy as a front man and let a ruthless cunt backstage do all the work. Thousand-year Reich? No problem! Sudeten Germans? Sudeten who? We don't believe in petty provincial distinctions – we're bigger men than that! Anyway – we're all at the same Party, aren't we?*

<u>The Sharks Lyric</u>:   (Sing-along, ditto)
> *Hey, we've got Konrad's back! No, not like that – the way Brutus had Caesar's! And who's got ours? Why, our friends the Nazis, of course, on*

---

[4] Note that while Henlein knows what he doesn't want, i.e. 'not to be part of Czechoslovakia' and 'not to be part of the Reich', he is on less firm ground when it comes to working out what he *does* want. See Ireland (Northern): Orangemen, their problematic 'Identity' and the Saying of No.

the other side of the border! See, they're not in a democracy and they're doing damn fine. Votes – who needs them? Fuck Democracy. And the Volk. And the Czechs. And the Slovaks and the Jews and hey – whoever said the Sharks and Jets were mortal enemies was writing the wrong play, buddy!

At this very point, adding insult to injury, the Group with which Little Konrad seems to have most affinity, the 'Traditionalist' Good Old Boys,[5] suddenly experience a rapid downturn in their Fortunes – thanks, in no small part, to the Social Darwinian machinations of the Nazi 'Radicals' both sides of the border. Meanwhile upstage left, a sinister silhouette has appeared....

Act III

Drumroll! A spot upstage front-lights the silhouette. Rapturous applause! The Boss has arrived, at the perfect Moment for a Takeover Bid!

The Boss Lyric: (Don't even think of singing along)
   Bide my time, let the dogs figure out how to take the meat from the bones. Let them figure out if there is meat, if it's the sort of meat I want to eat, and if so, when I might want to eat it, and how. Bit of salt, sir? Pepper? Knife and fork? Or maybe Sir would prefer to tear the whole thing apart with his fingers? Doesn't matter. When the time is right, I'll forget my vegetarian principles, baby, put on my napkin and dig right in!

Now our Spectacle twists further, wrenching the Guts of— (! / a—) ⅌o, visitors, it's fine, we've broken that circuit— everyone, even those in the Upper Circle. The Nazi Jet–Shark Alliance has moved centre-stage, ousting the Good Old Boys through their greater political and financial Leverage and a clearer picture of Their Brave New World. High noon turns to dust as our Hero's old mucker, Heinz 'Nancy Boy' Rutha, is arrested and found dangling from a Noose. In a blaze of Inglory, the rest of the Good Old Boys die, are made Redundant or Incorporated into Jet–Shark Institutions – see, for example, Hermann 'Butcher' Frank![6] Meanwhile, in the sinisterest of sinister corners, Alpha Jets Reinhard

---

[5] Yes, this is rather complicated: For 'Traditionalists', see 'politicians of the 1930s who want to help Germans in places where Germans live but who aren't necessarily bound by the ideology of hardcore National Socialism'.
[6] Later responsible for the massacre of Lidice at which c.5,000 Czechs died.

'Two-Face' Heydrich[7] and Heinrich 'Racial-Purist' Himmler[8] have opened a Trapdoor that leads under the stage to tunnel under the Bohemian borderlines. Their target? Sudeten Hearts and Minds!

What will Our Hero do now? Where else can he turn but to—

Again, that ominous drumroll (? /— **alert!** [*sense-kinaesthesis input* → *cognition-flash* '**Is that my heart? Is it beating?**—/ Ⓖood news, visitors, one of our curatorial systems is experiencing a fresh surge of power, so we'll just keep on— ☆ / *[circuit blazes]*

Quick! All eyes on the Big Bad Boss! In the Boxes, tears flow as the spotlight upstage following him prepares to move. We are – yes! Hankies! – re-enacting the 1937 November Letter,[9] when Little Konrad officially invites the Boss to step into the Centre of the Bohemian Stage.

Act IV

A glorious anthem, chock-full of brass and drumbeats, as the set turns, revealing a silhouetted landscape: the infamous City of Traitors. Following the Reich's Successful 'merging' with Austria, 'Czechoslovakia' now finds itself outflanked on all sides. The 'Sudeten' Germans have become Hysterical with Anticipation – maybe they will be next for *Anschluss*?

On his platform centre-stage, the Boss lifts his Arm, pounds his Fist and speaks of Ten Million Germans Outside the Reich! Our Hero, closely followed by King Shark 'Butcher' Frank, races upstage and kneels at his feet! SdP Flags unfurl all over Bohemia and Moravia! German-speaking militias[10] mobilise—

What's this? Little Konrad, petrified at what he has started, is doing a U-Turn! He has fled from the Boss and run offstage to his Allies in London to see if they can help!

Hurrah! / Boo!

Sound-effects: Noises off, in clipped Old Etonian Accents. Some lyrics about *Sorting This Mess Out Once and For All—*

Bang! Gunfire! It's the Czechs' turn to Mobilise!

---

[7] Later to approve the use of the gas chambers during the Wannsee Conference.

[8] Later to order the liquidation of the ghettos, the establishment of Auschwitz and the mass deportation of the Jews of Western Europe, amongst other things.

[9] For comparison, see Ireland: the Comber Letter, the Siege of Derry/Londonderry and their consequences.

[10] Sourced to a large extent from those gym clubs of the late nineteenth and early twentieth century. See, though it's really very tricky at this stage, *Lognote # 7*.

No! say the plucky Brits, hands up to stop the mess. We need a Peaceful Solution to the Sudeten Problem![11]

Poor Konrad! Look at our Hero, running all over the stage. He can't make up his Mind between Beneš, the Boss and the Brits! On his central platform, the Boss is Holding, Holding, Holding his long, ominous note—

Sorry? What's that? A Surprise Twist?

A Letter appears, as if by magic. Our Hero stops his faffing and takes it. In a trembling voice, he announces that Beneš has just offered the Sudeten Germans Everything they Want… within a Czechoslovak State.

Shock! Horror! Especially on the faces of the Jet–Shark Alliance! Fee-Fie-Foe-Fum! This wasn't what Dr Mengele ordered!

Furious that their Plans may be coming to Naught, the Jets and Sharks immediately incite Riots! In response, the Czechs get Trigger-Happy! Lots of People are Dying! (? !!!! ?/— **alert!** *[memory-input → cognition-flash* '**Am I**—/ '**Ands, am I**— ☆ / *[circuit blazes]*

Visitors, stay with us! Listen to that siren! It's not an ambulance ☆ / no, visitors, it's too late for that! It's the Army! The Czechs have brought in Martial Law—

What's that?

A voice, a reedy baritone?

Why, it's none other than Neville Chamberlain, stepping in with – sing along with the catchphrase, everyone! – 'Peace in Our Time'.

Hurrah! / Boo!

Finale

From this point on, visitors, we invite – no, demand – full audience participation. Why not? We've less than a Moment. Why not go in Style! It's going to be bloody marvellous. Our Hero, after all, has ensured immortality, if not for us, then at least for himself!

The Our Hero Final Aria Lyric: (Sing along: that's an order)
> *Juggling is wonderful. Juggling is fun. One day I'm a decent, moderate chap, respected by the Brits. The next I'm a Nazi. Hmm. Maybe I was always a Nazi, working for the Boss on the sly. That's what a lot of historians will think. Or maybe I wasn't. Juggling is tricky. Juggling*

---

[11] See for contrast: Irish Solutions for Irish Problems, Gladstone; see also Heydrich et al. at Wannsee and Final Solution, The.

is shit. It's not easy, holding up an umbrella that's so big and so hastily tacked together. And the Czechs don't like talking to chaps with umbrellas – unless, of course, it's an umbrella they've made themselves. Maybe a greater man would have cracked under the strain too. But I shouldn't worry, should I? After all, like Moses, I will lead my people home.[12]

He's right, visitors! The people of the Sudetenland are going to be German Citizens! Come on – join in! Clap your hands, stamp your feet, prepare to sing! Forget that unnecessary and rather distressing Epilogue, without which this *Kammer* might have never have seen the light of day![13] Leave all that behind! Instead, tune up for the rousing Song & Dance number popularly known as *The Munich Agreement*, whereby the 'Sudetenland' is ceded to the Reich as a Gau and Bohemia – as we know it – ceases to exis—[14] (!!!!!!!— ?— **alert! alert! alert!** [*sense-kinaesthesis overload* → *cognition-flash* '**Ah!**—/ / [*circuit diverts*] – 💣⃰ 💣⃰/ ! / ☹ ☠

> *[circuit breaks]*

---

[12] i.e. to the Reich.

[13] Aware that our *Raum* is now contracting at an exponential rate, we direct you to that infamous Dumb-Show presenting Tableaux of 'Fear & Misery' from World War II, again not written by Bertolt Brecht but featuring, among other horrors, the subordination of the Sudeten Borderlands to Reich policies; the persecution and genocide of the European Jews; the takeover of the Czech interior; the somewhat uncertain Czech Resistance *[this entry needs citation]* peaking in the assassination of Reinhard Heydrich, 'Protector' of Bohemia; the Nazi Reprisals at Lidice; and the Final Liberation of Czechoslovakia by the Red Guard and the Czech militias, culminating in a Rousing Group Photo of the Expulsions of 1945, at which point the 'entire' German population of the Sudetenland (don't even try to see *Lognote # 8* for exact figures), as if by magic, disappears.

[14] See, for contrast and similarities, Ireland: Ulster, partition of. At which point our parallels, at times so tantalisingly close, diverge indefinitel—

Singularities

He's back.

Crawling forward on his belly, a maggot creeping through the guts of the mountain. He keeps waiting to see things. The next corner he turns, he thinks—

He wakes just as the lights in the mine flicker off. Not after they go; but right in the moment. He can't figure out whether he has made himself wake, terrified of the death the blackness is about to bring, or whether the blackness itself is life, the waking moment.

David gets up, goes to the bathroom, and pisses. The yellow fluid glitters in the darkness, catching the bits of light trickling in from the hallway. His nose is tickling with the smell of almonds, the smell of gelignite.

His chest is tight. He pushes his hands against the sink, feels the force travel up to his shoulders. Give me strength, he thinks.

The Black Country, 1956. The year before, at nineteen, he'd fled from Ireland and got a job as a navvy, working underground, blasting earth with a team of other Micks and Jocks to make a tunnel for a hydroelectric dam. They'd kept the geli in a big steel box, a hundred yards away from the works. STORE IN A DRY PLACE. And there it was, smelling of almonds, sitting in six inches of water in the bowels of the earth, the wettest place in the world. The main blasts were electrical but the minor ones they did by hand. The cartridge was open, like a gun cartridge. You had to stick the fuse into the open end and then tighten the cartridge around it. Sometimes the fuse wouldn't go in easily, but if you tried to force it, it would blow. Everyone had a story about some gobshite who'd used pliers to sort it out and lost his fingers.

Welcome to hell, shouted an Aberdeeny the first day. He caught David's eye. Ye ken, Dublin? I wish I was fucking deed.

It took David days to figure out what the Scotsmen were saying. Cheenge the peents! screamed the ganger. David hadn't a clue what he meant. He went wandering, came back with two bags of stones. The ganger swore at him for twenty minutes. Change the points, he'd meant, change the points on the locomotives.

Once you got the cartridges loaded with the gelignite, you had to turn the electrics off before lighting the fuses. Afterwards you had to turn everything on again. Nobody wanted that job because you had to reconnect the electrics in the dark and if you got it wrong, you could fry. Everyone had a story about some gobshite who'd shocked themselves into Harpo Marx.

They called you by the name of your town. On the first day, David told them he was from Dublin. He didn't plan it; it wasn't out of fear that anything back home would catch up on him. There was nothing to be caught up on. The name of the capital just slipped out of his mouth and once spoken, it couldn't be taken back. He told himself it fitted better than Clonmel. There weren't any jackeens in the tunnel – if anyone asked, he'd say his people had moved to Dublin from Tipp. Nobody did ask. Hennessy, the closest he had to a pal, was tone-deaf, couldn't tell one accent from another. Hen was an engineering student, from Limerick. At night, when he'd a few scoops on him, he'd live up to his nickname, goad the other navvies into competing to see who could come up with the most obscene limericks, though he'd usually finish them himself.

There was a young man from Dundee
He never was able to pee
So they chopped off his cock
And gave him a frock
And now – yelled Hennessy – *he goes round with a gee!*
What's a gee, Limerick? shouted the Jocks.

David sucked on his naggin and laughed till his face felt like breaking. In the camp at night, they had to tie their wallets to their belts on twine and put them under their pillows in case someone would rob them. David was aware of Hennessy's angular shape on the camp bed beside his, the abrupt sweeps and falls of his gaslit silhouette; his smell of home.

One day a stream overflowed into the shaft, flooding the mine with water. Don't panic! screamed the ganger. Wait for the locomotive. But the locomotive driver ran off down the mine with the diesel and the carriages. They had to wait an hour to get out.

402

They fought all the time, the red-faced Paddies and the black-toothed Scots. They fought about drink, about women, about money; about moral superiority, about fighting, about the English, about independence, about brotherhood, about hate and love and death. Sometimes they hauled David and Hennessy out of their beds to adjudicate. Being a student, Hennessey was seen as having a certain scientific objectivity. Because David palled around with him, some of that leaked out onto him until, by the end of the summer, everyone thought David was a student too.

Hennessy was a talker. At night he'd talk about anything; his ageing father, his rugby-playing brothers, a girl he had an eye on. He was planning to go to Canada once he got his degree, though he'd heard there were opportunities opening up on the old sod. A new firm had set up in Dublin, a local office of a big international outfit. Mr Lyons, the man heading it, had vision. He was always on the look-out for talent. If you had a spark, Hen told David, Lyons would take you on as an office boy; might even pay for your college education.

Ah, said David, feeling fifteen again, burdened by the weight of Brother Sheridan's expectations, his mother's failed aspirations. His own sick-bed childhood fantasies long-forgotten. Who in their right minds would put him and a *spark* in the same thought?

He started to avoid Hennessy, drink more, spend longer at the fights, watching his heavyset compatriots flail at the stringier, faster Aberdeenies. Ding-ding. Round one to the man with the bright eyes and glowing cheeks. Got up himself one night, muddled with alcohol, and began swinging his fists, only to realise they were all laughing at him, his opponent included. Who would fight a skinny boy wearing glasses? So he sank back to the ground and drank some more.

There was a strange comfort in that life. Working with men, not speaking much, the hard physical graft. It seemed centuries away from Clonmel. The money was good too. They'd go out to local hops time to time, chat up the girls. David had his pick, charmed them with his shy looks and his spectacles, his Irish accent, his ability to play back their Brummie voices to them like he was one himself. Years later, as a father, waking terrified and silent beside Aisling in the wee hours, he would try not to imagine the David he could have been, staying to work the next stretch of dam, or going on to another tunnel, or a railway or a building site in Manchester or Birmingham. Yet another unskilled Paddy on the Railroads, sending the few bob home to his sisters, drinking the rest, the odd card to his decaying mother to reassure her he hadn't wasted the life she'd given him. And that would have been that. Graft, drink, the few bob, a girl every town until his looks ran out. Then liver failure in a men's hostel – a bitter, if quiet end.

That afternoon, he'd been put in charge of timing the explosions. He'd had to loop the fuses on nine of the sticks to shorten the delays. That would allow the explosions to go off in sequence, like a piece of music, giving enough time for everyone to get out. The loops were different sizes. Fifty seconds, forty seconds, thirty seconds….

He called time. The men retreated. The generators stopped. The lightbulbs on their wires fizzled into darkness. Silence, except for the drip of water and the breathing of the men.

Thud. Thud…. Thud.

Thud.

Thud. Thud.

Thud.

Silence.

He could smell burning and sweat and almonds. The heat of the other bodies near him. He could hear nothing.

The ganger raised his head, squinted. Frowned, shook his head. David's mouth was dry. Not all the sticks had gone off. Someone would have to go back to check. Nobody would want that job. Everyone had a story about some gobshite who—

The ganger's eyes slid past David, landed on Hennessy.

An image shot into David's mind. A girl on a bridge. *Charade.*

He stepped forward. I set them. I'll do it.

Ah, whisht, said Jimmy Gogarty from Mayo. You'll only make a hames of it, Mr Magoo. The others laughed. Gogarty was from Louisburgh, near the foot of the sacred mountain, Croagh Patrick. A hulk of a man, rippling with muscle; great at the fighting but useless at the limericks.

They watched Gogarty disappear into the darkness.

Thud.

The last stick exploded just as Gogarty reached it. The blast ripped up the left side of his body, taking off his arm.

The mess, the blood and bone sticking out from the side of his body, wasn't the worst. Nor was Gogarty's face, a white blur ripped open by the wound of his mouth. The worst was the silence. David couldn't hear Gogarty scream. All he could hear was a dead hiss, the aftermath of the explosion.

There were no accusations. Couldae happened tae any of us, said the ganger. A series of nods, solemn.

They clapped David on the shoulder, harrumphed, cleared their throats, passed around their naggins and talked about other, inconsequential things as the hiss faded into noise again and the night came down over the mountain, taking unconscious Jimmy Gogarty on his stretcher with it. They'd made more of a fuss during the Suez crisis, when a Glasgowman had told them he was a conscientious objector. They'd jumped on the Jock that night, nearly murdered him.

Hennessy, for once, was silent.

Couldae happened tae any of us. The first thing David had thought was *Load of shite*. The accident slapped him in the face with his own lack of foresight. A man had lost his arm because of him. If he hadn't been there to set the stick wrong, Gogarty would be intact. And he, David, was only there because a fellow in Liverpool had told him there was work in the Black Country. He'd had no better idea for himself than that. Get away. Work. How different was that to the life his Da had envisaged for him? Was this how he was going to live – hopping from one moment to the next, not knowing what he wanted, knowing only what he didn't?

She slinked into his mind again, the snaggle-toothed girl with the cloud of dark hair that he had used as his ticket out. Shame flooded him. That night, he had his first dream of the tunnel. When he woke the next morning, shouting, slick with sweat, he knew he was done.

Hennessy looked up from his breakfast. Thanks, he said. That should have been—

Me, said David. His throat filled with grit. He pushed it down. Tell me the name of that firm in Dublin, Hen.

Did you always want to be an engineer, Davey?

Multiple-choice question:

a) First answer (to a wife, attempted but interrupted on the night he was told he was going to be a father): his mother had other plans.

b) Second answer (to a ghost, while sitting on a train bound for a death camp): these plans inadvertently led to a first sighting of the Grail.

c) Third answer (a far trickier one, to his own reflection, on this dank February morning in 1977): while lost in the Black Country, he found a trail to Camelot, courtesy of two compatriots, Limerick Hen and one-armed Jimmy Gogarty.

🕐

Sleep is shallow and useless, like it's been for months. She wakes with a weight on her chest. Spikes are digging into the soft part of her upper body, not quite breast, not quite underarm. A deep rumbling sound, the squelch of tongue and spit on cloth. 'Caliban?' His whiskers brush her cheek, prickly and light. Her hands move, searching for his strong back, his soft fur, and then – whoosh.

He's gone.

☼

Breakfast is silent. Georgie watches David butter his toast, drink his tea.

They are just about to leave when the phone rings.

'Oh,' says David into the receiver. He frowns. 'That's a— No, no, I'm sure we can sort something out.'

He puts down the phone. He does it without looking and the receiver misses the hook, so he has to put it back again properly and this time he slams it. 'That's Mrs Lynch,' he says, though Georgie didn't ask him who it was. 'She's got a bug.'

Georgie kicks at the door, a jiggy, impatient kick.

Can I come with you instead? She could ask this question, but she doesn't, because she already knows the answer.

She can't come because today is a school day and there is swimming on afterwards and swimming is fun.

She can't come because David has got loads on and so do her aunts and she would just be in the way.

She can't come because something is happening in Clonmel that she is not supposed to know about and it would mess everything up if she was there.

She can't come because David doesn't want her with him. And nor do her aunts. And there's swimming on and, anyway, swimming is fun.

David is squeezing the bridge of his nose between his fingers.

'I can go to William Robinson's after school,' says Georgie. 'He's always asking me to come over.'

David stops squeezing his nose and looks at her.

💣

The countryside sweeps by. Hills, patchwork fields dotted with sheep and cows, scrubby hedges, bare-boned trees, the sudden lift of the road out of Dublin and into Kildare, the green stretch of the Curragh. David drives automatically, barely registering the shudder of the Cortina on the road, the jolt of the gear changes, the tinny crackle of the car radio. He was on edge when he woke – that bloody dream – but the minute he left Georgie off at school, it got worse. Now the muscles in his chest are wound so tight it feels like a nest of alien eggs down there, waiting to hatch. He knows what they're hatching: the compulsion. It's dying to get out, stick its claws into him.

He has been dreading this. For the last six weeks, since the night they rang with news of her stroke, he's tried to resist. Hoping to persuade his sisters to keep his mother where she belonged – at home, safe, comfortable, a place where she had at least some idea of what she was or used to be. Even just a while, he kept saying. Till—

But Maura was insistent: Davey, we've tried, but we can't.

What she didn't say: *This isn't up to you.* She didn't need to. He knows he has no claim on this decision; he surrendered all those claims years ago, when he fled Clonmel. Objectively, it makes a sort of sense. His sisters are ageing, their mother needs care. There is enough money. But since Maura's phone call on New Year's Night, David hasn't been able to stop thinking of – Eureka! – Archimedes. The converse of the Greek's principle: for every body taken out of a fluid, a space is left for the filling.

He feels the counter-arguments begin again, rattling around in his head like dice.

The pre-empt first: He's fine. Thought you should know. Or, if they ask: He's doing great, actually. Thanks for asking. Holding fast. Making friends. Eating like a horse, but that's healthy. Yes, the schoolwork has slipped a bit since Christmas – he knows Bridget will pry about that – but he'll bounce back, in time. He's safe, that's the main thing. I keep a good eye on him.

A good eye. How true is that? He had thought – stupidly – that given time, Georgie might start to settle. There was all that upset at Christmas, and then the changes of plan, and Annie getting ill, but David had thought somehow that if he could only hold fast, then maybe something would change. Instead, Georgie has just been slipping further and further away. David knows he's been doing his best. It touched a nerve, what she said to him at Christmas. It stung, of course – nobody wants to be told they're not good enough – but she was right, and since then, he's been making more of an effort. Telling Georgie things. Stories, bits about science, his own childhood. The Pre-War Shelf at the back of the larder, him and the lads in school taking it in turns to be Spitfires and Stukas, the shot-down German plane his mother's cousin found in the green hills of the Vee, the shining yards of aircraft insulation brought back and turned by his sisters into Christmas decorations. Asking questions too. How's school, old chap? That lad, Timmy, fancy asking him over for a spot of grub some day? Listening, or being all set to listen. Except Georgie won't talk or answer, and when he does, only the minimum. How do you listen to that, ask that questions? And if it won't listen, then what do you say?

There's no comfort in the fact that the backchat has stopped. Mrs Lynch's tactless insinuations about things going missing from her house. Those careful inquiries by Mrs Kelly's daughter about whether David had seen anyone hanging around the back door or heard any strange noises from inside the empty house or....

What are you implying? he'd wanted to shout. That my son is breaking into your tatty auld dump and stealing from it?

Those sly comments from Joanie Flynn, the hoor, saying how she used to hear Georgie talk to himself when he was playing out in the lane, putting on a high voice like a little girl's when nobody was there. How do you know there's nobody, you nosey bitch, if you can't see him? But even she's put a stopper in it. She hasn't mentioned Aisling in months. As for those other digs – *Haven't seen that girl around for a while, Lottie, isn't it? Everything alright there, David?* – they've dried up too. As if, David fancies sometimes, when the house is quiet and he's sitting in the kitchen with just a bottle for company, Joanie, and all those other women, with their questions and insinuations and well-meant offers, have given up on him. On Georgie, on the house, on everything.

He sees his dream again, those dark, shrinking walls. In the old days, when Aisling was still there, he used to wonder what it meant, but not anymore. It's clear as day to him now.

No. Way. Out.

His left hand moves, touches his jacket. The letter, in his breast pocket, burning a hole.

Hard luck, David, Art had said over the phone. It was close. But Niall's got the edge. Three mouths to feed.

The youngest, apparently, about to go to Bolton Street, follow the old man's footsteps. Bolton Street, David had thought stupidly. How had he missed that?

Don't take it personally, David. Another year, perhaps? But not now.

He had been taken aback at how fast his shock had evaporated; how real the relief had been underneath. As if, in spite of all the blathering to everyone, he'd known he would never have been able to shake off the feeling that if he had got that promotion, it would have been for all the wrong reasons. Only then reality bit in. Rourke and O'Hanlon and their quips about Also-Ran's. The smug smiles from everyone else in the office. *Poor old David. He had his heart set on it. He hasn't been the same since blah blah blah.* He would find himself buying into it then, playing the Great Pretender again, acting like it was all fine, no problem, troops, yet knowing all the same what had he in front of him if he stayed there, except a no-man's land fit only for muddling through, day in, day out. Putting up with all the shite. Festering, changing nothing, going nowhere, his child in a state bottling everything up, getting worse by the day, he twisting himself into knots, crawling down that fucking tunnel till kingdom come trying to curb his stupid panics, only to fail again and drive himself and Georgie up the same stupid walls, without any more thinking ahead than, Well, old chap, next day should be better, eh?

Then, in mid-January, the brainwave. He'd written the letter fast, faster than he'd written anything in his life.

What a pleasure it had been to meet in Munich, how highly Morgan Lloyd and Klaus Fuchs had spoken of Mike, how much David had enjoyed his presentation, how glad he was that they had managed to get some time to talk together over dinner.

Asia is where it's happening, David, Morgan kept saying as he'd refilled their glasses.

We're always looking for people in Hong Kong, said Mike, and Klaus had nodded, enthusiastic, and the conversation had gone on from there. The shortage of good people. Quick people, flexible people. People unafraid of innovation, said Klaus. Exactly, said Mike. Like you, Klaus, or – one of his considered, courteous pauses – David? Then later, in the bar in the Red Light District, after they'd had far too much to drink: I just want to say, David, and I know, Morgan's told me, you're in line to become a director in Dublin, so I suppose you won't have the inclination for a move, but if you ever....

David has never described himself as the wondering kind, a person who drifts around, fantasizing about possibilities. He ponders; that's his job. To tease out implications, analyse consequences before taking action. Figure out what might go wrong before it does. But that isn't the same as wondering. One takes facts and applies logic; if this, then that. The other follows the far more dangerous, open-ended path of imagination; what if....

Hong Kong.

He sees himself again, not-so-young Parzival in a hard hat, perched on a bridge strung like an angel's harp, while around him sprout his Grails, mile-high buildings reaching for the sky, wrapped around themselves like strange, science-fiction contortions.

What would it be like to raise Georgie there? The question had surfaced right after he'd left Mike and started the long wander back to his hotel, knowing sleep was going to elude him again, dreading the green leather chair, already worrying about what he'd asked Lotte to do, his attention starting to snag on the taut legs and sharpened nails of the cooing women. An idle speculation that popped in, then – Hey *Jungs*, want some fun? – straight out of his mind.

The second he'd finished the letter to Mike, it popped in again. What would it be like to bring Georgie there?

The first. The important. The only question.

What If….

A fresh start? Men together, having an adventure! Or—

Georgie plonked on a sofa, watching Asian cartoons on his own, eating himself to death.

Then, as always, David thinks of Aisling's grave. The granite headstone, the fading flowers. *For Mum*, calling to her child six thousand miles away.

The road sweeps on, grey and bumpy, through the misty countryside. David's fingers start twiddling the knob on the radio, looking for distraction: Gay Byrne, the news, Larry Gogan's phone-in competition, anything.

🕐

She calls Caliban again, but he doesn't come. This is the third day in a row he's done the same thing: woken her up, then disappeared. If it wasn't for the fact that his plate is always empty when she gets in at night, she'd be worried. She ladles out two spoons of catfood; then, as an afterthought, a third.

He sense it, Lotte. Growing in your belly. Don't want to share.

Share what exactly, Ands? Right now, there is nothing to share.

The ghost doesn't answer. He doesn't like her talking back to him.

She splashes cold water on her face; it doesn't feel cold, but in the mirror she sees the downy hairs on her cheeks stand on end. It is February 14th. Valentine's Day, 1977. She is approximately ten weeks gone.

She lights a cigarette, her first of the day, and inhales. It tastes of nothing, just bad. She realised she was pregnant the moment she started losing her taste for them. It happened the other time too, with the Captain. She'd stopped smoking then, obeying her body's wiser instincts, and fled to London, to Ands, asked him to help her get rid of it before Julia found out, because no matter how unspeakable the origins, it would still be *a life, Lotte, not your to remove, only the God*. Charlie had been there; had just started going out with Ands; had been brilliant, had sorted everything.

This time, even though the nicotine no longer gives her any pleasure, she's kept up the habit. She coughs. Her breath shortens. She wonders if she's becoming asthmatic. All she needs. The dampness, the greyness, that infernal, eternal greyness, would make anyone asthmatic. This place is killing her. She needs a mountain, a big sky, fresh air, heat and sunlight, another language, colour, conversation, not this small, religion-bound province.

So what you do, Lotte?

A couple of days ago she stopped outside a travel agency on Grafton Street and looked at the advertisements for package holidays and, beyond that, at the grubbier lists of ferry prices back to Britain. She stood like a fool, unable to do anything except look, and in her belly the time-bomb continued to tick. She only has another fortnight, if she wants to do it in a safe way. If she wants to do it at all.

Maybe it's not Dublin that's killing her. Maybe it's her own head. She thinks of Hamlet and his will, paralysed by fear of doing the wrong thing; or doing the right thing at the wrong time. At least Hamlet had Horatio to talk to; someone real, a friend to mitigate the madness.

But you, you have nothing, Lotte. Why you must always wait, for others to make the thing happen?

Fuck off, Ands.

Even her anger feels separate from her, as if it belongs to someone else. She stares at her reflection. In her white nightie she is a Schiele whore, angular and unkempt; a set of babies' teeth wound totemlike around her right wrist. Something glimmers behind her.

Slowly, slowly, catchee monkey.

She forces herself to turn, willing him not to disappear.

For a heartbeat it feels like he might stay. Then, he's gone, like he always is.

She lets out a sound; a gasp, a laugh.

Lotte, you lose your marbles. You stay here longer, you lose them for sure.

☼

Beside Georgie, William Robinson's body is a brick of heat. He is using a compass point to scratch a cartoon into the seamed wooden surface of their desk. He nudges Georgie. He's carved a prick and balls, beside his name which has been there since the second week of January, when he officially made his plea to be moved up a desk because, Mrs Allen – all innocent eyes – he couldn't see the board so well from where he was. Georgie grunts in acknowledgment. The compass disappears. She feels William Robinson's warm palm press against hers under the desk; between them a narrow spike of metal. It's her turn now, to draw prick-hairs springing from the balls in his cartoon. That's the deal: William Robinson does the main bit; she supplies the accessories. The reason he knows so much about pricks and balls and girls' parts is because he is the youngest of a family of five and his dad is a dentist who works from home, and in Mr Robinson's waiting room there are stacks of ladies' magazines that have a lot of stuff about things like that. Sex.

Making her eyes look sleepy and innocent, Georgie slides the compass up on top of her side of the desk and starts carving.

Behind her she can hear Timmy Nelson, snuffling like a pig. William Robinson has lots of names for Timmy Nelson. Pigface and Crusty-Nose and Puke-Teeth are the ones he uses most. They are mean but they fit Timmy Nelson and when Georgie closes her eyes and tries to picture Timmy, all she sees now are these names; a big snouty face and a nose covered with yellow pus-snot and green teeth, smelling of sick. When people close their eyes and think of her, she wonders, is all they see a huge ugly rage-monster, bile-green and bursting out of its shorts? She starts another prick-hair. William Robinson nudges her. His elbow is sharp in her side and red-hot like the rest of him. Mrs Allen is looking at them. There is a sad sort of look in her eyes which makes Georgie want to grab the compass and stick it in them and make the goo spurt out like in a horror film.

But that's the sort of behaviour that only people like William Robinson do, so instead she makes her face soft and stupid like she's about to cry. Mrs Allen sighs and looks away.

'*Anois* – Saoirse?'

William Robinson nudges Georgie again. Georgie glances over. Saoirse is staring down at her desk.

'She's a moron,' says William Robinson, speaking really low into Georgie's ear. 'She's so deaf, she should be on *Vision On*.'

Timmy Nelson snorts a laugh. Old Crusty-Nose has heard, even though he wasn't meant to. Georgie wishes she hadn't suggested going over to William Robinson's after school that day. But what else was David going to do?

'She likes you, Hulk,' says William Robinson.

'Huh?'

'Stinky.'

Despite herself, Georgie looks. Saoirse is staring at them, a doleful expression in her eyes.

Over the last week, Saoirse's supposed crush on Georgie has become the main thread of conversation in William Robinson's gang. Georgie doesn't like the way they keep going on about it but she knows that if she makes a big deal it will just get worse.

'She wants you to play with her,' says William Robinson. 'She wants to be your girlfriend.'

Georgie shifts on the seat part of her desk.

'Would you stick it in her?' says William Robinson. 'That's what you have to do if you're her girlfriend. Stick your prick in her fanny and wiggle it around.'

Timmy Nelson laughs again. Georgie sighs and concentrates on the next prick-hair. Today she's drawn them like the tendrils of an octopus, extending from the bubbly little prick that William Robinson has drawn. They don't really look like prick hairs. They look like the many tails of those pointless mermaids she used to draw, the ones she burnt to ashes when Jan came prying. But William Robinson doesn't seem to notice and even if he did, he'd probably think her prick-hairs were great, the real thing. That's how much William Robinson, dad a dentist or no, knows about science.

He laughs. 'Then you'll make a baby and it'll be really fat.'

'Saoirse!' says Mrs Allen more sharply. Saoirse flushes and answers. Mrs Allen shakes her head and turns to the blackboard to explain.

Dear Saoirse, says William Robinson, putting his mouth close to Georgie's ear. Thank you for inviting me to fuck you in the hole. Un-for-tune-it-lee, I have to say fuck off. That's because you are a stupid smelly cow and your lips stink of piss.

Georgie makes that grunting sound again. Her jaw is aching.

Even though like you I have no real Mom since yours went away to America to be a lesbian, I still hate you and I have my own friends.

'Right,' says Mrs Allen. 'Georgie, can you try the passage in the past tense?'

Passage, says William Robinson, so soft Georgie feels more than hears it. A-nal passage.

🕐

The morning moves slowly, golden syrup oozing out of a tin. Lotte tries to read; fails. She picks up Dante's *Inferno*, but can't get past the Third Circle, the gluttons, so she moves on to Plato's *Republic*, a battered brown paperbook she found in the Dandelion Market. Whoever owned it before her was a student, or a madman; the text is full of furiously underlined phrases and enraged

413

question marks. Justice is only justice when it's practised by the strong, says Thrasymachus. If weaker people were to do the thing the big guns do, we'd call them criminals. No, says Socrates. If the weak overcome tyranny, then they're the strong. That's real justice. But what about the ring of Gyges, says Glaucon. Aren't people just, only because they have to be? Wouldn't you do a spot of raping and pillaging, Socrates, if you could wear ring of invisibility, if you could do it and not be seen? Wouldn't anyone?

NO!!!!! says the enraged madman. Underlined three times. A fountain pen.

Lotte's eyes are aching. Ands' books were full of similar denials, but in his neat, rational script. As if that made them any less hysterical. What if you do something to be seen, Glaucon? And it never gets a witness? Is that justice?

The Rilke volume that David gave her at Christmas lies on the windowsill. She hasn't been able to open it since everything went tits up. She should get rid of it, really; someone else would get far better use of it. She'd had it with her the last time she'd gone to the Dandelion Market and had stood around, in a daze, unable to buy anything. It would have been easy to slip it onto one of the book stalls; she'd even thought that, fingered the delicate spine in her bag. But she hadn't been able to follow through.

To Lotte, for all you've done to us. Strange, and rather incorrect, as inscriptions go.

The problem with Rilke, Sybille had said once, is his sentimentality. Love, religion, desire, the spirit. Bourgeois *Quatsch.*

And Art, Sybille. Andrew mocking, looking lazily at them both. We must never forget how Rilke treasured Art.

She fingers the pearl beads wrapped around her wrist. They've been there for six weeks. An iconoclastic gesture, she'd thought – drunk, though she shouldn't have been, and alone and starting to get a little crazy on New Year's Eve – to take them out of their purse and wear them like any other piece of jewellery. But since they made their way there, she hasn't been able to get shot of them either.

Dust motes are dancing in the slivers of light coming in through the narrow windows. The floor is a grubby colour that hides the dirt. In the corner of the empty pub crouches a black phone box; it has a sinister aspect, hunkering on its own, like a man in a trench coat spying in the shadows. David sips the strong tea the barman made him with its shot of Jameson for the road. The place makes him uncomfortable. It is too full of his father's raging ghost. The smells, the taciturn man behind the counter, the silence, the two old boys from a farm up the road who will, any minute, make their appearance. He's sure it's just that, the suck of the past working on him, especially given the day that's in it, but the eggs in his chest don't believe him. They're crackling louder, the compulsion starting to insist. Maybe he should have held off on the tea; waited till he got into Clonmel. But he didn't fancy taking a shit on the side of the road and—

Keeping a good eye on him.

What class of fucking idiot would let their son go anywhere near a little cunt like William Robinson?

He stares down at his notebook; his calculations a nonsense swirl of matter and energy. The barman flips on the radio. Larry Gogan, wittering on about unemployment in England. And David is up, out of his cushiony seat.

🕐

'I'm sorry,' he says. 'I didn't know if you'd still be. You know....'

'Yes. Here.' She doesn't know whether she's relieved or disappointed that it's him; whether to laugh or spit at herself for jumping so fast to the phone.

His voice sounds different, distant over the pips and bleats of the telephone line. 'Sorry. I wouldn't call you, but....'

Oh, she thinks. Of course you wouldn't.

'You're probably busy. With the typing for the students and....'

He stops.

She doesn't say, Go on. She wants to make him work. Did she want him to call? Is this what she feels? Why she's so angry? Is she angry at him, poor, sad, fucked-up David Madden? This – Joanie Flynn's word – *saint*.

'I, eh, wouldn't ask you.... You must have other things on....'

Other things? She nearly laughs. Worse, she nearly says it: what in Christ's name makes you think that, David? And why in Christ's name would you care?

'It's, it's just Mrs Lynch. She got sick. And I, em, we made other arrangements.'

He's unwilling to speak of these other arrangements. Why? Should she care? He starts telling her how busy he is. Today. He has business in Clonmel, family stuff. He leaves a little gap as if inviting her to ask, Oh, Really, What Family Stuff, David? But she doesn't. You have some nerve, she thinks, treating me like this. Pushing me away from you, dropping me like I'm some

415

piece of rubbish got stuck on your shoe, then expecting me to jump back in as if nothing happened.

But nothing did happen, Lotte. And who did the pushing away?

'I mean, if it's a problem, that's, eh…. He has friends.'

'What friends?' she says, despite herself.

An intake of breath. 'That Robinson boy.'

William Robinson? thinks Lotte. The one Georgie used to talk about so much? She isn't sure what makes her feel more sad: the fact that Georgie has become proper friends with this boy without her knowing, or the fact that David doesn't know the first name of his child's new best friend.

'I wasn't thinking,' he blurts. Fast, furious, defensive. He takes a breath. 'Sorry. Really. I just think, he'd be safer with you. Just for today? I know we, eh—'

Please, David, she thinks, whatever you imagine you want to say, don't.

He stops.

Promise, Aisling had said in the hospital garden. *Promise me you'll stay and look after him, our baby. He's a good man, Davey, I owe him that much, and Georgie, our baby…. Ours…. That odd emphasis in her words. Please. I'm begging you, Lotte. I can't stand the idea of those bitches in Clonmel getting their hands on him.*

Okay, said Lotte, and was surprised at how calm her voice had sounded.

'Okay,' she says.

Neither of them speak after that but she can't hang up, and neither can he. Something like relief, or hope, is singing in the silence between them and it's not hers, she swears it's not hers, because why on earth would she be hopeful about this? Some tired, lonely middle-aged man asking her to come back and take care of his child; more than asking – expecting; pleading, even? But she doesn't know how to tell him, No, please don't get the wrong idea, I'm not doing this for you, for whatever you think might happen between us, for whatever you thought you walked away from that awful Christmas night on my doorstep, because how dare you patronise me like that, laughing at me, like I was the one making a fool of themselves, taking advantage of me, brushing me off when I was vulnerable. That's not it, I'm over that. I'm not staying for you, it was always for Aisling, and Georgie, and there are plenty of men I can have if I want, younger than you, and far more attractive, it was never about—

But is she sure, really? Is she sure anymore about anything?

One of them finally says okay, goodbye, see you then, and when she puts down the phone, she realises her heart is pounding.

Her fingers pulse, alive with electricity. The body never lies. A spark as they had made contact, after that dreadful Christmas lunch. Georgie had been coming back from the bathroom, green about the gills. Sick to the soul. You couldn't blame the poor kid. David hadn't seen. Lotte had reached for him, not able to stop herself. A spark as her fingertips met his arm under his jacket – skin, muscle, bone – and then they couldn't let go. She hadn't known, hadn't let herself. Till he started walking away. Then she looked down and saw them. Her silly fingers. Little limpets, holding on for dear life to a sinking ship—

Until it had twinged; the germ inside her revolting against the cigarette, and she realised the Poet had fucked her rightly.

She catches sight of herself in the little mirror. She looks gaunt. Ill. Crazy. Not the sort of person you want looking after your precious child. It was a rubbish promise; she was a rubbish person to ask. Aisling should never have put it to her. She should never have agreed. They are fine, David and Georgie. They've survived for the last six weeks without her. Six whole weeks without a woman's touch and they're still alive, still healthy, and Georgie is nowhere near Clonmel, miles away from being snaffled up by the ugly sisters. As for David—

Sorry. But you got me wrong, Aisling. And maybe she's got herself wrong too. Maybe she is relieved, and hopeful, but not for the reasons she thought; the ones David, poor exhausted, foolish David, might think. Maybe that phone call was all she needed to make a decision. Vacillating Hamlet, finally finding his backbone.

Today, before she cycles to the school to collect Georgie, she's going into the office of the Budget Travel Agency on Baggot Street where she'll buy a ticket for tomorrow's ferry. She'll figure out later what to do with Caliban. After all, he's a survivor.

💣

The net curtain twitches as he parks on the narrow road across from the house. Seen from this angle, as if he's some stake-out cop in an American television series, the place looks unbalanced, neglected, suspicious. He notices things he missed during the exhausted haze of Christmas. The grey render on the front is cracked; little spiderwebs trickle out either side of the main fissure like the tributaries of a river. Around them spreads damp, a dark, feverish grey. Moss is growing on the granite blocks closest to the footpath. The windows are grimy.

Did he do the right thing by calling Lotte? He can feel his mind trying to worry at him, tease out the consequences and ramifications, but he can't afford to do that now. Too much else to deal with. He made the call, she said yes, Georgie will be okay. For now, that's enough.

He reaches for his bag and, as if on cue, the front door opens. Maura stands on the step, behind her Bridget and Eileen. When shall we three meet again?

He hauls out his bag and locks the car.

'Ah, there you are,' says Maura. 'We got hungry waiting for you, Davey, so we'd the lunch already. But there's a bit left over. Eileen made a salad.'

'Sorry,' he says, and realises he doesn't sound in the least bit apologetic.

The hall is dark; bereft of the festive tinsel and pious cards, it feels too narrow and long. It smells of cat piss; his mother's cats, the strays she keeps letting in through her bedroom window. One of them gave birth to a litter under her bed at Hallowe'en, Maura had told them when he and Georgie came down for Christmas. Can you imagine that? The filth. If she didn't feed them, there wouldn't be a problem. But it was sorted fast enough, said Bridget. We shoved the mammy out onto the windowsill and Eileen packed the kittens into a sack quicker than three shakes of a lamb's tail.

Georgie had stopped eating. A sack?

Eileen coughed.

Why did you put the kittens—

David glared at Bridget.

We gave them away, said Eileen, patting Georgie's hand. It was the best thing for them. Sure we couldn't look after them ourselves. That way at least they'd be safe.

Liars, thought David. Bloody liars.

The kitchen is hot, misty with steam and his sisters' sweat. Under the smells of cooking food and turf is something chemical that rubs against the inside of David's throat. Air freshener. They have the fire blazing, the coppers shining, gingham oilcloth on the table. It's a lot better on the inside than it looks from the street. Maura has a new picture up on the wall. A little girl and a puppy, gazing soulfully at each other.

He finishes the salad – ham, tomatoes, hard-boiled egg and beetroot; a cold choice for February – and accepts the tea Maura pours him. Eileen serves the buns. Bridget has baked them. They aren't a good batch. The currants are burnt; little flies that sprinkle coal dust on David's tongue as he bites in.

The clock ticks.

This is the feel of his childhood. Grey light only half-attempting to fight its way in through the net curtains before it gives up the ghost and flees back to the sunnier side of town. The gilt rims on the good delf twinkling. The sounds of chewing and unspoken hostilities.

You ungrateful little runt, screams the ghost of his father, staring down from the silver-framed sepia of his wedding photo. All this I made for you and you tossed it away, threw it to a pack of women.

David clears his throat and the desultory small-talk fades into nothing. Maura puts her cup back on her saucer. She smiles.

'You're looking well, Davey. A bit of spring in your step.'

Spring? Some joke. Not wanting an argument, he nods.

'How's Georgie?' says Eileen.

'Great.' He pushes the last of his bun to one side. 'Is Mammy alright?'

'She's grand,' says Bridget. 'A bit snuffly now with the cold weather, but….'

'Does she know?'

'Ah, Davey,' says Maura. 'It's been years since she's known anything.'

Eileen and Bridget nod, murmur something he can't quite hear.

'Now,' says Maura. The others hush. 'I've rang the nuns and they're expecting her at three. That way she can get the tea in and settle herself for the night.'

'They've a telly there, Davey,' says Eileen. 'And a sunroom. Very fancy.'

'They've the English stations,' says Bridget. 'The BBC. You know how she loves the BBC.'

But only the radio, thinks David. D'you know nothing, Bridget?

'Are you sure we'll all fit in that car of yours?' says Maura. 'It looks terrible small.'

He laughs. They look at him.

'Maybe we should go in the Plymouth. Old times' sake.'

Maura smiles. 'Aren't you still the great fella for the jokes, Davey?'

He pushes back his chair and stands. Bridget and Eileen follow suit. He gestures for them to stay put.

'No. I eh… I just want to say hello to her on me own.' His voice has reverted, as it always does when he comes here, to the thick, gloopy vowels of his youth.

'Course you do,' says Maura. 'Girls, leave him go.'

The smell of cat piss grows stronger as he walks up the stairs. He thinks of the kittens Eileen drowned at Hallowe'en, little bits of bone and skin and fur, sinking to their watery death. Were they ever like

Schrödinger's magical animal, he wonders, alive and dead at the same time? Some of the holy pictures on the wall are at odd angles, as if they've been brushed by the wing tips of a rushing, distracted angel. He stops outside his mother's door. The architrave is still splintered. He touches the broken bit and closes his eyes. Inside, she is singing some kind of murmuring song to herself. A wordless progression of sounds that slip, lopsided, from her struck mouth. The sounds a child would make. The sounds Georgie makes at night, when he walks and talks in his sleep. He lifts his fist. The humming stops.

Davey, she says. Zhavey?

He prepares a smile, drops his hand, turns the knob.

🕐

After closing the door, she stops for a moment on the top step and looks around. Just in case.

In case what, Lotte? Your child-father is come back?

And if he was there, Blessed Eoin the Marxist, trudging around the corner, a duffel bag over his shoulder, eyes destroyed from the sights he'd seen, arms aching for comfort, would he be enough to change her mind, make her want to stay?

☼

It's Saoirse's fault. They are practising diving, down at the deep end, and Saoirse doesn't wait until Sarah Hannigan has finished but jumps in straight away. Sarah Hannigan lets out a shriek and disappears under the surface. William Robinson, standing on the edge with Georgie, swivels his gaze. It lands on Saoirse. Under his blunt fringe his eyes are implacable and Georgie thinks of an illustration in a library book, of a dark man on a horse—

No. Caligula, the crazy Roman Emperor, watching his pet lions fighting to the death.

On other days, that might be as far as it would go, because Mr Smith, the barrel-chested swimming teacher with hair like a white coxcomb, is right beside them and he's the one teacher William Robinson treats with anything other than contempt. But just then old Pig-Nose, Timmy Nelson himself, down at the shallow end with the rest of the bad swimmers, gets one of his fits and begins thrashing around.

420

'Stay where you are!' bellows Mr Smith to the good swimmers. He sets off at a run to the shallow end. 'Don't let that child move!'

Sarah Hannigan's head reappears above the water. She is gasping and red-faced. Saoirse resurfaces too and awkwardly begins to tread water.

Sorry, she says to Sarah, or at least that's what it looks like. I'm sorry.

Without a glance at Mr Smith's retreating back, William Robinson dives in. His dive is smooth, barely breaking water. Half boy, half alligator. He surfaces beside Sarah Hannigan and grips her arm. Georgie sees his mouth move. 'You okay?'

Sarah nods.

Stay out of the water, says a voice in Georgie's head. If I was you, I'd stay out. Georgie knows this voice is not real; it belongs to Elaine, who is not here. *Go away*, thinks Georgie, because that's the best way to get rid of Elaine's voice when she's not there. The trick works. Elaine stops nagging. And Georgie does not see – repeat, *does NOT see* – down near the bad swimmers, where Timmy Nelson is turning blue and flailing around, and Mr Smith is shouting for help, in the doorway that leads to the Ladies changing rooms, under the flashing blue blades of the swimming pool reflections and the light dappling in from the little window at the top of the wall, a small figure standing; skeleton-thin, tufts of blonde hair on its head.

'Ha ha.' The laugh is from tall Brian Woods, who is going to be a rugby player when he grows up, and it pulls Georgie's attention all the way back to the pool.

Saoirse is still asking Sarah if she's okay – thick Saoirse, still too concerned about whether it's her bloody balls fault to realise what's going on – but Sarah isn't looking at her. Sarah is gazing at the place where William Robinson used to be.

'I'm so—' starts Saoirse. Then she disappears, glug, under the water.

Brian Woods and Ian Jones start laughing. When Saoirse resurfaces, William Robinson comes up too. He's smiling and Saoirse is laughing with him, like the thick she is, like it's some joke she's in on.

'Oh wow, that was funny,' says Saoirse – or Georgie thinks she says it because she can only read Saoirse's lips – as Brian Woods slides in next. For such a large boy, he makes barely a ripple in the water. Then it's Ian Jones' turn but Saoirse doesn't notice him either, or the fact that they've formed a circle around her, William Robinson facing Sarah, and Brian Woods facing Ian Jones and they're treading water, arms waving, beginning to move around her, and the stupid bloody grown-ups in the seats aren't watching anymore, because they're all down near the shallow end, bustling around Timmy Nelson and—

'Nobody told me that bloody child was epileptic!' shouts Mr Smith.

'Stinky, stinky,' starts William Robinson, low and soft.

'Pissy, pissy,' Sarah Hannigan joins in.

'Shitty-Saoirse,' add Ian and Brian.

'Swim, Stinky, swim.' William Robinson changes the rhythm. He looks up at Georgie, his eyes shining. His eyebrow is cocked, and that only means one thing.

You're next.

Stay out of the water, whispers Elaine again. But Elaine is not – repeat *not; repeat NOT; repeat* – real.

Swim, Stinky, Swim. They circle Saoirse, smiling, and William Robinson's eyes are bright and full of joy, instead of empty and hungry like they usually are, and Georgie can tell his skin is so hot under the water it's making little trails of steam come up from it, curling, twisting shapes like dragons. The children's voices are light; they're following William Robinson's lead, and he's good at this, the way he's singing, light and chanty, making it sound like they're just having a game, a harmless game that they're all in on together. Down near the shallow end, Timmy Nelson is starting to come round, and the bad swimmers are looking gormless, their mouths open like eejits and their eyes wet as if the same thing could happen to them, and the adults huddled around Timmy Nelson are softening their shoulders with relief and love, because even though Timmy Nelson comes from a children's home and has no mum or dad and is technically way fuck-off worse than Georgie, people actually love him.

Stay out of the water, says Elaine.

But Elaine is not here. Elaine is not real; she's imaginary.

William Robinson pushes Saoirse on the shoulder. Ó Buachalla's daughter is starting to look anxious. About bloody time. Stop, she says.

The others start then. In turns. Push one shoulder under the water, then the next.

She's pissing! calls Sarah Hannigan, and they laugh. William Robinson looks at Georgie again. The light in his eyes makes his blank, cruel face seem almost beautiful. Or is it Brian Woods looking? Or Ian Jones? With all the splashing, the naked arms, the swimming hats, it's hard to tell.

Someone shoves Saoirse's head under the water. She bobs up again. She's crying now. Sorry, she keeps saying. Sorry. She looks up at Georgie and her eyes are desperate.

Stupid, thinks Georgie. What good is *sorry*? That's just going to make him angrier. Saoirse's thick but the thickest thing of all is if you keep saying *sorry* – especially when the damage is done, and especially to someone who does mean things to other people – you run the risk of making them feel like they're a goody, weak and powerless, and William Robinson, like Georgie, has a furnace inside him, of temper and rage and badness, and trying to make him feel like a goody will just make that furnace hotter, and then, God knows what will happen.

Mr Smith is helping Timmy Nelson to his feet. He glances towards the deep end, but the middle swimmers are playing havoc in the water, duck-diving and messing, so Georgie knows he's not seeing anything.

Blood pounds in Georgie's head. *Sink, Stinky, Sink*, the gang are singing now, while they shove Saoirse under and pull her feet downwards and yank off her togs and William Robinson pushes himself against her with his strong goldy-coloured willy, and it seems like they're singing to Georgie too, but another song. Come on, come on, they're singing, what are you waiting for? Join with us and we'll look after you. Join, and everything will be okay.

William Robinson looks up. He is staring right at Georgie and his face is bursting with something that almost looks like love – split open with light, like that picture in the National Gallery where the light splits open the mountains just as the world is about to end.

At O'Connell Bridge, Lotte gets a puncture. Swearing, she pulls the bike up onto the footpath, ignoring the angry looks from the passers-by. Of all the times in all the world....

The wind is biting at her face. The sky is blue but there are clouds scudding across it and she is freezing. She can't think of anything better to do so she kicks the bike, hard, in the front wheel, the one that isn't punctured.

'Useless fucking object!' She is shocked to realise she's shouting.

'Temper,' says a voice behind her, and when she looks up, she sees her brother.

☼

At the moment that William Robinson offers Georgie the closest thing he has to a heart, something frays. In her sense, her deepest-held conviction, that if you sit it out, long enough, patiently enough, silently enough – that if you Cope, it will all change For the Better.

423

Does it matter where this conviction originally comes from? Whether it's been eaten away for a while now, and this is the last strand fraying? Perhaps it's simpler than that; perhaps this is the point at which she finds another conviction. That if you sit it out, long enough, patiently enough, silently enough, all that happens is that things Get Worse.

There is only Worse. Better doesn't exist. It never will because—

William Robinson will never stop trying to make you into a copy of him.

Saoirse Ní Bhuachalla will never stop needing something from you that you can never give.

Lotte will never be your Mum.

Dad will never get happy again.

And Elaine will never fully disappear, even if you ignore her and stop feeding her and pretend she's not still living next door when you know full well you haven't done what she wants you to.

She turns. The circle are hammering it to Saoirse. The architect's daughter is screaming, hysterical now. But she only has herself to blame.

I *am* real, says Elaine, standing at the door of the Ladies changing room. You know I am. And you know what I want.

Bring. Her. Back.

Poor parentless Timmy Nelson forgotten, Mr Smith is racing up the side of the pool, blowing his whistle. His face is like a beetroot.

In all the confusion, nobody sees Georgie slip out.

The girl in charge of the clothes is not where she should be, behind the counter, so Georgie ducks under the shelf and rummages through the baskets. She hears the loo door opening while she's still searching, so – executive decision – she grabs the basket nearest her. Then she ducks out again and races into the changing room. She has, she reckons, approximately five minutes before the old people start coming in for the next hour and her classmates are sent filing out from the pool in disgrace. The clothes in the basket belong to some girl – Georgie's in too much of a rush to figure out who – but there are trousers instead of a skirt so it's not too bad. She pats herself down with a stripey towel and starts dressing. The girl is big, nearly as big as her, but rounder in the waist. The clothes are crap but they're better than nothing.

Black socks, red shoes. Red cords. Black poloneck. Turquoise shirt. Turquoise is called that because it comes from Turkey, right beside the place which shares the name Lotte gave her. Georgia, homeland of the Amazons.

In the bottom of the basket is a duffel coat and a pair of pink-rimmed specs and it's only then that Georgie realises whose stinky clothes she's put on. Too late to change. She swears under her breath and, reluctantly, forces on Saoirse's coat. It's too tight across the shoulders and her wrists stick out under the cuffs, but she guesses it's as good a disguise as any.

The door of the changing room opens. Georgie hears little old lady voices. Leaving Saoirse's schoolbag in the basket, she walks quickly towards the exit, doing her usual trick to make herself invisible, eyes lowered, breastbone sunk, shoulders hunched.

🕐

'D'you realise something?' says Lotte loudly, and to nobody in particular. 'I don't think I can do this anymore.'

The passers-by on the bridge turn and look at her. Most of them duck their heads and continue. Mad British woman talking to herself.

'Oh, fuck off,' she says, and pushes the bike from her. It totters, falls, clattering against a woman laden down with shopping.

'Here, you! Watch it!' says the woman. 'That's my foot....'

But Lotte is shaking her head, brushing the woman's protests away with her hand, and moving on.

Sorry, she thinks, and she's not sure who she's apologising to: the child she's leaving to the mercy of William Robinson, or the dead mother twisting in her grave, or the father too bound up in his pain to do anything about the bloody obvious under his own nose. Sorry, but you see, my dear Maddens, I'm a runner-awayer. Can't help it. It's part of my nature.

The traffic light signal is red. She takes a wild look, left, then right, then runs.

As she strides up Westmoreland Street, she imagines that she is discarding clothes with every step. Her coat, her scarf, her boots, her jeans, her sweater, her vest, her bra, her knickers, her skin.

The door of the travel agency swings open.

A slothful-looking girl dressed in a green uniform is sitting behind the counter. 'Hello, can I help you?'

☼

Her key is in her schoolbag, in the boys' changing room, but she lets herself in with the spare, the one Aisling put under the plant-pot for Lotte and that David never took away.

425

The room still smells of Aisling. There she is – fainter now, not strong like the first few days after she died and Georgie kept thinking her mother was standing right behind her and would turn around only she wasn't, which was weird because she'd been in that hospital for weeks – but yes, still there. Like perfume. The sun is coming in through the window and David has left it open and she can hear the sounds of Marino and, beyond that, Dublin; some kids are out on the Green, playing and shouting, and there are cars and the rattling sound of a train and….

Georgie walks to the wardrobe. The long mirror on the right-hand side reflects a frowning, long-haired, overweight person. Too big to be a small child; a girl, maybe, on the cusp of adolescence? Whoever she is, this person is dressed in clothes the colours a clown would wear and a duffel coat that's too short in the arms.

She pulls at the door. Aisling's clothes are still inside, hanging on what used to be her half of the wardrobe. Blouses, skirts, dresses, jeans, corduroys, coats. On the shelf above the rail are her jumpers, folded carefully, sheets of tissue between each to stop the wool from balling. Closest to the wall are two coats; Aisling's white mac, that she used to wear in summertime, and her Afghan, the coat David said made her look like a hippy, the coat she wore less and less as time went by, and in the end not at all.

Georgie shrugs off Saoirse's duffel and slides the Afghan off its hanger. It smells of Aisling and the long fur on the collar is like hair, reddy-blonde and fine. She tries it on. Not too big, not too small. Perfect, like the Baby Bear's porridge.

She closes the wardrobe door and her new reflection bounces back at her. She seems sturdier in the Afghan, more solid, less raggy. Even Saoirse's clothes look okay underneath. She looks, she thinks, almost like a grown-up.

Elaine has stopped talking since Georgie left the pool, but she's still waiting.

Coming, thinks Georgie, sending out the thought that way Aisling said you could do if you wanted good things to happen to you.

David always keeps spare money in the top drawer beside his bed, along with tubes of mints and hard sweets and his socks and underwear. Georgie digs, and finds three tenners rolled into a ball. Terr-if-ic.

On the dressing table glimmers a curve of silver and turquoise. Georgie leaves that where it is. She doesn't want to put it on, to see how the colours of the torque do the same beautiful things on her that they used to do on Aisling. Taking something precious from someone else just because you want it, even from someone dead, isn't the worst reason to take things, but it's not, as Lotte might have said, particularly admirable either.

🕐

It's happened again; she's angry and it's happening to and in somebody else. The bus conductor is staring at her as if she has lost her mind, and maybe she has, but it is not her fault that she has no change left for the fucking bus.

'Alright, then,' she says, loudly and rudely, and she sounds like her mother, Anna Bauer, whom she and Ands nicknamed Julia, when Anna forgot she was on enemy territory and that it wasn't good to speak loudly in a German accent in a country where people blamed you for the loss of those they loved. And drew you pictures at Christmas of concentration camps and told you, You killed all the Jews.

'I'll walk.'

Her face is flushed. Maybe I'm killing the baby, she thinks, with all this rage, and then thinks, Oh, what a shame. If I'm already killing the baby, I don't need to go to bloody London. I can go to Paris instead, join Jacques Mesrine. Wouldn't that be fun, Ands? *Viva la revolución!* Okay, Mesrine is just a gangster, not a shred of integrity to what he's doing, but honestly, Ands, do you think we're ones to talk?

'I'll need your name and address, love,' says the conductor.

She says something rude and then she's up and walking down the aisle and they're staring at her through their clouds of cigarette smoke, the hypocritical Irish, the silver-tongued poets, the scholars and the saints, this colonised nation of shopkeepers and warriors and quarrelling tribal thugs, and none of them, including the mealy-mouthed conductor, can think of a word to say to her.

She stops at the top of the stairs. 'You know what—' she starts, lifting her hands, thinking, Forgive them, Lotte, for they know not what—

The bus rounds a corner, far too quickly. Her hands jerk, looking for support. Her left hand misses the rail, flails. Her right jams, trapped in her hair by a silver link from the rosary beads.

💣

He still can't get used to her hairstyle, still expects to see the rigid, shining waves she'd always been so proud of, even though it's years, the third stroke really,

427

since Bridget hacked it off, moaning at the bother of washing and curling it. Now what's left lies soft and mousy around her pale face; the hair of a little girl, held neatly up with a clip. Gone too is the lipstick – that Rita Hayworth pillar-box red that used to make her look a film star – and her shaking hands are no longer bright with rings, sparks of John's Fire against the boggy greys and browns of the armchair. Her eyes are wandering, uneven, like those puzzle games where you have to tilt a box so that the little balls go into the holes. She has lost more weight since Christmas and the spare skin hangs off her bones in folds. Her ankles are thick and swollen, plump with water.

Davey, she says. She looks up at him and smiles and in that moment she is beautiful again.

David sits on the edge of the bed. She starts humming to herself again. A foxtrot.

Mammy, he says. She continues humming.

Mammy. This time louder. She looks up. Her eyes are vague and cloudy.

He smiles and takes her hand. It trembles in his. The skin is paper-soft, dry except for the damp, swollen palm.

She sighs. The bed shudders. She lifts her other hand and cradles David's between both hers. He closes his eyes. The room fills with the scent of her: perfume, honey and mushrooms. The trembling of her hands turns into a rhythmic patting, her fingertips beating the bones of his fingers like butterfly wings, pulling him closer to her. Her mouth against his ear; feathers.

He flinches. 'No.' He pulls away. 'I'm not Fergus. It's me, Davey. Your son.'

She blinks, puzzled. Then smiles: Georgie.

'That's right, Mammy. I'm Davey. And Georgie's my little boy. Your grandchild.'

She frowns. Then she says it.

Déjà vu. Shock first. Bitter cold. A pulling sensation in his chest, just above his heart, like something has ruptured. His eyes stinging, weightlessness, then

daviddontadditup

■ *o* ■ *u* ■ ■

No, Mammy, says Bridget out of nowhere. She must have come up the stairs behind him. Georgie *is* Davey's son. He's his son, Mammy. A boy. Not a little girl—

He turns, boiling with anger. Can you not just—

His mother whimpers. Colour flares in Bridget's face. I was only trying to help, Davey. She opens the wardrobe with a bang. 'We're going out on a little drive now, Mammy.'

David is up on his feet. How did he get there? Can't think straight. Can't breathe. A thought pushes through. Lotte. He needs to ring her. In Marino. Check Georgie is okay.

☼

She shoves her armchair up against the door so if anybody happens to come back here to check on her, it'll take a while for them to get in. She pulls out some clothes from her wardrobe and rolls them up into a long log shape, and sticks that under her duvet. She draws the curtains closed. This she knows is stupid, because if they do manage to break the door open, the first thing they'll do is try to wake her. But still.... Grabbing the canvas bag where she keeps her Lego, she shakes it, emptying it out, then stuffs in a spare pair of pyjamas, some underwear and a fresh pair of cords. Be Prepared.

The phone begins to ring downstairs.

'Coming!' she says, loud and clear.

🕐

Lotte totters, right wrist caught at her temple, left arm extended, a figure from a Victorian melodrama.

And, suddenly, she is exhausted – absolutely, utterly bone-tired, ready to sleep for hours, in long dreamless blocks like she hasn't slept in months. Twenty to be exact, since that awful morning Sybille's father, gentle Pastor Henkel, phoned from Germany with the news that they'd done it, the idiots. They'd made a big bloody statement on the top floor of a newspaper building, blown themselves up for their beliefs, their art, their convictions, the people. They'd recorded the whole thing with a camera they'd set up in an apartment across the street. He and his wife had received a letter from Sybille telling them there would be a film. Your mother will receive one too, he'd said. He'd *Du*'d Lotte on the phone, using the intimate pronoun you use with children; though when he'd said *your mother*, he'd reverted to the formal *Sie*. But there was no film, he said; the camera in the apartment opposite was still there but it had been emptied, and Sybille, in a coma, with half her face torn off – what a fucking botch job – couldn't tell them who, if anyone, had helped them, who had recorded it, from across the street.

What worries us most, he'd said, is if that person sends it to the press. You can imagine, the pictures. My wife, she will....

429

Lotte had made all the right sounds and nodded, though he couldn't see her, but all she could think was, Jesus Christ, I need some sleep, with the smell of the train on her, and the smell of the boat, Hook of Holland to Harwich, and the other train, and the stink of her false papers and the cast-iron alibi Charlie had promised her, and Jesus Christ, she thought, Jesus bloody Christ.

They'd got tired of their statements, you see; those big, ugly installations they'd set up in communes and warehouses all over Berlin, the ones that Lotte, for a joke, called their Anti-Fascist Wunderkammers, though Sybille never liked that description. A *Wunderkammer*, she said, was a collection. All collections are imperialist. They got tired of pulling pieces out of themselves – shit, blood, piss, semen, vaginal juices, sweat, tears, hair – and using it to scrawl incendiary statements on expensive Fabriano paper or embroider ironic folk art samplers on costly linen. Fascism Lives; Police State; Silence Kills; We Are All Pigs; Capitalism Must Die; Nothing Must Survive. They wanted something bigger, a proper statement. They needed back-up, they told Lotte, someone to make sure the explosion was properly framed in case they were delayed making their getaway. They would process the film afterwards, they told her; make stills from it, send it to the newspapers. Get their big bloody statement over to America, Britain, Vietnam, Palestine.

Lotte hadn't been able to resist some movement; a close-up here, a pan and tilt there. Something to make it more intimate, more human, more *real*. She'd got tight in on Andrew's eyes and he'd looked straight at her, through the lens, across the street. Even then, she hadn't twigged it. She watched them place the bag on the filing cabinet, fiddle with the kitchen timer. She'd bought it, you see; thought they'd run, like they'd said they would – she'd planned to film that too, and the twenty minutes of nothing, a silent room, before the bomb went off. She'd thought that, the silence, would be the most interesting piece of the whole film.

Stupid, stupid, Lotte. How blind you can be.

He'd stopped fiddling with the timer and looked at her. A strange light in his eyes, and she didn't even cop it then; that she'd seen that light before, when they were seven and he'd handed her a cobbled-together rosary savaged from a Holy Communion dress. Then he'd pushed the dial to zero. Bloody idiot.

One more tug. Her wrist rips free. She falls. As she does, even through the tiredness, she can see that there are good things. Things she hasn't noticed in months; a piece of graffiti on the stairwell of the bus, sunlight flashing through the windows, the pulsing of her blood under her skin. These are nothing to do with anybody else, nobody living or dead either, only her, and, God, she thinks, if she had her time over again, maybe she would even film them, and hey, she thinks, as her legacy, the unmade art in her, begins assembling itself into her own personal *Wunderkammer*, maybe this isn't such a bad way to—

☼

Georgie has to break the window because it's still jammed; she does it properly, like a real robber, putting a T-shirt across the glass and knocking against it with the hammer from her carpentry set. Then she taps gently against the fragments of glass sticking to the frame, gathers them in the T-shirt and puts the whole lot under her bed, pulling the curtains closed again so it won't look too suspicious. Gingerly, she crawls out over the broken glass onto the sill. The day is bright. The sun is shining and there are hints of warmth through the cutting cold of the wind. She closes her eyes. Below her she can feel her homeland, suburbia: grey roofs, green patches of garden, grey worms of back alleys and lanes, the tall leafy treetops of Griffith Avenue, Fairview Park, the Dracula crescent where Saoirse lives, beyond that Howth and the sea.

She takes care sliding down the extension. Getting onto the wall between her back garden and Mrs Kelly's is tricky because of all the glass they'd stuck there after Christmas, but she uses Saoirse's duffel, folded lengthways, to cushion the worst of it. She'll have to jump down before she gets to the apple tree because the duffel isn't long enough to cover all the glass. She steels herself and jumps, landing on the horrible bit of cementy patio with a thump. One of her ankles turns.

The window of Mrs Kelly's back door glares at her; an evil eye.

Her chest is tight, her stomach sick. Because Mrs Kelly's daughter has been here so many times, with people who want to buy the house, Georgie knows the house will be fragrant with detergent, cleaner than it was when she used to visit Elaine. But under the detergent she can already smell that horrible smell, of sugar and fat, that she got at Christmas. Steeling herself, she opens the back door and enters the poky gloom of the kitchen. Under the February sun, the place seems even more pee-coloured than ever. She's inside a toilet, she's in the bottom of where people put their waste.

The hall is empty of people, full of shape and noise. Its flowery carpet, ugly and startling. Small brown pieces of furniture, old lace, the smell of Pledge.

431

And, everywhere, dust; way more dust than should be in a place which is being cleaned every week.

Bile rises in Georgie's throat. She feels weak, hot, shaky. She is sweating, even her hands. Not good sweat like after running a race, but the other type. Smelly sweat, old people's sweat. The steps come to meet her one at a time. Orange cabbage roses in a sea of whirling black, hungry fangs of thorns. The room on the left at the top of the landing is open a little, the span of a child's hand. Light the colour of old ladies' knickers is seeping out onto the landing.

'Elaine?'

Georgie stalls, paralysed. Her heart is beating so fast, she thinks it's going to explode. Her foot moves. She pushes the door.

There are shadows on the far side of the room. A wardrobe, large, dark brown and imposing, like the one in the Narnia books, with a long black-spotted mirror down one of the doors. A lone bed, very small, is pushed tight against the wall, the same wall where the shadows are gathering. This is a bed reserved for guests; a grandchild maybe, or a daughter coming to stay the night with her ageing mother, or a next-door neighbour's child gone for a nap while her mum, poor love, is at the hospital. There are lace curtains on the windows, draped sullenly like the torn ears of a mangy dog.

Georgie forces herself to kneel down. The carpet is gooey to the touch. She closes her eyes and pushes her hand under the bed.

For a second, as her fingers brush the tufts, she almost expects to find a real girl. Elaine, disappearing to thinness, head scalped with a chemotherapy crewcut. But instead her fingers lock around a plastic head with rubbery cheeks. The room sighs. Carefully, Georgie extracts the thing from the dust and the cobwebs.

'Elaine?' she whispers. But Elaine says nothing.

Gritting her teeth, Georgie turns the thing upside down and feels inside it. Her fingers are shaking; they reach, find nothing, then—

Folded paper, softened with age. Her chest is hurting. She pulls out the paper; it's still crumpled into a ball. She smooths it, forces herself to look. On the side facing her is a newspaper article. *Progress Halted. Architect Furious.* Most of the article is a picture, a drawing by her father of his bank. A side-on view of a ziggurat, striped black and white. Right under that is a smaller picture, a grainy photograph of an enormous, wild-haired man standing at the crossing near O'Connell Street bridge. The way they've organised the page makes it look like David's drawing is lurching up behind him. The man's arms are folded and you can't make out his features, but Georgie knows who he is and what the look on his face means. The Black Knight guarding Astolat. Stony, blank, full of accusation.

November 1974, says the small writing at the top of the page. Two years, two months and twenty days ago.

Georgie's jaw clenches. She turns the paper over and sees—

A young girl, insolent and gap-toothed. Underneath the photo, words that a then seven-year-old would just about be able to understand. *Monaghan Bomb: Family to Leave their Home.*

If anything happened to Queen Bess, said Judith Conyngham, I would *die.*

It's important to know why you take things that belong to other people. There are three reasons: you can take them for yourself, which is weak, or for someone else, which can be okay sometimes. Or you take things for a bad reason: because you want to hurt the person the thing belongs to because they've hurt you.

There are lots of things Georgie could say. Sorry, Judith. I'm bad, a really bad friend. But there's a pain in her jaw which won't let her form the words. Anyway, sorry would just turn Judith into a goody, weak and powerless; and that was the one thing Judith wasn't – like Georgie isn't, or William Robinson, or Saoirse even, or anyone really, including a stupid fuck-off Mum who goes and dies on you.

Besides, it's all there, in front of her, in smaller, harder black type: *I don't want to hear sorry, said the young mother. Sorry won't bring her back.*

They'd been at their great-auntie's birthday party. Judith had gone out to the car because she was bored playing with the other kids and wanted a book. Her daddy had given her the key. She'd opened the driver's door and that's what made it happen.

What's weird is how young Judith seems in that picture, just a little kid, really. Because that's not at all how Georgie remembers her.

Georgie folds up the cutting and sticks it back inside Queen Bess's head and puts the lot into her bag. She does it carefully, not like she did that evening in 1974, the panicky, awful November night, two days before David's hearing, when she discovered the terrible thing that she'd done. She'd pulled her box out from under her bed, the box she used for keeping things she had no use for any more, like bits of jewellery taken from a mother's bedside table that a boy wasn't supposed to play with, or a matchbook stamped with the name of the North Star Hotel, smelling of a man's cologne, stuffed deep into the pocket of an Afghan coat, or silly pointless drawings of mermaids, or a borrowed library book with a picture of a Black Knight glaring an ominous warning, a warning she'd been too frightened by stupid madey-up ghost stories to recognise. The carpet had been clean that evening because Aisling had hoovered, but as Georgie pulled at the box, she'd felt something catch in the casters. She'd brushed her fingers underneath, but whatever it was – pig's ear, milk teeth – was in too deep and she was in too much of a rush, panicking, so she'd kept pulling and whatever it was finally dislodged itself, freeing the box. She'd hauled out the doll's head and stuffed the cutting inside and shoved the whole stupid mess into her schoolbag and raced up to the corner of the road and put them into the bin, and that, she'd thought, would be the end of that.

No evidence. No crime.

I was playing, she'd told David when he'd caught her coming back in. No. Not with a lane. I was upstairs.

She has no idea how they made their way out of the bin, Judith and Queen Bess, how they landed themselves here, in Mrs Kelly's spare bedroom. Does it matter? Or is all that matters what she's going to do next?

🕐

Go.

Then—

Shit. Time speeds up. The steps tumble past. Fear rushes into her veins. Her insides turn sour: vinegar and bile. Christ, she thinks, please don't kill my baby.

☼

Georgie leaves Mrs Kelly's, swiftly retracing a path that feels familiar but not, like something from a dream. Down the stairs, out through the kitchen, through the garden, out the back door and down the lane.

David hangs up. His head feels spongy and dense, stuffed with some inert, useless substance. Nobody answered, but that doesn't mean anything. They're probably still out, on their way back from school. Or swimming. Or whatever.

One step at a time like a good girl. His sisters are coming down the stairs. Maura first, leading their mother by the hand. Then Bridget, carrying a small case.

But she has more clothes than that, thinks David stupidly. Surely they haven't forgotten to pack her frocks.

Maura smiles and coaxes their mother down the last step. There you go, pet.

David glances back at the phone.

'Davey?' says Eileen.

He opens the door, ushers his womenfolk through.

They pile into the car, Maura in the front passenger seat, their mother in the back, flanked by Eileen and Bridget. Out of habit – Georgie's usually in the back seat – David checks the rearview, meets the bulky reflections of the women. Bridget catches his eye. She's glowering, pretending she's not. Raging about what happened upstairs— and at the thought, his own rage tinders again, sawing through the sponginess in his head. Let her stew, the weapon. It was her fault for barging in with her *stupid blindingly obvious so-called observations.* The phrase jabs at him. It's like a script, something he's learnt by rote, automatic, inauthentic. The rage crunches harder, grinding through him. He snaps the indicator on, moves off. His body feels deformed; buckling under the weight of his fury. Beside him, Maura is gripping her handbag as if it's going to jump out of her lap. Her hands are veined and the skin is mottled. She's getting old. *Oh well. Comes to us all in the end.* She catches him looking and gives him a brief smile. Her eyes are moist.

In the back, Bridget and Eileen are fussing over their mother, trying to get her seatbelt fastened. Safety first. What if, thinks David, and has a sudden image of the car skidding out of control, flying into a lamppost, killing them all in one fell swoop. A perfect solution. No more problems, no more panic, no more stupid anxieties. Lotte could move into Marino and look after Georgie. That way she could get the chance to settle down, God knows the silly girl needs it, and Georgie could finally get some decent looking after for a change, nobody could say he's been a model father, nobody could say he's been any sort of father at all—

Maura hisses, grabs his arm. An articulated truck is turning onto the Waterford Road. He swears, brakes. A bark of fear from Bridget. Eileen's voice rises, fluttering little miaows. He looks at the steering wheel. His left hand is soldered to it; his right bunched into a fist. Beside him, Maura is saying the Rosary.

His foot on the brake pedal is shaking. Uncontrollable. Things fall apart.

'Sorry about that, troops,' he says in his cheeriest fakest of fake Boy Scout voice. 'Nothing to worry about.'

And there he is, the International Man of Mystery, driving over the humpy back of the Gashouse Bridge, the Suir sludging beneath, and all he can think of is that desperate girl's word.

lambofgodyoutakeawaythesinsoftheworldhavemercyonus
charade

☼

The train hugs the coast as far as the park, then swoops inland, into the city. Through the window, Georgie sees empty gardens, empty streets, rooftops. The siding is wall-grey, dead-fern-brown; too early for weeds and leaves. Once they get past Howth Junction, they'll start to see the sea again.

Georgie unpeels the silver foil from the chocolate bar she got at the kiosk. She breaks off a square.

The woman sitting across from her is knitting a long, grey scarf. Her lips are pursed and her cheeks are hollowed and creased. She looks like she doesn't have any teeth.

The city spits them out again, into the flat northlands of the estuary, sea both sides of them. The woman knitting says nothing; just knits and makes funny sounds with her mouth. She has an odd habit of whooshing her tongue around inside her mouth as if hiding something. There are bananas in the big striped bag that she's put on the brown tabletop between them. They smell sickly.

The woman across clears her throat. It takes Georgie a second to realise that the throat-clearing is being addressed to her.

'Are you hungry, pet?'

The woman's voice is familiar; it is the sweet, sing-song cadence of the North. Of County Down and Granny Bell and Aisling. She is holding out a packet of boiled sweets. Lemon's; the name of the confectioner, not the sweet. She's holding them out to Georgie and she's doing that funny thing with her tongue again and Georgie realises she is moving it around her mouth to hide the gaps where her front teeth should be. That's funny, thinks Georgie, a lady with no teeth offering sweets, and the thought makes her want to laugh, not in a bad way, like when William Robinson is making fun of someone, just happy.

'Go on,' says the woman and smiles, darting her tongue up again to hide the gap.

Georgie puts her hand into the bag and pulls out the first sweet she lands on. The woman chuckles and takes a sweet for herself and they sit, in companionable silence, the woman with her half-finished knitting, a scarf nobody in their right mind would wear, and the child sucking and in between times looking out the window and trying not to let her hopes get too high and realising that it's been a while since she thought anything was as funny as the lady with no teeth offering her sweets.

❦

She was named after a flower. Lily or Rose or Daisy or something. You've lovely hands, she said on the dancefloor. *Très élégant.* You're a very handsome-looking fella. She had friends with her, she whispered, but she'd let him walk her home, if he liked.

David was nineteen, had been stuck working behind his Da's bar for two years. His mother had managed to force him through the Brothers, but the old man had drawn the line, as everyone knew he would, at university. Down the plughole they went, her dreams of her son the doctor. By then, Fergus Madden was on his own way out, shuttling between his lonely, stinking bedroom at the back of the house and the cancer ward in Waterford Hospital. Maura was drafted in to help David with the bar. She was great with the customers, quick at the numbers. They made a deal. David would give her a cut of his wages if she let him away on dance nights.

It was St Valentine's. The girl kept stumbling on the cobbles. She was a chatterbox, full of plans. University, teacher training. Then marriage, a good one. To a Professional. What about you? she said.

David made a vague noise and she'd laughed. A bright spark like you? Don't be hiding your light under a bushel. Everyone knows you're all set for college. Your mammy's been planning it long enough. God forgive me, but once your daddy's dead –he's not far off now, is he? – you'll finish up with that old charade and no one will stand in your way.

Charade? said David.

At the foot of the Gashouse Bridge, she pulled him into the shadows and started nibbling at his ear. He wished he was more expert, but she seemed to know what she was doing. She unzipped his fly.

Power surged in him. He lost all sense of himself.

Her hands flew up, batting. Fists first, then claws, scraping, then—

437

Grabbing him, forcing him in. Do it, she said. Was she crying? You know you want to. You're all the same.

Oh oh

oh

Gravity is the weakest of the four forces, Madden, Brother Sheridan once said. It is also the closest a scientific understanding can get to the mystery of death.

They arranged to meet the next day.

The Library, so. At four. I'll put manners on you. She smiled. Her teeth were scraggly. Tombstones, he'd thought.

🕐

Shit.

Andrew's face is screaming something at her and the stairs are tumbling, murmuring with the pebbly rattles of children's loose teeth, and his eyes are blazing, bloodshot, and his hands reaching towards her and—

Now, she realises, she has a choice. Now she can make a real decision.

☼

'I find Dublin very big,' says the lady with the grey scarf. 'What about you?'

Georgie shrugs.

'It's fierce confusing trying to find my way around. I only come down once the year to see my niece. She gets worried about me, with the soldiers and all that bother. Where are your people from?'

Georgie thinks. 'Lots of places.'

'Och, isn't that something?'

Georgie shrugs.

'You're a quiet wean. It's a good way to be.' The woman winks. 'You can do whatever you want and you don't get seen. Are you the oldest?'

Georgie nods.

The woman clicks her tongue against her missing front teeth. It makes a wet sound, squelchy. 'That's a job. Let me tell you, that is a real job of work.'

The wool continues to pull, twist, torque.

💣

She didn't turn up and he assumed she'd gone off him. Then the rumours started. Under the cover of the LambofGodyoutakeaway, Bridget muttered to

Eileen, *They don't know who got her that way. Her daddy's on the warpath.* That night, in the wee hours, David let himself into the bar. Pulled a pint, downed it fast, then another. The idea already ticking away in his mind; loads, timing, points of stress and fracture. Two weeks later, his father died. Just in time, but slow enough to make him sweat.

Right, said Maura, looking at David across the kitchen table. Anxious, working it all out. I'll swear to her da you were in the bar that night, Davey, and—

He'd shaken his head, fearful cuckoo in the nest again. The doorman saw us leave, Maura.

He let the silence fill between them; allowed it to do the talking. That was her weakness, he had thought. Maura always assuming she knew what was going on in her little brother's head. Later, he would realise his sister had been cleverer than that. She must have read the truth off him and simply smelt advantage in the situation. The crown prince out of the way; the business for the taking. As for the girl named after a flower, a publican's son was no Professional. But the whole town knew the Maddens had money, that although Fergus would be a belligerent, crafty fucker even on his death-bed, the wife, poor soul, was a soft touch. *God forgive me, but he's not far off now, is he?* Loads and timing. No wonder she had been so eager to get him inside her.

Charade. He looked it up in the dictionary before he left. A ridiculous pretence.

A singularity, said Brother Sheridan, is defined in two ways. One is the centre of a black hole, when gravitation distorts space and time beyond recognition. But singularities happen all the time, Madden; think of water, flowing down a plughole. One minute the event is there, the next it's over the horizon.

Did you always want to be an engineer, Davey?
Multiple-choice question (ultimate version):
a) a child in a bed
b) a man in a tunnel
c) a coward in a kitchen, looking for a fast ticket out: one way, no return.

In 1963, he saw Aisling for the first time. September, an Indian summer. He had reclaimed his life by then; left the navvying, moved to Dublin, cut down on the drink, graduated from office boy to apprentice, and was studying engineering in Bolton Street, courtesy of Arthur Lyons. He had been on a lunch break and, on a whim, decided to go through Trinity. She was coming through the front gate, in a white mini-dress and a cream coat with black buttons and the sun blazing through her hair. His heart had knocked against his chest and he had thought, this, this goddess, this must be mine.

She had pressed her mouth to his ear the first time they did it, on his single bed in the digs on Northumberland Road, just around the corner from Percy Place. She had asked a question – *Did you always want* – and he kissed her instead of answering and brought her to his room. My sister, he told the landlady. She had been about to scald him when Ash turned on her grand act, all how-dare-you Protestant doctor's daughter, and the woman retreated, cowed and simpering. Upstairs, in the balmy air of the Indian summer, they lay on top of the sheets, not under them, and made love, and the first time David understood properly what that meant, after the not-time on the bridge, and the sweat-and-bone animal fucks with the girls of the Black Country. He thought she was going to wreck it at one point by saying something, like You're my first or You're not or The boy I met in Greece last summer who I lost my heart to, the one I never talk about, he was called Denis, and he didn't want to wreck it either by talking about that scraggy-toothed girl saying, Go on, and him seeing splinters in an architrave and stopping in the nick of time, or the shame he had felt after for having used her misfortune as a way to rid himself of that damned grocery bar, all because he hadn't the balls or vision to face up to a dying man and say: No. Fuck you. I am going to make my own future. So he moved his ear away till they were looking into each other's eyes again, that off way – parallax – where you can't focus on both eyes at the same time, and tried to tell her, without speaking, that he loved her and, to the best of his ability, he always would.

Until Georgie, that moment had seemed the most real in his life. When he had been most himself; pure, free of pretence, before his fear and shame and covering up and her disappointment and rage and his suspicion and unravelling had set in. But it was a moment that had come out of dissimulation and evasion, and would lead to avoidance. He had set up a life with someone – stayed together, made a child, failed to weather the storms – that had had nothing but dissimulation at its core. How could that ever be pure?

'Thanks,' she says, because she can't think of anything else to say. Her voice comes out strangled, gulping.

The man grunts. Under the slippery wet of her armpit his shoulder is like granite.

'I'm sorry,' says Lotte. She's crying. Ridiculous. Another part of her doesn't give a damn. Her foot is twisted out at an odd angle and the base of her spine is throbbing. She has bruises along her left thigh. Her scalp where the chain-link of the beads tore her hair out is stinging. Her coat sleeve is ripped. In the corner of her eye she can see the hazard lights of the bus, blinking.

Stairs falling. She'd toppled, undone. Then—

What?

Still feels uncertain. A wind rushing past. If she was superstitious, she would have said, An angel, brushing her with its wing tip. Or just her own reflexes, or those of the tiny human – still living? – inside her, sending split-second synaptic messages. Twist, curl, protect. She thinks of the pregnant woman she saw fossilised in the ruins of Pompeii, making a shell of her back to protect her bump from the eruption's hellish flow.

The man in the black coat had moved faster than she would have thought possible. Too late to break the crunch between her tailbone and the ground; fast enough to catch the weight of her head in his hands.

In a parallel universe, she thinks, she's lying broken, useless, impaled on the railings like Cary Grant's little brother in *Spellbound*, except – silly her – there are no railings on a bus.

He's shushing her and she realises that she must have started gabbling again. 'You'll need to get this seen to.'

He looks vaguely familiar. Big mop of greying black hair, sideburns, bags under his eyes. Handsome, in an overused sort of way. He doesn't look like the type who should be on a bus. Maybe his Jag has broken down. She doesn't know why she thinks that. It could be his clothes. He's dressed well, if slightly too young for a man of his age. His mouth is heavy. His jowls too, though the sideburns hide them well. The hair makes him seem younger; that and the tight green shirt. For some reason she thinks of the Mayor of Casterbridge, gambling away his family, and as soon as she does, realises she's had that thought before, about a different person, though she can't remember who.

'Alright,' he says to the other passengers, crowded uselessly around the stairwell. They do nothing. He says something else in what must be Gaelic and the crowd move back.

'I'm pregnant,' she says.

He nods, unsurprised. The smell of his cologne drifts up to her nose and it's fresh and clean, bergamot and apples, and now he's young again, boyish, and that reminds her of Andrew and sets her off again, crying. He shushes her, half-distracted, like she's a cat yowling for milk, and she thinks of Caliban and, Oh, Jesus, I can't leave him, what was I thinking, and then she feels him—

Her?

It

they

Inside her, moving, jealous, and

Hope is in her, in the jagged scream of her ankle, in the smell of the man beside her, the shaft of brightness from the bus window, in the shadows on the stairs, even in her heart. Then something moves in the man's face, a curve of heavy, sensual lips, unspeakably familiar, and she *sees*—

Christ.

'Georgie,' she says, still not fully knowing what she's seeing and what's just imagination. Knowing only that she needs to get away from Donnacha Ó Buachalla and find David's child for him before the stupid bloody obvious happens with that awful William Robinson. Except as she tries to claw her way out of his arms, she keeps slipping on those stupids beads. Scrabbling, scrabbling, to get away.

Well, says the nun, she seems happy enough.

Thanks, sister. That's very good of you. David has never heard Maura's voice so shaky.

Some whispering follows, the type of communication women make with each other when they don't want men to listen.

They drive back to Clonmel in silence.

You'll be staying, says Maura when they reach the house. For a bite.

He looks at her, surprised. Then – Eureka! – remembers, and his guts turn to lead.

You'll crash that car without some supper in you. Maura pats his hand. A suck of breath. You're a block of ice, you craythur.

☼

Georgie gets off the bus at Massfort. Behind her lies a low stone wall, cypresses, the jutting grey finger of a church. In among that, the place where her mother should have been buried, but wasn't, because David said if Aisling was buried up North, he and Georgie would never get the chance to visit her.

Behind that, dusk and the black humps of the Mournes. The Binion Light is starting to flicker in the foothills. Car headlights swirl, speeding along hairpin bends. Mad Red Rooney, thinking he's in Monaco again. The narrow road to Cranfield is hidden behind an overgrown lump of hedge. Georgie hoists her schoolbag up onto her shoulders, and crosses over.

The path twists, unpredictable as those electrons David used to talk about over Sunday dinner. On either side stretch the flat fields, the sheep, the airfield that was used for landing planes in World War II, the caravan parks. At its end lies the beach, the sea, the Conynghams' house, empty since they decamped to Canada six months after Judith's death, so that, with everyone so anxious to *keep things from the child*, there was no evidence to tell Georgie what had happened to her friend, except for a cutting in the newspaper, and not even that, after she stuffed it into Queen Bess and got rid of them both, or thought she did. She thinks again of the barn with its unquiet ghosts and wonders what wee Adam is doing in Canada. She imagines the upstairs bedroom at the front of the two-storey grey farmhouse; the room that used to be Judith's and which – Georgie heard Granny Bell saying once, though she wasn't supposed to have heard – they kept as a shrine before they went to Toronto. Georgie can picture that. The room untouched, pink and frilly, Judith's clothes hanging in the wardrobe, her books gathering dust on her bedside locker. Her dolls crowding up against each other for company on the mildewing satin of her eiderdown. All save one.

Blackbirds are singing. Crows are cawing. Georgie's nose fills with clean country smells: cow poo and dead winter grass, rotten leaves, skeleton-thin trees. Seaweed and the lonely bones of mermaids.

She thinks that will be the right place for Queen Bess and Judith, the sea. Putting them into another lonely bedroom just wouldn't be fair. But the saltwater will clean off all the old dust and wash away that black type, and maybe even keep them afloat for a while. Besides, Judith always wanted to go on adventures.

Georgie swings her arm, lets go. The doll's head whirls up through the air, pauses for a moment, then drops. A splash. Gone.

For a second, almost, she thinks she hears Elaine. But Elaine has turned into nothing. She is everywhere and nowhere at once; whatever membrane separated her from the rest of existence has melted. Georgie + Elaine = Georgie plus. The bits of her that might once have been human have been vaporised, stripped of their material value. Memories only, fragments for a Golem to be cobbled together in Georgie's imagination, scavenged from the people she knows. Lotte's cheekbones, Aisling's illness, David's long limbs, Joanie Flynn's voice. Gone, all turned elemental. While the truest source was the only material fragment that the Golem never had: Judith Conyngham, blown to pieces on a pretty Monaghan street one glorious summer evening. Gone, Elaine, gone. Your hair the grass and your face the stones and your voice the wind and the sea and the swoosh of the lighthouse beam and the tinkling of the ghostly bearers of the Binion Light and the sad murmurs of unblessed babies and poor dead Black Protestant children, and the comforting crackle of the BBC in Granny Bell's sitting room and the shimmering, quivering hum of the Border stretching around this quiet land.

◦⋇

David stares at his fry: rubbery egg, scorched bacon, blackened sausage. He thinks of Georgie sitting at this table, eating the same burnt offering every morning till he's grown.

He places his hands on the tea table. Feels the ironed linen scratching against his palms; under it, the wood, pushing back. Give me strength, he thinks again.

'You shouldn't let her annoy you, Davey.'

He glances up. Bridget's eyes are simmering with a sharp, resentful intelligence.

Eileen looks over. 'Who?'

'Mammy said something silly to Davey up in the room.'

His jaw begins to hurt. 'Did she now?' The compulsion is starting again. He wills himself to fight it.

'Have your tea, Davey,' says Eileen. 'Don't mind Bridgie. She's only....'

'Davey.' Maura puts her teaspoon down and reaches across the tablecloth to take his hand. 'We didn't ask you here to bicker. You know what we're going to say.'

He looks down at the table, at their joined hands. Pain starts up again in his chest. He's mine, he wants to say, but can't.

'We've had a good chat about it, Davey. We've been thinking about it a while. Ever since you went off to Germany and left him all on his own.'

'I.' His voice is hoarse, rusty. 'That was only two days. I came back early, ye know that—'

Maura waves it away. 'With Mammy gone, there's a spare room now. And we could do with a bit of help in the grocery on the weekends.'

'He's only nine.' He shouldn't be answering her. He should be coming out with his own arguments, the ones he's prepared. *He's doing great. We're fine. I don't know what you're all so worried about.*

'We can keep an eye on him—'

'He's not yours, Maura.'

Bridget smirks.

'What are you grinning at, Bridget?'

'Davey, sit down.'

The compulsion again, stronger. 'I have to phone the babysitter.'

'It would be better for him here, Davey.' Maura reaches for him again. 'None of this nonsense. You'd know who'd be minding him. He loves staying here—'

'He loves Mammy, not here. He loves Mammy because—'

Bridget chuckles.

'Are you looking for a puck, Bridget?'

'Davey, think of the boy—'

'I am, Maura. I need to phone my own house because I am thinking of him right now. Are you going to let me do that?'

'We'd love having him.' Eileen, interrupting. Eileen, who never interrupts. 'He'd be no bother. And it would be good for him to have....'

None of them say it.

A woman's love.

'He needs to get away from that little houseen of yours,' says Bridget. He tries to cut across but she keeps going, bulldozing through all the things David already knows. 'Too many memories there. He needs a decent school. A boys' school. Toughen him up. He needs to get out more. Do some sports—'

'It would give you freedom, Davey.' Maura's voice is loud. Bridget stops. 'The chance to travel.'

Hong Kong, he thinks, and feels a treacherous pang in his heart.

The sisters glance at each other.

'They haven't treated you well in that place, Davey,' says Maura.

Bridget sneers. 'Promoting that half-wit Niall Rourke and him with only a second-class degree.'

David hears an animal sound, coarse and brutish. Is that him, laughing?

'You deserve better,' says Eileen.

'She's right,' says Maura. 'You're wasted here. You need to spread your wings.'

'You never were the sticking kind, Davey.' Bridget leans forward. 'No matter where you were, you'd need to be out working. What if something bad happens to him because you're not there? You'd never forgive yourself—'

'Shut your mouth.' David is on his feet again. 'You're talking shite.'

'That little fella is trouble waiting to happen.'

445

'He's not. He's as good as gold—'

'Oh? So who's looking after him today?'

Maura rises. 'Bridget—'

Bridget laughs. 'The English girl? That hippy?'

He shouldn't speak now. He should stay calm.

'You know fucking nothing, Bridget.'

'You owe us.' She's shouting now. 'You owe Daddy. He always wanted a boy to take over, only you were too much of a girleen to—'

'Fuck off, Bridget.'

'Davey, sit down—'

'That Aisling, with her airs and graces. Fooling everyone. But she didn't fool me—'

'Fuck right off, you hoor.' Face up against his sister's. So close he can smell her breath.

Her eyes widen. 'Oh, I'm right, Davey, and you know it. You're not able for him. Farming him out to god knows who, even on a day like this. You're dying for the chance to be shot of him. You call yourself his—'

His fist rises.

Now Eileen's up too, trying to ward him off, and Maura's grabbing at him to hold him back, but his fist is moving, heading for Bridget's face, and he's lost, floundering in her eyes, their eyes, their collective gaze, a grey so dark it's almost black. The same eyes as his own; the same as Georgie's. His son is everywhere, he sees – in this house, in these people. In the slant of his sisters' cheekbones, the bulk of their shoulders, the photograph of his father, jeering him on the mantelpiece.

Shit.

He tries to stop, but his fist has much momentum behind it. Bridget's head is tilting back, trying to angle out of the trajectory. Not enough. His bones meet hers. A dull, wet sound.

Eileen starts screaming.

'Davey!' calls Maura.

But he's off, fleeing again, down the stairs.

'Look,' he had said, surprising himself. They were at the top of the steps that led to her flat. Georgie was slumped in the car. All around them, the smells and lights of Christmas; everybody inside, playing Happy Families.

Lotte turned. 'Sorry?'

A choice. He could have gone back to pretending again, like he'd been doing since that dinner, like he'd done all his life with Aisling. He could even have looked at her blankly or laughed again, made out she was the one making the fuss. Instead, he shook his head. 'Em.' He felt himself frowning, searching for speech. 'It's....' Waved his hands, whipping up the space between them. 'This. It's not just you or—'

Me.

'But.'

She stared at him. He had thought he wanted to say something about Aisling and her idea of *help,* about him having played into that without knowing – or, after Germany, thinking it was his own doing – about how everything, all that had been going on between him and Lotte was down to Ash, had been her plan for when she'd be gone. Her way of trying to put things right, or even saying sorry. He'd wanted to say that he'd realised that at the dinner table, that he'd been had, that they'd both been, and that was why he'd laughed, not at her, but at the whole bloody mess—

But: Christ, he thought instead. You don't need to know this. He stepped back.

Lotte's breath, sharp. A beat. Then: a little twist of a smile. 'You know, David. Parenthood isn't something you're given. You have to earn it.'

He couldn't help it. He flinched.

Her face changed. She started to speak.

'Mind yourself,' he said, fast, before she could get anything out. A nothing goodbye, but it was the best he could do. He didn't trust himself to touch her, not even to offer his hand. Just turned and went back down the steps to Georgie.

I don't have to do this, he had realised that night, and for a while, he had thought it would release something in him, akin to forgiveness. Of Aisling, for what she had done or might have done. Of himself, for not paying attention sooner or nipping things in the bud or doing more to keep them apart. For not fighting his so-called friend for her or just fighting, full stop. For spending those last six to eight months mired in the madness of suspicion and self-recrimination, instead of looking after her when she needed it most, all because—

At this point, the *because,* it happens again.

Pain. Chest. Torn. Cold. Eyes hurting. Can't see. Can't think.

Déjà vu. Time spools back. Concentration! Are you Ready! If so! Let's—

Rauchen verboten. No Smoking. phone box!*cold smell stale tobacco vomit shivering panic* earlier → corridor!*something separating missing left behind* earlier → courtroom!*balloon weightless floating* later →

greenbaizechair!

Them ≠ Us

Us = ?
∴ ?
∴ ?

And he is back again, in the courtroom, staring at the architect, Donnacha Ó Buachalla.

Staring in horror because something has been scratching at the walls of his awareness since he woke, some wordless doubt that linked itself to a train of memories that started playing in his mind after he left the house, and he has just realised what it might be. He stares, but all he can see is a formless whirl of energy, inhuman, unrecognisable, cycling around a blanked-out word.

Not Donnacha Ó Buachalla. All Donnacha Ó Buachalla is, is a man. Bigger than average, like David's own child, with wild hair and mutable, mythical features, but still only human. This whirling entity is David's own demon, spawned when he ruptured the most fundamental part of himself by disowning the person he loves most in the world. A demon he will never be able to afford to name, because if he did, well – what would he be left with?

Not *ours*.

What to do, Davey? What else to do, except stuff the cat back in the box. Put it down to exhaustion. Drink. Turn a blind eye. Don't question. Try to contain. Avoid returning to the shunt-room. Attempt, at least, to move on.

A gap – what happened? – he nearly tripped. Now he's back in himself, running down the stairs. Mouldy walls, creaking wood, smell of his father. Door, car, road, Dublin. Georgie. He reaches the bottom step. His chest is bursting. Not just the left side. Whole thing. Heart. Lungs. The asthma. Terrible pain. Some sound comes out of him. A whimper. He reaches for the door, and as he does, the old black Bakelite phone in the hallway starts to ring.

He skids, stops, lunges back. Grabs the receiver.

'David?'

∴

Iris out. An old camera trick.

The edges of the frame darken, tunnel in around the man in the hallway, eat him up. One last glint. A pearl bead. A spectacle lens. A doll's plastic eye.

Blackness.

'Ausland/Otherland'. *Regie/Director: Sabine Wiedemann.*
Datum/Date: 16/03/20— Ort/Location: Aberystwyth.
Befragte/Interview Subject: '*Anna Bauer*' **(Sitzung/Session 4)**.

Note:
Subject has withdrawn permission for usage of footage from this session.

Fade

Be not afeard: the isle is full of noises,
Sounds and sweet airs, that give delight, and hurt not.
Sometimes a thousand twangling instruments
Will hum about mine ears; and sometime voices,
That, if I then had waked after long sleep,
Will make me sleep again: and then, in dreaming,
The clouds methought would open and show riches
Ready to drop upon me; that, when I waked
I cried to dream again.

William Shakespeare, *The Tempest, 3.2.146*
(Caliban's speech)

(((((✹)))))

Visitors, our Tour is Ending.
Single file, please
Stay Calm
and
Follow the signs for the

☆

𝕰xit

heavy black bar

Lognote # 10

A first-floor flat above a busy, cordoned-off street in East-Central London. We draw your attention to the sitting room which resembles – its owner might have joked sardonically, were she there to joke – a bombsite. The room's two windows, both overlooking the street, have been shattered, although the external wall holding them remains intact. As if swept by a sonic hand, objects have been tumbled off shelves, photographs and certificates hefted from their hooks, broken glass and books scattered on the floor. The main door to the flat, at the rear of the building, is locked and undamaged. A pile of unread post indicates that the owner has been away for some time. There is an animal's feeding bowl in the kitchen, but no sign of the beast.

Of primary interest, on the floor of the front room, is an Object: a heavy black banker's box. On its front, a label, on which is drawn a skull and crossbones, underneath which is typed: '*Notes for a Bohemian Wunderkammer: for Owen to unravel, if he wishes. LB.*' The typeface on the label belongs to a slightly faulty 1969 Olivetti Valentine. The lowercase 'e' is faded and the lowercase 't' is marginally higher than the other characters.

Inside the box are books and reference material, including a rather rare hardback entitled *Schöne Bilder der Verlorenen Heimat* ('Lovely Pictures from a Lost Home', Adam Kraft Verlag: 1970). Also: jotters, notebooks, sketchpads, loose A4 sheets, drawings, photographs, photocopies and computer printouts. The material has not been arranged according to a clear organising principle. Most of it seems to have been gathered in the 1980s, though there is evidence of sporadic collection between 1989 and the date of discovery (March 20—). Although there are sketches and notes for 'Curiosities', intended, presumably, for display in the aforementioned '*Wunderkammer*', no actual objects or exhibits, besides the Box, are present. One might therefore reasonably conclude that 'LB's *Wunderkammer*, unlike its specialist subject, does not – and never will – exist.

Some notes propose the use of 'twinned histories/herstories' between Bohemia and, we imagine, other disputed territories. These are sketchy;

random connections rather than systematic comparisons. No single 'twin' has been selected for investigation and most of the suggestions for Irish/Northern Irish resonances have been crossed out, suggesting an almost personal discomfort with this territory: *Don't want to overload ??Not my history.* ~~*Owen's*~~ ~~*(partly)*~~ *? Not that interesting. Shd forget*, etc.

Of final interest is a sheet of A2 card, on which is sketched text for a 'placard'. This invites 'tour visitors' to take as a parting gift a copy of a quiz which they can use to test their knowledge of Bohemian history (which has been expanded, we assume, following their 'tour' of the *Wunderkammer*). Note the scribblings in pencil (H5): *Not sure if this will work. Will anything? Is there a point?* etc. In the Box, there is no evidence of the 'quiz' alluded to in the text. We do invite you, however, to step into the shoes of those virtual 'visitors' and imagine the sort of questions it might have posed.

01:15:34–10:29:59

There is a long poem Rilke wrote once, or maybe it's more accurate to say it's a letter, addressed to a friend, a fellow artist who had died. Have you left something behind? he asks her. Something that tortures itself in the need to have you back? I'll ask you now: do you believe that, David? That things hold something of the person who is gone, that they fret, like abandoned pets, for their vanished mistress or master? Is that why you hung on to it so long, that gift you've sent me, so you could hang onto something of her? What, then, does it mean to you, to pass it on? What do you need me to do with it? What does it need of me? Should I even be asking you this?

In January 1999, three weeks after we'd landed in Glasgow, we went on an outing to Edinburgh. Martin had never been there. We took the train; I insisted. I had no *Lust*, as they say in German, to deal with Edinburgh's stupid parking restrictions and Mar's stupider road rage.

There are two railway lines between Edinburgh and Glasgow. On the outward journey, we took the high road. Sweet little railway stations; dark forested hills behind them, covered in snow, very picturesque. I found my heart aching for Germany. Edinburgh was lovely: fairy-tale winding streets, salt and sauce on our chips – salt and sauce, said Martin; fuck me, east coast shite! – a dusty tour around the castle. Dungeons, Margaret's Chapel, tea rooms. I hadn't realised, I said, that you Scots were so militaristic. Aye, said Mar, flatter the Highlanders into thinking they're indispensable and they'll do anything for you.

Cannons. Fluting educated accents. The view from the Rock was magnificent.

On the way back we took the low road. Factories, slums. More factories. More slums. We stepped out from the station and I gagged at the weight of the air. They'd named the wrong town Auld Reekie. Nothing going anywhere, least of all Glasgow, a cauldron of smog and chip grease trapped in a rocky valley. The citadel of Britannia. The Prague of the north.

Martin laughed, grabbed my arm. 'Gowawn, ye softie. It's not that bad.'

I coughed. On arriving in Glasgow, I'd come down with a chest infection. Martin said it was grief at having to leave Berlin. Grief? I'd said. For God's sake, don't be dramatic. Sorry, he said. Why? I said. It's fine. *Fine*: your word, David.

Anyway, I said, it was time for a move. It's not your fault.

Not his fault? That was a lie and he knew it, even if I didn't. Sorry, he'd said again, his face still a mess of green and yellow from where the Serbs had beaten him up for trying to run out on his poker debts.

Months, it had been building. Worse than the last time we'd run. Knocks on our door late at night. The phone ringing and nobody speaking on the other end of the line, just breathing. Cars following us down the streets of the Old East, foreign reg plates, two shaven heads silhouetted against a windscreen. Next time, they'd warned him, they'd do more than break a couple of teeth. They'd take his whole fucking face.

Glasgow was our holding chamber, our safe haven where we'd wait for the storm to pass – fucksake, said Mar, it was only a few thousand marks, it wasn't a fortune or anything – and figure out where to go next. An English woman I'd worked with in Lausanne was setting up a post-production company in Brighton; she needed a partner, someone who could drum up business, help manage things as well as cut. On paper it looked interesting; a change of direction. I had good people skills, the English woman had said. Why not take a leap of faith?

Why not? I said to Mar.

He'd shrugged.

What? I asked, irritated.

I thought if you wanted a change, you'd be thinking of doing something a bit more— He hesitated.

What?

Creative.

Creative? I'd said. For the last year we'd lived in Berlin, he'd been at me to do something different. Go to art college, learn to draw properly, make my own movies. The thought of it exhausted me, but I was done explaining that I was fine with the work I did; more than fine, that sometimes putting other people's stories together could be the most creative thing in the world, that storytellers need editors and it's important to know what side of the line you stand on – so I gave him the pat answer instead: How can I be creative with your debts to sort out?

He flushed.

For a month, we'd stalled. Mar pacing the same narrow floors he'd paced as a teenager, me lying in the Super-Ser-heated bedroom, coughing, and between us, Mar's mother Janet, anxious, small and dishevelled. Her flat was above the bookie's on Dumbarton Road, a stone's throw from the Partick Tavern where the Rangers fans congregated, another stone's throw from the Dolphin. On nights Celtic won, you could hear the Blue-Noses roaring to the tune of a samba: *Let's all do the Dolphin, let's all do the Dolphin!* Martin, for all his apology, his talk of *grief*, loved being back. Because despite his plans for moving on, going somewhere that would accept us as we were, Glasgow was *home*. He loved the violence humming under the surface, the looming architecture, the river, pretty Kelvin Grove park, the museum with its replica of the mysterious Ghost Shirt, the hills, the sausage rolls from Greggs. The lumpen betting shops, the scratchcards, the chips. The chips, the chips. But I was suffocating, stuck in the rickety bed with its fading brass-effect bedposts, covered in fleas. The fleabites on my skin were round, pink and raised and made me think of Hogarthian illnesses. French pox. Typhoid. Scrofola. All thanks to his mother's dog. Small, a terrier, just like the one in the whisky ads. Blind in one eye, a stump of a tail from where another, bigger dog had mauled him. A tumour in his arse.

He'll have to go, said Janet. Aye. But not just yet. Janet, matchgirl-thin, loose strands of sandy hair floating around her face, peering around the edge of the bedroom door. Alright there, hen? Can I get ye anything?

Hen, she called me, though I was still in drag then, still pretending to be a boy.

cough cough

No, thanks, Janet.

Stink of chip fat pouring out of the chippers, but not just there. Pouring out of the supermarkets, the art galleries, the cinemas.

Jesus! I said, the first time I saw the deep-fried Mars Bars on a menu.

Well, it's a lot better than being stuck up Marianne Faithfull's arse, said the chippy.

No argument there.

Anything, hen? said Janet, worried. A boiled egg? Maybe some chips? Would ye like that? I have the fat ready.

No.
cough cough
Grief?
I'm fine. Really.

Och, no, you're not. Would ye like some Christmas cake? I've got loads left. I made it myself. The icing's lovely. Marzipan. I can cut you a slab.

No, thanks. My head throbbing, thinking of deep-fried Christmas cake; melting, oil-drenched marzipan.

On the day after we'd visited Edinburgh, Mar made us supper. Nothing fried: poached salmon and steamed potatoes with broccoli and a cream sauce. I couldn't smell Janet's chip-fat but I could feel it everywhere, clogging up the atmosphere, coating everything, even us, with a film of grease. Janet had put a fresh oilcloth on the kitchen table. It was a prettyish pattern, flowers or something, except the colour separations had been done on the cheap, so the magenta and cyan overlapped, criss-crossing and pulling away from each other at weird places, reminding me of the *Great! Exciting! New! 3D!* comic books that boy, whatshisname, William Robinson, used to bring into class. Martin had laid the table properly and bought some wine, but the salt and pepper were in cardboard tubes and Janet insisted on putting out ketchup for her tatties. At that, I looked at Martin, but he wasn't sneering, or embarrassed, and I think it was right then, in spite of my better instincts, that I gave him my heart. The ketchup bottle was spotless, no red scum around the lid. The mismatched cutlery and the cheap condiments reminded me of home – Marino, I mean – after Aisling, when you and I had done our damnedest to mind our little fort on our own, but the oilcloth and the cleanness of the ketchup bottle were from an entirely different place.

Scout! That was the dog's name. Because, said Janet, I always thought my wee boy would be in the Scouts. But he never made it.

My aunties made me join the Scouts, I nearly said, but stopped.

Mar grinned. Boy Scouts, he said. That shower of jessies? Ye must be joking.

Janet tutted, then glanced at me and smiled. Her face so sweet in that instant, all the dishevelled worry gone.

You're good for him, hen.

Me in my new image: my sharp haircut, my TV-executive trendy-casual clothes. But she *saw*.

You know what you do when you're around her, I told him that night. I shouldn't have said anything, but the Super-Ser and chip fumes had drained my mind of oxygen. Everything felt very far away, and at the same time, too close. I was whispering in his ear. I had to whisper because I was afraid Janet would hear. The whisper tickled my throat, made me worry I would start coughing again. The curl of his body, cupped in mine, tensed.

No, he said. Meaning, don't tell me.

You…. I hesitated. You play. It's like you put on another face for her. The good boy. Mischievious. But still good.

He shifted away, leaving a damp gap between my belly and his back. Only an inch but, as the man says, in the bed those inches count.

That's a laugh, he said.

What?

Geo, enough for now, okay? I need some sleep.

No. What?

I…. He stopped, struggled. D'you not think I'm good?

What?

D'you not think I'm a good person then, Geo? Just because I've a, you know, just because I'm weak sometimes?

No, I didn't mean that. I meant—

What is it, then? Are you the only one who's allowed to be good all the time?

Christ. I'm not—

Geo the Sensible One. Geo the Ever-Practical. Geo the one who's always right—

I'm not—

Not like that?

I'm not some fucking— I couldn't find the word. I stopped, started. *Saint.* If you only knew—

Knew what? Your dark side, Geo? Don't make me angry, you wouldn't like me if I'm angry?

Oh, fuck off.

Geo. His voice changed. Look, I'm sorry. I just want—

No. Forget it. And I'd turned from him, given him my back, drawing up my legs and any hint of weakness away.

The chance of a male – or for the sake of exactitude, let's say, a person born with XY chromosones and a penis and testicles – contracting breast cancer is 1 per cent. Low, but if you take genetic mutation into account, possible. Was this the cost of heredity? I'd asked myself. The price of being seen as my mother's daughter? I had laughed at first, those horrible days of my first scare, before Breast Clinic Visit Number One, eighteen months ago. It's funny, isn't it? I'd said to Martin. Ironic. A tragic irony. But he wasn't laughing. Then I'd got angry, because it was typical, wasn't it? A tranny-tale if ever there was one, the he-she punished by her own body, her desire to be what she's not supposed to be. Just like the Little Mermaid; the price of getting those feet everlasting agony any time she took a step.

Fuck you, Hans Christian Andersen, I'd shouted. Fuck you to the hills, you Swedish cunt.

Danish, said Martin. Geo, we need to talk.

We hadn't, though. We'd just fought and retreated and frozen each other out.

You want this, I'd shouted. You want me to get cancer. Because then I'll have to stop taking the hormones, and my tits, whatever's left of them, will disappear and my stubble will grow back and my voice will drop again and I'll turn back into a fucking man—

Don't be thick, Geo. You got the laser for the stubble—

Jesus—

Stop it. You know what I mean. It's not any of that makes you who you are—

You want me to get sick like my father wanted my mother to die because she was fucking that stupid architect—

Geo, you silly bitch, stop that stupid tidying up and listen to me—

You calling me a bitch? Well, hurrah.

D'you want a slap?

Don't do that bullshit with me, Mar—

All I'm saying is if you think that's what I want then you're more stupid than—

Stupid? Me? When you're the one pissing our savings away, sorry, my fucking savings, on your poxy internet poker—

Geo, that's unfair. I haven't—

Haven't what? Done that since I caught you? Wow, how big of you. Or is that just classic addict behaviour? No, no, of course not. I'm sure you don't have any other tricks up your—

Fucksake, Geo. Don't—

Don't you—

And on. And on. Me zooming around our little house, our pathetic, inadequate little house in Inchicore, the Isle of the Snout, opening cupboards, cleaning presses, clearing out crap and dumping it in sacks, because when you're in shock, sometimes tidying up and clearing stuff out is the best way to manage things. Then they stuck a fine needle in me and liquid came out and it turned out to be a cyst, nothing more.

Quite normal, said the nice ladies at the clinic. Given your age and your medication history. Good, though, that you got it checked out. These things can play on your mind.

But by then, the damage had been done. We'd had our last fight the night before, on our way over to Sonia's for what was supposed to have been a reassuring supper. I'd picked Mar up from his new job; deep-frying chips and chicken wings in a pub near the Docklands, just around the corner from the fancy seafood place where he'd been on his way to making sous chef except the recession came along and jack-booted that dream to a pulp. It had been a Thursday. The traffic on the quays had been brutal, the parking spaces jammed. The closest I could get was the funeral parlour near the Five Lamps, not far from the North Star. I was late, so I texted him, and waited. *cu in 5*, he texted back. When he finally arrived, forty-five minutes later, he was coming from the wrong direction, the bookies on North Strand. By the time we reached Connolly Station we were screaming at each other again.

That's it, I'd shouted, fuck you, Martin Canney, fuck right off and rot in fucking hell.

I can't remember who forced the door open, who slammed it shut. What I remember is Mar, dwindling to a speck of nothing in my rearview mirror as I pulled away from the kerb and left him outside the Russians' or Poles' or whoever-they-were's amusement arcade, with their private rooms upstairs for those who wanted something a little riskier and no longer had access to their so-called loved ones' credit cards.

Traffic had been worse than brutal: shit. I'd gone through town and got caught in gridlock. At the bridge of the Grand Canal, near Northumberland Road, my mobile began to ring. I hadn't even looked at it to check if it was him. I was too angry. I'd just buzzed down my windscreen and lobbed the fucking thing, caller and all, into the canal. Out of my life, Mar.

That night I stayed in Sonia's; we drank too much and bitched about how shit love is, especially when it runs out, and I cried in her arms on her white leather sofa. By the time I got home the next afternoon, after the tests in the Clinic, Mar had cleared out, taking his stuff with him. But if he'd been looking for an invisible exit, he'd failed drastically. For months afterwards, I kept finding traces of him: a rolled-up T-shirt in an empty drawer, cheffing knifes under the sink, his underwear in the laundry basket, his shaving foam on a bathroom shelf. His smell on my pillow; his hairs in my brush.

Maybe you thought you were sparing me that when you swept me away to Clonmel and disappeared out of my life. No traces of you; no traces of Aisling. Just me, and my three ageing aunts. The only smell of what was gone my crazy Granny's perfume in the room where I slept. Sweet and rotting; like honey and mushrooms.

He had left a note on the kitchen worktop. *Hope you're okay.* Then, crossed out, but badly, so I could still see the false-start stammers of his good intentions. *Please ring, please txt, Let me know if you'r* Followed by a standard Dear Jane. *Sorry, Georgia. Can't do this anymore.* That was what infuriated me most; that pathetic *Sorry.* From him, of all people. As for *Georgia,* that was the thing that really saddened me, though it took me a long time to realise that was what I was feeling.

What were you going to say? he'd asked, the night I'd turned away from him in Glasgow.

I stayed silent.

You said. He spoke carefully, like he was talking to a child. You said if I only knew…. Knew what, Geo?

I had an imaginary friend once, I said, my back still to him. She lived in a lane and her name was Elaine. It felt weird to hear her name aloud. I hadn't intended to speak. It just came out, and then it kept coming.

It was that time I don't remember so well, when my mum was sick, but I remember her. I thought she was real, for ages, and then I thought she was a messenger, or something, come to help me fix this terrible thing I thought I'd done. Because I'd got angry with someone and wanted to punish them. But now I don't know….

I stopped, because it was happening again; those years blurring, shifting out of focus into parallax. One version that I could see, clearly, as if recording it with a camera; the other, the feeling part, blank.

Does it matter? said Mar.

I turned. He was lying on his side, propped up on one elbow. What?

What she was, or why you made her up? If you wanted to go back over it with a therapist or something—

Ugh.

I know. He took my hand. All I'm saying is I'm sure you could piece it together. But is she relevant anymore? I mean, she's not here, is she?

No. I brought her back.

As I said it, I felt that moment again; not just saw it, but *felt* it. That moment where I dropped a childhood friend's toy into the sea and stood looking out over grey water, and what I'd felt was *whole*. An hour later I would arrive in my grandparents' and all hell would break loose. My sick grandmother moaning in the upstairs room, my big, capable doctor grandfather shrunken and terrified, trying not to think of the B-Special boys he'd treated for chicken pox and measles roaming Ameracam Lane, looking for Fenians, big or small, to take out their own pain on, while you raged at the other end of the phone: Where did you go, Georgie? Where the hell did you go? Cursing Lotte for being irresponsible; and yourself, for being so stupid to trust someone so bloody, bloody useless. Though by then the rage was dissipating and you just sounded emptied-out. Defeated. I never understood why you got so upset at Lotte. She wasn't in our lives anymore, so it was my fault, for running away, wasn't it? Or yours, I later thought, for not being there to stop me.

Martin touched my face. So that's all gone. Isn't the only thing that matters what you do now, Geo?

I stared at him, thinking but that's exactly what *I'd* thought. Then he told me about the guy in *his* lane, the one at the back of his tower block in Govan, the guy who'd got *at* him when he was nine, and he was opening up, for the first time since we'd met, about his gambling, the pull it had on his soul, how he would do anything to get free of it, how, with me, for the first time in his life, he felt he could. And I was opening up about everything too, my fear that if I talked to a therapist I'd let slip about Elaine and then they'd think I was crazy and never diagnose me with Gender Identity Disorder, and I'd never get reassigned, but stay locked inside some stupid psychosis label like a piece of unwanted baggage. Trans rule number one: never, for your own sake, be seen as sad, bad or, worst of all, mad. And he talked about his father that he'd never known and the hole that absence had left in his mother's heart. And I found myself talking about you, and Aisling, for the first time properly, feelings and memories fizzing up in me, coming into sudden clarity, then fading again, like I was a radio getting tuned. And he— And I—

And both of us wound around each other, that night in Glasgow after Edinburgh, after he'd refused to take my turned back for an answer, our heads full of the stink of chip fat, our mouths full of marzipan, our bodies full of each other.

The next morning he'd told me that whatever I needed to do, however I needed to change, he would support me in it, stay the distance. You know, he said, squeezing my hand, Brighton's a good place. For us, for you, Geo, for what you want to be; after Berlin, it's the best in the world.

I laid Martin's coat on the edge of the balcony. It jutted like an opened accordion, too bulky to drape properly. I took out one of Jammy Noel's fags, lit it and inhaled. Across the green-lit road, beyond the train tracks and the sea wall, I could see out onto the strand up to the line where it grew dark, disappearing into blackness.

I lifted my palms to my face and breathed in the smell of almonds; then I placed them on Martin's coat. Under my touch, the sweaty, familiar leather seemed to shiver, an animal clinging for its life to balance. Had I ever dumped it, like I'd once dumped a doll's head, wishing to be shot of Martin's soul and all the pain I associated with him? Or had I just thought I had, and unconsciously, without realising, bundled it into a bag and shoved it up into our attic, thinking, That's done now, that's over—

but I'll keep a bit of him here, just in case I need him again

I dipped my face in its folds, searching for his smell. It had disappeared, but for a moment I had a sense of a dark shape standing behind me; something enormous, fierce and undeniably male. Armour-plated and black as night. Was it accusing me?

Things are only things, I told it. They're not repositories for souls, or ghosts, or people. And no thing, no matter how loved or despised, will bring back a person who's gone. Of course, you can wish someone ill, and curse them to hell, and you shouldn't do that, but if something bad happens to them, well, how on earth could that be the fault of a *thing*?

Light flickered: the TV, still fighting with itself over the story of the dead man in the canal.

I pushed. Exhaustion fell, claiming me.

I'd love to be able to tell you that I dreamt that night: of marvellous things, the sky opening, and gold and precious stones falling on me, and sweet music that would break your heart to hear it, but I can't remember dreaming anything. All I remember is being woken up by the siren on my smartphone, howling like a banshee on Sonia's bedside table. Though it took me a while to realise that was what it was, because as far as I knew, I had lost my phone in the wilds of Wicklow.

I pulled myself up and turned it off. The movement hurt. The phone's casing was gritty with sand. Weird, I thought. Even weirder was the fact that on the carpet, clearly visible in the golden morning light, I could see the marks of damp, sandy footprints, leading from the open bedroom door to Sonia's bed. I swung my feet out onto the floor and looked at them. Little strands of seaweed and sand sprinkles had gathered between my toes. I had a cut on my ankle bone; bits of seashell under my toenails. Oh, I thought. I'm a sleepwalker, and the thought landed with a funny, quiet weight.

3 New Text Messages, said my phone. 6 Missed Calls.

sight ↔ thought ↔ action

Mar? … *u ok geo been thinking abt u pls get in touch am there 4 u &* … Not a chance.

Instead, two calls from Sonia, checking up on me. Three from Brid; some garbled messages saying their in-house guy was going to do the Troubles series after all, very sorry about that Georgia, hope we can work again sometime blah blah blah. And one from Sabine Wiedemann, that TV director I'd worked with in Berlin. Sounding a little panicked, thanking me for the kind invitation to stay with her – when had I sent that? – but something urgent had come up, with the old lady she was interviewing in Wales, a family crisis, someone had been hurt or died or something in that terrible attack on London, and she'd have to postpone. She'd be in touch again once everything settled down.

Down my sternum, a dagger of dull red. The pain still there – but familiar, almost, like an invisible hand pressing into me. On my left hipbone the other bruise had risen, purple and green. I touched it, flinched.

I put on my face first, taking care around the cuts. They stung, but not as much as I'd expected, and the bandage on my scalp had held overnight. A small blessing. Then I tidied up Sonia's place – because that's what I do sometimes when I'm stressed and don't want the telly on, not even with the sound off – and I combed the apartment for Martin's coat, just in case I'd picked that up too when I'd been sleepwalking on the beach, looking to reclaim my mobile. But it was gone. There wasn't a sound from next door. I imagined all the party-goers lying in heaps on the floor, twined around each other like corpses in a history painting.

I could have checked the spyhole in the door before leaving in case those creepy twins were still lurking, but I was sick to my soul of being afraid. Recklessness can lead to trouble but caution is a bitch; once you start to feed it, it's hard to let it go. The floor of the corridor was littered with red beads. Pomegranate seeds.

Do you remember that myth Lotte told us – at Hallowe'en, I think it was, after you came back early from that conference in Germany – how the king of

467

the underworld tricked Persephone into eating pomegranate seeds and that was why she had to spend six months of every year with him in Hades, the land of the dead?

I walked past them, didn't even think of picking them up.

Outside, it was glorious; fresh, not too cold. The sea was choppy and the sun was darting off the waves. Little silver knives. I thought of mermaids, ones with tails, not feet, and grey hair, happily frolicking underwater, and – believe it or not – my fingers itched to hold a crayon.

This next thing is odd and maybe I've put two and two together and made seven, but as I was walking up to the Breast Clinic, a flash of colour at the Bring Centre near the level crossing caught my eye. Someone had sprayed a mural on the wall. It wasn't very good and looked like a rush-job, but it showed a map of Ireland, caricatured to look like a pig, painted garish pink and flipped ninety degrees so it was on its knees. A man in a bowler hat and striped trousers was fucking the pig up its arse. In his right hand he was waving a fistful of dollars; his right eye was a euro mark; his left a sterling sign. It was impossible to make out what kind of expression was on the pig's face. The gates were locked and there was nobody in the security cabin. They must have climbed over the wall during the night and done it then.

Rad & T.C. was their tag, inside a big anarchy A.

I remembered the twins again, from the night before; their bag clunking with canisters. A strange chemical smell. Rad. Wasn't that what he'd called his sister? As I say, I could be making seven. But something in me likes the sound of that: two eggs, separated at birth, whisked together again. It reminds me of a photograph I once saw, of babies on a picnic rug, though – this is odd, not like me at all – for the life of me, I can't remember where I saw it.

The news stand in the hospital foyer was full of headlines. They had begun to find bodies in the Underground; some names, many numbers. I stared at the names of the Tube stop and the street, but they were empty. There was lots about the security crackdown in Britain and the global response. The Chinese were getting in on the act now. It was unclear whether that was because they'd found out who was responsible, or because they hadn't. It was all very confused; some of the papers said the bombers were students, nationals from a former Soviet state; others said they were homegrown Jihadis. Eoin the Marxist, bless him, was still arguing for understanding. I bought an *Irish Times*, more for the sake of it than anything else. The canal story was on page 5. They'd released some information. The man had been homeless, like the young Dub on the arts show had said. Polish, in his thirties, known in most of the hostels. He'd been missing for a week. The police were still trying to identify how he'd died. Suspicious causes not ruled out. There was no mention of his face, or rats eating it. As for the mystery YouTuber, the cops had confirmed they'd found the person responsible but, due to their age, couldn't release details. A vagrant and a child, then, not Serbian thugs teaching a Glaswegian gambler with bad debts a harsh lesson. I felt relieved all over again, like I'd felt the night before when I'd seen the tiger on the man's back and realised it wasn't Mar, then stupid for having even thought that, then guilty for feeling relieved, then angry for just about everything. That familiar vicious circle. Speculation was rife about the YouTuber's motivations. In the Hooligan corner, arguments about how sick, desensitised and attention-seeking the youth of today had become. In another, clamourings of how this should be read as a statement, an attempt to push the reality of death into the faces of a society that itself was sick and desensitised. I remembered the beauty in the way the footage had been shot, the almost excruciating slowness of the camera movements. What patience had it taken, I wondered, to crouch there and simply watch a dead man be dead, in the bitter cold of a March dawn?

I sat in the waiting room and did nothing.

Thoughts came and went in my mind.

I thought of the Invader, the ginger cat waiting for me at home, and wondered if he'd still be waiting when I got back, and if he was, would I try giving him a proper name? Like Brad. Or Rick. Something manly.

Then I thought about you and the package you'd sent.

Valuable. A thought struck me, followed immediately by a *No. He wouldn't....*

Torque is a word with two meanings; one means a necklace and *the other means a force, pet, that makes things twist and turn and sometimes even change their shape. Dad uses that in his job; he'll explain it better than me, darling.*

Would you?

The morning after the court case, she came into my bedroom and woke me. Daddy's not well, she said. He was a wee bit silly last night. But you and me are going to make pancakes. We crept down the stairs so as not to wake you and headed straight for the kitchen, so we didn't notice the lounge door was closed. She sniffed – I remember that – then shrugged it off, puzzled. When she saw the package on the table, her face changed. Oh my God, she said. She took out the torque and held it up to her face. It was magical, what the colours of the metals and the stones did to her. Her eyes, her skin, the threads of silver and red-gold in her hair. Making her more real, somehow, but not too. A goddess, I'd thought. She heard something at the door, and turned, her face flooding with light. Relief; almost triumph. Davey, this is—

Beautiful, she was going to say.

She stopped. Then I saw him. I blanked. I remember staring at the grains of sugar in the bowl in front of me and starting to count them because I was terrified, for a reason I'd pushed to some sleeping, inaccessible part of my mind, that he was going to tell you both I'd done something very wrong and then you'd both leave me because you wouldn't love me anymore.

Well, he said. This beats the North Star, *bean an tí*.

I had a vague impression of her reaching out, a formal handshake. I'm Aisling, David's wife. Her voice very clear. And *this* – a touch on my shoulder – is our wee baby. Georgie.

Ah, he said. Understood. Then you were crawling down the stairs, pinched and cold and sick, and she began making a fuss of how well you'd looked after her while she was ill and what a thoughtful, beautiful gift it was, and all that.

Daithí is a diamond, he said.

You started laughing. An odd, hollow sound. You fucking panic, Donnacha. I glanced up. Beautiful, she said again, trying to draw your attention, but you hardly looked at her, and when you did, there was something so skittering and painful in your eyes I knew you couldn't see the magic your gift was doing to her.

She only wore it once. It stayed in the drawer during the months of her first recovery, the December parties, the spring evenings when he would come by to pick you up for a jar, those Sundays when he'd drop in for lunch and stay for dinner, those one two three weekday afternoons when he called and you weren't home yet, and he'd angle for a cup of tea, and I'd try to get out of the way as soon as possible, and that last time, in the lounge, just before Jan came over, when I saw them reflected in the mirror over the fireplace, he putting his hand on her hip, and she saying, No, Denis, please no, it's not right, her face bright with a terrible guilt – before I ran out the front door. Washing her hair afterwards, trying to get rid of the smell of his aftershave, though it still clung to our downstairs rooms, only you, God knows why, didn't notice. Your gift stayed unworn during the second scare too, when she lost both her breasts, and the chemo and radiation, right through the point we thought she was going to get better. The evening after she interviewed Lotte, she took it out of its box and put it on. You had come in late from work, exhausted, brittle, stretched so thin you were almost flat. She came up behind you and put her arms around your neck. You stiffened first, then let her in. You almost relaxed. You started speaking, but all I could hear was her, whispering. Lovely, Davey. Lovely.

She had put a scarf around her head to hide how her hair was growing out and somehow that and the torque worked well together, though they shouldn't have. She looked beautiful, you see, but ridiculous too, like a sad, skinny clown. No longer a goddess, but unbearably special. Later, when Lotte showed me that famous bust of Nefertiti, I saw Aisling. The thing I remember most is how it snaked around her throat, drawing attention away from her ravaged chest, highlighting the clean curve of her new bones.

I'm holding it now. She was right. It is lovely.

Glamour, said Lotte once. From the old English. Meaning: magic, a spell. Mermaids, monsters, Amazons. Here be Caliban.

'Now, Ms Madden?'

Thanks, I said, giving the nurse my brightest, most professional smile as I walked towards the obvious, my own torture chamber waiting for me.

Helen says in her letter that your sight is almost completely gone; that explains the handwriting. I was sad to hear that. I always liked your drawings. And a little frustrated, I admit, picturing you obstinately forming characters with a Rapidograph you might have got as a Christmas present a long time ago, waving off her help as you traced my name on the birthday card – thanks for the *Georgia* – through touch alone. I wonder what it will be like for you, listening to this. Whether I will sound like you expected, or anything you know. Will you hear yourself in me? Or Aisling? I wonder if you'll listen to everything, or fast-forward through the things that make you uncomfortable.

I don't think there's another story I could have told you. The past, of course, our last years together; maybe you'll think I should have gone back, tried to rediscover that time, *feel* how it was for you as well as me. For Mum, even. Edit it into an arc that makes sense. Ta-dah. But a lot of that is still a blur – emotionally, I mean. There was only so much I could unpack with Martin before things between us reached the point of no return. I'm still just a new radio, learning to tune myself in.

You'll guess by now. Inconclusive tests. Biopsy. A phone call, any minute, with the news. I'm not going to go into what that's been like, the last few days: waiting, not knowing. You can make your own mind up about that. Maybe there'll be times when you'll hear something in my voice that gives me away. I think knowing an outcome would have made this, talking to you, impossible. You know: the awful gush of relief, the sickly ooze of grief, they can get in the way. Whereas a limbo, that inbetweeny place where Schrödinger's cat is both alive and dead— Well.

Unforgiving, Martin once called me. I don't know. Blame and recrimination, recrimination and blame. Do I blame you for our separation? Do you still blame Lotte, for God knows what reason? Do I still blame myself? I might as well ask, who am I still angriest at, saddest at, me or Mar, for how things worked out. Does it matter? Or does all that matter what we're going to do next?

So, to this valuable thing, your gift. After much deliberation, I accept. I don't promise to wear it – that might be one jinx too far – but you can trust me to look after it.

Bis der nächste, as they say in Germany. Till the next, David.

'Ausland/Otherland'. *Regie/Director: Sabine Wiedemann.*

Datum/Date: 17/03/20– Ort/Location: Aberystwyth.

Befragte/Interview Subject: '*Anna Bauer*' (**Sitzung/Session 5**).

To start again, what it must take? Well, I suppose. That is the good question.

...

It was as this. With the Captain I left Bristol and went to Morecambe and then after I did the split, you know, divorce, from him, I left that place, and came to here. Aberystwyth. Not this home, but the other hotel, guesthouse, yes, on the prom? *Moranned*, it was called. I had money from the Captain, guilt-money, I make a joke sometimes, so....

To leave it? Bristol. It was just another crossing, a leaving, like all them I have talked about. Friends and others ask me, Anna, how did you feel to leave this place and that place and the other? And the truth is, I don't know. For others maybe, it is strange to leave a home and to leave another home and another.... But for me, there is only one home to leave, the first. Everything else is replacing it, *ersatz*, like instant coffee. There are so many journeys it is hard to remember. I think sometimes, as I remember, I am making like a jigsaw puzzle. Olivia, Doctor Brooks, spoke often of old stories. She told the children stories at bedtime and they listened. It was beautiful to see. I could not tell so many. My English was not so good – I still speak it with an accent, as you hear – and they did not want to hear stories in German because of the children in school, mocking them, you know. But this story Doctor Brooks told was of queen who is a twin and the children loved that – and so did I because I had a twin too, Peter, who died in the East, have I told you of him? – and the brother twin dies, and the queen is, how do you say, wild with sadness, because some wicked monster has cut the brother into pieces. And the queen must find all the pieces before the cock crows and mend them together again and then he will live.

And see now, talking to you, remembering this, because as you know, I don't have the chance to speak these stories, nobody is interested now, the names of the towns are changed, the Flight is forgotten, only some crazies on the, you know, Internet who want money from the Czechs. And – I almost forget – Lotte, for a while, though she thought I didn't know, but she was curious, yes, when her little boy, the Owen, was growing, that's natural, yes?, to gather the family history. At one time I thought, maybe she will make something of that, Lotte, it would be a lifework, perhaps, with meaning? Though I had fear also of what people might think, with the new Nazis and so forth. But now she is not so curious anymore, and apart of her, there is nobody. So it is strange, *komisch, gel?*, to remake them, the stories, to remember. And to tell the truth, some of what I say is so long ago I don't know if it is true anymore. But in the last days, as we have talked, I have started to fill with a sense that I am doing such a thing as the queen did, putting the pieces together again so the other one, the twin, will live. Absurd. It's like the English, the English I speak, it has started to slide from me, so I can hear me speaking, but more German is being said than English, as if I am making together again the pieces I was as a young girl. All the tone and the music in my speaking is returning to what I had at the beginning. And still the Czech words are hard in my mouth.

Excuse me? *Welcher? Also, meinst Du—*

Sorry? Again? Who am I putting together again?

. . .

Maybe me, my self. Or perhaps an other. Peter, my brother who died in the East, from the Russians, or Andreas, Andrew my son who died in that stupid action, or maybe it is something else, not a person. Just some thing that can live in the mind because I put the pieces together. Like Humpty Dumpty, who is not a real person, just an egg the soldiers have broke. Oh. Yes. Excuse me. It was falling off the wall that was when he broke and the soldiers tried to fix. But I always asked, when the twins were little, what made Humpty fall first? Andrew said, the soldiers, shooting. But Lotte said, maybe he wanted to jump. It made fun – you know, we laughed – to hear their answers. Children are wise.

But, *Du*, listen, you see, this jigsaw picture that is in my head. I – after we spoke yesterday and I would not tell of the raping – because you have many other women telling their story, another raping is, you know, of what use is that? And you will honour my request, *gel*? Not to show me saying that I will not speak, or to cut out a picture of me silent from that day, because that is just the same as to show me crying and telling a story – but after that, I thought, is there one piece in the jigsaw that is bigger, that is better, that is... Special? That will work a form of hex and glue all together. Make Humpty an egg again. Is there one story of leaving that is more in the centre than the others? I thought it was leaving the village, with the little van and the horse, but perhaps this is wrong. Perhaps the first leaving was when the Revolutionary Guard, the Czechs, the partisans, came and my mother shouted at me, run in the barn, Anna, and hide there because they're taking women. And I was so, confused, because before that she said it was the Red Guard who were monsters. The Czechs, she said, would be kinder.

Na. If you want to find the start, perhaps it is there.

But that is maybe only as children think, to believe that one piece of the jigsaw is the more important than the others. In truth, you need every little stick. If you lose one, no matter where, then all the game is, you know....

Yes. Spoiled.

In some way, the most exciting leaving was of Bristol. That was a motor car. I had made the wedding dress of grey silk, because of the twins, I would not pretend I was a virgin, and the Captain bought a beautiful corsage and I pinned it to my front. Andrew was in the boarding school. Olivia, the Doctor Brooks, gave him money for that. But Lotte came with us. That was good at the start but not so much later. Lotte did not like the Captain and he was, *tja*, he as they say, outlived his use to us....

You know—

Excuse me? Which came first—

Ah. So. Lotte is the younger by two minutes only. She came fast after his heels.

The Doctor? No. She wrote, many times, but I was very busy, and my English still not so good on paper and there was a guesthouse to manage, and so on. And then she died and, yes, that was as it was. She was very kind to us, to the children. She left them both money. So they could buy the flat in London, near the Tube stop, Farringdon, where Lotte and the dear boy, the Owen, my grandchild, lived for a while. They stay there still if one or the other visits England. That was kind of the Doctor, to give a living-place. Sometimes I am sad I did not write or visit, because she was good to me, the Doctor, and to the children, and she was our home for many years, very kind, there was a sort of love there. But that is how it goes. I—

No. No. Nothing.

...

You know—

My name? Oh, the nickname. Yes. You will laugh. It was Lotte's mistake. From Shakespeare, Doctor Brooks helped them read the plays. Lotte intended Viola from *The Twelfth Night*, who has a twin brother and a friend named Olivia, but she mistook it. Julia is in a second play; she dresses as a boy too, but she has no twin. I wanted to tell Lotte she was wrong, because I remembered the stories, but Olivia said, No, Lotte, she's a funny one, she does not like to be told she is wrong. And it was comical, yes, how Lotte understood I had a twin too, a brother, their uncle, though I never told them of Peter. I told Lotte only later, when she gave birth to her own twins and the little girl, you know, was dead, because Owen – so strong, yes? – had taken up all the room.

I had no photographs of Peter, you see. All they knew as children was Mutti lost everyone in the war and had her heart broke and did not talk about these things. It was an easier thing to say. Many of the girls, in Rochdale, they talked always of their home and their families and then they married POWs, Ukraine, Germans, Lithuanian. It was not like that for me. I talked to Lotte after she had the twins, spoke her some stories, though only a little. And now she is so rarely in England, always travelling, we are not so close as I would like.

Yes, this photograph, of the wedding, of us in the car, it is Lotte who made that. Can you believe? Twelve years old. That is a professional photograph. She was always very skilled at this work. Andrew had the ideas, but Lotte was always stronger at the making. Do you, I mean, is this good for the television? For the story you are telling?

Ah. To make me comfortable. I see.

How do I feel about what he done? You mean, Andrew? What do I think? Do I think he was a fool? Is this important for the story? Is your story not about the Nazi-time and the flight and the rapings and what came later? What do you search, a so... a linking, between one time and the next? You know, as I said before, many times, I think, and perhaps it is boring for your television programme, the important thing is to be kind. What Andrew done was perhaps a kind thought, to change things. But it led to a very stupid action. Because, in the end, that newspaper office, it still works, it still makes the newspapers. Nothing changes.

You know, and this is what I want to say. Sometimes I think, is there something missing in the person's, so you say, essence of them self, that makes them ready to do such a thing, a violent thing such as Andrew done? And I wonder, if that is a thing you carry from the mother, you drink up in the womb, that essence that is not there. Was that of me, was that missing also from me, because of what happened after the War, when the first lot came, during the wild flight? Remember, as we spoke yesterday, the first time, and I told you of how it was, leaving, how I could not reach into my soul to, um, sense as I felt then, and you wanted to ask was it because of what happened in the wild time? *Na.* I thought much about that last night. And, you know, I think sometimes, if I had the courage to do as my son, to strap the explosive around my waist when the partisans were coming, and do them in before it, *und ich auch*, and even the little horse that I loved and the animals in the barn, then maybe my children would not have—

But that is *Quatsch*. One must live. And what can I say? Sorry? Sorry, sorry? Sorry that I survive?

The only thing I am sorry of is I did not see faster what was happening to my girl. With the Captain. Because if I done that, if I knew that, I swear to *Gott*....

...

Ach, so.

What I really want to say is, when I left Bristol, in the motor car, with the Captain, I thought, this is it. This is my life. This is the fresh start. Now I will really live, a proper lady with a husband and family and a home of my own. In some way it was only the start of the end, but still, to have that, you know, hope.

Sabine, I have ideas! Why not make the camera take a picture of Redcliffe Way, from beside St Mary's, at the corner of Guinea Street, the spires is so beautiful? There is a concrete tower instead of the Lead Shot, and a flats there now on the corner, ugly, but perhaps still it may work, and you can put the camera in the back of a, you know, *Auto*, and have a child throw confettis. And the car will drive off, and that will be the ending of your documentary. The happy ending, with the girl in the car, looking back, waving. *Schönes Bild, gel?*

And now. I must go to the television.

[rises]

Yes. To catch the News!

Acknowledgements

A great many people helped in the making of this book.

For sharing their insights around transgender identity and experience, I would like to thank Florence L., Julia Ehrt, Lynda Sheridan, Quince Mountain, Richard Köhler, Robyn, Stephen B., and, in particular, Philippa James for her generosity, clarity and humour. Thanks to Louise Walsh for some great reading material and introducing me to Trish, who filled me in on life in 1990s' Berlin. Kurt Hartwig, Dr Siobhán Maguire and the Irish Cancer Society helped me research medical details; any technical or factual errors are my own.

While the design and planning history of David's bank is inspired by the Central Bank on Dame Street, and his firm inspired by Arup's international structure, the characters and politics of the organisation in this novel are fictional and fully my own invention. Any errors are also mine. I owe a big thank you to John Mulligan and to Engineers Ireland, particularly Alec McAllister and John Callanan, and the brilliant engineers they put me in touch with: Derrick Edge, John Higgins, Finbar McSweeney and Gerry Dunne. Also to Peter Debney from Oasys for the jokes, names, astounding technical detail and for so expertly introducing me to Mike Prince, Angus Low, David Taffs and Henry Bardsley, all of whom I am also indebted to. Thanks to my Dad, Gerhardt, for letting me borrow – and (heavily) fictionalise – his experiences of being a 'Tunnel Tiger' in the 1950s.

The novel owes its title and the first curiosity of the *Wunderkammer* to Hilda Natko, whose candid and detailed interviews helped me flesh out Anna Bauer. I can't thank her enough. I was guided to Hilda by her daughter Maria and Dr Inge Weber-Newth of London Metropolitan University, whose expert knowledge of German migrants in post-war Britain opened the door to Bohemia for me. For those interested in reading more, I recommend Elizabeth Wiskemann's *Czechs and Germans*, Ronald M. Smelser's *The Sudeten Problem*, Mark Cornwall & R.J.W. Evans (eds.) *Czechoslovakia in a Nationalist and*

Fascist Europe, Norman M. Naimark's *Fires of Hatred* and David Gerlach's doctoral dissertation *For Nation and Gain.* Botting's *In the Ruins of the Reich,* MacDonogh's *After the Reich* and Evans' encyclopaedic *The Third Reich at War* are also great starting points for those wanting to build their own picture of the 'Sudetenland' during and after the Nazi era.

Annie Warburton introduced me to Bristol. Thanks to her and Rachel Devitt for their hospitality and to all the Bristolians who spoke to me about their city, including Dave, John Marshall, Philip Barton, Richard Thorpe, Sue, Steve and, in particular, the kind family in No. 10 Guinea Street who let me nose around their home on a freezing January evening in 2009. I'm also very grateful to Kay Scorah and Jane Dowling, who helped me get a sense of growing up in 1950s-60s' England.

Edited excerpts from the novel have appeared in *Literary Imagination* (14:1, 2012, ed. Greg Delanty), *Spolia* (2013, ed. Jessa Crispin/Gus Iversen), *Colony* (2014, ed. Dave Lordan and Kimberley Campanello) – as well as *Young Irelanders* (2015, ed. Dave Lordan, New Island) and the dual-language anthology *Lost Between/Tra Una Vita E L'Altra* (2015, foreword Catherine Dunne and Federica Sgaggio, New Island/Guanda). I am grateful to all those editors, and to everyone involved in the Italo-Irish Literature Exchange (IILE), the initiative behind *Lost Between,* which led so fortuitously to the publication of this novel. Thanks particularly to Catherine and Federica, Gaia, Luigi and all the writers of *ònoma,* my six fellow-travellers – Afric McGlinchey, Bill Wall, Liz McManus, Noel Monaghan, Nuala Ní Chonchúir and Sean Hardie – and to Jack Harte, Jack Gilligan and Valerie Bistany, for championing and administering such a complex project.

I could not have embarked on, let alone completed, this book without the financial assistance of the Arts Council of Ireland, who grant-aided me in 2006, 2008 and 2011. Many thanks in particular to Sarah Bannan for her unstinting moral support. Also to Kenneth Redmond and his team at dlr Arts Office and Josephine Browne and Paula Gilligan from IADT, whose joint dlr/IADT residency in 2009/10 supported me on many levels – financial, creative and professional. Blue Mountain Center (NY) offered me a residency in 2008 at a crucial point in the book's development. Thanks to Ben Strader and Harriet Barlow for inviting me in, and to the late, great Eithne McGuinness for leading me there.

I owe a big thank you to my fellow-writers, students and mentees in Dublin and beyond, and an even bigger one to all my friends and family – especially Emer MacDowell, Helen Healy, Karen Hand, Ken Carroll, Kurt

Hartwig, Michelle Read and Una MacNulty for reading early drafts, and Anne Mary Luttrell for lending me her compassionate ear and her strong Kilkenny shoulder to lean on right from the start.

It's been a pleasure working with all the team in New Island, including Hannah Shorten, Shauna Daly, Mariel Deegan and Justin Corfield. Both I and the book are hugely indebted to Dan Bolger for his enthusiasm, rigour, creativity and editorial insights. Jonathan Williams, my agent, is due my special appreciation for his faith in this book and his unwavering professionalism.

Finally, enormous thanks to my parents, Miriam and Gerhardt, for their encouragement and love over the years. To Izzy for simply being, and to Seán, for everything.